Children
of the
Archbishop

NORMAN COLLINS

COLLINS

fontana books

First published 1951
First issued in Fontana Books 1960

To
Audrey and Patrick

CONTENTS

And he who gives a child a home
Builds palaces in Kingdom come.
And she who gives a baby birth
Brings Saviour Christ again to Earth.

JOHN MASEFIELD
The Everlasting Mercy

Introduction in a London Bus

THERE are too many of them. Too many. Too various. And, in their separate and divergent ways, all too supremely important.

Take just one bus-load, for example. An ordinary No. 14, type S, plying somewhere between Hornsey and Roehampton. It isn't even full, this particular bus. But, for all that, it's crowded. Packed solid. Overflowing.

Start anywhere you like. Right up in front, for instance, with the driver. His name's Sid Harris. He's been driving buses for nearly ten years. Ever since 1910, in fact. Even during the war—the Great War, that is—he was still hard at it. And, when he came out, he was a full Corporal in Army Transport. He still talks a lot about those days. It was the crown of his life, that fine September morning in 1914 sitting behind a slung tarpaulin windscreen—they were the old B-type buses in those days—driving forty-eight of Sir John French's men—thirty-two inside, twelve standing—to meet General Hindenburg's army just south of Arras. Naturally it was the peak, you will say. It was history in the making, raw stuff of empires, and all that. But that wasn't the way Sid saw it. It was the behaviour of his bus that impressed him—the way the engine boiled over but the old thing still chugged along for another thirty miles or so before seizing up. He's mad about buses, is Sid.

And not only about buses, either. He's got hold of the extraordinary notion that someone is going to die and leave him a fortune. It's a good enough idea in its way, only somehow it hasn't yet got round to the other person. The dim benefactor apparently knows nothing of it. Not that this makes Sid doubt the truth of it. Only last night as he was getting into bed he woke his wife up specially to mention it. " Not long now, Vi," he told her in the kind of voice that he always used when he was talking about his legacy. " You wait and see. Just you wait. May be there in the morning."

In short, poor old Sid's practically barmy about legacies by now. Barmy but, in a way, happy too. Happy from sheer, unrealised expectation.

Far happier than his conductor, Edward Musk. And that's funny when you come to think of it because Edward Musk

9

actually married money. When he took on Andrew McInerney's widow she was worth every penny of four hundred pounds. And Edward Musk got all of it. But he also got Mrs. McInerney. In consequence, when he isn't actually taking fares, he spends his time washing up; carrying trays; cooking little things in saucepans; opening the window; putting the cat out; letting it in again; turning the mattress; going round to the Public Library; buying little bunches of flowers; and generally trying to be as kind, loving, patient and thoughtful as one should be with an invalid. For Mrs. Musk is nowadays completely bedridden. It is something internal, something incurable. What's more, she's gone all religious. And Edward Musk, with the four hundred still untouched in the bank, and nothing to show for it except tracts and missionary magazines and holy pictures, is often so fed up that he wishes that he could do something to speed up Nature.

Not that he ever will. He's far too quiet and timid and spiritless for that kind of thing, is Edward Musk. It's simply that he'd like to. And what makes it all so queer when you come to think of it is that, if only he had known, he might have been able to pick up a hint or two just now from a two-penny-fare. But how was he to guess that the twopenny, Warren Street to Brompton Road, was a wife-poisoner? That even now the dark stranger, with all the deep cunning of the murderer, is on his way to buy another bottle of Emmott's Arsenical Insect Spray from a chemist in order to dispose of Number Two?

The other passengers aren't all so sensational as that one. Poisoners are special. But in their own ways the others are interesting, too.

There's the little faded, frightened-looking spinster in the second seat. She's a music mistress and she's just been giving a private lesson to the practically tone-deaf daughter of a family grocer in Clerkenwell. Half a crown for the hour is what she got for it. And how is she going to spend her money? Sheet music? Oratorios? A new case for her second-hand, two-guinea violin? Not a bit of it. She's saving up for a steamship ticket to Australia. Her brother's wife died just over a year ago. And ever since then the little music mistress has seen herself at his side, a big, motherly creature in a vast new world; a heaven-sent, full-bosomed auntie bringing up her four little nephews and three little nieces. She has only got £7 10s. so far towards the ticket, so

10

she hasn't told her brother anything about it yet. But she's in earnest all right. And because she's cut her personal expenses down to the bare minimum and is living on about twopence-farthing a week, the nervous flicker of the eyelids which was so bad when she was a child has come back again. At times she can't even see enough to read the headlines, let alone her music. And she isn't sleeping so well because of the nervous strain and excitement. That's why she's so jumpy that she can't bear to have people touch her. She nearly screamed out just now when she felt Edward Musk thrusting the change into her hand.

There's nothing like that about the man opposite. He's in a state of positively splendid equilibrium. He wears his ticket stuck into his hat-band and has thick, smooth lips, like slices of orange-peel. Through them, he whistles snatches of recent song-hits. His suit is brown with a broad white stripe in it, and his boots have cloth uppers. In his tie is a five-carat diamond. Or white sapphire. Or zircon. Or glass. Whatever it is, it's five-carat and defiant. When he fingers it—which he does constantly—it looks strange somehow, because his fingernails are so short and broken. But that comes from carrying his bag. He's a commercial traveller, and because he's in the fancy-goods line—pocket-mirrors and manicure sets and that kind of thing—the contents are full of points and edges. He's fifty-two. His name is Solly Green. He's got forty-five pounds in fivers strapped round his waist. There are two boa-constrictors tattooed across his middle. His wife hasn't seen him for seven years, and she hopes that she never sees him again.

He's living at the moment with a girl called Daisy. She's nearly twelve years his junior and calls him Daddy—only of course there aren't any children. Not by her at least. And that's a pity. Because perhaps a pair of little pattering feet would help to keep them together. But only perhaps. There were three pairs of little patterers all at once, remember, in his real home. And that didn't help. Quite the contrary, in fact. But it would be hard to find a formula for keeping Solly Green chained permanently to any woman. And poor Daisy, a ghost-designate already, is on her way out to join all the other ghosts in Solly's past, poor Olive, poor Pearl, poor Elsie, poor Mabel, poor Doris and poor all the rest of them. In the meantime, Solly is still whistling. And he can afford to. He is now representing a powder-puff with a small pink china doll in the centre for a handle. The doll is nude,

11

and its tiny hands cover up its embarrassed eyes most appealingly. It's all the rage with the trade, that powder-puff—though only with a certain class of customer, of course.

There's a very different kind of man beside him. A nice, neat young man with flat, fair hair and a closely trimmed moustache and a weak, receding chin. He's reading a book entitled *Heroes of Peace*. But he's really thinking about his fiancée, Miss Mills. They're going to be married next month and they've found a house in Stroud Green, within a stone's throw of the water-works. Miss Mills is a pale, pretty little thing of twenty-two, and she is looking forward ever so. Thank goodness that she doesn't know what is coming to her. Doesn't know that, by Christmas, Harold—it's still less than six months since she first called him by his name—will be dead and in his coffin with the wreaths and crosses piled whitely on top. It's only a hundred and sixteen days to Christmas. And on December 21st, this brand-new husband of hers is due to go under a District train at the Mansion House in an unaccountable fainting fit following on a nasty bout of influenza. By then—and this is the sad part—the pale, pretty thing his wife will be paler than ever but not half so pretty. She'll be feeling sick most of the time because there's a baby on the way. But in the meantime Harold, of course, knows nothing of all the misery he is bringing to Miss Mills. Contented and engrossed, he holds out his penny to Edward Musk. He is reading about Madame Curie and thinking about Miss Mills.

On the seat behind him is an elderly woman in black, obviously a grandmother. She is holding the hand of a solemn, preoccupied little girl. The solemn little girl sits bolt upright, her eyes fixed hard on space, her small mouth drawn into a thin, firm line. And there is something of the same fixity, the same preoccupation in the face of the grandmother. They sit there, the old woman and the little girl, holding hands and not speaking. They've been like this for the last five minutes and it is obviously some important, private silence that they're sharing. Then the little girl suddenly wrinkles up her nose and, as she does so, a tear runs down her cheek. Because the tear tickles, she puts out her tongue to intercept it. It is the tip of the pink tongue that the elderly woman notices. And when she sees what is happening she squeezes the child's hand harder.

Is there tragedy here, too? Has Papa got himself caught up in the machinery at the works? Or has Mummy died,

12

and does the little girl keep on remembering her? Or have they just been taking poor old Rover to be put down by the vet? No, as a matter of fact, it is none of these. The old lady and her grand-daughter have just been to a performance at the Finsbury Empire where there was a performing seal that the little girl loved very much and knows she won't see again. It's the seal that she keeps remembering, not her mother. And once they're home again Granny's brief authority will be over, and she'll just be a useless, lonely old woman again. That's what's on Granny's mind, and that's what she's so quiet about.

That about accounts for everyone inside the bus. And there's no one outside because it's raining so hard. Ever since lunchtime it's been coming down by the bucketful, and Sid Harris on his little seat in front is soaked right up to the elbows. He's got one of his mad theories, has Sid, that when it's wet it's always wetter up Putney way. And that certainly seems reasonable enough to-night because they're over Putney Bridge already and mounting slowly towards the Common. Meanwhile the rain is coming down like a bath-waste. In fact, Sid is just blindly cutting his way through water, darkness and reflections. Plunging through mirages. It's nearly nine o'clock already. But, before he can call it a day, he's got to take the bus back all the way to Hornsey to garage it. And then, just when he thinks that he's got a clear stretch where he can let her rip, the little bell above his head tings suddenly. He recognises it for Edward Musk's delicate professional touch and prepares to draw the bus up neatly and correctly alongside the next Request Stop.

It's a young woman with a baby in her arms who is getting out. We haven't seen anything of her simply because she was sitting in the back seat and, from the way she was bending forward over the infant, her face was in shadow all the time. Not that there's anything in the least unusual about her. Just any young woman of twenty-two or twenty-three in a raincoat and carrying a baby. She pauses for a moment and arranges the folds of the shawl carefully so as to protect the baby's face and turns up her own coat-collar before she reaches the platform. Then, noticing the raindrops that are falling on the baby's forehead, she opens the lapels of her coat almost as though she were going to feed the child and clasps it close up against her bosom. The child whimpers faintly as she does so. And Sid Harris applies the handbrake.

The young woman gets down carefully and is grateful when

Edward Musk helps her off the step. But even though she is getting wetter every moment she does not move off immediately. She stands there on the kerb in a dazed, stupid kind of way looking after the dull red lozenge that is the retreating rear lamp of the No. 14.

Then abruptly, as though remembering some forgotten purpose, she crosses the road, splashing through the puddles without even seeming to notice them. And with head averted from the driving rain, she begins to mount the steep slope of St. Mark's Avenue.

Well, that's that. The bus with all its load of human treasure has gone on. And the young woman whom we scarcely noticed is all that is left of it. But she's probably better than nothing: so perhaps we'd better follow. There'll certainly be no one else about on a night like this.

It's a quiet, neglected sort of thoroughfare up which she is going. There is a high stone wall on one side, and the hedges and front drives of substantial family mansions on the other. The avenue itself is composed of lime trees that climb up the hill one above the other and obscure the sky-line. Not that there's any sky this evening. The avenue is simply a sheer black chasm with the gas-lamps dotted faintly along it, more like clues to steer by than street-lighting. Because the rain is rushing down the hill so fast there are tracks of watery light leading up to each one of the lamp-posts. And it is outlined against one of these that we see the young woman, still pressing on her way, her body bent forward as she climbs.

Then, where the outline of the high stone wall is broken by the roof of a gate-house, the woman stops suddenly and glances behind her. Even though it's too dark to see her face, the gesture is revealing. It is furtive, anxious—almost as though she is apprehensive of being followed. But there is no one else in sight either way, and apparently she is reassured. For, without further hesitation, she opens up her coat and holding the baby in her arms long enough to kiss it on the forehead she places it gently and tenderly on the porchway of the gate-house. She pauses for a moment to make sure that the small bundle is secure there; that the rain can't reach it; that its shawl is keeping the chill of the stone away from it; that it can't roll over and smother itself. Then she reaches up for the heavy ornamental bell-pull and jerks it violently.

Somewhere inside the gate-house a bell starts to jangle

madly. And, as though frightened by the din that she has made, the young woman starts to run. Up the hill she goes, her heels showing under her bedraggled skirt. On up the hill and clean out of sight. Clean out of sight and not a chance of catching up with her. She's lost. Disappeared from view. Vanished. At this moment she's simply number ninety-nine in London's daily hundred mysteries.

So you see, it didn't do us much good following her. We're left behind all alone in the wet and darkness of St. Mark's Avenue with nothing except the black doorway and the empty street.

But not quite alone. There's the thin whimper of a child coming from that doorway.

And a moment later there is the creak of a bolt being withdrawn, and a shaft of pale, daffodil-coloured light shows up the polished brass plate of the Archbishop Bodkin Orphan Hospital, and reveals the white woollen bundle on the doorstep.

BOOK ONE

The Bundle on the Doorstep

CHAPTER I

I

THE GATE-HOUSE bell hung immediately above Sergeant Chiswick's chair in the porter's room. It was a small room, and an uncommonly large bell. Even when the wrought-iron handle outside was pulled ever so gently the bell inside blazed forth like a tocsin. It had a high, hysterical note, that bell. And, because it was suspended very delicately on its pivot, it always continued to ring even after the front door had been opened.

To-night, however, it was as if some new kind of musical bomb had exploded just over Sergeant Chiswick's head. At one moment, there he was, sitting quietly stirring a thick spoonful of condensed milk into his cocoa and, at the next, the bell had pealed forth and he had spilt half the contents of the cup—all the rich, frothy part—on to his knees as he got up. Then, mopping at his trousers to prevent himself from being scalded, he glanced apprehensively above him and saw that the bell was swinging through its full arc of a hundred and eighty degrees. He had seen it swing like that before and knew it meant trouble. Sliding his feet hurriedly into his carpet-slippers he started slopping off down the stone passageway.

He saw the bundle immediately, but he knew better than waste his time on it. Sergeant Chiswick was not a man to be fooled by runaways. If strange women on dark nights were going to dump unwanted babies on his doorstep he was ready to do his best to get even with them, catch them, hand them over to the law. Reckless of the weather, he went right into the middle of St. Mark's Avenue and shouted, " Hi, there! Hi!" as loudly as he could utter. And, having shouted it once, he shouted it again.

But it was no use. After the brightness of the porter's room, the night outside was as black as a cellar. And, though

17

he thought he saw the figure of a woman—a figure which in the course of time became transformed in Sergeant Chiswick's memory into that of someone wearing a large picture hat and an expression of almost unearthly tragedy—he was never really sure. All that he knew for certain was that his shirt and waistcoat were already soaked through, and that in the porchway behind him there was a baby crying.

It tickled up Sergeant Chiswick's lumbago, bending over to lift the baby. But by going right down on one knee he was able to gather it up all right. And pulling the door shut behind him with his foot he shuffled back along the stone passage to the Lodge. Because his arms were entirely filled by the bundle he opened his own door with his shoulder and sidled carefully into the living-room. The bell on the wall was still swinging—but the baby was crying so shrilly that Sergeant Chiswick hardly noticed the bell. Besides, he was busy undoing the shawl that was damp from the rain that had driven on it.

When he had unrolled the outer layer of the cocoon, he straightened himself and placed the baby in his own arm-chair. Then he stood back and inspected it. He was a good judge of babies and he reckoned this particular one to be somewhere round a fortnight or about three weeks—under a month certainly—and as well-nourished as a baby of that age should be. It was clean, healthy—not like some he'd seen—and despite the fact that its face was as wrinkled as a monkey's and flushed crimson by its crying—probably not bad-looking. It had more hair than most babies. Dark, shining hair. Sergeant Chiswick began to stroke it with his forefinger. No more sentimental than most regimental sergeant-majors, Sergeant Chiswick nevertheless suddenly felt strangely compassionate towards this particular baby. And more than compassionate: he felt positively paternal.

A moment later, he felt flattered as well. For, either because of his gentle, regular stroking of its skull, or because of the heat of the tiny room—Sergeant Chiswick lived for preference in an atmosphere that would have parched and withered up a cactus—or because of the pleasant tinkling that was all that now remained of the original bell-peal, the baby abruptly stopped crying. It lay there on its back in Sergeant Chiswick's own arm-chair, its face still flushed and puffy from its recent paroxysms, its nether lip quivering, its clenched fist slowly unfolding. Then opening its dark, unfocusing eyes very wide it stared straight up at its rescuer.

18

" Poor little chap," Sergeant Chiswick said feelingly. " You poor little unwanted old thing."

While he was addressing it, Sergeant Chiswick had temporarily forgotten his stroking. In consequence, the baby immediately started to crease up its face again. Wide white circles appeared around its eyes. Its mouth began to distend and the chest swelled up under the folds of the inner woollen shawl. But Sergeant Chiswick was too quick for it. Before the first yell could reach the surface, he had run his finger rapidly round the lid of the condensed milk tin and thrust a sweet, sticky fingernail between the baby's lips. Then hastily re-wrapping the shawl and tucking the fringe in carefully, he shored up the bundle with a couple of cushions on either side of it, and went off in search of Mrs. Gurnett.

Mrs. Gurnett's room was on the far side of the courtyard, past the boys' lavatories and the statue of Archbishop Bodkin. It was the Cranmer block where Mrs. Gurnett was quartered. And to get there Sergeant Chiswick had to make a hundred-yard dash from this, the Latymer side.

The Putney rain was still coming down just the way Sid Harris always said it did. The expanse of shelterless asphalt in front of him became a pool, a lake, a reservoir. But Sergeant Chiswick could not afford to stop now. Taking off his jacket and putting it over his head like a poke-bonnet he made a dash for it.

And there was no relief even when he had reached the high Gothic doorway on the other side. The green front door marked MATRON was already shut fast for the night, and there was nothing for it but for him to stand there in the wet, tugging at the bell-pull. This bell-pull was a miniature, domestic version of the bell-pull that hung outside the gatehouse. And as Sergeant Chiswick pulled, there reached his ears from somewhere inside the Cranmer nunneries a faint treble jingling like distant sheep-bells. It didn't sound half loud enough to satisfy him, and Sergeant Chiswick pulled again, harder this time.

A moment later a window on the second floor was raised violently and a female head appeared. It was too dark to see very plainly and, in any case, the rain was getting in his eyes. All that he could make out was a blur against the white window curtain. But the voice was Mrs. Gurnett's all right.

" Well?" it asked.

Sergeant Chiswick tilted back his head and screwed up his features as the rain beat down into his face.

"There's beener narrival," he said.

A gust of wind sweeping across the courtyard tore the words away from his lips and swept them into the far corner of the courtyard.

"What's that you say?"

"A baby. Somebody's just left one."

"Where?"

"On the doorstep."

There was a pause.

"Stay where you are. I'm coming down."

The head withdrew itself and the window was slammed down again. Then, a second later, a light appeared. Mrs. Gurnett was dressing.

I I

It was her mouth that was Mrs. Gurnett's most remarkable feature. Thin and bloodless, it curved downwards like the new moon inverted. There was disgust in that mouth. Bitter, unconcealed disgust. Disgust at the very pattern of life as human beings lived it—the unbridled desires of men, the wantonness of women and young girls, the whole displeasing unnecessariness of sex. And all because of a nuptial flight of her own that long ago had been so full of Spring, so brief, so disastrous.

It was thirty-two years ago when it had all happened. But she remembered every minute, every incident, every single detail of the shame as clearly as though even now the waxed tip of Mr. Gurnett's ginger moustache was still tickling her cheek-bone through the open meshwork of her veil. And she remembered other things as well—the tainted metal of the ring, the breathless tobacco-laden kisses, the hotel at Ramsgate with its private bathroom, that horrible slot machine on the pier on which Mr. Gurnett spent no less than sevenpence on the second day of the honeymoon, going back to it again and again until his bride had felt like jumping fully-clothed into the sea from sheer humiliation. And then the awful third day—the arrest, the charge of bigamy, the hysterics and the last glimpse of Mr. Gurnett with his wonderful white teeth gleaming and tears in his deep, bed-

20

room eyes as he was whisked away to the Police Station in a growler.

Lesser women would have been broken by such an experience. But not this one. She had rallied, struck out, tried to save her own honour. Pawning the only present that Mr. Gurnett had ever given her—a dressing-set in imitation tortoiseshell—she had bought herself a complete set of widow's weeds, and had returned to London, tragic, shattered and with a mythical funeral in the background. It was only the name that haunted her. Much as she would have preferred to become plain Miss Lippitt again, widowhood, even false widowhood, was indispensable to her good name. Swathed in her own deceit, Mrs. Gurnett she remained. And she had prospered. Worked her way upwards to matronship of an Orphanage. She was independent again. Still heartily and unfluctuatingly opposed to sin, she had lived for twenty years largely supported by the fruits of it.

She had reached the bottom of the stairs by now, and was drawing back the bolts that secured the door. A swirl of rain eddied in on her and the gas-jet in its glass cage jerked and bounded. But Mrs. Gurnett promptly thrust out her head full into the fury of the storm.

" Did you get her?" she demanded.

" Too quick," Sergeant Chiswick answered. " She'd got away."

" Ugh!"

Mrs. Gurnett had spoken. And, in speaking, she had uttered the very sound that such a mouth was made for. But this was no time for recriminations: there was a baby that needed looking after.

" I'll call Nurse Stedge," she told him.

Nurse Stedge's room was at the far end of the bottom corridor. She was a light sleeper and, as Mrs. Gurnett approached, the door opened obediently. A tall, giraffe-necked woman, Nurse Stedge stood there in the gas-lit passage, her black emergency bag—the one with the curved pins and the nappies and the pair of blunt-nosed scissors in it—clasped ready in her long blue hand.

" Come along," Mrs. Gurnett told her. " We're wanted."

Mrs. Gurnett led the way, Nurse Stedge fell in behind and Sergeant Chiswick, who had temporarily crept into the shelter of the hall, followed up the rear. Together the three of them went out into Sid Harris's weather.

They had got as far as the entrance to the courtyard, and were just turning into the covered part, the cloisters, where a bracket gas-lamp was gleaming, when they were nearly bumped into by someone. It was Canon Edward Mallow, the Warden. He had not seen them coming because he was walking with head down, violently opening and shutting his umbrella in an endeavour to shake the drips off.

At the sound of footsteps, however, he looked up in surprise.

"Ah, Mrs. Gurnett," he said. "Going out I see?"

As he looked up, the light from the gas-bracket fell full on him and showed a round, pink face with very wide-open pale blue eyes. It was the face of an elderly and puzzled cherub.

And, as he looked, his expression of puzzlement increased. "Nothing wrong, is there?" he asked.

There was something in the quiet and gentle undertone of the Canon's voice that came as bitter and corrosive poison to a woman of Mrs. Gurnett's temperament.

"Sergeant Chiswick's got a new baby in his room," she told him. "That's what's wrong."

"A baby?" Canon Mallow repeated as though the whole idea of a baby in the Archbishop Bodkin Hospital came as a surprise to him. "Ah, yes. I thought I heard one crying as I came in. Where did it come from might I ask?"

"Orf the doorstep, sir," Sergeant Chiswick replied. "I just found it."

"How dreadful," Canon Mallow answered. "In all this rain, too."

He had turned by now and was walking back with them towards the gate-house.

"The mother got away," Mrs. Gurnett interjected suddenly. "Chiswick wasn't quick enough."

"And he hasn't told the police yet," Nurse Stedge reminded them.

Cannon Mallow, however, made no movement. Indeed, by simply standing there in the doorway, he impeded them.

"But don't you see?" he said. "It's providential. It means we've kept our numbers up. We're back on the 500 mark again."

They made quite a crowd, the four of them, in the small, stuffy room with the flowered wall-paper and narrow Gothic windows. Like everything else in the Archbishop Bodkin Hospital, the room was bleak, ecclesiastical, uncompromising. Even the wall-paper—upside down bunches of peonies, tied round with knots of lavender ribbon—had faded with the years into no more than a faint, autumnal background; and the coronation group of Edward and Alexandra, painted in brightly varnished colours on the lid of a biscuit tin marked Family Assorted, assumed in its setting the formal, devotional air of a rich and rather splendid icon.

But already Nurse Stedge was getting down to her work. With the uncontradictable authority of her calling, she pushed in front of everyone—even in front of Mrs. Gurnett—and began to undo the baby's shawls. It was obvious from the number of them, and from the skill with which they had been wrapped, that whoever it was who had left the baby had taken good care that no harm should come to it. Some-one a short while ago had loved that baby a very great deal. Probably still did love it, in fact.

Immediately the baby felt Nurse Stedge's fingers, it began to howl louder than ever, expressing a gaping, toothless rage to heaven. But Nurse Stedge was familiar with the habits of babies. She had a way with them. Twisting and turning the bundle on her lap like a bobbin she soon had it stripped down to a flannelette vest and nappies. And as soon as the small dappled shoulders were bare she inspected each bicep critically.

"Ah," she said, "not vaccinated."

"Or christened, probably," Canon Mallow added.

"Or registered," Mrs. Gurnett said, snapping her mouth to again when she had spoken.

"Or wanted," added Sergeant Chiswick in an undertone.

But meanwhile Nurse Stedge was steadily burrowing deeper. Then, as she loosened the vest, she said "Ah" again. She had come on something. There was a length of ribbon fastened round the baby's neck and on the end of the ribbon was hung a piece of card. Mrs. Gurnett realised at once that this was important. If there was a name on it, it might even clinch matters: it might be evidence. Therefore, feeling that she had been kept out of the mystery quite long enough already, she abruptly thrust Nurse Stedge to one side and removed the card herself. Holding it up to the light, she examined it. And she was right: there was a name on it.

Across the card in large, irregular letters, appeared the one word, SWEETIE.

But that was all there was. The unknown writer had used an ordinary HB pencil so there wasn't so much as a split nib or an unusual coloured ink to provide a clue. The letters had been deliberately printed in capitals to defeat the calligraphists. The cardboard was of the kind that is found in the cheapest of cheap boxes. And cheap cardboard boxes are thrown away every day in their tens of thousands.

Canon Mallow, however, was not content until he had examined the card himself. He took it from Mrs. Gurnett's fingers. Then, slowly, with a maddening and unspeedable slowness he changed into his other pair of spectacles—his reading ones—and scrutinised the card as though he expected invisible writing to spring to life as he looked at it. Finally, he turned it over and inspected the back as well. But " Sweetie " was still all it said.

"Extraordinary!" Canon Mallow remarked. " Really most extraordinary."

But Mrs. Gurnett and Nurse Stedge were used to ignoring Canon Mallow at such moments. They were already engaged in the ultimate and profounder intimacies. And they were clicking their tongues disapprovingly over what they found.

Sergeant Chiswick, therefore, addressed himself to Canon Mallow with the air of man turning to man in too exclusive a feminine society.

" Whilst they're gettin' on with 'em, sir," he pointed out, " one of us 'ad better ring up the Station. Shall it be me or you, sir?"

Canon Mallow frowned slightly.

"The Station?" he inquired. " Now?"

"Police Station, sir," Sergeant Chiswick explained.

Canon Mallow's frown cleared away.

"Ah, yes, to be sure. The Police Station. We mustn't forget the Police Station."

Having disposed of that point, Canon Mallow shook his head thoughtfully.

"The sadness of it," he said slowly. " The tragedy."

Sergeant Chiswick stroked at his moustache in a manner

which indicated that he too was of the sensitive sort who recognised sadness and tragedy when he met them.

"'Ardly a month old," he continued in the same vein. "And such a fine little lad, too."

"Girl," said Mrs. Gurnett, suddenly turning her small fierce eyes contemptuously in Sergeant Chiswick's direction.

"And under the week," Nurse Stedge added to complete the picture of Sergeant Chiswick's ignorance.

But Canon Mallow merely smiled. "I thought it was a very odd name for a boy," he said. "If it's a girl, that explains it."

As he said it, he bent over the child.

"Poor little Sweetie," he said. "Let me give you a kiss."

Mrs. Gurnett and Nurse Stedge both stepped forward to prevent him.

"You don't know what that baby's got the matter with her," Mrs. Gurnett said sharply.

"And the child requires attention," added Nurse Stedge decisively.

Canon Mallow, however, suddenly found that he had no patience with either of them. Picking the baby up, he kissed her in the centre of her forehead.

"You're one of us now, Sweetie," he said. "And I hope you're going to be very happy here."

CHAPTER II

I

BUT DON'T begin getting wrong ideas about the place. Don't imagine that there were mysterious women tugging away at the bell-pull of the Archbishop Bodkin Hospital every single night. Dismiss entirely the mental picture of unwanted babies landing up on the doorstep as a kind of regular daily delivery.

That wasn't a bit the way things were in St. Mark's Avenue. If anything, life there was rather on the quiet side; just the fiddling day-by-day affairs of a big institution.

Admittedly, an ornamental weather-vane was blown from its moorings in the autumn gales of nineteen twenty-three and crashed through the skylight into the probationer nurses' sitting-room; and, in the January of twenty-six, something —a shot from an airgun probably—went clean through the windows of the laundry, in one side and out the other, without harming a soul.

But that is about all on the structural side. And there wasn't very much more among the inmates, either staff or children. One of the girls' mistresses, a Miss Dewchurch, resigned to look after her invalid father; and a Miss Seedworthy (whose own father incidentally was causing quite a bit of anxiety within the family circle) came in to take Miss Dewchurch's place, no one could say how permanently. An Old Boy, one Charlie Spencer, got himself sentenced to three years' hard labour on a charge of burglary—two other charges of housebreaking, and one of receiving, being taken into account, and the sentences allowed to run concurrently. A present Bodkinian, Ginger Woods, aged three, in a sudden fit of temper threw an ink-well at another inmate. And a red-haired and rather short-sighted little girl, Lettice Moon, died from complications following a sharp attack of measles. But that's nothing, really. Not among five hundred.

As for Sweetie, she had settled herself in very nicely. Or, rather, they were always on the point of thinking that she had. But she was a highly strung sort of child: a perfect little angel on Monday, she would be all tantrums—stampings and pinches and rages—by Tuesday. And, just when she should have been taking her place among the others, it was discovered how secretive she was. She didn't seem to be like the other children. She was awkward and acquisitive. Not over sweets, which she didn't seem to care about. But over things like toys. There was one particular pink rabbit that she seemed to regard as her own, despite the fact that there was an absolutely clear rule that was explained to all the children in the Hospital that every toy was to be shared in common.

They had removed the rabbit from her they couldn't remember how often. But somehow she always contrived to get it back again and was usually discovered somewhere by herself, talking to it, kissing it, putting it to sleep. Obviously, there was affection and to spare inside the child; and it was largely a matter, as Canon Mallow told them, of developing it, making it grow outwards, teaching her that there were more important things than pink rabbits in the world.

As it was, there was only one person of whom she seemed

fond. Really fond, that is. And even there it showed what a queer, contrary nature the child had. Because it wasn't Nurse Stedge or Mrs. Gurnett or anyone who did things for her all the time. It was one of the Hospital visitors who came only on Thursdays when the nurses had their time off.

What's more, it didn't even seem a particularly good choice. For, instead of choosing Mrs. Lamprett, who was a doctor's widow, or Miss Giles, who had a brother who was a magistrate, or even Mrs. Chapman, who spent her whole life visiting infirmaries and children's homes and prisons and things, she chose Margaret, who was a nobody. No family, no background, no position. Merely one of the maids in the household of Dame Eleanor Pryke, Chairman of the Archbishop Bodkin Board of Governors.

It had, indeed, come as rather a surprise to some people that Margaret at her age should want to spend so much of her spare time in looking after other people's children. But it was all put down to the splendid seriousness of purpose with which Dame Eleanor infused anyone with whom she came in contact. Even to enter into Dame Eleanor's service was to become a kind of social missionary. And there was no finer training for marriage, Dame Eleanor had repeatedly and emphatically declared, than practical babycraft.

That was presumably why Margaret was there. Because it was obvious that she was one of the marrying kind all right. Placid, sensible, well set-up and undeniably good-looking, it was assumed that she was just getting her hand in, preparing herself for life and babies of her own.

Dame Eleanor was pleased to see things turning out that way. She thought highly of Margaret; sufficiently highly to have taken her back into her service after the girl had gone away to look after a sick father or a sick mother or a sick someone—Dame Eleanor could remember nothing of the details, except that they were sad—who had eventually been considerate enough to die, and so release her again.

And Sweetie had taken to Margaret from the very start. Indeed, when Sweetie was in one of her difficult moods, Margaret was the only one who could do anything with her. Even having her about the place seemed to pacify the child; and Thursday in consequence came to be regarded as Sweetie's quiet day. If she had been forced to choose between Margaret and the pink plush rabbit, it is even possible that she would still have chosen Margaret.

And that's really about all that there is up to date to say

about Sweetie; certainly nothing very sensational so far. But for that matter there was nothing very sensational at the time about the whole Archbishop Bodkin Hospital. One death (from measles) among all those children is a fairly low average; and one weather-vane blown away isn't much when you remember that the Victorian builder put up twelve of them altogether—and in the most exposed places, too.

No: during Sweetie's first three years at the place everything went on as quietly and placidly as it had done during the preceding three centuries.

Then something really did happen. Canon Mallow retired. The Canon himself had seen it coming on for some time— ever since he had joined the Hospital seventeen years ago. Sixty was retiring age, and it was the age of sixty that he had now reached. That was all there was to it.

But for those who remained, for the under-sixties, there was unrest, speculation, anxiety, turmoil in the outcome. Even for Canon Mallow himself there was undefined uneasiness that he could not quite dispel. And the more he thought about to-morrow's interview with his successor—the last interview that he would ever hold in his own study—the less somehow was he looking forward to it.

After all, seventeen years is a long time.

CHAPTER III

I

"There. I think you'll find that's everything."

Canon Mallow tried to smile reassuringly and folded his hands across his waistcoat. One by one he had ticked off the items on his fingers—the bank pass-book, the current ledger, the sundries, the file of birth-certificates, the medical reports. And now, relieved of all responsibility, he was facing his successor across the wide expanse of bare, polished mahogany.

Because it was his reading glasses that he was wearing he could not see Dr. Samuel Trump very plainly. Could hardly see him at all, in fact. But he still remembered quite enough about him. And as he sat there, peering and frowning slightly, he could still discern—though only smudgily, mistily, like something seen through a damp window-pane—the large, egg-shaped head; the sharp grey eyes, deeply set and very close together; the massive caterpillar eybrows.

It was not, however, merely the shape of his visitor's head that was worrying Canon Mallow: it was the way up it was. The pointed end was on top. And, rising above the high, the almost too-high, clerical collar, it looked exactly as though it had been carelessly inserted upside down into a clean white egg-cup.

But perhaps that was only the effect of seeing the head silhouetted so sharply against the light. Canon Mallow had always meant to move his desk round so that the light should not fall full on to his face. And more than once he had called in Sergeant Chiswick and his predecessors and asked them to do something about it. But when it actually came to it, he had never been able to decide where else the desk should go. And in the evenings, of course, it was exactly right where it was. Or, it would be, if only he could have remembered to put a new bulb into his reading-lamp.

But this was dreadful! While he had been thinking about himself, he had forgotten all about his visitor, and the very last thing that he wanted was to appear off-hand or discourteous. So, putting his two hands on the table-top, he prepared to rise politely. But it was a low chair and a high table-top. And, when finally Canon Mallow had struggled up, it was rather in the manner of a child pulling itself on to its feet in a play-pen.

"Well," he said, smiling vaguely into the light as he emerged, "and now shall we go round and see the rest of the Hospital?"

"But the laundry accounts," his successor reminded him. "Weren't you going to show me the laundry accounts?"

The voice that had spoken was nasal and rather high-pitched. There was a serrated, metallic edge to it, as though, inside the egg, wheels were rasping. Canon Mallow decided that he did not like the sound of it. It was not a sort of voice at all for carrying on a conversation. It was simply a sharp, effective instrument for asking questions and requiring answers.

Canon Mallow smiled again; apologetically this time.

"Ah, yes, of course," he said. "How silly of me. They're all here. The figures, I mean."

He opened the large leather volume with the vertical cash columns, and pointed triumphantly to figures in red on the last page.

"There you are," he said. "Nearly two hundred pounds out. It was worse last year."

"And how long has it been going on?"

"The laundry?"

"No," replied his successor. "The loss."

Canon Mallow paused thoughtfully for a moment.

"Oh, as long as I can remember," he replied. "You see, it's always made a loss, our laundry."

"Then it must stop."

"The laundry?" Canon Mallow asked again.

"I am still referring to the loss," Dr. Trump told him.

But Canon Mallow only shook his head.

"I'm afraid it's not so easy as that," he explained. "I've often tried to stop it. But it's the cost of things, you know. Soap powder. And soda. And starch, and all that. They're what run away with the money. And, of course, the coal. There's a tremendous coal bill."

"Other laundries pay," the visitor remarked severely.

"Do they?" asked Canon Mallow, and hesitated. "Oh yes, of course," he added. "I suppose they must do. Or people wouldn't go on running them, would they?"

Dr. Trump ignored the question.

"Is our machinery out of date?" he asked.

Canon Mallow considered this point carefully.

"I don't think it can be that," he said slowly. "Because you see we don't use machinery. Not really. It's just wash-tubs and ironing-tables and things. Oh, and mangles. I suppose you might call a mangle a machine. But I don't think a mangle ever really goes out of date. Mangles are all very much the same, aren't they?"

"Is the turn-over sufficient?"

"Sufficient for what?"

"To make a profit."

Canon Mallow paused again.

"Well, put like that, I don't see how it can be. Because if it was, we wouldn't be making a loss, would we?"

"We might, or we might not."

Dr. Trump's lips came together again and remained pursed up after he had spoken.

"Do the girls work hard enough?" he demanded at last.

At that, Canon Mallow flushed.

30

"Good gracious, yes," he said. "You wouldn't find a nicer lot of girls anywhere in England. And in that heat, too. And all the steam. Why, they're a lesson to every one of us."

"Then I for one would like to learn," the visitor answered. "Let us go to the laundry first."

The man was certainly losing no time. Everything that Canon Mallow had been told about him was obviously correct. And as he stood there, he could hear again those words that Dame Eleanor had spoken with such confidence.

"Samuel Trump is the successful candidate," she had informed him. "And the Board has made an excellent choice. Truly excellent. You need have no fears about leaving the Hospital in *his* hands. One of the shrewdest men in our Church. Quite one of the shrewdest."

"And the greatest of these is shrewdness." The words, uninvited, had formed themselves inside Canon Mallow's mind and become a slogan. He shuddered. This was worse than irreverence. Much worse. It was blasphemy.

Hurriedly, he pulled himself together.

"We'll go into the steam-room first," he said. "Just to show ourselves. Then we'll get out again. We won't spend long in there. It's so hot."

And they certainly hadn't spent long. It was all over, including the accident, inside half a minute. Not that it had been Canon Mallow's fault. Or Dr. Trump's for that matter. Accidents aren't usually anybody's fault. And, as for this one, it had just happened.

Anyhow, they were back in the little office by now, and Canon Mallow was bending over him.

"You're sure you're all right?" he asked anxiously. "You don't think you've broken anything?"

Dr. Samuel Trump raised his head, and his eyes—his small, too deeply inset eyes—met Canon Mallow's blue, wide-open ones. Then pursing up his lips he deliberately turned away again and continued to massage his right ankle.

"Sprained, possibly," he replied at last. "But broken, no."

He spoke briefly as if he wished to erase the whole unseemly incident from his mind. And, straightening himself, he began scrubbing vigorously with his knuckles at the

31

disfiguring patch of soapy water on the sleeve of his new black jacket.

But Canon Mallow was far too solicitous, too deeply concerned, simply to drop the subject.

"Because you did come down an awful bump, you know," he went on thoughtfully.

"Fortunately I grasped something," Dr. Trump replied. "Otherwise . . ."

His voice trailed away significantly, with a hint of ambulances and anæsthetics in the silence that succeeded it.

"There used to be a light there," Canon Mallow remarked quietly, almost as though speaking to himself.

"And there is going to be a light there again," Dr. Trump assured him. "A bright light."

"It's a wonder you weren't killed," Canon Mallow went on. "It is really."

"It would not have been my fault if . . ." Dr. Trump began. But, instead of continuing, he beckoned Canon Mallow over.

"Forgive my not rising," he said. "The ankle, you understand. But I wish to ask you something."

Canon Mallow smiled politely.

"Of course," he answered.

"When I fell," Dr. Trump said slowly and accusingly. "Did you hear anything?"

Canon Mallow's eyes opened even wider in astonishment.

"Why, everyone must have heard," he answered. "You came a tremendous wallop."

Dr. Trump frowned: his eyebrows were now like something taken from a box of Carnival Novelties and gummed on to him.

"I don't mean *after* I had fallen," he went on in the same accusing tones. "I mean *as* I fell."

Canon Mallow himself was frowning now.

"I don't think so," he said. "Did you?"

"I did," Dr. Trump answered. "I heard laughter. A laundress's laughter."

"Oh that," Canon Mallow answered. "That was just hysteria. They're a very highly strung lot, those girls. And it was a bit sudden, you know. At one moment there you were saying how glad you were to be here and at the next you'd vanished. Simply vanished. It was enough to make anyone . . ."

He broke off and ran his handkerchief across his forehead on which the steam from the wash-house still glistened. It had been a deplorable business, this visit to the laundry. First the heat and humidity of the steam-coppers—Dr. Trump, he could not help noticing, had emerged looking as if he were ready for ironing himself—and now the disaster on the stairs. Canon Mallow was afraid that Dr. Trump would think badly of the Hospital Laundry for ever. And he was anxious, desperately anxious, for everyone's sake that somehow or other he should soothe him.

"Feeling all right?" he asked again.

Under Dr. Trump's tremendous eyebrows, the eyes themselves seemed to contract still farther and come together until they were one single eye, fixed centrally and gleaming like a jewel in the forehead of an idol. Then the jewel blinked suddenly as a sharp spasm of pain passed through the idol's ankle.

"I am perfectly well, thank you," Dr. Trump replied.

"Sure you wouldn't rather go back?" Canon Mallow persisted.

"Quite sure," Dr. Trump said firmly. "I wish to see everything. Now. Before it gets too dark."

"Well, just as you say," Canon Mallow answered. "But mind yourself. It's all stairs and corners."

The route from the laundry office lay along a worn asphalt pathway that stopped abruptly at a brick wall with a narrow Gothic doorway in the middle of it. The wall was high and a crest of broken glass ran along the top. Canon Mallow paused. It may have been the act of pressing down the latch that reminded him. For he suddenly recalled that he was conducting a visitor.

"This leads through into the boys' side," he said pleasantly, like a guide indulging in the professional small talk of his calling.

"From the girls'?" Dr. Trump asked pointedly.

"That's right," Canon Mallow replied. "Senior boys one side. Senior girls the other."

"Is it not kept locked?"

Canon Mallow shook his head.

"There used to be a key once," he said.

"What happens at night?"

Canon Mallow looked blankly towards him.

" Why nothing," he replied. " They're all asleep by then."

But while he was speaking, Dr. Trump had removed from his pocket a small black notebook.

It was a new notebook and at the top of the first page, Dr. Trump wrote the single word " key."

I I I

"And what would you like to show me next?" Canon Mallow suddenly heard Dr. Trump addressing him. " You are still Warden here—until to-morrow remember."

Still Warden? Why, yes ; he supposed he was. But he hadn't thought out any formal itinerary: he was just going round the place in the way in which he had always done. He was about to suggest the sick ward, because the children always liked to see a new face—even possibly Dr. Trump's—when the top of the Founder's Tower caught his eye.

It was the most imposing feature of the Hospital, the Founder's Tower. Nearly eighty feet in height and pinnacled in Victorian Gothic, it rose proud and dominant, like a vast and gritty *bombe-glacé* in two contrasting shades of brick-work. Supported in the structure were a clock with four faces, the Big Bell, an ornamental bronze weathercock and a narrow balcony enclosed by a frilly railing, bearing an iron-founder's version of the acanthus leaf.

The balcony was the highest point to which any ordinary sightseer could climb. Or, rather, could have climbed until Canon Mallow had closed it. The trouble was that the steep spiral stairway, lit only by arrow slits, made some people giddy. And, after a sister of one of the governors had been brought down feet first one Easter Sunday, he had shut up the whole thing. And this was a pity because, at one time, the Canon had hoped that by charging sixpence or even threepence for admission he could, especially on public holidays, have made the Founder's Tower practically self-financing.

Not that anything of the kind had ever actually happened. For a start, there had been few visitors. Then, as no proper receipt books were kept, no one knew how many the few amounted to. And, in the end, Sergeant Chiswick, who had always pocketed the price of admission along with the tips, was relieved rather than resentful when he found that he would never again have to climb the hundred and fourteen steps in order to be able to rescue someone who was overcome on one of the upper landings.

The moment which Canon Mallow chose to draw Dr. Trump's attention to the Tower was an auspicious one. The late afternoon sun, slanting through the limes of St. Mark's Avenue, lit up the pile with a warm amber light as though the bricks themselves were glowing; and, on top, the bronze weathercock blazed like a firework.

Canon Mallow balanced himself on his heels and peered upwards. Because he was wearing his reading spectacles—he had left his others somewhere in the study—he could see no more than a dim blurred streak stretching upwards into the sky. But he had seen it often enough before. And with a wave of his hand he indicated it.

"That," he said, not very revealingly, " is the . . . er Tower."

"The *Founder's* Tower," Dr. Trump corrected him.

Within the past twenty-four hours, Dr. Trump had read the handbook of the Hospital carefully and thoroughly—starting at the beginning and marking the important passages in pencil as he came to them—and he knew all about it; knew more than Canon Mallow, that was obvious.

"Just so," Canon Mallow answered casually. "The Founder's Tower. We usually call it ' The Tower.' "

Dr. Trump's eyebrows rose a little.

"A pity," he said. "Our Founder's memory is a trust handed down to us."

"Oh, I'm not worried about that," Canon Mallow replied easily. "It was children the Archbishop cared for, not towers. He never even knew about that tower. It was after his time."

"But not after ours . . ." Dr. Trump began, and then stopped himself. There was no point in stressing it. He paused.

"Can I go up?" he asked.

Canon Mallow seemed surprised.

"Well, you *can*," he said. "But I shouldn't if I were you. You see, it's all been shut up for years."

"Shut!" Dr. Trump repeated.

"That's right," Canon Mallow told him. "I closed it after Miss Larkin got taken ill up there. It's a long time ago now."

"I take it that you would have no objection to my going up," Dr. Trump asked.

"Objection?" Canon Mallow said in astonishment. "Good gracious, no. That is if your ankle's all right. After all it's your tower now. Or it will be to-morrow. But do be careful."

The reply was so charming, so placating, that Dr. Trump felt mollified completely. His face lit up for a moment in a warm, natural smile.

"Then perhaps you wouldn't mind waiting for me," he said.

There was delay—the kind of delay that smelt of inefficiency—while Sergeant Chiswick found the keys. And Dr. Trump was not pleased to discover that the stout wooden door had warped so badly that it required the combined efforts of himself and Sergeant Chiswick to open it. He was so much displeased, in fact, that he declined Sergeant Chiswick's suggestion that he should go up with him. He would mount alone, he said.

And he was not sorry that he had got rid of the man. There was something exciting—yes, strangely exciting—about being alone in the Tower in this way. It was the first time in his life that he had ever owned a Tower; and he did not want to share the experience with anyone.

He was even more pleased to be alone when he found how out of breath he was. Badly out of breath. Winded, in short. And this shocked him. It showed that, apart altogether from his injured ankle, he must be out of condition. And as he mounted, he began prescribing his own treatment.

"I must do exercises," he told himself. "Regular exercises. Hip bending. Touching the toes. Lifting the knees to strengthen the stomach muscles. Prone falling. Swedish clubs. I must be fit."

The prospect of the exercises pleased him. There was that note of self-discipline, or martyrdom almost, that was distinctly gratifying. And, above all things, it could be entirely private. If he was careful to put the Swedish clubs away again in the wardrobe afterwards, no one was to know that he had ever needed this toning-up process.

When, at last, he reached the balcony he was blinded as well as breathless. The early evening sun was shining full into the top doorway like a light-house beam. Dr. Trump put up his hand to shade his eyes. And, as he did so, he placed his other hand upon the railing. It trembled. But its flimsiness did not alarm him. He was too pleased at having got there. He was right on top of everything by now.

And the view was certainly reward enough. The Hospital, spread out beneath him, was like a toy farm. He could see the sports-field, the kitchen gardens, the girls' playground, the boys', the high raking roof of the main hall, the little dolls' house that was the Warden's Lodge set on its own strip of bright green baize, the entrance gateway, the laundry block. And around all, ran the great wall. Fifteen feet high, and without a break except where the spiked gates were let into it, it enclosed the landscape.

On the outer, the barbarian side, stood the little houses, row upon row of them. Grey-roofed and regular like furrows in a winter wheatfield they stretched away into the distance, their tiny chimneys smoking. And beyond them glinted in places small fragments of mirror that were the river.

" But this is magnificent," Dr. Trump told himself. " It shall be my first task to re-open this Tower. My very first——"

Then Dr. Trump cast his eyes to the ground beneath him. There directly below, stood Canon Mallow so violently foreshortened that the tips of his toes were emerging from underneath his chin. His pink round head looked ridiculous with the fringe of white hair surrounding it. Ridiculous, yes, that was exactly the right word. Not that it mattered any longer. The man was already on his way out. Practically packed up and ready for despatch. His foolishness, his futility, his fumblings did not matter any longer. By to-morrow the Hospital would be in other and far stronger hands. In Dr. Trump's hands, in fact.

Then, obscured by a cloud, the sun disappeared abruptly. It grew colder. Only the coolness of the breeze remained. Striking against his forehead, it chilled him. Dr. Trump shivered. It was as though inside him the sunlight had gone out too. And it was he himself who had extinguished it. He had recognised his earlier mood of exaltation for what it was —pride. Arrant spiritual pride.

" Oh God make me humble," he said devoutly. " Make me worthy of my new vocation."

37

CHAPTER IV

I

AND, EAGER as he was to get started, it seemed to Dr. Trump next day as though he would never get rid of Canon Mallow after all. The man was so abnormally slow and absent-minded. He did things, even quite little, unnecessary things, like showing Dr. Trump where the gas-meter was, twice or even three times. He pottered. And, above all, he wasted his time with the children.

Indeed, from the way he said good-bye to them you might have thought that they were his own children. Two of them, in particular. One of these was Ginger, the small boy who had thrown the ink-well: Dr. Trump had already been sizing him up as someone who would be all the better for not having too much notice taken of him. And the other was Sweetie. Also an exhibitionist kind of child, Dr. Trump had noticed. With the sheer genius that such natures possess for attracting attention, little Sweetie was on everybody's lips practically all the time. She seemed to cause more commotion than the other four hundred and ninety-nine put together.

It was silly, doubly silly, therefore, of Canon Mallow to make such a fuss over saying good-bye to her. He had even taken her up in his arms and kissed her, finally giving her a farewell sixpence just as he was leaving. Dr. Trump had promptly confiscated the sixpence: but there had been nothing that he could do about the kisses.

Anyhow, all that was over now. He had really said good-bye to Canon Mallow for the last time. In point of fact, he had thought that the first time was the last time. But he had not known then that, at the end of St. Mark's Avenue, Canon Mallow would suddenly tell the taxi to return to the Arch-bishop Bodkin Hospital because he had just discovered that he had come away with all the keys.

Seven-sixteen a.m. Seven-sixteen precisely on Monday, the 24th of September, nineteen hundred and twenty-four. And there, alone under the sheets of the double bed in the front bedroom of the Warden's Lodging lay the new Warden, Dr. Trump, propped up against the pillows and sipping his early morning tea. It was his one personal indulgence, this tea, drunk scalding hot and—since it was solitary drinking—punctuated between the gulps with loud exhalations like long drawn out sighs.

But even in his self-indulgence he did not entirely lose control. Not once, for example, had any housekeeper of his ever found him sleeping when she entered. There was indeed, a strict drill in such matters—the knock on the door, the pause, the slow, deliberate "Come in." And by the time the woman was actually inside his bedchamber, Dr. Trump would be sitting up, wide-awake, tidy (he kept a small pocket comb on the bedside table especially for the purpose) and smiling. It was a recurrent fear of his, especially when he had been overworking, that he might die in the night suddenly and without warning. And then . . . he shuddered to think what awfulness, what grim, unposed mortality would greet his domestic in the morning.

But last night had proved to be one of his lucky ones; he had not died during the course of it. He felt remarkably well, in fact. And those quiet minutes before he rose at seven-thirty were probably the best in the whole day for clear thinking. This very morning, for instance, he saw things clearly and distinctly as a whole—with himself as a separate and important part of the whole. He was a cog, a breathing sentient cog in a vast, intricate machine of life. And for a cog he was not doing so badly. Seven-fifty per annum was not exactly a flea-bite. Especially when there was an eight-roomed house thrown in. And, of course, washing.

Nor was it nothing for one particular cog to be responsible for the entire well-being and livelihood of five hundred and forty-five other cogs, forty-five of whom were full-sized adult cogs. Five hundred and forty-five. What a total! And all supported by private donations, too.

Not that he was convinced that every one of the forty-five was really deserving of such charity. Sergeant Chiswick, for example. The Sergeant, he could not help noticing, was elderly. And he looked as though at one time he might have been a drinker. He seemed inclined, moreover, to be sullen. And worse than sullen: he was a mumbler. Dr. Trump could not always hear what he was saying. Whereas with Mrs. Gurnett, he had more than once heard only too plainly. The woman, in short, was downright rude. Only yesterday when he had inquired why the milk bill was so large, all that she had said was that if he knew of anything else other than milk on which to bring up small children she would be glad to hear of it. He had not forgotten that reply, even though he had done nothing more at the time than merely raise his eyebrows. And Mrs. Gurnett was not going to forget it either. In due course, when Dr. Trump was ready, she was going to apologise for it; apologise—or go. Because it wasn't even as though he had asked why the bill was *large*. He had asked why it was *so* large.

Then there were the others, the masters. Mere names at the moment—Jeffcote, Prymore, Rushgrove, Dawlish and the rest. And the women—Mrs. Glubb, Miss Wynne, Mrs. Entwhistle, Miss Sattell: as yet, also mere names. He had not yet had time to get to grips with any of them, the male or female, as human beings; had not explored, probed, analysed them. Already, though, he recognised that there was some pretty promising probing to be done.

Take Mr. Prevarius, the organist, for example. A trifle too much inclined, perhaps, to the arpeggio and the cadenza, but an excellent church organist nevertheless—and entirely in Dr. Trump's power. Helplessly and inextricably bound. And why? All because of what had happened thirteen years before in a fortune-teller's booth at a charity garden party under church auspices near Banbury.

There was a complete dossier of the incident attached to Mr. Prevarius's private file locked away in the filing-cabinet marked STAFF CONFIDENTIAL. By now, Dr. Trump knew that dossier by heart; yes, practically by heart; knew why the name on the index tab was simply Mr. S. Prevarius and not The Rev. Sidney Prevarius, B.D.; knew why the correspondence which had opened with a humble and contrite letter of apology had closed with affidavits, depositions, statements witnessed by Bishops; knew, in fact, as much about the whole shameful incident as though he had been there in the rectory meadow on that sunny August afternoon.

Elderberry wine was at the bottom of it—that much was admitted on both sides. But who had taken it—the visiting curate or the swarthy fortune-teller? The man or the woman? Here evidence rioted in conflict, and even the public analyst's report on a specimen of the brew was ruled inadmissible, because the Vicar's sister had confessed that dismayed by its too obvious potency, she had speedily diluted the remainder.

Shorn of its divergencies, the story was all too plain: too sordid; too heavily laden with original sin. The Rev. Sidney Prevarius, having sportingly paid his sixpence, had gone inside the booth, ostensibly to have his palm read. Such operations are normally silent or, at most, muttered. But a moment later on this occasion a shrill scream had penetrated the canvas flaps, and this was followed by a gasp—some said a drunken oath—and a loud crash as, first, a folding-table folded too completely and gave way and then, in the mêlée, the little tent itself shut up and collapsed.

By the time the rescue party—two church workers and a cow-hand—had disentangled the guy-ropes and lifted up the billowing canvas an astonishing sight greeted them. The curate and the brunette daughter of a Rural Dean were locked together in a fierce and terrible embrace: her gipsy costume had been ripped open and he had been bitten in the right ear. On the grass at their feet lay a book of raffle tickets, the fortune-telling crystal, a dead goldfish—squashed practically flat, like a bright pink plaice—with its shattered bowl around it and, key evidence for the defence, a custard glass with elderberry wine stains in it.

Both sides were adamant and unbudgeable. He had borne down on her, she claimed. She had flung herself on him, he contended. She had been secretly tippling when he entered. He had drunkenly tottered, cup in hand. She was desperately struggling to escape when the table gave way. He was fleeing from temptation when he had caught his foot in the tent pole . . .

None of it mattered now, however. The findings were ultimately in favour of the Dean's daughter and Mr. Prevarius, bearing an imperishable scar on one lobe, was reduced to organist in a charity institution.

As Dr. Trump sipped noisily at his tea he smiled inwardly. He suspected that it might have been for all the wrong reasons that his predecessor had ever taken on such a man. There had probably been sentiment behind the decision. But

41

how right! An organist without references was a pearl among employees. If Dr. Trump ordered him to do anything—stoke the boilers, sweep out the nave, black his boots even—the man could not possibly afford to refuse. And his £110 per annum was an investment. For never in any conceivable circumstances would Mr. Prevarius be bothering him for an increase.

But Dr. Trump had more than the providential ruin of Mr. Prevarius on his mind. He had Dame Eleanor. A remarkable woman, Dame Eleanor. A figure. An institution. Almost, in fact, a syndicate. Chairman of the Board of Governors of the Archbishop Bodkin Hospital, she was also Founder of the G.C.S.—Guild of Christian Soldiers—President of the Unmarried Mothers Reclamation Society, Treasurer of the Junior League of Innocence, Campaigns Director for the Abstinence Crusade of Great Britain, and Organising Secretary of the National Association of Voluntary Part-Time Church Workers, the NAVPTCW; she moved speedily and impressively from meeting to meeting, punctual, precise, pugnacious.

From 9.30 a.m. when the two typist corporals attached to headquarters staff of the Christian Soldiers marched into their barracks in Dean's Yard, until ten or eleven at night when the Abstinence Crusaders soberly concluded their late sessions, she was on the go all the time, granting interviews, signing papers, stopping things.

And it was not only her range of works that made her so powerful: it was her connections. One brother was a judge and another was a bishop. Her sister, now dead, had been Principal of a Ladies' College. She herself was the daughter of an underwriter and the granddaughter of an admiral. One uncle was a major-general and another (deceased) had been an actor. Thus she was able to speak with full tribal authority—saying " Edmund doesn't think so " or " Augusta would never have heard of it "—whenever commerce, war (on land or sea), advanced studies, the stage, theology, or the law came into the conversation. And there was ever present the threat that at the first whiff of argument the entire family was ready to rally around her.

Not that Dr. Trump had the slightest intention of attempting to argue with the lady. Didn't he at this moment owe her everything, even the cup of tea that he was holding to his lips? Wasn't she the patroness who had raised him high above the others when the rest had failed? Wouldn't it therefore be sheer commonsense at least for the time being to agree, to conform, to acquiesce regardless of where her strange exalted views were leading her, him, all of them? Did it really matter so much if ecclesiastical embroidery were made compulsory throughout the girls' side from the age of five? What was the harm, the damage to these future citizens, if stool-ball instead of cricket persisted in the other playground?

Dr. Trump slid out of bed and thrust his feet—his thin, spatulate feet—into his new bedroom slippers. They had been an extravagance, those slippers with the little fluffy bauble on each instep. On the other hand, his old ones—his very old ones—were clearly impossible. They smacked too much of the intimately squalid, and would have given the servants the wrong ideas about him. Like his new walking shoes they had been bought not from vanity, but simply to uphold his new position. He felt that he owed them to the late Archbishop.

And, on the lowest showing, the new slippers were so much warmer for praying in. This, however, was a point on which he had battled with himself. Was it right to be comfortable? Was it *good*? He had tried it both ways and still the answer was unclear. If he jumped out of the sheets in the manner of the saints and went straight down on his knees on the little strip of Axminster beside the bed, his toes were left dabbling on the cold oil-cloth. In consequence his prayers tended to be scamped and fidgety. On the other hand, if first of all he cleared his head with hot tea and then wrapped himself up snugly, he could manage ten, fifteen, even twenty minutes of really hard praying, out loud if he felt like it. And he had finally decided in favour of the hot tea and camelhair. There was, moreover, no doubt about it: he had been praying better than ever of late. More fervently. More comprehensively. More . . . more imaginatively.

But this morning he was disappointed in himself. His thoughts, instead of fastening themselves upon the rightful object of all prayer, concentrated on Dame Eleanor instead. And once there, nothing could displace them.

43

The Board Room of the Hospital was a rather imposing chamber. Panelled up to waist-height in a highly polished red wood that might have been sawn from the trunks of old pillar-boxes, it rose soaring and majestic to an arched Gothic roof that was held together by criss-cross metal stretchers from which three gas-burners of orthodox ecclesiastical pattern were suspended.

The windows, like the roof, were pure Gothic and all three of them were glazed in frosted glass with a thick border of amber, crimson and Prussian blue squares. It was thus impossible at any time of day to see out of the windows. And, even in the cold light of early dawn, the room was flooded with a mysterious multi-coloured magnificence like a private sunset.

The chairs, too, owed much to the Gothic inspiration. Unusually high and narrow, with hard wooden seats, their backs rose up sheer and pinnacled. And a ridge of deeply embossed carving that ran across them at shoulder-blade height made lounging unthinkable. There were in all eight chairs of this design with an even taller, almost thronelike, stall for the chairman. This last was a notable and important piece of woodwork. Rising to a height of nearly five feet, it carried three pinnacles as against the mere two of the others, and had arms as well. This chair, together with a long deal table and a plain stool at the far end for the secretary, completed the furnishings.

This morning only five of the eight chairs had occupants. On Dame Eleanor's right sat Dr. Trump himself. Next to him with his hands nervously gripping the table edge as though to preserve his balance, was perched the Rev. Philip Chigwell, a pale, apologetic creature, curate of St. Mary Magdalene, Putney Hill. Beside him, ancient, stertorous and surrounded by a perpetual aura of medicated camphor, was placed Mr. Chitt, a retired tract publisher. On the other side of the table, the company was similarly arranged. Opposite Dr. Trump was seated Canon Larkin of the National Orphanage Council, a hard-scalped and highly respected administrator, who was acknowledged to be something of a wizard with charity finance. And last of all, facing Mr. Chitt, sat Miss Emmeline Bodkin, last living descendant of the founder and herself already in her seventy-second year: her electrical acoustic aid in its leather carrying-coat was on the table before her.

Dr. Trump ran his eyes round the assembly and smiled inwardly: he could see at a glance that with the possible exception of Canon Larkin, he had nothing to fear from any member of the Committee. And even Canon Larkin, tactfully and adroitly handled, might prove a friend, an ally, a supporter.

It was his first board-meeting and he wanted to make a good impression on everyone.

"Could we not begin by opening the window? That is, unless Dr. Trump wants us to be all boxed-up."

It was Dame Eleanor who had spoken, and Dr. Trump rose hurriedly.

"No, no. Not at all. Quite the contrary. I mean, yes, yes. Just as you prefer."

He was already half-way over to the window by the time he had finished speaking. Then deliberately he checked himself. It was silly this confusion on his part simply because Dame Eleanor had spoken. She would think him servile and undignified if he hurried. Possibly even unworthy. This, he recognised, was a moment when he should proceed majestically.

But before he had reached the window, Dame Eleanor had spoken for the second time.

"Where on earth's the man off to now?" she demanded of the meeting at large. "Why can't he ring for someone?"

Dr. Trump blushed. To hear himself referred to in this way was dreadful. He must, he realised, be making the worst possible impression: Dame Eleanor would surely despise him. There was, therefore, only one thing to do: assert himself. Accordingly, squaring his shoulders, he advanced boldly and opened the window to its full extent. Then triumphantly he returned to his place.

"So much quicker doing things for oneself . . ." he began.

But Dame Eleanor interrupted him.

"Too much," she said. "We might just as well be sitting out in the playground."

The blush that had begun to fade immediately remounted to its full scarlet and suffused his neck. He rose again and went back over to the window. In an absurd childish fashion, he was, he realised, afraid of Dame Eleanor. Whenever her dark eyes were turned on him, he felt himself a mere choir-boy again.

It was from her grandfather, the admiral, that Dame Eleanor had inherited that particular glance of hers. And Dame Eleanor took after Grandpapa in more ways than one. The overlong nose, the nervous tic of one eyelid, the sideways corner of the mouth, the pleated and protruding chin, all belonged as much to the bridge as to the board-room. And it was as though deliberately to avoid any possible mis-understanding that she allowed herself to wear so ostentatiously feminine a hat. Small, veiled and frivolous, it was perched on the neat white hair, like a butterfly resting on a spent flower.

But already Dame Eleanor was glancing down at the agenda. And, at the first item, she froze.

"Bathroom," she said incredulously. "The place is full of bathrooms. What do they want another bathroom for?"

Dr. Trump cleared his throat.

"This one is for the isolation block," he replied.

He had learnt by heart the particulars of this item and was now confidently reciting them. Hadn't he sat up half the night going over the details?

"The nearest bathroom is in the junior girls' block across the courtyard," he went on. "And in wet weather . . ."

Dame Eleanor tapped sharply on the table with her pencil.

"Why should the doctor choose this moment to start bathing fever patients when it's raining?" Dame Eleanor demanded.

There was a pause. Dame Eleanor turned sharply in her chair.

"Well, Dr. Trump, why should he?" she insisted.

"Canon Mallow thought it was necessary," Dr. Trump began weakly.

"Canon Mallow managed without it for seventeen years," Dame Eleanor reminded him. "I can't see why he should want it now."

A dutiful titter, the regulation murmur of applause that runs round a board-room when the chairman has been witty, greeted this last remark of hers, and everyone turned tormentingly towards Dr. Trump. Dr. Trump smiled, too: a faint, dutiful smile. He could see that things were not going to be easy. The board was bunching against him like a pack of wolves.

46

"Postponed for further examination," Dame Eleanor said sharply.

She glanced rapidly round the table as she finished speaking, and five heads nodded in turn. Canon Larkin pursed up his lips approvingly. Then Dame Eleanor turned again to the Agenda.

"Now we come to a new kitchen boiler," she remarked. "You seem to want everything new this morning, Dr. Trump."

"What was that, Dame Eleanor? What is it that Dr. Trump wants?"

The question came from the elderly Miss Bodkin at the far end of the table. In the dim world of sound, she was perpetually groping, stumbling, falling. And this morning her electrical apparatus was not functioning at all helpfully. It needed a fresh battery, perhaps, or it may have been that something was wrong with one of the little valves.

"Everything new, Miss Bodkin," Dame Eleanor told her.

"Everything blue?"

"No. *New.*"

"New what?"

"New everything," Dame Eleanor retorted.

Miss Bodkin shook her head, defeated. For all that she could make of it, it might have been so much gibberish that Dame Eleanor was talking at the other end. There was nothing for it, therefore, but for her to withdraw altogether from this world of shadows. But she was reckoning without the bright light of old Mr. Chitt. Leaning forward suddenly he placed his mouth right up against her patent acoustic box on the table.

"Boiler!" he shouted.

Miss Bodkin jerked back, startled. The instrument had not managed to make the word out; it had come simply as an explosion, a concussion right inside her head.

"Good gracious," she said, looking resentfully in Mr. Chitt's direction.

Dame Eleanor glanced down at her watch. Because she wore it pinned closely to her bosom she had to contort herself to see the face. And what she saw alarmed her. At this rate, her other meetings—the Junior League of Innocence, the Unmarried Mothers, the NAVPTCW—would all be upon her before the ancient Miss Bodkin had understood. She turned to Dr. Trump.

47

"Write it down for her," she said.

Dr. Trump caught Dame Eleanor's eye and smiled understandingly. Then taking out the gold-sheathed fountain-pen that had been presented to him by the troop of the Boys' Brigade that he had once commanded, he wrote rapidly in his large, cursive script on a piece of scribble-paper.

"Would you mind passing this to Miss Bodkin?" he asked Mr. Chigwell.

"I'm so sorry," Mr. Chigwell replied meaninglessly, and passed it.

Meanwhile Dame Eleanor's eye had roved suspiciously farther down the Agenda.

"We had better come back to this one later," she observed. "It seems to be a general extravagance competition this morning. What is the meaning of item number three, Dr. Trump?"

Dr. Trump consulted his own copy of the Agenda.

"Improved facilities in the senior girls' lavatory," he began.

"I can read, thank you, Dr. Trump," Dame Eleanor told him. "I want to know what it means?"

"It was the Matron who asked for them," Dr. Trump explained.

Dame Eleanor turned her glance full on him.

"That still doesn't tell me what it means," she replied.

Dr. Trump felt Canon Larkin's gaze fastening itself on him as well, and his blush returned.

"It's . . . it's fittings, I believe," he said miserably.

Dame Eleanor was now glaring at him.

"Basins or pans?"

Before he could reply, however, Miss Bodkin had spoken.

"Why does Dr. Trump want a new boiler?" she asked.

"He doesn't," Dame Eleanor snapped back at her. "Not now."

"Oh, but he does," Miss Bodkin persisted. "He says so here in his own handwriting."

Dame Eleanor tapped hard on the table with her pencil.

"Order, Order," she said. "We're dealing with item three now. Senior girls' lavatories."

Miss Bodkin uttered a deep sigh.

"But why should they want a boiler in a lavatory?" she asked. "It seems a great deal of money."

"They're not going to be given one," Dame Eleanor assured her.

48

For a moment the little box responded nicely. And the information appeared to pacify Miss Bodkin.

"Oh, I didn't know it was being given," she replied. "That's different. Is it Dr. Trump who's giving it?"

She turned her head in his direction as she said the words, and smiled gratefully on behalf of her ancestor. Dr. Trump shook his head and made a gesture of disavowal with his hands. Already, however, Mr. Chitt had anticipated him. Leaning forward once more towards Miss Bodkin's apparatus, he addressed it loudly.

"No boiler," he shouted.

This time her acoustic instrument worked perfectly.

"Then why has Dr. Trump changed his mind?" she insisted. "It all seems very sudden."

Dr. Trump recognised this for his opportunity. He would sort out this misunderstanding and Dame Eleanor would admire him for it. Rising from his place, he went down to the far end of the table and pointed with his forefinger at the items on Miss Bodkin's Agenda paper.

"Not item two, Miss Bodkin," he said, speaking slowly and clearly as though Miss Bodkin were lip-reading. "Three. *Three.*"

There was a brief pause.

"Three boilers?" Miss Bodkin asked. "All in one lavatory?"

It was then that Canon Larkin intervened. He had a fine rich voice that in its time had filled cathedrals. Clearing his throat, he spoke over the head of Mr. Chigwell.

"We've left the question of the boiler," he explained. "This is something new."

Miss Bodkin's frown of puzzlement returned.

"But it can't just be something new," she pointed out. "It must be a new *something.*"

"Basins," Canon Larkin boomed back at her.

"Or pans," Dame Eleanor interjected. "Dr. Trump doesn't seem to know which."

Canon Larkin pursed up his lips again.

"Then I move that the matter be put back till the next meeting for Dr. Trump to investigate," Canon Larkin replied tersely.

"Do you hear that, Dr. Trump?" Dame Eleanor asked him. "*Investigate.*"

"I will ask the Matron," Dr. Trump replied.

49

He resented Canon Larkin's attitude and was deliberately cold in the manner of his reply.

But Dame Eleanor would have none of it.

"Nonsense, man," she said. "Go and look for yourself. You're in charge here."

She paused and continued to stare hard at him. Dr. Trump found himself wriggling. Then Dame Eleanor resumed.

"I'm afraid, my friend, you're being hoodwinked," she told him. "They're taking advantage of you."

Dr. Trump's hands were tightly clasped together. The knuckle joints showed white under the strain.

"You mean about the . . . the lavatories?" he asked anxiously.

"And about the boilers. And all the rest of it. You're here to curb expenditure, Dr. Trump. Not to encourage it."

Everyone turned again in his direction, and looked accusingly at the spendthrift. Even Miss Bodkin turned too and thrust out the black acoustic box in his direction for the least whisper that might reach her. Like an echo from across a valley she had just caught the one word "boilers."

"It's always the same with an unmarried man," Dame Eleanor went on. "They're on to him in a pack. They were with Canon Mallow. What you need is someone who can see through them."

"You . . . you mean an assistant?" Dr. Trump asked eagerly.

"I mean a wife," Dame Eleanor retorted. "Someone to put an end to all this nonsense. What this place needs is discipline."

CHAPTER V

ALONE IN his study—the desk was the right way round by now and the electric light had a new bulb in it—Dr. Trump was reading a letter. He had only just begun it, but already a twinge of irritation had run right through him.

"But why did he have to write at all?" he asked himself. "Surely he must realise how busy I am. How can he imagine that I care how he spends his retirement?"

But Canon Mallow could easily have imagined it. After all

50

such a lot of interesting things had been happening to him. For a start, because he had been forced to go back with the keys of the Hospital, he had very nearly missed his train. And, in the result, there was less than two minutes to spare at Waterloo. Less than two minutes, that is, after the caboodle of luggage—the two tin boxes, the leather trunk, the wicker hamper, the hold-all, the suitcases and the religious pictures—had been safely stowed away in the guard's van.

On any showing, it had been cutting things pretty fine. Too fine, in fact. Because, in his excitement, Canon Mallow had forgotten that his book and his tin of tobacco were in the suitcase and there was no way of getting at them until the train reached Portsmouth. In consequence, there had been nothing for him to do the whole way down except stare out of the window and sit polishing and re-polishing the two presentation pipes that nestled together like unborn twins in the velvet and morocco leather fastness of their case. He had tried them in his mouth once or twice, carefully turning his head away so that the other occupants of the carriage should not see that he was only playing at smoking. But it was no use: without tobacco even the best of pipes, even selected straight grains with a silver band round the waistline, taste simply of fresh varnish and wet vulcanite.

And, while he was sitting there, he had wondered more than once why he was going to Portsmouth at all. In a sense, he knew, of course. It was because you can't go to Seaview without going to Portsmouth first: that's where the ferry starts. But why Seaview? Why the Isle of Wight at all, in fact?

The answer was simple. It was all because of a cutting from an ecclesiastical newspaper which advertised a room in a house called Balaclava. It sounded such an extraordinarily nice sort of room, overlooking the garden with a view of the sea beyond—Canon Mallow had already pictured the whole thing, the sloping lawns, the blue ocean set in a little bay, the white yachts, the glinting dancing waves, the great liners passing. And that was not the end of it. There was full board and service as well, all thrown in for three guineas a week.

But that wasn't a bit the way things worked out. Because, just when the sea air and the change and the cup of coffee on the ferry had made him feel better than he had felt for years, he suddenly folded right up. As the landlady opened the front door of Balaclava to receive her visitor—and having caught the train and the steamer and the tram and the taxi and all the rest of it, he was dead on time—she was confronted by a mass of luggage with the two pictures on top, and a sagging clerical figure who asked if she would mind if he sat down on the front steps for a few moments because he had come over a bit faint.

After that, she got him straight up to bed without giving him a chance of taking so much as a glimpse at the garden. And, once in bed, Canon Mallow remained there. Thursday, Friday, Saturday all passed quietly and uneventfully, except for minor interruptions like cups of tea and Bovril, and toast and hot-water bottles. Not that he was thirsty or hungry or even cold. Just tired. Tired out, in fact. And beautifully sleepy. He kept pulling the bedclothes up closer to his chin and saying to himself: " Just another forty winks and I'll get up and take a look at the place. No point in rushing it. Far better to have my sleep out."

It was the same, too, on Sunday. It wasn't until after lunchtime on Monday that he felt fit enough to put on his dressing-gown and slippers and sit for half an hour or so in the arm-chair by the window.

He saw then that he hadn't missed much by not sitting out in the garden: it was very small, and appeared to be mostly wire trellis and crushed sea-shells, with two rustic seats that did not look as though they had been seriously designed for sitting on. The sea was there right enough: it was an inverted triangle between two roof tops, and it was khaki coloured. Besides that, it was raining. Quite fast, too. While he had been skulking in bed there must have been a real thorough drenching on the island . . . Then he pulled himself up abruptly. "Good gracious," he exclaimed aloud. "I haven't written to Dr. Trump. There's such a lot I've got to tell him."

In the end, it was towards the end of the week—Friday, in fact—when Canon Mallow finally got down to the letter. And, even then, he did not really feel equal to it. In consequence, it was a rambling, disconnected sort of letter, not a bit like the urgent, incisive note that he had meant to send.

" *Dear Dr. Trump,*" it ran, " *I would have written sooner but for the fact that I unfortunately caught a slight chill and have been confined to bed ever since. I am now about* again though still a trifle shaky, and have seen enough of Seaview to be able to tell what a delightful little place it is. The pier by Priory Bay is, I am told, the only suspension pier in the whole country, though I believe Brighton once had one. Considering the time of year, the weather is quite mild though the mornings are very sharp. Yesterday before breakfast I saw someone bathing.

With so much on your hands I am sure that you must be very busy. I should have warned you that one of the ropes in the gymnasium is very frayed and not to be relied on. I think it is the one on the left by the door, but no doubt you could check this: we certainly don't want an accident and I meant to mention it before I left. Also, the contract for the liquid soap we use in the laundry comes up for renewal in January and Canon Larkin thinks that we might get a reduction. No doubt he will speak to you himself, but it's worth remembering. The matter, however, about which I really wanted to write to you is the little boy whom we all call Ginger. I've always been interested in him because, as you will discover, whenever anything goes wrong it's usually safe to assume that Ginger is at the bottom of it—at least so I always found. Not that he is, in the least, mischievous, only adventurous. He is exactly the kind of boy who really needs a father to steer and direct him and I would be particularly grateful if you could spare the time to keep a personal eye on him. High spirits of his kind are far too precious to be wasted and I am not sure if Mr. Dawlish really appreciates them. Provided that Ginger is guided rather than driven I am confident that he is a leader in the making and that is exactly what our country needs. There are one or two other matters which I meant to refer to when I was writing, but I cannot at the moment recall them. I will write again when they come back into my mind.

Wishing you every success in your important work and assuring you at any time of any help that I can render,

Yours sincerely,

Edward Mallow.

PS.—Give my love to little Sweetie. I have a particularly soft spot in my heart for Sweetie and I feel sure that she will grow into a very charming little girl who will be a credit to the Hospital."

It was only after he had sent the letter that Canon Mallow

began to have doubts about it. For a start, he wondered whether Dr. Trump would be interested in the bit about the suspension pier. And hadn't he been a bit untactful in referring to the Hospital as though he were still a member of it? But what was worse, he began to wonder whether he had really done Ginger much of a service by drawing attention to him at all. Might it not even prejudice him, and make Dr. Trump suspicious and unduly on the alert where Ginger was concerned? He could not now remember exactly what it was that he had said. And because the letter had been posted he could not refer to it. He began to wish now that he had not sent it at all. And wasn't that reference to Mr. Dawlish a bit disloyal to an old colleague? It made the man sound like a monster.

As for Dr. Trump, he sat at his desk with the letter in one hand and the other tapping irritatedly on the arm of his chair.

"Can't the man understand that he is a back number already?" he asked himself. "Is he proposing to pester me indefinitely?"

CHAPTER VI

In the bed a child is lying. She is an angry child. And because she is angry she is taut and rigid, with her fingers clenched. Her arms are bent, and her rounded fists are faintly visible over the top of the bedclothes. On her cheeks the splashes of tears still glisten in the light of the one gasmantle that has been left burning. But she is not crying now. She is far too angry to cry. She just lies there alone, angry and unsleeping.

All the other children in the ward are asleep. Have been asleep for hours. The sound of their breathing fills the room, rising and falling in unison as though even in sleep they are well trained and disciplined. This one little girl is the only rebel among them. A fiery and self-consumed anarchist, not quite three feet high.

Usually at this time of night if she wakes up she is frightened. The ward looks so long. And wide. And high. It seems to extend for ever, going on and on from the glow of light of the one gas-burner into a world of complete outer darkness. It is black night itself that reigns at the far end.

And when the lights are out children in the other beds look strange somehow. Not like children at all. One of them, the little girl with thick curly hair, is a sheep-dog. Next to her, with the snub of her nose just showing, is a pig. And, in the bed beyond, the little girl with the clothes humped over her, is a bear. A sheep-dog, a pig and a bear. They are horrid companions for bedfellows. And once seen they are generally too frightening for her to be able to go off to sleep again.

Luckily she can't see the little girl opposite her. That one is a particularly alarming little girl: she breathes growlingly and turns into a leopard as soon as the lights go out. She is probably a leopard at this moment. But the angry little girl isn't bothered by her to-night because she is lying on her back and her feet make two mounds in the bedclothes that cut the leopard clean off from sight. Besides she is far too angry to feel frightened by anything to-night.

How can so small a child be so angry? What is it that makes her draw her legs up to her chin and then thrust them straight out again, thin and bony, towards the bottom of the bed? It is injustice. A cruel injustice that she has had inflicted on her. An injustice from which there is no appeal because everyone, the other little girls, the day-nurse and the night-sister are all in a conspiracy against her.

The cause of the trouble is a pink plush rabbit. There isn't more than this one pink plush rabbit in the whole world. That's what makes it so precious. And how would you feel about it if just such a rabbit had been taken away from you by force? How would you feel if you had been held screaming while thick fingers prised open your arms and snatched your cherished, your favourite, in fact your one and only piece of personal property from you? Well, that is just what had happened less than six hours ago to this little girl.

It is because she is all alone and unbefriended that she has got to do something about it herself. And she means to do it. First she has to get out of bed. This isn't easy because the bedclothes have been tucked in so tight. But at last she manages it and, businesslike and deliberate, she slides down on to the floor.

Now that she is standing up you can see what a skinny child she is. Her black hair is plaited into two rats' tails that stick out over her shoulders and her small face is grave and anxious-looking. She goes over to the hook where her clothes are hanging—the blue cape and red hood of the Hospital—

but they are too high up for her to reach. She can't even reach up to the shelf that holds her vest and knickers and the rolled-up black stockings. There is nothing for it, therefore, but to set out as she is in her long flannel nightgown.

The only things she can reach are her shoes which are on the floor underneath the shelf. And, without stockings, these feel ice-cold and sloppy as she puts them on.

Then she sets off down the main avenue of oilcloth between the double row of beds. It is to the far end of the ward that she is going, away from the light; and this means passing quite close to the sheep-dog, the pig and the bear. In her sleep the bear girl is growling faintly and, under the bed-clothes, her limbs are moving as though she is getting ready to spring.

But the little girl gets past her safely. She goes on, slop-slopping in her big clumsy shoes. At the far end of the ward is the door—the door leading to the corridor with the door of the playroom on the other side. It is in the cupboard of the playroom that the pink plush rabbit has been put away. And it is to this cupboard that the little girl is going.

The door opens silently and the moonlight shining in through the slanting window in the roof makes the corridor bright and empty-looking. It is a specially cold kind of light that the moon gives, and the little girl suddenly realises that she is shivering. Her teeth are chattering and her nightgown that had seemed so warm in bed now doesn't seem to have any warmth in it at all. But she keeps on across the corridor. And then, for a moment, she pauses to listen. Someone is breathing. Slow, heavy breathing as though the person who is breathing ought to have her nose blown for her. It is the night-sister's breathing. And she is in the conspiracy, the night-sister. She is on the other side. An enemy.

The door of the playroom opens just as easily as the door of the night-ward; and the little girl goes in. The windows here face full on to the moonlight and the room looks even colder and emptier than the corridor. But it is easy to find the cupboard and straightaway the little girl begins to drag a chair over to it. She doesn't pause to think about the noise she is making because, in a moment now, the pink plush rabbit will be in her arms, and everything will be all right again. She can feel the feel of him already.

But the cupboard door is locked. All that she can do is to rattle it. And that makes the chair wobble. And rattling and wobbling won't do any good. Realising suddenly that she has

56

lost, it all comes back to her—the injustice, the wickedness, the true sin of what has happened. Only it is not simply despair this time. It is revenge that is eating up her heart inside her.

She can't hit the night-sister because she is too big. It is Susan that she can hit. And she means to do it. Because Susan was behind it all. If Susan hadn't cried because she had toothache, the day-nurse would never have thought of giving her the pink rabbit to comfort her. And the night-sister wouldn't have let her have it afterwards while she was waiting for her bath. It wasn't even as though Susan usually played with the pink rabbit. She is a thief, is little Susan. A mean, nasty, horrible thief. And she is going to be punished.

So the little girl goes back in her direction. Slip-slop in her big walking-shoes she goes across the empty corridor and back into the night-ward with the solitary gas-mantle burning at the far end. It is easy to find Susan's bed. It is the second one from the end, next to the pig-girl's. And as soon as she gets there she goes up to Susan, the girl with the toothache, and does the most dreadful thing she knows. She pinches her in the face with her finger-nails.

Then appalled by the awfulness of what she has done, she bursts out crying. She simply stands there in the dim ward, her pig-tails sticking out and her outdoor shoes, her clod-hoppers, showing under the hem of her nightgown, crying at the top of her voice. The ward looks bigger than ever now. And because the little girl has left the door open there is a draught, and the shadow of the gas-bracket keeps twisting round like a big worm on the ceiling. She isn't angry or revengeful any more, this little girl. She is simply cold. And miserable. And very frightened.

Susan is awake too. She doesn't know what has happened. But at the sound of the little girl's crying, and because her face hurts her, she cries too. Then the pig-girl starts. A moment later there is the sound of someone in the corridor and the night-sister comes in pulling her dressing-gown around her. She catches sight of the little girl by the bed and whisks over to her.

"You bad, naughty little girl," she says. "How dare you get out of bed. I declare you're more trouble than all the others put together."

She snatches hold of her under the arm-pits and starts back down the ward with her. The little girl is too wretched to resist and just hangs there in her arms boo-hooing.

57

" I'll tell Matron about you," the night-sister goes on. " You're a wicked child and you've got to be punished."

When she reaches the little girl's bed she thrusts her back under the bedclothes and tucks them down so tightly that escape is impossible.

" And stop that silly noise," she says. " You'll wake up Dr. Trump."

Then she goes across to comfort poor Susan and the pig-girl.

The little girl turns her head to one side and lies there watching her. The moon has moved round a bit and her pillow is full in the moonlight now. We can see her face quite plainly. And we have met her before. Known her practically from birth in fact. She's the little girl who was left on the doorstep, the one who helped to keep the numbers up.

She's Sweetie. And she's getting on for four. Must be just about four, in fact. Within a week or so either way.

Could be her birthday to-day, for that matter.

CHAPTER VII

I

EVERYTHING that Dame Eleanor had said to Dr. Trump had rankled. There had been two more board-meetings since then, each one as bad as the last. And the words of advice, of instruction even, with which he had come away remained in his mind, pricking and wounding him like a hedgehog.

" I'll show 'em," he told himself vulgarly. " I'll show 'em whether I can run a children's home, or not." And then remembering his vocation, his calling, he re-phrased his intentions: " With God's help, I will redouble my efforts. I will reveal myself as not unworthy."

The trouble was that he was feeling tired. It had been a long session, and the ledgers spread out on the big mahogany desk in front of him went back a full ten years into history, right back to nineteen-seventeen, in fact. As he had turned over the pages, his nostrils had been filled with the leathery mustiness of sheer antiquity. But even now he couldn't feel sure that he had really got to the bottom of it, that he wasn't being bamboozled about the shortages.

There they were, accusingly set forth in his clear, angular handwriting, and he started to read them through again:

137 pairs boys' cotton underpants
224 girls' vests (small)
139 girls' vests (medium)
127 girls' vests (large)
218 girls' nightdresses (medium)
136 . . .

But after that he could restrain himself no further. Spearing downwards with his pencil point on to the cotton underpants, he raised his eyes and addressed Mrs. Gurnett. She was placed exactly opposite to him, bolt upright upon the hard carved chair on the far side.

"They can't have vanished," he said. "They can't have walked away. They can't have been eaten. Therefore they must have been lost. Or stolen."

"Or worn out," Mrs. Gurnett snapped back at him.

There was an interval during which Dr. Trump's dark, deep-set eyes stared unwaveringly into Mrs. Gurnett's resentful grey ones. Then he spoke again.

"If they were worn out as you put it," he said, "why weren't they entered in the replacement ledger?" He paused. "One hundred and thirty-seven pairs of anything is . . . one hundred and thirty-seven pairs, you know," he added with indisputable logic.

The crescent of Mrs. Gurnett's mouth turned down lower still at the corners. Her shoulders were squared defiantly and her hands lay tightly clenched in her lap. The whole body was held rigid and immovable. But, to relieve her feelings, she was twiddling her thumbs. It was a habit that annoyed Dr. Trump and made him determined, at some suitable moment, of course, to speak to her about it.

"It's over ten years," she replied stoutly. "Don't forget that."

Dr. Trump drew his breath in sharply.

"If it was over a hundred years, one hundred and thirty-seven pairs would still be one hundred and thirty-seven pairs," he replied, wishing that Dame Eleanor could hear him. Then he braced himself. "I'm afraid there has been carelessness."

"Meaning me?"

The words had come darting out at him like a stab from a

jack-knife. He was astonished, positively astonished, that there could be so much malice and vindictiveness in any woman. But he was ready, and more than ready for the assault. He parried the blow neatly, not even showing that he had been aware that he had been struck.

"Meaning the system," he replied quietly. "The entire miserable system my predecessor left behind him."

He paused and, sitting back in his chair, held his pencil horizontally like a handlebar.

"What is lacking," he said, "is supervision. Real, proper, thorough supervision."

As he said the word, it struck him suddenly as being a beautiful word. There was an augustness about it that overwhelmed him. And, warming to the subject, he resumed.

"With adequate supervision, things will no longer disappear," he observed. "And the supervision will certainly be adequate, because I intend to provide it myself. In future I shall do *everything.*"

He waited long enough for the meaning of the words to penetrate into this deeply obstinate woman and, as he sat there, he wished again that Dame Eleanor could have been there to hear. And not only Dame Eleanor, Canon Larkin. Yes, certainly Canon Larkin. Even Miss Bodkin. It was, in fact, one of those supreme moments when Dr. Trump wished that everyone could hear, wished that the entire world might know that a new supervising Messiah had been born to them.

But he had been forgetting about Mrs. Gurnett. He was quite shocked to see her still sitting there, regarding him with a fixed and painful hostility.

"Everything," he repeated pointedly.

"Then you don't need me," Mrs. Gurnett replied firmly.

Dr. Trump started. This was alarming, most alarming. The very last thing that he wanted was a resignation. One resignation might lead to a spate: there could be no end to it. Ultimately he might even find himself left simply with that dreadful Mr. Prevarius. Besides, to the uninitiated—the Board, for example—it would look as though he couldn't manage people.

"But I do," he assured her quietly. "Who am I to decide whether . . . cotton vests are worn out or not?"

Mrs. Gurnett, however, merely grunted. There was no recognition, no response at all, to the generousness—the deliberate over-generousness—and humility that he had just displayed.

"Do you still want to supervise?" was all she asked.

And here Dr. Trump recognised his opportunity. Now that he had shown that he could be magnanimous, the moment had come to demonstrate that he could also be resolute. And firmness, he knew, paid handsome dividends always, none handsomer.

"I do," he replied. "That is why I have been asked to come here."

It was presumably because of this last remark that, forty minutes later, there was a knock on the door. It was one of the laundresses—a big, strapping girl almost indelicately over-developed, Dr. Trump could not help noticing—who stood there. She had a large bundle in her arms. Ah, the study antimacassars, Dr. Trump told himself. But he was wrong. They were not antimacassars; they were twelve pairs of girls' vests (large), with a note from Mrs. Gurnett asking him to put his hand inside any one of them and decide whether they should be thrown away or not.

As he read the note, Dr. Trump instinctively stepped back from so unsavoury a parcel. Thrust his hand into a large girl's vest, indeed. The very idea was odious, utterly odious. But wasn't it also ironical? Wasn't there something of the heartache of the saints, the practical ones, in such a situation? To think that all his reading, his study, his prayer, his contemplation, should have brought him to this, simply because he had turned—administrator.

Spreading out his hands in the manner of someone shoo-ing chickens, he addressed his visitor.

"Take them away, foolish girl," he said sharply. "What do you suppose I am—a rag-merchant?"

Then, when the over-developed laundress had left him, he sat down to write one of his considered, carefully-worded letters to Mrs. Gurnett. It was a good letter and it looked well, too, on the note-paper with the black gothic-type line, Warden's Office, at the top.

But, best of all, was the last sentence that began: "*I do not ask for an apology because no offence was, I am sure, intended. Nevertheless, if after reflection you yourself without any prompting from me should feel . . .*"

Yes, Dame Eleanor had been right. More than anything else—more than the new lavatories on the girls' side, the extra lighting in the Great Hall, the re-pointing of the Cranmer block, the moulded hygienic flooring of the nursery wing, the raised pedestal for the Archbishop's statue, or even the re-opening of the Founder's Tower itself—what the Hospital really needed was discipline.

And the more he said the word over to himself, the more beautiful it sounded. There was almost a semi-spiritual ring to it. Discipline—order—beauty—truth; he saw the whole thing at last as a kind of sacred and devout procession.

And like all the great verities there was so much contained within the word. It embraced everything: the laundry accounts, the "Keep off the Grass" notices; the fire precautions; early morning handkerchief drill; silence in corridors; smoking, other than in the masters' common room—Dr. Trump had wondered if later perhaps the principle could not be carried further and the whole ash-laden nuisance be extirpated for ever; the proper care of fingernails throughout the whole school; the length of the girls' hair; the exact hours for choir practice—Mr. Prevarius, Dr. Trump had noticed, seemed to have a somewhat Chinese sense of time; and, of course, above all behaviour in the classroom—attention during lessons; no note-passing; no decoration on the covers of exercise-books; no paper darts; no blotting-paper pellets that had been soaked in ink-wells; and, certainly, no ragging.

He had examined the masters specifically on this kind of point, deliberately not mincing his words. Could they or could they not keep order? he had bluntly asked. Did they or did they not experience trouble as soon as their backs were turned? And he was bound to admit that the answers that he had received had not been entirely reassuring.

Admittedly Mr. Prevarius's reply—" Oh, no trouble at all, my dear sir. A boy who is truly occupied, mentally and physically, is never any trouble "—had been all that he could have hoped for. But, unfortunately, he did not believe Mr. Prevarius.

And as for the rest of them, they were such a wretched

lot. Mr. Dawlish, for instance, had created a most unfavourable impression. Dr. Trump had been compelled to ask him to remove what appeared to be egg-stains from his waistcoat. Also, though it was really too absurd to have to correct a grown man in this way, he had been forced to ask him to clean the lenses of his spectacles and make himself look generally more energetic, more sprightly, more commanding.

It was then that the truth had come out just as Dr. Trump had always thought it would. Mr. Dawlish *did* have trouble. And there was one small boy, Ginger—the boy whom Canon Mallow had mentioned—who apparently gave most of it. Dr. Trump resolutely made a note of him while he allowed Mr. Dawlish—dirty, smeary Mr. Dawlish—to continue. Then as Mr. Dawlish paused for breath—he was naturally a wheezing, disjointed kind of speaker—Dr. Trump interrupted.

"Keep your eye on him," he said sternly. "If there is anything further of this kind, I am quite ready to make an example of Master Woods if necessary."

The conversation came back to him at this moment as he sat in his study soaking his ginger-nuts in his tea before eating them. There was nothing actually wrong with any of his teeth. He was quite satisfied in his own mind that, if he wanted to, he could bite cleanly and incisively through any ginger-nut that the manufacturers might set before him. It was simply a sensible precaution, this softening process. Besides, it slowed up the meal and assisted thought. At this moment, for instance, while he soaked and sucked, he saw the future most plainly. Saw a chastened and reformed Master Woods after what would obviously have to be the inevitable caning.

He had never caned anyone before and he, somehow, wasn't looking forward to it. To lash with the tongue until the victim quailed and whimpered—that was one thing. But to flog with a flexible stick—that was somehow too much like admitting intellectual defeat. Nevertheless, if discipline demanded it of him, he would tan the hide off every boy that he had under him.

He had finished the last of the ginger-nuts by now and, carefully stacking up the tea things, he went over to the corner cupboard that was also his armoury. There in the corner stood the cane. After a moment's hesitation he took hold of it and proceeded to examine it. It was both thicker

63

and more springy than he had imagined. Altogether, in fact, it looked a brutally effective sort of instrument.

Then, idly at first, he began swishing with it. But that taught him nothing—except perhaps to avoid the dangerous backlash, the recoil. If he really wanted to experiment, he would have to hit *something*. A cushion possibly.

And why not a cushion? There was one, a red velvet one, on the settee in the corner. And, crossing the room with the cane tucked smartly under his arm, he picked it up and arranged the cushion carefully across the seat of one of the chairs. Then he removed his coat and rolled his sleeves up. He was engrossed, utterly engrossed, in this piece of practice by now. And he spat on his hand before attempting to get his grip right.

"Six of the best, I think we said," he observed to the empty air above the chair. "And if the treatment is not effective it can be repeated."

"Six of the best!"

There was a classic ring about it, and he repeated the words, louder and more menacingly.

Then he began.

"One!"

Pause.

"Two!"

Pause.

"Three!"

He was breathing more heavily by now. And the veins in his forehead were beginning to pulsate. But he persisted.

"Four!"

It was just as he was about to deliver the fifth blow—the cane was raised and his teeth were clenched fast in readiness —when he heard somebody address him. And it was not merely the sound of his name that had startled him: it was the voice that had spoken it. It was Mr. Prevarius's.

And Dr. Trump remembered now. He had been so grossly dissatisfied with the look of Mr. Prevarius's register that he had told the obnoxious man to bring it over to his study for inspection.

"It *was* nine-thirty you said, wasn't it, Doctor?" Mr. Prevarius was asking, his eye upon the study clock which now showed nine thirty-one. "I trust that I am not interrupting you."

CHAPTER VIII

I

THE EPISODE of the caning had pleased Mr. Prevarius. All the week he had felt better because of it. And now he felt best of all. That was because it was Wednesday: and Wednesday was Mr. Prevarius's half-day.

From 11.30 when he had finished with the Mixed Juniors —boys one side, girls the other, with Mr. Prevarius himself at the piano in the middle—the rest of the day was his own. There was, therefore, really no reason why at 11.35 or so he should not have shot off down the asphalt walk towards the front entrance. He was a free man, until 10.30 p.m. when the gates closed. But was he? The last time he tried to slip away before lunch he had run full into Dr. Trump. And Dr. Trump had raised his eyebrows. Merely that. But they were remarkably expressive eyebrows, and Mr. Prevarius had understood.

Therefore, he now stayed, sullen and unnecessary, and ate his Wednesday lunch at the high table in the Great Hall with Dr. Trump seated idol-like at the head. But Wednesday was more than Mr. Prevarius's half-day: it was also the cook's. In consequence, it was cold corned beef and tapioca pudding that was always served. And, as he ate it, Mr. Prevarius thought longingly of the dainties that he would be eating before the night was out.

To-day in particular the tapioca seemed more nauseating than usual. It oozed. It gleamed at him. It adhered. At this very moment his teeth, his tongue, the entire roof of his mouth were all glued solidly together with the stuff. Then, accidentally, he caught Dr. Trump's eye at the far end of the table. Removing the spoon, which came away from his mouth with a tell-tale kiss-like sound, he smiled obediently at his Warden. The smile was not returned.

"To-morrow. And to-morrow. And to-morrow," Mr. Prevarius remarked cryptically to himself. "But not necessarily, thank God, the day after that. Then just watch the balloon go up."

And, dutifully scraping his plate, he sat there with head bent, waiting for Dr. Trump to say the closing grace.

But he was free now all right. And, as the iron gate clanged behind him he allowed himself a little two-step of sheer delight. For a moment he became young again. His life still had a future. Then he remembered: he had no future. The elderberry wine had seen to that. No future and Dr. Trump had asked to see him to-morrow about extra choir-practice. His pace slackened. He slouched rather than walked and his music-case—it was a large, limp leather one of the kind carried by mistresses in select girls' schools—swung despondently at the end of his long thin arm.

He did not recover his spirits, in fact, until he had got to the bottom of St. Mark's Avenue. That marked the 74 bus route. In one direction it led merely to the river and places where people went for walks. There was nothing there for Mr. Prevarius. But in the other direction it led to London, the real London, the London of the West End and the Marble Arch; the London of decent restaurants and obscure, snug cafés; the London of mysterious women in shadowy door-ways and little snatches of overheard, fascinating conversations; the London where he wasn't known and could move freely; the London of pleasures and obscurity; the London of Mr. Prevarius's accommodation address.

It was to this address that he was going now and he could hardly wait to get there. There would be something for him —he felt sure of that. But what? Perhaps . . .

" Fares, please."

It was Mr. Musk's voice that had spoken in his ear and Mr. Prevarius started.

"Oh, a fivepenny, please," he said. "From the . . . er Clock Tower."

Then as the ticket was punched and handed to him, Mr. Prevarius relaxed. It was not strictly true that bit about the Clock Tower. From where Mr. Prevarius had got on was really a sixpenny. But on an income like his, he had to be careful. Not that Mr. Musk noticed. Mrs. Musk had, if anything, been rather worse lately. There were now her delusions as well as her pains to contend with.

By the time the bus had reached Oxford Street, Mr. Prevarius's spirit was riding high. But it was an anxious spirit, nevertheless. There was a keyed-up, highly-strung sort of feeling inside him as though at any moment something would snap. And when the bus drew up near Bourne and Hollingsworth, he was biting his nails from sheer excitement. He was within a couple of hundred yards of his destination by now and in five minutes he would know. As he hurried down Berners Street, the slouch developed into a lope.

17a Leak Street was the address for which he was making. He had written it so many times at the top of sheets of cheap note-paper that he knew it by heart. At times, he almost felt that he really lived there. Not that there was anything in particular to commend Leak Street. It lay in the very heart of the north island of Soho, and the traffic that flowed along the broad rivers of Oxford Street and Tottenham Court Road knew nothing of these forlorn, forgotten jungles. The street was full of small dejected shops, and there were children playing in the gutters.

No. 17a itself was a disappointment, a disappointment in a street of disappointments. It was only half a shop and the slice of window that it had retained was filled by a board of small advertisements. To recover his breath, Mr. Prevarius paused and started to read: " Reliable woman wants work, mornings only "; " Deal chest of drawers, cheap "; " Feathers any quantity, distance no object "; " Artificial flowers, experience not necessary "; " Widow where child aged three not objected to . . ." Mr. Prevarius winced. Whichever way he turned, the sadness of life seemed to be pressing in on him.

Then he went inside past the rack of magazines and periodicals and stood there, peering across the counter that had bottles of ink and toy balloons displayed upon it. The little grey-haired woman with the knitted cardigan pinned across her bosom came out of the back room and smiled at him.

" Good-afternoon, Mr. Cavendish," she said.

Mr. Prevarius smiled. He enjoyed the sensation of being somebody different, someone else. And then the irony of it occurred to him: he didn't know the little old lady's name himself. While he had assumed a pseudonym, a nom-de-guerre, a false address, this ancient creature by remaining where she was in her own shop had beaten him at his own game. She was utterly anonymous.

" Good-afternoon, Mrs. . . ."

" Sixpence, please. Threepence on each," she replied. And in her hand she held out two envelopes addressed to B. Cavendish, Esq.

He had only one plan now: to read the letters. But he was careful, deliberately careful. He wanted to do nothing that might appear rushed or over-eager. Therefore he paused for a moment and addressed the little old lady a second time.

"And a bottle of ink: the twopenny size, please," he said.

"Blue-black?" the little old lady asked him.

"No. Plain blue, please. The pale kind. And two thin nibs."

He opened the letters in the entrance to a side courtyard. It was a sordid spot of cats and dustbins and the sound of quarrelling. But Mr. Prevarius was too much excited by his letters to notice his surroundings.

Not that the first did anything to cheer him. It was from a leading impresario and said merely that the concert trade was down at the moment, and that only pianists of European reputation were being given bookings. The other, however, was decidedly better. So much better, in fact, that Mr. Prevarius whistled. Then he straightened himself.

"Charing Cross Road," he murmured. "Couldn't be better. We will go and visit him."

II

No two streets in London are exactly the same. And when you see the Charing Cross Road you feel glad they aren't.

It's a queer, disordered sort of thoroughfare, the Charing Cross Road, narrow at each end with a bulge like a tuber down by the National Portrait Gallery and a circus where five other streets come together just after the thing gets started. No real continuity, nothing consistent; not even straight. And it suffers from the same lack of purpose in its occupations. It sets out quite openly to be the principal book-selling pavement in the capital—and not just new books, novels, paper-backs, whodunits and trash of that kind, but good solid books; stuff that has stood the test of time; sermons, classics, histories; all original binding, half-calf, 24 vols. uncut. Then, just when the victory of culture and antiquity seems conclusive, the present-day keeps breaking in, raucous and irreverent, like a red-hot blast from Broadway. As well as the bookshops, there are five theatres, three cinemas, an underground dance hall, a fun-fair, a shop that sells nude photographs, little half-shops specialising in surgical unmentionables, one or two milk-bars and a great plate-glass emporium full of tenor saxophones, castanets, harmonicas, conductors' batons, chromium-and-mother-of-pearl squeeze boxes, and sheet-music.

Especially, sheet-music. It is on sheet-music, in fact, that the real fortune of Charing Cross Road is founded. There are reams of it, coming off the presses every day ; acre upon acre of minims and crotchets and quavers and strict tempo love-ditties. It is the staple export of the place, like ships from Clydeside or lace from Nottingham. No matter what goes on at street-level, the upper storeys are dedicated to sheet-music. There are suites of rooms where the conversation is of nothing else but hot numbers and lyrics and plugging and close harmony and song-hits. It is one of the lower slopes of Parnassus, this Tin-Pan-Alley of ours, with Terpsichore or her agent, always one flight up.

As Mr. Prevarius looked down the Charing Cross Road, his eyes lit up. After St. Mark's Avenue and the Hospital, it was like finding himself on another and a brighter planet. At the corner of Old Compton Street, for example, there was a coloured gentleman in a white trilby, arm in arm with a lady with a lot of yellow hair. Really, it was magical. It was like getting on the Underground at Oxford Circus only to find that the next station was Marseilles or New Orleans. But still not half so astonishing as to think that Mr. Prevarius really had business there.

He padded rapidly along in his spongy crêpe soles, his black clerical-looking hat pushed on to the back of his head, his music-case swinging agitatedly in the crook of his left arm. And when he reached Arcadia House he was breathless. But it was more than breathlessness that made him utter a deep sigh as he turned inside. It was happiness. Sheer happiness. This, he told himself, was life ; real life ; a secret life of which Dr. Trump and his other tormentors knew nothing.

And right on up to the fourth floor he climbed, past the office of a man who engaged midgets, and another who booked bands, and a third who dealt in juveniles, until he came to a frosted-glass door lettered with the words " Spike Jerome, Music Publishers." Then he went inside.

The hall was also the waiting-room. There were three chairs in office-oak, a square of cord carpet, a pedestal ash-tray and a polished deal table covered with song sheets, like periodicals set out in a club library. The walls, of thin, white-painted woodwork, had panels of frosted-glass mounted above them, and the sound of two or three different conversations all came through at once. A small bell-push on the farther wall was prominently marked: " Ring."

Mr. Prevarius hesitated for a moment. Then he obeyed the notice. But because a telephone bell rang at the same moment, Mr. Prevarius was kept waiting. He was unprepared, in fact, when one of the glass panels was shot suddenly upwards and a girl's head appeared.

" Gottenerpointment?" she asked in a slow, husky drawl as though she had only just got off the boat at Southampton.

" Not exactly," Mr. Prevarius told her. " But Mr. Jerome wishes to see me personally. I have his letter here. ' Cavendish ' is the name."

" Okay," the girl told him. " Takerseaplease."

The glass shutter descended and, through the frosted-glass, Mr. Prevarius could see the girl still sitting there and apparently polishing her nails. He was sorry that she had shut herself off again so suddenly because she looked interesting. Not that there was anything very strange in that. To Mr. Prevarius, all blondes looked interesting.

Because there seemed no immediate prospect of seeing her except through frosted-glass, Mr. Prevarius began to look around him.

He went across to the fumed oak table and began turning over the music library—" Grandmamma's Straw Bonnet," " Honolulu Lulu," " Clinging to the Stars," " You are my Torment," " The Girl with the Icicle Eyes," " Miss Fortune," " Perfume for Two," " Bewilderment." But it was all old stuff. Nothing to fear from that. No serious competition. No discoveries . . .

He was lost in his own thoughts when the shutter lifted for the last time and the girl addressed him.

" Misterome's ready now," she announced indistinctly. She was putting on lip-stick this time and her voice was more muffled and out of focus than ever. " Goritin."

Mr. Jerome was only a small man. Small and bald and harassed-looking. But he wore a vivid American tie as though in an effort to persuade people that he was really a carefree trans-Atlantic sort of dare-devil. And he carried a

70

cigar between his lips for apparently the same reason. During the whole time Mr. Prevarius was there he didn't see him get so much as a puff out of it: Mr. Jerome just kept transferring it from one side of his mouth to the other, and spitting out the portions of leaf that had become detached on the way.

But he knew his business. Shut up there in his little glass and plywood cell with the walls plastered with signed photographs of sleek, ferociously smiling men and drooping, romantic women, he wasted no time in idle courtesies. He got down to things right away.

"Sit down, Mr. . . . er . . . er . . ." he said. "I like that last number of yours."

"'Four o'clock Doll,' you mean?" Mr. Prevarius asked him.

Mr. Jerome nodded.

"It's got something. Catchy little piece if we can get the boys interested."

The cigar suddenly began coming apart so alarmingly that he had to interrupt himself to get rid of the fragments.

"You in a band yourself?" he asked, as soon as he could speak again.

Mr. Prevarius shook his head.

"Not at present," he replied evasively.

"Pity," said Mr. Jerome, frowning. "Know anyone in the B.B.C.?"

"Only on er . . . er . . . the religious side," Mr. Prevarius admitted.

Mr. Jerome was not impressed.

"Wrong department," he said. "Wouldn't help. Have to do everything myself."

"Perhaps I could ask to see some of them," Mr. Prevarius suggested.

Mr. Jerome, however, did not seem impressed.

"Better leave it to me," he advised. He paused.

"Of course, I shall lose money on this, mind you," Mr. Jerome went on.

"I'm sorry," Mr. Prevarius replied, not knowing what else to say.

"Have to keep the royalties low to pay for advertising. No good unless it's properly promoted."

Mr. Prevarius tried to nod understandingly.

"No, no. None at all."

"America O.K.?" Mr. Jerome inquired.

"I understand so," Mr. Prevarius assured him, wondering why Mr. Jerome had changed the subject so suddenly.

"No ties?"

"None whatsoever," Mr. Prevarius replied, still wondering what Mr. Jerome was talking about.

"Any split?"

"Any what?"

"Split. Any helpers? Did you go to anyone for the orchestration?"

"The words," Mr. Prevarius replied slowly, "and the music are mine and mine alone. I . . . I wrote them myself, in fact."

"You'll have to sign the usual," Mr. Jerome told him.

"Naturally," Mr. Prevarius replied. "Would you like me to sign it now?"

The idea appealed to him because he wanted to know what sort of a thing the usual really was.

But Mr. Jerome was not to be rushed.

"Got to get it typed first," he said. Then he looked up. "Berkeley Cavendish your full name?" he asked.

Mr. Prevarius turned his round dark eyes full on him.

"Berkeley *de Vere* Cavendish," he replied slowly. "But I drop the ' de Vere ' for professional purposes."

CHAPTER IX

IT WAS Sweetie's problem. When you are four, the days of the week don't stand out very clearly. Sometimes there seem to be eight of them and sometimes only six. You count up as carefully as you can. And then you find that you have missed a day like Tuesday altogether, or done something silly like counting Sunday twice over.

It had been like that this week. According to Sweetie's calculations it should by rights have been Wednesday. But instead of prayers and arithmetic, and then break and singing and Scripture and needlework, it had turned out as prayers and arithmetic, and then break and *English* and *geography*. And that showed that it couldn't be a Wednesday. Then when the afternoon came and Margaret turned up at the Archbishop Bodkin Hospital, Sweetie realised that it couldn't be Tuesday either. It *must be* Thursday.

And that was lovely. Because as soon as Margaret had

taken off her coat and hat, she would begin the games. But even before the games started, Sweetie was quite happy just standing there watching her. She was so smooth and peaceful-looking. It made Sweetie want to rush up and bury her face in Margaret's skirt. But that would have been silly. The other little girls would have laughed at her. And Sweetie couldn't bear being laughed at.

But Sweetie reminded herself that the other little girls weren't to know what she was *thinking*. Thoughts were private. You could do what you wanted with them. They were a sort of obedient dream. You could have happy endings every time if you wanted things that way. Or you could make yourself so miserable that you nearly cried. Or you could just think about being grown up. That was one of the best thoughts of all. And she had decided, quite firmly and definitely without any chance of ever changing, that as soon as she was old, really old like Margaret, she would wear a long black coat with a little piece of brown fur round the collar and a hat with a thin strip of veiling along the brim and brown kid gloves that she would take off slowly, finger by finger, and then fold them up and put them down beside the hat on top of the piano. It had to be a piano. A dressing-table or a chest-of-drawers wouldn't have done. Because when Sweetie grew up she was going to be exactly like Margaret in everything.

But to-day there was something worrying her. And she knew what it was: it was the English lesson. Not that it was exactly Miss Wynne's fault. Miss Wynne hadn't really got any faults. She was just a flat, grey thing in a drooping knitted suit. She taught lessons. For a long time Sweetie had wondered whether Miss Wynne really knew what she was saying during lesson time. And to-day Sweetie was quite sure that she didn't know. If she had known, she could never have repeated such a horrible story. It was called Snow White. And it was the first time Sweetie had ever heard it.

"So the cruel Queen said to the poor woodman: 'Take my step-daughter out into the forest and kill her,'" Miss Wynne had recited in the same rolled-out, expressionless voice that she used when she was talking about capes and peninsulas, or Moses and Jonah, or simple addition. And Sweetie had shuddered. Because by then Sweetie had already been Snow White herself. From the very first description of her, Sweetie had known that she was the one that Miss Wynne was describing.

73

And Miss Wynne had asked someone to take her away and kill her. As she remembered it, she shuddered again. It was all too dreadful to think about. And none of it could have happened if only her mother hadn't died.

But by now Margaret was speaking, and Sweetie had to listen.

"We'll start with Nuts-in-May," she was saying. "And I shall play for you."

Margaret didn't play very fast. But she played very nicely, Sweetie thought. And, while she played, she talked.

"We don't want all the big ones on one side," she told them. "If we have it like that, everyone will be pulled away."

It seemed a very sensible sort of remark to Sweetie. So she went over and joined the little ones. She knew that, when it came to pulling, she could pull harder than anyone. But Margaret didn't seem to think so. She had stopped playing.

"You go back where you were, Sweetie," she told her. "That only makes it worse. We want some *big* ones to go over."

So Sweetie crossed the floor again, and went on thinking about Snow White's cruel step-mother. The only nice part in the whole story had been the bit about the dwarfs. Sweetie decided that she would like to have seven little men of her own to look after her. One of them could clean her shoes. And one of them could bath her. And one of them could bring her meals on a tray. And one of them could play the piano. And one of them . . .

But Margaret was speaking, and Sweetie couldn't go on thinking about the little men any longer.

"Wake up, Sweetie," she was saying. "Bridget's waiting. She wants to pull you away."

"Pull her away. Pull her away," Sweetie thought. "But if I start pulling I shan't be able to go on thinking about the little men . . ."

"You're not trying, Sweetie," Margaret told her. "You're day-dreaming."

But by then it was too late. Bridget had pulled, and Sweetie had gone over. So far as she was concerned, the game was finished. And she hadn't liked touching Bridget because her hands were so sticky. They had made Sweetie's hands sticky, too. She wiped them on the back of her dress.

It was the saddest of all games that came next. It was Poor Jenny. And Poor Jenny always made Sweetie want to cry, no matter how happy she was feeling. Because even before the music had started Sweetie wasn't just pretending: she *was* Poor Jenny.

And this time it was worse than usual. Because there really was something to be sad about. She kept remembering Snow White and how the cruel step-mother had tried to kill her with a poisoned comb. That was a dreadful thing to do. And it wasn't the end of it. For when the seven little men had taken the comb out of her hair, that awful step-mother of hers had given her a poisoned apple to eat.

"We'll make Sweetie play Poor Jenny," Margaret said suddenly, "because she looks so serious to-day. Only she'll have to play harder than she played Nuts-in-May. She wasn't trying then."

"I'll try now," Sweetie promised.

And she meant it. She went into the middle of the room and knelt down on the floor, covering up her eyes with her hands. She was going to be the best Poor Jenny they had ever had. Then Margaret would be pleased with her again. But with her eyes shut it was Snow White that she began thinking about, not Poor Jenny. It was silly of the mirror to have gone on talking about Snow White, Sweetie decided. Because if the mirror hadn't said anything, the cruel step-mother wouldn't have got angry. Then Snow White could have lived for ever with her new friends.

No mother would behave like that, Sweetie was sure. Only step-mothers. And then Sweetie remembered that she hadn't got a mother herself. Nobody in the Hospital had got a mother. They weren't like other children. Other children went to school and then went home to their mother where they belonged. But the children in the Hospital were at school all the time. If a step-mother came inside the Hospital she could have poisoned them one by one without anybody minding. Already Sweetie could feel herself swelling and burning and growing thirsty.

She tried not to think about it. But it was no use. And the music only made it worse. *Bump, bump-y, bumpy bump, bump,* Margaret was playing slowly and carefully. And all the time Sweetie was thinking about Snow White. Then, quite suddenly, Sweetie decided that what she wanted was a mother. The thought had never occurred to her before. With all the children there were in the world there weren't enough mothers to go round: she could see that. But all the same she wanted one. She wanted a mother who would put her arms right round her and hold her close and run her fingers through her hair and tell her that nobody would ever send her away. At the thought that there wasn't anyone to do it, Sweetie began to cry. And once she had started she went on crying.

She was crying so hard that she didn't notice at first that the music had stopped. But, of course, when the *bump, bump-y, bumpy, bump, bump* stopped, the children all stopped, too. The first thing Sweetie realised was that everything was quiet. Quieter than she had ever known it before. And her own crying sounded suddenly very hard.

Then Margaret spoke.

" Are you really crying, Sweetie?" she asked. "Whatever's the matter?"

At that, Sweetie looked up. Because of her tears the room looked all misty and swimming. Even Margaret seemed wobbly. But Sweetie could see that she had got up from the piano and was coming over to her. And that was nice.

" I don't want to have a step-mother," Sweetie began. " I want . . ."

But before she could say any more, Margaret had come over and put her arms around her. Sweetie could feel her running her fingers through her hair and telling her that she wouldn't ever have a step-mother, not ever.

All the other little girls were staring at her. But Sweetie didn't mind. She just stayed there, her arms close up against Margaret, still crying.

CHAPTER X

I

MARRIAGE! Dame Eleanor had returned to the subject more than once. And apparently she was quite serious about it: a married Warden was better in her view than an unmarried one. Part of Canon Mallow's trouble, she had repeated, had been that he was a bachelor.

And gradually Dr. Trump was beginning to see the whole subject in an entirely different light. Instead of regarding courtship as something merely cloying and frivolous, he saw it suddenly as noble and uplifting; a necessary and even agreeable first step to a state that was ordained and sacred. In short, he realised that it was his *duty* to get married.

But to whom? And by what means? As he stood beside his bedroom dressing-table, skilfully shaping his nails with the pair of curved scissors—when they were not in use he kept them for safety's sake jabbed into a cork that he had removed from an old medicine bottle—he turned over the various schemes that came into his mind. By joining a tennis club, for instance? He had noticed from his own observation of Church tennis clubs that the intervals between play were often distinctly amatory. But he didn't play tennis, and it seemed such a roundabout approach to matrimony to go out and buy a pair of rubber-soled shoes and a Slazenger. Or attending dances? There were studios in Baker Street that he had seen advertised which specialised in teaching the novice in six simple lessons. But could he be *sure* that he would become proficient enough for people not to notice what he was up to? He could not in his position afford to risk being pointed out as a wolf, a prowler. Or a foreign tour perhaps? The Swiss lakes or Holland in tulip time. The very nicest women visited that sort of place. His own Precentor at St. Neott's College, a man of the highest probity and attainments, he remembered, had met his own wife, a Miss Plimsoll, during an Anglican Travel Association fourteen-day all-in tour of the Scandinavian Capitals. Yes, there was certainly something in the idea of carrying the search abroad. Too much, in fact. There was the Channel. And ever since early childhood when he had once been taken down the Thames on a pleasure-steamer from Westminster to Greenwich, he had suffered from an unfortunate tendency to throw up at the mere sight of moving water.

As he reflected on this, he felt saddened. It seemed that matrimony was a charmed circle into which it was not merely difficult but almost impossible to enter. In consequence, he was moody, preoccupied and jumpy.

He was still in this state of gunpowder alertness to sex, as he emerged from his study that evening to make his rounds of the Hospital. He was strictly methodical in these matters, and to-day was the turn for the Latymer block. Because it had been raining earlier—not Sid Harris's kind of rain, merely a flimsy, tissue-paper kind of stuff—he took his umbrella and put on a pair of rubber overshoes. Then, notebook in hand in case he wanted to jot down any little things, he set out.

The first entry was completed before he had gone a hundred yards from his lodging. There was a flower, a dandelion, lying in the centre of the main pathway. There could be only one explanation—a child had dropped it. And then, while he was wondering whom to blame—the child for its carelessness, or the gardener for not tidying up after the children had passed—the solution, the simple dynamic solution occurred to him. Out came his notebook. "Close the main path to children," was what he wrote. Drastic, perhaps. But after all, what would Dame Eleanor or Canon Larkin think of the place if they found dying dandelions littering the footways?

By the time he had reached the nursery wing, he had noted also that the lid of one of the water-butts needed screwing down so that the smaller children could not drown themselves, and that what appeared to be a portion of a home-made kite was caught up in one of the gutters of the Cranmer block. Then, notebook still in hand and pencil at the ready, he pushed open the frosted-glass doors of Latymer and looked about him. At first sight he took the place to be deserted. Not that this was surprising. It was nearly eight o'clock by now and it must have been a good two hours ago that the toddlers had all been bathed, dosed where necessary, and put to bed.

Everything was ideal, therefore, for a visit of inspection. And, tingling with suppressed excitement, he set to work. First, he tried two of the cupboards and, finding them locked as they should have been, he turned his attention to the rocking-horse. It was too large to be put away: he saw that. And apparently the makers had provided no cover for it. He was just turning over in his mind the feasibility of an instruction that the rocking mechanism should be securely padlocked when not in use, when he heard footsteps coming up the corridor on the far side. This surprised him because so far as he knew everyone was off duty by this time. Withdrawing quietly into the alcove behind the dolls' house—it was a large dolls' house, practically cottage-size, in fact—he remained there watching.

And he was not kept waiting. The door opened and the figure of a woman stood before him. Because it was dusk he could not see her at all clearly. Indeed, he could make out no more than the general outlines, the darkness of the hair, the white blouse, the black skirt and stockings. All that he could see was that it was not Hospital uniform that she was wearing—that was broadly and distinctively striped, with a starched collar and cuffs. He could only assume, therefore, that one of the nurses was gallivanting around in her off-duty costume. Perhaps, after all, he was on to something.

But there was no attempt at secretiveness. When the newcomer had reached the centre of the hall, she casually put up her hand and pulled the dangling brass chain of the chandelier. There was a *plop* as the gas-mantle lit itself and then she stood there, clearly revealed and ignorant of the fact that she was being spied on. To his astonishment, Dr. Trump saw that it was Margaret.

What was more, as he peered round the dolls' house chimney stack, she struck him as being a rather agreeable kind of woman. She was tall, dark and . . . and dignified—no, that wasn't the right word—placid. She was the sort of woman whom he could imagine presiding gracefully over the nursery tea of a large family. Yes, that was it. What he saw in her was essentially maternal, strangely, movingly maternal . . . But he was allowing his thoughts to run away with him. What was she doing here at this time of night?

Apparently she was proposing to put up paper-chains. She had a whole bag of them with her and one by one she was taking out the things, red, blue, green, yellow, a veritable profusion of gay rubbish. Dr. Trump held his breath. Unperturbed and unself-conscious, she went about her work, fastening the strips on to the cupboard with drawing-pins, twining them through the chandelier—thereby, Dr. Trump noted, adding the danger of fire to damage to the woodwork —and then fastening them on to the cupboard opposite. She was quick and businesslike about it and as she climbed up on to a chair to secure one of the streamers, Dr. Trump noticed what a remarkably well-turned leg she had. But this was dreadful. Unless he was careful, he would find himself playing the part of Peeping Tom.

She had drawn something else out of her bag by now and was up on that chair again fixing it, whatever it was. Then, when she had got down, Dr. Trump was able to see it quite clearly. There hanging from the chandelier was a piece of coloured cardboard bearing the words " Happy Birthday, Sweetie."

It was only the briefest of glimpses that he got of it because the next moment Margaret, her work done, had pulled the little chain that extinguished the light.

The room was now in total darkness and Dr. Trump had to memorise the notes that he would otherwise have been making. There were quite a number of them, too: take down the card with Sweetie's name on it; remind Mrs. Gurnett that the child's *real* name, her hospital name, was Bertha; ask who had authorised the party.

But at that moment, his thoughts were interrupted by a most alarming sound. He heard a key turning in the lock and realised that Margaret had locked him in.

It was while Dr. Trump was climbing out of one of the windows—which was not easy because he had to balance himself on the sill like a window-cleaner and close the sash down after him to avert suspicion—that a remarkable thought came to him. He saw himself in a deep arm-chair in a comfortable drawing-room with Margaret seated on the hearthrug at his feet. He was toying lovingly with the lobe of her ear and, as he toyed, he was saying teasingly: "And do you remember, my pet, that first evening when you locked your poor hubby in?"

Then, holding his breath, he jumped.

As he landed, a voice spoke to him.

"Good-evening, Doctor," it said. "A little like rain again, I fear."

As he spun round he saw the bright glow of a cigarette end. He must practically have jumped on top of the man. And he recognised the voice. It was Mr. Prevarius's. But it was not the voice alone that worried him. It was the grin that lay behind it. And as he stood there the grin came wrapping round him like a serpent.

I I

As Dr. Trump woke next morning he was already hating Mr. Prevarius. Even in his dreams the man had remained with him all night like a bedsore. And now that dawn had come, the image of his skulking there in the bushes with his grin and his cigarette end, reappeared in all its rank offensiveness. After all, what was the man doing there at that time of night? What indeed? It was Dr. Trump's clear duty to find out. But how—since in the circumstances he could hardly be expected to re-open the subject—could he ever hope to know? With a moan of sheer helplessness over the unfairness of events, Dr. Trump did something that he had not done since early childhood: he turned over and lay face downwards on the pillow.

And to-day should have been such a happy day. All the week he had been looking forward to it, fondling and caressing the occasion in his mind. And why? Because Dame Eleanor had invited him to tea: tea at The Cedars, Putney Heath, at 4.30.

It was enough to make any man contented. For Bishop Warple, the Suffragan Bishop, was to be there. And already Dr. Trump saw the scene as clearly as though he were peeping through the keyhole. The gleaming crested silver of the teapot. The shining milk-jug and sugar-basin. The flickering spirit flame beneath the kettle. The priceless Crown Derby. The three-tier cake stand. The polished fire guard with the flames respectfully warming the ecclesiastical gaiters. The bowl of pot-pourri on the occasional table. Himself eating an anchovy roll. The ancestors enframed around the walls; the pretty maid in frilly uniform; the rich tapestry curtains. The conversation, lofty but still genial. The elderly spaniel slumbering on the rug . . .

Not that he had ever actually been inside The Cedars. It was precisely because it was his first visit that it meant so much. It stood for social recognition. Once arrived there, he had so to speak—arrived. He was, indeed, so much preoccupied by the thought that at breakfast he scarcely touched the lightly scrambled eggs that his housekeeper had provided. And, even in Chapel, his thoughts tended to stray away from Zerubbabel, Prince of Judah, and the two thousand one hundred and seventy-two children of Parosh, and concentrate irresistibly on afternoon tea. After all, he told himself, this would be the first time he had ever actually sat down with a Bishop as—but, yes—as an equal.

Over lunch, it was the same—thoughts far away and no appetite. And then, for Dr. Trump, began the real torment. How to get there? That was the problem. If he were chauffeur-driven like Dame Eleanor, it would have been easy —a word whispered through the partition and he would have been delivered on the doorstep. But Dame Eleanor knew that he had no car. Then a hire-car perhaps. But hire-cars are expensive, and the very last thing he wanted was to appear extravagant or ostentatious. A taxi possibly? But supposing the butler opened the front door as he drew up, mightn't he look just a trifle foolish and last-minutish fumbling for sixpences and threepenny pieces when he should have been handing in his hat and gloves?

It was then that the idea came to Dr. Trump that he would walk. There was something manly and vigorous in the idea. It wasn't far to The Cedars—not more than a mile-and-a-quarter. And if he allowed himself plenty of time—say half an hour or thirty-five minutes he could positively stroll. He liked the picture of himself as he entered the drawing-room unconcernedly, his face aglow with sheer animal well-being.

And as he put on his new black silk dickey—it was real silk with a rather pleasing moiré finish—it occurred to him that he would let fall some chance remark about fresh air and the joy of sunlight just to show them the kind of man he really was. Bishop Warple, he remembered, was strongly in favour of exercise in all its most violent forms ; and he could scarcely forbear admiring a similar taste in others.

The first set-back occurred punctually at 3.55, just as he was ready to leave. He had already adjusted the angle of his hat in the mirror and was reaching down into the hall-stand for his umbrella when he discovered that it was not there. Then he remembered. And, as he did so, a bomb of ice exploded in his stomach. He had left his umbrella and his overshoes in the day nursery. They were tucked neatly away behind the dolls' house—not so neatly, however, that a cleaner would not have found them by now. And, once found, how could they be accounted for? Really it was sickening—yes, positively sickening—the way everything was conspiring to ruin the whole delightful afternoon.

But Dr. Trump was not to be deflected. He went over to the windows and studied the weather. There was certainly no call for overshoes. And none that he could see for an umbrella. The sky was clear except for a cloud or two over Walham Green way, and there was a pleasant breeze blowing. It was, in fact, the very afternoon for a saunter. And, re-garded in that spirit, an umbrella was positively superfluous.

Without further delay, therefore, Dr. Trump set out, his neatly folded kid gloves held firmly in his hand. He did not hurry ; and, as he walked, he looked about him. Really the gardens of the Hospital were charming, quite charming. And, since he had excluded the children from the front paths, everything looked distinctly fresher and more pleasing. The grass-edges, in particular, showed improvement. There was now a geometrical, even cliff-edge, abruptness to the lawns that appealed to his whole sense of beauty.

Because he was gratified, he allowed himself a pleasantry as he passed Sergeant Chiswick's gate-house. The man was sitting on a wooden chair just outside his own front door and Dr. Trump hailed him.

" Ah, basking, I see," he observed.

Sergeant Chiswick rose hurriedly.

" Sorry, sir," he replied.

But Dr. Trump merely flipped his gloves back at him.

" No, no, my good man," he said, " pray continue as you were. It is sunny. And it is Sunday. Therefore—bask."

He smiled inwardly at his own good humour as he mounted St. Mark's Avenue. It was really quite extra-ordinary how the human touch ingratiated one with the working classes. He was sure, for instance, that Sergeant Chiswick would look back on those few words and remember them cherishingly.

But already there was something else that was occupying Dr. Trump's thoughts. His shoes, his new shoes, were troubling him. There was some invisible constriction across the instep. Not to put too fine a point upon it, they were too tight. And the farther he walked, the tighter they became. It was now as if red-hot bars had been inserted just below his arches. There was only one thing for it if he could get as far, and that was to sit down and ease them. At the corner of St. Mark's Avenue and Wendover Gardens—right at the Putney Heath end, that is—a thoughtful Borough Council had placed a park seat. It was a pleasant spot, much sought after by lovers, with a telephone kiosk at one end and a wire-mesh waste-paper basket at the other.

It was while he was resting on the seat with his shoes unlaced and supported only by his toes that the rain began. A mere few sultry drops at first coming from an apparently clear sky, they startled him. He could not believe in them. He suspected birds. But it was rain, all right. And, while he sat there, hurriedly lacing up his shoes once more, the down-pour started. There was no doubt about it this time. It was the genuine stuff, tropical typhoon by nature, that Sid Harris had always believed in.

Because there was nowhere else to shelter, Dr. Trump moved into the telephone kiosk. Except for the panel of glass that was missing in the door panel, it was dry, bone-dry, inside. But bare. There was merely a dog-eared directory and a cardboard notice " Out of Order " on the little shelf where the instrument should have been. Then a terrible thought came to Dr. Trump. He looked down at the damaged apparatus and wondered whether he might himself be suspected. Suppose there were a policeman watching. How was he to know that he would not be haled before a magistrate as a destroyer of Post Office property, a hooligan, a tamperer?

He had been inside the kiosk for a full five minutes before he looked at his watch. And, when he did so, he started. It showed four-sixteen. At this rate, he would have to make a bolt for it the very moment it stopped raining. And, what was worse, it showed no sign of stopping. At four-twenty it was still fairly lashing down and it was not until four-twenty-two that it showed the least hint of slackening. But every minute was precious now.

The rain meanwhile had lost its first fury and had set in steadily and thoroughly in the fashion that is good for lawns. It was patient-looking rain and there seemed no reason why it should stop before nightfall. Dr. Trump looked at his watch. Good heavens! It was four-twenty-five already. This was frightful. Rain or no rain, if he was to get there at all he would soon have to make a dash for it.

He started off like a road-racer, his arms swinging. But he had heard four-thirty strike just as he had left the kiosk, and no amount of hurrying could save him now. The most that he could hope for was that he would not be so late as to be conspicuous. He still trusted that he could slip in unobtrusively, saying: " Forgive me, Dame Eleanor. I sheltered for a moment to allow the worst to pass."

But he had under-estimated the length of Wendover Gardens. And of Gresham Crescent. There seemed to be no end to either of them. He went plodding on, wincing every time his foot touched the ground, and getting steadily wetter. He was really wet by now. And his dickey, his new black silk dickey, was apparently not so superior as he had thought it. It was steadily working up into a fan-pattern of sodden pleats and creases. Soon it would be merely a crumpled black bib.

Then Dr. Trump heard the sound of a car and wondered if it could possibly be a taxi. The car itself was still coming down Evelyn Avenue ahead of him. Dr. Trump hurried forward. He and the vehicle reached the corner simultaneously and his hand was already raised to summon it before he realised his mistake. This was no ordinary car. It was daffodil yellow picked out in vermilion, and on the side, the words "Tootie-Fruitie" and "Only best cream used in our ices" were lettered in coach-builders' scroll-work.

After one glance, Dr. Trump hurriedly dropped his hand again, and pretended that he had merely been adjusting his hat. But it was too late. He had been observed. The appalling object drew up in front of him. And, as he tried to slip round the back of it, a voice called out to him.

"You wanta me," it said.

"Thank you, yes. I mean no," Dr. Trump replied with a brief, chilling smile that was intended once and for all to get rid of the man. Italians, however, are a warm-hearted race, not easily chilled. And Mr. Rapporto—his name was displayed conspicuously on the door panel—was already concerned about Dr. Trump's welfare.

"I driva you," he went on. "You getta wet."

As he said the words, he swung the yellow and vermilion door wide open and beckoned invitingly.

Dr. Trump shrank back against the railings.

"No really, thank you," he said firmly. "I must not detain you."

Mr. Rapporto gave a loud guffaw.

"You notta detain me," he replied. "I goa home already."

"Good afternoon," answered Dr. Trump, and started to walk on again.

But it was no use. Mr. Rapporto followed and drew level.

"I makea no charge," he said. "I no likea see you getta wet."

"Good afternoon," Dr. Trump answered for the second time.

Then Mr. Rapporto grew angry.

"What issa the matter with you?" he demanded. "You afraida I kidnap you?"

This time Dr. Trump did not attempt an answer, and his silence aggravated Mr. Rapporto still further.

"Perhaps I notta good enough," he shouted. "You snobba. You afraida your friends seea you."

Mr. Rapporto had raised his voice alarmingly.

"Please. Please," Dr. Trump said firmly.

Immediately Mr. Rapporto stopped the car.

"That'sa better," he replied. "Getta in. I no wanta da thanks."

Dr. Trump hesitated. Inside, the car looked even more repellent than from the outside. It was full of cans and flat cardboard boxes. And now that it was alongside him he was aware of a sticky, sickly smell that came pouring from it. It would be like sitting inside a blanc-mange.

On the other hand, the rain was coming down harder again. And if he was ever to reach The Cedars he would have to get there somehow. Besides he could not afford to risk any more of that dreadful shouting. And, once in the car, it would not be so bad. After all, if he entirely covered up his clerical collar with his hands no one would even notice him. It was simply that the act of getting into the contraption was so shaming. And to avoid prolonging the shame he hurried. He was impetuous. He sprang.

As he sprang, Mr. Rapporto cried out: "Minda da cornets."

But it was too late. There was the sound of crunching as though a hundred egg-shells were all being crushed at once. Dr. Trump hurriedly shifted his position. But it was too dark inside the little front compartment. He could not see properly what he was doing. His feet came to rest on something soft and yielding and again there was the sound of crunching.

"My Goda!" Mr. Rapporto exclaimed. "Da wafers too. Firsta da cornets. Thenna da wafers."

Dr. Trump remained calm.

"I will pay for what is broken," he said coldly.

Mr. Rapporto let in the clutch.

"You paya all right," he said. "You ruina me."

Dr. Trump drew his knees up under his chin.

"Why you jumpa about so?" Mr. Rapporto asked. "You smasha so much."

Dr. Trump did not reply. And Mr. Rapporto changed the subject.

"Whicha church?" he asked. "What timea da service?"

Dr. Trump tried to smile.

"There is no church. And no service," he said. "That is, I am on my way to tea."

Mr. Rapporto nodded.

"Wherea she live?" he asked.

Again Dr. Trump tried to smile. But this time no smile would come.

"The Cedars, Putney Heath," was all he said.

"O.K.," Mr. Rapporto answered. "You holda tight."

There was, however, nothing of which to take hold. Dr. Trump sat there, insecure and miserable, conscious that with every jolt of the car he was flung against other boxes all as fragile and as yielding as the two that he had just demolished. He said nothing. He merely bit his lower lip and closed his eyes.

It was because he had closed his eyes that he was unaware how far they had come. After one particularly abrupt and vicious lurch, he took one quick and anxious glance around him and saw to his consternation that they had reached the front gates of The Cedars. Immediately, he sat bolt upright.

"Thank you, thank you," he said. "This is far enough."

But Mr. Rapporto took no notice.

"I finisha the job," he replied. "I no letta you walk. I likea you."

At this, Dr. Trump recognised that if the worst were to be avoided he would have to assert himself.

"I wish to be put down," he said firmly. "In fact, I . . . I insist."

But Mr. Rapporto was a common sort of man. All that he did was to spit out of the window.

"Soa what?" he asked. "I insista too."

As he said it, they turned the corner of the drive, and the house—white and spacious—came into view.

"Let me out," screamed Dr. Trump. "Let me out."

"You driva me nuts," was all that Mr. Rapporto replied.

The daffodil and vermilion vanlet came finally to rest between an elderly and upright Daimler and a princely and highly-lacquered Rolls. As Dr. Trump sat there he could see the reflection of his own vulgar ice-cream cart in its panel. He looked away and made ready to go bounding up the steps. Then he stopped, frozen with horror as the front door was opened for him.

"Da cornets," Mr. Rapporto was calling after him. "Anda da wafers. You paya me now."

As Dr. Trump entered the drawing-room he gave a start of sheer surprise. It was all so exactly as he had imagined it— the silver tea service, the spirit lamp beneath the hanging kettle, the ancestors around the walls, even the spaniel slumbering on the rug. His peep into the future had been perfect and complete. He felt himself relaxing.

Dame Eleanor rose as he came in.

"You're late, Dr. Trump," she said. "We've eaten everything."

Dr. Trump smiled: he had rehearsed the answer to this one.

"Forgive me, Dame Eleanor," he said. "I sheltered for a moment to allow the worst to pass."

But it was no use.

"Worst of what?" Dame Eleanor asked.

"The . . . the rain," he replied.

"Hasn't been raining here," Dame Eleanor told him. "You must have imagined it."

As she spoke the words, Dame Eleanor darted a knowing glance in Bishop Warple's direction.

The Bishop returned the glance. His face was sharp-featured and avian. And, as the mouth creased into a smile, the thin lips opened as though to release a shrill stream of bird-song. But all that emerged was a titter.

"Won't do, you know," he said, turning towards Dr. Trump, and waving a thin episcopal forefinger. "Have to think of a better excuse next time."

A feminine and supplementary titter from the window seat made Dr. Trump glance apprehensively in that direction. And, what he saw bewildered him. For now that he looked closely he could see that Bishop Warple was in two places at once: he was there on the window-seat as well as in front of the fireplace. The face clearly outlined against the sky showed the same needle-pointed features, the same bright malignant eye, the same peckish tilt of the neck. Then, noticing the difference in the crest, he realised that he was looking not at the Bishop but at some lesser female Warple.

She, for her part, however, was looking even harder at him. And because she was looking so fixedly, so intently, he felt himself growing self-conscious. The blush returned. And, when he spoke, he stammered.

The next moment, a tall sad-looking man by the fire addressed nobody in particular.

"It rained once at Roehampton," he said slowly. "I remember it. Cats-and-dogs at one end and bright sunshine at t'other. Most extraordinary."

Dr. Trump smiled gratefully.

"It was like that to-day," he said.

88

The sad-looking man fixed his attention on him like a magistrate.

"Were you there?" he asked.

"I was caught in it," Dr. Trump replied.

"At Roehampton?"

"No. At the top of St. Mark's Avenue."

"Don't know it," the sad-looking man answered. "This was years ago. I was playing tennis at the time. Lawn tennis."

There was a temporary respite while Dr. Trump sipped his tea and the others talked among themselves. The sad-looking man had just remembered something about a waterfall that he had once seen in Norway—and Bishop Warple was making signalling motions to his double in the window-seat. He was inviting her to come and join them. Dr. Trump felt better. The tea was warming. And so was the fire. Too warm, in fact. It was making his trouser legs steam. And as they steamed they emitted a strong smell like wet sheep.

Bishop Warple drew in his breath sharply.

"Someone's scorching," he observed.

And it was not only the Bishop who had noticed it. The spaniel was now awake and curious. He tottered to his feet and came lumbering over. Then, after sniffing for a moment, he growled.

Dame Eleanor seemed surprised.

"The last person Rover did that to was a pickpocket," she said. "It was in a crowd. Rover detected him instantly."

"We had pickpockets once at Roehampton," the sad-looking man observed. "A pair of 'em. Cleaned out the lockers. Never caught 'em."

He broke off suddenly and contemplated the cloud of vapour around Dr. Trump's shins.

"Fellow *is* wet, you know," he remarked to the room at large.

But it was another and a gentler voice surprisingly close to Dr. Trump's ear that took up the theme. A movement beside him caused him to turn his head and he found himself looking full into the pale greenish-grey eyes of Miss Warple.

"Why you're soaking," she said.

"Not really," Dr. Trump assured her.

"But you are," Miss Warple went on. "You ought to go home and change. You'll catch your death of cold. Why don't you?"

89

Here at last was someone being deliberately nice to him and Dr. Trump responded.

"I think perhaps I should," he replied, "but really I assure you I won't, thank you. I mean it's nothing. Just dampness."

Miss Warple drew closer.

"That's the way pneumonia starts," she told him. "Neglecting to take precautions."

But before Dr. Trump could reply, Dame Eleanor had spoken again.

"What are those two whispering about?" she asked, darting another of her quick malicious glances at the Bishop. "More tea, Dr. Trump?"

"Thank you, yes," Dr. Trump replied. "I mean, no. That is, I still have some."

"Well, when you've finished, why not take Miss Warple into the garden and let her show you the rhododendrons," Dame Eleanor suggested. "That is, if it's stopped raining."

Again that hideous glance was exchanged, and again Dr. Trump tried to show that as a good fellow he did not in the least mind being laughed at. But slowly and chillingly he became aware that it was no ordinary piece of mockery this time. Dame Eleanor was wearing the expression of someone who has brought off a lucky coup at cards. And the Bishop was nodding his head up and down like a mandarin. They were evidently congratulating each other upon something. And with a sickly faint sensation, Dr. Trump guessed that he was the object of it.

"Oh do," Miss Warple said. "I love rhododendrons."

Miss Warple, however, did not manage to get as far as the rhododendrons that she loved so much. Dr. Trump was still sitting on the springy edge of the couch trying to appear comfortable and at ease with his teacup and saucer in his hand when the door opened and Margaret came in. Dr. Trump looked up for a moment and his expression changed instantly. At the memory of the last time he had seen her—spied on her, rather—and of his thoughts afterwards, he blushed. Blushed a deep fiery red that would not die away again.

"Perhaps we oughtn't to look at the rhododendrons after all," he heard Miss Warple saying. "I'm sure you've caught a chill."

CHAPTER XI

I

AND IT'S really about time we met the girl, this Margaret of Dame Eleanor's.

But it's difficult to tell with parlourmaids. Particularly with good ones. They are as professional and impersonal as waiters. Their private lives may be anything. Or nothing. And it is the same with their thoughts. You never know what they are thinking. Their eyes reveal nothing. They may be dreaming of abstruse love affairs, or simply concentrating on the coffee spoons. You can't even be sure whether their expression changes once they have carried out the tray. And that is because no good parlourmaid ever allows herself to be caught off guard for a single instant. The mask goes on with the apron. And, if it comes off anywhere, it is on the other side of the bedroom door, right up at the top flight of stairs where the carpet stops and the strip of plain lino begins.

As for ladies' companions, they have to be more impersonal still. You simply can't have a woman with views of her own. And habits—even quite innocent ones like always folding the newspaper out flat before reading it, or making a point of going over to see if the radiator is turned off properly—can become quite as irritating as views. The whole secret of a good ladies' companion is always to be there and never to be noticed. If you are aware of the woman even for a single moment, if you can't entirely forget her mere physical presence in the room, it is a clear sign that you should get rid of her.

That, at least, was Dame Eleanor's view. And, in consequence, she had worked her way through a whole regiment of women in her time. One by one they had proved themselves human and therefore ineligible. Unexpected failings, pronounced and therefore fatal characteristics, had successively revealed themselves. There had been Miss Ridley, for instance: forty-two, strictly C. of E., excellent references from a titled family—she had developed Christian Science; Miss Arbuthnot, thirty-nine, well connected, musical in a quiet, inoffensive way—there were her perpetual colds; Miss Perriter, twenty-six, mousy, almost abnormally silent and a thoroughly competent letter-writer—her preternatural fear of burglars rendered her too unrestful. With Miss Stanley, aged forty-four, it was the Second Coming, and with Miss Gibbs, aged thirty-three, it was her teeth. So the list went on; always some unsuspected defect that made further employment impossible. Dame Eleanor, in fact, had just about come to the end of her tether and had decided on promoting Margaret.

At any rate, she felt that she would know what she was doing. It would be no shot in the dark this time, with a lot of valueless references to ponder over. Margaret had been with her for the best part of seven years. Admittedly, the first two of them had been spent almost exclusively in the kitchen. But Dame Eleanor was a keen manager: she had kept an eye on her even then. And when the girl was first allowed to appear at table, naturally she had watched her more closely.

At first she had not been quite suitable. There was too much life in her. She had radiated a crude, animal health. And, with the food that Dame Eleanor provided, she looked as though she were fairly bursting out of her clothes. But Dame Eleanor and the housekeeper between them eventually managed to quieten her down and get her to do her thick hair so that tendrils of it did not keep escaping from under the lace cap. Her parent's death, too, helped matters enormously. She went away buxom, red-cheeked, immature. But, brought face to face with the grimmer realities of life, she changed completely. By the time she came back, she was almost anæmic-looking; and quieter. Dame Eleanor took one look at her, and made her a parlourmaid straight away.

Even so, she had not taken any great pains with her because she was so sure that the girl was bound to get married and leave her. But either Margaret was unusually aloof, or the youth of Putney had less classical tastes. Whatever it was, Dame Eleanor's forebodings came to nothing. Margaret had no young man; showed no interest in young men in general; did not even, so far as Dame Eleanor could observe, exchange glances with them. Except for those excursions to the orphanage on Thursday afternoons, Margaret remained as firmly resident at The Cedars as though she had been brought up there. The only time that she had ever asked for an extra day off duty was at Christmas when she wanted to help arrange the Hospital decorations.

Of course, with a girl of Margaret's background for companion, it would be inevitable that Dame Eleanor would have to do more things for herself. She wouldn't be able to throw unwanted correspondence across the breakfast table to her as she had been in Miss Perriter's day. And Margaret didn't really understand little things like seating-plans for dinner, and which blooms to cut from the hot-house, and whom to admit when Dame Eleanor had said quite definitely that she was out.

On the other hand, she was restful. After a day spent with the GCS, the NAVPTCW and the Unmarried Mothers, it was positively soothing to get back to Putney and find Margaret waiting for her. In fact, she had by now grown to rely upon her entirely. She even intended to make some small token recognition of her dependence—say " £100 if still in my service at the time of my decease "—in a codicil to the will that Messrs. Thring, Thring, Goodfellow and Thring of Lincoln's Inn held for her.

There had, in fact, been only one tussle between them during the whole of the seven years—and that took place during the week succeeding Margaret's promotion. Clothes, Margaret's clothes, were the cause of the trouble. The foolish creature did not seem properly to appreciate her new position: she simply went on wearing housemaid's uniform. And when Dame Eleanor told her, quite definitely, that this would have to stop, she was greeted by a most astonishing revelation. Margaret had no money.

At first, Dame Eleanor was totally unable to believe this. The girl never went anywhere. Her walking-out clothes were of the simplest. She didn't bet. She didn't drink. She didn't go to theatres. She hadn't got a family. Her only sister was married and provided for. She had no brothers. For seven years she had been fed, housed and paid a regular weekly wage—lately she had been getting as much as twenty-five shillings a week—and for all that she had to show for it she might have been giving her services free. Dame Eleanor was astounded.

In the end, she advanced the money herself. Enough to buy two plain black dresses for house wear and a blue costume with a white blouse for public appearances. Miss Ridley, Miss Arbuthnot, Miss Perriter, Miss Stanley, Miss Gibbs and the rest of them, had all had plain black dresses and a blue costume. But where Margaret's money had gone still fascinated her. She could conclude only that the girl had some indigent relations somewhere that she was supporting. It was typical of her class to behave in that way. One of the chief failings of the poor was that they never knew where to draw the line with relatives. They went on helping them long after they had shown themselves unrescuable.

Then, suddenly, sharply, Dame Eleanor remembered her own son, and her lips tightened. God knew she had done enough to set him on his feet again. And God knew also that she had gone on doing it after he had proved that it was no use. But it had been nearly five years before she had stopped his allowance. By now he had either made a man of himself or gone under. She didn't know which because it was so long since she had heard from him. She prayed for him every night. But that was the only contact she had.

II

Dame Eleanor had just been settled in. Her detective story from the circulating library was on the table beside the bed, with a volume of memoirs underneath just in case she lost patience with the detective story and cut things short by jumping straight away to the last chapter. A little to one side, with her reading-glasses on top of it, stood a small volume of Radio sermons, entitled "The Voice In Your Ear," and a prayer-book—these were for reading last of all, a kind of final late extra, just before she put out the light.

On the other side stood the water-carafe, a small bottle of sleeping tablets, some aspirins, and an inhaler. The telephone, Dame Eleanor's diary, a small writing-pad, a propelling pencil, an electric torch (in case the mains failed) and a police-whistle stood on the lower shelf of the table.

Margaret had prepared the cup of malted extract herself and seen to it that the two Bath Olivers were crisp and unbroken. She had made sure that the hot-water bottle wasn't leaking. She had opened the side-window exactly six inches, and had drawn back the curtain so that it shouldn't get wet if it came on to rain. She had closed the door of the adjoining bathroom so that the noise of the pipes should not penetrate into the bedroom. She had turned off the gas-fire at both taps. Last of all she had switched off the two shaded lights on the dressing-table and said "good-night."

Dame Eleanor, her head swathed in a muslin mob-cap, her two strawlike plaits resting on her shoulders, was now sitting up in her bed-jacket that was quilted like a diver's. Since she had left home at 9.15 that morning on her way to the Crusade Headquarters until she had returned at 10.30 p.m. from an evening rally of the Anti-Vice Association this was the first moment that she could really call her own.

But not her own entirely. That worthless son of hers kept coming into it again. When she was tired like this she was always defenceless against him. He had a peculiarly destroying effect, too; a sort of bleakness that hung round her for days after she had been thinking about him. It all became clear to her. She knew why it really was that she spent all her time on these committees—simply because she hadn't got Derek. If she had still had him by her, there would have been grandchildren, a whole new life, to occupy her. And she wanted grandchildren more than anyone would believe. She was crying now. Yes, actually crying. And angry as well. Her detective story had slid off the bed and was lying there, crumpled and ignored.

"Oh God," she said fervently. "Help me to forget. Make him a good man, God. But *please* help me to forget."

But it wasn't really Dame Eleanor we were meeting. She only came into it because of that sudden outburst about Derek. It was Margaret that we were trying to get to know. And now that Dame Eleanor has been put down for the night, Margaret is a free woman until 7.15 to-morrow.

Margaret doesn't go upstairs to bed these days. Her bedroom is now at the end of the passage on Dame Eleanor's floor. It is a pleasant room with flowered wall-paper, and a Wilton carpet only a little faded—it had done service earlier in one of the guest-rooms—that had been cut to fit the walls. Margaret is very proud of the carpet. It is the first time she has ever had a carpet in her bedroom. The stain where Miss Arbuthnot had spilt her hand-lotion and the burn where Miss Gibbs's electric-fire had toppled forward are scarcely noticeable the way she has arranged the rug and the easy-chair.

But to-night she is not thinking about the carpet. She has a letter to write. There is no desk in the room and whenever she wants to write a letter, which is once every fourteen days, she has to use the dressing-table. The ink and the paper and the pen are in one of the small drawers close at hand. But before she starts her letter she takes out a newspaper that she keeps specially for the purpose and spreads it out on top of the embroidered linen runner. She does not want any tell-tale blots or splashes to reveal what she has been up to.

From the way she arranges the paper and then pulls the dressing-stool exactly into position, it is obvious that she is not an easy letter-writer. Nor does she hold the pen as though writing were natural to her. She writes with her fore-finger bent as though only enormous pressure will produce any words at all. But she knows what it is that she wants to say and she remains there, bent over the dressing-table, her image in the mirror leaning forward to meet her, for five, ten, fifteen minutes.

Then she sits back and slowly reads what she has written. There is one place where she had left out a word; and there is only one word "believe" that she did not know how to spell. Bending up her forefinger again, she inks in the "i" and the "e" so that no one could know which one really came first. And last of all she opens her handbag—it is a plain black bag with a snap-clasp that Dame Eleanor had given her last year for Christmas—and takes out a Money Order for two pounds. She studies it closely for a moment to make sure that it has been filled in properly and then pops it in the envelope. After she has written the address and stamped the envelope and made sure that it is stuck down properly, she sits there, thoughtfully staring out of the dark window.

Two pounds! If Dame Eleanor could have got hold of the envelope she would have known where Margaret's money went to. But Margaret has no intention of her knowing. And she is taking no chances. When she gets up, she puts the letter in her handbag and puts the handbag under her pillow. No need for such precautions, of course. Just one of those silly things that people do when they have a secret.

BOOK TWO

Boy Meets Girl

CHAPTER XII

I

THERE MUST have been something to Margaret. More, that is, than there is to most dark-haired rather handsome women who have made their way upwards from housemaid to lady's companion. Because Dr. Trump found himself thinking quite a lot about her. At odd, foolish moments he even wondered whether the difference in their two stations in life was insurmountable.

Ultimately he decided that it was not only insurmountable but unthinkable. But that didn't prevent his mind from returning to the thought at quite unsuitable times—in the middle of sermons, for example, or even when at prayer; and always when he least expected it.

Then something occurred that put it out of his head altogether—it was the burglary, or the breaking-in or the false alarm, or whatever you care to call it. But no matter what it was—and certainly no one was murdered or assaulted; nothing was found to be missing—it left the Hospital jittery and on edge for several weeks afterwards. Dr. Trump even authorised the purchase of a fierce Alsatian to go the round with Sergeant Chiswick—but the strain, the eeriness of those midnight patrols must have proved too much for the animal: one overcast night it ran away and was never seen again.

To explain the mysterious affair that kept the whole Hospital awake and on its toes from midnight until dawn, it is no use going to Dr. Trump or to any of the authorities. The only person who could have given a satisfactory explanation was Ginger Woods—Ginger for the opening of the incident, and Sweetie for the finish.

Even then, it started only because Ginger had always wanted a weapon. Not any particular kind of weapon. Just a weapon. Something sharp to stab or slash or jab with. Once, more than a year ago—and then for something less than a week—he had been the owner of a penknife. But it had been taken from him—confiscated in class by Mr. Dawlish. The knife was still in Mr. Dawlish's possession: Ginger knew that, because Mr. Dawlish brought it out sometimes and used it for scraping round inside the bowl of his pipe. The bowl of Mr. Dawlish's pipe was old and clogged-up, and every time it was used, the blade came away blunt and messy.

Ginger resented this, resented it with a bitterness that Mr. Dawlish with his stained moustache and his misted glasses and his unbuttoned waistcoat had never realised. As Mr. Dawlish saw it, the penknife was safer with him than with Ginger, and that was an end of it.

But, from Ginger's point of view, it was different. There were only three penknives in the whole of the boys' side. Only three, and one of them was being used as a pipe-cleaner. It made him mad just to think about it. Not that it mattered so much now. Because of some freshly entwined initials that had appeared mysteriously on one of the lavatory doors, Dr. Trump had forbidden penknives entirely.

That was why Ginger was so pleased with his new weapon, his bow-and-arrow, his invention. And it was a real weapon this time, something that should be able to kill, or at least maim, at anything up to twenty-five yards. He had been unusually lucky to get the pieces, and luckier still to have the opportunity of putting them together. In the entire Hospital, only one other boy, Spud Carter, knew anything about it and Ginger had pledged Spud to secrecy by promising that he could have a turn with it when it was finished.

In point of fact, it was going to be finished after tea to-day. That was what made this afternoon so important. He had got the string—better than string, in fact, blind cord—in his pocket. And that was all that was needed. The frame was a bamboo curtain rod that should by rights have belonged in one of the masters' dormitories. The shaft was a long slither of wood that had been lying about on the manual side. Not that the shaft was just a slither of wood any longer. Ginger had pointed it by rubbing it up against the brickwork of the storehouse at the far end of the playground, and he had feathered it as well. His last two cigarette cards were now neatly folded at right angles to each other and rested in a slot at the hilt.

Ginger had already made one or two surreptitious practice throws and knew that the flight was true. What is more, the brickwork had proved a good sharpener. If you pressed down hard enough on the point you could draw blood.

I I

The fact that the weapon was there meant almost as much to Spud as it did to Ginger. Usually there was nothing much to do in the tea-break. The whole of it had to be spent in the walled playground and, because of the windows, nothing larger than a tennis-ball was allowed. Moreover, under a new order of Dr. Trump's, a master had to be on duty the whole time. Anything worth doing was therefore definitely ruled out.

Indeed, on the face of it, to-day looked exactly like any other day. Mr. Dawlish, with his coat-collar accidentally turned up as though he were in the midst of a private winter of his own creation, was mooching up and down, his feet dragging and his eyes suspiciously slanting from side to side on the look-out for horseplay, or smoking behind the boiler sheds, or worse. Ginger and Spud went by him, deliberately sauntering and saying nothing. They knew that as soon as they had passed he would turn and look over his shoulder. That was why they kept up this aloofness until he was at the far end of the playground and out of sight behind the Senior block. Then Spud spoke.

" Fink it'll work? "

" Wot'l work? "

" Our bowanarrer."

" 'Oo says it's ours? "

" You did."

" I didn't."

" You said I could 'ave turns."

" 'Aving turns don't make it yours."

" But I can, can't I? "

" You can, if you shut up."

" Shut up yourself."

There was silence. The two boys walked on together. Equity had been maintained. And also friendship. But, because Spud was not seeking to press his point of ownership, it was a clear victory for Ginger. And both boys knew this.

When they reached the boiler-sheds, Ginger went flat on his face and began reaching under the steps for his treasure. It was there all right—the curtain rod and the pointed strip of wood. Ginger was relieved. Underneath the steps of the boiler-house was his private hiding-place.

Before Ginger attempted to string the bow, however, he stationed Spud as a look-out.

" An' wotever you do," he told him, in an unnecessary whisper, " don't 'oller. If you see old Dawly coming, stamp with yer foot. Free times."

" Don't forget I'm 'aving second turn," Spud warned him.

" I never said nothing about second turns," Ginger answered. " Wot I said was *a* turn."

" You said ' turns.' "

" I never."

" You did."

" If you don't do wot I say we shan't neither of us 'ave a turn."

" Oh, orl right."

" An' don't forget. Stamp with yer feet. Free times."

It was the fact that the genius of Ginger had devised a code that finally persuaded Spud to do what he was told. Simply to have been a look-out would have been unworthy, humiliating. But a code promoted the occasion. It was deeply gratifying to Spud to be able to look round the crowded playground and reflect that he spoke a language that no one else knew. There was a kind of magic in the fact that he could talk to Ginger simply by raising up his foot.

All the same, after a bit it was tedious just standing there. He couldn't even lean against the wall. Dr. Trump was very hot on lounging. And if Mr. Dawlish spotted it he would be sure to come all the way down the playground to jaw him.

" 'Ow you gettin' on?" he asked.

" You shut up," came the answer.

" Nearly finished?"

" Shut up, I said."

" Want any help?"

" Not from you."

This time Spud was offended.

" What's wrong wiv me?" he asked angrily.

" You talk too much."

" Wot about you?"

" Don' innerup. I'm working."

The last was, as a matter of fact, untrue. Ginger had

100

stopped working five minutes ago. His weapon was finished and he was just squatting there on his haunches, gloating over it. After all, it was *his* bow-and-arrow, and he wanted to have the first shot without Spud bothering him. But at the last moment vanity overcame him.

"Come an' 'ave a look if you like," he said casually. "Then get back like I told you."

The bamboo curtain rod was certainly elegant. It was bent into a firm crescent and the blind cord was taut and twangy. Ginger began to point out the several beauties of his craftsmanship.

"See them knots," he said. "They're nortikul."

"Wot's nortikul?"

"Same as wot Scouts use," Ginger replied contemptuously.

"You going to fire it?" Spud asked.

"'Course I am," Ginger replied. "Wot you fink I made it for?"

"Wot you going to aim at?"

Ginger looked round the playground with a marksman's eye. There was the door of the boiler-house immediately in front of him. Freshly-painted in a deep chocolate brown, it looked inviting enough. But too large. It would be no real test of his skill; at that distance he could scarcely miss it. He looked farther. On the other side of the door stood two dust-bins. They were just about right, except that he feared that he might make a noise if he hit them. Mr. Dawlish would be sure to come nosing if he heard anyone playing around the dust-bins. Admittedly, there was a tree to the left of the dust-bins. It was a large plane tree, simply standing there to be shot at. And Ginger eyed it critically. Already he could see the arrow sticking in it, buried up to the feathering in the living wood—or at least, quivering there. But even though he could see it in his mind's eye he wasn't sure that he could hit it, in actual fact. And in front of Spud he could not afford to miss.

It was while he was pondering that Mr. Dawlish took up his place in front of the school door and blew his whistle. It was a wheezy sort of blow because Mr. Dawlish always carried his whistle loose in his pocket with his pipe, and the whistle was all bunged up with fluff and fragments of tobacco. But the thin shriek reached Ginger's ears all right.

He turned angrily to Spud.

"There, you see?" he said. "That's wot comes of talking."

Spud wrinkled up his nose.

"Garn," he answered. "You're 'fraid."

"I'm not."

"Then shoot wiv it."

"Wot at?"

"That tree."

The tree looked farther off than ever. Ginger turned his back on it.

"Don't be soppy," he said. "A kid could hit a tree."

The playground had half emptied already, and with every moment the conversation was becoming more urgent. Both boys were desperate.

"Shoot at the wall."

"An' break my arrer?"

But Spud did not reply. He was gazing intently up into the sky at a fat-breasted Putney pigeon that was coming towards them, travelling flat out towards Wimbledon on its own peculiar business.

"Bet you couldn't kill that pigeon."

"Bet I could."

"Bet you couldn't."

"Gotter go in now."

"Told yer yer couldn't," Spud replied exultantly. "It's a rotten bowanarrer."

It was this last remark that goaded Ginger. He was so furious he narrowed up his eyes and stuck his bottom lip out. Then, just as the pigeon passed over him, he braced himself and released the shaft.

The pigeon was safe enough. It did not even know that it had been a living target. But if Spud was right about Ginger's aim, he was wrong about the weapon. It was an excellent bow-and-arrow. The almost surgically pointed shaft rose higher and higher in the sunlight, then turned in the air and, spinning like a bullet, passed out of sight over the row of broken bottles into the girls' side.

The two boys stood there aghast, looking after it.

"Now you've done it," said Spud

III

"I've lost my arrer. I shan't never get annuver arrer as straight as that one. It was the best arrer in the world. My bow isn't any good now. Not wivout my arrer, it isn't. It

*didn't half fly lovely, that arrer. Bet it's sticking into some-
fink. Bet I could find it if I got over. Bet I could climb that
wall . . ."*

It was the voice of Mr. Dawlish that interrupted him.
From the far end of the dormitory it came, tired and droop-
ing, drifting like a pall of smoke across the pattern of
Ginger's thoughts.

" Goo'night, boys. Goersleep. No talking."

As Mr. Dawlish turned away, Ginger's head came up from
the pillow. He had been waiting for this moment. And he
had never known Mr. Dawlish to be slower. For some in-
scrutable reason it was to-night of all nights that Mr. Dawlish
had chosen for inspecting the lockers. The stale smell of
tobacco from his clothes still hung about the bedside shelves
where he had been on his knees, prodding, prying, probing.
But he was going now. Really going. With a last look round
to see that everything was quiet—Ginger's head was flat again
on the pillow as he turned—Mr. Dawlish closed the door
behind him. For a moment his shadow was framed flicker-
ingly on the glass panel of the dormitory door. Then the
shadow dwindled and moved off. There came the sound of
Mr. Dawlish's footsteps, *slouch, slouch, slouch,* as he shuffled
off down the worn oilcloth of the corridor.

Ginger listened carefully. The *slouch-slouches* grew fainter.
Mr. Dawlish must very nearly have reached the stairs by
now. The third step was faulty. It had a squeak in it as
though there were a mouse trapped underneath the board.
And, as Ginger listened, he heard it. *Plomp, plomp, eeyk* it
came. That meant that Mr. Dawlish was practically down on
the lower landing. The inmates of Colet Dormitory were now
left on their honour for the night.

This suited Ginger perfectly. Rapidly, but still cautiously,
stealthily, he thrust one foot out of the bedclothes. The sock
was already on it. Then the other foot followed, similarly
socked. It was Ginger's private good fortune that he
possessed this extra pair of socks that neither Mrs. Gurnett,
nor Mr. Dawlish knew anything about. And, in their way,
they were a very special pair of socks: they had once
belonged to a little boy who had *died*. But he needed more
than socks for his purpose. And everything else had to be
removed from the locker. This meant causing a disturbance
—which was what he most wanted to avoid. That was why
he slid out of the bedclothes through the gap that his feet

had made and then crouched on the floor beside the bed, peeling off his pyjamas. He had managed to open the locker cupboard and was drawing on the blue jersey that Mr. Dawlish had checked so carefully less than five minutes earlier when Spud's head came up from the pillow of the next bed.

" You going like you said?" he asked.

" Shut up," Ginger answered.

" You'll get copped," Spud warned him.

" If you don't shut up, I'll bash you," Ginger replied.

Satisfied that he had silenced Spud, Ginger went back down on all fours and proceeded to crawl under Spud's bed. Spud was all right really. It was simply that he talked too much. Ginger hadn't got any quarrel with him. At least, not now that Spud had promised to lend him his gym shoes, he hadn't. And Spud's gym shoes were important. They were a brown pair whereas Ginger's were white. And white was altogether too conspicuous a colour for where Ginger was going.

But even if Spud wasn't giving any further trouble, there were ten other boys in the dormitory. They were something to be reckoned with. And from the moment Ginger had slid on to the floor it was as though an electric current had passed from bedstead to bedstead. There were creakings, stirrings, murmurs. Eventually all ten heads came up from their pillows.

Then the whisperings began. At first they were just vague silly stuff, these whisperings. Not one piece of hard foundation among the whole lot: Spud was the only one who knew Ginger's secret. But, even so, it was obvious that the whole dormitory knew that something irregular and illicit was afoot.

" What's going on, chaps?"

The question came from a pale, thin boy over by the door. During the daytime he always wore thick glasses. And, without them, he suffered from a prematurely senile anxiety that he was somehow being kept out of things.

" Ginger's wet his bed."

There was a general giggle at this, a ripple that ran up and down the whole length of the room. Ginger stood there tingling. He knew the boy who had spoken. It was a very small boy called Midge. And Ginger knew that, in ordinary circumstances, Midge wouldn't have dared to say such a thing. It was only because Mr. Dawlish was in his sitting-room on the floor below with one ear cocked up listening for any sounds of scuffling that it had been safe for Midge to speak at all.

Ginger bent over and spoke to Spud. He brought his face up so close to Spud's and spoke so fiercely that Spud did not attempt to argue.

"If anyone else speaks, tell 'im Ginger says he'll come and bash him. Pass it on."

He waited long enough for Spud to repeat it, just to make sure there was no mistake about the message. And, as a brilliant afterthought, he added: "Everyone's got to say it over to the chap he got it from. Pass that on, too."

Then, secure in this manifestation of his own authority, Ginger sat down again and began lacing up Spud's gym shoes. The unpleasant memory of Midge's insult was gradually evaporating. In its place, there came a suffusing satisfaction as he heard his message, his orders, being passed on from bed to bed.

All the same, now that the moment had come, Ginger did not any longer feel himself quite the breed of hero who had planned the expedition. He went over to the window and looked out. The night was black and impenetrable. A kind of chill unfriendliness hung over everything. And there was a wind blowing, too, with just enough rain in it to make the slates wet and slippery.

But he had boasted too much to Spud about what he was going to do for there to be any turning back now. He had even humped up the pillow to look as though he were still in bed. His whole reputation depended on going through with the plan.

"S'long, Spud," he said in as casual-sounding a kind of whisper as he could manage. "When I get back I'll tap free times on the window."

Spud sat up on one elbow and looked admiringly at Ginger.

"Goo' luck," he said.

Ginger was enjoying this moment, wanted to taste the full glory of it.

"An' better be quick about openin' the window," he said. "I'll be in a hurry. Don't you go to sleep while I'm gone."

As Ginger lowered himself from the sill he gave a little shiver. It wasn't that it was really cold, or that his blue jersey wasn't thick enough. Simply, that after the shut-up closeness of the dormitory, the night out here on the leads seemed suddenly hostile and noisy. The wind was swooping over the Colet Block with the sound of waves breaking. As it came purling over the roof it set one of the cowls on the chimney screaming. And Spud's gym shoes slid about on the wet tiles like skates. Ginger had to hold on to a drain-pipe to keep himself upright. This was surprising because he'd been out as far as this often enough before to recover things like shoes and vests and toothbrushes that had some-how got themselves slung out of windows. But then he hadn't been wearing rubber soles. He had been barefoot. And bare-foot is always safer.

The first part of the journey was the easiest. It lay along a four-inch catwalk with the steep roof of the wash-house rising up on the far side. There was nothing to worry about here. Except Mr. Dawlish. His room looked straight out on to the catwalk. And Ginger could tell from the slanting square of light on the wet roof that he hadn't got the cur-tains drawn. If he should happen to be looking out now the whole game would be up. Up before it had even started. That was why Ginger had to go down on all fours and crawl. Then even the top of his back wouldn't be showing. And, even if Mr. Dawlish had his nose pressed up against the window-pane, he would never know, never even suspect, what was creeping past him in the darkness.

To make doubly sure that he was not observed, Ginger went down as low as if he had been playing Indians. He thrust his arms out in front of him and kept his stomach pressed flat against the catwalk. It was a gutter really, that catwalk. And his jersey soaked up the water like blotting-paper. But he didn't let that worry him. It only showed that he was crawling properly.

From the far end of the wash-house roof there was a ten-foot drop. But that was easy because there was a drainpipe running down the angle of the wall. Ginger had climbed that pipe before. He knew exactly where the footholds were. It was as simple as going down a builder's ladder. And as quick. Less than a minute after he had passed Mr. Dawlish's room, he was standing upright on the ground with the blank wall of the wash-house sheltering him.

This, however, was where he had to be careful. The windows of the Cranmer Block looked straight out on to the playground. And there were lights in three of them. Broad shining trackways, like flat searchlights, stretched out across the wet asphalt of the playground. Because of them, Ginger had to keep up close to the wall, fairly sliding along beside the brickwork. And to get where he was going he had to pass right alongside Mr. Rushgrove's room. This wasn't so good because Mr. Rushgrove wasn't a bit like Mr. Dawlish. He hadn't got spots on his waistcoat and a wet dribbly place on his chin even when his pipe wasn't in his mouth. Mr. Rushgrove didn't smoke at all, in fact. He looked after the games and went three times round the playground in running shorts every morning before breakfast. In fact, Mr. Rushgrove was just the sort of person that Ginger most wanted to avoid. It would be like having a mastiff on his heels.

And there was one nasty moment. A thoroughly nasty one, a moment when Ginger really thought that he had been copped. He had left the Cranmer Block safely behind him and was about to slip along the narrow alley between the Ridley Block and the end of the Juniors' lavatory when he heard Mr. Rushgrove's door opening. And, at the same moment he heard the sound of footsteps approaching. This was the worst possible place for such a thing to happen. It was nothing less than a trap, this alleyway. The walls ran up a blank twenty feet on either side of him—it was a chasm, in fact—and behind him lay the open front door of the Cranmer Block with Mr. Rushgrove's room just inside. The nearest thing to a hiding-place was a wooden box about three feet high that projected some nine inches from the wall. It was where the stop-cock of the lavatories was housed. And behind the box Ginger crouched down. He gathered his legs up under him like a cat and turned his head to the wall so that his face shouldn't show up white in the darkness. Then he waited.

The footsteps came nearer. And the voice. But it was only one voice. The voice of Mr. Prevarius talking to himself.

"Shouldn't be long now," he was saying. "Not so long as

it has been. Not by a long chalk. Then to hell with Dr. Trump and the whole bloody lot of them. To red-hot . . ."

Unless Ginger got away now that the alley was clear he might just as well have stayed in bed. He was within thirty feet of the girls' wall by now. He could see it jet-black against the dark sky, stretching as far as the eye could reach, the Great Wall of Putney, with a crest of broken glass mounted on the top. It was the sort of wall that would make a cat think twice before attempting it.

But there was one place Ginger knew about where a plane tree grew close up alongside the wall. It was a shabby elderly specimen of a plane tree, with its skin coming off in slabs and patches, and its lower boughs lopped back unmercifully. The poor thing just stood there, maimed and mutilated, waiting for kites and paper darts to get caught in its branches. To Ginger's eyes, however, it was more than a plane tree: it was a staircase. There was a piece of rope hanging down from the stump of one of the lower limbs. The boys used it for swinging and Ginger knew that if he swung himself hard enough he could get himself right up into the tree. Then the rest was just plain climbing.

At the third attempt he was successful. He got one leg firmly over a branch and then moved on up the tree like a racoon. The wall seemed higher than he remembered it. He had to go on scrambling upwards before he could see over the top. And even then there was an unpleasant blank-looking gap between the farthest branch and the brickwork. It was about four feet of nothingness that Ginger had to get over somehow. Just slippery, peeling bark on one side and broken bottle-tops on the other.

" Cor lumme," Ginger said to himself as he surveyed it.

But, as there was nothing else for it, he went on, wriggling himself cautiously along the branch from notch to notch. He wasn't actually afraid, just a bit dubious about whether he was going to get over or not. And, in the end, it wasn't Ginger who decided it. It was the branch. While he was still thinking quietly about things, the branch slowly began to sag. It was only a small branch. But, even so, it didn't give way all at once. Instead, it dropped in a series of little jerks as though it were vainly trying to recover itself. And, as it sagged, it creaked. Every few seconds it emitted a sharp cracking sound. Then, just as the whole thing began to fold over like a lily, Ginger jumped. He landed square on the broken glass. And, relieved of his weight, the branch sprang up into the darkness.

"Got there," said Ginger.

Then he broke off suddenly. He had just put his hand down to his leg and found that it was wet. The serrated edge of a bottle had slit him right along the calf and the blood was running down on to Spud's gym shoes. Ginger could feel it like a warm, crawling caterpillar.

"Wish I'd brought a bit of rag," Ginger began thinking. "Wish I'd thought of it."

But there was more than this one cut to worry about. Now that he came to take stock of things he found that both his hands were bleeding. And, suddenly for no particular reason, he wanted to cry. It wasn't the cut on his leg, or the way his hands were bleeding, or the height or the blackness of the night that depressed him. It was the sheer unfriendliness of that wilderness of broken glass, that narrow graveyard of Bass and Batey and Schweppes and Guinness and the rest of them.

So far as he could make out, the girls' playground was simply bare asphalt like the boys'. This surprised him because for some reason or other he had always imagined that on the girls' side of the wall it would be grass. Smooth mown grass. But he was wrong. There was nothing soft to land on anywhere. And it was out of the question trying to wriggle along the wall. The points of the glass dug and jabbed at him every time he moved. So, because he had no intention of being sawn to pieces, he decided to jump. Jump straight down into the darkness.

To cut down the height of the drop he worked over to the edge and took a grip on one bottle stump more firmly embedded than the rest. Then twisting himself round he dangled there for a moment and let go.

"Now I really done it," the thought came to him as he was falling. "Now I'm for it if I can't get back."

Then the hard playground rushed up to meet him, and he landed. He was now in forbidden territory where no boy of the Archbishop Bodkin Hospital had ever been before. And, once he was on the ground, the night seemed thicker ebony than ever. He could only grope along, scooping a way through it with his out-stretched hands. Unless he actually trod on the arrow, felt it right under the sole of his foot, there would be no chance of finding it in this black asphalt pit.

"Better start looking all the same, I s'pose," he said to

himself. "Silly going back again wivout ever having looked for me arrer."

And hesitatingly, peeringly, without any real plan or purpose, and with a tingle of sheer excitement in the tips of his fingers, he set off across the lake of puddles looking for his piece of wood.

V

It was then that the trouble started. And it was the moon that set things off. Up to this moment, unseen and skulking, the moon suddenly appeared brightly shining, in a ragged window of cloud high up in the heavens over Hammersmith. The whole playground was lit up as though gas-lamps had been turned on. The outline of the Nightingale Block and the Victoria Wing appeared from nowhere, erected magically out of cardboard. Ginger could see every detail, even the toy fire-escape that zig-zagged downwards from the Junior Girls' to the entrance of the Infants' Recreation Room.

But what was more important was that anyone looking into the playground could see Ginger. And, at that moment, Nurse Stedge was standing at the window, her long giraffe-neck craning out. She had said her prayers and was twisting up her thin tail of grey hair in readiness to pop a hair-net over it when she thought that she observed a movement. Something black among the shadows. A man!

The plait slipped from her fingers and began to uncoil itself. But Nurse Stedge was past noticing or caring. All her life she had been dreading this. In a flash she saw herself gagged and bound with her nightdress torn and dishevelled while an armed thug callously rifled everything that she possessed, her handbag, her corals, her snap-shot album, her writing-case. And how could she be sure that fettered and defenceless as she was, the brute would stop short at material treasure? To preserve her honour before consciousness ebbed away, she snatched up her camel-hair dressing-gown and rushed along to Mrs. Gurnett.

Mrs. Gurnett was already asleep. Lying flat on her back with her hands folded like a Crusader's upon the prominent projection of her bosom, she was dreaming about Ramsgate. But at the piercing words of " Matron! There's a man in the grounds!" the pier, the kiosks, the pavilion, the little

110

cafés, all vanished and Mrs. Gurnett was out of bed with a bound.

Alongside Mrs. Gurnett's stockiness, Nurse Stedge felt safer. But only for a moment. For Mrs. Gurnett's orders were callous and terrible.

"Then go and tell Sergeant Chiswick," was all she said.

"Go?" Nurse Stedge faltered. "Across . . . across the playground with *him* there?"

"Then go round the back way," Mrs. Gurnett replied tersely. "And if you see anything, scream. I'll be here."

"Yes, Matron," Nurse Stedge replied meekly.

As she stood there, she was desperately working out in her mind the most roundabout route to the Sergeant's lodge. On her own calculation it would take at least five minutes.

"Well, hurry up," Mrs. Gurnett told her heartlessly. "He may be dangerous."

As soon as Nurse Stedge was gone, Mrs. Gurnett went over to the window to keep watch. The moon meanwhile had gone in again. Beneath her, Mrs. Gurnett could see nothing but inky blackness in which a whole regiment of men could have lurked without being detected. Then, out of the darkness, came a scream. Nurse Stedge's scream. It rose shrill and cutting, like a band saw, out of the still night air. And Mrs. Gurnett's heart gave a sudden bump as she realised that she had sent this faithful, frightened woman to her death.

Heaving up the big sash-window in front of her—she had forearms like a lumberjack's—she yelled : "Murder!"

Ginger had heard both the scream and Mrs. Gurnett's agonising cry. And he was frightened. Really frightened this time. He didn't know what was happening. Didn't even know that it was connected in any way with him. What he did know was that the police would be on the scene in no time. There would be flash-lamps, truncheons, trampling feet, pursuits, cordons, scuffles, handcuffs.

"I'm going back," he said. "I want to be in bed. I want to be next to Spud."

But the scream. What was it that had so alarmed Nurse Stedge? As it happened, it was Mr. Prevarius. His evening stroll over, he was on his way back to his room when he saw Nurse Stedge coming towards him, one hand outstretched for protection against unseen assailants, the other tightly gripping the neckband of her dressing-gown. Ad-

111

mittedly, in the darkness, Mr. Prevarius could not tell that it was Nurse Stedge. Could not even see that it was a lady in fact. But he should have been more careful, more considerate of other people's night-time jumpiness. He should definitely not have stepped out suddenly from a doorway and said: "Boo!" In the result, he had a fainting woman on his hands.

And it was not only Mrs. Gurnett who had heard the scream. Mr. Rushgrove had heard it. He was just finishing his trunk-bending exercises at the time. And, grabbing hold of a rounders bat, he tore off just as he was in vest and singlet ready to beat up all-comers.

Nor was Mr. Rushgrove alone in his intervention. Dr. Trump himself had been roused. He was not in bed: he was still finishing a sermon. He had just started the last page and had taken his shoe off to scratch his foot when he *thought* he heard a scream. Then, because Mrs. Gurnett's window was just opposite his own, he was nearly knocked out of his chair by the cry of murder. Scuffling into his shoe again and pressing his glasses more firmly into place, he set off down the stairs unarmed except for a police whistle. This was no time for *him* to think about weapons. He felt simply that he owed it to Dame Eleanor to be the first on the spot to calm, to assert authority, even if necessary to effect arrest.

All the same he had the forethought on the way to summon Sergeant Chiswick. The first that Sergeant Chiswick, who was naturally a heavy sleeper, knew about it all was when Dr. Trump hammered on his window with the mouthpiece of the police whistle and shouted: "Show a leg, man. There's violence."

By now, Nurse Stedge had recovered sufficiently to be able to speak. But only to Mr. Rushgrove. It was significant that she could still not bring herself to utter a word to Mr. Prevarius. But, encouraged by the sight of the rounders bat and Mr. Rushgrove's huge biceps, she told everything. Above all, she urged him to hurry. She was terrified lest the intruder, the burglar, the sex-maniac should already be loose among the innocents, pilfering, slaughtering, slashing to right and left among the cradles.

And by now it was a powerful enough sort of posse that had assembled. Mr. Rushgrove led, only because no one else could keep up with him. Then came Dr. Trump, his bare

112

fists clenched in readiness and his police whistle firmly clenched between his teeth. Next, Sergeant Chiswick swinging a truncheon. And finally Mr. Prevarius, sauntering nonchalant, incredulous.

Nurse Stedge, dismayed by the thought of her negligée before so many men, had returned to her bedroom to dress properly in readiness for the kill. She was not a sadistic woman. But, even so, she gave a little shudder of joyous anticipation as she heard the key inserted into the padlock of the green spiked gate that led into the girls' playground.

Ginger heard it, too. As it happened, he was only just on the other side of the gate at the time. And, at that moment, the moon again disentangled herself from a skein of cloud. Immediately the wet asphalt became as shiny as a mirror: it was as though a gigantic polisher had been rubbed across it. And because the moon was riding high there weren't even any shadows. Just nowhere at all for a small boy to hide himself. Simply bare, unclimbable walls with broken bottles on the top and a great empty floor of black looking-glass.

Mr. Rushgrove saw Ginger as soon as he entered. And Ginger saw Mr. Rushgrove. But only for an instant. As Mr. Rushgrove stepped into the playground the moon re-buried herself. It was blackness again. Already, however, Mr. Rushgrove was off the mark like a sprinter. And so was Ginger. Then the moon began playing tricks on them. Blazing forth at one moment like a beacon, she hid herself coyly at the next. It was like hunting by flashlights. No sooner was Mr. Rushgrove hotly on the trail than he lost it again. But the shouts of Dr. Trump and the pounding feet of Sergeant Chiswick were enough to warn Ginger that they were closing in on him. He was flat up against the Junior Girls' block by now, alongside the Infants' Recreation Room and the darkness in front of him was full of charging figures. This was the end. There was no escaping this time. They'd get him in a moment.

Then he saw the zig-zag fire-escape. He didn't know where it led to. Didn't know whether there would be any outlet that way. Didn't know whether they had seen him and would follow. It was simply that with the instinct of any hunted, anxious animal he began climbing; intended to go on climbing, in fact, until he could climb no farther. The steps were of iron-lattice. He mounted them two at a time. The night was now blacker and stickier than ever. He could

113

see nothing. But he could feel. And by the time he reached the sixth landing the ladder gave a shudder. That meant that Mr. Rushgrove was bounding up after him.

Until that moment Ginger had intended to go right on up to the roof if he could get there. But just as he was rounding the next bend he saw an open window a couple of feet above him. And he jumped for it. Because he was desperate, his fingers were firm, like hooks. They grabbed on the wet woodwork. And, with a heave, he drew himself up and got one leg over the sill. He had just got the other leg over and was lowering himself on to the floor inside when he heard Mr. Rushgrove, breathing deeply, go thumping up past him in the darkness.

"Cor!" said Ginger devoutly.

But he could hardly stay where he was. It was a girls' dormitory. If they found him here they would probably send him to prison or something. And already the disturbance had roused the whole block. As he crouched there he saw the glass panel in the door suddenly spring into brightness and knew that the corridor light had been put on. Someone was coming. It was the night-sister. He could see the shadow of her cap upon the panel. And there was nowhere to hide. Just iron bedsteads and little wooden lockers. There wasn't even another door at the other end.

Then, in that dim dormitory, with the long line of beds, all exactly like the one that he had left on the other side of the Hospital, he felt a hand come out from nowhere and touch him. He was so frightened that he was very nearly sick. But, when he turned, he saw that it was nothing to be afraid of really. The hand belonged to the little girl in the bed beside him. And, as he looked, she removed her hand and put her finger up against her lips warningly. Then as he looked closely he saw a fringe of dark hair across her forehead and a pair of eyes that looked enormous over the edge of the bed.

"Are they after you?" she said in a low whisper. "Better get in by me. Then you can hide."

And, as she said it, she lifted up the corner of the bedclothes in readiness.

That was Ginger's first meeting with Sweetie.

114

The whole incident remained unexplained and inexplicable.

By the time the police arrived, Ginger had quit Sweetie's bed and gone back down the fire-escape. Because he was a bit rushed, there was no time to say good-bye properly. And, in the circumstances, Sweetie did not attempt to detain him.

" I'm going," Ginger announced suddenly ; and all that Sweetie replied was : " I won't tell."

That was the whole of the leave-taking. It was simple, brief, sufficient. And, in comparison with the outward journey, the way back was quite absurdly easy. When Sergeant Chiswick had unpadlocked the spiked gate, marked " Girls Private," he had left it open after the posse had passed. Ginger just slipped through as quietly as an errand boy. Less than five minutes after leaving Sweetie's bed Ginger was back in his own bed and Spud's gym shoes were in the locker where they belonged.

It was only Spud himself who was the trouble.

" D'yer get it?" he asked hoarsely.

But this time Ginger's reply was so astonishing that Spud did not ask anything further.

" You shut up," Ginger answered. " There's been a murder."

It was getting on for 1 a.m. when the hunt was finally called off. But even with the departure of the policeman, the incident was not over. It was too momentous for that. When the whole year came to be reviewed in perspective, it remained the central incident of nineteen-twenty-seven.

Not that the twelve months had been entirely uneventful in other respects. A strange fungoid growth like subterranean mushrooms began pushing up the asphalt of the infants' playground and an area nearly the size of a tennis court had to be re-laid at a cost of eleven pounds six shillings. That was in February. Then towards the end of April, measles swept through the junior girls like cholera, leaving only Sweetie spotless and untouched. Sweetie herself mysteriously developed the ailment three days after the incubation period was over when, of course, the isolation business had to begin all over again. July was the next month for trouble : Mr. Rushgrove, demonstrating how a cricket ball should be hit, contrived to put it clean through the net and laid out a senior boy who had been hoping to make Mr. Rushgrove miss simply by staring at him: two front teeth was the price of such behaviour, and Mr. Rushgrove had to be warned by Dr. Trump not to hit so hard. The late summer and early autumn passed quietly. But October was a trial. The boiler on the girls' side went wrong again. And one of the laundresses, the big over-developed one who carried messages for Mrs. Gurnett, absent-mindedly put down a practically red-hot smoothing iron on top of a pile of nurses' uniforms and burnt a neat heart-shaped hole through all six of them. Then in November came the snow, and Dr. Trump was forced to prohibit snowballing.

And finally, right at the turn of the year, actually on New Year's Eve itself, there was one of those unhappy, unavoidable affairs, that strike a cold note and leave everyone edgy and miserable. They lost one of the girls through meningitis. Sweetie was in the Infirmary at the time and saw it happen. Knew all the details in fact as plainly as if she had died herself.

She was six at the time.

CHAPTER XIII

IT IS always strange in the Infirmary. Not just shadowy. Mysterious. Interesting. Full of puzzles. It is another world. Different faces. Different uniforms—everyone in the Infirmary wore white and looked like seagulls with big stiff butterflies resting on top of them. Different sounds. The beds in the Infirmary were mounted on rubber wheels and squeaked when anybody moved them. A different smell. Particularly a different smell. A smell like petrol, only it isn't petrol. Petrol, with soap and carbolic mixed up with it. It was the cleanest smell that Sweetie had ever known, as though the air itself had been sponged down and rinsed through with the stuff. Also, it was horrid.

Sweetie wasn't very ill. Just a temperature that kept running up and down, and a bit of a sore throat. But Mrs. Gurnett had decided that she would be better in the Infirmary: then they could tell if it was going to be anything.

Even though she wasn't very ill, she was very bored. Bored because there weren't any toys in the Infirmary. Dr. Trump had decided on that point. He wasn't going to have a lot of dolls and teddy bears and golliwogs, he said, going in and out of the Infirmary, spreading germs over the whole Hospital. The point had been explained to Sweetie and because everyone was very serious about it, she accepted it. But it was sad having to leave the pink plush rabbit behind her. And she supposed that Dr. Trump *was* right about the germs. She had been in the Infirmary for two days now and she had only seen one germ the whole time. That was when they were making her bed and she had watched the germ, soft and white as thistledown, detach itself from the edge of the new blanket and go whisking off into space. Only one germ, and two nurses to catch it if they had been quick enough.

But to-night something important was going on. So important that Sweetie felt out of it. There were six other children in the ward. And one of them, quite a small girl, was very ill, too: Sweetie could hear her scratching. Scratching and scratching all night long. That wasn't the one, however, that they were worrying about. It was a big girl, a girl of nine or ten with thick red hair, who was the centre of everything. She had been in the next bed to hers when Sweetie had first been brought in. But they had moved her now right up to the end of the ward away from everyone. Sweetie knew why, too. It was Sweetie's own fault. It was because she would keep talking to her. Even when the red-haired girl didn't answer, Sweetie went on telling her little things just so that she wouldn't feel miserable. And now she must be terribly lonely, completely cut off from everything with three empty beds between her and anyone she knew.

Then, as though that weren't bad enough, they put a screen round her. That was cruel, Sweetie thought, and it made her angry. It was wrong to punish any child so severely simply because she had been caught talking—and sometimes only just listening—after they had told her to be quiet. And Sweetie could tell that the red-haired girl minded. She could tell that from the sound her breathing made. It was very noisy breathing, as though she had been crying and had got herself all stopped up inside.

The breathing was the loudest sound in the Infirmary, except for the scratch, scratch, scratch two beds away. And it seemed louder still because everything else was so quiet. It was night outside. Everyone else in all London was asleep. Everyone except engine-drivers, that is. Sweetie could hear them all the time, banging into things and blowing whistles and letting off steam. Engine-drivers were different. They went to bed all day and then started shovelling coal into their engines as soon as it began to get dark. She had never actually seen an engine. But she knew all about them from books. And she had never heard an engine in the daytime. Not even one.

The night-nurse had shifted the screen a little, and Sweetie could see through the gap where the hinge was fixed. There was a light on the other side and she could see the big girl's red hair quite plainly. And her face. But something had happened to her face. It was red, too, like her hair, and one of the nurses kept sponging her forehead. While Sweetie watched she saw the nurse pour something into the girl's mouth straight from a teapot.

"I suppose they're sorry now that they've been so nasty to her," Sweetie thought. "They're trying to make up for it."

Then the doctor came. This was very interesting, because she had never seen the doctor come at night-time before. He was dressed in his ordinary clothes, dark thick sort of clothes, and he carried his bag, the one that he always took whenever he came. And as Sweetie looked at him she realised that doctors were even more extraordinary than engine-drivers. They never went to bed at all. Just had their tea and went out to see people like the red-haired girl, who had been asleep when they had called during the daytime.

She couldn't see what the doctor was doing. And that was because his back was in the way—if he had been over on the other side she could have seen perfectly. But he was there for a long time and she thought, though she couldn't be sure, that he was sticking something into her. The shadow on the wall looked as though he was. Not that shadows are anything to be relied on. Just now when he had come in, the doctor's shadow itself had looked like a giraffe that reached right up the side of the ward and bent over, when it came to the ceiling. And this was silly because the doctor was only quite a short man, shorter than Mrs. Gurnett, shorter than the night-sister; one of the shortest doctors in the whole world. But she was still sure that he had stuck something into the red-haired girl. Because when the shadow had made the prod the red-haired girl had given a little cry, a sort of whimper

118

as though someone was hurting her. And shadows never hurt anybody.

But something else was going on. The doctor came into sight again from the screen and walked back down the ward towards Sweetie. He looked cross, Sweetie thought. Or worried. Or else he had lost something—it's difficult to tell what grown-ups are thinking when they're frowning. And she didn't want to look too closely because she was supposed to be asleep.

She very nearly was asleep when the doctor came back. But this time it was more interesting than ever because the doctor had got Sergeant Chiswick with him, and this surprised Sweetie a lot because she had never guessed that Sergeant Chiswick was another person who didn't ever go to bed. Sergeant Chiswick was carrying something she had never seen before. It was round and long and heavy and it was metal. Then she recognised it. There was one of them in the room where the dentist came to see if your teeth were all right, and it was something to do with having a tooth out so that it didn't hurt. So that explained everything: the red-haired girl had got toothache and the doctor had borrowed something so that he could pull it out. Perhaps Sergeant Chiswick was going to help. Perhaps he always helped because he was so strong from carrying buckets and things.

And soon there was somebody else as well. The night-nurse had left the room for a moment, but she took a long time and when she came back she had Dr. Trump with her. This really was extraordinary. Because Sweetie had never seen Dr. Trump in the Infirmary before. And she had never even imagined that he had to help as well when a tooth was being pulled out. But second teeth she knew were awfully firm and perhaps they got stuck sometimes.

There was now a new sound in the Infirmary, a faint, high, hissing sound like a far away kettle boiling. And a new smell. Another petrolly kind of smell, only sharper. And the shadow on the wall was fixing something over the little girl's nose. It was a box. A box with a tube to it. Which was rather thoughtless really. Because if he held it there much longer the little girl wouldn't be able to breathe.

Then, interesting though it was, Sweetie dozed off because she was so sleepy. And when she woke up again everything was different. At the end of the bed Dr. Trump was down on his knees in that long dressing-gown of his as though he were praying. The doctor was putting things away in his bag again. But what the night nurse was doing was the strangest thing that Sweetie had ever seen. She had got hold of the sheet and was lifting it up over the red-haired girl's face. Right up so that her face was completely covered.

" She'll smother if they leave it there," Sweetie thought. " She won't be able to breathe."

Sweetie never knew whether she had really seen them carry the red-haired girl, still with her face covered up, out of the ward and away to some other part of the Hospital. Either she had seen it or dreamed it. Dreamed it probably, because she was *very* sleepy by now.

But a little later on she certainly asked for a drink of water. And the night-nurse seemed surprised to find that she was still awake.

" Have you been awake long?" she asked suspiciously.

And because she sounded so suspicious, Sweetie lied to her. " I've just woke up," she said. " I was thirsty."

That seemed to satisfy the night-nurse. She went away again and Sweetie lay there thinking. It had been a long drink of water that she had taken and she felt thoroughly wide-awake again. It was while she was awake that she heard the night-nurse say something to Mrs. Gurnett. She didn't hear all of it, but she heard enough.

". . . not that they ever notice anything," was what she said. " Half the ward could die and the other half wouldn't know anything about it."

Then Sweetie knew what had happened. And with the knowledge she didn't even attempt to go to sleep again. She was too excited. She knew about dying. And she understood it. So that was the way it happened. And because that was the way, she was careful to push the bedclothes down, right down, so that they couldn't possibly ride up over her face if she did go to sleep.

CHAPTER XIV

Dr. Trump's own plans for marriage might easily have come to nothing. But in the end, it was Miss Warple who precipitated matters.

Ever since that Sunday afternoon at Dame Eleanor's when

he had first met his Bishop on equal social terms, Dr. Trump had been a regular visitor to the Warples. That he was welcome was obvious. But so also was practically everybody else. For, Bishop Warple was possessed of a positively ferocious cordiality. Small as the Bishop was, his left arm had a way of sidling round the back of any newcomer while his right arm was still engaged in the preliminary handshake. Total strangers, indeed, sometimes recoiled from its intensity. Nevertheless, it was irresistible. And, in the result, guests came pouring into the bleak red-walled drawing-room with its snapshots of Lebanon and Galilee and the more studied, cabinet-groups showing Walter Warple in his college days as oarsman, cricketer, fencer, cyclist, footballer, hockey player; even as tennis champion, complete with a narrow-handled racquet, shaped like a long, thin gourd.

On Wednesday—particularly on what the Bishop always referred to as his midweek—the salon was always packed solid like a waiting-room. Young, adolescent-looking curates, battered despondent ministers from East-End parishes, swarthy missionaries home on furlough, lay deaconesses, church helpers—the whole miscellaneous company of ecclesiastical well-wishers—were all there.

More than once, in fact, Dr. Trump had wondered whether he was possibly cheapening himself a little by going among them so indiscriminately. He had not liked it, for instance, when a shabby toothless old vicar from somewhere down Hoxton way had said to him: " You properly settled in at the Hospital? Ought to be very snug there: Mallow was." " Snugness," Dr. Trump had been forced to reply, " is not my aim in life. I . . . I am a worker!" But just imagine having to say such a thing. Fancy having to defend oneself to someone who looked like a rather gruesome verger.

There was one reason, however, why Dr. Trump continued his visits. And that was because, after the cocoa tray and the cake-tiers had been cleared away, the Bishop always asked him to stay behind for a cosy, informal chat. Then everything was changed. It all became quite, quite delightful. There were usually just the three of them: the Bishop himself, Dr. Trump—and Miss Warple, at once girlish and birdlike, perched on the fancy-beadwork pouffe.

No Mrs. Warple : that was significant. But Mother was an invalid: this much had been conveyed to Dr. Trump at an earlier meeting. Mrs. Warple lived mysteriously in the perpetual purdah of her bedroom. And the soirées, the conversaziones, the little informal get-togethers had to jog along without her. Indeed, it was the continued absence of Mrs. Warple that had thrown such a heavy load on to the shoulders of her daughter. It was Miss Warple who had to snap quietly at the maid for not putting a mat under the hot-water-jug, and was compelled to break off suddenly from conversations because she had just noticed that a curate, a vicar, a missionary, a boys' club secretary was without his cocoa or his fairy-cake.

To-night had promised to be just such another evening. Dr. Trump had been looking forward to it all the week, fairly licking his lips for more revelations of episcopal intrigue at Lambeth, more disclosures of archidiaconal plot and counter-plot. But it was obvious to Dr. Trump as soon as he arrived that the Bishop was far from being at his best. Earlier in the week Bishop Warple had caught a chill at an unveiling ceremony. And he had now withdrawn almost entirely from the world, enclosing himself in a thick impenetrable cocoon of peppermint and eucalyptus. He was completely impervious to society already, and it was apparent that by to-morrow he was in for a real stinker of a common cold.

Shortly aften ten o'clock therefore, as soon as the last of the casuals—a saturnine, Dracula-like prison chaplain from Brixton—had moved moodily off into the darkness, Bishop Warple announced loudly and abruptly that he was going to bed.

Dr. Trump rose obediently. But Miss Warple intervened.

"Go on telling me about your House Captain plan," she pleaded. "You know we were interrupted."

And so, after the Bishop had left them, carrying with him his inhaler, his screwed-up handkerchief, and his tin of lozenges, Dr. Trump found himself sitting there, directly under the hockey group, alone with Felicity Warple.

Because Miss Warple was so keenly, extraordinarily interested in school discipline she instinctively moved over on to the couch beside him. It was a long, unyielding sort of couch and there was a good eighteen inches or more separating them. To Dr. Trump's relief Miss Warple made no attempt to close the gap. On the contrary, she sat round sideways so that she could see him while he was talking. But in a way this was worse. For she had such a strangely penetrating look in her eyes, an intense gimlet stare, that it was like

122

sharing a settee with a basilisk. And Dr. Trump found himself faltering beneath it. He grew nervous. He changed the subject first to sacred music and then to infant diet, then to girls' sports. But it made no difference: Miss Warple was equally interested in all of them.

And then, to his astonishment, he discovered that she had not been listening at all. With those hard avian eyes focused somewhere right inside his skull, she suddenly addressed him.

" Dr. Trump," she said shrilly. " You'll have to go."

The remark was so unexpected, so uncalled for, that Dr. Trump drew back as though he had been stung. Then he took firm hold of himself. He would not, he determined, allow himself to be rushed, stampeded, ejected in this way. Therefore, he rose slowly and with dignity, disentangling his long legs like a snake uncoiling.

" I was actually upon the point of departure," he said coldly. " In fact I . . . I am already going. Good evening."

But it was evident that more than an over-stayed welcome lay behind it all. For Miss Warple continued as shrilly as ever.

" And you mustn't come here any more. Ever."

Her voice rose to a high flute-like scream as she pronounced the last word, and Dr. Trump felt a wave of icy coldness pass across his stomach. This was no ordinary behaviour. It was hysteria, even madness possibly. Terrible thoughts began to race through his brain. Perhaps, if it were madness, it was inherited. Perhaps at this moment in a barred room upstairs, Mrs. Warple . . .

But this was no moment for idle conjecture. There was only one thing for it: to get out of the house quietly before the attack became too violent.

Sweating visibly he began to move rapidly towards the door. But Miss Warple was there before him. Stretching her arms out to their full width, she leant against the panels as though crucified. Her small flat bosom was rising and falling, and two hectic spots showed against the paleness of her cheeks.

" Not ever," she repeated.

Dr. Trump realised now that at all costs he must remain calm. If he were to lose control of himself even for a moment they would both be gibbering and grimacing at each other. Therefore, he parried.

" Just as you say," he replied. " Just as you say."

" Then you admit it?" she demanded.

"Admit what?" he asked, still trying to edge inconspicuously in the direction of the door-handle.

"That they're talking about us," she replied. "Everybody's talking. You know they are."

The answer was snapped back at him so viciously that he instinctively stepped back again. So it *was* madness. Complete and fully developed. It was voices that the poor girl thought that she was hearing. Now more than ever was it necessary to humour her.

"Quite so," he answered. "Quite so."

"So I'm going to put an end to it, if you won't," she said.

"But first we must know who they are, mustn't we?" he explained soothingly.

Miss Warple's eyes hardened.

"Dame Eleanor. *And* Canon Larkin," she told him. "*And* Mummy. *And* Daddy. It's everybody! They're talking about us all the time."

She sank down in a chair as she was speaking and began crying. The thin features were puckered-up and drawn, and the tears ran down in twin rivulets on either side of the sharp nose. Dr. Trump glanced from Miss Warple to the door, back to Miss Warple, and finally to the door again.

And it was here that he made his first mistake. For instead of making a dash for it now that Miss Warple was no longer standing in the way, he moved slowly and with dignity, talking as he went.

"I entirely fail to comprehend your meaning," he said with gravity. "I . . . I cannot conceive why our names should have been coupled."

A fresh sob rose up from the couch.

"Then they're wrong," Miss Warple moaned. "You . . . you don't like me."

"Oh but I do, I assure you," Dr. Trump replied, still backing. "I value our friendship most highly."

The Westminster chimes of the grandfather clock in the hall struck 10.15. The clock had been a parting presentation from the Bishop's old parishioners in Birmingham. A lot of money had been spent on it, and the bell-notes had a silvery mellowness about them that suggested riches and position and security. The music entered Dr. Trump's soul and lodged there. Remembering the wretched *ting, ting, ting,* of his own timepiece at the Hospital, a strange mood of madness entered into him. His ego enlarged like a balloon and he saw himself as someone of power and importance, a man of destiny

124

who could afford to trample even bishops' daughters underfoot. The emotion, however, was complicated by an entirely different feeling when he remembered how secure it would make him with Dame Eleanor if he married into the Bishop's family. But really the idea was unthinkable. Only this morning when shaving he had found himself thinking about Margaret again. And how could any man propose to a spinster whose head was buried in a sofa cushion?

And it was here that Dr. Trump made his second mistake. Curbing his ruthlessness, he returned to his mood of dignified benevolence.

"Hadn't we better shake hands and be friends?" he asked suavely.

Miss Warple struggled to her feet. Now that she was standing up again, she looked terrible, as though she had been crying for months on end. Her eyes were pink-rimmed and sunken, and her mouth quivered.

"Leave me alone," was all she asked. "Can't you just leave me alone, now that it's all over."

"But don't you want me to be your friend?"

"And is that all that you want to be?"

"Isn't it sufficient?"

Miss Warple did not reply. Instead the tears welled up again and the moan restarted.

Dr. Trump had never before been in such close, such intimate contact with a young woman in tears, and he was astonished to find that he was suddenly consumed by a great and overwhelming pity. A moment later this was transformed into a devouring sense of guilt to think that he should have been responsible for so much misery. And this, in turn, resolved itself into the fierce conviction that somehow or other—how, he still could not imagine—he must comfort her. The wild words that she had spoken had gone sailing past him like the wind. After all, he was older than she was, and a man: he could afford to be magnanimous.

"Felicity," he said at last, speaking like an elder brother.

"Samuel," Miss Warple replied, not in the least like a younger sister.

"I . . . I don't like to see you crying," he told her gently.

And it was here that Dr. Trump made his third, his consummate mistake. For while he was speaking he opened his arms appealingly as one might to soothe a child.

And as he did so, Miss Warple sprang into them

125

CHAPTER XV

I

ON THE night of his engagement, Dr. Trump scarcely slept at all. He began with an uneasy pacing of the room alternating with spells of despondent moodiness stretched out, nearly recumbent, in his wicker chair. Then, finding that sleep was farther away than ever, he went down to the kitchen and made himself a cup of cocoa.

Usually this was a beverage that had a magical, almost anæsthetising effect upon him. One sip of the liquid chocolate, and his eyes would begin to close, his breathing grow slower. But this time, it was different. It may have been that he had put in half a teaspoonful too much of the powder or, in his distress, had carelessly allowed the milk to catch. Whatever it was, to-night the cocoa had the reverse effect. It was like strychnine. First of all, it woke him up. Then it upset him. He felt wakeful, fidgety, sick. Even when he tried a short prayer, it was unavailing. He had to get up hurriedly halfway through, and go over to open a window.

The chief of his misgivings during that dreadful night when he wondered exactly what it was that had occurred—whether he had boldly proposed or merely timidly accepted—was concerned with Felicity's potential motherliness.

Everything now seemed to turn upon that point. Did she or did she not want children? And if so, how many? Dr. Trump then found himself asking of what sex—not so much because he thought that Felicity could do anything in particular about it as to see whether her views coincided with his own. And, as for him, his mind was *quite* made up. Four was to be the number: two boys and two girls, with a boy for the eldest. He was unprepared to make even the slightest concession. One of each, for example, would simply have been trifling with the problem.

Would Felicity be willing? Would she be capable? Above all, would she be *enthusiastic*? And, looking back on the whole astonishing incident in the Bishop's study, he saw now that he should have asked her; should have established his basic point right from the very start. There was only one thing for it and that was to ask her at the earliest possible moment before things had gone any further.

Sitting bolt upright in bed, he put the light on and looked at his watch. It showed 3.15, and he put the light out again. Even cutting things to their finest there was nothing that he could do for another four and three-quarter hours. It was at eight o'clock that he would phone her—the Bishop, he knew, was an early breakfaster and he assumed that Felicity would be having breakfast with him—and, gently but firmly, he would put his point of view. The suspense meanwhile was terrible. But a natural feeling of delicacy, a kind of sixth sense in negotiation, told him that he could not very well ring up any girl before 8 a.m., snatch her from a running bath-tub probably, to present her with such an ultimatum.

There could, however, he repeated to himself, be no possible compromise, no half measures. From the first moment when he had begun to think about such things—it must have been when he was just turned fifteen—he had pictured himself in the guise of a patriarch. Even the details had been clear to him. He had seen himself most clearly standing on an ancient rectory lawn, possibly even a deanery lawn, and to an admiring group of lesser-fry, vicars, curates and lay church-workers, he was saying: " My eldest is at Eton: the younger is at Radlett. The girls are both at Cheltenham. My wife's old school, you know . . ."

That reminded him. He must find out where Felicity had been educated. It might give depth and detail to an otherwise vague and shadowy picture. Because now that he came to think about it, he realised that he had never properly thought about this remarkable woman, his mate, the mother-of-four. As a young man, the nearest that he had ever come to visualising her was in the image of the golden-haired cashier in the tea-rooms beside the theological college where he had done so well, so strikingly well, in Old Testament studies. Not that there had been any suggestion of calf-love about the episode. On the contrary, keeping his heart well under the command of his head, he had deliberately transferred his patronage from The Blue Bird to The Copper Kettle where the service was slower, the cakes flat and apparently unleavened, the tea almost undrinkable, but the elderly proprietress a regular fellow communicant at the parish Church of St. Ninian's.

And only once since then had the possible mother of his children crossed his thoughts not merely as a mother but as a woman. Indeed, it still astonished him to remember that evening in the children's playroom when he had seen Margaret putting up the decorations. Moreover, it was essentially as a mother that he had seen her. He still thought what a strangely moving picture she had made with the whiteness of her blouse showing up the blue-black lustre of her hair . . . But this was terrible! Simply terrible. He was appalled at the course that his thoughts had taken him. Why he was being practically unfaithful to Felicity before he had even bought the engagement ring.

And, all the time, he was saying to himself: " But I should be so happy. So ecstatically happy. It is all that I could have dreamed of. I am betrothed. And to a Bishop's daughter."

But he could not make himself feel happy. Not the least bit happy. Even now, looking back on it, last evening had been like a nightmare. When Felicity Warple had flung herself upon him and he had been confronted at point-blank range by the arrowhead sharpness of her nose, the cold possessing eye, the upstanding quiff of hair, reason had nearly departed from him. It was as though the Bishop himself, possessed and out of his true senses, had leapt into his arms. Dr. Trump reeled as he remembered it.

And, at the thought that next morning he would have to meet the man face to face after having entertained such dreadful thoughts about him, he became distraught again. For there was no avoiding it. The way things had turned out it was his clear duty to see Bishop Warple as soon as possible. He still had to *ask* him for his daughter's hand in marriage.

I I

It did not make things any easier that the Bishop's cold was no better. On the contrary, it had thickened rather than cleared. In consequence, Bishop Warple had given up all thought of going out to-day. Bundled up in a crimson dressing-gown, with his feet thrust into a pair of bedroom slippers, he was sitting in front of the gas-fire in the bedroom. An egg, rather messily decapitated, stood on the breakfast tray beside him, and his cup had been absent-mindedly put down upon the tray-cloth instead of on the saucer. A copy of *The Times* open at the cross-word with the single solution, ANEMONE, filled-in in pencil, lay at his feet. And on the arm of his chair rested two clean handkerchiefs and a nose-dropper.

At the sight of Dr. Trump he flushed. When he had heard the housekeeper announce Dr. Trump's name he had assumed that the man was somewhere on the other end of the phone. And he was now waiting gloomily for the woman to switch the call through to him. This was bad enough in itself. But to see Dr. Trump actually standing there on the threshold was far worse. It was, in fact, intolerable. And he said so.

Drawing his dressing-gown across his pyjama legs, he waved his visitor away.

" I'b sorry," he announced, " bud I'd dod seeing addywud. Dod dis bordig."

" But I must see you," Dr. Trump replied. " I am here on business. Personal and intimate business."

Bishop Warple looked up in astonishment. Dr. Trump's voice sounded different. It was like having a blackmailer in the room. He resented the imperiousness. And he intended to tell him so. But he was reckoning without his cold.

" Yaa-chew! " was all that he could utter.

The sneeze was unexpected. Nevertheless it had the effect of unnerving his visitor.

" At any other time, I would have waited," Dr. Trump began, " but this is . . ."

" Yaa-chew," Bishop Warple interrupted him a second time.

". . . vital to both of us," Dr. Trump continued. " And . . . to Mrs. Warple."

At the mention of Mrs. Warple, the Bishop looked up in astonishment. He was still mopping himself with his hand-kerchief and his eyes had moist red rims to them. But at least he was listening.

" Wod's thad? " he asked.

Dr. Trump recognised this for the right moment. And he wished to do justice to it. Drawing himself up to his full height, he towered over his bewildered Bishop. But now that he was face to face with his future father-in-law and he remembered his awful thoughts, his courage abruptly left him. He was timid and confused.

" I have come . . ." he started in a high, unnatural voice.

" Go od," Bishop Warple said impatiently.

" I have come . . ." he resumed.

" Go od," the Bishop said for a second time.

"I have come to ask your spouse's hand in marriage," he blurted out at last.

"By spouse's!" Bishop Warple repeated in amazement.

"Your daughter's spouse I should say," Dr. Trump hurriedly corrected himself.

And then, because that still didn't sound right, he tried again.

"In short, I wish to marry your daughter," he finished up miserably.

A perspiration had broken out all over him while he was speaking and he was now looking down at his boots, not daring to catch the Bishop's eye. But the Bishop was self-occupied. With his handkerchief spread over his hand as if he were conjuring, he was waiting helplessly for the next sneeze that was slowly mounting to its climax.

"Yaa . . . yaa . . . yaa . . . chew!" he roared at last.

In the pause that followed, Dr. Trump screwed up all his courage and spoke again.

"Did you . . . er . . . did you hear what I said?" he asked.

The Bishop nodded. He had heard all right. But he still didn't know what to make of it. Even if he had been in normal health, Dr. Trump's words would still have taken him aback.

"Does . . . does by daughter dow?" he asked.

Here Dr. Trump smiled a trifle self-consciously.

"Indeed, yes," he said. "It was, in fact, she who asked me."

CHAPTER XVI

I

SWEETIE often wondered about the little boy who had visited her so suddenly in the middle of the night and had then gone away again without even saying good-bye.

He had been a very rough sort of boy, she remembered; and his feet had kept getting on top of hers as they lay together. Also he had been wet. Like a used bath towel—though he could scarcely be blamed for that because of all the rain that was coming down outside. But it was his rudeness that she minded about most. After all, it wasn't a lot to ask of anyone that he should say thank you to a complete stranger who had taken him into her bed simply because the police were after him.

All the same, she would have liked to meet him again if only to see what he really looked like. As it was, she could not remember properly. The most that she could be sure about was that his nose turned up rather than went straight; and that his hair stuck out in a kind of fringe from his forehead and didn't lie down flat the way other little boys' hair did. But even the way his hair stuck out, she was ready to admit, might have been because he had got himself a bit ruffled coming up the fire-escape. She had often looked down from the dormitory window at the criss-cross metal of the escape, and it was certainly a terribly long climb.

By now Sweetie had pretty much given up all hope of ever meeting him again. The Hospital was so large that there were hundreds and hundreds of other little boys to get him mixed up with. And the wall down the centre was so high that, even if she knew his name and called out to him, he wouldn't be able to hear.

It was only on Sundays in fact that the boys and the girls ever came together, and that was in chapel. But the boys all looked different then because of the white collars that they were wearing. And Sweetie expected that she must look different, too, because the last time that particular little boy had seen her she had only been wearing a nightdress.

Not that it mattered very much, either way. She had almost forgotten him. And he had probably forgotten all about her, too.

In any case, she had more than little boys to think about now. She was getting to be a big girl; she was six already. Getting on for seven. And she was going into the first grade to-morrow. This meant upheaval. A different teacher. A different dormitory—so that even if the strange little boy should happen to come back to look for her she wouldn't be there. And a different uniform.

It was the uniform that was the most important. The infants in the Kindergarten wore anything that would fit them; washed-out cotton frocks in the summer and woollen jerseys in winter. Nobody—not even Dr. Trump—seemed to mind about the infants. They were too small to disgrace anybody. But, once in the junior school, all that was changed completely. By then the Archbishop Bodkin uniform was compulsory.

It hadn't altered since 1668, this uniform. Winter and summer alike, it was the same. A pillar-box colour red flannel blouse with a narrow white collar, stiff like a bank clerk's, a blue serge skirt with a leather belt and brass buckle for a waistband, black lace-up boots and black stockings, and a blue cape and hood lined with the same pillar-box flannel. It was picturesque, historical, uncomfortable. Visitors were particularly affected by it. And Dr. Trump himself, carried away by so much orphan pageantry, had once enthusiastically declared that if he had his way he would make the uniform compulsory for all children everywhere.

Sweetie would have been ready to agree with him. She had lain awake at night thinking of that broad leather belt with its brass buckle. It was the most beautiful kind of belt in the world. The spike on the buckle was sharp enough for making holes in bits of paper. And the lace-up boots: they were worth keeping yourself from falling off to sleep just so that you could go on remembering them. They came up right over your ankles and the laces were as long as from your nose to the tips of your fingers. If she could only have that leather belt and those boots it seemed that nothing else would matter. She would be like all the other girls and could never be unhappy again. Besides, the red of the blouse was her favourite colour. It was the very hottest sort of red there was.

That was why it was so exciting to be standing at last in the clothes queue, with the pig-girl and the girl with thick curly hair like a sheepdog's and the fat one who looked like a bear. It was the first day of term, and the store room of the junior school had been turned into a shop. The various parts of the uniforms—the scarlet blouses, the skirts, the belts, the lace-up boots, the black stockings were piled up in heaps on the counters.

There were fifteen customers altogether. Fifteen infants from the Kindergarten all standing in a straight row waiting to be bewitched into real Archbishop Bodkin foundlings. Mrs. Meedle was in charge. Sweetie hadn't met her before. But come to that, she hadn't met her assistant, Nurse Savidge, either. They belonged to the other part of the Hospital: they didn't have anything to do with the Kindergarten at all.

Mrs. Meedle was nice: Sweetie could tell that at once. She was so fat that she looked soft all over. Her wrists had
132

creases in them. And because she was so soft she must also be kind. Sweetie wondered whether Mrs. Meedle ever nursed people. She would have liked to be nursed by Mrs. Meedle. But she supposed that Mrs. Meedle would be too busy. Everybody in the Archbishop Bodkin Hospital was always too busy for things like that. If you really wanted to cuddle on to somebody's lap you had to hurt yourself first, quite badly. A bruise wasn't enough. There had to be blood, as well. In fact, the only person who had ever really cuddled Sweetie was Margaret. And then only on Thursdays.

As for Nurse Savidge, she was quite different. She was hard. Everything about her was hard. She wore steel spectacles and a fountain pen stuck into a hard metal holder. On her chest she carried a small hard-looking brooch. She was straight, too, right from her waist up to her chin; and her legs were so thin that even if she had tried to make you sit on her lap her knees would be too sharp to be comfortable. Not that she ever would want to cuddle anybody. She didn't even look as if she had ever been cuddled herself.

Nevertheless Sweetie admired her. She had never seen anyone so quick with a tape-measure. When the infants first filed into the store room, the tape-measure was hanging over her shoulders like a necklace. Then, as the pig-girl came in front of her, first she whisked off the cotton frock that the pig-girl was wearing and began measuring so rapidly that Sweetie couldn't understand how she could read the figures on the tape.

"Twenty-six," she began calling out to Mrs. Meedle. "Twelve. Twenty-four."

And before the pig-girl knew what was happening she had been pushed sharply in the small of the back by Nurse Savidge, and Mrs. Meedle was easing the blue serge skirt on over her head.

Because Sweetie was last in the line she had plenty of time to watch what was happening. She should as a matter of fact have been third in the row, but she had got late on the way. She had stayed to watch a pigeon. The pigeon had been interesting. It had a smooth grey back like polished stone and a purple bib that changed colour as the pigeon turned its head. Its nose was especially interesting. There were white lumps growing on it that made the pigeon look brave and handsome, and its eyes were the colour of red ink. Sweetie would have been ready to stand there all day looking

133

at it, if it hadn't flown away. When at last she caught up with the party, they had all gone inside and she had to stand right at the end of the line behind the others.

Even though Mrs. Meedle was gentle, she was quick, too. The pile of uniforms grew smaller, and the pile of cotton frocks and strap shoes grew beside it. In Canon Mallow's day, Mrs. Meedle used to have her mouth full of pins as she nipped the blouses in over the shoulders, or marked the place on the side of the skirt with a piece of chalk where the buttons should go. After all, the uniforms weren't new. They weren't even second-hand. They were third, or fourth, or fifth, or sixth-hand. And little girls, even all of the same age, aren't by any means all of them the same size. That was why the workrooms had been kept so busy.

But Dr. Trump had put an end to all that. On his orders, three of the seamstresses had been dismissed and the other two were now engaged solely on necessary repairs. In the result, the uniforms looked more uniform than ever. It was obvious that the blouses and skirts and cloaks were all exactly as they had left the manufacturers and that the occupants had, one by one, been firmly fitted in afterwards.

It was the bear-girl that caused the trouble. Sweetie had always known that she was a very fat little girl. But she had never known quite how fat she was until she had seen her standing there in her vest and knickers while Mrs. Meedle went searching through the pile of skirts and blouses trying to find something that would fit.

It was at this point that Mrs. Gurnett came in. She had just met Dr. Trump as she crossed the playground and he had smiled at her as he said good-morning. There was nothing actually wrong with that, she supposed ; nothing that she could reasonably flare up about. But she didn't like it all the same, didn't like being the recipient of a smile that said as plainly as if the words had been actually spoken : " You are an elderly, obstinate and rebellious woman but, by sheer unrelenting firmness and politeness, I will tame you." It was because his fixed and concentrated smile had hit her full in the eye like a pellet that Mrs. Gurnett was out of sorts as she came in.

She caught sight of the bear-girl straight away.

"Why is that child standing there with nothing on?" she demanded. "She'll catch her death of cold."

"She's so enormous," Mrs. Meedle replied. "There's nothing to fit her."

"Then get something from Grade II," Mrs. Gurnett retorted. "She can't go about naked just because she's fat."

"But anything that goes round her'll be too long," Mrs. Meedle pointed out.

"If Dr. Trump wants to have the children falling over their hems, that's his affair, not mine," Mrs. Gurnett retorted.

"Then we'll have another go with this one," Mrs. Meedle said hopefully. "Perhaps there's a pleat we could let out."

She turned to Sweetie as she was speaking.

"And just you wait there," she said. "You aren't going to be any trouble, I can see that. You're just a little slip of a thing."

It was Nurse Savidge who supplied the scissors. They were something else in steel that she carried about on her. Hitched to a black silk ribbon, they were worn stowed away inside the waistband. And with them she began to open the box-pleat that ran down the back of the scarlet blouse. Then she stopped.

"It's no use," she said. "It'll have to be a Grade II."

She turned to the bear-girl.

"Stay where you are," she said firmly. "I'm coming back."

The bear-girl stood there without moving. She was not a particularly bright child. But, at least, she was obedient. She was ready to stand anywhere for hours if she was told to do so. Behind her, however, was Sweetie. And Sweetie was impatient. She wanted to get into her uniform. Also because she liked Mrs. Meedle, she wanted to be helpful. She wanted to save her all the trouble that she could. So she took up the scissors herself. They were very sensible scissors with long sharp points. If she really got to work with them she was sure that she could make the bear-girl's blouse so that it fitted perfectly. Then everybody would be pleased—Nurse Savidge, Mrs. Meedle, Mrs. Gurnett, Dr. Trump; and, of course, the bear-girl.

"Stand still," Sweetie said to the bear-girl. "I'm going to do something."

"What?" asked the bear-girl.

"Make your blouse so that it fits," Sweetie told her.

"How?" asked the bear-girl.

"With my scissors," Sweetie told her.

"Oh," said the bear-girl.

She was surprised that Sweetie should have any scissors. But she didn't care to argue. Sweetie was such a masterful little girl. And there was always trouble if anyone tried to stop her doing anything.

All the same she gave a shudder as Sweetie pushed the scissors up inside her blouse from the bottom. And she nearly cried out because the point pricked her. But Sweetie was very firm and decided about it all.

"Don't wriggle," she whispered, "or I'll hurt you. Then Mrs. Meedle'll be cross."

It is difficult cutting things from the inside. Very difficult. But it was the only way in which Sweetie could do it if other people weren't to see what she was doing. And Sweetie wanted it all to be a surprise. She wanted Mrs. Meedle to come back and find that all her work had been done for her. That was why she went on cutting, slowly, carefully, putting her tongue out a little because she was concentrating so hard. Then she reached the top. And as she made the last snick, the bear-girl's blouse fell apart over her shoulders and Sweetie found herself looking at the bear-girl's naked back. She must have made a mistake somewhere: Sweetie realised that. And she saw that she had cut clear through the bear-girl's vest as well. Now Mrs. Meedle wouldn't be at all pleased. She might be very angry, in fact.

That was why Sweetie put the scissors down again on the table.

Even so, Mrs. Meedle might have been ready to forgive her. But what Mrs. Gurnett couldn't forgive, however, was that Sweetie wouldn't own up. But how could she? "Who's the naughty little girl who's done this? Is it you?" Mrs. Meedle demanded, staring straight at Sweetie. And Sweetie could only shake her head. She was trying to explain that she wasn't naughty. Just helpful.

Then everyone got cross at once. And, because they were cross, Sweetie started to cry. And worse. She got cross, too. She hit the bear-girl for getting her into so much trouble.

That was why Sweetie was sent to Dr. Trump.

I I

It was serious, deeply serious, when anyone was sent to see Dr. Trump. And for an infant who had only that day gone into the junior school, it was unheard of. There was a gasp from Mrs. Meedle when Mrs. Gurnett threatened it.

The other children, the pig-girl, the girl with the sheepdog hair, the bear-girl, stood round silent, fascinated, appalled.

"I mean it," Mrs. Gurnett went on. "Over to Dr. Trump you go."

It was Mrs. Meedle who was the first to speak. She came forward and put her hand on Sweetie's shoulder.

"I'm sure she didn't mean to do it," she said. "She's just a very silly little girl who didn't think. You can't send her to Dr. Trump for being silly."

Mrs. Gurnett faced Mrs. Meedle angrily.

"I'm not sending her. I'm taking her," she replied. "If you want to be responsible for a size one vest that can't be worn again, I don't."

There was a pause, and no one spoke again.

"Come along," said Mrs. Gurnett.

It was quite a long way from the Junior Girls to Dr. Trump's study. The route led, first across the bare asphalt of the playground, then through a doorway into the vegetable garden and along a gravelled path, next through the doorway into the main block, past the Senior Girls' sewing-rooms and finally into the kept enclosure of the Warden.

Throughout the walk Mrs. Gurnett stumped along hard, her face flushed and indignant, her eyes fixed unblinkingly ahead, her lips drawn down into their uncompromising crescent. Because she was going so fast, Sweetie had to run to keep up with her. But it was not Mrs. Gurnett's intention that Sweetie should keep up. Mrs. Gurnett intended that Sweetie should follow: it would make the important fact of her disgrace more apparent. But Sweetie understood nothing of this. The faster Mrs. Gurnett went, the faster Sweetie followed. Soon they were both nearly running. And when it became obvious that she would have to break into a sprint if she was going to avoid the child, she slackened. It was for just this moment that Sweetie had been waiting. With a final spurt she caught up with her and took her by the hand.

"Leave go," ordered Mrs. Gurnett.

"I'm sorry," Sweetie answered.

"Not half so sorry as you're going to be when Dr. Trump hears what you've done," Mrs. Gurnett told her.

"Will he be angry?" Sweetie inquired.

"Very," Mrs. Gurnett replied.

"Oh," said Sweetie.

It seemed that the whole hospital was angry this morning.

137

People were living just to be cross with her. The unfairness of it made her miserable.

And because she was miserable she tried to take Mrs. Gurnett's hand again.

They had reached the Warden's corridor by now. Dr. Trump's study stood at the far end of it. Down the corridor they went, Mrs. Gurnett still leading. Then at the door she stopped.

"Wait here," she said.

She raised her hand to knock on the door. But before her knuckles had touched the panel, the door opened. Dr. Trump stood there with a small red-headed boy beside him. The small boy was rubbing his eyes with his fist.

"Let that be a lesson to you," Dr. Trump was saying, swishing the air with his cane as he was speaking. "Let us see who gets tired of this treatment first."

The small red-headed boy looked up and saw Sweetie standing there. And he resented her. He didn't like to be seen crying. Then he recognised something about her. It was her eyes. They seemed so much larger than the eyes of other little girls. For the moment, he forgot all about Dr. Trump.

"Hallo," he said.

Sweetie's eyes opened still wider.

"Oh hallo," she answered.

That was Sweetie's and Ginger's second meeting. It was the 7th September, 1928, on which it took place. Sweetie was six, and Ginger seven. As friendships go, you couldn't exactly call it a ripe one. Only just beginning, in fact. And with five hundred children in the Hospital and a high brick wall dividing the sexes there was no guarantee that it would ever get any farther.

For five hundred is an awful lot of children.

138

THE KITCHENS of the Archbishop Bodkin Hospital were long, low and rounded like converted railway tunnels.

At first glance they seemed to have been carved laboriously out of the still living rock. It was only closer inspection that revealed that they had been merely scooped out of London clay and then enthusiastically bricked in to exclude all but the last remnants of the sunlight. The windows, six in number and set high so that no one should be able to see out of them, had first been reduced practically to the size of port-holes, and then heavily barred across with metal strips that any prison governor could have pointed to with pride.

Up to six feet, the walls of the kitchen were painted a deep bottle green; next a dado of dark chocolate ran round the whole interior; and finally, the upper walls and ceiling carried a coat of smooth slaty distemper. The whole effect was both serviceable and sedative. And also strangely smothering. It was as though the decorator had risen temporarily from some submarine existence to choose and supervise his colour scheme.

At this moment—10 o'clock a.m. on the morning of Wednesday the 3rd—Mrs. Gurnett was standing at one end of the kitchen beside a small table that was bare except for a pair of kitchen scales and a metal spike on which was impaled the day's collection of tradesmen's bills and store accounts. She was not looking at them, however. She was not even thinking of them. Instead, she was gazing down the long line of white scrubbed tables at which the kitchen staff were working. They all looked exactly alike, these women, dressed in the blue-and-white-striped working uniform of the hospital. And facing each other across the table tops they conveyed the air of a cotillon of wardresses.

But Mrs. Gurnett was not thinking even of the women. She was adding up figures in her head. Private figures. Figures that no one except herself and the bank manager knew anything about. It was the mystical number "four hundred and fifty-nine" that kept swimming before her eyes. And, as she gazed at it illuminated as brightly as if in neon, she was reasoning silently within herself.

"Not yet," she cautioned. "Not before it's the full five hundred. I mustn't do anything that I shall regret later. There's only me to consider. But once I've burned my boats, where am I? Who's going to step forward if anything goes wrong?"

For a moment her eyes re-focused and she could see the kitchen staff once more. One of the women had paused and was scratching her head with the end of a long wooden skewer that she had been using. Mrs. Gurnett decided to speak to the woman about it. But not now. For the time being she was continuing with her secret thoughts, her confidential plans for her own separate and exciting future.

"It'll take three years," she went on to herself. "Every month of it. And only if I'm careful at that. But if it isn't then, it's never. I shall be too old for it. No patients of mine are ever going to say that I can't do justice by them."

At the thought of patients of her own, not mere Archbishop Bodkin weaklings but real paying patients, with laundry and cotton wool as extras, Mrs. Gurnett's soul became suffused with a warm inner radiance. She saw it as the one thing in life worth living for—her own private nursing home, with her own private operating theatre, her own private sterilisers, her own private nursing fees. Even the words on the brass plate set above the gate-post—THE LAMORNA NURSING ESTABLISHMENT: RESIDENT MATRON: MRS. GURNETT—were plain to her. She had decided already in favour of engraver's script for the lettering, because it looked less cold somehow than the Roman.

"That is, if I can stick it for another three years," she reminded herself. "There's my limit and I can't go beyond it. It's in his hands as much as in mine."

As she stood there, dwelling already in the brilliant but uncertain future, she became aware that the kitchen hands had stopped their work and were staring intently in her direction. At her? Apparently. But why? It was none of their business how long she chose to stand over them. And then she became aware of someone who was beside her. And, turning sharply, she found herself face to face with Dr. Trump.

"Ah," said Dr. Trump, his face creased in readiness for the smile he always used on such occasions. "I fear I startled you."

140

Mrs. Gurnett's chin stiffened and the crescent of her mouth descended sharply.

"Did you want something?" she asked.

Dr. Trump's smile remained fixed and purposeful.

"I wish to see the kitchens," he replied.

Mrs. Gurnett did not move.

"Well, there they are. That's all there is of them."

"Then perhaps we might go round them together," Dr. Trump suggested.

"Now?" Mrs. Gurnett asked. "Just when there's lunch to get."

"And what better time could there be?" Dr. Trump inquired.

Mrs. Gurnett was about to tell him. Then the figure of five hundred pounds rose up before her, clear and tantalising, and she checked herself.

"I'm ready," was all she said.

As the two of them advanced along the centre gangway, a rigid and unnatural silence descended upon the room. And, at the realisation of what this sudden hush portended, Dr. Trump smiled. A genuine and unpremeditated smile. A smile of sheer gratification at this latest proof of his tremendous presence.

He turned to Mrs. Gurnett.

"And are they happy at their work?"

"I'd soon hear about it if they weren't," she replied.

"Then let us put it to the test," Dr. Trump proposed. "Let us speak with some of them."

He paused opposite one shapeless aproned figure and addressed it. As he spoke, the girl turned round. She was a large, vacant-looking girl with a flat, white face across which tendrils of pale hair were straying. By now Dr. Trump was wearing his smile again.

"And what might your name be, may I ask?" he inquired.

The girl appeared puzzled as though there were a catch in the question somewhere.

Mrs. Gurnett came to her assistance.

"He asked you your name, Annie," she explained.

"Annie, sir," the girl repeated in a whisper as though imparting a closely guarded secret. She had somehow the air of a lunar visitor who had been captured and held for questioning.

"Well, Annie," Dr. Trump went on, "and what is it that we have here?"

"It's a rice pudding," Mrs. Gurnett interjected.

But Dr. Trump motioned her to stop.

"I want her to tell me herself," he explained.

There was a pause.

"Well," Dr. Trump insisted. "Tell me."

"S'rice," the girl confirmed, still in the same hoarse whisper.

"And do you enjoy making rice pudding?" Dr. Trump inquired.

This time the girl merely smiled back at him nervously. She had never had this question put to her before, and needed Mrs. Gurnett to help her with the answer.

Dr. Trump overlooked her silence.

"And are rice puddings all that you make?" he went on.

The girl gave the same nervous smile. It was evident that, under so exacting a cross-examination, she was getting rattled.

"It's apples to-morrow," Mrs. Gurnett reminded her.

Dr. Trump took up the cue.

"And do you like making apples?" he asked. "Apple pudding, I mean."

Again the smile. Again the look of complete bewilderment.

"You are, in fact, happy?" Dr. Trump asked her point-blank.

It was this question that really floored her. She could not make head or tail of it, could not understand this insatiable questioner who was interested only in enjoyment and happiness. So she smiled again and wiped her forehead with her apron sleeve.

Dr. Trump smiled back at her.

"That's all I wanted to know," he said.

As they moved off Dr. Trump turned to Mrs. Gurnett.

"She doesn't appear to be a particularly bright sort of girl," he said quietly.

"She isn't," Mrs. Gurnett replied.

"Then why employ her?"

"Because she's cheap," Mrs. Gurnett snapped back at him.

"How much?"

"Ten shillings a week, and her keep. She's an old Bodkinian, remember."

Dr. Trump's eyebrows came together with a little wriggle. He was frowning.

142

" How many of them are there?" he asked.

" Who?"

" These hired girls."

" Six," Mrs. Gurnett replied. " There should be more.
I've asked for them."

Dr. Trump ignored the second half of the answer.

" Six at ten shillings a week?"

Mrs. Gurnett nodded.

" A hundred and fifty a year!" Dr. Trump observed disapprovingly. " And could not the older girls in the Hospital
perform these simple duties?" he inquired.

" Cooking isn't simple," Mrs. Gurnett replied.

" But parts of it are," Dr. Trump pointed out. " The . . .
er washing up, for example."

" The children do the washing up, you mean?"

" Precisely."

Mrs. Gurnett sniffed. " There'd be breakages," she said.
" They'd need too much looking after."

" But," Dr. Trump reminded her, " that is what you are
here for . . . to look after them."

" I couldn't hold myself responsible," Mrs. Gurnett replied briefly.

There was a pause. A long awkward pause.

" We shall see," Dr. Trump replied enigmatically. " We
shall see."

They had now reached the end of the main kitchen and
were facing the entrance to a small inner dungeon, where a
single electric light was burning.

" And this?" asked Dr. Trump. " Are there more rice-
puddings being made in here?"

" This," said Mrs. Gurnett, " is the scullery."

" Ah," Dr. Trump exclaimed cryptically, as though he was
cherishing special plans for the sculleries.

After the heat of the kitchens, there was a sudden, unnatural chill about the scullery. The earthenware sinks, the
slate draining boards, the bare lavatory-like tiles all seemed
to have been refrigerated in the builders' yard before instal-
lation. And despite the naked electric light bulb that blazed
over the taps there were corners of the room still left in
darkness. Dr. Trump almost bumped into a solitary figure
seated in a low chair, with a sack of potatoes on one side and
an enamelled pail on the other.

" I beg your pardon," he said gallantly.

" Thash all right, shir," the woman replied.

Now that he could see her he realised how old she was. It was a toothless old crone who was sitting here in the twilight, amid a litter of potato peelings.

"And are *you* happy in your work?" he asked. "Do you like . . . er peeling?"

The old woman paused for a moment and looked up to catch Mrs. Gurnett's eye.

"Sho, sho," she said. "I'm shatishfied. No complaintsh here."

"Good," said Dr. Trump. "Then we will leave you."

He had just noticed that a small heap of freshly peeled potatoes was lying in the old woman's lap, and the apron that she was wearing looked as though other things had lain in it before. He was relieved to think that potatoes are not eaten raw.

"Come," said Dr. Trump to Mrs. Gurnett. "We must not detain the lady."

"Thash all right," the old woman replied, without even looking up again. "Taksh more than thish to shtop me."

Back in the warmth of the kitchens, Dr. Trump turned to Mrs. Gurnett.

"And what is her pay, might I ask?"

"Fifteen shillings," Mrs. Gurnett replied. "Mornings only. She lives out."

"And is peeling potatoes skilled work?" Dr. Trump went on.

"Not particularly," Mrs. Gurnett replied.

"Then why pray do we employ a paid peeler?" Dr. Trump demanded.

"To avoid waste," Mrs. Gurnett told him briefly.

This time Dr. Trump's eyebrows gave another little squirm and then climbed up high on to his forehead.

"Could anyone, even a child," he asked, "waste fifteen shillingsworth of potato peelings in a week? It seems unlikely."

Mrs. Gurnett was silent for a moment. Then she faced round angrily.

"Well, anyway," she said, "it's all the old thing's got. Just that—and her old age pension."

"Quite so," Dr. Trump replied. "But we must remember whose money it is that we are spending. If it were yours or mine I would say nothing."

"Then what do you want me to do—sack her?"

144

Dr. Trump spread out his hands in a gesture of deprecation.

"Oh, no," he said. "This is clearly a matter for the Board to consider. I am only their servant, remember. Not my own master."

I I

It was on the first Thursday of the month that the Board meetings were held. And, as the calendar moved round towards this one, Dr. Trump found himself growing steadily happier with every day that passed. By the first Tuesday of April he had his speech word perfect; and, on the Wednesday night, he could not sleep for thinking about it.

Appropriately, Dame Eleanor placed the item first on the Agenda: " *Proposed economies in catering and management* (Dr. Trump)," was how it read. And the meeting proceeded, wrapped in Canon Larkin's approving smile. Even the minute was exactly as Dr. Trump would most have liked to see it. " *Agreed,*" the paragraph ran, " *that to provide more practical instruction in domestic science and housewifery, girls in senior grades to assist in kitchens under close supervision from Mrs. Gurnett. Estimated saving for financial year 29/30 £175 per annum. The Board thanked Dr. Trump for his proposals.*"

Sweetie was seven when the Board, prompted by Dr. Trump, came to that decision. And the sevens, of course, were no more than juniors: they weren't affected. But there is less than five years to go before Sweetie reaches the senior school. She is already more than half-way, in fact, along the pilgrimage towards the scullery and the potato pail. And perhaps it is just as well. Domestic service has always been the one great opening for old Bodkinians from the girls' side.

CHAPTER XVIII

GINGER WAS in trouble again and Dr. Trump was standing upon the faded hearthrug of his study, his arms crossed and his chin held high in readiness to receive him.

Twice before he had drawn himself up to his full height

only to relax again as the footsteps had gone on past the door and down the corridor. But on this occasion something told him that the time had come. And he was right. On the panel of the door came the knock for which he had been waiting. And it was just as he had expected—a knock as timid and nervous as though a moth were fluttering there.

Dr. Trump's eyebrows contracted.

" Come in," he said.

He had been practising for this moment, and he assumed the rasp that he had in readiness.

Slowly the doorhandle began to turn. And, because it did not turn fast enough to please him, he repeated his invitation.

" Come in," he repeated, the saw-edges of his voice grating.

It was a rather formal looking Ginger who entered. He was wearing the short black jacket and narrow trousers of the Bodkin uniform. It was a rigid and formal sort of uniform at the best of times and this small boy in particular looked uncomfortable in it. Tight even according to the regulations, the jacket gripped so closely across the chest and shoulders that the short arms stuck out sideways in penguin fashion.

Dr. Trump frowned. He mentally registered the danger signs of overfeeding, and proceeded to examine the boy more closely. Then he breathed more easily. The trouser ends were short of the boot tops by a clear two inches and this was distinctly reassuring. It showed that growth and not excess nourishment might be at the bottom of it all. But the effect was nevertheless displeasing: it made it hard somehow to be proud of the boy.

And then the face—so blunt, so formless, so . . . so animal. Even the hair was—ah, that was the right word for it —rebellious! The boy, in short, was a goat, a he-goat among his placid flock ; a creature requiring all the attention of the shepherd. Dr. Trump paused and glanced out of the window : he felt a sermon coming on. Then he recovered himself. There was work, serious work, for him to do.

" Shut the door, boy," he said. " That's what doors are made for."

There was a pause.

" And come over here," he added. " I have no wish to shout across the room at you."

The boy moved slowly forward, his heavy boots dragging. The floor in that part of the room was polished and the hobnails grated like scrapers. At the sound, Dr. Trump winced.

"Are you under the impression that my study is the playground?" he asked, carefully keeping his voice level and unalarming.

"No, sir."

"Then pick them up properly. Not like that."

"Pick up what, sir?"

"Your feet, boy. Your feet. Don't grind with them."

Ginger had now come into position, and was standing obediently to attention.

"I'm not, sir."

Dr. Trump deliberately did not answer. At all costs he wished to avoid losing his temper. The whole interview had been carefully designed and would, he felt sure, prove very effective. He went over to his desk and began glancing through the papers.

"Have you come to receive a Conduct Star?"

"No, sir."

"Or a Woodwork Certificate?"

"No, sir."

"Then perhaps it is a Games Badge, is it?"

"No, sir."

"Oh, so what is it?"

"I was sent, sir."

"Of course you were sent. Boys don't walk in here whenever they feel like it. Who sent you?"

"Mr. Dawlish, sir."

"And why did Mr. Dawlish send you?"

"Because I spoke in prayers."

Dr. Trump paused. His eyebrows now made a continuous line across his forehead.

"You spoke in prayers! And what did you say, may I ask?"

"I said 'look,' sir."

"Indeed. And why did you say 'look'?"

"I wanted to show someone something."

"During divine service?"

"Yes, sir."

"Go on. What was this something?"

"It was a cigarette card, sir."

"Have you still got it?"

"Yes, sir."

"Then give it to me."

Ginger hesitated. For a moment, a single challenging moment, Dr. Trump feared that he was going to refuse. But

147

apparently the boy thought better of it. Forcing his hand down into his trouser pocket, he brought out a thin sheaf of cigarette cards secured by a rubber band. Then very carefully he began to select one of them.

But Dr. Trump was too quick for him.

"Give them *all* to me," he said. "All!"

Only when he finally had them in his hand did he realise what remarkably dirty cigarette cards they were. There was a juvenile sordidness about them that appalled him. Even so, he forced himself to examine them. They appeared to belong exclusively to a Common British Butterflies Series and this at least allayed the worst of the doubts that were in his mind: he had feared film-stars. Holding the cards by his fingertips he carried them over to the fire.

He was about to speak but the small boy interrupted him.

"It isn't my rubber band, sir," he said.

"Very soon it won't be anybody's rubber band," Dr. Trump informed him, and loosening his fingers he dropped the package into the flames.

"There!" he said.

Then he turned towards the boy once more.

"And do you mean to tell me that you wanted somebody to look at those things when you should have been praying?"

"Yes, sir."

"Why?"

"I just remembered them, sir."

"Weren't you thinking about your prayers?"

"No, sir."

"Why not?"

"I couldn't hear, sir."

"You couldn't hear!" Dr. Trump's nostrils dilated. "Are you accusing me of mumbling?"

"No, sir."

"But you are!"

"Yes, sir."

"So!"

Dr. Trump drew back a little. He had never encountered such insolence before. And polite insolence at that. The boy had actually behaved as though he were trying to agree with him. It was either stark honesty or abominable effrontery. And Dr. Trump could not afford to choose the wrong alternative. Already the interview had gone along quite different lines from those which he had intended.

148

"I shall cane you," he said briefly. "I have caned you before and I intend to cane you again."

As he went over to the cupboard where the canes were kept, he reflected that caning Ginger was becoming quite a habit with him. He had entirely lost his earlier nervousness.

"Get ready," he said over his shoulder. "Across that chair."

By the time Dr. Trump got back, Ginger was certainly ready. Startlingly ready in fact. Dr. Trump averted his eyes in sheer distaste. Ginger was becoming thoroughly professional too.

"Six of the best I think we said," he remarked lightly.

"You didn't say anything, sir."

The voice came from lower than knee level. And it disconcerted him. He was sidling round now to get himself into position. Then, when he was satisfied at last, he began rocking on his heels and swishing the cane in the air like a golfer making ready for a drive.

"Now."

The contours of the target stiffened instinctively, and Dr. Trump swept his arm back with all his force to its farthermost limit. He was a tall man and the big mahogany table was less than three feet away from him. The corner with the edge, bevelled like a sabre, caught him right across the knuckles.

"Ow!" said Dr. Trump, and dropped the cane.

Then he saw something that reminded him that he must recover the cane immediately and get on with the job. For Ginger was watching him. Still in that unspeakable position, he had twisted his head round and was staring open-mouthed at his tormentor. Not that he was grinning or smirking. Dr. Trump would have known how to deal with that. This was worse. Far worse. For so far as a red-haired urchin can display any emotion, Ginger was displaying it now. To his horror, Dr. Trump saw that it was pity that was revealed in that aghast, upturned face.

"Are you all right, sir?" Ginger asked.

CHAPTER XIX

IT WAS a Wednesday; one of Bishop Warple's mid-weeks.

"And now," he was saying as he looked at his watch, "no doubt the invalid will be ready for us."

The Bishop's habit of referring to his wife in this way had already conjured up alarming pictures in Dr. Trump's mind. He saw Mrs. Warple as someone—almost something—lying there, emaciated, grey, inert. In pain probably. Voice a mere whisper. Each breath drawn only with difficulty. Strength just sufficient to extend a limp, feeble hand towards her future son-in-law. He was, in fact, dreading the encounter and feared that, at any moment, he might break down under the sheer emotional strain of it. Nor did Bishop Warple's next remark do anything to reassure him.

"Perhaps my little Felicity had better go up first to see if everything's in order," he suggested. "We don't want to surprise the invalid, do we?"

As he uttered the last words, he gave Dr. Trump's arm a coy, affectionate squeeze and dropped a word of explanation in his ear.

"Her nerves," he said vaguely. "Any sudden shock, you understand."

"Just so," Dr. Trump replied. "I'll be most careful."

"I'm sure you will," Bishop Warple answered. "But we can't afford to take risks."

Dr. Trump shook his head. He was by temperament decisively opposed to risks. And above all he was anxious to avoid them on this occasion.

"You don't think it might be better to postpone it altogether?" he began hopefully. "Perhaps some other day . . ."

But Bishop Warple would not hear of it. "No, no," he said. "That would never do. Not after we've told her."

There was now an awkward strained silence, broken only by the sound of Dr. Trump's breathing. A heavy breather at all times, Dr. Trump in moments of agitation always became louder and more stertorous. And on this occasion he was suffering from a slight cold as well. In consequence, every inhalation was accompanied by a shrill, fluting sound. It was as though he was whistling to himself as he stood there.

The Bishop eyed him. He simply could not make out how

150

the man did not realise what an irritating sound he was making. It would be like having an oboe for a son-in-law. Then, when the Bishop could stand it no longer, he changed the subject.

" Getting the house all done up in readiness?" he asked.

Dr. Trump's breathing abruptly changed. He unclasped his hands and relaxed.

" Felicity was choosing wall-paper patterns this morning," he replied. " I mean . . . we were choosing together."

" Same thing," the Bishop assured him. " You'll find that out soon enough."

He gave a little chuckle as he said it and squeezed Dr. Trump's arm a second time. Dr. Trump smiled back obediently. But inwardly he shuddered. Why, he asked himself, did the Bishop have to be so . . . so worldly? All Bishop Warple's remarks about marriage had the same lightheartedness, even facetiousness. There was a comic postcard quality about them.

But any further thoughts of resentment were interrupted. The Bishop was looking at the clock.

" Might as well go up now," he said. " But we mustn't stay too long. We don't want to overtire her."

There was a screen inside the bedroom door and Dr. Trump tip-toed gingerly round it. As he did so, he was conscious of two things: the overpowering heat of the room—a large gas-fire was burning fiercely though it was still only early September—and the richly medicated atmosphere. It was like stepping into a chemist's warehouse. Immediately, he was enveloped in an odour of eau-de-Cologne, lavender water, menthol, friar's balsam, camphor, hot-water bottles, disinfectant, toothpaste. It was the very attar of sickrooms. And, as he raised his eyes, he found himself confronting the invalid—a large spongy-looking woman in a brightly flowered bed-jacket. There was a soft, almost transparent waxiness to her complexion that he found oddly disturbing. If the temperature of the room went up by even two or three degrees it seemed to him that she might start melting before his eyes into the bedclothes.

" Come in, Dr. Trump," she said.

As she said it, she thrust out her hand. Dr. Trump took it timidly. And immediately he regretted having done so. For he found himself being pulled irresistibly forward. But it was too late. With a sudden jerk Mrs. Warple had kissed him.

151

"How-do-you-do," Dr. Trump asked awkwardly.

He was still attempting to withdraw his hand. But Mrs. Warple had no intention of letting go.

"We're going to be great friends, I can see that," she went on. "You must come and sit with me."

"Indeed, yes," he replied faintly. "Many, many times."

Considering her delicate state of health, the strength of Mrs. Warple's grip was really most surprising. But so also was her whole appearance. It was evident that, unlike most chronic invalids, she had not let herself go. It was unmistakably lip-stick that she had on. And she was wearing jewellery. Large imitation pearl ear-rings were fixed to each ear, and she had a string of the little objects round her throat. From the close range at which he was inspecting her, Dr. Trump decided that she must be brave, very brave. Obviously undefeatable, in fact. But somehow not spiritual.

He drew back and found Felicity whispering in his ear.

"She likes you," she said simply.

Dr. Trump did not know what to say. He only wished that the note of relief, of surprise even, in Felicity's voice had not been quite so pronounced. But he was not paying attention to Felicity any longer. He was staring instead at Mrs. Warple. For instead of reaching out for her smelling-salts, or even for her Bible, Mrs. Warple had taken a cigarette from a common cardboard packet that lay among the bed-clothes. And, when she had lit it, she blew out a thick cloud of smoke and sank back among the pillows.

This time it was Bishop Warple who whispered. He had anxiously been observing Dr. Trump's face. And, when he caught his eye, he spoke.

"The doctors advised it," he said in a strained half-voice. "For its soothing qualities. Nerves you know. She takes no pleasure in it."

"Quite so," Dr. Trump agreed.

Mrs. Warple, however, appeared to be making the best of it. She blew out another cloud and half closed her eyes.

"You don't know what it means taking my Felicity away from me," she said in a deep melancholy-sounding voice. "She's all I have now."

Before Dr. Trump could reply, however, Bishop Warple had come to his assistance. He advanced to the foot of the bed and laid his hand upon the mahogany end-piece.

"My pet," he said sweetly. "You have me."

" Not always, I haven't," Mrs. Warple contradicted him. " You're always going out somewhere."

" But only on my duties," the Bishop tried to reason with her. " I haven't done what you might call enjoy myself for years . . ." He stopped himself abruptly and started to re-phrase the sentence. " I should say . . ."

But by then Mrs. Warple had turned to Dr. Trump again.

" You're a lucky man," she told him. " If Felicity serves you, the way I've served her father, you'll have nothing to complain about."

" Oh, but I know I'm lucky," Dr. Trump replied.

He reached out gallantly to take Felicity's hand as he said it, but Felicity was not there. She was busy arranging Mrs. Warple's pillows.

" Besides," he went on. " *I* want to serve *her*."

Mrs. Warple, however, had closed her eyes and seemed no longer to be listening.

" Some men seem to think women were created simply for waiting on them," she observed to no one in particular.

Bishop Warple smiled and shook his head.

" Ah, Samuel, I'm afraid the invalid knows us all too well. We men are all poor sinners, even the best of us."

" Quite so. Quite so," Dr. Trump politely agreed with him.

He was shifting restlessly from foot to foot as he stood there. The one thing that he wanted was to escape. Already in this temperature he could feel himself perspiring. There were little trickles running down his back. And he began to fear that he might be the one who would melt, dissolve, trickle greasily away.

" And nobody thinks of the hours I spend alone here," Mrs. Warple went on. She had opened her eyes by now and had fixed them on the ceiling. " Hours and hours while nobody comes near me."

Dr. Trump drew in a deep breath. A happy thought had come to him. Here before him lay his opportunity to ingra-tiate himself, to demonstrate his thoughtfulness.

" Why not have a wireless?" he asked. " The talks, you know. And the music. And, of course, the sermons."

There was a shocked hush at the suggestion.

Mrs. Warple did not even trouble to reply. The Bishop looked down at his gaiters. And it was Felicity who spoke for all of them.

" Not with Mother's bad head," she said reprovingly.

"Alas, no," the Bishop added sadly. "We tried it. It was no use. It's up in my study now."

"Oh don't bother about me," Mrs. Warple said suddenly as though she had been screwing up her courage to speak at all. "I don't count any longer. I'm just a poor old invalid. I'm better out of the way so that happy people can forget all about me."

An expression crossed Bishop Warple's face as though he had heard all this before. He pulled out his watch rather conspicuously and began fiddling with it.

"Good gracious," he said, as soon as he could be sure that everyone would hear him. "My ordinands. I must be going. I am already overdue. I am late, in fact. Very late. Very."

The thought of being left behind there after Bishop Warple had gone came over Dr. Trump in a panic. He realised that he too must do something, and do it quickly.

"And I gave my word that I would not overtire you," he said. "Next time perhaps you will allow me to stay longer. Much longer. There is so much to tell each other . . ."

The Bishop had already begun to make his way towards the door, and Dr. Trump started to follow. But Mrs. Warple was too quick for him. She snatched hold of his hand again. Again the soft, damp octopus embrace.

"I don't know why Felicity should want to leave here," she began. "She's got everything she wants here. Nobody ever tells her anything. She rules this house . . ."

"Ah," said Bishop Warple in a tone of great relief, "I hear the nurse coming."

In the corridor outside Dr. Trump nearly bumped into the woman. She was carrying Mrs. Warple's supper tray. The corridor was narrow and the tray was a wide one. As he flattened himself against the wall, Dr. Trump found himself inspecting the contents like a restaurant supervisor. There was a small casserole of soup ; a silver dish from under the cover of which escaped an appetising odour of onions ; and the two halves of a meringue glued together by a layer of whipped cream.

But it was at none of these that Dr. Trump was looking. His eyes were fixed on a bottle of milk stout that stood black and irreverent-looking, beside the china toast-rack.

Bishop Warple caught Dr. Trump's eye for the second time.

"For medicinal purposes," he said. "She needs the nourishment you know."

CHAPTER XX

I

Mr. Prevarius was back in Charing Cross Road again. He went there quite a lot nowadays, and every time he got out of Leicester Square Underground Station it did something to him. He felt better, younger, springier. And, above all, more creative. His mind enlarged suddenly. Tunes, with the accompanying words already attached to them, came into his head from nowhere. He saw glimpses of a musical comedy that he was going to write one day. He hummed brief snatches of a new cantata. He planned an opera.

Altogether it was as though the air that blew up Shaftesbury Avenue was oxygen, pure oxygen. Everything that he saw delighted him. The bird prints and the maps of old London. The bookshop that was preoccupied with world revolution. The one almost next door that was dedicated to reconciled and acquiescent-looking nudes. The stark simplicity of the Welsh Chapel. The monographs on the ballet. And the gentleman's outfitters. Particularly, the gentleman's outfitters. Fairly intoxicated by now with the sheer exhilaration of the place, Mr. Prevarius plunged inside and bought himself a saffron necktie with magenta spots. Then carried away by the charm of the little emporium, he purchased a pair of braces with horses' heads on them and a yellow bandana handkerchief with a design of horseshoes, to go with the tie and the braces.

Within limits, he could afford to be self-indulgent nowadays. Because, compared with himself on the first timid visit that he had paid to Mr. Jerome, he was now in a different class of men altogether. He was a success. A hit. A somebody. Not that all his numbers had rung a bell, of course. "Handbag Hankie," in particular, had failed to strike even the faintest chord in the public consciousness. It might just as well never have been written. But the other little piece, "Four O'clock Doll"—the title had come to him last Christmas during choir practice for "The Messiah"—had got there all right: only this morning he had heard a milk-boy whistling it in Putney High Street. And another composition of his, in an entirely different vein this time—a number entitled "Desolation"—looked as though it was going to repeat the success of "Four O'clock Doll." No matter how much the Rev. Sidney Prevarius might be kicked around inside the Archbishop Bodkin Hospital, here in the Charing Cross Road, Mr. Berkeley Cavendish was on the up and up.

It was significant that Mr. Spike Jerome, his publisher, no longer kept him waiting when he called. And, on the whole, Mr. Prevarius rather regretted it. Because he was getting on rather nicely with the daffodil-haired young lady in the front office—the one who was so conscious of her fingernails. He had already discovered so far that her name was Desirée, that her mother was a widow—her father, it appeared, had been something in the Indian Army—and that she had been destined for a career as a doctor. Then Papa had died, once of cholera and once of a native spear thrust—there appeared to be two versions—and Desirée had been forced to take up shorthand-typing to keep the home together. The only other information about her that Mr. Prevarius had been able to acquire was that she was thirty-two round the bust—the point arose naturally out of a conversation about jumpers—that her hair was really that colour, and that she liked open-toed shoes and sun-bathing.

But it was no use allowing his thoughts to wander in that direction because Mr. Jerome, his cigar gripped firmly between his teeth, was ready and waiting for him. With no more therefore than a hasty "ta-ta" coming almost on top of the welcoming "cooee," Mr. Prevarius left Desirée and went inside.

Mr. Jerome's smile was already in full display. And the flashes of gold bridgework made Mr. Prevarius feel as though he had stepped clean out of Charing Cross Road into one of the bazaars of old Damascus. There was a strangely hypnotic effect about such a smile, and Mr. Prevarius found himself smiling back at it.

"Got some good news for you, Mr. Cavendish," Mr. Jerome said with a quick roll of the cigar from left to right.

"You mean about 'Handbag Hankie'?" Mr. Prevarius asked eagerly.

But it was the wrong question. At the mere mention of that unplayed, unsung, unloved number, the shutters came down on old Damascus, and the cigar was smartly transferred from right to left again.

156

"'Handbag Hankie,'" Mr. Jerome said contemptuously. "Forget it. Give it a rest. Bury it. It isn't worth crying over. This is something important. It's 'Lullaby Lady' I'm talking about."

Mr. Prevarius had recovered his poise by now. He was not going to give Mr. Spike Jerome any further opportunity for rebuking him. Besides, "Lullaby Lady" was frankly an experiment, a little piece that he had tossed off with no vulgar thought of profit. He cared nothing for it.

"'Lullaby Lady,'" he said. "Oh that. I was thinking of withdrawing it."

"Oh you was, was you?" Mr. Jerome remarked, taken off *his* guard this time. "Well, you won't when you hear. I've placed it. It's in panto."

"But there is no pantomime in May," Mr. Prevarius objected.

"There will be when December comes," Mr. Jerome told him. "*Puss in Boots*. End of the first act. Principal boy number. Words on the screen. Audience singing the chorus. All the children joining in. Everything lovely."

"Well, well," said Mr. Prevarius. "Let us see if we can agree about the royalty scale . . ."

But in this he had gone too far. Mr. Jerome fixed his teeth more firmly in his cigar and leant forward across the little desk.

"We haven't touched on the financial side," he said severely. "It's only placed, subject. The lyric needs tidying up—something topical, you know. And they don't like the chorus. They've got their own man on that—subject to your approval, of course. And they want it re-orchestrated. Sid's looking after that. And Olly's rearranging it."

"Sid and Olly?" Mr. Prevarius inquired vaguely.

"They're under contract," Mr. Jerome explained. "You can't cut them out so it's no use trying."

"I was only wondering . . ." Mr. Prevarius began.

"Then don't," Mr. Jerome told him. "If you break with them, you're through. As it is, they'll expect something."

"How much?" asked Mr. Prevarius.

"Twenty-five each and fifty to you."

Mr. Prevarius paused. It was at moments such as this when he wished that he was a better business man, a stronger character altogether; someone with teeth.

"They're on to easy money, very easy money," he said slowly. "Who represents them?"

Mr. Jerome shifted the cigar into position again somewhere underneath his left ear.

"I do," he said.

But, even with fifty per cent of his new earnings about to go to Sid and to Olly, Mr. Prevarius felt that strange excitement—a kind of electric stimulation running right through nerves and sinews—that is known by all artists on the verge of achievement. And Mr. Jerome had shown himself the large-hearted gentleman that he really was. With scarcely any cajoling from Mr. Prevarius, who kept mentioning that he was thinking of moving over to Chappell's or Francis, Day and Hunter, Mr. Jerome had agreed to advance him twenty-five pounds against future royalties. And this put an entirely new complexion on the whole affair. Mr. Prevarius found himself cordially liking Sid and Olly.

But in the midst of his exhilaration, a wave of something colder, of sheer mortal loneliness, swept over him. It was dreadful that one so gifted and successful, so conspicuously in funds, should be left without a friend in London. Eight million people—and not one among them who cared whether he went under the first bus.

His self-sorrow was still mounting as he passed through the outer office, but a glimpse of the daffodil-coloured curls over the top of a filing-cabinet made him pause. He walked over to the little frosted window, marked "Enquiries," and tapped playfully on the glass.

"Cooee," he said again.

After what seemed to him an unnecessarily long pause, the window shot up and the young lady looked out.

"You again," she asked. She was using a chamois leather buffer this time.

"I again," Mr. Prevarius told her.

"Well?"

"I've just been given two theatre tickets for to-night," Mr. Prevarius began.

But the Colonel's daughter stopped him.

"Not in there you haven't," she told him. "He never gives anyone anything."

Mr. Prevarius smiled.

"Well, what would you like to see?" he asked.

The young lady was at work on the little finger by now.

"That's more like it," she said.

"Well?" Mr. Prevarius asked.

"Well what?"

"Well, what is it to be?"

"Please yourself entirely," she said. "It's no affair of mine." She had now picked up a nail file, and was at work like a real craftsman. "I never go out with accommodation addresses, thank you."

"Accommodation addresses?" Mr. Prevarius paused. "Oh, but I only use the box number for business purposes," he told her.

The young lady removed a fragment of loose nail with her teeth.

"I didn't imagine you lived in it," she said.

"And does it matter to you where I live?" Mr. Prevarius asked hopefully.

"It couldn't matter less," the young lady replied. "All the same, it's usual for gentlemen to say."

She was hard at work with the polisher again by now, and Mr. Prevarius could see only the thick cluster of curls— daffodil in colour, chrysanthemum in construction—a mere six inches from him, but with the wire mesh of the inquiry desk in between.

"And it's useful," she added, after a pause. "That is if you ever want to find them again."

She looked up as she said it and Mr. Prevarius found himself gazing deeply into the pure cornflower blue of her eyes. The eyelashes, he noticed, were long, black and romantically clotted with mascara.

I I

Accommodation address or not—and Mr. Prevarius certainly had no intention of allowing the words Archbishop Bodkin Hospital to cross his lips—she was there beside him. Or rather, opposite. It was a corner table, from which Mr. Prevarius had asked the waiter to remove the flowers, and leave merely the pink-shaded standard lamp. They had both drunk two Martinis already, Desirée had restored the lipstick that was now smeared round the edge of her glass, and Mr. Prevarius had his foot pressed up hard against her.

"I shouldn't be here at all really," Desirée was saying. "I broke another date just to come. Ed'll be furious."

It was the second time she had said it and Mr. Prevarius made the same reply as before.

" What the eye doesn't see," he observed, " the heart can't grieve."

Really this evening promised to be quite amusing. Besides, he was making such a lot of new acquaintances to-day. Apart altogether from Desirée herself, there had been Sid and Olly. And now Ed.

" Ed your boy-friend?" he asked.

" Not likely," Desirée replied. " He's married."

Mr. Prevarius reached out and took her by the hand.

" Wise little girl," he said. " Taking no chances."

Desirée disentangled her hand so that she could go on applying the lip-stick.

" You married?" she asked.

" Married?" Mr. Prevarius repeated. " Oh dear me no. Nothing like that about me. I have no ties of any kind."

" That's what they all say," Desirée replied. " I'll have the asparagus."

Mr. Prevarius was disappointed. He disliked the way Desirée had switched the conversation suddenly from romance to asparagus: it made her appear heartless and callous. But perhaps she was only being cautious, refusing to allow the riptide of their passion to sweep them both away. And, instead of attempting to force the pace, Mr. Prevarius took the hint from her own aloofness and decided to proceed by other means. He beckoned to the waiter.

" A bottle of the Widow," he said. " Very cold. And keep it iced."

Over dinner, Mr. Prevarius learnt a lot more about Desirée —Manners was the surname. And her life story was certainly remarkable. First, there was the old place in Sussex with all the horses. Then there was that unfortunate father of hers whose third death had apparently occurred when the liner that was bringing him back from Ceylon foundered on the rocks off Capetown. Her mother had gone down at the same time with Desirée's baby brother clasped in her arms. From this, Mr. Prevarius gathered that it must have been another son of the same ill-omened marriage whom Desirée was now helping through Sandhurst. And Desirée herself seemed to have been educated almost everywhere—in a convent in Switzerland, privately by a governess in the Mannerses' rambling old mansion in Sussex, in India and alternatively in Ceylon, and at a finishing school in Cheltenham. She had sung. She had danced. She had once spoken French like a native, even though she had forgotten it all now. But the very moment her brother Terence had passed out of Sandhurst and been appointed to his ship, she was going to chuck up everything and go off to Paris where she guessed that she really belonged. There was also an only partially explained kid sister who, like all the Mannerses, had contrived somehow to pack a lot into a short time. At this very moment, she was studying law, dancing in a ballet at Monte Carlo, on tour with an opera company up at Oldham and engaged to a Guards Officer with pots of money and another of those old places that keep turning up all over Sussex.

As the meal proceeded, indeed, the champagne served to break down all her accustomed reticence. She was in trouble with her dressmaker. And, until her thrice-dead father sent her next month's allowance, she frankly didn't know where next week's rent was coming from. Mr. Prevarius put his hand into his pocket while she was speaking and fingered tenderly the crisp one-pound notes that Mr. Jerome had given to him. He felt that, even if she didn't know he did. And he was glad that it was only her *pied-à-terre* in London and not the place in Sussex that was temporarily bothering her.

The meal had been a good one—lobster, duck and crêpe-suzettes—and the moment had come for coffee and liqueurs. He was disappointed that Desirée had chosen crème-de-menthe, and felt that Cointreau might have been more lady-like. But the crème-de-menthe could not have been more effective if he had prescribed it himself. It did everything that could have been expected of it. By the time she had lapped up the last emerald drop with her tongue, she sat back and said: "What do we do now?"

Mr. Prevarius cunningly suggested a theatre. But it was too late for any theatre: he knew that. Shaftesbury Avenue was already well into its third act. And until Mr. Prevarius got his new glasses he didn't want to go to a cinema because films made his eyes ache. Dancing, too, was out of the question because he was wearing crêpe-rubber soles.

"I only wish that I could suggest continuing our little conversation at home," Mr. Prevarius said plaintively. "But, alas, we should be interrupted. I share bachelor chambers with a friend, you see."

"Oh that's all right," Desirée assured him. "Please don't

apologise on my account. I'd hate to disturb your friend. Besides, I wouldn't *dream* of going back there. I scarcely know you."

" Then you must let me take you home," Mr. Prevarius told her. " On that, I insist. Yes, positively insist. Anywhere you say and we can go on talking in the taxi."

" Well, don't imagine I shall ask you in, because I won't," Desirée said firmly, speaking exactly as her father, the Colonel, would have wished her to speak. " I've got my own reputation to think of just as much as you."

" Just so," Mr. Prevarius assured her. " I shall imagine nothing, and then I can't be disappointed, can I?"

While Desirée had left him for a moment and Mr. Prevarius was settling up with the waiter, a mood of airy recklessness came over him. He felt like a disembodied spirit with mischievous tendencies. The whole thing was like magic, a fairy-tale. He had made a compact and sold his soul—not to the Devil, but what was far more profitable, to Mr. Berkeley Cavendish. He was re-born. The vast Babylon of London was spread out before him, rich in mystery and in temptation. Somewhere in one of its hidden corners, Balham probably, Desirée had her bower and after he had left her there—the terms of that could be arranged in the taxi—he could slip away again, into the shifting multitudes, unknown, unnoticed, unconcerned: so safe that he would not even have to feel furtive.

When Desirée was safely inside the taxi, her two hands folded demurely in her lap, Mr. Prevarius turned smilingly towards her.

" Where to?" he asked. " Where does milady want?"

" Medina Road," Desirée said sleepily. " Twenty-three B. Tell him to go to Putney Underground and I'll tell him from there."

" Putney," Mr. Prevarius repeated in a flat, hollow-sounding voice. " Did you say Medina Road, Putney?"

" That's right," Desirée answered. " It's just off St. Mark's Avenue at the bottom. You needn't sound so worried. It's only four-and-six."

It was just on twelve-thirty when Sergeant Chiswick was roused by a gentle tapping on his window. He rose and found Mr. Prevarius standing there, on the pavement, making silent signalling motions in the direction of the front door. And

162

because it was so late the whole of their conversation had to be conducted solely in whispers.

"I missed the last train," Mr. Prevarius explained softly.

"Quite so, sir," Sergeant Chiswick replied, holding out his hand for the tip.

Mr. Prevarius put half a crown into it.

"The Warden was asking for you earlier," he said slowly. "Wanted to see you as soon as you came in."

"What time was that?" Mr. Prevarius asked.

"Just after ten o'clock, sir."

Mr. Prevarius added another half-crown.

Sergeant Chiswick saluted.

"Thank you very much, sir," he said. "You can rely on me, sir."

It was blackmail, of course. Five bobs' worth of the darkest blackmail. But worth it, if Dr. Trump really had been inquiring.

And, in any case, it wasn't Dr. Trump who was bothering him now. It was Desirée. There she was practically on his own doorstep. From his bedroom window he could actually see the terrace of mean little houses where she had her miserable bed-sitter. By his one act of indiscretion, which he reminded himself had sprung from nothing lower than the anguish of sheer loneliness, he had placed his whole future in jeopardy.

"Why couldn't it have been Balham, or Streatham, or Belsize Park, or anywhere else?" he asked himself. "Why did it have to be Putney?"

CHAPTER XXI

I

DR. TRUMP had made up his mind. Mr. Dawlish would have to go.

Admittedly, the decision itself was a recent one. But the steps leading up to it had been slow and inevitable. In the first place, it was Mr. Dawlish's appearance that had counted so much against him. As a non-smoker himself, Dr. Trump disliked all smokers. But a dirty smoker was more than dislikable: he was downright disgusting. And it had to be admitted that Mr. Dawlish was dirty. Positively frowsty, in

163

fact. There was ash all over him. Then there were his shoes. Other masters somehow contrived to keep their shoes clean. But not Mr. Dawlish. He would come slopping down the stairs in the morning with shoes that looked as if he had spent the night in the kitchen garden. It was a key-point, the shoes: Dr. Trump had noticed before that clean shoes and self-respect always went together. He knew now at the first hint of shoe-trouble, to look out for the other danger signs. And in Mr. Dawlish they were all there—unpressed trousers, bulged pockets, ragged fingernails, creased tie, untidy collar, badly shaven chin. In short, the man was a specimen of advanced social disintegration. An outcast.

And an example. That was the dreadful thought. Dr. Trump squirmed every time he reflected on the influence that Mr. Dawlish must be having on the boys who were under him. The young of both sexes, as Dr. Trump had once described it at the Annual United Kingdom Convention of Christian Education Workers, are merely so many innocent mirrors miraculously reflecting what they absorb. And supposing that it was the image of Mr. Dawlish that was reflected? What an advertisement that would be for Old Bodkinians. Come to that, what an advertisement for Dr. Trump.

But, in any case, it was not Mr. Dawlish alone who was occupying Dr. Trump's thoughts. Mr. Dawlish himself was no more than a pawn, a solitary pathetic piece in a complicated and majestic game. For what Dr. Trump was working on now—had been working on for the last six weeks, in fact—was nothing less than complete reorganisation.

The idea of reorganisation had come to Dr. Trump suddenly when he was getting into his bath. And it had so entirely taken possession of him that he had simply lain there —with the nailbrush and the Sorbo sponge floating round him—while the water slowly cooled off below blood heat.

In consequence—since he was a morning bather—he was late for breakfast, late for Hall, late for his daily session with Mrs. Gurnett. But, rushed and harassed as he was, his soul was aflame within him. He now saw reorganisation as something apart and almost holy. For the time being at least, it seemed more beautiful even than discipline.

Nor had he merely toyed with the idea. With commendable thoroughness, he had already got down to details; hard facts, figures, personalities. There were fourteen members of the teaching staff altogether, drawing salaries that averaged three pounds ten a week, and all found. A hundred and eighty-two pounds a year apiece. Two thousand five hundred and forty-eight altogether. With food, heat, light and laundry on top, say a round three thousand. No wonder that the balance sheet was such a nightmare.

But under the reorganisation things would be different. For a start, he was going to reduce the teaching staff from fourteen to nine. There would of course be difficulties, grave difficulties, confronting him: he saw that. But wasn't it the very essence of life's challenge that problems should be encountered and overcome? And now that he saw it all on paper, in his own handwriting, how simple the solution really was. Larger classes: that was the first thing. Instead of segregating the children rigidly into arbitrary age groups, there would have to be more latitude. The bright sevens would go in with the backward nines. And there would have to be doubling up—Scripture *and* games; singing *and* woodwork ; cooking *and* needlework—that kind of thing. With, of course, less spare time. The present half-day a week would obviously have to go. And why not? Was it reasonable, was it proper, was it even honest, that Christian philanthropists should be asked for their alms, and the widow for her mite, that able-bodied men and women, whose lives should have been dedicated to the cause of teaching, should once a week for an entire afternoon lounge about in their rooms or in neighbouring cinemas in utter idleness?

There remained merely the question of which ones should go. And here Dr. Trump reminded himself that a good administrator had to be impersonal. Motives like sympathy and compassion that were admirable in other connections were entirely irrelevant here. And more than irrelevant: they were wicked. There was, indeed, only one criterion that could fairly be applied—age. It was, in short, the elderly, the infirm—and, of course, the difficult—who must be the first to go.

Three out of the five had been easy. First, there was Mr. Dawlish. Then Mr. Jeffcote, who was 63 and had trouble with his eyes. It was obvious that *he* couldn't double games or woodwork with anything. Then Mr. Prevarius. It certainly wasn't age in this case. At most, the man was no more than an abominably well-preserved 50. With him, it was something that went deeper even than time: it was his moral attitude. Whenever Dr. Trump had been with Mr. Prevarius for any period he felt as though he had been in the presence of someone not entirely, not scrupulously, clean.

On the women's side, it was the question of Mrs. Gurnett that had troubled Dr. Trump most. That she was obstinate, unco-operative, even openly hostile, had been apparent from the start. But who was there to replace her? Dr. Trump had to admit that, at the thought of actually dismissing her, he grew apprehensive. Not, of course, that he was afraid of the woman—that would be ridiculous. It was merely that he recognised her position, her influence, her long seniority. Who knows but that, with the corner stone removed, the whole edifice might not come toppling?

So, in the end, Dr. Trump left Mrs. Gurnett untouched and decided on Miss Wynne and Mrs. Glubb instead. And with good reason. Both were on the verge of sixty. Neither was well. Each again had private sorrows that were interfering with her work—with Miss Wynne, it was the death of her mother that had affected her and, with Mrs. Glubb, it was a goitre. So far as Mrs. Glubb was concerned, indeed, this was doubly unfortunate, for her ailment was both unsightly and incurable. Dr. Trump therefore decided that, in the interests of everyone, he had better act now and immediately. There was no provision anywhere amid the Archbishop's benefactions for elderly invalids and nursing cases among the staff. What he had to do might be painful but it was certainly his duty.

There it stood then, the final list of the condemned. On the men's side, Mr. Dawlish, Mr. Jeffcote, and—admittedly Dr. Trump licked his lips as he came to this one—Mr. Prevarius. And from among the women, Miss Wynne and Mrs. Glubb. Moreover, now that his mind was made up, there was nothing to be gained by hesitation. Unscrewing the top of his presentation fountain pen, Dr. Trump began to write:

"The Warden presents his compliments to Mr. Dawlish and would be obliged if Mr. Dawlish would attend in the Warden's study at . . ."

Dr. Trump had cancelled all other engagements. The entire morning from 9 a.m. till lunchtime was set aside for the dismissals. And when the first knock came on the door he was ready.

"Oh God," he had prayed fervently less than five minutes earlier, after going over the last of the staff files, "make me worthy of my task. Make me strong. Let neither pity nor weakness blind me or deter. Let me be ruthless in my righteous cause."

Even so, it did not prove easy. He had been forced to change his original order and it was Miss Wynne whom he was seeing first. The accident of sex embarrassed him. Because it was a woman that was being sacrificed he tried to make things easy for her, to be ruthless in a kindly, almost paternal fashion. And, in the result, he rather overplayed his hand: he was too disarming. For the first few minutes of the interview, in fact, Miss Wynne simply did not know what he was driving at. And then, when she discovered, she burst into tears.

"You mean you want me to leave?"

"Not until the end of term," said Dr. Trump gently.

"It's the same thing," Miss Wynne replied.

"Oh no," Dr. Trump corrected her. "It is not yet even *half*-term. There is no element of . . . er . . . urgency."

There was a pause while Dr. Trump sat there looking at her. As he did so he noticed with distaste that her skin was yellow rather than pink in colour, and that it had a loose, puckered appearance that he had seen previously only on the breasts of slaughtered fowls. There was no doubt about it, Miss Wynne was elderly all right. Deuced elderly. He even began to wonder if she had been keeping her real age from him. There, abruptly, the silence was broken.

"It all seems so unfair," she blurted out suddenly. "First Mother's death. And then this."

"But I," said Dr. Trump, drawing back a little, "can hardly be held responsible for your poor mother's death."

"No, but you can for her daughter's," Miss Wynne snapped back at him.

And before Dr. Trump could reply—a grave, crushing sort

of reply that would make further rejoinder impossible—Miss Wynne had snatched up her handbag and, with her handkerchief pressed hysterically against her face, had flounced out of the room, leaving him there.

Dr. Trump sighed and sat for a moment staring at the ceiling. Then he braced himself again—did no one ever pause to consider his feelings at such a moment?—and, taking up the little brass bell with a Swiss milking scene engraved on the side of it, rang for Mr. Jeffcote to be sent in.

And how differently Mr. Jeffcote responded. Even if Miss Wynne was not a lady, at least Mr. Jeffcote was a gentleman. He sat with bowed head listening silently while Dr. Trump talked. And, instead of resenting it, when Dr. Trump came to the real reason for his dismissal—failing eyesight—he seemed positively contrite about his affliction. He apologised. And, more than apologised. He confessed. His near-blindness, he admitted quite openly, was something that he had been seeking to conceal.

Pressed by Dr. Trump as to why he had not come forward like a man and said openly: " I am going blind: you must get rid of me," he explained that he simply could not afford to do so. Up to eighteen months ago, it turned out, he had been making a regular monthly allowance to an invalid sister seven years older than himself, and in consequence he had not been able to save a single penny. There was nothing for it, therefore, but to go on, even though from the back of the classroom he could not so much as see the blackboard. In short, it was sheer poverty that had made him so dishonest.

Dr. Trump pondered. It was only, he reflected, in actually getting rid of people that he had to banish all thoughts of compassion: afterwards, there remained much to be said for it. Besides, Mr. Jeffcote had been so respectful throughout. So respectful, when he might have been so difficult.

He took all these factors into account. Then going over to Mr. Jeffcote, he put his hand on the man's shoulder.

" But do not imagine," he said, " that I, or the Governors of this Hospital, would wish anyone with nearly thirty years' service to go out into the world unprovided for. There is unfortunately no pension scheme. That was an oversight on the part of my predecessor. But there is still perhaps something that I can do."

" Yes? " asked Mr. Jeffcote eagerly, screwing up his pale,

failing eyes as he looked into the light. "What is it, please?"

"Our bishop, Bishop Warple," said Dr. Trump, looking at his watch, "is an . . . intimate of mine. He is also Honorary President of the St. Nicholas Alms Houses in Wimbledon. I cannot promise anything, of course, but I will drop a hint, a broad hint, next time we are together."

There was a pause.

"Thank you," replied Mr. Jeffcote feebly.

"And, in the meantime, take my advice," said Dr. Trump, still speaking in the same mild but manly voice, "and avoid all unnecessary reading. That could only make matters worse."

As for Mrs. Glubb, she astounded him.

After the seemliness and humility of Mr. Jeffcote's behaviour, it was as though Mrs. Glubb, near-invalid as she was, had rushed at him with a bread-knife. And this time it cannot be charged against Dr. Trump that there was anything wrong with his method. On the contrary, for Mrs. Glubb's benefit he chose an approach that was really midway between the one that had deceived Miss Wynne and the one that had knocked the stuffing out of poor Mr. Jeffcote. And, for all the good it did, he might have spared himself the pains. For no sooner did Mrs. Glubb catch his meaning than she flared up and insulted him. Her eyes, already grotesquely large and protruding because of her misfortune, blazed up suddenly, and she moistened her lips before speaking.

"I knew it," were the words she uttered, "I knew it the first moment I caught sight of you. You want to get us old ones out so that you can get your own friends in."

Dr. Trump rose while she was still speaking.

"That, my good woman," he said coldly, "is a lie."

But he was allowed to go no further.

"Don't you start good-womaning me," Mrs. Glubb told him. "I'm not going to stand for it."

"And I," said Dr. Trump, "have no wish to prolong this interview. Good-morning."

"You mean that you are through with me?"

"I mean that you are through with us, Mrs. Glubb. You give me no alternative. You may leave as soon as you are ready."

After Mrs. Glubb had withdrawn—and the way she

slammed the door made the pictures of the Holy Land and the Old Boys' football team rattle on the thin deal panelling —Dr. Trump found that he was trembling. It was as though a powerful electric current was passing right through him. And it made him despise himself to think that any member of his staff, a woman moreover, could have upset him in this way.

He rose slowly and took a long drink of cold water from a glass on the side-table. It was only when he had half-finished it that he realised that the water was stale and rather warm: it could not have been changed this morning. With a frown of displeasure, he went back to his desk and wrote the single word " carafe " on his pad. Then, bracing himself a second time, he rang for Mr. Dawlish to be sent in.

And this time it was all exactly as he had expected. If Dr. Trump had ever been assailed by doubts, one glance at Mr. Dawlish would have been enough to overcome them. The pathetic creature had again dropped something messy and disgusting on his waistcoat; haddock it looked like. What was more, as soon as he began to speak he condemned himself out of his own mouth: in short, he was a grumbler.

" Canon Mallow would never have done this," he said, as soon as he had heard Dr. Trump's ultimatum.

" But Canon Mallow is no longer Warden here," Dr. Trump replied. " Canon Mallow does not enter into it."

" And it's always the old ones who catch it," he went on. " Years of service—and then this."

" I didn't invent *anno Domini*," Dr. Trump said pointedly.

" And it isn't as though the Hospital paid enough for the rainy day when it comes," Mr. Dawlish muttered. " Same now, as when I came here."

Here Dr. Trump saw his opening. And, like a leading counsel, he pounced.

" I am unaware that you ever asked for any increase," he said.

" If I had, I shouldn't have got it," Mr. Dawlish answered in the same flat dissatisfied voice that had always annoyed the Warden.

" That," Dr. Trump replied, rising, " is another matter. We are not discussing fancy. We are face to face with fact . . ."

Even with the surprises, such as Mrs. Glubb's unreasonableness, Dr. Trump's sense of timing had been immaculate. Four of them were gone already, and it was now 11 a.m. precisely. He rang the little Swiss bell again. But this time it was not to summon a victim: it was for his elevenses. And while he stirred his Ovaltine and broke the Marie biscuits into small pieces so that he could eat daintily and without making crumbs, he pondered on the morning's work.

"Mallow would never have had the guts to do it," he told himself. "That's what a job like this needs—guts."

The coarseness of the word privately rather delighted him, there was something so essentially masculine about it, so strong, so robust, so—so gutful.

And he would certainly need all his strength for the next interview, the one with Mr. Prevarius. This, in fact, was going to be the set piece of the whole morning. And, when it was over, the Hospital, Dr. Trump told himself, would be a purer place.

At first Dr. Trump had resolved to finish his elevenses before seeing Mr. Prevarius. But Ovaltine made with freshly boiled milk conserves its heat amazingly. And he saw no reason why, for Mr. Prevarius's sake, he should risk scalding himself. He liked his Ovaltine and wanted to be able to sip it slowly and worthily. Moreover, he asked himself, wasn't there something impressively unperturbed about such behaviour? Wouldn't it, more than anything else, show Mr. Prevarius the unassailable contempt that he felt for him if he went on sipping throughout the interview?

Therefore, with his cup no more than tasted, he rang his fatal bell for the last time. Only on this occasion he was unaccountably kept waiting. It was as though Miss Phrynne had not heard him. He was, in fact, about to ring again when he heard Mr. Prevarius's voice in the corridor outside.

"Thank you, thank you, Miss Phrynne," he was saying. "My hands are full, you understand. Otherwise . . ."

A moment later, the door opened, and Mr. Prevarius stood there, smiling.

"I am not too early, I hope," he began, gazing upon Dr. Trump with a smile that every moment was mounting to a leer.

"Come in," Dr. Trump replied coldly. "I am waiting."

"And I have brought my own mid-morning snack along with me," Mr. Prevarius answered, stepping out of the shadow of the doorway. "I thought that you would not mind if we shared our modest refreshment together."

In his hand was a cup and saucer. From above the rim of the cup a thin veil of mist was rising. Dr. Trump did not trust himself to catch Mr. Prevarius's eye. Instead, he glared at the offending object.

Mr. Prevarius intercepted the glare.

" Milk," he explained. " Plain boiled milk. I rarely change. Cocoa, sometimes. But, in the end, I always go back to plain, pure milk."

" Sit down," said Dr. Trump.

" Thank you, thank you," Mr. Prevarius answered. " You are more than kind."

Dr. Trump paused. Now that he could see Mr. Prevarius clearly he disliked him more strongly even than he had realised. For a start, Mr. Prevarius had suddenly become almost atrociously well-dressed. He was wearing a double-breasted black jacket and striped trousers, with an open butterfly collar. The impropriety of it shocked Dr. Trump. It was the sort of clothing that a bank manager or a Harley Street specialist might have worn, or a county solicitor. But, for a music master in an orphanage, it was frankly presumptuous.

" You know why I have sent for you?" Dr. Trump began. Mr. Prevarius nodded.

" How difficult it is," he admitted, " to guard even the best kept of secrets. And now to think that this one should have leaked out, too."

" Secret?" Dr. Trump asked, unwarily.

Mr. Prevarius's eyes opened still wider in astonishment.

" Why, yes. The B.B.C. Do not tell me now that I have confessed it that you had not heard."

" Explain yourself."

" Our choir, the broadcast."

" Broadcast!" Dr. Trump's nostrils dilated as he said the word.

" What broadcast?"

" Then you had *not* heard," Mr. Prevarius replied gleefully. " But you have a right to know. The B.B.C. is anxious that our choir should sing to all Great Britain. In a series, you understand. ' Voices of Children.' The National Programme, I believe."

" And . . . and when is this to be?" Dr. Trump inquired. Despite himself he could not help being interested.

Mr. Prevarius paused.

" Next term," he said slowly. " Somewhere in the second

172

half. Sir John Reith is still considering. The date is not yet fixed. Merely pencilled in. June the 3rd, I fancy."

Dr. Trump did some rapid thinking. The date was certainly very awkwardly placed. It would mean enduring Mr. Prevarius's company longer than seemed possible. But just think of it! The Archbishop Bodkin Choristers on the B.B.C. It was terrific. Looked at in round figures, it was probably worth a thousand pounds in unsolicited donations . . .

Mr. Prevarius, however, interrupted him.

" But I see that you are dubious "—Dr. Trump heard the words as though they were coming through a thick curtain—" you are thinking of the effect on the children. Perhaps you are right. The experience may be harmful."

Dr. Trump started.

"Harmful?" he said. "On the contrary, if they are brought straight home again by the bus they can come to no possible harm."

" I meant to their voices," Mr. Prevarius explained. " If I thought that a single treble, even one isolated alto, had been over-taxed by the strain of public appearance . . ."

" Nonsense," said Dr. Trump. " Think of the choirboys in Cathedrals. They're at it all the time, week-days as well. Of course our children shall sing."

" As you say, of course," Mr. Prevarius agreed politely. " Exactly as you say. But really I cannot hold myself responsible."

" I shall accept full responsibility," Dr. Trump told him.

" Besides," Mr. Prevarius continued, " if I move across to St. Christopher's . . ."

Dr. Trump started.

" St. Christopher's," he repeated incredulously. " You mean you are thinking of leaving?"

" There have been approaches," Mr. Prevarius admitted. " Nothing definite has been settled, of course. Naturally I would want to consult you first. But I must confess, the offer is attractive. Their pension scheme, you know. And the organ. Three manual. Music plays such an important part at St. Christopher's. The Principal there simply adores it . . ."

But Dr. Trump was not listening. He hated St. Christopher's almost as much as he hated Mr. Prevarius. The way St. Christopher's foisted itself upon the public was nothing less than shameless. St. Christopher's Home of Refuge—he

173

saw the words everywhere, on hoardings; on little highly-coloured cardboard buttons sold by well-meaning ladies on flag-days; in newspaper headlines. "St. Christopher's Boy Saves Centenarian from Drowning," "Old St. Christopher's Girl Wins Queen's Prize for Needlework," "Royal Duke Visits St. Christopher's"—it was sickening, downright sickening. And now St. Christopher's was proposing to steal his broadcast.

"Then you don't feel that the publicity would be distasteful?"

Dr. Trump did not reply immediately. Publicity had suddenly become one of life's truly beautiful words. It had taken its place alongside discipline and reorganisation.

"Publicity distasteful . . .?" he began.

III

That afternoon, Mr. Prevarius sat down to write a letter. It was addressed to the Director-General, B.B.C., and there were half a dozen sheets of pale mauve note-paper in the waste-paper basket before it was finished to Mr. Prevarius's entire satisfaction.

"*My dear Sir*," it ran, "*I am in sole charge of the music in a recognised educational establishment and wish to offer the services of my choir in connection with a new series (which I suggest might be entitled ' Voices of Children') suitable for the National Programme.*

"*The use of the choir would, of course, be entirely free and, as for myself, I am ready to rely without demur upon your generosity. Certain of the settings are my own and these, too, I assume would be paid for at the usual rates. If you would like to have me call upon you in order to discuss the matter more fully . . .*"

174

YOU CAN make all the rules you like, take every precaution, erect barricades, and put broken bottles along the tops of walls, but you still can't prevent two people seeing each other if they have really set their hearts on it. Or even if one of them has.

Take Sweetie and Ginger, for instance. Sweetie was getting on for nine by now, and the first promising moment had come when Sweetie discovered that by climbing up on to the top of the water butt outside the junior girls' lavatory, she could see into the boys' playground over the crescent of the gate that curved downwards in the middle.

It wasn't much of a view—just a narrow half-moon of playground—and it was difficult at first to distinguish Ginger from among the two hundred and fifty other Bodkin orphans who exercised themselves on that particular stretch of asphalt. But size, of course, was a help. And behaviour: there were generally two or three boys following Ginger. But it was his hair that was the certain, the infallible, feature of identification. First, the colour, a fine flower-pot red; and then, the peculiar ridgelike structure that made it stand up in front like a saint's halo that had slipped forward. As soon as Sweetie saw that she knew that she had found the right one.

Then, the problem was simply how to attract his attention. Calling " Cooee " was no good because everyone was always calling out " Cooee." She couldn't whistle because her front teeth weren't firm enough. And it would simply have been asking for trouble to shout out his name for everyone else to hear. So, in the end, she resorted to an accomplishment of which anyhow she was extremely proud. She had learnt it from Annie, the slow-witted Bodkinian who was still about the place ; and it consisted of inserting the forefinger between the front lips while emitting a high-pitched ululation. A " Red Indian Love Call," Annie had told her it was, and Sweetie had been practising it for some time. Now that she was proficient, the love-call could cut through the uproar of the break-period like a skewer.

Not that it got her very far to begin with. The first time Ginger realised that he was the object of this singular alarm-note he was openly resentful. He came over to the gate and told her to shut up. He even added, speaking quietly but with the utmost distinctness through cupped hands, that if she didn't get down he would bung a brick at her. But when she was there the next day, and the day after that, and the day after that as well, he saw that it was hopeless. Threats weren't going to get rid of her and he must try something else instead. But he was still cautious.

"Wodjerwant?" he asked.

"I can see you," Sweetie told him.

"Of course you can see me," Ginger answered. "But wodjerwant?"

"Only just to see you," Sweetie replied.

The extreme silliness of her response persuaded him that it would be pointless to continue the conversation: at this rate they would never get anywhere.

"You're barmy," he said shortly. "You're soppy."

Considering the snub, Sweetie was quite philosophic. She had seen him again and she had got him to take notice of her, which was all that really mattered. The only thing was that he might have been a bit nicer, she felt. It wasn't easy to get on to the top of the water butt, and he might at least have said "Hallo." But the device had worked, worked splendidly. Because next day when Sweetie climbed up, Ginger was there waiting for her. Admittedly, he moved away as soon as she came into sight, but it showed that he was thinking about her, for he came back twice more, each time covering his face up with his hands so as to be unrecognisable, just to see if she was still looking.

She often wondered how many times he turned up after that, because she wasn't there herself. This wasn't due to any slackening-off on her part but simply to the fact that the cover of the water butt caved in as she was getting on to it. It was a tall butt with the better part of five feet of water in it, and it was very nearly the end of Sweetie. By the time Nurse Stedge heard her threshing about inside she had gone down for the third time. And though she was able to support the drowning child with one arm, it required Sergeant Chiswick's strength to withdraw Sweetie. After that, Sweetie spent three days in the Infirmary, and Dr. Trump had "Danger" notices and barbed wire fixed to all the water butts.

It was largely because she was kept in the Infirmary that

she had so much time on her hands. And she spent most of it in thought. Barbed wire, she knew, would make that particular look-out point impossible. Besides, water butts would be too conspicuous after what had happened: everyone would be watching them. So she decided that she would write to Ginger instead. She would use an ordinary piece of exercise-paper, fold it into a paper-dart and simply shoot it over the top of the dividing wall. Then Ginger could read it and send his reply by the same route. A whole barrage of correspondence could pass between them in this way. But again there were difficulties. In the first place, somebody might see it all happening and stop it immediately: then there would be more trouble and more no sweets. Secondly, she couldn't be sure that Ginger would reply: he might simply catch the notes and keep them. But it was the third difficulty that was the greatest of all: she couldn't make paper-darts, never had been able to, didn't even know how to begin.

But even if she could think of no means of actually sending the letter it was still fun writing to him; and, sitting up in bed in the Infirmary, she wrote " For Ginger," " For Ginger," " For Ginger " over and over again, all down the piece of paper that Nurse Stedge gave to her just to keep her quiet.

And that is as far as it would ever have got if it had not been for Annie, who had taught her the love-call. A simple-minded, if not actually deficient creature, she had the bright scarlet thread of true romance running right through her nature. Sweetie did not even have to explain what she was up to: Annie spotted it at once.

" Is Ginger your boy-friend? " she asked.

Sweetie considered the question.

" Not really," she said, " I don't think he likes me."

" But do you like him?"

Sweetie was silent again.

" Yes," she said at last. " Very much."

" Well, you write your letter and I'll get it to him," Annie promised. " Only don't tell anybody. Cross your heart."

Sweetie crossed her heart.

" I'll write it now," she said, licking the pencil in readiness.

She took some time over it, making several false starts before she was satisfied. Then, when it was finished, she doubled the paper over so that no one else should see. She had done her work carefully and, to avoid any possibility of mistake, she had used block capitals throughout. It was a perfect little letter and said everything that she had wanted to say. She sat back exhausted, and waited for Annie to come round again.

Naturally, Annie wanted to read what was written and Sweetie didn't in the least mind showing her: she was rather proud, in fact. What she was absolutely unprepared for, however, was to find that Annie didn't think much of it.

"Is that all you're going to say?" Annie asked.

Sweetie read the letter again from start to finish.

"That's all," she said.

"Aren't you even going to sign it?"

Sweetie looked up. She was worried now. Perhaps there was something wrong with the letter after all.

"Do you think I ought to?" she asked anxiously.

"Well, he won't know who it's from, if you don't," Annie told her.

But Sweetie only smiled.

"He'll know, all right," she said.

And, with that, she handed the letter back again. All that it said was: " FOR GINGER."

After Annie had taken the letter Sweetie felt strangely flat. Flat and empty. She didn't actually regret having written. But she wondered nevertheless whether it might not have been better to wait a bit longer to see if Ginger would write to her first. The news of her disaster in the water butt would be certain to have gone right through the whole Hospital by now. And, if he really cared, Ginger would have been quite certain to get in touch with her somehow. After all, it was for his sake that she had nearly drowned herself.

And waiting to see if there would be any reply was the worst part of all. She became moody and suspicious. She decided that she didn't like Ginger after all. She hated him. And she began to doubt whether Annie had even delivered the letter. But, in this, she did less than justice to a born go-between. In affairs between the sexes Annie was at the highest fulfilment of her nature. She was deriving a vicarious and sublimated form of pleasure from the whole episode. Even if it did not amount to much—couldn't in the nature of things ever hope to add up to anything—it was still serving the cause. And it was starting off all right. She recognised that Sweetie had got the right stuff in her.

She had even thrust the message, for what it was worth, right into Ginger's own hands. And she had been forced to invent an entirely unnecessary journey to the boys' side to do

178

so. This had taken some arranging. But not half so much as bending down and pretending to pick up the piece of paper so that, if anyone was watching, it would look as though Ginger had dropped it.

She even managed to say under her breath: "I didn't write it. It's from Sweetie."

And this was very thoughtful of her. Because, when he read it, Ginger realised that if she hadn't explained, he wouldn't have had the least idea where it had come from.

Anyhow, Ginger found it an awful bore getting it. It worried him. And he resented it. Why couldn't she leave him alone? Why did she have to climb up on things, hollering at him? And now, why did she have to send him a piece of paper with " FOR GINGER " written on it? At odd moments during the next three days, he pondered on her inexplicable behaviour. Perhaps she was a bit mad, he decided.

And then a little incident occurred that made him see things in a new light. One of the seniors—a big fellow of practically fourteen—was found over in the laundry section talking through the window to one of the junior laundresses. The ironing section was absolutely forbidden territory to the boys of any age and because of this flouting of authority, Dr. Trump caned him immediately. Caned him, despite the fact that the boy was almost as tall as he was.

That made Ginger think. If he had been discovered over in the girls' side and at night too, his punishment might have been anything. Prison, most probably. Or, at any rate, a reformatory. And Sweetie had saved him from that without even so much as a thought for her own reputation. Clearly, he had cause to be grateful.

So, simply because Dr. Trump had caned one of the seniors, Ginger wrote his reply. He did it during Geography, right under Mr. Dawlish's nose. In the circumstances, it wasn't as carefully written as Sweetie's. And, by the time he had got it into Annie's hands, it was pretty dirty-looking bcause there had been other things in the same pocket. But Sweetie didn't mind about that. It said all that she could have wanted it to say.

In Ginger's bold and manly handwriting, it read: " FOR SWEATY."

CHAPTER XXIII

I

It WAS Felicity Warple herself who had prompted Dr.
Trump; and more than prompted—goaded. For the past
fortnight she had spoken of practically nothing else. The
Warden's Residence, she declared emphatically, was unin-
habitable. And something, she added, would have to be done
about it before she could be expected to set up house there.

At first Dr. Trump had assumed that it was mere eagerness and excitement that made her behave in this way.
Admittedly, in Canon Mallow's day, the Residence like so
much else in the Hospital, had been sadly neglected, simply
allowed to go to ruin, in fact. But Dr. Trump had already,
he thought, put all that to rights. He could see nothing
wrong with it now. There was new brown linoleum right
through the ground floor, with a pleasing and artistic change-
over to green on the landings; and the dado that he had
found as a muddy coffee was now rich, shining chocolate.
Even the woodwork on the banisters had been repainted—
and properly done, too; the original graining of the oak
showed up most plainly. And when the morning sun shone
in through the squares of stained glass in the fanlight over
the front door, the whole effect was glossy, beautiful, even
opulent.

Nevertheless, it did not satisfy Felicity. Everything in
white was what she wanted. White and chintzy, with painted
parchment shades to all the lights. It made all the difference
having the right kind of lamp-shades, Felicity explained: it
didn't matter a bit how dark and opaque they were, provided
that all the rest of the room was bright and gay and flowery.
It rather added to the effect, in fact.

Also, she had once girlishly confided in Dr. Trump, there
were her china rabbits. She had a unique collection of them,
it seemed. Rabbits of all ages; and of all sizes. With ears
erect; and laid back. Asleep; and scratching themselves.
Prone; and prancing. Staring piteously upwards; and wink-
ing humorously. Realistic; and stylised. Painted in full,
natural colours; and in plain porcelain. In family groups;

and solitary specimens. She had been collecting them ever since she had been a child, and they had come from as far away as Bournemouth, Bangor and Rosyth. By now there were thirty-seven of them, and she was simply aching for a home of her own where she could show them properly. She even had some tiny china toadstools to go with them.

With every day that passed, Felicity was thinking more and more about her future home. It was still a good three months before she would be occupying it, because despite his natural eagerness for matrimony, Dr. Trump remained decisively opposed to short engagements. But, from the way Felicity spoke, it might have been to-morrow. And, carried away by her enthusiasm, she insisted on paying frequent visits. Simply to get the feel of the place, she said; so that she could lie awake afterwards planning and deciding where everything should go.

From the far-away look in her eyes, Dr. Trump guessed that she was planning something at this very moment. There were just the three of them—Felicity, the Bishop and himself —all seated round the fireside in the Bishop's study. It was a singularly bleak February day outside, and Dr. Trump had allowed himself to be pressed to a third cup of tea and the second half of a toasted teacake. Because it was a Saturday afternoon, the Bishop was momentarily a man of leisure, and he was certainly at his most affable. Dr. Trump had already heard two delightfully intimate stories about his late Archbishop—the kind of stories that he would be able to repeat as though he, too, had been a frequent visitor to Lambeth—and a quite astonishing anecdote about a visiting American divine and his behaviour in a London club.

As he sat there, Dr. Trump was conscious of a most delicious warmth; a dual warmth, both physical and spiritual. The fire was toasting his ankles and spreading up his legs, and his mind was filling with pictures of eventual advancement when he, too, would be able to drop into his club on his way back from Church House to drink a glass of sherry and gossip casually with his brethren from the other Sees. Altogether, it was exactly the sort of afternoon that Dr. Trump would have liked to have go on for ever.

But apparently his Felicity was restless already. Indeed, during her father's last story about a minor and otherwise forgotten Archdeacon who when nervous had always developed a highly comical impediment in his speech, Dr. Trump

181

noticed that she was not listening at all. And as soon as Bishop Warple had finished laughing over his own impersonation of the tongue-tied Archdeacon, Felicity turned accusingly to Dr. Trump.

" You haven't forgotten, have you?" she asked.

"Forgotten, my dear," Dr. Trump inquired. " Forgotten what?"

An expression of pain or irritation—Dr. Trump feared that it might be the latter—crossed Felicity's face.

" That means you have," she said tersely.

" But I don't understand, my love . . ." Dr. Trump began. " Was it something I promised?"

" It was something we'd arranged to do together," she told him with a gulp in her voice. "That's all it was. But it doesn't matter, if you don't remember."

" Was it . . . was it something to do with the house?" Dr. Trump asked cautiously.

"We were going to measure for curtains," Felicity replied.

She gave a little sniff as she said it and Dr. Trump was afraid that she was about to cry. And her next remark did nothing to reassure him.

" Not that I mind," she said, staring hard into the fire. " If you don't care how the place looks I'm sure I don't."

Bishop Warple rose hurriedly and caught Dr. Trump's eye. "Well, I must leave you now," he said. "I have my correspondence to attend to."

I I

On the way round to the Hospital, Felicity was a different girl altogether. She almost apologised. But her father's stories, she explained, sometimes drove her almost to distraction. And, if she ever had to hear the story about the stuttering Archdeacon again she really thought she'd scream or smash something.

For a moment Dr. Trump was too stunned to be able to say anything. He had never imagined that anyone, least of all the Bishop's daugther, could think of it in that way. Besides, he had thought the impersonation of the Archdeacon very funny and clever; and all the more subtle somehow because it was a Bishop who was doing the impersonation. Really, women were the most puzzling of creatures.

Felicity, however, had entirely failed to notice how deeply she had shocked him. She was prattling on again already about the curtains.

". . . with a deep valance," she was saying, "and proper drawcords they ought to be lovely. The real trouble with chintzes is that people don't line them properly."

She spoke as though this were a deep secret known only to herself, and a small inner circle of chintz-lovers; and Dr. Trump did not feel entitled to make any comment.

"And another thing," she went on. "We must have proper runners. Ordinary rings are quite hopeless."

There was a pause. A brief one.

". . . and central heating," Felicity was saying. "The house is like an ice-well. They'd better put a hot towel rail, too, in the bathroom while they're at it. We can't be expected to use the bathroom as it is. It hasn't even got a built-in bath."

Dr. Trump drew in a deep breath.

"Everything shall be exactly as you want it," he said.

Felicity smiled up at him gratefully.

"As you want it, too, Samuel," she told him.

The afternoon had, if anything, grown colder. The sun had been shining brightly earlier in the day. But it was now lost behind low grey clouds that looked as though they might be concealing snow. Dr. Trump made a mental note to make sure that Sergeant Chiswick had closed all the windows. He didn't want the man simply to be shovelling coals into the boiler unnecessarily.

He and Felicity had reached the corner of St. Mark's Avenue and were walking alongside the wall of the boys' playground. The bricks themselves seemed to be radiating a hard, bitter cold. And when Felicity suddenly shivered and Dr. Trump looked down at her, he noticed that the tip of her nose—her thin, distinctive Warple nose—was a bright shell pink.

"Oh dear," thought Dr. Trump, "poor circulation."

The discovery annoyed him. He still felt a trifle self-conscious when he went anywhere with Felicity in public. And in particular, he was anxious that she should always look her best. The thought that other people—enemies like Mrs. Gurnett and Mr. Prevarius—might make disparaging remarks behind his back was quite unbearable.

Not that any improvement in Felicity's complexion would

entirely have removed his embarrassment. The real cause lay deeper. It lay in her very presence. There was, he was bound to admit, something essentially frivolous in the very sound of the word *fiancée*.

It pleased him still less that she should have chosen that moment to take his arm. But, worst of all, she snuggled. Dr. Trump was afraid that such a gesture might be misconstrued. But it was all right: there was no one about, and all that she wanted to do was to keep warm.

Not that the Hospital was any more sheltered than the street outside. The arch of the gate-house led straight into the open cloisters, and there was bare playground on either side. Even the green-painted door with the brass plate, " Warden's Residence," did not conceal anything better. There was merely a narrow gravel path with a strip of grey-looking grass on either side of it. But cold as she was, Felicity's spirits rose. She began planning again.

" And as soon as we've got settled," she started off, " we shall have to do something about this garden."

" Do something?" Dr. Trump asked in surprise.

" Flowers," Felicity told him. " It all needs digging and then planting."

" I see," said Dr. Trump.

" You don't sound very excited," Felicity said to him.

" Oh, but I am," Dr. Trump assured her.

Then a happy thought crossed his mind.

" The older boys shall do the digging," he volunteered magnanimously. " And the little girls may plant the flowers."

They had reached the Residence by now and Dr. Trump with his free arm contrived to get the front door open. It was a relief to shut the wind out,-and he was just about to remove his overcoat when Felicity suddenly threw her arms around him.

" I loved what you said just now," she told him.

" About what, my love?" he asked.

There was a note of caution in his voice as he addressed her because he had detected a tenseness, a sudden ardour, that alarmed him.

" About the garden," she said simply.

" And why about the garden?"

" Because we want it to be all pretty and flowery," she confided. " We want the garden to be one big nursery."

Dr. Trump shuddered involuntarily. Now that he was

actually about to embark on marriage, those four children that he had made her promise him seemed somehow excessive. Three would possibly be suitable. Or even two

But he concealed his feelings.

"One big nursery," he repeated, and kissed her ice-cold face.

CHAPTER XXIV

GINGER WAS sitting at a desk in the front row of the empty schoolroom, writing. He had already finished two pages. And the rest of the paper—eight pages more of it—lay by his right hand in readiness.

Eight pages is a lot. Writing as fast as he could, one page in ten minutes was as much as he could manage. Because writing had never been one of his good subjects. He didn't hold the pen properly or something. And it wasn't interesting, either. Not what he was writing. Simply "I must not spit," "I must not spit," line after line, all down the page.

What was more, he didn't even want to spit. Not in the slightest. The sudden, uncontrollable desire for spitting, the inexplicable impulse to prove that he was the longest, straightest, wettest spitter in the whole Hospital had passed away completely. No trace of the spitter remained anywhere in his whole make-up. At this moment, spitting seemed entirely valueless and without merit: it was potty, barmy, kids'-stuff. He couldn't imagine why he had ever cared for it.

Boring holes in things was something different. Boring holes, in fact, was what was now occupying his entire leisure attention. He had even managed to take time off from writing the interminable words "I must not spit" to make two holes, deep ones that came out the other side, in the lid of the desk at which he was now working.

It was, however, not so long ago—eleven o'clock that morning to be precise—when spitting had seemed all-engrossing. Because he had felt so strongly about it, he had issued a challenge. And Spud had accepted it. Nor would any real harm have been done if Spud had been ready to admit defeat. But he hadn't been ready. Decisively, overwhelmingly outspat, beaten by a good eighteen inches in fact, he had issued a counter challenge. In front of everyone, he had bet Ginger that he couldn't spit into the open classroom window. And in the face of such unreasonable defiance there was nothing for Ginger to do but take up the challenge.

It was a good six feet up to the window. And clearly there was nothing for it but to step back a full couple of paces and trust to sheer lung-power. Taking up his position, and screwing up his lips in readiness, Ginger prepared for his bombardment.

Not that he was successful immediately. The first two rounds merely flicked the lower window-panes. But the third was a beauty. Perfectly globular even at the height of its trajectory, and gleaming like a pearl in flight, it entered the open portion of the window and landed audibly on the floor within.

Faced by such consummate mastery of a difficult and notoriously exacting art, even Spud let out a cheer. And Ginger, carried away by such acclamation, took up his position once more to repeat his achievement. It was this vainglory that was his undoing. For while he was still standing there with his eyes closed, sucking hard at his cheeks in preparation, Mr. Dawlish's head appeared at the open window.

Considering the danger and indignity of his position, Mr. Dawlish behaved very moderately. He withdrew. Then, when the peril had passed—and, when it came, the shot was no better than an outer—he re-appeared quickly before Ginger could possibly have had time to re-load. Emerging from the side door that led straight into the playground, he took Ginger by the ear, and conducted him back into the classroom. And once he had got him there he handed Ginger a piece of blotting-paper and indicated with his foot the exact spot on the floor where he wished him to blot.

That done, Mr. Dawlish went over to the window once more and stood there looking out, while he absent-mindedly ran a long discoloured pipe-cleaner backwards and forwards through the chewed stem of his pipe. The incident had not seriously disturbed him. There was no point in raising his voice or losing his temper: he had realised that long ago. The infinitely varied beastliness of boys was something that no longer even seriously troubled him.

Not that Ginger had got off lightly. There were twenty lines to each of the school pages and the ten pages that Mr. Dawlish had set him would mean that by the time he had finished he would have written the words " I must not spit "

exactly two hundred times. It was cruelty of the most refined and devilish kind. Already his hand was aching, and
the ink that was all over his index and second fingers was
making various sore places and scratches hurt and tingle.

While he was sucking his fingers, a new thought came to
him. Supposing he bored a hole right through the lid of the
locker, he might be able to lift up the lid and spit *through* it.
It was an agreeable and entertaining project, a graceful varia-
tion of his earlier barbarous pastime. But, unfortunately, it
came to nothing. To make a hole that was sufficiently large
for his purpose would have been to court immediate discovery. So he explored other possibilities. Going through
his pockets, he found a button, the end of a comb, a small
piece of rubber, the crinkly metal-top off a lemonade bottle,
a piece of string—and his gimlet. With patience he was at last
able to make a series of holes in all the solid objects. And
the rest was simple. Passing the string through the holes, he
now had a neat bunch of treasures. Then he resumed his
writing-exercise.

It was going better now. He seemed to be getting along
faster. And the mechanical nature of the labour drugged him.
He found that while he was writing he could think about
other things as well—railway accidents, and massacres, and
torture, and starving to death on uninhabited islands, and
executions.

Another happy idea came to him by the time he had got
to the fifth sheet. If he held two pens in his hands at the
same time perhaps he could fill two lines at once. The idea
was attractive and daring in its novelty. But, like the hole
in the locker lid, it too proved a failure. Something always
went wrong with one of the pens and the two nibs kept col-
liding. There was nothing for it, therefore, but to slog along
in the slow old-fashioned fashion. One boy; one pen; one
line at a time.

"Bet Spud couldn't have spat into the window," Ginger
told himself. " Bet he couldn't have got it right inside, even
if he'd climbed on to the window-sill. But he hadn't enough
spit in him to do it properly."

It was some time later—just after Ginger had managed to
prise out the two screws that held the locker lid in position
—when Dr. Trump came into the room.

He came quietly, discreetly, unostentatiously, passing

silently down the corridor like a prowling panther. But not so silently or panther-like that Ginger had not heard him. Sitting there as he was, with his gimlet at the ready, he suddenly became aware of danger. Real danger. Danger, immediate and unavoidable. The muscles at the back of his neck tightened for a moment and he thrust his gimlet hurriedly into his pocket. Then reason conquered fear. Taking out his collection of treasures and the gimlet, he dropped them into the locker behind him.

By the time Dr. Trump entered, Ginger was diligently writing once more. Dr. Trump stood in the doorway regarding him. It was a hot afternoon and the windows of the classroom were all closed. Even from where he was standing, Dr. Trump was unpleasantly aware of the distinctive odour of small boy. He would have liked to turn back into the airy corridor again. But clearly there was something here close at hand for him to investigate. His afternoon's snooping had not been entirely fruitless.

"What are you doing?"

Ginger got up politely.

"Writing, sir."

"Writing what?"

"Words, sir."

Dr. Trump's eyebrows came closer together, and he pursed up his lips. In the entire Hospital there was no one else, child or master, who could produce quite Ginger's effect upon him. Sooner or later he was going to lose his temper with him: he could feel it in his bones. In the meantime, however, he must control himself, must show that it was beyond the power of any boy to aggravate him. Therefore he continued icily.

"What words?"

"Words Mr. Dawlish told me to write, sir."

"Why did Mr. Dawlish tell you to write them?"

"Because he wanted me to, sir."

Dr. Trump's breathing deepened, and the whistling sound began high up in his face where the nose joined the eyebrows. Ginger recognised this for the alarm signal: Dr. Trump was getting ratty.

"Are they words that you couldn't spell?" Dr. Trump asked in the same hard, frozen tone.

"No, sir."

"Are they words of which you didn't know the meaning?"

" No, sir."

" Then why are you writing them?"

" Because I was told to, sir."

Dr. Trump's patience snapped suddenly. Snapped even before he knew it.

" Read them out to me," he shouted. " All of them."

" They're all the same, sir."

" Then read any page."

" I must not spit," " I must not spit," " I must not spit," Ginger began. " I must not spit . . ."

" That's quite enough, thank you."

Dr. Trump stood there confronting him. He had closed the door behind him and crossed the stuffy classroom so that Ginger should be within arm's length if he wanted to shake him.

" So you are a spitter, are you?" he asked as soon as he felt that the silence had been long enough to be effective.

" No, sir."

Dr. Trump shot out his hand and gripped Ginger by the shoulder. He had hard, strong fingers and he hurt. But Ginger knew better than to resist. He just stood there limply, while Dr. Trump shook him.

" Don't lie to me," Dr. Trump commanded, his voice rising and growing louder. " Don't try to cover up your filthiness by lying."

" I'm not, sir."

" And don't contradict me."

" No, sir."

Dr. Trump let go of him.

" I shall remain here until you speak the truth," he announced quietly.

He paused impressively.

" Did you or did you not spit?" he asked.

" Yes, sir."

Dr. Trump's breathing was now so noisy that Ginger wondered if he could hear it himself. Perhaps he's going to have a fit, he thought. Perhaps he's going to start foaming. But Dr. Trump was never more master of himself.

" So you did lie to me," he declared triumphantly. " You are a spitter."

" No, I'm not, sir," Ginger answered. " I've stopped."

Dr. Trump had gone away again and the room was quiet

189

once more. Ginger had got to see Dr. Trump in the morning; and that meant another caning, he supposed. It wasn't fair, not coming on top of all those lines. But it might have been worse. A lot worse. If Ginger hadn't taken precautions, he'd have lost everything, his entire treasure trove.

Because the last thing that Dr. Trump had said to him was: "Turn out your pockets."

BOOK THREE

The Night of the Fire

CHAPTER XXV

I

THE WAY things were going, with the Warden's Residence re-painted throughout entirely in white, and with the fish-servers, for which the staff had collected, actually at the silversmith's for engraving, and with the banns already read for the first time—the year would have been memorable for Dr. Trump's wedding alone.

But, when it came, the perspective of things was different. When, at last, Felicity Warple passed up the chapel aisle on Bishop Warple's arm, and Dr. Trump waited nervously behind the cleaner's cabinet ready to step forward and claim his bride, the event was not the crescendo for which everyone had been waiting. There was an air of bathos and anti-climax that was unmistakable. And that was not surprising considering what people had just been through.

For, by then, the Hospital, St. Mark's Avenue, even the whole neighbourhood, had endured the ordeal of a fire. *The* Fire, as it was now known.

In the ordinary way nowadays there is nothing particularly alarming about a fire. Some passer-by notices a glow, or spots a thin spiral of ascending smoke, or even merely smells burning, and he or she—usually it is *he*—rushes off to summon the brigade. Women are by nature reluctant to make such public exhibitions of themselves and are less good at smashing glass in street-corner fire-alarms. But either way it is the same. Immediately the firemen come sliding down their slippery pole, straight from bed into the engine. The apparatus they bring with them is of the most modern. Pressure huge, jets enormous. The discipline of the men is exemplary, their courage superb. The very ringing of the bell spells confidence. And there is always the knowledge that close behind—a kind of faithful Sister Martha to scurry

191

round and mop up the mess—will come the Salvage Corps. More, in fact, could not have been done to make modern fires orderly, undangerous, even comfortable. Even so, when there are five hundred children inside a blazing building, the situation seems somehow different. Nerves are subjected to unheard-of strains. Authority is everything. Panic is always just around the corner.

And, when the Archbishop Bodkin Hospital suddenly lit up the night sky of Putney on the 23rd of May, 1928, it was Dr. Trump's testing time. Between 1 a.m., when the Brigade arrived, and 2.15, when the Superintendent reported that the fire was under control and everyone could safely return to bed—the Warden had been both hero and victim in his own domestic drama.

From the very start, from the first clanging of the alarm bell, Ginger regarded it as *his* fire. And he was possibly right. Even probably right. Almost certainly right, in fact. As proof of his rightness, he could have led any fireman to the exact spot among the charred and smoking ruins and shown him exactly where in his opinion combustion had begun. If cross-examined, he could have substantiated his case. He could have convinced a Grand Jury. And the extraordinary thing is that among all the investigators no one asked him, no one so much as thought of Ginger. He was ignored completely. The fire was explained away to everyone's satisfaction, and attributed to other causes. And, in the circumstances, Ginger saw no reason to disabuse the theorists.

Up to the moment when it publicly declared itself, the fire had been Ginger's especial secret. And it was Sergeant Chiswick who had made him a present of it. The Sergeant had been cleaning out the clinkers in the main boilers and carrying up bucketfuls of the stuff to throw on the slag-heap behind the boiler-shed. He had made eight journeys already and, when he went down for the ninth time all that he really intended to do was to give the boiler-room a sweeping. At the last moment, however, he had decided to put the rod through the furnace once more to see that everything was really clear. And it was this that had given Ginger his opportunity. For the furnace was now working perfectly. It was nothing but red-hot nuggets of fire that came dropping through the bars when Sergeant Chiswick poked. And because there wasn't so much as a trace of clinker in the whole

192

firebox the little gems of coke came pouring through like fiery hail. There was such a hail-storm of them indeed that Sergeant Chiswick decided to scoop them up in one final bucketful and start clean for the morning.

Then, his work done, he set the bucket neatly against the wall, turned his back on the slag-heap and made his way back to his porter's lodge and the racing editions.

Even now, everything would still have been all right if it had not been for the extreme dullness of one of Mr. Dawlish's lessons. It was a history lesson and Mr. Dawlish had been going on and on about the barons. Ginger had given up listening long ago; so long ago, in fact, that he could not remember when he had last heard anything. It seemed that, so long as he could remember, Mr. Dawlish had always been talking about barons. And in the end, merely to escape from barons, Ginger put his hand up.

Of course, he knew enough not to let the gesture go at that. He was careful at the same moment to suck his breath in noisily between his teeth, screw up his face hard and wriggle his fingers frantically in the air as though every moment's delay were painful and unpredictable.

At first, Mr. Dawlish took no notice of him. He knew that nothing was ever so urgent as a boy would make it. Also, he was opposed to these sudden departures. Idleness, rather than nature, he had long ago learnt, was at the back of most of them. On principle, therefore, he kept Ginger waiting before he let him go.

And as soon as he had got outside, Ginger felt wonderfully better. He had already made it apparent from his manner that this was not merely one of those brief, passing calls that scarcely even interrupt a lesson. He could afford to saunter. And, though it was necessary when he passed the window of the classroom that he should be proceeding in the general direction of the lavatory, once out of sight he could afford to go slower still.

As he sauntered, his mind wandered idly. It was, in fact, almost a complete blank by the time he reached Sergeant Chiswick's clinker-heap. But he knew at once that this was something really worth looking at. And, for the time being, all other thoughts left him. Clinker in all its aspects became entirely absorbing. He picked up a piece shaped like a swollen pancake, examined it critically and threw it away. Then, as it fell, he noticed that in the heart of the little cloud of dust that it raised there was something that glowed dimly like an opal.

This was a discovery, and like an inquisitive rooster he made his way across the slag-heap to the glowing thing. By the time he had scuffled around in the ashes he found that it was only quite a small cinder, a tiny nodule of hot coke not much bigger than a walnut. But it was hot all right. As soon as he picked it up he dropped it, and he stood there sucking his fingers wondering what to do with such a hostile treasure. It wasn't the sort of thing that he could put in his pocket. But left to itself out there in the cold it would surely die.

It was while he was standing there pondering, that he noticed that the soles of his feet were getting hot. Really hot; not just warm. And as he looked down he saw that he was standing on a whole heap of the little fiery opals. There must have been twenty or thirty vividly living fragments in among all the dead dark slag.

"Cor," said Ginger, as he realised tht he had stumbled on a whole treasure heap.

The problem of saving them had now assumed different proportions. It was no longer a matter of protecting one tiny defenceless morsel from extinction. He now had a small furnace to take care of; to look after; to keep quiet about. He was still working things out in his mind when he caught sight of Sergeant Chiswick's bucket upside down against the wall, and he let out a sigh of sheer relief. This at least was somewhere to put his find until he could think what to do with it. And, even pressed as he was for time, he still did the job carefully, lining the bucket with bits of warm slag so that the cold metal shouldn't chill off the fiery pieces. Because Sergeant Chiswick hadn't left a shovel handy and because cinders were too hot to pick up in his fingers, Ginger had to use his shoe. As soon as he had extracted everything worth keeping, he picked up the bucket and made his way towards the one private hiding-place he knew, the corner under the stairs of the laundry stores where he had kept his pet bow-and-arrow.

Considering how few spare moments he had during the day, his store-cupboard and hiding-place was reasonably well filled. There was the bow, now broken; a bottle; a length of iron tubing; a bird's wing; a biscuit tin badly holed on one side; some nails that Ginger had straightened; and a lump of coal. When he had added the lump of coal to his collection there had been no clear plan in his mind as to the

use to which one day he would put it. The discovery of the
live cinders was his vindication. It just showed how, in the
restricted economy of the Hospital, almost anything would
eventually come in useful.

And the biscuit tin was handy, too. Ginger brought it
out, straightened it and broke the lump of coal into small
pieces, by means of the iron tubing. Then, into the nest of
virgin coal he tipped his collection of cinders. He had
worked quickly all the time, not daring to slacken for a
single moment. And, even now, he was afraid he was too
late. The cinders were turning grey in front of his eyes.
But blowing revived them, and he squatted there beside them
simply keeping the poor things alive. When he felt giddy
and could go on no longer, he moved the biscuit tin close
up against the door where the draught would fan it and
started back to the classroom.

He had been so busy that he hadn't been able to fit in a
visit to the lavatory at all.

Inside the classroom it was exactly as he had expected:
Mr. Dawlish was still going on about the barons. He heard
the word " Runnymede " before he even got the door closed
properly behind him. Not that it mattered so much now. He
was thinking about his firebox instead. He was therefore
quite surprised when Mr. Dawlish addressed him.

" Where have you been all this time? " he asked.

" I've been to the lavatory, sir."

" Look at yourself."

Ginger inspected himself carefully.

There was ash all over him and his hands were black from
the coal. Even his face was smeary.

" Sorry, sir," said Ginger. " I fell over."

He managed to get down to his biscuit tin once more
before he had to go to bed. And by now it was really exciting. A miracle had occurred. He could see the glow of the
firebox before he got to it. The whole thing had been converted into an incandescent cube. It possessed a strength
and fury of its own. It was alive, in fact. And because
there was now no danger of extinguishing it he scattered the
rest of the raw coal on top, pressed it down with his heel and
left it hopefully to itself for the night.

That was the last that he ever saw of his biscuit tin. Or of
his bottle, or length of iron tubing or any of the rest of it.

Or of the store room itself, for that matter. By the time morning came the whole appearance of the side of the Hospital was different. There was, in fact, a gap, empty and smoking, where the store-room had once stood.

II

It was Miss Phrynne, the Hospital Secretary, who was the first to smell burning. This was at 10.15, just as she was going to bed. But, as she had always smelt gas or burning or something at bedtime, she did nothing about it. Simply turned off the light and went to sleep. Some thirty minutes later—at 11.5, that is—Mr. Jeffcote, who was leaving next week anyway, thought that he detected something that he described afterwards as " a vague, hot sort of smell." He even got up to look out. But, without his glasses, he could see nothing. In front of him was merely a blurred, cubist design of walls and roofs, and when he did see a sudden glare breaking through the darkness it turned out to be merely a car coming up St. Mark's Avenue. Satisfied that it was nothing, Mr. Jeffcote mixed himself a mild dose of milk of magnesia, and went back to bed.

No one else in the Hospital suspected anything until midnight, and then it was only a kind of false premonition that did not really count. Exactly at 12 o'clock however, Nurse Stedge awoke gasping because she had dreamed that the Latymer Block was on fire, and that a great brute of a man was taking liberties with her as she was being carried down the fire-escape. She was always surprised that such a nice woman as herself could have such lurid dreams—she had one or two of them nearly every night—and so she too kept quiet about it.

But it was Dr. Trump who was most mortified by lack of faith in his own forebodings. He had been working late and at 12.35 when he had finished next Sunday's sermon, written a letter of complaint to the Water Board because the domestic supply tasted of chlorine, glanced through the advertisements in the *Church Times,* and moved single-handed a small book-case that Felicity had told him would drive her mad if it were left out there on the landing, he went outside for a breath of fresh air.

The night was still and rather chilly. Dr. Trump stood on his own doorstep, thinking about the responsibilities of his impending marriage, when a new and more urgent thought entered his mind. Why should he not take his electric hand lamp and set off on a tour of the whole Hospital?

The idea was certainly attractive. On any showing, it was almost inconceivable that he would not come across something—even a window left unlatched—that he could report to somebody to-morrow. He was, in fact, on the very point of starting off when he pulled out his watch and examined it in the light that was streaming out through the open front door. Then he hesitated. It was now twenty minutes to one—a ridiculous time at which to go prowling. If someone like Mrs. Gurnett saw him, she would probably conclude that he was a burglar and telephone for the police. He therefore turned back indoors, and resolved to make a thorough inspection—kitchens, laundries, isolation block, everything—at 9 a.m. the following morning.

And by the time he had locked up, undressed, said his prayers, got into bed, and closed his eyes, the alarm had sounded.

At first, Dr. Trump simply did not believe it. The ringing of the bell meant nothing to him. In fact, he sat up on one elbow in a sudden dazed sweat of anxiety, imagining that it must be Sunday and that, in some inexplicable fashion, he had overslept himself. Then the one word, "Fire," shouted distantly in Mr. Dawlish's voice, reached his ears. In a bound Dr. Trump was out of bed buttoning on again the clothes that he had just discarded. It would have been quicker simply to put on an overcoat on top of his pyjamas: he realised that. But he realised also that in an emergency, a state of general alarm, people would look to their Warden to spread authority and calmness. And if he knew that pink and white stripes of poplin were showing under the hem of his black ecclesiastical overcoat he would feel neither.

Because his dressing had taken longer than he had realised, there was plenty of movement in the Cloisters when Dr. Trump emerged through the Warden's Gate. He almost cannoned into Sergeant Chiswick, who was still buttoning up his trousers as he ran in the direction of the playground. And, a moment later, he met Mr. Dawlish coming at the double to rouse him.

Dr. Trump's first thought was of the unsuitability of Mr. Dawlish's attire; and he congratulated himself on his own forethought in the matter of clothing. For Mr. Dawlish had not even put on an overcoat. He was wearing his ordinary short jacket over his pyjamas. And the pyjamas themselves were too short for him: they revealed his ankle bones. There was a wild look in his eye as he rushed forward.

"Get the Brigade, sir," he said hoarsely. "Get the Brigade."

He was on the point of collapse as he said it, and stood there, gasping. Dr. Trump looked at him, pityingly. The man was making a miserable spectacle of himself and, unless he pulled himself together immediately, he would be spreading panic and alarm all round him.

"Go back to your room before people see you," he ordered. "Go back and get dressed."

As he said it, Dr. Trump started forward again. He was still determined not to run, not to do anything that would excite emotion. But when he turned the corner by the Ridley Block and distinctly saw a glow, he forgot all discretion. He broke into a run. He sprinted. And, catching his breath as he ran, he began shouting out "Fire! Fire!"

The sight as he drew nearer was truly dreadful. At first glance, the entire laundry block looked as though it was past saving. No flames were actually visible but from the glare that showed through the upper windows, the whole interior was incandescent. Moreover, the fire was audible. From inside the building came a dull roaring sound in the midst of which shrill cracklings could be heard.

A shadowy group of figures was already assembled. And their presence irritated him. He felt that by rights he should have been first. But he conquered his irritation.

"Is everyone safe?" he demanded.

It was Mr. Jeffcote who answered.

"There's no one in there," he said. "It's the stores."

"Well, do something, man," Dr. Trump replied tartly. "Don't just stand there, gaping."

While he was still speaking, he heard the sound of running feet in the darkness behind him. They were heavy feet and, pounding on the hard asphalt, they rose above the roaring of the fire. There was a harsh trundling noise as well. Dr. Trump turned hurriedly. Emerging from the gloom, came the Hospital's own fire-fighting apparatus. An ancient post-office red affair, mounted on a bicycle undercarriage and with long graceful arms for pumping, it was being hurtled to the scene by Mr. Rushgrove, the games master.

This was Dr. Trump's opportunity.

"Stand clear," he shouted. "All hands man the pump."

By now, one by one, the whole staff was assembling. And

Sergeant Chiswick had re-appeared. He was staggering along under a load of flat and ragged-looking hose and was shouting out instructions over his shoulder as he paid out the hose behind him.

"Don't pull too hard, gentlemen," he was pleading. "We don't want to tear it."

Up to that moment, Dr. Trump had hoped that the Hospital staff could attend to the fire unaided. It seemed so amateurish somehow to have to call on outside assistance. But those words of Sergeant Chiswick's unnerved him. The sooner the Brigade was summoned, the better for everybody.

III

Dr. Trump was certainly in no mood for tolerating delay, either from the Exchange or from the Fire Station. As he stood there in the lobby of the porter's lodge, frantically joggling the hook of the receiver up and down, his patience suddenly boiled over. And, when the Exchange answered, he fairly bellowed into the mouth-piece: "You'll hear more of this in the morning. You mark my words, you will."

"More of what?" a voice asked him.

"More of this delay," Dr. Trump roared back at him. "Don't argue with me. There are five hundred lives in peril."

And if the Exchange was dilatory, the Fire Station was positively imbecilic.

"Yes, sir, The Archbishop Bodkin Hospital," a man's voice answered. "We'll be there inside five minutes. Which entrance?"

For a moment Dr. Trump gasped.

"Which entrance, you fool?" he retorted. "Do you think we stand on ceremony at a time like this?"

It was not, however, until he had slammed back the receiver and paused for a moment to wipe his brow that he realised the enormity of what he had just done in summoning the Brigade at all.

"Oh dear," said Dr. Trump aloud. "This is dreadful. Quite dreadful. It'll be in all the papers to-morrow."

It was while Dr. Trump was telephoning that the roof collapsed. First, it bulged upwards in the middle as though a huge invisible hand were pushing at it. Then, as suddenly,

199

the hand was removed—withdrawn mysteriously into the fiery depths—and the roof went down after it.

The spectacle was now magnificent. The fall had broken the cross-timbers into kindling wood, and these were caught in the up blast and now went sailing away into the cherry-coloured sky like meteors. One of them passed, comet-wise, over Dr. Trump's head just as he re-emerged into the playground.

But there were more than flaming particles to occupy his attention when he returned. Mr. Rushgrove had got the hose connected and, with Mr. Jeffcote on the other end of the pump handle, was trying hard to work up the pressure. There was now a watery as well as a fiery peril. And Dr. Trump was unsuspecting as he strode towards it.

The first indication that the pump was working properly was when a jet of ice-cold water suddenly shot out of the nozzle and caught him across the ankles.

" Aaah!" Dr. Trump exclaimed involuntarily.

In the excitement of the moment, however, Mr. Rushgrove did not even pause to see which way the jet was pointing. It was sufficient for him that there was a jet at all. " Harder!" he yelled. He was now jerking up and down so energetically that Mr. Jeffcote, who was only a short, slight man, found himself being carried right off the ground and into the air by the sheer force of Mr. Rushgrove's down strokes.

And the effect on the jet was terrific. First it described a wide arc, pursuing people. Next it whip-lashed and made complicated patterns and wave forms in the smoke-laden air. Then it rose vertically like a water-spout and sprayed the assembled company. And finally, gathering itself up in frenzy of intensity, it exploded. The brass nozzle, a solid eight pounds of well-turned metal, abruptly went careening off through the lurid darkness, mortar-bomb fashion.

Dr. Trump crouched almost double as he heard it go whistling over him. He was, in fact, still crouching when the cascade descended. And, with no nozzle to restrain it, the water came down in a broad spreading gush. In a moment Dr. Trump feared that he had been saved from the fire and the unknown projectile only to be drowned in his own playground. Then, as suddenly as the deluge had started, it ceased entirely. Even the squeak and rattle of the pump stopped. And, as he got to his feet, Dr. Trump saw why. Beside the over-turned instrument, Mr. Rushgrove and Mr. Jeffcote lay sprawling on their backs. The long and graceful handle had snapped clean in half.

For a moment, Dr. Trump stood there silent and aghast. Then recovering his voice, he asserted his authority.

" Evacuate the Hospital," he ordered hoarsely. " Everyone downstairs in three minutes."

At a high upper window in the Bede Block a man was craning his neck out to its full extent in order to get a better view. It was a long neck and the view that its owner was now getting was all he could wish for. He had, in fact, seen everything—the manning of the pump, the dowsing of Dr. Trump, the collapse of the apparatus—and twice he had nearly fallen out of the window in his excitement.

Now that the drama in the playground was temporarily ended, he transferred his attention back to the burning store-room. He had been watching this on and off for the last ten minutes. And from the height at which he was standing he could see right down into the blazing shell. Not a detail was hidden. He might almost have been directing the fire instead of merely contemplating it. And the way things were going, the wall of the adjoining laundry would soon be ablaze as well. After that, there was really no telling. The flames might even advance majestically and consume the main buildings.

" Fascinating. Absolutely fascinating," Mr. Prevarius reflected. " I wouldn't have missed this for anything."

I V

At this point it is important to see things in their true perspective. Admittedly, the laundry store-house was already gutted, and the despatch department in jeopardy. If a wind had sprung up, the whole laundry block would probably have been doomed anyway. On the other hand, the store-house and the laundry block was at the remote apex of the Hospital area. Beyond the laundry lay the junior boys' classrooms— entirely empty at night-time. And beyond the boys' classrooms spread a broad expanse of unignitable asphalt, with the dormitories, the real death-traps, on the far side. Nothing short of a spark carried on a strong gale could possibly have laid them open to any danger at all. And, up to the present, there was not even a breeze. The night, in fact, was unusually calm for late February.

The decision to evacuate the Hospital was thus one that had called for the highest moral courage. Drenched and breathless as he was, Dr. Trump had been compelled to choose without an instant's hesitation between a remote and terrible possibility and the present and immediate likelihood of having a sick bay filled up by to-morrow evening with cases of common cold. He dared not think what Mrs. Gurnett was going to say to him. And, with a quick catch of his breath, he realised the awfulness of what he had just done. The assembly point for fire drill was the main playground. This meant that within the next two-and-a-half minutes nearly three hundred boys of all ages would be dragged from the safety of their beds and led defenceless into the very jaws of the conflagration.

Clearly, there was not a moment to be lost. Summoning up the last vestiges of his strength, Dr. Trump gave his second order of the day.

"Open the gateway into the girls' playground," he said. "Mr. Dawlish will remain here to direct the boys through."

He paused.

"Boys over on the South side," he added. "Mrs. Gurnett will keep her girls to the North."

A moment later, the first of the evacuees came out. They were Mr. Pippett's class, the very junior ones of seven and eight. Because they had been roused and rounded up so suddenly they wore the vacant expression of astonished cherubs. They gaped. But Mr. Pippett gave them no time for wonderment. He was tirelessly turning, and yapping at their heels like a sheepdog. And, in consequence, the flock scampered. Only one or two of them were crying, but Mr. Pippett himself beamed. He had beaten the clock by nearly twenty-five seconds and glory shone on him. As he passed Dr. Trump, he tried to catch his eye. But Dr. Trump was preoccupied.

"Don't hang around, Mr. Pippett," he said. "No blocking up the gateway."

It was some time before anyone else emerged. No records were broken this time. Mr. Rushgrove came second with six minutes exactly. Mr. Jeffcote came next with seven-and-a-half. And, by the time Mr. Dawlish appeared, the ten-minute mark had been passed and eleven minutes was coming up. It was as much as Dr. Trump could do not to box Mr. Dawlish's ears as he went by him.

Meanwhile, under Mrs. Gurnett's supervision, the girls' side had been cleared more rapidly. Sergeant Chiswick had been sent through to ensure that in the darkness the ranks of sexes did not get mixed. And when Dr. Trump had at last returned from waiting for the fire-engine, everyone had assembled.

"What do you propose to do now you've got them here?" Mrs. Gurnett asked pointedly.

"Count them," Dr. Trump snapped back at her. "Call the roll immediately."

The firemen who had finally succeeded in getting their hoses through the courtyards and alleyways were by now shouting orders to each other so loudly that the calling out of names was impossible. At last Dr. Trump could stand it no longer and went through to tell them to make less noise. As a result, the Fire Superintendent was rude to him, and Dr. Trump threatened to report the Superintendent. He even demanded that the man should stop what he was doing— winding up a fire-tower or something—and apologise. But the Fire Superintendent took no notice, and a moment later stepped on to the rising platform and was out of ear-shot.

By the time Dr. Trump returned, the roll-call had already been taken.

"All present?" Dr. Trump asked curtly.

"One missing," Mrs. Gurnett replied. "It's Sweetie."

"She can't be missing," Dr. Trump replied. "Call the roll again."

He stood there stamping his feet with irritation. It was maddening, positively maddening the way carelessness came breaking in even at times like these. He was therefore all on edge when he turned to Mr. Dawlish.

"Are all yours all right?" he demanded.

"All except one," Mr. Dawlish replied. "It's Ginger. We're just re-counting."

"Then count faster," Dr. Trump ordered.

V

The big staircase looked very empty and lonely when Sweetie reached the end of it. Even though she was ten she didn't like empty, lonely places; not even in the daytime. At

203

this moment, all the lights were shining and no one was about anywhere. It was emptier than she had ever known it. Not that she had expected to meet anyone. Five minutes ago she had been in the midst of them all as they had come pouring down the stairs. But that was what had been so silly —the speed with which they had all left. Nurse Stedge hadn't given them time to get a thing. And if the place were going to be burned down Sweetie wanted to be quite sure that her drawings were safe. It was her drawings that she was going back for now.

Tightening her lips, she began to climb. There were eight landings altogether. In the stillness, her feet sounded as loud as if she had been stamping. In the emptiness, too, the echoes started. It was as though there were dozens of other little girls, all stamping, racing up after her.

And really there didn't seem any need for all this hurry. There wasn't the least sign of burning anywhere. She could quite safely have left her drawings where they were. But as she had come all this way back for them she felt that she might as well get them. She was, in fact, just gathering them together into a bundle when she heard someone on the stairs.

At first, she scarcely dared to look. Perhaps it was burglars. Burglars always came at night: she knew that. And sometimes they carried pistols and murdered people. But somehow the person on the stairs didn't sound like a burglar. He was whistling, and Sweetie knew that real burglars never whistled. So she forgot that she was frightened and turned round to look. And, when she looked, it was all right. Because it wasn't a burglar who was out there: it was only Ginger.

" What's the matter?" she asked, as soon as she had got the window open. " Are they after you again?"

" I heard you was missing," Ginger answered. " So I came up to look for you."

He did not add that he regarded himself as responsible for the fire, and therefore had the matter of human life upon his conscience. But it would have been superfluous.

For Sweetie merely smiled at him.

" That was very nice of you," she said. " I've got what I came for. We can go back down again now."

With that, she took his hand.

And that was how it was that when Nurse Stedge, distraught by now with anxiety, reached the entrance to the Latymer Block, she met Sweetie and Ginger coming out hand-in-hand. They were not even hurrying. With their heads bent close together, they were in close and intimate conversation about something—Nurse Stedge could not guess what. All that she knew was she suddenly felt out of it, almost as though she were eavesdropping. And, in her annoyance, she suddenly lost her head.

"Come here at once, you wicked children," she screamed at them. "Do you both want to be burnt alive?"

Which was absurd, of course, because the fire never got round to that part of the Hospital at all.

CHAPTER XXVI

I

AFTERWARDS, it seemed to Dr. Trump that the fire itself had been the least of the disturbance.

By next morning the ashes were not even warm. Merely wet. The Brigade had gone on for hours pouring water into the ruins, and the basement of the laundry was now an unsavoury-looking black marsh with bits of charred wood-work floating on the surface. Then, with the dawn, the visitors began.

The men of the Salvage Corps were still floundering about in the slops retrieving bits of Hospital property—door-knobs and things—from the puddles, when the gentlemen of the Press arrived. At first, Dr. Trump refused indignantly to see them: he ordered that they should be sent away again immediately. But, in doing so, he misjudged the measure of Fleet Street. For one by one the reporters politely raised their hats, went off, and came in again by the side entrance. And with the instinct and training of their kind they tracked down Mr. Dawlish like a pack of beagles. He was surrounded by six of them, all with open notebooks in their hands, when Dr. Trump suddenly came upon them. And to Dr. Trump's dismay he heard Mr. Dawlish saying with a note of self-satisfaction that he had never detected in his voice before: "When I first noticed that the building was ablaze . . ."

To Dr. Trump this was insufferable, yes, it was positively

insufferable, that Mr. Dawlish, while actually under notice of dismissal, should become a popular hero. And the unmistakable flash of a camera showed that all the vulgar tributes to popularity were at this moment being paid to him. Dr. Trump stepped forward to intervene. But it was too late. Already his future father-in-law, the Bishop, was advancing towards him, striding daintily through the debris like a giant penguin.

"I learnt at breakfast of your trouble," the Bishop said simply. "I have come."

And, having come, he wanted to see everything. He stood at the edge of the crater and peered down. He asked whether arson was suspected. He poked at the brickwork with his umbrella. He crushed a charred ember with his heel and remarked that fire consumed all things. Then, abruptly, he took out his watch.

"Well, I must leave you now to tidy up," he said. "I fear that things at home are far from well this morning."

For once, Dr. Trump forgot to say how sorry he was. At the moment, however, he was too much preoccupied by the Press men who were still crowding round Mr. Dawlish to give so much as a thought to his future father-in-law. And he did not even show the excitement natural to a good fiancé when the Bishop turned and remarked over his shoulder: "Felicity said she'd be round later. She's coming as soon as she can get away." Instead, he merely waved distractedly and prepared to thrust his way into the group of reporters. But it was no use. Before he had gone more than a couple of paces, he was hailed. And the voice was summoning and peremptory. It was Dame Eleanor's.

Dr. Trump turned.

"How kind of you to come in the midst of our trouble . . ." he began.

But Dame Eleanor was in no mood for politeness.

"Whose fault was it?" she asked.

"The cause of the fire is unknown," Dr. Trump replied guardedly. "The Salvage men are still hoping to discover something."

"In all that mess?" Dame Eleanor asked him.

Dr. Trump nodded.

"They are looking for a cable," he explained, adding unnecessarily, "an electric one."

"Well, it's too late now even if they find it," Dame

Eleanor answered tartly. "The harm's done. Is the insurance all right?"

"I . . . I trust so," Dr. Trump told her.

"It'd better be," Dame Eleanor replied grimly. "You're responsible, you know."

"Quite so," Dr. Trump replied. "Oh quite."

And in his agitation he forgot all about Mr. Dawlish and the news-hawks. The one thing that now mattered was to check the policy.

Dame Eleanor, however, had not yet left him.

"Margaret was round here before breakfast," she said. "There's loyalty for you. That's how I heard . . ."

It was still only 9.25 when Dame Eleanor departed. And Dr. Trump braced himself for the day's work before him. There was so much to be done—insurance, salvage, police, and his complaint to the local Fire Station. The children, too, would have to be quietened down and brought back to a sense of proper discipline. The staff needed steadying. Sergeant Chiswick would have to be cross-examined. There was Mr. Dawlish's story to be probed into—for all that Dr. Trump knew, the man might simply be seeking to conceal something. And, above all, fresh arrangements would have to be made about the laundry.

"Even if the Juniors have to lose their playroom," Dr. Trump told himself, "we must get the ironing done somewhere. Nothing must be allowed to stand in the way of the orders."

And, at the prospect, his spirits began mounting.

"No one in authority, no administrator," he told himself, "is ever really put to the test until things begin to go wrong. What is needed now is clear thinking and action. I shall cancel all the day's appointments. Religious instruction, the catering accounts, the sports fund, everything. I shall shut myself away entirely."

He was still repeating this last piece of determination when he entered his study and found a telegram on the table.

"Just read this morning's Stop Press," it read. "Earnestly praying all well and no casualties stop. Returning London immediately stop."

The telegram was signed "Mallow."

It seemed to Canon Mallow that the train had never been slower. He sat in the corner of the third-class compartment, still clutching the fatal sheet of newspaper. "FIRE IN ORPHANAGE," the Stop Press ran, "WING OF BODKIN HOSPITAL, PUTNEY, GUTTED LAST NIGHT. CAUSE OF FIRE UNKNOWN." And every time he raised his eyes from those three lines of black and inky type he became more conscious of the slowness of the train. There it was ambling through the fields when he was wanted urgently, desperately in town. He was so much concerned, indeed, that when the train reached Waterloo he sprang from it before the driver had really got there. Two porters caught him, and a ticket inspector who had seen it happen came along all the way from the barrier. If Canon Mallow, he said, had been anyone other than a clergyman he would have reported him. People who jumped from moving trains injured other people more often than they injured themselves and the railways were getting pretty hot on it; it was, in fact, Canon Mallow's last chance at train jumping.

Canon Mallow was upset by the whole incident, and apologised. "You must forgive me," he said. "My home was on fire last night. It says so here. And all my boys and girls, five hundred of them, you understand." But when he tried to find the newspaper, it was gone. Knocked from his grasp when he had collided with the porters, probably. So he wasn't altogether surprised when he saw the ticket inspector turn away and tap his forehead significantly.

"Quite so, sir," said the inspector. "Now you go along quietly. You'll find everything's all right."

Naturally as soon as he had got through the barrier, Canon Mallow went straight up to the bookstall to buy the evening papers. For some extraordinary reason, the news of the fire wasn't on the front page at all. There was a lot about a railway accident in Italy and a murder in Stoke Newington and a killer-dog in Sussex. But still nothing about the Archbishop Bodkin Hospital fire. It was not, in fact, until he turned to page three of one of the papers that he came upon anything at all. And then it was only a paragraph entitled "Laundry Blaze."

Canon Mallow was astounded that with so much human life hanging in the balance, the orphanage should have been called a laundry. It was all of a piece with the callousness that made the public Press so distressing.

He concluded afterwards that it must have been because the newspaper paragraph had upset him that he left his umbrella in the Underground. But he could not be sure. It was quite possible, for instance, that he might have left it in the train coming up to Waterloo: he did not actually remember having it in his hands when he had fallen from the train. Or he might even have left it propped up against the bookstall when he went to buy the papers. He had been in such a rush all the time that he couldn't be certain of anything.

And the loss saddened him: it was a break with the past being separated from that umbrella. The handle was that rare thing, an absolutely straight piece of cherrywood, and the silver band was of the ingenious kind that pushed down and fastened on to the ribs when the thing was folded up. But what made the loss all the more heartbreaking was that it was the Old Bodkinians Association that had given it to him to celebrate his fifteenth year as their President.

He would rather have lost anything than that umbrella.

Canon Mallow was craning his neck out of the taxi as it approached St. Mark's Avenue. And, certainly from the front, everything looked reassuring enough. All the same, his nerves were fairly tingling as he stood in the deep, mock-Gothic gateway, tugging at the ornamental bell-pull.

"Please God all the children are safe," he kept repeating to himself. "Let them be all right. I can't think how it can have happened. Not with all the staff there . . ."

He had turned his back on the Hospital and was gazing up the avenue in contemplation. That was why he did not notice when Sergeant Chiswick opened the door to him. He was not in point of fact at that moment thinking about the missing children at all: it was the lost umbrella that was preoccupying him. And he jumped when he heard Sergeant Chiswick's voice saying loudly in his ear: "Why it's you, sir."

Canon Mallow spun round.

"Is everyone all right?" he asked quickly. "Are the children safe?"

He could tell at once from Sergeant Chiswick's expression that nothing was seriously wrong and he continued breathlessly.

" Then there's nobody been killed?"

" Bless you, no, sir."

Canon Mallow paused. The alarm, the urgency dissolved inside him. He felt flat and empty. There was possibly even something a little absurd in the way in which he had come hurtling back from the seaside. But he was still not satisfied.

" What caused it?" he asked. " We didn't have any fires in my time."

Sergeant Chiswick leant forward.

" Something in the electricity, sir," he said. " One of the firemen told me. It's the wiring. Ought to have been seen to years ago."

Canon Mallow clicked his teeth disapprovingly.

" I'll speak to Dr. Trump about it," he said. " We can't risk another one. We may not be so lucky next time."

He was already beginning to move off in the direction of the Warden's Residence, when Sergeant Chiswick stopped him.

" Dr. Trump said on no account was he to be disturbed, sir," he explained apologetically.

But Canon Mallow only smiled at him.

" You needn't worry about that," he said. " I don't think that he'll count me as a disturbance."

Here, however, he was wrong. At first the maid—she was a new one whom Canon Mallow had never seen before—refused even to take his name up. And then, when she had been persuaded, she returned with the news that Dr. Trump could not be interrupted now, but would hope to see Canon Mallow later if his business permitted.

Canon Mallow was momentarily taken aback. And then, when he had reflected on it, he saw how reasonable it was.

" My compliments to the Warden," he said, " and tell him that with his permission I will take the opportunity of looking up a few of my old friends."

When the door of the Warden's Residence had closed again—and it seemed strangely like having his own front door closed in his face—Canon Mallow went back through the side door into the Cloisters. And straight away he noticed one or two rather puzzling innovations. In the first place, there was a placard fixed on to the pillar nearest to the Residence: and when Canon Mallow had slipped his glasses up on to his forehead he saw that it read: " NO TALKING OR RUNNING IN THE CLOISTERS."

" I wonder why," he asked himself. " I do hope no one's ill."

There was something different about the lawns, too. They were now surrounded by a low trellis of wire and, attached to the wire at the point opposite the entrance to the Latymer Block, was a notice bearing the words: " CHILDREN ARE FORBIDDEN TO WALK ON THE GRASS."

" Oh, I suppose they must have sown new grass seed or something," Canon Mallow reflected. " But it's funny. It always looked all right to me."

He was still reflecting on the enclosure of the lawn when he saw a familiar figure approaching. It was Mr. Dawlish. His head was bent forward as he walked because he was doing something to his pipe. In consequence, he did not see Canon Mallow until he was almost upon him. But when he did so, the effect was remarkable. He came forward and pressed Canon Mallow's hand with undisguised emotion and seemed, though Canon Mallow could not imagine why, almost to be upon the brink of tears.

" Ah, Canon," he said. " It's good to see you. Things aren't a bit the same since you left, you know. Not a bit the same."

And, without warning, Mr. Dawlish unloaded himself of his second piece of news.

" They're getting rid of me at the end of this term," he said.

" Getting rid of you," Canon Mallow repeated in amazement.

Mr. Dawlish nodded.

" Nine weeks' notice last Friday," he said. " Nine weeks, after seventeen years," he said.

" But . . . but why didn't you write and tell me?" Canon Mallow demanded.

He realised as he said it that writing would have been of little use. Even if he had heard, the most that he could have done would have been to appeal to Dame Eleanor. Or to Bishop Warple. But Dame Eleanor would have been bound to support the decision of her own Warden. And, as for the Bishop, he could hardly be expected to turn against his future son-in-law.

Mr. Dawlish, however, was making no demands on him.

" Not that I'm grumbling," he said. " It had to be."

" Oh, don't you worry," Canon Mallow told him. " Perhaps it won't happen."

As soon as he had said it, he realised how silly it was. But he felt somehow that it was his duty to comfort the poor man.

"Just don't think about it," he went on. "We none of us know what God has in store."

And with that, Canon Mallow went on his way towards the laundry block. And as soon as he got there he saw at a glance how terrible things must have been. The charred rafters were outlined against the sky, and the area where the ironers used to work had disappeared altogether: it was now simply a pit, half filled with blackened rubbish, chairs, tables, ironing-boards, gas-rings, clothes-baskets, sinks, lamp-brackets and lengths of twisted iron tubing.

"Thank God that it happened at night," thought Canon Mallow devoutly. "Otherwise someone would have been hurt for certain."

He shook his head as that awful possibility occurred to him, and turned to go away in search of Mrs. Gurnett. He knew that he could be sure of a sensible account from her. But as he turned he realised that he was not alone. Peering in through one of the empty window frames on the far side was a face. And as soon as the face saw Canon Mallow it disappeared.

"Is there anybody there?" Canon Mallow asked.

No reply.

"Was someone looking through the window just now?"

Still no reply.

Canon Mallow raised his voice a little.

"Come here, Ginger," he said. "I want to speak to you."

For a moment, the silence continued, unbroken. Canon Mallow frowned. Had he been mistaken? Did the fringe of carroty-coloured hair that he had seen really belong to somebody else? Then he heard a slithering sound, the sound of heavy boots clambering about on rubble.

"Coming, sir," a voice said.

Because the middle portion of the wall had collapsed, it took Ginger some time to get round to Canon Mallow. And when he arrived Canon Mallow looked at him in astonishment: until he had been again brought face to face with Ginger he had forgotten quite how dirty a small boy could get himself. Not that it would have been difficult this time. The whole place was like a charcoal-burner's. But he looked pleased to see Canon Mallow.

"What are *you* doing here?" Canon Mallow asked.

" Just looking, sir."

" Why aren't you in the classroom? "

" I'm on the way to the lavatory, sir."

Canon Mallow shook his head.

" This isn't the way to the lavatory, is it, Ginger? "

Because Ginger didn't answer, Canon Mallow dug him gently in the ribs with his forefinger.

" It isn't, is it, Ginger? "

Ginger grinned.

" No, sir," he answered.

Canon Mallow looked away from him and stared down into the ruins.

" Most extraordinary," he said, speaking aloud in the way that had now become a habit with him. " Not even a clue as to what caused it."

Ginger looked down at his feet. Then he moistened his lips. This was the moment for his big confession.

" Sir."

" What is it, Ginger? "

" I know what done it," he said.

" Do you, Ginger? "

" Yes, sir. It was me."

" Are you sure? "

Ginger nodded.

" Have you told Dr. Trump? "

" No, sir."

" Then tell me."

" I took some cinders there."

" Cinders, Ginger? "

" Yes, sir. Out of the boiler."

" Did you steal them, Ginger? "

" No, sir. They was old cinders. They'd been thrown away."

" And what did you do with them? "

" I put 'em in my tin, sir."

" What tin? "

" My biscuit tin."

" What made you do it? Did you want to set fire to the place? "

" No, sir. I just wanted to keep them."

Canon Mallow put his hands on Ginger's shoulders and moved the boy round so that he was facing him.

" Now look at me and speak the truth. You're quite sure you didn't try to set fire to anything? "

" Quite sure, sir."

Canon Mallow seemed relieved.

" Then don't you worry any more," he said. " Because it wasn't your cinders, you see. It was a short-circuit in the wiring. The firemen have said so."

So that was the end of that. And while he was speaking, Canon Mallow was searching in his pocket. He liked Ginger and he wanted to give the boy a little present.

" Here's some pocket money for you," he said.

It was a shilling that he was looking for. He hadn't got a shilling, however. All that he had was half a crown. Half a crown was too much: he couldn't even afford it. But now that he had shown it to the boy, however, he didn't see very well how he could put it away again.

" Don't go and spend it all at once," he said. " Keep it and buy yourself something useful."

" Thank you, sir," Ginger told him.

" And now hurry up and go to the lavatory," Canon Mallow told him. " You've been waiting a long time."

As Canon Mallow moved away, he suddenly remembered that there was a rule against the boys having loose cash in their hands. Twopence a week was all that was allowed, and any accumulations had to be paid into individual savings accounts. It was something like that: he couldn't remember the exact details because it was such a long time since he had made the regulation.

III

It was not until quite late in the evening when Canon Mallow was able to see Dr. Trump. The Warden had been kept busy all day and now looked tired, Canon Mallow thought. In the circumstances, he didn't like to tackle him about Mr. Dawlish. But the poor man was so obviously distressed about having to go that he saw no alternative. And naturally that set them talking.

In the end, Dr. Trump ended the conversation quite abruptly.

" I don't want you to miss your last train," he said.

Canon Mallow looked at his watch, then at the clock on the Warden's mantelpiece, and then back at his watch again.

" I . . . I've missed it," he said.

"Have you anywhere to sleep?" Dr. Trump inquired coldly.

Canon Mallow confessed that he had not.

"Then you had better stay here," Dr. Trump told him.

"Oh, thank you, thank you," Canon Mallow answered. "You are most kind. And do you think that possibly you could find me some pyjamas? You see when I left this morning I didn't know that I should be staying. And if I might use the phone. Otherwise, they'll be worrying about me." Canon Mallow paused. "It's lovely being back here again," he said at last. "As I am stopping, perhaps you wouldn't mind if I came into prayers in the morning. I could stand right at the back where they wouldn't notice me."

CHAPTER XXVII

I

THE MORNING of Dr. Trump's wedding dawned clear and cold; and, though the weather forecast predicted fog and low temperatures, by the time the happy couple were ready to depart, it was fine and sunny with a hint of real summer in the air.

Fine and sunny; the hired car a Rolls, and his bride a bishop's daughter. But, even so, Dr. Trump was not happy in his heart. And that was because there had been so many little things to upset him. Ridiculous, undignified, distasteful things.

On the previous afternoon he had made one of his customary tours of inspection. Only this had been an unusually thorough one. He had wanted to make sure that everything would tick over smoothly during his . . . his absence: "honeymoon" was a word that somehow he simply couldn't bring himself to use. And when he had reached the kindergarten playroom he had found Margaret there. The children were all gathered round her and she was showing them something. And really it was remarkable, quite remarkable, how pleasing she looked. There was that placid Madonna-like quality that he had noticed the first time he had set eyes on her. Not beauty exactly. Sheer womanliness rather. Motherliness, even. And everything that went with it—gentleness, affection, purity. With her dark shining hair and the pale oval of

215

her face, she might have stepped straight out of the Old Testament. It might be Ruth herself, for example, that he was looking at. "She's . . . she's good enough for a stained-glass window," he told himself. And then, shocked at the course his thoughts were taking, he had stopped abruptly. Really it was too dreadful the way the old Adam kept breaking through. There he was on the eve of his own wedding-day gloating over the physical attractions of another woman. He was disgusted at himself. And when Margaret saw him there and smiled at him, his emotions were entirely under control again. He merely gave her a curt nod and reminded her that the fire-guard needed fixing.

Then, on his own marriage morning, with the bride practically setting forth, he was forced suddenly to cast off the spirit of a bridegroom and become a schoolmaster again. In short, he was forced to cane Ginger again. Fairly paste him, this time, for what was nothing less than a savage and unprovoked assault.

And it had all been so unexpected. Up to that moment, indeed, Dr. Trump had been in a singularly benign and jubilant frame of mind. A little nervous, perhaps ; but still jubilant and still benign. As he fitted his new black moiré dickey around his neck he had caught his own eye in the mirror. And it was with profound respect that he took notice of himself. Not that he was exactly handsome—he was ready to concede that much ; not handsome in a vulgar, actorish way, that is. But there was something in the bone structure of his forehead that was more than handsome: it was truly *fine*. And his eyebrows gave a kind of dignity and nobility to the whole. Altogether, it was the sort of face that essentially looked down from places—from public platforms, from pulpits, from magistrates' benches, from gilt frames in the Royal Academy, from distinguished strangers' galleries.

When he had wriggled himself into his clerical frock-coat and inserted in his buttonhole the white carnation that had been standing ready in the tooth-glass on the dressing-table, he stood back for a moment to take stock of the entire effect. It was distinctly gratifying. Considering that he was forty-three, his figure was certainly a credit to him. It was something that he should be able to wear the same frock-coat that he had worn twenty-one years previously when he had gone back to St. Asaph's to receive his doctorate. Admittedly, he had not worn it often in the meantime. Doctorates are not picked up every day, and social fashions had declined rather

216

than improved in the interim. Indeed, after two clerical occasions when Dr. Trump had found that he was the only person present in a frock-coat, he had wistfully hung the garment up in his wardrobe and given instructions that it should be sprayed for moth every springtime. At this moment, except for three small holes ingeniously repaired by the invisible menders, the suit was as it had left the tailors. And, if Dr. Trump did not attempt to button it, there was nothing even to hint at the passing of the years.

He was, in fact, feeling at his best, his absolute best, as he strolled out into the cloisters on that fine April morning. He had just acknowledged with a polite, though distant, half-bow the rather self-conscious smile that Mrs. Gurnett gave him as she passed, when he noticed a crowd of boys huddled in the far corner. This in itself was unusual, since talking was prohibited within the cloisters, and small boys in number are usually unable to remain silent for any length of time. Dr. Trump therefore expectantly cocked his head to one side to listen. And it was exactly as he had anticipated. There was a low buzz of conversation that reached him right across the width of the courtyard.

This was defiance of the Archbishop Bodkin rules. Dr. Trump therefore walked over in their direction. He did not hurry. And he was still inclined to be indulgent. A frown here, a cuff over the ears there—and so far as this morning was concerned the incident would be over. But, as he drew nearer, he was horrified to hear the distinctive chink of a coin, and his blood ran cold. Gambling? Was it possible? Here in the open cloisters!

He was just about to address them, to call them sharply to their senses, when trouble broke out somewhere inside the group. The coin chinked again and immediately he heard Ginger say: " Gimme back, or I'll pay you." This in turn was answered by a defiant sound like " Garn," and the next moment Dr. Trump winced as he heard the distinctive whack of a well-delivered blow.

Then he spoke.

" Every boy to remain where he is," he commanded. " No one is to move."

And within the little circle of stone figures Dr. Trump found what he had expected. Ginger, with his collar burst open, was standing opposite a boy with white face and a brightly bleeding nose.

" I see!" said Dr. Trump. " Fighting!"

217

There was a pause.

"Whose penny did I hear fall?" he asked.

Because no one answered and because Dr. Trump knew that any moment his bride would be arriving at the church, he could contain his temper no longer. Reaching out, he gripped Ginger by the ear.

"Was it your penny?" he demanded. "Was it, boy?"

"No, sir," Ginger answered.

Because the reply irritated him still further, Dr. Trump gave Ginger's ear a sharp tug. For an instant Ginger was caught off balance and, as he moved, he revealed the coin that he had been concealing with his foot. Dr. Trump detected it instantly.

"Is that yours?" he asked.

"Yes, sir."

"Ah," said Dr. Trump gloatingly. "So you lied to me."

By then, Dr. Trump had already decided to cane Ginger. For lying, there was only one punishment, six crisp ones with his middle-sized cane. But Dr. Trump was still unprepared for it when Ginger answered back.

"I didn't lie, sir. It isn't a penny."

"Then what is it?"

"It's half a crown, sir."

"Half a crown," Dr. Trump repeated, in an aghast tone of voice as though half-crowns were blasphemous. "Half a crown! And where did *you* get half a crown, pray?"

"Canon Mallow gave it to me, sir."

"Canon Mallow!"

Dr. Trump could not attempt to conceal the irritation in his voice. He would write to Canon Mallow protesting. And, in the meantime, there was Ginger to be attended to.

Dr. Trump turned on him.

"You know you're not allowed to have any money," he said sternly.

There was a pause.

"Pick it up," Dr. Trump ordered.

Ginger picked it up.

"Now give it to me."

"It's mine, sir."

"Give it to me, I say."

He screwed Ginger's ear as he said it and Ginger painfully handed over the half-crown.

"Come with me," said Dr. Trump, still not letting go of Ginger's ear.

The walk to the front gate was not a long one and Dr. Trump walked rapidly. Once there, he paused triumphantly before an iron-bound collecting-box mounted on the wall. On the side of the box, the words "For the Hospital" were lettered. And twisting round Ginger's head so that he could see exactly what was occurring, Dr. Trump dropped the coin noisily into the box.

As it fell, Ginger kicked him.

In consequence, Dr. Trump caned Ginger harder than he had ever caned any boy before. Or rather, he caned Ginger harder that he had ever caned Ginger before—after the last caning Dr. Trump had noticed wryly that the corporal punishment book was practically dedicated to Ginger. Only three other boys, in fact, had been caned in the whole time Dr. Trump had been there. And it was because he caned Ginger so hard—fairly lamming at him, in fact—that he split the seam on his right shoulder. Tight at the outset, it suddenly ripped open like a banana, revealing the soft white interior. And, as it tore apart, the bronze clock on the mantelpiece struck 10.45.

It was while Mrs. Gurnett was stitching up the frock-coat and Dr. Trump was standing in his shirt-sleeves looking out of the window and tapping impatiently with his foot, that he pondered on the difficulty that he had experienced in selecting a best man. At a pinch, one of the unmarried masters, he supposed, would have done—Mr. Rushgrove, or Mr. Pippett, for example; not Mr. Prevarius certainly, or dirty Mr. Dawlish. But to have had a member of his staff would have savoured too much of compulsion. And it was odd now that he came to think about it that he had no real friends of his own. No friends! Good gracious, whatever sort of man did that make him sound? He shuddered to think. And then, as he saw things in true light once more, he smiled indulgently. It was all so simple when looked at properly, so perfectly understandable. He had been too *busy* to make friends.

That was why he had so gratefully accepted when the Bishop had offered him his own Chaplain as best man. It had seemed a most admirable solution. Not that he actually liked the fellow. He was inclined to be just a shade too familiar, to presume too often on his new-found intimacy. Dr. Trump felt perfectly well able to snub him, of course, if occasion demanded; had already done so once or twice, in fact. But that had been for another reason. It was because this conceited young Chaplain chose to regard himself as a born organiser. And ever since Dr. Trump had been saddled with him, the Rev. Edgar Parker had been ringing him up every minute of the day with one footling question after another. Had he got the ring? Had he got a buttonhole? Had he got a present for the bridesmaids? Were the Press to be admitted to the church or only into the porch and churchyard? Did he know that the train to Torquay left fifteen minutes earlier on Saturdays? Were the friends of the bride and bridegroom to mingle or sit separately? Had . . .? Did . . .? Were . . .? Was . . .? Should . . .? Could . . .? Would?

At last Dr. Trump had been able to stand it no longer and he had given instructions that he was permanently out to Mr. Parker. There was, in fact, only one supreme merit about the man. He did know the Church of England service backwards. With him there as a leader and exemplar, the congregation would know exactly when to stand and when to kneel. There would be none of those absurd half-postures like imperfectly practised physical exercises that Dr. Trump had noticed so often when heathens and agnostics attend the service of Christian matrimony. Mr. Parker would be able to put the congregation through its paces like a drill sergeant . . .

"I've done it," Mrs. Gurnett remarked suddenly. "It won't show if you don't bend."

"Thank you," Dr. Trump replied coldly. "I have no intention of bending." And then feeling that the occasion called for something more forthcoming, altogether more spontaneous, he suddenly turned his special smile full on her.

"How helpless, truly helpless, man is without woman," he observed. "You have indeed been more than kind. The coat itself, as you see, is practically new."

It was while he was sliding stealthily into the coat, keeping his shoulders well back so that there should not be even the slightest pressure, that a letter was brought into him by Miss Phrynne. He glanced at it idly and recognised Mr. Dawlish's handwriting. Again his face softened into an indulgent smile.

"Dear old Dawlish," he reflected; "how kind, how generous of him to send me his good wishes."

And then, as he opened the letter and began to read, his

220

face clouded. He drew his lips in sharply and the flute-like breathing began immediately.

" *Dear Dr. Trump,*" was what he read, "*I have natur-ally been giving a great deal of thought to my future. At the time of my interview, you told me that you wished me to leave the Hospital in nine weeks' time. Since the inter-view, however, I have re-read my letter of appointment and find that I am entitled to twelve weeks' notice with the alternative that I can leave at once if it is more con-venient. In the circumstances I feel that the latter would be preferable because it would give me more time to look around. With your permission, therefore, I would like to leave at the end of the current month as it will take me that time to tidy up . . .*"

Dr. Trump could read no farther. He crushed the offend-ing letter in his hand and dropped it into the wastepaper basket. Abominable! Truly abominable! The miserable man was simply trying to skulk out of his responsibilities by quoting some foolish phrase that Canon Mallow must have written. Dr. Trump would see his lawyers immediately. But how? He could hardly call a conference in the vestry when he should be signing the register. And to-morrow would be worse still: he would be in Torquay by then. Dr. Trump ground his heel into the carpet as though it were Mr. Dawlish himself that he was destroying. Why, oh why, of all times did the man have to choose this particular day for his rebellion?

The door opened quietly and a face appeared round it. It was Mr. Parker's face. But this time, Dr. Trump was ready for him. He got his question in first.

"Did you remember to stipulate no rice as well as no confetti?" he asked. "Very often, you know, the specific injunction against the one is taken to imply tacit approval of the other."

I I

The wedding was now over and bride and bridegroom, changed into their going-away clothes, were standing self-consciously among their guests. Champagne—a great deal of it, Dr. Trump noted—had been handed round, and the tiered white ice-berg of a cake had been divided into small sections like window-wedges. Everyone else was now wearing the expression of arch benevolence that is peculiar to weddings and for the eleventh time Dr. Trump had replied. " Oh Torquay. For a fortnight. Felicity adores the sea. The swimming you know. And the . . . er . . . ozone."

But he was not at that moment thinking of Torquay. Or the fortnight. Or even of the sea. He was thinking only of Felicity.

" Quite extraordinary," he was reflecting, " that she should have chosen puce. By itself extraordinary. But with that complexion really astonishing."

Because of his bride's colour scheme, even the champagne could do nothing to raise his spirits though he sipped away valiantly, and smiled obediently whenever he had caught the Bishop's eye. It was not, however, merely Felicity's going-away costume that had upset him. Too many other things as well had gone wrong since he had crossed the threshold of St. Mark's for mere champagne to be able to dispel them.

In the first place, there had been the regrettable sudden illness of the organist—something that he had eaten, it was said. In consequence, Mr. Prevarius had been roped in, *volunteered* so Bishop Warple assured him, to assist. And Mr. Prevarius had played execrably. Simply execrably ; almost as though he were doing so on purpose, in fact. Very loud and very fast, with fistfuls of grace notes and arpeggios that Handel and Sullivan had never authorised flung about all over the place. The Wedding March, in particular, had been murdered ; played with a kind of saucy insouciance that would have been more in keeping with a parade of Pearly Kings. The majesty and jubilation had been lost entirely, and an irreverent and offensive cockiness substituted for it, as though the abominable creature were leering at the bridal pair in his little mirror. And for no conceivable reason the Bishop had invited the monster back afterwards. At this very moment he was over at the buffet stuffing himself. Even as Dr. Trump looked, Mr. Prevarius was dipping his bridge roll, which was a little hard, into his champagne and sucking the end noisily like a schoolboy.

But Mr. Prevarius had been no more than one of Dr. Trump's mortifications. Two other mortifications had travelled all the way up from Swansea specially for the wedding. They were relations of Dr. Trump's ; poor, ageing and obscure. Dr. Trump's only relations, in fact. It would be

222

untrue to say that he had forgotten about them because Auntie Flo and Auntie Caroline never allowed Dr. Trump to forget. They were proud, very proud, of their successful nephew. And they were always writing to him, keeping him in touch with himself as it were, posting him extracts from newspapers where the name of Archbishop Bodkin's Hospital happened to be mentioned. Indeed, it often seemed to Dr. Trump that these two old ladies must have organised a sort of amateur press-cutting agency to keep track of him. At times it had become distinctly trying. Do what he might, Dr. Trump could not escape the sensation that he was being spied on. Round every corner of his life either Auntie Flo or Auntie Caroline seemed always to be peeping. And in their last letter, they had even threatened that they might sell the shop and come to live near him.

He had not, of course, invited them to his wedding; had not considered doing so. And, looked at frankly, how could he possibly have done so? For the fact had to be faced, that, through no fault of his own, their ways on life's stream had drifted steadily apart. Or rather they had drifted while he, Samuel, had cleaved his way against the current, drawing farther and more decisively away from them with every stroke.

He could now scarcely remember—possibly because he had always been anxious to forget—the tiny shop with its stacked-up newspapers and balls of string and bottles of cheap sweets, to which Auntie Flo had taken him after his poor mother's funeral. And, in the circumstances, he had already forgiven himself as he had uttered the white lie that he had no living relatives.

" You take me as I am, Felicity," he had said. " Myself alone. No living kith or kin that bears my name."

But that was what made it so devilish awkward—almost as though he had been deliberately lying to Felicity—when the two Miss Lewises, one elderly, one ancient, came tramping up the aisle to do honour to him.

He had spotted them out of the corner of his eye the moment they came in. And he recoiled at the recognition. It was bad enough that they should have come at all. But in those clothes! They had evidently fitted themselves out specially for the occasion, combing the smaller shops of Swansea for their finery. And the effect was deplorable. Auntie Flo's hat had obviously been designed for a much younger woman, and Auntie Caroline had bought a blouse that any sensible barmaid would have avoided. But it was the steel-framed spectacles that were worse: completely out of fashion, but devilishly efficient. He could feel them probing into him like exultant gimlets.

Even so, he would not have minded if only these two old ladies had shown the good feeling not to declare themselves. But Swansea to Putney is a long way. And Auntie Flo was determined to get her money's worth: she wanted to embrace her brilliant nephew, nothing less. Nor was Dr. Trump left in any doubt as to her intention. Just as he was getting into the car he heard her voice—strident with purpose, high and cracked with age—saying to Mr. Parker: " Well, even if he hasn't invited us, I'm still his auntie, aren't I?"

But by then Dr. Trump was too angry about something else to waste time reflecting on the shame of his own past that had followed and caught up with him. And that was because of the confetti that was in his ears and nostrils, and the rice that had run down inside the hard, unyielding collar. Either Mr. Parker had entirely forgotten his instructions, or had deliberately defied him.

For with no warning, the bombardment had suddenly begun. Under the twin influences of sex and ceremony, even quite sedate sensible sort of people had become overpowered by the sense of carnival. They had produced little cartons of confetti from their handbags, flung stinging charges of rice full into his unprotected face. Dame Eleanor herself had gone lunatic. She had her own personal brand of nuisance to bestow—little silver paper bells with serrated edges that clung like burrs to his clothing. And all the while, roaring out through the Gothic doorway of the church, there was that dreadful *tootle-ee-oot-tee-toot* played *ff* by Mr. Prevarius upon the organ.

The ordeal, moreover, showed every sign of mounting rather than subsiding. For no sooner had they left the church than Felicity began talking about her mother. She was, in fact, so much concerned about her mother that Dr. Trump found himself wondering whether she could really have been attending properly while the service was still on. In the first place, Dr. Trump now learned to his astonishment, that it somehow hadn't seemed like a proper wedding at all without Mummie. But if Mummie had been there, so Dr. Trump was led to understand, she would undoubtedly have broken down. And this seemed extraordinary because Felicity explained in the same breath that Mummie had simply been living for to-day; it was the one thing that had been keeping her alive. Indeed, only the arrival of the bridal car at the episcopal home saved Dr. Trump from saying something that he would unquestionably have regretted: another hundred yards of that awful journey and he would indignantly have demanded whether it was his wedding or Mummie's that he had just been attending.

But even if Mrs. Warple had missed the ceremony, she was undeniably mistress of the reception. Wearing a blue silk dress with a lace jabot and hung with a double row of her most dubious-looking pearls, she had availed herself of the invalid's privilege of remaining seated. On a high upholstered chair she was enthroned like an aloof female Buddha. And as Felicity came into sight the dams and flood-gates of emotion opened. There in full view of the arriving guests, Mrs. Warple let herself go. She wept. As Dr. Trump looked at her, he acknowledged respectfully that Felicity had been right: in a small church such an outburst would have been disastrous. It would have drowned even Mr. Prevarius's playing.

As soon as Mrs. Warple was sufficiently recovered, the Bishop brought the guests over to her one by one. And, not knowing any better, he brought Auntie Flo as well. Just as Dr. Trump was brushing aside a local reporter with the words: " Torquay is the destination. Not Switzerland as we had hoped. And then only for the briefest spell. The Hospital requires me back. So much to do, you understand. So many responsibilities . . ." Auntie Flo was saying to Mrs. Warple: " Well, I'm his auntie. I ought to know. I tell you if he sets foot in a boat he's finished . . ." And when Mrs. Warple, making polite social conversation, remarked how proud Auntie Flo must be to see her nephew to-day with his bride beside him, the answer came back, prompt and horrifying: " Proud? It's like black magic. When I remember the nights I sat up rubbing his poor chest I never thought I'd live to see him standing at the altar."

It must, Dr. Trump reflected afterwards, have been the deplorable effect of the champagne on a constitution unaccustomed to it that had made Auntie Flo so suddenly and so remorselessly reminiscent. On the subject of her nephew she became as a woman inspired: she was eloquent. She forgot nothing—his first manly trousers; his weak chest; his tantrums; his indigestion; his flat feet, particularly his left one that had always turned inwards at the ankle; his bicycle accident; his disastrous experiment in shaving; his bouts of bronchitis that succeeded even the least of chills; his fear of large dogs; his abnormal longing for a silver watch in a local pawnbroker's; his dislike of other children of the same sex; the sweetness of his singing voice; his affection for clergymen; his powers of application and the diplomas, medals, prizes, exhibitions, scholarships and whatnot that had all followed.

Twice Dr. Trump plucked her by the sleeve—the second time quite hard—and tried once more to show her the presents. But she was not to be distracted. Her colour had risen and with her veil slipped back across the brim of that awful hat she faced the world on more than even terms.

With a newly discovered confidence she now assailed him. Why had he never been back to see them? Had he forgotten his own auntie? Did those who loved him and cared for him and thought about nothing else mean so little to him? How could he bear to leave empty his own bedroom above the shop that was just as he had left it, just as he would want to find it whenever he returned? And when, even to her ears, his assurances of an early visit and prolonged stay sounded empty and deceitful, Auntie Flo turned on Felicity. There was room, and a welcome for both of them. She offered her own bedroom if only they would really come.

But Dr. Trump had ceased to listen. Instead, he was looking at the faces of the listening group. And if it had not been for the foxy alertness of the unwelcome reporter he would—weak digestion, flat-feet, affection for clergymen and all—have wiped the smile clean off Mr. Prevarius's face with one crisp and uninhibited clip across the jaw.

III

The hour had come at last. Felicity had turned off all the lights, except for the pink-shaded one above the bed. And Dr. Trump, who had just remembered that he had not put his shoes outside, was walking self-consciously back into the bedroom, fiddling with the tassels of his new dressing-gown.

But, instead of getting into bed, Dr. Trump—to Felicity's great astonishment—passed straight through the bedroom and out on to the balcony again.

The air there was cooler, and Dr. Trump shivered slightly.

Nevertheless, it was a pearl among evenings. Night had already descended on the bay and the moon shining on the water made a pathway that vaguely suggested a subject for a sermon. But Dr. Trump at this moment had no appetite for sermons. He stood biting his lips and gazing at a distant star.

Behind him from the bedroom a soft voice called.

"Samuel," it said.

Dr. Trump started guiltily.

"Yes, my love."

"A penny for them, dearest."

Dr. Trump turned and began to remove his dressing-gown as he re-entered.

"I was just thinking," he said. "So far there hasn't been a single answer to the advertisements. And with Dawlish wanting to go, it'll be extremely awkward if no one else applies."

CHAPTER XXVIII

ESPECIALLY in the dawn-light, the new laundry block looked most impressive. The insurance company, having failed to find any flaw in the policy, had finally paid up like gentlemen. And, in consequence, an expanse of bright yellow brick now showed violently among the grey, smoke-laden walls of the rest of the Hospital. Nor was the laundry block all. There was also the new fire-engine. Of the latest model and with centrifugal action, it was painted pillar-box red like its predecessor, and stood at the Latymer end of the cloisters, roped off from passers-by and with the notice "DO NOT TOUCH" fixed on to the front of it.

But a great calamity like a fire can hardly be expected to pass off with nothing more to show for itself than some clean brickwork and a fancy-looking, stream-lined fire-engine. Indeed Dr. Trump by now had taken every precaution. He had ordered new fire-escapes. And the whole Hospital was now girded and festooned with extinguishers—one in each dormitory and classroom; one in each corridor; one in the board room; one in the masters' common room, and one in the mistresses'; one in Dr. Trump's own room, just behind his chair; three in the Warden's Residence; and one

227

in the chapel. After some thought, Dr. Trump had decided on the pulpit as the most suitable place for the chapel extinguisher. In the result, if a conflagration should break out during divine service Dr. Trump could, without abandoning his position, merely strike the knob sharply and direct the jet into the very heart of the inferno.

It was really the extinguisher in the masters' common room that was the most important because, as Dr. Trump frequently upbraided himself, he had practically *invited* his own staff to make a bonfire of the whole place. He had already issued one of his orders on the subject of smoking in bedrooms. Over the mantelpiece in every master's room there now hung a printed card in bold letters: SMOKING IS EXPRESSLY FORBIDDEN IN BEDROOMS, AND OFFENDERS WILL BE DEALT WITH SEVERELY. MASTERS WISHING TO SMOKE ARE PERMITTED TO DO SO IN THE COMMON ROOM BUT ARE ONCE AGAIN WARNED OF THE DANGERS OF CARELESSNESS. *Signed* Samuel Trump, Warden.

And on his tours of inspection Dr. Trump now always made a special point of pausing long enough to sniff outside each door. Of abnormally keen powers of smell, he prided himself that if the dirty habit were secretly being practised anywhere behind closed doors he would be able to detect it immediately. The only difficulty was that Mr. Dawlish's room was so soaked and impregnated with tobacco that it was difficult to decide how recently the weed had been burning.

For Mr. Dawlish was still there. The other victims of Dr. Trump's re-organisation, his purge, had duly passed outwards into limbo. Mr. Jeffcote, practically blind already, was reduced to addressing envelopes for an agency at the rate of 10d. a thousand; Mrs. Glubb had found a post—but only at £52 a year—in a home for backward children in St. Leonards; and Miss Wynne, her goitre growing steadily worse and more disfiguring, was with an aunt at Hendon. But Mr. Prevarius and Mr. Dawlish remained.

In fact, when Dr. Trump had come to review the matter it became more and more distressingly apparent that Mr. Dawlish was well-nigh irreplaceable. There was simply no one else in the whole Hospital who could teach so much English, History, Geography, Arithmetic and Scripture to children of all ages from six to fourteen. And the size of class did not seem to worry him either. Sixty was the present number, and Mr. Dawlish, still as dirty and tobacco-stained

228

as ever, took it all as calmly as when the class had been only half the size.

As for Mr. Prevarius, he was still there because Dr. Trump had set his heart on that B.B.C. broadcast. Admittedly, up to the present there had been nothing to show for it. But, according to Mr. Prevarius, he was engaged in a practically day by day correspondence with Sir John Reith, who was ready to cancel anything—symphony concerts, plays, even the news bulletin itself—to fit it in, and it was thus only a matter of waiting for the happy moment.

In the meantime, Dr. Trump had been strict and business-like. Mr. Prevarius now combined the Old Testament and a little English Grammar with music-teaching, and there were no more free periods anywhere in Mr. Prevarius's calendar. Dr. Trump had, indeed, considered throwing in the New Testament as well. But, remembering the incident of the elderberry wine, he had finally decided against it, and had added commercial script and simple book-keeping instead.

And so, except for the doubling-up of classes on the girls' side, life in the Archbishop Bodkin Hospital continued very much as it had done before Dr. Trump's major re-organisation.

Or, at least that was how things were before Mrs. Gurnett fired off her bombshell. That was something that threw everything into chaos ; something that, as Dr. Trump told her, he found it quite impossible to forgive, especially at such a moment when Mrs. Trump's condition was naturally causing him so much concern.

CHAPTER XXIX

BUT NOW look at it from Mrs. Gurnett's point of view. Just think what it meant to her.

The letter had come at the ordinary time—it was round about 8.15 when the postman usually reached the Archbishop Bodkin Hospital—but until this moment, Mrs. Gurnett had not had more than a chance to glance at it. Admittedly, she had already raced through it no fewer than five times. Once when it had arrived ; again immediately after breakfast ; once at eleven during the break for a mid-morning cup of tea ; once during the lull after lunch while the washing up was going on ; and once surreptitiously in the lavatory at about

229

5.30. But she was still not satisfied. Up to the present, she had not managed to do what she called *getting down to it properly*.

But this was different. She was in her own room, now. The nickel-plated alarm-clock on the mantelpiece showed 10.25 p.m., and Mrs. Gurnett noted the fact approvingly. It meant that, short of anything sudden and dramatic, there would be no more interruptions for to-night. Mrs. Gurnett therefore moved her chair round so that the light was better, unbuckled her belt, eased off her shoes until her toes were only just poking into them and started to re-read what had been written.

Started to re-read, and then stopped because the past was suddenly so recent and so overwhelming. It was terrible, frightening, the way it all came sweeping back over her. She remembered everything—her shame, Mr. Gurnett's trial and imprisonment, her own imaginary widowhood. It was all so recent, yet so remote—like reading in the evening paper of some other woman's misfortune. And now, out of the blue, to receive this letter telling her that Mr. Gurnett was dead.

It was twenty-three years almost to the day when she had last seen him. And that had been when he had turned in the dock with the warder's hand already resting on his shoulder, and had blown her a kiss where she was sitting. Twenty-three years, but she could still see every detail of the scene—the rather large check of the suit that he had on, the black silk cravat worn somewhat wider than was customary among gentlemen in his social position, the solitaire pearl tie-pin, the militarily waxed moustache, and, above all, his large, dewy black eyes that he had once brought so close to hers.

And Mrs. Gurnett remembered something else as well. She remembered how the first, the *real* Mrs. Gurnett, had sat just below her in the body of the court. And, at that distasteful memory, the crescent of Mrs. Gurnett's lips hardened and she drew in her breath involuntarily. That one glimpse was all that she had ever had of her rival, her forerunner. But it had been enough. The tendrils of fair fluffy hair escaping round the straw hat-brim, the china blue eyes, the pink and white complexion all betokened the essential cheapness and frivolity in Mr. Gurnett's false nature. It was as though somehow he had earlier got himself entangled with a wax doll. And it had shown that she was well shot of such a
230

monster, this cheap Italian-looking bedroom-monger who could blow a kiss to another woman with his own lawful wife looking on.

Then to receive this, to learn when it was already too late, that he had loved her all the time. It was staggering, incredible; like re-writing history. To think, after all, that those playful whisperings that had raised a blush every time he turned towards her, had come not merely from the tongue, but from the heart. To realise that if it had not been for that snivelling blonde milk-maid whose eyes had been pink-rimmed right through the case, Mr. Gurnett would have been with her all through these years, his lusty tenor laugh ringing through the house, his Homburg hat and yellow gloves on the hall-stand, his heavy breathing on the pillow beside her at night-time. Mrs. Gurnett sat back for a moment and wiped away a tear.

Not that she had felt like this about the matter from the start. Her first emotion when she opened the letter had been one of sick horror, of disgust. When she had seen the name Albert Nathaniel Gurnett set out in the cold script of the lawyer's typewriter, her first instinct had been to tear the letter up, destroy it instantly, so that no matter what message was contained within it she could not possibly be drawn back down into those depths, that cesspool.

But, when she read its astonishing message, she paused. Two hundred and eighty-nine pounds! It was a fortune. And apparently this incalculable and misjudged man had decided to leave it all to her. Not that she was going to do anything rash like accepting. For all she knew, Mr. Gurnett might not really be dead at all: the whole thing might be simply a trick, a ruse to get her back to him. But even if he were dead *could* she, *ought* she, to accept the money? Wouldn't it reduce her to a level as low as his if she calmly put the cash into her handbag and called the whole thing quits?

She paused, easing her toes inside her half done-up shoes. Then she began to see things differently. All the money in the world wasn't enough to put right the wrong that he had done her. Mr. Gurnett must have known that. But it was something that he had tried, it showed that she must have been on his conscience. And who was she to refuse a dying man, a dead man even, his last wish? Besides, there was something very touching, something that made a lump come into her throat, at the thought of him far, far away—Bridlington was where the letter came from—remembering her as the death mists had closed around him. In that moment, she forgave him ; and, having forgiven him, there could be no point in refusing what he had been so anxious to bequeath.

Her reply took some time to write because she wanted it to be as formal and correct as the letter that the lawyer had sent her. And, when she had finished it, she still had to make a copy of her own so that she would know if the firm was a sharp one and tried to do her out of anything.

Then, her work done, she sat back. Her face softened and the hard crescent of her mouth began to relax and draw downwards no longer. After all those years of waiting, of saving every penny, everything was coming right at last. Compared with the sixty-three pounds that she had been wanting, this was affluence. The Lamorna Private Nursing Establishment, resident matron, Mrs. Gurnett, would be able to have its own white-tiled operating theatre, its seven-guineas-a-week surgical wing, after all. In short, dear, dead, derided, misunderstood Mr. Gurnett had put her on the road to affluence.

And then, as another thought crossed her mind, Mrs. Gurnett uttered a loud " Ah," and this time—the first time for years—the corners of her mouth tilted upwards.

" This means that I'm a free woman," she said exultantly. " I'm as good as he is now. As soon as I've actually got the money, I can tell that Dr. Trump just what I think of him."

CHAPTER XXX

I

MARRIAGE, Dr. Trump was discovering, is not necessarily the quiet and placid haven that sentimentalists make it out to be. The last twelve months, indeed, had been appalling: simply one confounded rush after another.

And it was not his fault. It was Felicity's. She was organising him. Taking him in hand completely. Re-making him. And, with every fresh outburst of wifeliness, Dr Trump shuddered as he remembered Mrs. Warple's words from the sick-bed. " She runs this house," was what Mrs

Warple had said to him. At the time he had not realised that the words were not merely a statement, but a warning.

For a start, there were his friends. He had got to make some, Felicity said; and quickly. And not merely any friends: they had got to be of the right kind. At first Dr. Trump had agreed. He had been indulgent, even cordial. It seemed a capital idea to have a lot of the right kind of friends. Come to think of it, who could possibly want the wrong kind? But he soon saw that there were snags, disadvantages to the process. Friends took up such a terrible lot of time. And while these new and, he still hoped, beautiful friendships were ripening and developing, the candidates had to be fed.

Already, the Trump household accounts were rocketing; positively rocketing. The grocer's bill for one week had shown two botts. claret, one bott. sherry, one bott. invalid port—the invalid port was for a well-known lay evangelist —as well as little expensive oddments like one jar olives and half-pound salted almonds. Indeed, late at night, as Dr. Trump went over the bills, he decided that the price of friendship might in the end prove so high that he would have to call the whole thing off, revert to solitariness.

There were, of course, compensations. Invitations were a two-way affair. And though, for the time being, Felicity could not accept, Dr. Trump was by now a regular luncher and diner-out. Ever since his ordination, for instance, it had been one of Dr. Trump's ambitions to receive a luncheon invitation to Lambeth. And now it had happened: " Lambeth Palace," he had been able to say to the taxi-driver as he left the Bodkin Hospital.

Admittedly, the top sparkle, the sheen, of the affair had been removed when Dr. Trump saw the seating plan. No matter how he reviewed it, he could still not understand how he had come to be placed one from the end on the left-hand side. But his neighbours, if not exactly distinguished—no rings, no large amethyst-studded crosses reclining on scarlet —were at least stimulating. They were two missionaries from Illinois. And very plump, milk-fed little missionaries they were, too. Their bright concave spectacles flashed like the head-lamps on a smart sports car, and their gold fountain pens and fancy wrist-watches added that indefinable note of the exclusive coach-builder. It was the World Kingdom of Apostolic Churches—a body of which Dr. Trump had not previously heard—that they represented, and they were in the course of a lightning nine-day tour that was to include London (England), Paris (France), Geneva (Switzerland) and Rome (Italy) on the way.

Dr. Trump was right between them, with their national president, Professor Zollberg on his left and Mr. Sussman, their organising secretary, on his right. And after a few moments of plain caution and resentment, he sat there speechless and entranced. It was propaganda and publicity that was Mr. Sussman's speciality and, as Dr. Trump listened, he felt himself being reborn into a richer and more charitable world. Doors began to open all round him, and the future that lay beyond seemed at once immense, wonderful. He even wondered how the Church had contrived to crawl through those impoverished early centuries before Mr. Sussman's services had been available.

" So it's money you want, is it, Doc?" Mr. Sussman inquired.

He leant forward as he said it and came so close that Dr. Trump had the uncomfortable impression that the little man had climbed on to the cloth and was now sitting on the table-top facing him.

" The needs of the Hospital are certainly very pressing," Dr. Trump admitted guardedly. " Very pressing indeed."

" Well, name it," Mr. Sussman instructed. " Put a figure to it."

" It's about . . . about eleven thousand pounds," Dr. Trump told him.

Mr. Sussman turned towards his national president.

" Say, what's that in dollars, Professor?"

Professor Zollberg took out his pen.

" Times four," he said. " I calc'late that as forty-four thousand."

Mr. Sussman shook his head.

" Wrong sort of sum," he said. " Ask for fifty thousand. Sounds bigger."

" It *is* bigger," Dr. Trump pointed out.

But already the organising secretary was hard at work organising.

" What's your literature like?" he asked.

" Our literature?" Dr. Trump inquired. " You mean . . . er . . . English studies."

" Naw. Naw," Mr. Sussman told him. " Appeals literature. Brochures. Pamphlets. Booklets. Hand-outs. Giveaways. Just how do you set about it?"

"We appeal twice yearly," Dr. Trump replied. "With an ..... er .... Roneo-ed letter. And, of course, *The Times* and *Telegraph*. In the personal column, you know."

"Who signs the letters?" Mr. Sussman demanded.

"Oh, Dame Eleanor," Dr. Trump answered. "It is always our Chairman who signs."

"Is she Royalty?" Mr. Sussman persisted.

Dr. Trump drew in his breath quickly.

"I am afraid not," he admitted.

Mr. Sussman took up the point at once.

"Oh don't imagine that I've got anything against the lady. It's just that I wonder whether she's big enough for you. Whether she's got the name."

Dr. Trump said nothing.

And it was now evident that Mr. Sussman was really warming up to his subject.

"Have you studied Appeals Research?" he asked. "The statistical side, I mean."

Dr. Trump paused. He would have liked to be able to say "yes"; that he had graduated in Appeals Research; that the standard work on the subject was one that he had written himself. But somehow he did not feel that Mr. Sussman would believe him: those head-lamp spectacles of his would see through anything. He was compelled therefore to humiliate himself for the second time.

"No," he confessed awkwardly. "I am afraid I have never had the time. I am not ... er ... a professional appeal-maker. I am a theologian."

He was pleased with this arrow as he fired it. But he might have saved himself the trouble. After all, Mr. Sussman was only trying to help, and there was no call for rudeness. Not that it mattered: the armour of the organising secretary was perfect and impenetrable. He brushed the sentence away like a fly and went straight on.

"Seventy-eight point four per cent of all donations to charity," he said, emphasising each syllable by prodding Dr. Trump with his thumb, "are the result of photographs. Children on crutches. Blind babies. Old people in wheel-chairs. It has been definitely established by the psychologists ..."

But Dr. Trump never knew what it was that the psychologists had been so definite about. For, at that moment, his neighbour—a gaunt, wolf-like prebendary with whom so far Dr. Trump had not exchanged so much as a single word

235

after the original snarl of greeting—leant right across him and addressed Mr. Sussman.

" Quiet, please," he said reprovingly. " His Grace is trying to address us . . ."

All the same, Mr. Sussman's words had not been wasted. Within Dr. Trump's mind the seed germinated and took root. Little prickly feelings inside kept reminding him of his new mission, his self-appointed task. And exactly eight days after the planting, Dr. Trump got out pen and paper and began cultivating the first tender shoots.

This title had come as one of the happiest of his inspirations. First he printed the words, " THERE IS A HOME FOR LITTLE CHILDREN " in block capitals half-way down the page. Then, after contemplating the beauty of the design for a few moments he deleted the words " THERE IS." Yes, that was it —" HOME FOR LITTLE CHILDREN "—that was what the booklet was to be called. And above the words he drew two large balloon-shaped frames for the photographs of the two prettiest children in the Hospital. His own likeness he decided would go inside ; nothing formal or studied—just a simple picture of himself with his hands outstretched appealingly, or a casual snap taken unaware as it were, showing him romping on one of the lawns with the toddlers.

And, as he worked, he became a kind of super-Sussman : ideas for new phrases, new photographs, new captions, came pouring in on him. He seethed and bubbled with creation, and began furiously making notes on the cover of his sermon pad. " Big Friend " was what he was going to call himself throughout, not Warden. There was something altogether too chilling, too prison-like about his official title for the purpose of this heart-breaking little booklet. How easily it flowed, too. " Big Friend tastes the breakfast porridge " ; " Big Friend leads the Sunday sing-songs " ; " Big Friend visits the tiny sick ones " ; " Big Friend talks to his small friends " ; " Big Friend shows the way " ; " Big Friend says a prayer " ; " Big Friend asks *you* for *your* help."

What was more, even the format of the booklet was plain to him by now. It was to be sixteen pages of large note-paper size, and the back of it was to be in the form of a banker's draft, perforated so that the charitably-minded could simply fill in the particulars, rip it off, and pop it in the post-box.

Already Dr. Trump was itching to get down to the letter-
236

press itself. For it was here that the subtlest touches of all, the real conscience-tweakings, could be got in. And in his fine, angular script Dr. Trump began to write: "Dear Other Friend," it started, "Do you carry a tear in your heart?" But here Dr. Trump paused. It wasn't a sermon that he was writing and how could he be sure that the reader would understand him? He meant, of course, the crying kind of tear, not the torn sort. But as, apparently, there was no means of conveying this simple fact without the aid of the human voice, he drove his pen through the entire sentence and began again more simply. "I have lately become the father of five hundred children . . ." But this was clearly impossible, and he hurriedly put his pen through that, too. Then he thought of another approach, the direct, manly one: "Were you ever an unwanted child? Was it your shame to have no father's name on your birth-certificate?" But this would never do: it sounded somehow so gratuitously insulting. How could he possibly expect generosity from people who opened a perfectly nice-looking letter only to find that it contained a lot of nasty allegations from some unknown clergyman? So out went that sentence as well. For a moment or so he toyed with the notion of: "Our beds are full, but our pockets are empty." But that had the unmistakable note of a begging appeal that he most wanted to avoid: most recipients would not even trouble to read any farther. And the variant, "Last week I could not pay the milk bill," was even worse. So he made one more shot at it. "Dear Other Friend," he wrote, "Wouldn't you like to 'adopt' a Little Friend? Big Friend has five hundred Little Friends to choose from—sweet, appealing little girls and fine manly little fellows. Perhaps yours is there waiting for you . . ." Then, remembering the somewhat misty parenthood of some of the five hundred, Dr. Trump decided that perhaps the last sentence was just a shade unfortunate. It sounded too much like a police trap. So down came the pen once more obliterating, scratching out, erasing.

By lunch-time Dr. Trump was moody and preoccupied. When Felicity told him quite clearly and distinctly that the editor of the *Missionary Times* and his wife were coming, he merely nodded. Indeed, he particularly did not want to be interrupted at that moment. He could feel the mood coming on him and the perfect first sentence, at once arresting and provocative, was forming in his mind as he sat there.

"Would you like to become a surprise father or a surprise

mother?" he was going to say. "If so, all that you have to do is to ring Putney Hill 1236 and Big Friend will make everything easy for you."

II

The letterpress was now finished. And, by the time Dr. Trump reached the last page he had acquired a profound respect for the Mr. Sussmans of this world. But there it was at last, five and a half quarto pages all neatly typed by Miss Phrynne on the office Oliver, and with the initial words of each paragraph underlined in red. There now remained only the photographs. And here Dr. Trump showed the deep resourcefulness of his nature. He did not go to any of the local firms, the Putney regulars who exhibited wedding groups and football elevens and newly-married couples in their windows. Instead, he wrote to a firm entitled " Child and Camera " whose shop window he had seen somewhere off Baker Street. And he was imperious and commanding. He told " Child and Camera " to come to him.

The letter was acknowledged next day on a strange-looking heliotrope-coloured postcard signed in green ink with a name that Dr. Trump could not read. But at least it was civil. It announced that the mysterious writer would be there on the following day at 3 p.m., and looked forward to making the Warden's acquaintance.

Dr. Trump spent the greater part of the morning getting ready for him. He removed one of the " DON'T WALK ON THE GRASS " notices so that there would be a place for the toddlers to romp. He brushed up his old Norfolk jacket and grey flannels in case the photographer felt that his new black was a trifle too formal for the setting of some of the pictures. He rearranged his desk so that Big Friend could be seen at work with the presentation desk calendar, the travelling clock, the silver inkwell and the chromium blotter all showing. And finally he asked Felicity to arrange a large bowl of flowers on the side-table. Then, conscious that there was nothing left unprepared, he sat back and re-read what he had written. He was still reading when three o'clock struck on the carillon-clock—it was " Men of Harlech " to-day—and " Child and Camera " was shown in.

Dr. Trump's first impression of his visitor was, he was

bound to admit, distinctly unfavourable. The man might have been connected with the Black Bourse, or even with the international drug traffic rather than with juvenile photography. He was so undisguisedly foreign. Mr. Zibbo, his unreadable name turned out to be; and he was Hungarian. He was short, bald, and spectacled. They were very large spectacles that he wore and he seemed to be focusing for an exposure even when he was merely looking at Dr. Trump. And there was an abruptness, a kind of fanatical suddenness about him, that Dr. Trump found most disconcerting.

After one particularly offensive stare he made little smoothing motions in the air with his hands.

"Plees to be natural," he said. "There iss nothing for nervousness."

Dr. Trump drew himself up in his chair.

"I assure you that I am not in the least nervous," he told him. "I am . . . er . . . entirely natural."

But Mr. Zibbo only shook his head.

"Now it iss worsse," he said. "Much worsse. Breeth plees."

Dr. Trump carefully restrained himself from replying. Really, this little monster who was staring at him was nothing less than impossible. Another question like the last one, and he would send "Child and Camera" packing, and go to one of the reliable local firms.

But Mr. Zibbo was not easily put off.

"Breething iss mosst important in life," he went on. "It iss the mosst important thing of all. I learn that in Vienna. Now I breeth always. Like thiss. I show you how some time. Now we look at the children, plees."

On their way over to the Latymer Block, Mr. Zibbo became intimately autobiographical. He had begun specialising in children—delinquent ones especially—in Buda, he said. Then in Rome he had found the material for his book, *Children in Focus*. Dr. Trump had heard of it, no? He would send him a copy. Two guineas, yess? Dr. Trump had written many books himself, no? Mr. Zibbo was writing another one. It was to be all about photographing children. Dr. Trump would like to order a copy, yess? It would be three guineas this one, with every photograph signed. The children were all Armenian. Next year, Mr. Zibbo was going to China. Chinese children had very photogenic heads.

By now they had reached the grass plot from which Dr.

239

Trump had removed the "DO NOT WALK ON THE GRASS" notice. Dr. Trump paused.

"It is here," he said, "that I propose to be taken romping with the toddlers."

Mr. Zibbo spread out his hands.

"Toddlers, yess," he said. "What is ' romp,' plees?"

"Play merrily," Dr. Trump told him. "Go down on all fours. Sing."

"You go down on all fours?" Mr. Zibbo asked.

"Only for the purposes of this photograph," he replied.

Mr. Zibbo spread out his hands again.

"We see," he said guardedly. "We think about it."

Dr. Trump was particularly pleased by the scene that met them as he opened the door of the Ridley Block. The junior girls were ranged in a long line ready to go through to fancy needlework. There was not so much as a tremor anywhere in the whole length of the column, and the effect of so much Archbishop Bodkin uniform seen against the high Gothic windows was beautiful, spiritual, like something out of a Church pageant.

"There," he said proudly. "These are our little ones. Why not snap them now and then we can go across to the woodwork room. You'll find everything ready."

But Mr. Zibbo was not impressed.

"I photograph children," he said. "Not seely clothes. I photograph them naked in the sun. To-day eess not hot enough. I only look. Then next time everyone naked, plees. Then I make my picture . . ."

After that, it was L. Tuckett & Son, Artistic Photographers, from the High Street, who took the photographs. And very creditable they were, too, considering that they were all done one morning by the aid of flash-light bulbs. There was only one serious shortcoming and that was in Mr. Tuckett's choice for the two portraits on the cover. Indeed, when the proofs reached Dr. Trump he could hardly credit it when he saw Sweetie and Ginger framed side by side on the front cover.

But by then the cost of composition, proof-correction, resetting and all the rest of it had become so alarming that he was forced to let it go. There was simply no alternative. When he raised the matter with the Board, Dame Eleanor made it perfectly plain to him that the Board was not prepared to sanction another penny for the pamphlet.

In her view, a Roneo-ed letter signed by the Chairman was the right vehicle for an appeal, and she intimated that this was how it would be next time.

CHAPTER XXXI

I

MR. PREVARIUS was not really paying much attention to Hospital business at the moment. He had just met with more success. Or rather with two successes—one as Sidney Prevarius, B.D., the other as Berkeley Cavendish, author and composer of " Lullaby Lady " and " Four o'clock Doll."

The first was in connection with " Infant Innocence," a two-part song for children's voices. Published by an obscure house in St. Paul's Churchyard, it had already been sung at half a dozen choir festivals and been commented on favourably by *The Church of England Newspaper* and *The Musical Times*. Thoughtfully dedicated to " My friend and master, Samuel Trump, D.D.," its publication had done Mr. Prevarius nothing but good within the Hospital—even though the Warden was still waiting impatiently for something firm in the way of a date for the broadcast.

Mr. Berkeley Cavendish's little piece, on the other hand, had done him good in a wider and more prosperous world. Entitled " Switchback," it was being played by West End dance-bands, and in the halls of Camberwell and Poplar. The American sheets were coming out next month and there was a French version, " L'Amour en cendres," ready for the autumn. A catchy little tune, da-da-da-dee-dee, and good words, had done the trick. The words, indeed, were pure inspiration from nowhere and had occurred to Mr. Prevarius during one of Dr. Trump's sermons. They ran lightly off the tongue as follows:

> *Life is a switchback*
> *And I can't hitch back*
> *My wagon to your star.*
> *You've gone away too far . . .*
> *I'm on my own now*
> *And all alone now*

Casting till I die
Lassos at the sky.

In the original version there were eleven other verses besides. And when Mr. Prevarius had cut them down to the conventional half-dozen, what he had was the cream, the real money-maker.

It was, indeed, the success of "Switchback" that changed Mr. Prevarius's life in more than one direction. He had already developed a rather pretty taste in dress, currently favouring something double-breasted in black, with a lavender waistcoat and lightish check trousers, but he had simply nowhere he could put it on. Or rather, having put it on, he had to take it off again. And he had grown to hate the gentlemen's lavatory at Charing Cross—the attendant always looked at him so suspiciously every time he changed from dark clericals into magenta and spats.

Mr. Prevarius decided therefore that he would rent a room. A *pied-à-terre*. A hide-away. A bolt-hole. A den. Even possibly a love-nest. And he began looking around. He considered Albany, but dismissed it as too expensive. Shepherd Market? Too distracting. Bloomsbury? Rather damp and boarding-housy. Westminster? There was the nuisance of those everlasting bells. Old Hampstead? Too far, and full of children. Regent's Park? Admirable, but what did he want with a 999 years' lease and twelve bedrooms? So in the end he compromised with 23a Deirdre Gardens, a cul-de-sac just off the Fulham Road.

No one could exactly describe it as fashionable. The steam laundry at the bottom saw to that. But 23a was mercifully at the right end. It was in fact next door but one to a public house, the "Duke of Clarence." And the large block nearly opposite that had been converted into studios added just that note of Latin Quarter and Bohemianism that Mr. Prevarius felt so much that he needed.

No. 23a was kept by two elderly maiden ladies, the Miss Lewises. They were newly arrived in the neighbourhood, and were proposing to make a living by letting rooms. In his first interview—on the doorstep—they inquired which room he was after. And Mr .Prevarius discovered that he could have the choice of the second floor front or the small third floor back. There was 3s. 6d. a week difference. But the success of "Switchback" had made him carefree of money, even spendthrift. He took the second floor front and paid a month's rent in advance.

The matter of references, however, presented some difficulty. The Archbishop Bodkin Hospital was clearly out of the question. And he was not anxious to give his music publishers in the Charing Cross Road—because being known ties a man down somewhat. So, in the end, he compromised. He gave the name of Berkeley Cavendish *as a reference*. And inquiring politely the next time he visited his little Soho newsagents to see if there were any letters for him, he was able to send the Miss Lewises an entirely satisfactory and reassuring sort of reference; even a rather magnanimous one.

Unfortunately, however, multiple lives tend to be rather confusing. On the doorstep he had, for example, described himself on the spur of the moment as a travelling university examiner from St. Andrews. The name, he added, was Gordon—Archie Gordon. His wife, his wee wifie as he remembered to call her, might from time to time be visiting London with him—and that should solve things, he told himself, so long as he remembered to stick to the same girl. He himself, he explained, would be in London every Thursday for his examinations. Altogether, it was a little masterpiece of invention. It gave him no fewer than four personalities—as a choir-master, as song-hit writer, as university examiner—and as wolf.

And if the Miss Lewises needed any further proof of his intentions, the scale of the refurnishing that he embarked upon spoke for his permanency. It was only the *kind* of furniture that left them puzzled. And this itself was largely fortuitous. It was simply that a second-hand dealer in the Fulham Road had marked down a whole collection of miscellaneous Chinese junk—lacquered fretwork chairs, a deeply-embossed decorated altar, carved stools, a pair of shields, joss-stick holders and a war-mask—and Mr. Prevarius bought the lot. That, and a really good divan from a shop opposite, completed the room.

Not that Mr. Prevarius was yet content. There was still the piano. And here he fairly let himself go. Getting trade terms through Mr. Spike Jerome, he bought a boudoir grand. It was a pleasing piece in ebony—Mr. Prevarius would have preferred satinwood as going better with the flowered curtains that he had planned, but the red lacquer furniture plainly indicated something darker—and there was all the fun
243

in paying for it, of knowing that the money was really in the bank.

The only little set-back occurred when he suddenly recalled that at No. 23a Deirdre Gardens he wasn't the gentleman who had signed the cheque. He was Mr. . . . Mr. . . . who the devil was he? Yes, Gordon, of course; it was Cavendish who had been kind enough to give the reference. But with what Christian name? Alistair? Alexis? Adolphus? Augustin? He had forgotten.

"I . . . I am sending it as a present to a friend. A surprise, you understand," he said vaguely. "I will phone up and complete the address later."

Mr. Prevarius passed his handkerchief across his forehead as soon as he got outside. This was altogether too dreadful. He had never suspected that multiple identities would prove so bewildering. And why, oh why, had he told the innocent Miss Lewises that absurd story about being a university examiner? Why wasn't the story that he had told Desirée, about being a director of something, good enough?

To get things sorted out and tidy, Mr. Prevarius slipped into a tea-shop and over a cup of coffee and a bun made a few notes on the back page of his diary, just to clear his mind. In his rather charming, backward-sloping hand he inscribed:

Sidney Prevarius, B.D., Archbishop Bodkin Hospital.
Berkeley (de Vere) Cavendish), c/o Moulton's Newsagency, Leak Street, Soho, director.
—— Gordon, 23a Deirdre Gardens, W.9. University examiner.

That done, he felt better. But twice the diary came out again. The first time was when almost immediately he remembered that his Christian name was Archie. And the second time—it was so abrupt and unpremeditated that he spilt coffee all over himself—was when he snatched open the diary to destroy the incriminating evidence of all the names on one piece of paper.

Phew! His forehead was really sopping this time. And to make certain that the waitress could not piece the bits together afterwards, he dropped them into the ash-tray and set fire to the remains. There was quite a little blaze, because he had not noticed that the edge of his evening paper was so

close to the ash-tray. But with the waitress's help he got it
out before the lamp-shade caught . . .

The delivery of the piano must, he realised, have created
considerable excitement in the quietness of Deirdre Gardens.
Things like that cannot very frequently have happened
there. The Miss Lewises were very nice about it. They
merely asked if next time he was going to order something
that meant the whole window frame had to be removed in
order to get it in, they should be warned first.

But Mr. Prevarius assured them that it would not occur
again. In any case, the Chinese altar was rather larger than
he had reckoned on. And, with the four-foot six divan
there wasn't space for another upright chair. Besides, all that
he was now thinking of was bringing Desirée—his wee wifie,
he must remember to call her—to his hide-out.

And she, he hoped, would be coming quietly up the stairs
in the ordinary way.

I I

Mr. Prevarius had been the tenant of the second floor
front of 23a Deirdre Gardens for nearly six weeks before he
decided to avail himself of its unique, its dizzy and delightful privileges.

The furnishings were complete by now. An imitation
leopard-skin rug lay before the hearth; a gilded plaster
Cupid smiled from the top of the Chinese altar; and the
parchment lamp-shade with its gay hunting scene of jolly,
pink-coated riders and russet-coloured hounds in pursuit of
a shrinking and deceitful-looking fox, cast a discreet and
intimate circle of light upon the outsize divan.

The only thing that Mr. Prevarius was not sure about was
the joss-stick burner. He had only tried it with joss-sticks in
it once. And that time he had made the mistake of not
opening any of the windows. In consequence, he had been
nearly stifled. For days afterwards his clothes—his Deirdre
Gardens clothes—had been impregnated with a smell that was
reminiscent of cheap handbag sachets and penny packets of
cachous.

Perhaps, Mr. Prevarius told himself, they hadn't been the
best joss-sticks. The real Chinese—the Chinese who lived
in China, Asia—could not, he felt certain, have used this

kind and have survived so long. But he was reluctant, nevertheless, to give them up altogether. There was something so . . . so *recherché* and exquisite about opening the door and saying quietly: "Not scent, my dear. Incense. An old Oriental custom. But still beautiful beneath our grey Western skies, do you not think?"

And now the moment had at last come for putting all this battery of charm and luxury to the supreme test. He had phoned up from the call-box at the corner of St. Mark's Avenue and made his date with Desirée; he had bought a bottle of champagne and had even made arrangements with the fishmonger next door for the delivery of some ice. Finally, he had laid the scene with the Miss Lewises.

"To-night," he had said, "I am hoping that my wife, my wee wifie, will be with me. That is, of course, only if the bairns are better. Puir Angus and little Jeannie have been real bad. But if all is well we should be rolling along . . . reaching London, that is . . . somewhere round about eleven. It is the night train—er, the late train I should say—that Mrs. Gordon will be catching."

And by 10.55 everything was proceeding exactly according to plan. He and Desirée had enjoyed a pleasant evening together at the Plaza, with a bite at the Café Royal afterwards, and they were now in the taxi together, her head on his shoulder, as they passed Sloane Square.

"I don't know why I ever gave up the stage myself," Desirée was saying dreamily. "It's the only life for a girl."

"Or the concert platform," Mr. Prevarius corrected her.

"What's that?"

"But think of your singing lessons," Mr. Prevarius replied, allowing his hand to stray affectionately towards her knee. "When you left the convent in India you took up singing. Your father, the colonel, had set his heart on it. Don't you remember?"

"That was afterwards," Desirée told him, rather vaguely. There was a pause and she shifted the conversation.

"How's business?" she inquired.

"Oh, so-so," Mr. Prevarius answered. "Mustn't grumble, you know. Up one moment and down the next. But that's what life's like—all rough and smooth."

"What sort of business *is* it?" Desirée went on. "Somehow I can't actually see you doing anything."

In the darkness of the cab, Mr. Prevarius smiled.

"No?" he parried. "But I didn't always write songs, my dear."

"You're a director of something, aren't you?" Desirée persisted.

Mr. Prevarius hesitated. He was almost beginning to regret that he had ever brought her. After all, there must be hundreds of other girls, thousands probably, who would be ready to be given a night on the tiles without getting so confoundedly inquisitive.

"Yes, I am a director of something," he said finally. "If not a large concern, at least an old one. In the City, you know. One of the smaller issuing houses."

He leant forward and tapped sharply on the glass of the taxi.

"Here on the left," he said. "Next door but one to the pub."

Then he turned towards Desirée again.

"You must forgive bachelor quarters," he said. "They're simple—but sufficient."

III

Considering the lateness of the hour, 23a had an unusually wakeful air about it. To Mr. Prevarius's surprise there were lights blazing in the hall, in the Miss Lewises' sitting-room and in the large basement kitchen down below.

He was even more surprised, however, when the front door opened just as they reached the top step and Miss Lewis the elder stood there smiling at them.

"Come on in, dear Mrs. Gordon," she said. "Indeed to goodness how tired you must be after that terrible long journey. But you can just relax now. There's no need to lift a hand whatever . . ."

Her face dropped a little, Mr. Prevarius thought, as Desirée stepped into the brightly lit hall and Miss Lewis caught sight of her. It had occurred to him earlier that evening that Desirée was wearing an unusual amount of make-up, and the large black beauty spot on one cheek was by way of being a mistake. But he had entirely failed to make allowances for the extremes of hospitality of which the emotional Welsh race is capable. For already Desirée was being snatched from him and led upstairs by the ancient Miss Lewis.

"It is into my room you must go, Mrs. Gordon, to put off your travelling clothes," she said. "Then you can unpack everything you need . . ." She broke off abruptly. "But what have you?" she asked. "Where are your bags, indeed?"

Mr. Prevarius started. He hadn't thought of bags.

"Oh those," he said hurriedly. "A misunderstanding at the station. Sheer carelessness on the porter's part. The stationmaster has been told. But you know how it is—all gold braid and inefficiency."

"What's going on here?" Desirée asked him.

But by now Mr. Prevarius was close enough behind to give a playful warning pinch.

"The luggage. At Paddington . . . I mean King's Cross," he explained hurriedly. "You remember, dear. We shall simply have to rough it as we are."

They had reached the door of Miss Lewis's bedroom by now, and it was suddenly opened and closed again in Mr. Prevarius's face. He was alone on the landing, and Desirée and Miss Lewis were closeted inside.

As he stood there, he felt the sweat breaking out on his forehead again. There was Desirée shut up with the landlady, not knowing that she had just come down from St. Andrews, not knowing that her husband was a university examiner, not knowing that she had two wee bairns—even Mr. Prevarius could not remember their names—not even knowing that she was Scottish.

And when he opened the door of his little snuggery, there was another shock in store for him. The golden-hearted Miss Lewises had done their utmost for him. For amid the exquisiteness of ebony and lacquer, a small nasty table with a hideous tablecloth had been wheeled in; and up against it were two horse-hair chairs. But it was the way the table had been laid that distressed him most. Two kinds of sandwiches, a Swiss roll, a seed-cake, a plate of ham, an obviously tinned tongue and a great bowl of egg-salad were arranged around a large earthenware tea-pot. Mr. Prevarius's bottle of champagne stood indignantly in the mid-centre.

He was still standing there gloomily contemplating this ruin of so much beauty when Desirée and Miss Lewis returned.

"And how relieved indeed you must be that the bairns are better," Miss Lewis began immediately. "Mrs. Gordon did not credit how you had been worrying yourself. Like a sick man with the toothache, I told her. But all that's over and forgotten now."

"Quite forgotten," Mr. Prevarius answered truthfully.

"But it's your meal you're wanting," Miss Lewis said tactfully. "Make a good start and I'll bring up the potatoes while Mrs. Gordon is pouring out . . ."

The interruptions were too frequent to allow of much intimacy while the meal was proceeding, and Mr. Prevarius and Desirée ate in silence. There was an apple tart that Miss Lewis had been keeping hot for them. And some cheese and radishes. And another jug of hot water in case the tea was getting stewed. It was not, indeed, until Mr. Prevarius had given Miss Lewis a hand with the table and had bumped it downstairs for her that there was even the slightest promise of an uninterrupted moment alone with Desirée.

"It's kind you are," Miss Lewis told him. "These corners, indeed. I could never have moved it without you. My sister helped me to bring it up."

"And she is in bed now?" Mr. Prevarius asked enviously.

"Indeed to goodness no," Miss Lewis told him. "She is out telephoning."

Mr. Prevarius asked no further questions. He was still trying to repair the ruins of the evening. Going back into the room, he extinguished all the lights except for the hunting scene. Then he lit the fresh consignment of joss-sticks that he had just bought. They were his first mistake, because they immediately brought Miss Lewis upstairs again to say that she could smell burning. And, even when she was satisfied, Desirée said that the smell gave her a headache and Mr. Prevarius had to extinguish them.

It seemed then that rest had at last come to them. Desirée lay in Mr. Prevarius's arms, staring up at the jolly-looking huntsmen, and Mr. Prevarius sat gazing into the gas-fire and humming. Desirée was still inclined to be suspicious and resentful, but Mr. Prevarius was busy in the rôle of comforter.

"Just an innocent deception to protect milady's honour," he explained to her. "No woman can afford to be too careful. And my little story about the children should allay all doubts. It was only for your sake that I thought of it . . ."

They were interrupted by a loud knocking on the door.

It was Miss Lewis again, and her excitement was uncontrollable.

"It's the luggage, indeed it is," she said triumphantly. "All this time you've been here my sister has been telephoning. They think they've identified it, indeed they do. The Lost Property is open all night, so Mr. Gordon can go back for it. They're expecting him. I'll sit here and talk to you till he returns." Miss Lewis paused breathlessly. "Oh, the relief it'll be to you to have your own things again."

CHAPTER XXXII

I

DR. TRUMP'S first child—and, as it subsequently proved, his only one—had been born at six o'clock that morning. In consequence, Dr. Trump was beside himself. He was enfolded in a bright new bliss. A son too! Sebastian Samuel they were going to call him. And at the mere thought of what it meant to have an heir, Dr. Trump kept repeating the names over and over to himself like a kind of spell.

He stood there in his purple dressing-gown in front of the bedroom fireplace gazing down at the tiny form, the pink crumpled face, the pigmy hands of the baby that had just been placed within his arms. And, as he gazed, he radiated. His face and dressing-gown both glowed. Compared with Felicity, pale among the pillows, Dr. Trump was like something that had stepped down from a stained-glass window.

"My nose. My forehead. My ears," he was thinking. "Felicity's expression somehow—but that, of course, may change. My hands. My fingernails. And undeniably my chin."

And then the happiest thought of all came to him. The child was the grandson of a bishop! But even this sacred and paternal moment was not left inviolate. From nowhere, angry and disturbing memories of Mrs. Gurnett came crowding in.

For Mrs. Gurnett's own lawyers had played themselves to a standstill with the Bridlington firm, and there was nothing more left to confirm or acknowledge. Less lawyers' fees, the money now stood to Mrs. Gurnett's account. And it had all happened exactly as Mrs. Gurnett had intended. The moment the money was actually hers, she resigned. What was more, two of the nurses—both silly, rather hysterical creatures—decided that they would go too. No real reason for it; just a sense of drama. Then a kitchenmaid, practically a half-wit, caught the fever of resignation and started packing in sympathy. Thus, in a stroke, there were four vacancies for Dr. Trump to fill—the post of matron and three lesser posts.

Naturally there was a governors' meeting to discuss the situation. But Dame Eleanor on that occasion was in one of her pooh-poohing sort of moods.

"Well," she said brightly, "there's nothing else for it. Dr. Trump will just have to manage as best he can, until we find the right people. Luckily it's the summer term. We don't have epidemics in the summer."

"We don't have epidemics in the summer": it was more than once on the end of Dr. Trump's tongue to remind Dame Eleanor of those words of hers.

Not that it would have done any good. Merely have led to unpleasantness and recriminations, and that kind of thing. But the temptation was there all right. And, on any showing the time sequence was certainly remarkable. It was in June when Dame Eleanor uttered the fateful sentence. And by the August, the whole Hospital was properly in the thick of one.

It all started off quietly enough. Indeed, right up to the Tuesday evening Nurse Stedge felt confident that she had the whole situation comfortably in hand. Simply an outbreak of snuffly summer colds: that was all it was. She had dealt with summer colds before, and thought practically nothing of them. What really worried her was that Dr. Trump had set August aside for redecorating the infirmary and, now, with three new cases in it, the painters would have to be put off again.

It was one of the little ones, Evelyn Parker, who was the first to be brought in—and then only because she had complained of a headache, and kept saying that she felt sick. That was on Tuesday, just before lunch. And by tea-time Sweetie had joined her. But only just. There was nothing in her symptoms that really justified being excused geography and sewing. It was simply that she said that her eyes hurt and insisted vaguely, without being able to say in which part

251

of her, that she ached. Nurse Stedge, indeed, was frankly dubious about the whole affair: she suspected that it was simply Sweetie up to her tricks again.

And then strange things began happening to little Evelyn. The first hint that it might be more than a passing chill was her temperature: already a hundred and one, and still rising. But Nurse Stedge had met temperatures like that before and, even now, did not intend to be intimidated by this one. She gave the child a generous dose of the Hospital's No. 1 mixture, and let Nature have her chance. But though the No. 1 mixture did everything that could have been expected of it, the child seemed no better. Her pulse was up by now and, only twelve hours after the runny nose and the streaming eyes, the pains in the legs began.

The pains, indeed, gave Nurse Stedge the first clue—a false one as it happened—as to the real cause of the trouble. It was Wednesday by now and Monday had been rainy—the one rainy day in a whole succession of hot, sunny days. Nurse Stedge diagnosed rheumatism, even rheumatic fever possibly. And she diagnosed wrongly.

By the time Dr. Arlett came in next day the pains in the legs had got better: there was scarcely any pain at all, Evelyn said, just a sort of limpness. And there was a tingly feeling in the small of her back. Dr. Arlett looked at her throat, felt her neck for glands, examined her chest and back for any sign of rash, listened to her breathing—and for all the good he had done he might just as well have examined Nurse Stedge instead. Baffled and frustrated, he said that Evelyn was to be kept in bed until he had been in again to-morrow. Not that he was unduly worried. As a family doctor with a large practice, he had been baffled plenty of times before. And he knew that children, in particular, made a habit of running up and down the thermometer in a way that the text-books had never properly got round to.

It was round about lunch-time when Dr. Arlett called. And, after he had left, Evelyn spent most of the afternoon sleeping peacefully enough. By tea-time, Nurse Stedge began to feel a bit worried. And at seven when the night nurse took over, she definitely didn't like the way things were going. In all her experience of children she had never known a child have such difficulty with its breathing. And, when Evelyn's skin showed waxy underneath the flush, she took matters into her own hands and sent for Dr. Arlett again.

And only just in time. Because Evelyn was unconscious

when he arrived. The pulse, after racing furiously like a tiny engine with its governor gone, had suddenly become feeble and intermittent. At moments Nurse Stedge could hardly feel it at all: it simply faded away beneath her forefinger. And the breathing was no longer quick and stertorous. It was now vague and casual like the pulse; and shallow. The small flat bosom scarcely rose and fell. Evelyn was simply lying there inert with her eyes and mouth half open, and the fingers of her hand, which was half-clenched, twitching as though she were trying to pick up something.

Dr. Arlett immediately recognised the condition for what Nurse Stedge had only feared it was. In the nine hours since he had last seen her, Evelyn had passed from the state of a sick child into a dying one. She was now insecurely attached to this world at all. At any moment she was ready, quietly and without turmoil, to exchange the green distempered walls of the infirmary with the little iron bedstead and the bare linoleum, for the space between the stars and the heavenly staircase. The thermometer standing up in a half tumbler of water on the table, and the bed-pan with napkin decently over it on the chair beside the bed, did not belong to her way of things any longer.

Dr. Arlett was not in the ordinary course of life either swift or nimble. But, looking back on it afterwards, Nurse Stedge thought that she had never seen anyone open a medical bag so quickly and get out a hypodermic syringe. It was coramine that Dr. Arlett had brought with him and, raising the sleeve of the nightdress that Evelyn was wearing, he inserted the needle in the upper arm. Not that the child gave any sign when the point of the needle entered the skin between Dr. Arlett's two fingertips. She was too far away already to worry over what was happening in the life that she was leaving so rapidly behind her. She merely lay there, quietly concentrating on dying. And the pauses in her breathing were longer and more frequent. There were moments when she did not breathe at all.

Nurse Stedge was the first to speak.

" I think she's gone, sir," she said.

Dr. Arlett took out his stethoscope. He remained there for the better part of a minute bending over the small silent body from which the flannelette nightdress had been folded back. Then he straightened himself and pulled the sheet right up over the white face.

" You'd better ask Dr. Trump if he can come here," he said. " And tell Chiswick to bring the stretcher."

At the far end of the ward, two dark eyes were watching. They were very alert, observant eyes, and they knew enough to close themselves every time Nurse Stedge or Dr. Arlett came near. It was the second death that Sweetie had witnessed, and she felt that she knew all about dying by now. But knowing about things is different when you're nine, very nearly ten. She lay there staring up at the ceiling.

" Perhaps I've got what Evelyn had," she told herself. " Perhaps I'm going to die, too."

I I

Anyhow, that was how it started. Margaret had just left the Hospital at the time—it was a Thursday, remember—and the first that she knew about it was when Dr. Trump rang up Dame Eleanor to tell her what had happened. Margaret did not even take the call herself: after bedtime the phone was plugged straight through to Dame Eleanor's bedside. So it was entirely second-hand that the news reached her, just as she was about to give Dame Eleanor her good-night Horlicks. And when Margaret heard, she did not believe it. She had been in the infirmary only a few hours ago sitting on the end of Sweetie's bed and talking to her. Little Evelyn had seemed perfectly all right at the time.

" Mind, girl," Dame Eleanor had been forced to say to her quite sharply. " You're pouring the Horlicks all over me. I wouldn't have told you if I'd known that it was going to upset you so."

And it was the same next morning. Margaret seemed preoccupied and restless. She had the unprepossessing appearance—at once drawn and puffy—of someone who had not slept at all well, and at the end of breakfast she asked if she might slip round to the Hospital for a moment. At first, Dame Eleanor was inclined to refuse. But, on second thoughts, she allowed it. After all, Margaret spent all her spare time at the Hospital and it was only natural, Dame Eleanor supposed, that she should feel herself one of them. It was all of a piece with her loyal nature that she should want to be there as soon as anything went wrong.

254

" But remember: no hanging round the children," she told her. "Whatever it is, we don't want you bringing it back here."

Not that it was herself that she was thinking of: it wasn't. It was her committees, her meetings, all the thousand and one other things that depended on her. To-day was going to be one of those days when she would be rushing about committee to committee from the moment she left The Cedars until she returned there, a tired, crotchety old woman, round about seven.

Even then, Dame Eleanor did not know how quickly and alarmingly things were going to develop. By the middle of the morning a boy called Roger in Standard Seven, the going-out form, went down with the same symptoms. They were all there—slight sore throat, mild summer cold, moist eyes, pain in the back and legs and a soaring temperature. But this time Nurse Stedge was on the look-out. After one glance at him, she was on the phone for Dr. Arlett. Nor was Dr. Arlett any slower: he seemed to have been on the other end of the phone waiting. Putting aside two measles, a blood poisoning, and a malignant tumour (second visit), he was round at the Hospital inside ten minutes.

And on this occasion he was in time. The boy did not even appear to be unduly ill. But Dr. Arlett was not so easily reassured this time. In fact, he was looking for trouble. Ever since little Evelyn's death, he had been reading up poliomyelitis and he now knew exactly what to go for. Not that it helped him. Because, though the text-books knew all about the symptoms, apparently they knew nothing about the cure. But, at least, he wanted to be quite certain about the symptoms. And his test of the boy's reflexes revealed that there were none. He went through the correct motions again and again, striking with his little rubber hammer beneath the knee-cap. And he could hardly believe it when he found that there was no response: just nothing at all to show for all the trouble that he was taking.

There were no signs of the paralysis spreading. Not a trace of anything in the back—the fatal part. The breathing was strong and regular, throat muscles firm and hard. The mysterious germ, in fact, had done its damage and spent itself. But it was sufficient for Dr. Arlett. It was Case Number Two all right. The Medical Officer of Health would have to be got hold of immediately.

And Case Number Three—Sweetie—was apparently just waiting for the symptoms to develop.

Faced with the new seriousness of the situation, Dr. Trump did not hesitate. He rooted Dame Eleanor out of her Unmarried Mothers and demanded to know whether he should close the Hospital. But here it was obvious that he was at a disadvantage. Because the one thing that no orphanage can do is to close—it is of the very nature of orphanhood that there is no home to go back to. Dame Eleanor advised, therefore, that the Hospital should remain open, but the children should be kept as far away from each other as possible.

Not that even that was easy. But on this point Dame Eleanor was adamant. She insisted that until the epidemic was over, the boys and girls should be kept entirely apart. The fact that one case already had come from either side of the Hospital did not affect the decision. There was to be complete and absolute segregation, she said. She spoke as though everything depended on it.

And she added wearily that she would be round later the same evening.

CHAPTER XXXIII

AS SHE rang off, Dame Eleanor realised how tired she was. And more than tired: played out completely. A kind of self-sorrow which had become rather more frequent of late had suddenly descended upon her, and all that she wanted to do was to put her feet up and close her eyes. And was there anything so very extraordinary in that? There were plenty of women half her age—yes, literally half her age—who would have taken a couple of aspirins and packed themselves up in bed long ago if they'd had a headache one-tenth so vicious and jangling as hers.

But she couldn't do that kind of thing. They needed her round at the Hospital. If she hadn't been tied up with so many other things, she'd have been there already and got back again. But on a day like this, it had been impossible. Not a single free moment until after dinner.

That was the trouble. She was too busy. Too much going

on. Too many things depending on her. Too many meetings.
Too many letters to write. Too many people to see. Too
much and too many of everything. It wasn't as though she
were running the machine any more. The machine was
running her.

She asked herself sometimes why she had ever allowed
things to get that way, why hadn't she simply refused when
she was asked to take on any more. And she asked herself,
too, why she didn't struggle harder to break away now
before it all got any worse. Why didn't she resign? Leave
those innumerable committees to find some other woman
fool enough to kill herself on their behalf. Why didn't she?
She had done her bit, no one could deny that. Why didn't
she? Could anyone please tell her why?

As a matter of fact, she knew. Knew perfectly well. And
it wasn't simply that she cared more than other people, had a
keener sense of duty. No, it went deeper than that. Much
deeper. Somewhere right at the back of her mind, she knew
that, even now, if she eased up for a single moment, she
would begin thinking again about that precious son of hers.
It wasn't easy to forget a son. On the day when he had
sailed away for ever, she had felt as though she, not the boy,
had been the one who had gone voyaging into a world where
England was half-way round his globe and the stars themselves were upside down.

Merely to go on living had called for a new kind of
courage, had demanded a faith above earthly things; even
above mother love. Faith! Yes, that was it. She had clung
to faith. The Church meant everything to her now. The
Church—and rescuing people. The only time she so much as
mentioned her son's name to herself was when she prayed
for him. Not that it was really painful any more, so long
as the name came back to her that way. It is hard to go on
saying the same prayer, night after night, for years on end
—ever since November, 1913, in fact—without the sharp
edges getting a bit rubbed away in the process.

He had been such a handsome-looking boy, too; handsome, but weak. There had been something about the way
one lock of dark hair fell across his forehead while he was
talking—he was always tossing it back, only to have it come
forward again—that had made it impossible to deny him
anything. And apparently it had been impossible for other
women, too . . . But this was the very thing that she had

set her mind against: this dwelling in the past was the one weakness she had taught herself to fight.

And turning back now was out of the question. She had made a new life and she intended to go on with it. Go on, until she dropped. If only she weren't so tired, so perpetually tired. Often she had presided at meetings, started things going, made decisions, jerked other people into activity, when she had been so tired herself that she had scarcely been able to crawl along there at all. And she hated tiredness. It reminded her how old she was. "I ought to have been interred years ago," was a thought that constantly recurred to her. And every time it brought with it the same damp chill, the mouldiness.

That was why she was so grateful for Margaret. Margaret made her forget all that. The woman understood. And she was devoted. It was obvious, in fact, that apart from the Hospital she had no other serious interest in her whole life. She simply lived for Dame Eleanor, treating her in the way which in large families the best kind of unmarried daughters look after their mothers. Dame Eleanor would not have minded, would rather have liked it, in fact, if Margaret *had* been her daughter—and now that Margaret was dressed properly, she certainly looked quite respectable enough to be a daughter.

Dame Eleanor had already definitely determined to increase Margaret's bequest in her will. A hundred and fifty, she had decided, would be about the right sum. There was no point in *showering* money on servants, especially on servants like Margaret who had shown that they were spendthrift with their money. Something substantial, however, was certainly called for: she owed it to the girl. As the car drew up at the front porch, she was even wondering whether the bequest should not be two hundred.

She could tell that there was something wrong as soon as she entered the house. The broad hall with its big vases of flowers looked normal and welcoming enough. But Dame Eleanor *knew*: she could feel the whole place tingling with hostile currents.

"Margaret! Margaret!" she began calling. "Where are you? I want you, Margaret."

And it seemed afterwards that she had known all the time that Margaret would not be there. Dame Eleanor was prepared for it, yes, positively prepared, when the housekeeper

258

came towards her bringing an envelope in Margaret's handwriting.

But even then Dame Eleanor did not waver. She simply put the unopened envelope into her hand along with all her papers and things and said sharply: "Hurry up the dinner, please. I've got to go out again."

Because of Margaret's deceitfulness, her unforeseen and unimaginable disloyalty, Dame Eleanor saw nothing for it but to dismiss her altogether. Altogether, and immediately. Nor did the awkward and rather halting sort of letter that Margaret had left for her do anything to make her change her mind. ". . . *I feel awful having to go off like this,*" the letter ran in the clumsy housemaidish handwriting, "*but another of the children is ill and with Mrs. Gurnett gone there is no one to look after her. I am very sorry and the moment she's better I do want to come back and . . .*"

But Dame Eleanor only shook her head. She had liked Margaret, had raised her from the kitchen, had lavished gifts on her—the very shoes that Margaret had on her feet at the moment were a pair that Dame Eleanor had worn only once because the instep was too high—had been fully prepared to do a great deal more than merely pass on second-hand footwear. But the foolish girl had, so to speak, decided to fling her gifts in her face and go off blindly on this self-invented mission of mercy.

Well, if that was how she wanted it, Dame Eleanor would say no more. She wasn't her keeper. And Margaret would very soon learn which side her bread was buttered. It would take just about one week, Dame Eleanor reckoned, for Margaret to discover that the staff quarters of the Archbishop Bodkin Hospital weren't quite so agreeable as one of the guest bedrooms at The Cedars. And if Margaret seriously imagined that she could whisk back to The Cedars as soon as she got tired of a lot of children being sick all over her she was mistaken. Because Dame Eleanor intended never to have her in the house again.

What was more, she intended to attempt no further experiments with kitchenmaids. They were the wrong material. They hadn't got it in them. They didn't know the meaning of words like "loyalty" and "service" and "responsibility." These were upper class words that had taken generations to instil.

And to make sure that she didn't weaken, didn't get taken

in a second time by those dark appealing eyes and that gentle loving manner, Dame Eleanor decided to act first thing in the morning. Even so her hand trembled quite noticeably as she put the letter down. Why, she asked herself, had Margaret had to do this thing to her? Wasn't she as important as one of the Archbishop Bodkin inmates? Didn't Margaret realise that while she was nursing one solitary child she was neglecting someone who had devoted her whole life to the care of children? Someone who without a share of this world's attention simply could not keep up under the strain of it?

"It would serve her right," Dame Eleanor told herself, "serve her absolutely right, if I were to drop dead to-morrow. And I may do, with no one to look after me."

CHAPTER XXXIV

I

BUT Margaret was too busy to worry about her future with Dame Eleanor. Too busy to worry even about herself. Too busy to worry about anyone except Sweetie.

Sweetie had certainly got the disease all right. And more than merely got it. She was now a classic case—it was as though she had been reading up the symptoms and was now practising them. Dr. Arlett was at her side constantly.

Nor was this all. For Dr. Arlett, as visiting physician to a Hospital that was apparently riddled with infantile paralysis, was something of a celebrity in his own right: he could call on whom he wished. And though Sweetie hardly noticed them—with her temperature already up at one hundred-and-four, she was more than a little hazy about her immediate surroundings—there was at one time the Medical Officer of Health for the Borough; a Dr. Bengin from Harley Street, who was something of a connoisseur of high fevers; and a doctor from one of the teaching hospitals, who was secretly convinced that all polio was waterborne and was always anxious to get his head inside cisterns.

Their presence, however, was of no assistance to Sweetie. Her temperature continued to rise swiftly and devouringly.

260

She became delirious. She gabbled nonsense. She fought them away when they tried to test her reflexes. She slept. And by 10.30 that night, when the bedside conference broke up, the three doctors exchanged glances. They knew exactly what to expect by the morning. And they warned Nurse Stedge about it.

Nurse Stedge, who was fond of Sweetie, nearly broke down from sheer misery and anxiety and loss of sleep as soon as they had gone. It seemed so unfair, somehow, that it should have come now and that she should have had to face this crisis alone; alone, and desperately short-staffed.

From sheer nervous exhaustion—and she had been all of a jitter ever since poor little Evelyn's death—she went sick herself. Nothing serious, as it turned out, just a sore throat and a temperature. A touch of summer laryngitis perhaps. But it was near enough to the other thing to scare everybody, Nurse Stedge included. And it left Margaret in practically sole charge. Between Friday and Monday Margaret got rather less than twelve hours of uninterrupted sleep.

And it was a revelation. She had never loved anything so much before. She felt as though she had been waiting all her life for that moment. Everything about it was perfect, and she felt that she would remember it always—the way she smoothed back the hair from Sweetie's forehead; the smallness and hotness of the hand that had held hers; the last exquisite moments when Sweetie fell asleep still with Margaret's arm under her. And the kisses that she had given her. Gentle, bedtime kisses of the kind that would have been impossible by day with the other children all looking on.

The memory of it would not leave her. Nothing that she had ever known before had been so complete and satisfying.

"It ought to be like this always," she kept saying. "I can't ever leave her again. She belongs to me."

There was one evening in particular. The worst was over by now, and Dr. Arlett had only been to see Sweetie once that day. Margaret was simply sitting beside her. She wasn't asleep—wouldn't allow herself to drop off just in case Sweetie did want anything—but she was resting. Had never felt more restful in her whole life, in fact.

And Sweetie felt restful, too. She wasn't even sleepy any

more. She was just lying there, looking at Margaret. She liked looking at Margaret: it gave her a warm, safe feeling. And Margaret had noticed that she was awake. She asked Sweetie if she wanted anything. And, simply to be polite, Sweetie said a glass of water.

It was nice feeling Margaret's hand as she raised Sweetie's head to give her the drink. It was nice, too, the way Margaret smoothed her forehead after she had put her back down again. Sweetie felt that she could go on like that for ever. And it may have been the stroking feeling that did it: it is difficult to be on your guard when someone is stroking your forehead. Whatever it was, the words simply slipped out of her.

"I don't want to die," she said suddenly.

And Margaret laughed at her. But it was not the kind of laugh that hurt. It only showed that Margaret wasn't afraid of dying the way Sweetie was.

"You're not going to die, silly," she said. "Why do you think you are?"

And Sweetie told her. All about having seen the doctor pull the sheet up over Evelyn's face; and about that other night in the infirmary, when she had been small and had seen the other little girl die. She told Margaret everything. About the screens. And about the way the doctor had taken his coat off. And how the doctor had fixed something on to the little girl's nose. And how Dr. Trump had come into the ward in his dressing-gown.

By the time she had finished, it was getting late. Sweetie had been talking for nearly an hour and she felt hungry. She told Margaret so and Margaret heated up some milk on a gas-ring and gave her some dry biscuits that she had in a tin all ready, just as though she had been expecting Sweetie to sit up and ask for them.

And then just as Margaret was putting Sweetie down for good, the most extraordinary thing happened. She bent over to kiss her good-night—one of those things that Nurse Stedge always forgot. But instead of kissing her the way Sweetie expected, Margaret went on kissing her, kissing her over and over again, on her forehead, on her hair, on her eyes, on her nose, on her mouth, on her chin, everywhere. And when she stopped for a moment Sweetie saw that Margaret was crying. Really crying, with proper tears.

"Oh, Sweetie darling," she said. "You do need me so. I mustn't ever leave you. Not even for a moment."

Sweetie didn't know quite what to say. She was still breathless from all those kisses.

"Well, I won't ever leave you either," she replied.

CHAPTER XXXV

I

GINGER HAD been growing restless. Restless, even for him. He felt enclosed. And, in consequence, he became dreamy and unable to concentrate. Lessons simply didn't exist any more—he heard dates, the names of rivers, numbers, tribes of Israel, and gems of English poetry; and they were too faint and far away for him even to think about.

And, because of this enclosed feeling, his social nature deteriorated. He was rude to Spud. He punched out at people for no apparent reason when he came near them. He let a door fly back deliberately just as Mr. Dawlish was going through it. And worst of all—what any practising child psychologist would have spotted at once as the real danger signal—he avoided his fellows. For the last couple of days he had spent the breaks simply mooching round the playground by himself, or—another unmistakable symptom of a rapidly advancing neurosis—inflicting pain upon himself. For minutes on end he would stand up against the grey wall of the Hospital conscientiously kicking at it with the toe of his regulation Archbishop Bodkin boot.

In others words, he was fed up. Not about anything in particular. He hadn't been caned lately, or got into any fresh kind of trouble. He was just fed up with everything. And he was planning to run away. He had considered such a course before. Had considered it carefully in all its detail. And in the end, he had broken the problem down into its three essential elements. First he had to have money. Then he needed clothes. And finally he must decide on somewhere to go. All three points presented difficulties. The half-crown that Canon Mallow had given him was more money than he had ever had before, but Dr. Trump had stolen it from him: all that he now had was threepence-halfpenny that had been acquired with pain and perseverance over the preceding six months. But threepence-halfpenny wasn't much. He supposed that it was enough for him to go by bus somewhere. Buses, however, were not what Ginger wanted. He wanted to put a length of shining railway track between him and the Archbishop Bodkin Hospital; preferably, a length of shining railway track with a waiting boat at the far end of it.

Then there was the question of clothes. Suppose they started looking for him, they would find him at once if he had on the Archbishop Bodkin uniform. But here Ginger had his own private reserve again. There was a pair of flannel trousers, rather large, that had got left behind somehow when the builders had been there, and a blue woollen jersey that had been circulating mysteriously round the Hospital for years.

But when it came to choice of destination, Ginger was frankly beaten. The only places in London that he could remember were Whitehall, Paddington Station, St. Paul's Cathedral and Buckingham Palace, and he could not imagine what he would do in any one of them. Apart from them the only other place he had ever heard of was Bombay. But that was out of the question: it was in South America somewhere.

All the same, it gave him an idea. Suppose he didn't run away entirely. Suppose he just made one or two little trips outside the grounds so that he could find his way about—discover at which end of Whitehall St. Paul's and Paddington Station happened to lie; establish where the big boats really sailed from, and all that kind of thing. What he wanted was simply to get the layout of the place in his head: that was essential. Because, living the kind of life that the Archbishop Bodkin Hospital provided, he realised that he knew no more about London than an intelligent Eskimo.

The one thing that he did know was about the boats. Not once but a hundred times had Mr. Dawlish taught them: " London is not merely the capital, but also the greatest port. Liverpool and Southampton are only . . ." It was one of the bees in Mr. Dawlish's bonnet: he was practically potty about ports. But it sounded promising all the same.

And, thanks to Dr. Trump, the Hospital was no longer the prison that it had been. The new fire-escapes had changed the whole architecture of the place. As they were being erected Ginger had studied them carefully. And appreciatively. Even though he had no very definite scheme in his head, no plan, he could n t believe that so many perfect

264

footholds, spanning walls and roofs, could not eventually be put to some useful purpose.

There was one fire-escape in particular that seemed to offer almost limitless opportunities. Starting on the landing just outside his dormitory, it zig-zagged down on to the leads below, a mere twelve feet or so from the pavement of Ryecroft Gardens, just where they led into St. Mark's Avenue. The twelve feet itself was nothing, nothing to a boy of Ginger's size. It wouldn't hurt much even if he fell. But Dr. Trump hadn't let things go at that. He had, apparently deliberately, made matters easier still. For the fire-escape in rudimentary form had been extended downwards by means of three steel rungs let into the stonework. From the bottom of these, Ginger reckoned, his feet would pretty nearly be touching the ground.

Admittedly, getting back wasn't going to be so easy. But he supposed he could manage it somehow. He could leave a piece of rope dangling down, if he could get a piece of rope. Or he could give Spud a whistle and get him to come down the fire-escape himself and haul him in. Something or other would turn up—he was sure of that. The important thing was to get out.

Even for a short jaunt, a mere half-hour outing, however, it took a bit of planning. And if Spud were to play the part of reserve rescue obviously he would have to be told date, time, route, alarm signal, everything. But this, in itself presented difficulties. Because the fact had to be faced that Spud was a talker. Devoted as Spud was to Ginger, obedient to his various whims, Ginger was still not entirely sure of him, not absolutely convinced of his hundred per cent reliability. He had once caught him out, passing on to another boy, whose company Ginger had subsequently forbidden him, something that Ginger had told him in confidence. And, though Spud had denied indignantly that it was secret, Ginger had given his arm an extra twist and had made the mental resolution to be more careful in the future.

Because it was so important this time, Ginger took considerable trouble about Spud's conditioning. He began by giving him a piece of coconut toffee that he had been hoarding for weeks. Wrapped in its original paper as it was, the toffee was still misleading. And that was because Ginger had twice removed it and started to lick before some sixth sense had told him that it might be needed. In consequence, it had a bent, worn sort of look but it was still recognisably coconut toffee with straight shreds from the tropics imprisoned in the creamy amber.

As Spud sucked, Ginger unfolded his plan. And, at the end of it, Ginger made Spud swear an oath. It was a ready-made oath, invented specially for the occasion. And as it proceeded it got better. Indeed, by the end, it was on the top level of oaths; memorable, impressive, infinitely binding.

". . . and if I ever tell anyone," Ginger was saying.

". . . ever tell anyone," Spud repeated after him.

". . . I hereby give my friend Ginger full permission . . ."

". . . hereby give my friend Ginger full permission . . ."

". . . to cut my throat from ear to ear . . ."

". . . to cut my throat from ear to ear . . ."

". . . and stab my heart in."

". . . and stab my heart in."

So that was that. And everything was ready for Ginger's little sally. It was only in the rehearsal of the alarm signal that danger threatened. And that was because Ginger's rehearsal was too loud. Not that it was his fault exactly. He had only just learned how to make that particular kind of whistle and, until his fingers were actually in his mouth, he never knew quite how shrill the escape of air was going to be. This time it was terrific. There was a peculiar band-saw sharpness to the edges that left the ears tingling. But it was too loud. Definitely too loud. It reached over wall and roof-top to the Warden's study. And after Ginger had emitted it for the second time just to make sure that Spud would be certain to recognise it, Dr. Trump broke off from his sermon and made the note " Playground noises " on his pad.

It was, in fact, this incident that gave Dr. Trump the basic idea for a brilliant new reform—silent breaks. And a fortnight later, after Dr. Trump had pondered, he introduced it. Henceforth, shouting, singing, whistling, cat-calls and so forth—were expressly forbidden in the main playground. The children were free to play, play for all they were worth, he emphasised; but they must in future play *discreetly*.

Tuesday was the night set aside for Ginger's experiment. Tuesday at twenty-two hundred hours. And, by the time the moment of departure came, the whole dormitory knew all about it. This was not Spud's fault, however, so much as Ginger's. And that was because of the thick streak of the actor in Ginger's nature. It was one thing to pull on a blue jersey and a pair of dirty flannels that nobody knew anything about. That was good: there was the authentic charm of midnight plot and secrecy about it. But what was ten times as good was to get ready in full view of everyone so that curiosity was roused to fever pitch, and then dismiss the whole affair as though it were nothing.

"You shut up," he said one by one to the other boys as they questioned him. "You keep your nose out of other people's business."

It was the ability to be able to say that, to feel the aura of mystery growing and expanding round him, that added the real flavour, the exquisiteness, to his adventure. Moreover, there was even an extra spice for which Ginger had not been prepared. Just as he clambered over the parapet he happened to look up at the dormitory. There were four windows to it. And at every one of the windows were faces, white, smudgy, goggle-eyed, admiring faces.

It was, indeed, the excitement of seeing them that made him lose his grip. And, viewed from above as Spud saw it, the effect was distinctly dramatic. At one moment he was there, suspended over space, and at the next he had disappeared. Only the slightly squeaky thump of gym shoes on hard pavement indicated that he had landed and not simply vanished.

And the pavement was certainly hard all right. It came up and hit Ginger like a hammer. The sheer pain of the blow—it felt as though his left ankle had been snapped sideways—brought him back to his senses. Up to that moment he had been too eager and excited to consider the consequences. But now as he leant up against the Hospital wall and massaged his leg from the shin right down to his foot he suddenly wondered why he had done it, why he had ever come down at all. If he were discovered he would probably get the worst caning that Dr. Trump had ever given him.

In the meantime, he decided, the best thing would be to clear off quickly in case anyone were looking. That was where his gym shoes helped. Even though his ankle was hurting, he could still run. And on soft padding feet he set off down Ryecroft Gardens towards the High Street. There weren't many people in Ryecroft Gardens at the time but, even so, he was careful. Running was conspicuous, it drew attention to you. And if people became too curious they might run after you. So now that he was out of the direct view of the Hospital windows he sauntered. Putting his hands in his trouser pockets he strolled along as though he were taking a late evening breather before turning into bed.

It all seemed so easy and natural, in fact, that he nearly headed straight into disaster as he reached the corner. He and Mr. Dawlish arrived there simultaneously. And it was only Ginger's scaling clothes that saved him. Mr. Dawlish looked straight at him. Or rather he looked at and *through* him, and passed straight on. But it taught Ginger a lesson. After that he was careful.

Not that it was easy to be careful in the High Street. There was so much light about. After the gas-lamps of Ryecroft Gardens with their incandescent mantles bubbling away inside their small glass boxes, it was like stepping into the beam of a searchlight to reach the High Street. There was light everywhere, a sort of hard brilliant daytime. And the shops. Ginger stood entranced before them. One of them had nothing but ladies' hats in it, dozens and dozens of ladies' hats, each one stuck up on a thin chromium stalk. And the shop next door was even better. It was ablaze with cheap jewellery, rings, brooches, bangles and watches, all glittering and shining there. Ginger spent some time looking at that. He even held out his own wrist to see how one of the men's watches would appear on it.

He would have liked to spend more time looking at the watches but there was a policeman on the other corner, and the last thing that Ginger wanted was for the policeman to begin getting interested in him. So with a final wink from the diamond engagement rings, he left Aladdin's Cave behind him and went on past a grocer's that made him feel hungry with its window full of biscuits and pots of jam and tins of cocoa, past a men's tailor's with nothing but lengths of cloth showing (very dull), past a chemist's with tooth-brushes

268

and combs and feeding-cups and bath sponges (mildly interesting) until he came to a public house.

There was something special about this because it was still open. Night-time, but still open. It hadn't got a window exactly. Just a big sheet of frosted glass. But there were designs cut in the glass. Flowers and bunches of grapes and true-lovers' knots. And there were the shadows of people's heads inside. There must have been some kind of a ledge inside the window because Ginger could see the shadows of glasses as well, a whole row of them. But the best thing of all was the music. Inside, someone was playing a piano. Playing it very fast; faster than Ginger had ever heard a piano played before. And louder. Whenever the door—which was of glass, too, with the same design of flowers and grapes and love-knots—swung open, the noise of the piano burst all over him like a silver-and-gilt waterfall.

And with the music came another sound as well, a roar of voices as though everyone inside was shouting at the top of his voice—not quarrelling, just shouting. And above the shouts, the sharp clink of glass, and the rattle of the cash register.

Altogether, it was easily the noisiest place Ginger had ever found, and the jolliest. When he got a glimpse of the inside, he saw that it was also the brightest. There were lights everywhere arranged in festoons with little paper shades on them, and the whole of the wall was of mirror with shelves of coloured bottles in front of it. It was easily the most beautiful interior that he had ever come upon, and the only thing that he didn't like was the smell, a hot, stagnant, used-up kind of smell that made him wonder how all these noisy, jolly people could stand it. But the sheer beauty of the place was staggering.

The words, "Time, gentlemen, please," came to him suddenly through those tantalising swing-doors. And, at the same instant, the little clusters and festoons of lights were extinguished. People poured past him as he stood in the passageway under the "No betting," "No Children Admitted," "No drinking on the footpath" notices. There was a finality to the whole incident that left Ginger saddened and at a loss. The curtain had come down and the magic was no longer there. But the moral of the moment was lost to him. He should have recognised it for the signal that it was time for all decent people to be getting to their beds.

269

And, instead of that, there he was still looking for adventure.

Then a remark dropped casually over the shoulder disturbed him. He was standing doing nothing in particular when he saw a woman nudge her companion as she was going out with him.

"Just look at the clothes that boy is wearing," she said. "He might be an orphan."

An orphan! This set Ginger's nerves tingling. It was everything that he had wanted to avoid: he was conspicuous again. So he decided that it was time to be moving on. And quickly, too. Determined to put as much distance as possible between himself and the woman, he crossed the road to the railway station. And then a stroke of sheer genius came to him. Going over to the paper stand outside, he bought an *Evening Standard*. Admittedly, it was expensive: when he had paid for it he had only got twopence halfpenny left. But it should have allayed all suspicion. The one thing that orphans don't do is to buy expensive evening papers.

If Mr. Dawlish had been more thorough in his invigilation, he might have come upon an unusual group in the lavatory at break the next morning. At the far end of the water closets, five boys were assembled with Ginger in their centre. He had a copy of last night's *Evening Standard* in his hands, and the other boys were looking admiringly from it to him and back at the newspaper again. Then the bell sounded. Ginger folded up the paper and restored it to his pocket.

"Givicher for a ha'penny when I've finished it," he volunteered. "I can get er nuvver one whenever I want it."

CHAPTER XXXVI

I

SWEETIE WAS better by now. Recovered completely, so far as anyone could tell. She was out of the infirmary again, and playing with the others as though the fear of death had never troubled her.

What is more, she did not appear to have any particular

need of Margaret. And Margaret hadn't really got much time left for Sweetie either. She was living just the kind of life that Dame Eleanor had predicted: up at 6.30 in a little bleak cubicle of a room with only a straw mat between her feet and the chill of the bare oilcloth, and in the ward shortly after seven because there was no night-sister at the moment and Nurse Stedge, who was sleeping up there for the time being, wanted to get on with her own job.

It was then that Margaret's day really began—sheets to be changed, faces and bodies washed, bed-pans carried, temperatures taken, meals collected. And there were all the things that Nurse Stedge needed when she came round again at about ten-thirty—little bowls of hot water, lint, bandages, enemas, syringes. Sometimes, if one of the children was really ill, Margaret did not get proper meals at all—just a cup of tea and a couple of thick slices of bread and butter taken up there in the ward with the children.

By the time she got back to that top bedroom of hers she was tired, so tired that she could only throw herself down on the bed aching all over—aching back, aching arms, and legs aching from the stairs. But she was not unhappy. Far from being unhappy, in fact. It was not the tiredness that worried her. It was simply that she hadn't been able to do enough. "What those children need is a mother," she kept telling herself. "They want someone to look after them. It's not simply Sweetie, it's every single one of them."

But here she was lying to herself. It *was* simply Sweetie that she was thinking of. And because she was thinking of Sweetie she made excuses to see her. Clumsy, awkward excuses. And they were not enough, these brief intermittent glimpses. Sweetie in class, her head bent over the exercise book ; Sweetie in the playground talking solemnly about something that Margaret was too far away to hear ; Sweetie on her knees weeding in Dr. Trump's garden. It was for something more than this that Margaret was asking. And sometimes the words formed themselves inside her.

"I want her for myself," she kept saying. "I want her. There's no other way for it. I want her. I want her for myself."

Nurse Stedge, however, knew nothing of this unprofessional silliness. So far as she was concerned, she was fully satisfied. And more than satisfied. Margaret, in her opinion, was a treasure, a downright treasure. It wasn't simply that

271

she liked children. She apparently liked doing things for them, and liked going on doing those things endlessly, hour after hour, and day after day. Nurse Stedge had never seen her cross or put out or ruffled about anything. She was the real stuff that nurses are made of, the kind that you can't get in the hospitals nowadays. And every time she saw Margaret in the ward she had the same feeling. "If only she had the training," she told herself. "If only she'd got her diploma." But training or no training, Margaret was the best infirmary nurse that Nurse Stedge could remember. And the all important thing was that they had got her. While Dr. Trump was still inserting advertisements for wardmaids and investigating the testimonials that came in, Margaret was getting on with the job.

And what testimonials. As Dr. Trump flicked the papers over with his forefinger, he could feel himself recoiling. There was Hilda Venn—a tendency to spasticity rendered her unsuitable for intimate association with young children; Doris Long—kleptomania was her trouble; Kathleen Grimes—he could hardly bring Kathleen back after what had happened in her East Grinstead post; Janet Thomson—out of the question: it didn't even say whether her baby had been born yet; Olive Green . . .

Dr. Trump sat back in despair.

"We must indeed count ourselves fortunate in having Margaret," he reflected. "I only wish that Dame Eleanor wouldn't look at me as if I had tried to lure her here."

I I

Tired as she was in her first week at the Hospital, Margaret wrote another of those mysterious letters of hers, a letter that showed how her life was divided down the very middle, and that there was a part of it that failed entirely to fit into the regular pattern.

One half was all simple and straightforward: it was the sunny half that contained everything that was pleasant and comforting about her—the way she had cared for Dame Eleanor, her love of children in general, her special devotion for little Sweetie. The other half, the midnight half, was the one that contained the mystery.

And those letters of hers certainly stirred it all up again.

". . . *when I don't hear from you I get worried. You know I do, so you ought to write just so that I can be sure that nothing's happened . . .*" That is what the last few lines on the first page happened to say. You can't see the opening because her hand is across it. And that's strange, too, when you come to think of it. There's something secretive about it, as though she's afraid that someone may come up and peep across her shoulder while she's writing. A whole history of furtiveness is revealed in that single gesture.

And, when she turns the page over, it's the same thing all over again. She shields the paper with her left hand while she writes down the words. She is a slow writer and it takes her some time to get to the bottom of the sheet. Then she blots it, rubbing the ball of her thumb vigorously across the blotting-paper in the way a school child does.

It is the envelope next, and there is the same deliberate caution about that too, the same shrouding with one hand while the other one is writing. Nor is that all. For as soon as she has blotted it—again that heavy-handed scrubbing on the blotting-paper—she turns it face downwards on the dressing-table. No chance of seeing anything there. Not even so much as a hint of the address.

But at least something more of the letter is now left showing. And what appears is even more puzzling than the first part. The emphasis now is all on money. There is more than a hint of something unwelcome, of compulsion possibly; but it clearly isn't blackmail. The tone is all wrong for that. There is more the suggestion of an indigent relative, someone who keeps going only by means of loans and allowances and a little bit extra at Christmas. And you may remember that this is exactly how Dame Eleanor diagnosed the trouble. So perhaps the old lady was right after all.

Because this is what the letter says: ". . . *so don't rely on getting something every month in future. I'm not at The Cedars any more. I'm only getting a pound a week now and it may be less when they get someone again. Don't ask me why because I can't tell you and don't write to The Cedars whatever happens. I still hope . . .*"

That is all that is visible because Margaret's arm covers up the rest of it. And she makes no move to fold the letter up and stuff it into the envelope. Just sits there, staring into nothing the way she always does when she has been writing to the mysterious someone who is draining her money away from her shilling by shilling.

273

And there is clearly something more than the sheer bitter expense of it that is disturbing her. She is crying now. Her eyes are quite wet as she goes on staring into nothingness—at a face probably. And she does not move until a tear runs right down her cheek. When the tear reaches the corner of her mouth she puts out the tip of her tongue. Then hurriedly, as though ashamed of herself, she folds the letter abruptly and thrusts it out of sight into the envelope. But she isn't finished with it yet. Because now she does the most extraordinary thing of all. She picks up the envelope and kisses it.

CHAPTER XXXVII

I

THE STRAIN of being Mrs. Gordon had proved too much for Desirée. Ever since the evening when she had sat in the front room of No. 23a Deirdre Gardens talking to Miss Lewis, while Mr. Prevarius had been pretending to go to King's Cross, she had been less forthcoming. All that he was allowed nowadays was to see her home. And it was because of the unforthcomingness—almost, in fact, the holdingbackness—of Desirée, that Mr. Prevarius took his bold and purposeful step: he put his affairs, his personal and heart-rending affairs, into the hands of a marriage bureau.

Not that he proceeded rashly and unguardedly. Indeed, from the moment when the idea had first occurred to him, he took every possible precaution. For a start, he selected his marriage bureau carefully and with circumspection. This, as it turned out, had been a longer process than he had expected simply because, once he really got down to a study of the subject, he found that London was positively bristling with marriage bureaux. On the face of it, everyone else in London was at least as lonely and unwanted as he was. Across the vast empty spaces of the human heart came their miscellaneous cries, their call-signs, their throbbings. There were even entire newspapers, periodicals, monthly magazines, devoted to this particular form of yearning. And Mr. Prevarius bought the whole lot. Dropping casually into a small newsagent's in Fulham that seemed to specialise in adult misery and its remedies, he emerged with a large sheaf of the publications.

Even getting it back into Deirdre Gardens without either of the Miss Lewises asking what it was—the trouble with the confounded thing was that in a sordid way the bundle looked vaguely eatable—was difficult enough.

Naturally, he turned to the Female Wants Section first. And really it seemed as though his problems magically were at an end. There was no need even to compare the rival claims of the prospective clients. The pages were full of optional fascinations. They were so orderly and well-edited that a maharajah could confidently have ordered an entire columnful. As for Mr. Prevarius with his more modest needs, he might just as well pick his charmer with a pin.

A pin! The idea seemed entirely excellent. " To think," he reflected, as he removed the pearl tie-pin from the black silk stock that he was now affecting, " that with one wave of the hand it is a human heart that is imprisoned. But which heart? What is it that guides the dart? An inch, half an inch, to left or right and the true measurement of distance is between misery and bliss. A fraction up or down, and it may be a harridan or a wood nymph who is chosen. Such indeed is life with all its rich and glorious uncertainty."

And smoothing out the paper upon his knee, he began making circling movements with the fatal and decisive pin.

" Bzzz—bzzz!" he murmured half playfully as he kept the pin suspended in its gyrations over the eager, awaiting columns. But there was, indeed, more than mere playfulness. There was also an ecstasy of suspense. " Bzz-bzz, bzzz-bzzz-bzzz," he went on like an air-liner arrived too early at its airport. Then suddenly the note changed. " Zzzz!" he said as he desperately plunged the pearl tie-pin into fate.

The buzzing sound had been so low that the Miss Lewises were not quite sure whether they could hear anything or not. They were merely aware of a faint, insidious vibration as though in another room a bee had been trapped behind lace curtains. But the note changed suddenly. " Ouch!" was the sound that reached them from the front bed-sitter, as the pearl tie-pin driven impetuously downwards penetrated the folded sheets of newspaper and went into Mr. Prevarius's knee.

The sudden sharpness of the pain brought him to his senses, and a spasm of a different kind of pain crossed his face as he

275

remembered something. So far he hadn't said a word to Desirée about his researches into ditching her. How could he? She wouldn't have understood. There would have been a scene. Probably an ugly one. She might even have put her head into a gas-oven, with his name mentioned in an open letter to the coroner. Besides, he didn't yet know that he was going to get what he wanted. For the present, it was much better that they should just tag along as they were until he had checked up more thoroughly on the state of the market. Only when he had other arms to fly to as the storm broke round him, would he convey the news to her.

The matrimonial paper itself had been trampled underfoot as he sprang from his chair in sudden pain. And when he came to examine the page he could find nothing. Not even the trace of a puncture. The lethal pin had been vertical in its descent and had been jerked back again too quickly to have left even the slightest mark.

But Mr. Prevarius was not so easily defeated in the pursuit of love. He was both curious and resourceful. And as soon as he held the paper up to the lamp he could see the tiny hole of light immediately. The only trouble was that the type from the other side showed through and he might as well have been reading gibberish. So, carefully keeping the tips of his fingers over the pin-point, he brought the paper back on to his knees again and began to read.

Then he fairly bubbled over with excitement. His stroke, blind and unguided, had come down plumb centre in the middle of a four-line insertion, that he might almost have inserted himself in the " FEMALE COMPANIONSHIP WANTED " columns.

Young lady, good figure, early twenties, genteel, attractive natural blonde, it ran, *musical and artistic tastes, fond of dancing and the theatre but "Homey," wishes meet refined gentleman ample means age no object similar tastes view matrimony.*

But really it was amazing! He had harpooned his dream-girl at first stab. And phrase by phrase he kept re-reading the description, running his tongue across his lips as he did so. " Good figure . . . early twenties . . . attractive natural blonde . . . fond of dancing " . . . similar tastes . . . Phew!

It was almost too good to be true. His head was reeling. Sitting back in the chair, he closed his eyes, trying to visualise the elusive but obviously willing creature.

It was while he was sitting there that vague misgivings began to come seeping in. Did genteel young ladies really advertise themselves and their attractions in this way? Looked at coldly, it seemed rather mercenary. And how could he be sure that if he sent his reply rocketing back to the box number he would not eventually find himself face to face in a dreadful waiting-room somewhere with a shameless baggage, a hoyden, even possibly a trollop?

CHAPTER XXXVIII

I

MARGARET HAD been in the Hospital for nearly three months before Dr. Trump found a new matron to replace Mrs. Gurnett.

But when he found her, she was perfect. The post had been advertised in all the right places—*The Nursing Times, The Charitable Institutions Gazette, The Homes and Settlements Record*. But though there were plenty of other candidates, they were all passed over when Miss Britt appeared.

Robust, reliable women who had nursed hundreds and whose first glance at a chest rash was worth a three-guinea Harley Street consultation, were turned down in favour of this highly-qualified ice-queen from North Staffordshire who had been successively Assistant Matron of a Home for Backward Girls in Stoke-on-Trent, a Hostel for Deficient Children in Nottingham, a Settlement for Problem Cases in Burnley, and lastly a Farm Community for Delinquents near King's Lynn.

She was tall, pale, chilly to the touch, and silent. In her interview she emphasised that she had two interests—providing proper school meals—here she held up one of her diplomas to prove it—and supervising the *minds* of the children that she was feeding. This was proved equally by her other diploma. And it was certainly obvious that she knew everything about children. Everything that is except how to set about having any of her own. But with so many cheerful millions all providing her with subjects, she seemed perfectly content with things as they were.

Otherwise, she would probably have done something about her appearance. Her hair, for instance. Thin, sandy-coloured and already prematurely streaked with grey, it fitted her head so closely that it might have been applied with a stick-on transfer; and, considering its smallness, the knob of hair at the back seemed unusually full of pins. Then again her spectacles. Very few women look well in rimless spectacles, and Miss Britt's had a hard, purely scientific glitter to them. And pens. Fashion has been very unkind to women in the matter of pens. The two still don't seem to go together somehow, and, in consequence, women's pens usually have to be carried about in handbags along with the latch-key and miscellaneous small change. But Miss Britt refused to accept this disability. She carried hers, openly clipped to the breast pocket of her blouse—a fountain-pen, a propelling pencil and a plain white handkerchief all ready to hand and all permanently on view.

The watch, too, was like a man's. Was a man's, in fact. Miss Britt wore it boldly and conspicuously like a knuckle-duster that had slipped up over the wrist. And somehow the glasses, the pen, the propelling pencil and the watch did not seem to go with children: they did not belong to the world of nurseries and celluloid ducks. But that only goes to show how misleading appearances can be. Because Miss Britt belonged to children and to nothing else. She had *studied* them. Studied them with a clear, appraising eye that is usually brought to bear on another species. She knew everything about them—their comfort, habits, their fantasy world and their repressions, their over-compensations and their revenge motives. It was as though, after ten thousand years, the race had reluctantly yielded up its secrets.

It was Miss Britt's conviction that a properly balanced diet was the primary requirement of a truly happy childhood. And her first researches into Archbishop Bodkin meals appalled her. When she called for diet-sheets, there were none. For nearly three hundred years, it appeared, successive matrons had simply been buying in enormous quantities of meat and vegetables and flour and lard and stuff and then cooking it. In consequence, the carbohydrates had won an easy pernicious victory. And as for Vitamins B and D, it was sheer good fortune if one ever went down a Bodkin throat at all.

But Miss Britt altered all that straight away. The old arrangement of stew and rice pudding on Mondays, liver and jam tart on Tuesdays, and so on throughout the week, was discarded. And, in its place, was substituted a modern menu, as closely balanced as a hairspring and fairly reeking in all the vitamins. Raw vegetables was the basis of it—with raw fruit as well in season. Cabbage, lettuce, carrots, potatoes, turnips with plenty of cheese, all carefully shredded into digestible-sized fragments and with a little lemon squeezed over them, replaced the unhealthy slabs of meat and potfuls of boiled vegetables that had been served previously.

It was against the boiling of vegetables that Miss Britt had set her face most firmly.

"If you served the vegetable water and threw away the cooked vegetables," she told the assembled kitchen staff in her high clear voice, "you would be doing the children more good. As it is, the drains get the best part and the children get the rubbish. In future we must do things differently. Quite the other way round, in fact."

I I

Then, as soon as Miss Britt was assured that her charges were at last being properly fed, she turned her attention to the infirmary.

And, remember, that she was no stranger to infirmaries. That was why she spotted immediately that there was something strange about Margaret. Nor did it take Miss Britt long to discover what it was. The woman, in short, was an impostor. A well-meaning but totally unqualified impostor. The fact that she *was* well-meaning had nothing to do with it. Miss Britt was forced to point out this fact to Nurse Stedge, who obstinately kept on repeating that she couldn't get along without her.

"We shall see," was all Miss Britt replied. "We shall see."

And having said it, she decided that she would speak to Margaret herself.

The interview with Margaret did not take very long because Miss Britt was so expert, so sure of herself.

"Everyone tells me how good you were during the epidemic," she said, "and the last thing we want is to lose you. It's only that we can't afford to have unqualified nurses. Children are so precious, you see."

"I know they are," Margaret replied.

But Miss Britt had misunderstood her. Already she was speaking again in that high, senior-prefect voice of hers.

"I was sure you would," she said. "I don't really know you. But everyone's told me I could rely on you." She paused. "And that's not all," she said. "The Warden has spoken to Dame Eleanor. And she's quite prepared to have you back."

There was another pause and then Miss Britt's clear steady voice resumed.

"Apparently the new companion hasn't proved a success," it went on, "and Dame Eleanor wants to make a change anyway. So everything's turned out for the best, hasn't it?"

"But I don't want to go back," Margaret told her.

Miss Britt smiled. It was a faint, sun-in-February interviewish kind of smile.

"I'm sure there are plenty of other posts open to you," she said. "From what Dame Eleanor told the Warden, she thinks most highly of you and she'll be ready to give you an excellent reference. I'm sure the Warden would, too, if we asked him."

Margaret stood there without speaking. Her eyes were fixed full on Miss Britt's smiling ones, but she herself was not smiling. She was still thinking of Sweetie. Thinking a lot of things about Sweetie.

"I want to stay here," she said.

It was only then that Miss Britt's smile faded.

"But, as I explained, that's impossible," she said. "Our nurses *must* be qualified. They must have their diplomas."

As she came to "diploma," her voice rose slightly. It was as though she were saluting the word, almost curtsying to it. And it was obvious that she thought she had brought the discussion to an end. Otherwise, she would not have removed the cap from her fountain-pen and reached out for the greengrocery bills.

But Margaret had not finished. She stood there unmoving. A tall pale figure—she was noticeably paler than she had been when she first came to the Archbishop Bodkin home—those large, dark eyes of hers fixed on Miss Britt.

"If I got my diploma could I stay?" Margaret asked.

Miss Britt smiled again. A genuine smile, this time. The extreme silliness of the question had amused her.

"Diplomas aren't as easy to get as all that," she said. "Otherwise everyone would have one. Diplomas need study and application and hard work."

Margaret leaned forward.

"If I work hard," she asked, "could I get my diploma? I mean really hard. I don't mind how hard I work as long as I can stay here."

It was, Miss Britt decided, not amusing any longer. It was pathetic. There was a streak of stupid obstinacy in the woman that was like a peasant's. And she remembered now that Margaret had been a country girl. Evidently there were some things that she just couldn't understand.

"It's out of the question," Miss Britt told her. "We can't have you until you're qualified. And even if we could, we're not a training college. It's no use thinking about it. You came here in an emergency. And now the emergency's over, well . . . there just isn't anything to stop for."

"But the children . . ." Margaret began.

"What about them?"

"They need me."

This was really too much. And Miss Britt resented it. She snapped the top back on her pen and screwed it up hard.

"It's not for you to worry about the children," she said sharply. "They're my responsibility. And now," here Miss Britt got up from her desk and went over towards the door, "I'm afraid I've other things to attend to."

But still Margaret had not moved. She really was pathetic now, because she seemed to have no self-respect left to her.

"Isn't there anything else I could do?" she asked. "I don't mind what it is. Cleaning. Anything. I don't mind if I'm just a ward maid."

Miss Britt did not reply immediately. There was something so earnest about the woman that she didn't want to hurt her feelings.

So all that she said was: "I won't give you my answer now. Come back in the morning when you've thought more about it. Remember, being a ward maid is very rough work. People should've been brought up to it."

"I was brought up to it," Margaret said bluntly.

And then Miss Britt did one of those things that only those who have been used to authority can do. She went up to Margaret and laid her hand on her arm.

281

"Love of children is a very beautiful thing," she said. "God intended women to love children. But there are other ways of doing God's work besides nursing. What you ought to do is to get married. Get married, my dear, and have children of your own."

CHAPTER XXXIX

MR. PREVARIUS had overcome his misgivings. Had bunged in a reply the same evening, in fact. Nevertheless, when the time for the appointment came round, he was doubtful whether or not to go through with it. For a start, the box number had turned out not to be that of the young woman herself, but merely of a marriage bureau. And when Mr. Prevarius arrived and saw the collection of brass bell-pushes beside the door he thought for a moment that he must have mistaken the address.

He was surprised, too, even disappointed, by the informality of the office arrangements. It was a man in his shirt-sleeves who opened the door. And when Mr. Prevarius inquired diffidently for the Eros Agency, the man said, " Oh, 'er," and jerked his thumb upwards, adding: "Second landing."

It was so dark going up the stairs once the front door had been shut behind him that Mr. Prevarius found himself groping and fumbling. Indeed, only the thought that somewhere at the top of this shadowy and unprepossessing staircase a genteel young lady of good figure might be waiting for him made him persevere. Otherwise he would have turned tail and run. But he had reached the second landing by now, and facing him was a white-painted door that bore the words " Eros Agency. Please 'ring."

It was one of those cheap clockwork bells that are screwed on to the back of the woodwork. As soon as Mr. Prevarius had touched it, he sprang back again because the buzzing right under his fingertip was so sudden and so near.

But there was no time for nervousness now. The door had opened and he realised that he was being inspected by a young woman. She was not even a nice young woman. There was too much of the tired slug about her, a limpness ; a moistness even. She was, in fact, about the plainest young woman whom he had ever seen.

" Namepleasehaveyouanappointment?" the young woman said in a flat, weary-sounding voice.

" I have," Mr. Prevarius replied. " For 2.30. And the name is FitzWinter. Algernon FitzWinter. Captain Algernon Fitz-Winter, retired."

There was no mistake, not a trace of hesitation this time: he had been practising it all the way on the bus. But all the same he had imagined himself saying it to someone a little more personable. He had imagined a rather gay receptionist at such an agency. And then he understood: it was precisely because it was just such an agency that it had such a receptionist. Anything better would have been snapped up immediately by a disappointed client.

" Wouldyoutakeaseatinthewaiting-room," she asked. " It-won'tbelongnow."

The poet in Mr. Prevarius was stirred.

" Poor thing," he reflected. " Poor unlovely and unwanted thing. Always the bridesmaid. How many many romances must she have seen blossom—always out of reach."

The waiting-room itself was uncomfortably reminiscent of a dentist's: Mr. Prevarius began thinking of drills and forceps and bent, spiky metal things. The words " rinse please " rose up within his mind. The main difference was that this room was darker. Much darker. The walls were green. And the heavy brown velvet curtains had not been looped back far enough to admit much light. What did penetrate was drained and filtered by coffee-coloured muslin. The light, in consequence, was pale and watery as though the Eros Agency had its waiting-room somewhere at the bottom of the Sargossa Sea.

It took Mr. Prevarius some time to adjust his eyes to the dimness. And, as he did so, he became aware of another occupant, a female occupant, already seated there. He looked harder, and then relaxed. This was not the dream-girl. The woman was past middle-age and wore a battered, peevish expression like a sub-postmistress in Christmas week. " Surely she must be waiting for something else," he told himself. " She . . . she can't be thinking of starting up again at her time of life." He paused. " But who knows?" he reflected. " Nature is very wonderful."

And trade in the Eros Agency was certainly pretty brisk. The sub-postmistress was called almost immediately, and she was replaced at once by a large fattish man in a check suit

283

who sat with his bowler hat covering the lower part of his face as though he were afraid of being recognised. Then a plump blowzy woman in a thick veil, with wisps of reddish hair escaping from under a picture hat, was shown in. And Mr. Prevarius was still thinking that there might be something doing if only the fat man would lower his hat and the blowzy woman would lift her veil, when he heard his own name called.

It was as a matter of fact called twice, simply because he hadn't recognised it the first time.

But he was careful not to appear eager and ill at ease. He felt that he needed all his wits about him for the interview that was coming.

" Probably a dago," he told himself as he followed the epicene receptionist into the audience chamber. " Only a dirty dago would get mixed up in a job like this."

He was still prepared to find himself in the presence of something olive-skinned with almond-shaped eyes and long side whiskers, when the door opened and he saw a little old lady seated at a writing-table. She looked up as he entered and smiled at him.

" Pray be seated," she said. " I heave your faile heare."

" My God," thought Mr. Prevarius. " A woman. I hadn't reckoned on that."

Nor had he reckoned on such refinement of voice and such perfect poise and efficiency. He was still studying the smooth white hair, the shining spectacles, the cairngorm brooch, the black lace choker, when the little old lady spoke again.

" The preliminary fee is faive guineas," she said. " A further faive for an introduction. And a fainal fifteen for satisfaction."

" Isn't it rather a lot?" Mr. Prevarius asked cautiously.

But the old lady only smiled.

" Not to our clayents," she replied. " Our clayents are exclusively of the twenty-faive guinea class."

" Do you take a ch . . ." Mr. Prevarius began and stopped himself. He had only just remembered that Captain Fitz-Winter hadn't got a bank account.

" Aither a cheque or benk notes," the old lady said. " Whichever is moare convenient."

Opening his wallet, Mr. Prevarius slowly counted out five one-pound notes and passed them over.

"End faive shillings," the old lady said. "Faive guineas is our fee."

Mr. Prevarius put two half-crowns on the table.

Then the old lady smiled again.

"Are you naeval or military?" she inquired.

Mr. Prevarius thought for a moment.

"Military," he said. "Seventh Rajputana Light Foot. Since disbanded."

"Then you would perheps laike someone who knows India?" the old lady suggested. "We hev several clayents on our books at the moment."

"I'm not particular," Mr. Prevarius answered truthfully.

"Hoew about a Major's widow from Cawnpore," the old lady persisted. "So much in common. Such links. Such reminiscences."

"Too old," said Mr. Prevarius bluntly.

"But I haven't mentioned her age," the old lady pointed out. "She is only forty-naine. And extremely well presairved. Really quaite remarkable."

Mr. Prevarius shook his head.

"I am still a boy at heart," he said simply. "Almost a young man. My life is dancing, the theatre, music . . ."

"Music in the army?" the old lady asked him.

"Certainly," Mr. Prevarius told her. "I was . . . er . . . a bandmaster."

"I see," said the old lady. "Then you wish for a romantic match."

Mr. Prevarius nodded.

"I do," he said. "Very."

But really this was becoming positively embarrassing. It was like discussing sex with his grandmother.

"End haeve you prayvate means?" the old lady asked.

Mr. Prevarius shrugged his shoulders.

"Not riches," he said. "Not affluence. But a pittance. A thousand a year, shall we say? A round thousand."

"A thewsand a year," she said. "That does maeke metters easier."

"But naeturally," said Mr. Prevarius simply.

There was a pause.

"And now may I see the young lady I came about?" he asked.

"Bay all means," the old lady replied sweetly. "I shall be moast heppy to arraenge it."

" Then where is she?" Mr. Prevarius demanded.

The time for play-acting was over now, and his voice sounded hoarse and desperate.

" Oh, we doan't keep our clayents here," the old lady reminded him approvingly. " Not on the premases. I shell hev to wraite to her. That will be a further faive guineas. Faive for the original registration, remember. And a separate faive for the introduction."

BOOK FOUR

CHAPTER XL

I

THE Sweetie and Ginger correspondence had been continuing only fairly promisingly when it broke down altogether. There were two reasons for its sudden and complete collapse. First, Ginger got sick of it. And secondly, Annie, tired of acting as courier in an affair that was obviously getting nowhere, withdrew any further offers of assistance. By then, there had been six letters in all: the original interchange and four more unanswered ones from Sweetie.

Indeed, if it had not been for Dr. Trump's Vocational Training, it is hard to see how Sweetie and Ginger would ever have managed to meet again. As it was, for a period of nearly three months they simply had to get along without seeing or hearing from each other. And then they were suddenly brought face to face. It was over on the laundry side that the encounter took place. In the damping and pressing room to be exact.

Naturally everything was under the strictest possible supervision. The girls had the room entirely to themselves, and it was only when the hampers had to be dragged in and out that the boys ever came into the room at all. And Sweetie had not got so much as a single thought of Ginger anywhere in her mind. She was thinking instead of any number of other things, important things like how she was going to grow her hair until it was right down to her waist; how it was that soap never tasted as nice as it smelt; how Nurse Stedge had a sort of little moustache almost like a man's; how nice it would be to run a tea and serve only cakes and biscuits instead of scones and bread and butter; how Tuesday was pale blue in colour while Wednesday was chocolate brown; and why bathwater always started turning round like a corkscrew just before it ran out.

Also, in her way, she was concentrating. She liked Vocational Training. It meant that she had to dip her fingers into a bowl of water and sprinkle a few drops on to each of the garments that were in the basket beside her so that they would come out smooth when the iron went over them. She wouldn't have minded going on doing it all day. Every day, in fact.

As it was, she had just sprinkled the first one when the swing-door that led through into the main laundry was shot open from the far side. In the doorway there appeared the hindquarters of a small boy. It was a familiar posture, this bending-down one, because the delivery-hampers were too large to be carried; and the boys, particularly the smaller ones, always dragged them backwards using their rear-parts as a kind of gentle battering ram when they reached the swing-door.

And as all hindquarters look very much alike, and as the door was banging open and shut every few minutes, Sweetie did not even pause to wonder who it was who was concealed behind the tight seat of the trousers. It was not, indeed, until the trousers had slacked off a bit and the small boy had got himself again into an upright position that Sweetie saw that it was Ginger. And, as she did so, her heart gave a sudden thump inside her. It was the first time her heart had ever done such a thing and its behaviour surprised her. She quickly recovered herself, however.

"Hallo," she said.

"Oh hallo," said Ginger.

There was a casual, almost deliberately disinterested note in his voice. Not a trace of embarrassment, she noticed; no hint of shame at his unfaithfulness.

"I didn't know you were here."

"Well, you can see I am, can't you?"

This was better, definitely better: he was beginning to sound defensive now. Even so, she thought that he might have said something more, something about being glad to see her.

"I wrote you a letter," she said.

"I know," Ginger answered. "I got it."

"Well, why didn't you reply?"

"I did."

"You didn't."

"I did."

"Well, only to the first one."

"They were all the same."

"But you could have answered them, couldn't you?"

288

Ginger shook his head.

"Couldn't be bothered."

At the reply, Sweetie was so angry that she forgot herself. Putting her entire hand into the water-bowl beside her she shook a whole fistful of drops full into Ginger's face.

"You stop that," Ginger said. "I haven't done nothing to you. I didn't start writing those potty letters."

Sweetie drew herself up.

"I think you're a very rude little boy," she told him. "I hate you."

That was as far as their conversation ever got because it was the moment for Miss Gurge, the laundry supervisor, to come round. A red-faced, heavily-breathing woman with a mouthful of small, sharp teeth, Miss Gurge had the air of a large hot bulldog. Only the grey hair that strayed across her forehead from underneath the white uniform cap suggested something different—a sheep-dog possibly. Whatever it was, there was the distinctive air of canine fierceness; a hint of brass studs encircling a stout leather collar. On their first meeting Dr. Trump had taken one look at her, and had not even troubled to ask whether she experienced any troubles about discipline.

The *woof-woof* of her voice had started up already.

"I can 'ear talking," she said. " 'Oo is it?"

She knew perfectly well already, of course. Knew without even looking that it would be Sweetie. For Sweetie was always talking, always saying something or other. The child seemed incapable of ever remaining silent for more than two or three minutes on end. If there was no one else to talk to she spent whole periods talking quietly to herself about nothing.

"An' you," she went on. "You with the red 'air."

This was too much for Ginger. He stood where he was and stuck his underlip out. He had been quietly getting on with the job that he had been given and now Sweetie had got him into this mess. He had messes enough of his own in any case, without Sweetie's stepping in to help him.

" 'Oo's in charge of you?" she continued.

"Mr. Dawlish, mam," Ginger answered.

"Well, go straight back an' tell 'im you've been caught talking to one of the girls," she said. "If you don't tell 'im yourself, I will. I'll be dealing with Sweetie myself."

With that Miss Gurge took hold of Sweetie by the shoulders and stood her up against the wall. Right up against it, too. So close that her toes were touching the skirting-board. If she put her tongue out she could lick the distemper. She did try it once or twice simply to test the experience. But it was an unpleasant one. The wall was wet, slightly greasy and flavoured very strongly with soap.

" An' no talking," Miss Gurge had said over her shoulder as she departed. " No talking an' no moving. Just you stay there till the end of the lesson. There's half an hour, so you'd better get used to it."

It was on the other side of the swing-door that the trouble started. Ginger went straight back to Mr. Dawlish and reported himself. By now, he displayed a natural grace in such matters, a kind of easy charm that came from sheer experience in the situation.

". . . so she told me to come and tell you," he finished up.

" Who's ' she '?"

" Miss Gurge, sir," Ginger answered, wondering whether it was possible that Mr. Dawlish hadn't been listening and really didn't know.

" Well, don't do it again," Mr. Dawlish told him.

That was the end of the matter so far as Mr. Dawlish was concerned. He was prepared for anything when Ginger came up to him, and it was a relief to find that on this occasion it was merely a trifling affair of talking. Also, Mr. Dawlish wasn't feeling well ; it was the heat of the laundry, probably. He disliked the whole idea of Vocational Training. It was a nuisance. A damn' nuisance. And if making better citizens depended on dragging dirty clothes baskets about a laundry floor, he wished that Dr. Trump would come down in person to show them all how to set about it.

But if Mr. Dawlish was casual and disinterested, there was someone who wasn't. And this was Edward, the fourteen-year-old, who had once been *caned* for talking to a junior laundress. He was somewhat of a hero, in consequence, and he listened carefully to the whole conversation. Then he turned to the boy next to him.

" Ginger's got a girl," he said. " Pass it on."

It took about five minutes for the message to go right round the room. But, as the word spread, Ginger became aware that people were looking at him. There were nudges, glances, titterings and giggles. And after a while, Ginger could stand it no longer. He turned to the boy next to him.

" Wosermatter wiv you?" he asked.

290

There was no answer. His neighbour was a small timid boy who was not in the least anxious to get drawn into an affair with Ginger.

"Dunnowodiermean," he said simply, and continued to apply himself to folding up wet blankets as though the whole operation fascinated him.

Then, seeing that his revelation was in danger of falling flat, Edward started it up again.

"Ginger's got a girl," he began chanting softly between his teeth. "Ginger's got a girl. Ginger's got a girl . . ."

At that moment Mr. Dawlish had to step outside for his own purposes. He took the precaution of appointing a monitor before he went but unfortunately he chose Edward. And, as soon as Mr. Dawlish had left, the tall boy took up the refrain louder and more clearly.

"Ginger's got a girl," he declaimed. "Ginger's got a girl. Ginger's got a girl."

It was an annoying kind of voice that he possessed, and the intonation was offensive, too. He made two syllables out of the last word, "Gu-url," every time he said it, and Ginger flushed.

"You shut up," he said.

"And suppose I don't?"

"I'll come and bash you."

"All right, come and do it," Edward replied. He felt confident and contemptuous. With his height, his weight and his reach he saw nothing to be alarmed about in Ginger. And just to show his feeling of superiority he taunted Ginger as he advanced towards him.

"Gu-urlie," he said. "Gu-urlie."

But he had reckoned without Ginger's temper. For, at the first insult, Ginger sprang forward. He gave a sort of bound. And, shooting out his fist, he reached Edward's nose. There was a distinguishable crunching sound. Edward stood motionless for a moment thrusting his tongue out over his upper lip. It came away salt, and he knew that his nose was bleeding. Then he got down to business.

"I'm going to give you a hiding," he said.

By now, all work in the laundry was suspended. And, sensing not merely a fight but a good fight, all the boys gathered round leaving an empty space between the wringers and the airing racks. It was in this open space, this soap and water arena, that Edward let Ginger have it. There was nothing very skilful or scientific in his method. It consisted simply of shoving Ginger away hard with one hand and then hitting quickly before he could recover his balance. By the time they had been once round the ring, Ginger's left eye was closed up and his mouth had been cut.

Even now the fight might have ended more or less peaceably. Ginger was so much smaller that the older boy was getting bored with the whole affair. One further round of shove and jab, and he would have been more than ready to call the whole thing off. But the crowd, in the mysterious manner of crowds which somehow magically acquire a corporate existence, a personality, had suddenly turned against him.

"Hit someone your own size," it began saying. "Hit someone your own. . . ."

There were thirty-two boys in all engaged on Practical Instruction at that moment. And they were all saying the same thing. In short, the crowd had turned ugly. And Edward found himself at a disadvantage: he did not know how to withdraw himself. Every time he dropped his hands, Ginger came at him again; and every time he punched back, the class resented it.

What was worse was that the audience was now definitely supporting his opponent, a bad state of affairs, as every boxer knows.

"Come on, Ginger," they were shouting. "Hit him."

It was, in fact, one of these war-cries that gave Ginger the opening that he needed. The voice that had spoken was Spud's. And it was so sharp, so strident and edgy, that Edward turned his head to see where this sudden yell of defiance had come from. As he did so, Ginger jumped in for the second time. He caught him hard on the point of the chin. So hard, indeed, that he hurt his own knuckles. He felt as though he had the point of the monitor's chin permanently lodged there between the second and third fingers.

After that, there could be no possible question of withdrawing. The crowd was cheering. Cheering Ginger. And some of them were booing as well. Booing Edward. Also, Edward was in pain, considerable pain. So he went right in to finish Ginger. And it was not difficult. The two blows that he landed in Ginger's face were enough to leave him dazed and stupid, an open undefended target for what was coming. Ginger went over on his back, and lay there winded and unmoving.

There was now the sudden and tremendous silence that follows an unpopular knock-out. The crowd had seen injustice done and a feeling of deep moral indignation ran through everyone. Also, there was a subtler, more intangible emotion. The whole classical tradition demanded that it should be the little fellow who was victorious. The booing started up again.

II

One of the strange things about a fight is the way that news of it spreads, and spreads quickly. Sudden danger to a queen bee in a busy beehive does not produce more excitement than a fight in a big institution. Ginger had hardly got in his first blow, in fact, before Sweetie in the damping and pressing room knew what was happening. And it had nothing to do with the noise that the boys were making: the rumbling of the big wooden mangles in the next room would have suppressed all trace of it if rogue elephants had been fighting next door. No, it was a tremulous psychic message that came vibrating through the brickwork, and announced unmistakably that there was mischief somewhere in the camp.

Sweetie got the signal straight away. "S O S," "S O S," "S O S," the messages came piling in. "S O S," "S O S," "S O S."

So clearly she had to do something about it. And quickly. It was not exactly that she was disobedient. At that moment she merely forgot all about her punishment, all about the Archbishop Bodkin regulations, all about Miss Gurge. She simply concentrated on the distress-call and made straight for it.

She was small, very small, remember, and she got through the crowd round the door like a rabbit running through a brier-bush. And the circle of spectators in the main laundry, the front-row five-guinea ones, didn't hold her up either. Because they were too close together to run through, she scratched her way between them.

It was obvious that the big boy had killed Ginger. But even so she remained a woman. A man in such circumstances would have waded straight in, using his fists. But a woman is different. A woman always requires a weapon. And Sweetie immediately started looking round for something sharp. As there was nothing—no daggers or scissors, not even a fork left lying about—she chose the next best thing. Something heavy. It was a tailor's iron which stood on the raised pedestal of its own little gas ring. And when Sweetie picked it up, it had not even occurred to her that it might be hot. At any rate, it was a weapon. And snatching it off the gas-ring she rushed over with it and thrust it into Edward's back.

The effect was terrific. Simply terrific. It was like nothing that she could possibly have anticipated. Instead of a mere thud as the iron landed there was first an angry fizzing sound like a freshly opened ginger-beer bottle. And, at the next moment, a great cloud of steam went sizzling upwards. Then Edward let out the loudest yell that Sweetie had ever heard.

It was that yell that Mr. Dawlish heard as he made his way slowly back towards the laundry. He extinguished his pipe, thrust the day's newspaper quickly into his pocket, and hurried.

When he got there he thought at first that it was Sweetie who had hurt herself. For over by the window, Miss Gurge was bandaging Sweetie's hand where the handle of the hot iron had burnt it. And it was only then that he saw that Ginger had a black eye and Edward, his monitor, had a great scorched hole in the middle of his jacket.

CHAPTER XLI

I

BECAUSE OF the enormity of what Sweetie had done—and branding a fellow inmate with a practically red-hot iron was not something that could be overlooked—Dr. Trump reflected carefully on her due punishment.

For the time being everything was at least under control. The victim, Edward, was in the infirmary, lying face downwards with a pad of collodion on the afflicted part. And Sweetie herself was confined to the dormitory. She had been there for two hours already and Dr. Trump had expressly forbidden anyone to approach. But he couldn't leave her there for ever because she would starve. Or throw herself from the window. Or scream for help. Or set fire to the bedclothes. Anything, in fact, to attract attention and create confusion. Because it had to be recognised, he told himself, that she was that kind of child.

And so, pacing up and down his room, Dr. Trump considered the problem. Expulsion? That was naturally the first thought. But on reflection he saw clearly that it was impossible: orphans are as secure as judges: there is no getting rid of them, no matter how appalling they may be. Or call in the police and have her sent to an approved school? But the scandal, the publicity, the notoriety. He could just imagine the glee that such an action would cause in St. Christopher's, and he winced at the mere idea of it. A good, sharp caning? No, for some reason, the deceased Archbishop had refused to countenance corporal punishment for female orphans: either his saintliness or his bachelorhood had made him most emphatic on that point. Dr. Trump bit his lip in irritation. And then he had a happy thought. Solitary confinement! He would sentence Sweetie to three days' silence and imprisonment. He would be perfectly humane, of course. Meals, plain ones, would be served regularly and there would be the necessary personal supervision. But, beyond that, nothing. No company. No conversation: he would instruct the maid not to utter a single syllable, when bringing the food in to her. No books. No toys. Nothing.

There was a small room on the ground floor of the Matron's own block. It had a high barred window, and was used for storing things. With the addition of a bed it might have been expressly designed for the incarceration of children.

Above all things, it was set in the very centre of the Hospital buildings. And there in the silence of her little cell, with no interruption from the outside world, Sweetie could ponder and repent. When she emerged, he had no doubt that she would be chastened. And if she wasn't, if pride and wickedness were still raging inside her, then she could go back inside again. On that Dr. Trump was determined. He was not going to allow a little thing like a child's obstinacy to stand in his way when the good name of the Hospital was at stake.

And now that his mind was made up, Dr. Trump rang for Miss Britt.

". . . and if three days is not enough, we will repeat the treatment," he concluded. " There is no need to make a secret of it. The more the other girls know about it, the more powerful the example. And, above all things, remember: no talking. It is in silence that the child's conscience will begin prickling."

It was in the bit about telling the other girls, however, that Dr. Trump made his great error. Because in no large institution is there ever such a thing as the truth. Passing from lip to lip, it becomes distorted. At second remove, even the simplest and most elementary fact is scarcely recognisable. Somewhere round about this stage, elaboration and improvement begin. Next, invention comes in. And from then onwards sheer fantasy takes over.

In this instance, confusion was aided guilelessly and without effort by the slow-witted Annie. It was not that she consciously falsified. She simply misunderstood. Deep in the recesses of her mind, where the wheels turned slowly and some of the cogs were entirely missing—she got hold of the notion that Sweetie was being shut away *for ever*. And putting two and two together, and remembering some of the more dreadful stories that she had heard of medieval convents, she became convinced that they were bricking Sweetie in. Not caring, however, to repeat so grisly a story at the top of her voice she went round the Hospital whispering it. And this gave colour and a kind of awful authenticity to the myth.

Within half an hour of the sad little procession that had been seen crossing over towards the Latymer Block—Miss Britt leading, Sweetie in the middle and Nurse Stedge bringing up the rear with a pillow case—the ghastly rumour was all over the ironing and pressing room. From there, borne like a spark, it reached the kitchens. Then back to starching and despatch. And finally on to the big hall where the other girls were having supper.

It was 4.45 precisely when Sweetie heard the key turn in the lock behind her, and not more than five-thirty before the entire female side of the Hospital was discussing the outrage in awed whispers. Only the closing accident of night prevented the news from spreading over into the boys' side until the following day.

Everyone seemed to be talking about it, however. And there was one little incident to upset Dr. Trump considerably. Quite changed the course of things, in fact.

He was standing quietly in the corner of the cloisters, having just made his evening inspection, when he heard voices

—the voices of Mr. Dawlish and Mr. Prevarius. It was Mr. Prevarius who was speaking as they approached.

". . . anyhow, if she's shut up there, she'll probably hang herself, or something," Mr. Prevarius was saying in an off-hand, casual sort of tone as though it didn't really matter. "And then there'll be a beautiful big inquest and we shall all have our names in the papers."

II

Because the unpleasant little incident had upset him, Dr. Trump was quite unable to sleep. In the cream and lilac bedroom, with Felicity's pet china rabbits ranged along the mantelpiece, he tossed anxiously. He counted sheep, he prayed, he recited narrative poems, he went through Old Testament characters in alphabetical order, he did cube roots. But always into his unquiet mind the unpleasantness kept returning. And doubts, too. Perhaps he *had* blundered. Perhaps Sweetie's punishment was just a shade too austere, too reminiscent of the Spanish Inquisition.

But, confound it, the child had got to be punished some-how, hadn't she? He couldn't let her off altogether. With this thin layer of consolation in his mind, Dr. Trump was at last drifting into slumber when suddenly he sat up again, bolt upright. Suppose something *were* to happen to Sweetie while she was shut away there? Suppose she cried herself to sleep face downwards on the pillow and was smothered? Suppose . . . no it was too dreadful to put into words. At all costs, further mischief must be prevented. So, springing out of bed, Dr. Trump began dressing hurriedly.

Hurriedly but not silently. Before he had reached the door, Felicity spoke to him.

"Now you've woken me up too," she told him. "You'll ruin your digestion if you go on pouring cocoa inside you whenever you can't sleep. You know it only gives you heartburn."

Heartburn, indeed! It was the good name of the whole Hospital that was at stake. And as he slipped out of the front door, his Boy Scout inspection lamp in his hand, he began praying again; really praying this time.

"Oh God, don't let anything happen," he kept saying. "Don't let me be too late."

297

It was rather eerie crossing the big courtyard by Latymer. The Hospital was silent except for the sound of the wind in the ornamental weathervanes, and Dr. Trump shivered. Compared with the chill in the night air, his bed seemed unusually warm and inviting. He felt that if only he were back there now he would be asleep inside two minutes. But things were too urgent for regrets about his bed. And as he drew near the Matron's block he saw something that banished all thoughts of sleep. Over in the shadows, right up against the wall and immediately under Sweetie's window, was a figure. A figure strained to its uppermost so that its fingers could rest upon the sill.

He knew now that it was some sixth sense that had warned him. Even so, he did not swing the beam of his lamp directly on to the figure. Instead, he extinguished it altogether and crept silently forward, keeping carefully in the shadows himself. He wanted to be right upon the interloper before he pounced.

And as he drew closer he could hear that words were passing. The figure was saying something. It was carrying on a whispered conversation.

This itself was bad enough after he had forbidden all conversation. But what amazed him most were the words that were being spoken.

"Don't be frightened, Sweetie," the figure was saying. "If you wake up, remember I'm here. I shall be here all night. If you call I shall hear you."

Dr. Trump knew by then who it was that was speaking. And there was really no need for him to switch his lamp on suddenly and point the beam accusingly full at her.

But, as it happened, it was the most important single thing he did that evening. For the light showed Margaret up perfectly. Indeed, it was so bright, the beam so powerful and well-focused, that the small boy up on the roof-top just above him could see everything.

The small boy was Ginger. He had been out for about half an hour on one of his little jaunts, just having a look round at things in general. And because he was cold and bored, he was on his way back to bed again, when Dr. Trump had suddenly chosen to press the special Rover-type safety switch.

"Leave that window immediately," he heard Dr. Trump

say to Margaret in a toothed, rasping kind of voice. "The child is alone by my orders. I shall deal with you in the morning."

Then, taking a key out of his pocket, Dr. Trump went inside. He was there for so long, that Ginger did not wait for him. With his colossal piece of news fairly bursting inside him, he was on his way back across the roof-tops.

Sweetie did not stir as Dr. Trump entered. With her cheek supported on her hand, she appeared to be sleeping blissfully. He stood motionless beside her. And it was impossible for him mentally not to compare his own tortured night with this deep, peaceful breathing. Certainly the little girl did not *look* wicked. On the contrary, the air of infant innocence was pronounced and unmistakable. As also was the sheer natural beauty of the child. The darkness of the hair and the pearly —yes, transparency was the word—the pearly transparency of the skin—were really quite remarkable. It was like gazing down on a little figure carved out of alabaster. Indeed, the emotion that he experienced was so powerful that he felt an entire sermon taking shape as he stood there. "On Forgiving a Sleeping Child" he would call it.

And wasn't it possible, he asked himself, that already he had achieved his purpose?

III

Ginger woke Spud up as soon as he got back to the dormitory, and told him everything that he had seen. But Spud did not believe a word of it; simply did not believe a word. And as soon as the dressing-bell went next morning, Ginger made a few discreet inquiries. He tried Sergeant Chiswick. But Sergeant Chiswick had spent a quiet night dreaming of the chancy fortunes of the turf, and knew nothing. He could not even quite make out what Ginger was driving at. And Ginger was unable to enlighten him because he could not very well admit that he had been enjoying another of his little jaunts upon the tiles.

After the blank that he had drawn with Sergeant Chiswick, Ginger tried Mr. Dawlish. But here again he drew blank. Mr. Dawlish wasn't even interested. He simply told Ginger that he must have been dreaming—there had been no one flashing

299

a torch about in the playground—and mooched off, smelling rankly of tobacco. So, finally, Ginger tried Annie. And from her, of course, he got everything.

Moreover, the news that she recounted was so startling, so melodramatic even to someone of Ginger's lurid tastes, that for a moment he was left stunned. Then at the thought of Sweetie, bricked up there, Ginger decided that it was time to act. Act, and act swiftly.

He began by calling a meeting. As soon as the Scripture lesson had dragged wearily through the misfortunes of Esau, and the mid-morning break had arrived, he signalled to Spud, and the two of them made their way to the space where the boiler house had once been. It was a good place for conferences, quiet, private and secluded. And as soon as they were settled, Ginger wetted his finger and drew it across his throat.

"There's one of 'em locked in," he said in a low whisper. "It's Sweetie."

But Spud was not impressed.

"You're potty about Sweetie," he answered.

"I'm not," Ginger replied. "I'd do the same for any of them."

"Do wot?"

"Rescue her."

"How?"

Ginger paused. The question was important. Fundamental, in fact. And, for the moment, Ginger had no answer. But he could hardly admit it. And more to play for time than for any other reason he replied: "Get the cops."

"How?" Spud asked him, still intent upon establishing the practical details.

"Go and fetch 'em, of course," Ginger answered. "I can git out, can't I?"

"But yer can't git in again," Spud replied callously. "Not in the daylight."

"Well, we can shart, can't we?"

Spud shook his head.

"Nobody wouldn't take no notice," he said. "Sharting's potty."

"Well, chuck a note over the wall," Ginger suggested.

Spud paused, considering.

"Wot'll it say?" he asked.

"It'll say what's going on," Ginger told him. "That's wot it'll say."

"Who's going to write it?"

"I am."

"When?"

"Juring jography."

"Where?"

"In the lav. of course. Where d'yer fink?"

The message was well phrased. Written in pencil in large capital letters on a sheet of paper torn haphazard from a notebook, it carried the authentic notes of desperation and despair.

"HELP, HELP," it read. "I AM DIEING IN A PRESON. HELP SEND A POLISEMAN. HELP." And because it was written in the first person, Ginger signed it "SWEATY."

Ginger was determined to deliver it at the very feet of the law itself. It was now eleven o'clock and at eleven forty-five the day's patrol of St. Mark's Avenue regularly took place. Provided that Mr. Dawlish could be persuaded to excuse him again—not that twice in one morning was going to be easy—he would take up a commanding position in one of the tallest plane trees and allow his amazing document to flutter down before the policeman's very nose.

As it happened, Ginger experienced no difficulty whatsoever in being excused. At the first sight of his wriggling body and painfully distorted features, Mr. Dawlish jerked his thumb over his shoulder and, without even being asked, indicated that Ginger was to leave them.

Indeed, it was the excess of leisure that was Ginger's undoing. For it gave him time to improve upon a plan that was already well-nigh perfect. Instead of allowing the paper to drift down lightly on the breeze, he weighted it. And he weighted it too heavily. When it finally left his hand, there was a good half-pound of brick-bat wrapped up inside it.

And all unsuspecting, P.C. William Glubb advanced up the avenue to meet it. A large, robustly-built man, he moved slowly. There was a kind of courtly and majestic indifference about him that indicated that crime was to be approached on his terms and in his time, or not at all. And this morning he did what he had always done: when he reached the corner of St. Mark's Avenue and Ryecroft Gardens, he loosened his collar and stood there, idly shifting his weight from one massive black boot on to the other. He braced his shoulders,

301

spread his legs a little wider apart and placed his clasped hands behind his back.

Then Ginger threw. It was a good twenty-five feet from the plane tree to where P.C. Glubb was standing. And, naturally, Ginger did not want to miss. Therefore he threw hard. Really hard, with all his strength behind it. Hard and straight. His aim was deadly and unerring. At one moment there was the policeman with the top hook of his collar undone and his mind laboriously trying to work out the details of his pension: and at the next, a flying brick-bat had carried away his helmet.

With one glance at the scene of havoc below, Ginger got down out of the plane tree as quickly as he could manage. And back into Mr. Dawlish's class-room. The class-room at that moment seemed the safest place. But none too safe at that. Not to put too fine a point upon it, Ginger was scared. Even Mr. Dawlish noticed that there was something wrong with him. The boy seemed to be muttering to himself. But Mr. Dawlish was too far away to know what the words were. And he would have been more concerned still if he could have heard them. For Ginger was saying the same thing over and over again.

" I've killed a policeman. I've killed a policeman," were the words. " I've killed a policeman. I've killed . . ."

CHAPTER XLII

I

IT WAS the arrival of the policeman, very red-faced and carrying his dented helmet, that finally tipped the scales of Dr. Trump's temper . . . Not that he was to be blamed for his little outburst.

Taken all in all, it had been an unusually trying morning. And after such a shocking night, too. Twice he had wakened suddenly, dreaming that Margaret was breaking into the detention room by force. And once it was not a dream at all: it was a nightmare. Instead of playing gaoler, he was now the prisoner. Shut inside the little cell, he was vainly groping round the walls searching for escape. And he was suffocating. Indeed, it was not until a hand gripped his shoulder and a voice, Felicity's voice, said into his ear: " Stop lying on your back. You're snoring," that he was released from the nightmare. By then, moreover, it was six-thirty—too late for any serious thoughts of snuggling back down among the bedclothes.

And by nine o'clock Dame Eleanor was on the phone. This did not surprise Dr. Trump greatly because Dame Eleanor was an inveterate telephoner: she snatched up the instrument whenever anything occurred to her. But this morning he was more than her equal.

"Good-morning, Dame Eleanor," he began. "A truly beautiful morning . . ."

But that was as far as he was allowed to get.

"What's going on there?" Dame Eleanor demanded. "What's this I hear about locking children up in store-rooms?"

Dr. Trump drew in his breath sharply and involuntarily. So Dame Eleanor had heard! That could mean only one thing—treachery on the part of a member of his staff. Nevertheless, he kept his voice carefully controlled and modulated.

"I think your informant whoever he or she may be has unintentionally misled you," he said. "I decided to release the child at least a quarter of an hour ago."

But he was wrong in imagining that any reply at this moment would satisfy Dame Eleanor. Unlike Dr. Trump, she had not enjoyed her breakfast. No sooner had she sat down to it, in fact, than Margaret had arrived.

And it had been only Margaret's downright insistence that had got her inside the house at all. At first, Dame Eleanor had refused to see her. Simply refused point-blank without giving any reason. But when Margaret had declined to go away again, had said that it was a matter of life or death, Dame Eleanor had finally admitted her. And, once she had heard, Dame Eleanor gave up all thoughts of eating. She simply sat there, food untasted on the plate. And the moment Margaret had gone—it had as a matter of fact been rather nice seeing her—she had asked for the telephone to be brought to the breakfast table.

She was talking at this moment from behind a pot of lukeish-warm coffee and a toast-rack in which the little pieces, once so hot and crisp, were now leathery and useless.

". . . and children burning each other with hot irons, I never heard of such a thing in my life," she was saying. "It's disgraceful. The whole place must be bedlam. Thank goodness, I've got Margaret there to tell me what's happening . . ."

So it was Margaret! He was still pacing up and down his study wondering why so admirable a woman should suddenly have turned viper, when the maid knocked at the door to say that Sergeant Chiswick and a policeman wanted to see him.

II

It was not, indeed, until after Dr. Trump had paid over thirty-one-and-sixpence in cash for a new helmet, and had written out a cheque for two guineas for the Police Orphanage, that Dr. Trump was able to reconsider his own position.

And clearly it was the worst possible. Dame Eleanor had been short with him. And more than short: rude. She had practically said in so many words that he had lost her confidence.

Moreover, the internal situation was developing most awkwardly. Things were being whispered in the kitchens and repeated in the laundry. With ugly rumblings as well. Miss Phrynne reported as much. There were, she said, signs of open friction. "A distinct nastiness in the tone of some of their remarks," was how she put it; "even downright unpleasantness in Latymer."

Altogether, it was as Dr. Trump realised, likely to prove the supreme test of his own personality. To quell rebellion —that was his next task. And he was not going to flinch from it. The hand that ruled the Archbishop Bodkin Hospital would be one of iron; firm, cold, inflexible. But supposing other people were cold and inflexible, too? Dame Eleanor, it seemed, was distinctly taking Margaret's part in the matter. He did not want to face an entire institution organised against him. That would be dreadful. It would provide such opportunities for trouble-makers like Mr. Prevarius.

And then the brilliant idea came to him. He would forgive Margaret, too. And not merely forgive her—which would be construed as weakness. He would openly proclaim her forgiveness from the pulpit on Sunday. The effect, he was confident, would be terrific.

And so it was. Taken all in all, it was probably the best sermon that he had ever delivered. "Dare to be a Daniel" was the main theme, with bits on the side about the red badge of courage and inner voices speaking clearly. Most of the congregation—particularly the lower grades—could not make head or tail of it. But there was one passage which everybody understood. And that was when Dr. Trump referred to Margaret by name: "One of our number, our dear Sister Margaret," he said, "misguided and misled by her emotions as she may have been, has nevertheless shown herself ready to risk everything when she thinks that justice is at stake. That is truly Christian, truly British, and truly in accordance with the great traditions of this Hospital. It is not therefore a matter of forgiving our dear sister for a trifling breach of the rules, but of thanking her. She is our example and we are proud to have her with us. To one of our number, a little one, Margaret has shown herself all that a mother could possibly have been. . . ."

It was at this point that the growing and involuntary murmur of applause was shattered by a sudden loud and inexplicable roar from the Chapel organ.

Mr. Prevarius apologised afterwards for the fact that it was his elbow that had caused it. He had, he said, been listening so intently with his chin supported by his hand that he entirely failed to notice that the bottom ledge of the music rack on which his elbow was resting was simply not strong enough to bear his weight.

"Held in enthralment," was how he described his state. "Quite, quite bewitched by your eloquence, dear Doctor."

CHAPTER XLIII

I

MR. PREVARIUS'S dream-girl had replied at last. And as soon as Mr. Prevarius saw the mauve envelope with the silver deckle-edges and the name Captain Algernon FitzWinter on the front, his heart turned over.

And now that he looked closely he could see that the hand-writing itself was every bit as intriguing as the envelope. For a start, the ink was heliotrope. And heliotrope on mauve gives just that note of elegance and easy grace that might be expected from a genteel young lady of artistic tastes.

Then the handwriting itself. It was rather large and back-ward sloping with very large twiddly bits to the under-the-line strokes. Mr. Prevarius had read enough scientific graphology to know what that meant—a dreamy nature, smothered impulses, deep and as-yet-unattainable desires. Judged solely in terms of handwriting, his unknown correspondent was practically an open petrol tank waiting for her Fairy Prince to strike a match.

Because of the exquisiteness of the moment, the sudden relief after the suspense of wondering whether she was going to reply at all, Mr. Prevarius did not open the letter immediately. Paying his threepenny collection fee and buying a ninepenny cigar with the change, he passed up Charlotte Street in search of a quiet public house. And then, when he had found what he wanted and had lit his cigar and then taken the first sip of the brandy-and-soda that he had just ordered—then, and only then, did he open the letter and begin to read.

And the shock of what he saw made him very nearly upset glass, table and everything. "*Dear Fairy Prince,*" the letter started. Fairy Prince! They were the very words that had occurred to him while he was still standing in the doorway of the newsagent's. It showed an affinity of taste beyond all imagining. And from the way it went on, he could see that with Desirée he had simply been banging his head up against a brick wall.

"*I was thrilled by your wonderful letter,*" the letter ran. "*You cannot imagine how I dreaded opening something from a man whom I had never seen. But I could tell at once from the handwriting that you were someone good whom I could trust.*" How extraordinary, Mr. Prevarius reflected. That was my *disguised* handwriting: in the ordinary way, it's quite different. "*But it will still be an ordeal meeting you for the first time. Will you forgive me if I am frightened. Remember, it is my life you are playing with— if you are playing. If I were older perhaps I would not mind so much. But you must know how defenceless I feel. So please, even if you don't like me, be kind and gentle*

306

when we meet or I shall run away. Would 3.30 on Sunday next, the 27th, Cannon Street Waiting Room (First Class) be convenient. You will know me at once because I never wear anything but lilies of the valley."

Never wear anything but lilies of the valley! No, no, of course, she couldn't mean that. But already his eyes had strayed to the last line. "*Your Beggar Girl*," was what he read.

Sunday! Mr. Prevarius should have remembered that it was the very hardest day of all on which to get away from the Archbishop Bodkin Hospital. By rights he should have been accompanying the entire choir—boys on one side, girls on the other—in chant and sacred song at the precise moment when he was to keep his romantic assignation in the First Class waiting-room.

And, in the end, it was nothing less than a forged telegram —Mr. Prevarius carefully kept his thumb over the office of origin when showing it to Dr. Trump—reading CATHEDRAL ORGANIST GRAVELY INDISPOSED CAN WE RELY ON YOU FOR AFTERNOON MISSION SERVICE AND FULL CHORAL EVENSONG BEST REGARDS Signed EXETER that settled the matter. But Dr. Trump had a great respect for bishops. He was indeed flattered rather than resentful that it should be *his* organist who was sent for all the way from the West Country, and he excused Mr. Prevarius immediately.

Directly after breakfast, therefore, Mr. Prevarius was already on his way out through the front gates on his way round to Deirdre Gardens to get changed into his courting clothes. He had given some thought to the costume. Had, indeed, spent whole singing periods with the class all round him yelling their heads off, pondering over what a retired Indian Army officer would wear in this climate.

Finally after a visit to a gentleman's outfitters at the back of Covent Garden, he had chosen a blue double-breasted blazer with plain brass buttons, rather lightish flannel trousers and a pair of brown and white half brogues.

It was only at the last moment that he remembered the tie. And going back he had picked out something in green and magenta stripes with a black adder's-back zig-zag running across it at intervals. It was, the assistant said, the withdrawn version of a Sydney rowing academy's club colours. But Mr. Prevarius doubted whether the love-maiden would spot anything wrong with it. And, even if she did, Mr. Prevarius supposed that there could be queer coincidences in club ties as in other things.

Dressing in Deirdre Gardens was easy. Within twenty minutes he had changed completely. And with a quick word of explanation to the Miss Lewises that he was off to Oxford for an old students' collegiate garden party, he was on his way. It was still early: there was a good two hours before the appointment. And he decided to take a bite of lunch on the way.

But his lunch came as an entire disappointment to him. His nerves were too much on edge for him to be able to eat anything. Drink, yes. Food, definitely no. By 2.15 he was out on the pavement again having drunk two Martinis, a large Pimm's, and a brandy, with only half a roll, a sardine and one side of a Sole Meunière to absorb the lot of it.

It was at that moment that he remembered his buttonhole. A red rose he had said. It was to be the symbol by which she would know him. And, as he made his way towards Piccadilly Circus, he kept repeating to himself:

The red rose stands for passion and the white rose stands for love
Oh the red rose is a falcon and the white rose is a dove.

But as soon as he had passed down Great Windmill Street into Shaftesbury Avenue he realised that something was wrong. There were three separate flower-sellers, and he could have had his choice of scarlet roses, pink roses, white roses, even saffron yellow tea-roses. But there was not a dark red rose among the lot of them. Evidently, the passionate had been out doing their shopping early.

He ran one dark rose to earth in the end on the steps of the National Gallery. And the old lady who was in charge of it let him have it for ninepence. It was not much of a bloom, rather blackened at the edges of the petals, and with a pin thrust through its heart to prevent complete collapse, but he had passed the stage of being fussy. It was recognisably a dark red rose, and it would have to do.

It was two forty-five already, and Mr. Prevarius was in a fever of anxiety lest he should be late.

"Cannon Street, three o'clock," he said to the taxi-driver. "I'll make it five shillings if you get me there."

Not that it was difficult. There was no traffic in the City on Sundays, and Cannon Street was nearer to Charing Cross than he had realised. There was six minutes to spare when he arrived and, in the circumstances, it seemed silly to pay five shillings for a one-and-threepenny trip. He compromised in the end on half a crown and entered the station so quickly that the taxi-driver's abuse was wasted on the station-yard. Indeed, the single word "bandit" was all that Mr. Prevarius could catch.

Once inside the main hall, Mr. Prevarius carefully slackened his pace. The moment, the supreme moment, had come: he might even be under observation already. He must appear dignified, soldierly, even nonchalant. The very last thing that he wanted was to be seen bounding in like some hot Pan bursting from the bushes.

But, as it turned out, it was quite all right. He had the First Class waiting-room entirely to himself. Sitting down in the far corner, he removed his hat—a new white Panama with the hatband also in the distinctive colours of the Sydney rowing club—placed it on the knob of his ebony cane with his yellow gloves in the dent down the middle—pulled up his lavender silk socks—and waited.

By three o'clock, he was still waiting. And at five past, and ten past, and quarter past. He was by now so nervous, so anguished by the suspense, that he inadvertently pulled one of the gilt buttons clean off the blazer simply through fiddling with it.

"I've been had," he told himself. "She isn't coming. It was a put-up job. A hoax. There may even be blackmail in it . . ."

And then through the plate-glass panel of the door, just below the frosting and above a poster of brilliantly sun-drenched Cliftonville he caught a narrow glimpse of a female bosom, supporting an out-size bunch of lilies of the valley. At the sight, all self-control went from him and he sprang up.

Then the door opened, and there stood Desirée confronting him.

CHAPTER XLIV

I

Dr. Trump was pacing up and down his study.

The sermon, the truly magnanimous sermon, had tided things over for the time being—and it had been gratifying having Margaret with tears in her eyes thank him for allowing her to remain—but Dr. Trump was not deceived. All was not right yet. Something else, something dramatic and momentous, was needed to wipe away all memory of the Sweetie incident. That was why Dr. Trump was unusually reserved and inaccessible. He was thinking. And out of those profound, intense imaginings emerged—the Pageant.

It was still only faint and shadowy. A spectral affair of children in gay costumes dancing on the lawn, and perhaps a Masque with words specially written by someone—himself possibly—performed in the courtyard up against the cloisters. And a hidden choir, singing from behind the bushes. And a bright marquee, with a buffet and tea-urn inside. And flags and bunting. And photographers. His mind inflated and grew bouyant at the prospect ; it soared.

And instead of being dismayed at the thought of all the detail, Dr. Trump was eager ; positively on tiptoe to begin. Not that there was any real hurry. The three-hundredth anniversary, the tri-centenary of Archbishop Bodkin's birth was still fifteen months away. But what a birthday Dr. Trump was planning for him.

And in the meantime, there was so much else to do. The laundry van, for instance. The present one had been bought in 1912, and it was horse-drawn. From the moment of Dr. Trump's first glimpse he had disliked it. There was something so antiquated, so decrepit about the thing. And the horse looked older than the van. It could barely totter to the top of St. Mark's Avenue. What Dr. Trump had set his heart on was a motor van. Something that, going through the streets of Putney, would remind the inhabitants that things were stirring inside the Hospital.

And there was opposition—violent in Dame Eleanor's case —when Dr. Trump chose daffodil yellow for the colour scheme. But there it was ; and no one, not even Dame

Eleanor, was prepared to sanction a further twenty-two pounds for repainting. So daffodil yellow it remained, a 23 h.p. tribute to Dr. Trump's vision and persistence, with his own name neatly lettered on the side as Warden of the Hospital, and, in law, the owner of the vehicle.

Then there was the Founder's Tower to be considered. The Founder's Tower, in fact, had been a reproach to Dr. Trump ever since he had been there. It was now nearly seven years since he had promised himself that he would re-open it. And, of course, in the meantime the structure hadn't been improving. Two hundred and twenty pounds was what the builders now wanted in order to put the upper balcony into proper repair, and it had required all Dr. Trump's eloquence to get the Board even to consider it. Miss Bodkin, in particular, had been difficult because right through the discussion she had thought that it was another tower alongside the old one that Dr. Trump was proposing to build, and she could not see why. But all that was over now, and at practically any moment the scaffolding would begin going up.

II

Apart from the laundry van and the Tower, there was only one other notable event during the course of the whole year. And that was Canon Mallow's illness. Considering that it all took place more than a hundred miles away—Canon Mallow was still living at Seaview on the Isle of Wight—it caused an extraordinary commotion.

It was all Canon Mallow's fault, too: that much was agreed on both sides. A walk along the front without over-coat or muffler, on a day when sensible people were wrapped up against the local *brise* that came round the corner by Bembridge—and there Canon Mallow was, flat on his back with pneumonia and the local doctor talking grimly about adequate nursing in readiness for the impending crisis.

It was the adequate nursing that did it. The landlady said flatly that it was something entirely beyond her own powers, and that it would be impossible to house a trained nurse as well as Canon Mallow in Balaclava. Not that this was entirely true. The season had not yet started—it was only March remember—and the first floor front was entirely empty. No, it was not impossible; but undesirable. For among the delicately adjusted values that determine the fortunes of seaside boarding-houses there is nothing, absolutely nothing, that sends things crashing faster than a death on the premises.

So Canon Mallow, bundled up in a large cocoon of blankets, left Balaclava, and travelled by ambulance as far as the Creevedale Nursing Home at Ryde. By the time he arrived he was ill, very ill. The doctor prescribed sleeping tablets. But Canon Mallow refused to take them until he had written a letter. And then, when he found that he was too weak to write himself, he allowed one of the nurses to write it for him. The nurse who had expected something rather more dramatic—an appeal, for example, from an only living relative to come at once to his bedside immediately, was openly disappointed.

For what Canon Mallow dictated was as follows:

" Dear Dr. Trump. In case you should need me suddenly"—the idea that the Hospital might find that it could not get along without him was something that was constantly in his mind—*" I am dropping you this line to say that because of a congestion in my chest I am moving into the above nursing home. The doctor thinks that I shall be here for about a month. After that, I shall go to a convalescent home somewhere. I hope that Mrs. Trump and yourself are both well. Please give my regards to the staff and ask them to remember me to any of the children that still know me. Particularly Sweetie and Ginger. With kind regards, Yours sincerely, Edward Mallow."*

He was able to manage the signature himself. And then satisfied, as though it were something really important that he had achieved, he took his sleeping tablets and dozed off.

Dr. Trump was annoyed rather than gratified by receiving the letter. Its extreme unnecessariness displeased him. How, in any circumstances, could the Bodkin Hospital possibly require Canon Mallow suddenly? And the reference to Sweetie and Ginger. It coupled their names together in a way that he disapproved of most strongly: he would certainly not pass that bit on.

It was Miss Phrynne who carefully read all letters before filing them, who passed the news of Canon Mallow's illness round the Hospital. And the effect was remarkable. Everyone—that is the older ones, the pre-Trump era appointments —promptly wrote to him. And Mr. Dawlish, dirty, unsentimental Mr. Dawlish, decided to start a small subscription list, a mere bob apiece affair, so that the staff could send a small token—a basket of fruit, or a book or two for when he felt like reading again.

In the end, one pound sixteen was collected, and Mr. Prevarius made the diplomatic error of asking Dr. Trump if he would like to subscribe. *Like* to? The answer to that was obviously no. But how could he refuse? It would look mean; grudging; even possibly un-Christian. So reluctantly Dr. Trump forked out his bob along with the rest of them.

And then something else occurred that annoyed him. It was a phone call from Dame Eleanor asking if it were true that Canon Mallow was ill, and if Dr. Trump was satisfied that everything possible was being done to look after him properly. As though Dame Eleanor of all people did not know how deeply occupied he was. As though she imagined that whenever elderly clergymen on the Isle of Wight caught a chill he could go chasing off to see that the sheets were aired and the stopper had been properly screwed down into the hot-water bottle. He replied briefly and coldly saying that he was entirely satisfied. If anything untoward occurred he would, he added, get in touch with Dame Eleanor immediately.

Then, on the very day when Mr. Dawlish was wasting Dr. Trump's time showing him what had been bought with the money—a folding bedside-table with an adjustable flap—Miss Phrynne showed herself at her most tactless. She had written to Mrs. Gurnett, she said, and Mrs. Gurnett was proposing to go down to the Isle of Wight to see for herself.

Dr. Trump could hardly believe his ears. The waste of time. The money squandered on the fare. The busy-body nature of the whole expedition. For some reason, the whole incident rankled deeply. He realised now that he resented Canon Mallow.

Going over to the window, he stood there drumming with his fingers on the glass, and observed that one of the "keep off the grass" notices was crooked.

Down below, Mr. Dawlish was crossing over from Latymer to the boys' playground. In the shelter of the buttress he stood long enough to light his pipe. When at last he had got it going properly, and an expression of depraved animal

313

satisfaction had come over his face, as he sucked the smoke inwards, Dr. Trump saw him toss the used match-stick idly over his shoulder.

Immediately Dr. Trump shot back the catch of the window. " Mr. Dawlish," he called. " Mr. Dawlish. You'll find you've dropped something. *There,* man, *there!* Just behind your foot."

The abduction of Canon Mallow—for that was what it amounted to—was carried out swiftly and efficiently.

Less than twenty-four hours after Mrs. Gurnett had arrived in Ryde, Canon Mallow, wrapped up like a mummy in thick fleecy blankets was being transported northwards at Heaven knows what expense in a vast private ambulance.

Not that the removal had been easy. Or rather, not that it would have been easy for anyone other than Mrs. Gurnett. In the ordinary way, matrons of nursing homes do not surrender their patients. The whole idea of surrender is foreign to them. For matrons are aloof and unassailable. Even the night-sister is respectful to them. Matrons are rarely contradicted, never challenged. But that, it must be remembered, is only because matrons are not frequently brought face to face with other matrons.

Aud though at first Miss Tremlett of the Creevedale Nursing Home was confident, even contemptuous, when she heard that the afternoon visitor to No. 3 had a complaint to make, she very soon came to realise that this was no casual encounter.

A foxy, red-haired woman with two bright spots of colour on her cheek bones, Miss Tremlett made her way quickly and purposefully—her low rubber-heeled shoes squeaking on the polished oilcloth—towards the unexpected trouble centre.

That it was not Canon Mallow himself who had complained, she was certain. Male patients were never like that. Even strong men in the prime of life became extravagantly, idiotically grateful for the most trifling attentions—for a fresh bed-warmer, or an aspirin tablet, or even for a drink of water. It was women who were the mischief makers ; and women visitors were worst of all. Miss Tremlett hated them.

At the thought of the indignity of a complaint, the spots of colour in her cheek bones began burning like twin dabs of rouge. And by the time she opened the door, the corners of her mouth were drawn down, and the phrase "Don't you think that perhaps we're upsetting our patient?" was all ready on her lips.

Then as she stepped inside her eyes met Mrs. Gurnett's. She stopped short. She wavered. For the female figure who faced her was that of another woman-hater, someone not in the least likely to be impressed by mere technique. And there was a massiveness about her that made Miss Tremlett feel lightweight and chittish. As Miss Tremlett looked she realised that the visitor had been in no need to set her mouth for this interview. The visitor's mouth had been tucked grimly down at the corners for years.

But this was not the worst. For before Miss Tremlett could speak, the visitor had addressed her.

"Hadn't we better close the door?" she asked, in a phrase as polished as Miss Tremlett's. "We don't want draughts as well as pneumonia, do we?"

And with the use of the plural, that adroit, commanding "we," Miss Tremlett recognised that this was no amateur bout. It was professional up against professional. And the weight was in favour of the challenger. . . .

The preliminary skirmishes took place at the bedside. The real stuff, the clinches and the body blows, went on in the privacy of Miss Tremlett's private room. And Mrs. Gurnett did not spare her. Air-bubbles in the water-carafe on the side table, the used teacup not removed from the sick room; fluff behind the dressing-table; the position of the bed; the uncovered basket of fruit; the hole in the pillow-case—Mrs. Gurnett left nothing unmentioned. And when, beaten down and sagging, Miss Tremlett referred to her bill for professional services already rendered, Mrs. Gurnett retaliated with talk about the Town Hall and the County Medical Officer.

In all, the match lasted for forty-five minutes—and less than two hours afterwards, Canon Mallow was being carried downstairs to the waiting ambulance.

It was a long journey from Ryde to Bedford, and Canon Mallow slept most of the way. Because of his high temperature—he was still somewhere away up above the hundred—he could not think very clearly. He was, indeed, rather confused by the whole occurrence. Creevedale had seemed very

315

nice to him, even though they had been a bit slow whenever he had rung the bell for anything.

But he did not question that Mrs. Gurnett was right. In his experience, she had always been right about everything. And it was so nice of her to take the trouble. With all those children on her hands—but, no; he was forgetting. She wasn't at Bodkin any longer. She was . . . What was it she was doing? He couldn't remember. But whatever it was, he was still sure that she was right.

And Mrs. Gurnett was sure, too. Through the whole long journey she sat on the inadequate canvas-backed chair that was provided for the attendant and gloated. Whenever Canon Mallow stirred, she covered him up again. And, each time she gave the bedclothes a little pat as well. When the ambulance-driver asked her thoughtfully if she would like him to break the journey for her own convenience, she ordered him sternly to drive straight on.

It was late—really late: getting on for midnight when they reached Bedford and drew up before the Lamorna Nursing Establishment in Bunyan Gardens. But everything was exactly as Mrs. Gurnett had directed. The light over the porch was burning and the night-sister opened the front door as the ambulance came to rest. No. 1—the big room with the bow windows—had the gas-fire on in readiness and the bed was positively padded with hot-water bottles. Fresh water stood in the carafe on the side-table. And there was a large screen at the foot of the bed so that the window could be wide open without so much as the first flicker of a draught.

Mrs. Gurnett insisted on doing most of the settling-in herself. And the night-sister noticed that she had never seen this large, rather grim-looking woman so gentle and solicitous. When, after the tucking up, the time came to switch off the light, leaving only the night-light burning, Mrs. Gurnett stood there for a moment smiling down on him.

Then, tired as she was, she said something that surprised the night-sister.

"If he needs anything, send for me," were the words she uttered.

And she meant them. She was, in fact, conscious of one thing and one thing only. She had got back under her own roof the nicest gentleman she had ever known.

CHAPTER XLV

I

THE EVENT that shook Dr. Trump's life was sudden and unanticipated. It came with a fierce and dreadful emphasis that left him stunned, resentful and rebellious. There seemed something so entirely *unnecessary* in this disturbance of the pattern that he had designed for himself.

There was not even any accounting for it. The weather was warmer, considerably warmer, than it had been when Canon Mallow had caught his careless, vexing chill. And, in comparison with Canon Mallow who was moving appreciably towards the shadows, Bishop Warple was in the very prime, the mere mid-afternoon of life. A suffragan Bishop to-day— who knows what to-morrow might have held in store?

And now—nothing. A yawning, horrid blank simply because the clay at Highgate Cemetery had been damp after another interment, and Bishop Warple had stood about on it for too long burying a lay preacher.

What was so maddening, too, so absolutely infuriating, was that the deceased had been someone of practically no importance; merely one more zealous church worker among so many. And to think that the course of Dr. Trump's life, the very course of ecclesiastical history, possibly, should have had to be re-written because of him. It simply did not make sense.

Not that anyone detected at the time that Bishop Warple had done anything other than got his feet wet. Even Bishop Warple himself did not suspect it. He travelled back to Putney, his mind full of plans—for a revised Church hymnal for the blind; for a Mission drive that would somehow or other help to utilise the services of a young coloured deacon who had been foisted on to him; for the establishment of a diocesan re-building fund; for everything, in fact, that overloads the thinking of a busy bishop.

On the following morning, he was snuffly, but continued with his duties. The day after that he retired to bed. And forty-eight hours later—a mere four days after the first funeral—Dr. Trump was sitting again in the chintzy drawing-room where Felicity had proposed to him. Only this time the curtains were drawn, and it was not Felicity but a solicitor who was sitting there beside him.

The intervening moments—that brief, disastrous gap between funeral and funeral—had by now become fused within Dr. Trump's mind into one dark and desolating whole. As for the events themselves, they had been so swift and terrible that, in retrospect, he recalled only certain of them; mere isolated signposts all pointing ominously towards the grave.

For even on Friday it had still seemed nothing, this ailment of the Bishop's; a sort of summer cold with general lassitude and marked irritability. Dr. Trump had, indeed, spent from 7.30 p.m. until 10 on Friday evening alone with the Bishop. And so lightly had he regarded the whole matter that he had taken the invalid nothing—not even a grape or a bunch of flowers.

And apart from his querulousness, Bishop Warple had seemed lively enough. He had even suggested a game of chess. As it happened it had proved a bad, desultory kind of game in which both of them lost their queens through sheer carelessness. But at least the *intention* of chess had been there; Dr. Trump clung to that. And afterwards they had drunk cocoa ; chatted mostly on secular subjects—as Dr. Trump could not subsequently help remembering, the Bishop's worldliness had become magnified rather than diminished in the face of impending dissolution ; and tried to do *The Times* crossword. Altogether it had been a pleasant, rather lazy sort of evening.

At 10 o'clock, when Dr. Trump announced that he must be going, he left the Bishop sitting comfortably in his chair. He was just going to glance through this week's *Popular Cycling,* he said, and then toddle off to bed. There was nothing in the least surprising about his choice of reading: indeed, it was reassuringly normal. A keen amateur cyclist in his undergraduate days, Bishop Warple had maintained a lively interest in the subject. He read himself to sleep every Friday, the day on which *Popular Cycling* appeared, with details of patented spring handlebars and built-in hub dynamos and other refinements that had come in since his time.

It was 10 o'clock when Dr. Trump left him. And at three in the morning—a mere five hours later—the phone rang and Dr. Trump found an hysterical Mrs. Warple on the other end of it.

A bedroom telephone extension was something that, on principle, Dr. Trump did not allow himself. But to-night, as Dr. Trump, rubbing the sleep out of his eyes, found himself stumbling down the stairs barefoot—in his agitation he had accidentally kicked his bedroom slippers too far under the bed to be able to recover them—he envied people who merely had to thrust an arm out of the warm bedclothes. And the chill of the ornamental tiling in the hall was so intense that he could not concentrate properly.

"Yes . . . yes," he said, shifting from one icy foot on to the other. "What is it? Dr. Trump here. Who wants him?"

He paused while the telephone crackled back at him.

"Mrs. Warple!" he said, in astonishment. "You . . . mother dear!"

The voice at the other end was so agitated and confused that he could not follow it.

"The Bishop . . . yes . . . yes," he said at last. "You say he's thinking. At this time of night! But surely he must be thinking *something*. What is it exactly that he's thinking about?"

Dr. Trump removed the receiver six inches from his ear because Mrs. Warple was speaking no longer: she was screaming at him. And then the awful truth came to him: the word was "sinking." And his spine went as cold as his feet as he realised the significance of it.

Then promptly his manliness, his sense of authority, asserted itself.

"I'll be round immediately," he said. "Stay where you are. Fetch a doctor. Don't move. Keep calm. I'm just leaving."

And with the word "sinking" tattooed upon his mind, Dr. Trump ran back upstairs to tell Felicity.

It was a good fifteen minutes' walk and the roads were empty of human beings. But not of cats. They stood scowling in gateways and skulking about from amid the shadows. After one peculiarly large tabby had appeared suddenly beneath their feet from nowhere pursued by a lean hunting tom, Dr. Trump remarked upon it.

"How little," he remarked, "is one aware of the nocturnal existence of the ordinary domestic cat . . ."

But he got no farther.

"For goodness' sake don't start talking about cats," Felicity interrupted him. "Just hurry."

319

And after that, Dr. Trump, snubbed and offended, walked in silence by her side through the lonely streets.

The doctor had already arrived by the time they got there. And Dr. Trump took a liking to him at first sight. He seemed so exactly right: dignified, experienced, not easily rattled, respectful. Everything that he said was quiet and reassuring. There certainly was inflammation, he admitted: but only the merest trace of it—a spot the size of a pin's head. And with care and a little nursing even the pin's head would vanish and Bishop Warple would soon be back again, marrying, confirming, organising.

It was an hour or so before dawn when Dr. Trump shook the doctor warmly by the hand. And by sunset he realised that he had made one of his rare misreadings of human character. For the man was nothing less than an impostor, and Dr. Trump was already considering reporting him to the General Medical Council. If a common suburban doctor imagined that he could afford to let Dr. Trump's father-in-law slip through his fingers like that he was going to be shown his mistake.

But already it was too late. All that was eternal in Bishop Warple had departed from them. He lay there motionless upon his bed, not even having stirred from his last sleep. His day's correspondence and his Bible were beside him and, over on the dressing-table stood the copy of *Popular Cycling* with the article on spring-forks pathetically turned down for future reference.

As Dr. Trump stood there, gazing down on him, he was disappointed in himself. Even shocked. Irresistibly his thoughts rushed pell-mell into the black future. With Bishop Warple gone, there would be no more of those little Lambeth luncheon parties. Personal introductions count for so much with busy people like prelates, and Bishop Warple had been wonderfully good at pushing his own son-in-law. And now . . .

But how truly disgraceful! To be guilty of thoughts like that when he should have been at prayer. It was downright appalling.

Going down on his knees, Dr. Trump asked for forgiveness. He was sincere, contrite, fervent. But his prayers were still all about himself.

"Oh, Lord, drive all vain ambitions from me," he began in a torrent rush of emotion. "Chasten my mind and subdue it. Cleanse me of self-interest and purge me of unworthy thoughts. Make me meek. Make me humble . . ."

He felt better when he got up again, and decided to spend the rest of the evening comforting Mrs. Warple and Felicity.

I I

As for the funeral itself, it was everything that Dr. Trump could have wished; and he felt that Mrs. Warple should have been pleased, too.

A couple of bishops—only one of them a suffragan, like the deceased—a well-known dean and quite a cluster of minor canons were among the mourners, and the sheer quantity of flowers was enough to make the verger comment. Dr. Trump's own tribute—white lilac with a centrepiece of daffodils and grape hyacinth—looked quite dwarfed alongside the mammoth structures of roses, gladioli, and Arum lilies that had kept arriving from the florists during those first dreadful days of loss and sadness.

By the time the chief mourners, consisting of Mrs. Warple, Felicity and himself, had regained the first carriage Dr. Trump allowed himself for the moment to relax. A thoroughly satisfactory funeral, he kept reflecting; satisfactory in every way. It was merely a pity that he had not for once been able to give Dame Eleanor a lift in a car noticeably more magnificent than her own. Little things like that—as courtesies he liked to think of them—are always remembered; and, in the long run pay dividends.

Even so, there was much for which to be thankful. Mrs. Warple's behaviour, for example. Throughout the whole ordeal it had been exemplary. Her few tears had been not only natural, they had been seemly. Also, she looked distinctly better in black; quieter and more subdued.

Not so her daughter. Felicity in black, Dr. Trump had decided gloomily, looked simply terrible. Like a small, weird nun. And the very moment it was proper, he proposed to whisk her back again into tweeds and jumpers. But he was too experienced a husband to say anything about it at a moment like the present. Instead, he murmured something to the effect that though Mrs. Warple had lost a husband she must not forget that she had already gained a son. And then, more to fill up the sentence than for any other reason, he added: "You will always be at home with us."

A moment later Dr. Trump's hand was clasped violently by Felicity's. It was a small, rather bony hand. And the strength in it was astonishing. It was like finding oneself snatched up by an eagle. Dr. Trump winced. The next moment, however, the thought of mere physical pain meant nothing to him. For Felicity had taken his words at their face value.

"That's it! Stay with us always, Mother dearest," she said eagerly. "You can have Samuel's study, and he can have the little room upstairs. We'll send round for the rest of your things in the morning."

It was because of that—because at one stroke he had got his mother-in-law and lost his study—that Dr. Trump did less, considerably less, than justice to himself at the funeral reception. He was vacant and staring, like a man stunned. He spoke to no one, not even the bishops. And his behaviour did not pass unnoticed.

"I'm afraid poor Trump's taking it badly," the dean remarked to one of the canons as they were on their way back together. "I didn't know the fellow had so much feeling in him."

CHAPTER XLVI

I

SWEETIE WAS eleven now. A ripe age: the age for serious decisions, as Dr. Trump had just reminded her.

She was standing on one side of his desk on the small square of red carpet, and he was seated on the other. And because she was so short, she was at a disadvantage. Whenever Dr. Trump leaned back he disappeared from sight altogether, cut off from her by the top of the little rack in which he kept his note-paper and his "Urgent" labels.

But every time he bent forward he was near, frighteningly near. And his eyes were too close together: it was like a folded-up pair of scissors staring at her. He was ugly, Sweetie decided. So ugly, in fact, that she was sorry for him. Very sorry. It must be dreadful, she thought, having to go about looking like that.

And dreadful, too, being so cross always. He didn't look

as though he had once been happy—in all his life. Half his time he was furious about something or other. He was furious at this very moment. Really furious. And all because of things that other people had said about her.

The report lay there on the desk in front of him, propped up against the blotter so that he could glance at it quickly again if he felt his anger beginning to subside. And the bits that he had read out to her didn't seem to be too bad. They were true, too, most of them. And very sensible. Sweetie hadn't realised in fact that other people knew so much about her.

" Arithmetic: poor, does not try," Dr. Trump was reading out aloud for the second time. " English: backward, cannot spell ; History: fair, does not remember dates ; Geography: poor, does not concentrate ; Music: a pretty singing voice " —here Dr. Trump paused: the rest of the line read: " Excellent, altogether a very charming melody maker." It was Mr. Prevarius who reported on singing and Mr. Prevarius's choice of words nauseated Dr. Trump. Then his eyes passed farther down the sheet and he began reading aloud once more. " Scripture: fair, does not seem interested ; Needlework: disappointing, cannot sew buttonholes ; Cookery: poor, careless on the practical side ; Physical training: good, easy posture. Conduct: fair, unintentionally impertinent."

The bit about physical training had slipped out as he was reading but he managed in time to introduce a quick note of contempt into his voice as he uttered it. Then he sat back and folded his hands in front of him.

" Not interested in Scripture," he repeated. " Are you aware what those words imply? You, a pupil of the Archbishop Bodkin Hospital, and you have the impudence not to be interested in the Holy Scriptures!"

" I'm sorry, sir."

" You should be more than sorry," Dr. Trump snapped back at her. " You should be ashamed. And more than ashamed. You should be contrite. Are you contrite?"

Sweetie nodded her head. It was safer than answering, because she did not know what the word meant. But she gave a quick little sniff as she nodded, just so that Dr. Trump would know that she was ready to cry if he wanted her to do so. Once she really started to cry she knew that it would be all over, and she could get back to her class-room again: Dr. Trump never kept any of the girls very long once they were crying.

But he evidently did not mean her to cry yet because he was still repeating bits out of the report. " Backward . . . fair . . . poor . . . fair . . . disappointing . . . poor . . ." he was saying. " Do you realise that in three years' time you will have to earn your living in the world?"

" Yes, sir," Sweetie answered.

There was no conviction in her voice, however, because she did not really know how people did earn their living. It was one of the things that nobody had ever told her. She wasn't tall enough to serve in a shop like some of the girls who had gone out into the world: she wouldn't be able to reach things off the shelves properly. But perhaps she would grow, shoot up suddenly. At least, it was worth hoping.

And then Dr. Trump settled the problem for her.

" All our girls get situations, unless they are bad girls," Dr. Trump told her. " But no one wants to take an idle, careless, clumsy creature. Who do you imagine "—here Dr. Trump flipped the report contemptuously with the back of his fingernails—" would want to take a girl with nothing in her favour except an easy posture and a pretty singing voice?"

Sweetie could not imagine, so she remained silent.

" Answer me," Dr. Trump insisted.

Then she saw what he was driving at, and she was grateful to him. It made everything so simple.

" The man who is going to marry me," she replied.

But from the expression on Dr. Trump's face, Sweetie realised that she must have been mistaken. All that he said was " Pah." So perhaps she was too short even to get married. Already, however, Dr. Trump was speaking again, and that took her mind off things.

" Do you know what I should do if I were to do my duty?" he asked suddenly.

" No, sir," Sweetie answered truthfully.

It was a surprising sort of question, because until he had asked it she had imagined that Dr. Trump always did do his duty.

" I should turn you out on to the streets," he told her. " Turn you out so that you waste no more of the money that is being spent on you."

That startled her. The prospect was both fascinating and alarming. Apart from the Sunday afternoon crocodile and the regular nature walks she had never been outside the Hospital in her life. Not once, since she had come there. And certainly not alone. It seemed a drastic sort of treatment

for not being able to remember dates and sew buttonholes.
What would she do at night-time, for instance? But apparently, it was all a false alarm. For Dr. Trump was addressing
her again.

" I shall not, however, turn you out," he went on. " I shall
ask for you to be kept here. And I shall ask for you to be
observed. From now on someone will be watching you—
always. And at monthly intervals, I shall ask for a report.
If that report . . ."

Dr. Trump had closed his eyes for a moment while he was
speaking: it was a habit of his when he was collecting his
thoughts and arranging them. But when he reopened his eyes
he was amazed to find that Sweetie was no longer attending.
She was peering fixedly out of the window, her face puckered
up with the intensity of her stare.

" Are you listening to me?" he demanded.

"Yes, sir."

"What was I saying?"

"About a report, sir."

" Then why were you looking out of the window?"

" There's a bee, sir."

" A what?"

"A bee, sir. It's got shut in."

" We'll soon see about that."

Dr. Trump got up hurriedly and snatched hold of the
massive brass-knobbed blotter that stood upon his desk.
What made it all so simple was that the bee was now stationary. It was blankly and angrily contemplating the bright
sunny world from which it was cut off by this mysterious
transparent barrier. And Dr. Trump's blotter landed right on
top of it. When the blotter came away there was no bee—
only a bright smear upon the window-pane.

" There," said Dr. Trump triumphantly.

But he could scarcely believe his ears.

"You beast," Sweetie said to him. "I wouldn't have told
you if I'd known."

I I

And Dr. Trump was not by any means satisfied when he
received Sweetie's letter of apology for her rudeness.

" I am sory I was rude," it ran. *" It was bad to call you*

*a beest. I am sory. I must not shout at old people. Shout-
ing at old people is rude. I am sory. I did not know you
hated bees. I should have knowed. I am sory."*

He dropped the sheet of note-paper into the wastepaper
basket. Really it was heartbreaking, simply heartbreaking,
the ignorance and stupidity of the child. He did not hate
bees. On the contrary, he rather liked them. And he was
not old. The phrasing, the handwriting and the spelling of
Sweetie's all depressed him equally. He rose and began
walking up and down the room.

"Really it's maddening," he told himself. "Sweetie and
that boy Ginger are more trouble than the rest of the
Hospital put together. They'll be the end of me, these two."

And though he did not actually utter the words there was
the authentic note of despair, of prophecy almost, about
them.

CHAPTER XLVII

I

MRS. WARPLE was now a permanent resident in the Warden's
lodgings. And, all during those long months of planning and
devising and arranging, when Dr. Trump's mind should have
been fully concentrated upon the Pageant, the presence of
his mother-in-law ominously hung over him, distracting and
destroying. Even at night—sometimes, indeed, especially at
night, when he was wakeful—he was aware of her in a sullen,
uneasy way as though she were a low thundercloud that
threatened at any moment to burst over him.

Not that Mrs. Warple had at first given the slightest cause
for complaint. She had been exemplary. That is, as exemplary as any permanent invalid can be. There were, of
course, the "little cups of tea" as Felicity always referred to
them—though to Dr. Trump's eye they looked exactly the
same size as other cups—that she was constantly taking to her
mother. There were the packets of cigarettes for her nerves.
There was the breast of chicken, the only part of the meat
that Mrs. Warple in her weak condition could tolerate. And,
as Dr. Trump scraped gloomily at a leg, Felicity would

come downstairs happy and radiant, to say that Mrs. Warple could just manage the other side.

Also, there were her library books. Indeed, to keep Mrs. Warple's mind off her own inescapable tragedy, Felicity was for ever going out for fresh reading material. Dr. Trump had already taken out an " On Demand " subscription, and he shuddered every time Felicity passed him on the stairs with new loads, all at 2d. a day extra.

But this was not the worst. For as Dr. Trump noted gloomily, Mrs. Warple was growing stronger every day. She now had what she called her " good spells." And when these were on her she went round the house from room to room, interfering, managing and rearranging things. She had been up three whole days last week.

And because of Mrs. Warple, Dr. Trump spent more time than ever in his makeshift upstairs study. Not that he was unhappy there. On the contrary, the Pageant was already opening in his mind like a flower. And new buds on the parent stem were unfolding every day. He had already thought of a Physical Fitness Display by the Under Fives, a Breeches Buoy Deep Sea Rescue Demonstration on the tennis court by the Senior boys, and First Aid and Folk Dancing Sections for the girls—all in addition to the great central theme of Charity Through the Ages. This, he had decided, was to be treated in the boldest manner with the staff as well as the children participating. He had already marked down Nurse Stedge for Queen Bess, Mr. Dawlish for Robin Hood, Margaret—because of that extraordinarily queenly bearing of hers—for Boadicea, and . . . and yes, of course, himself for St. George.

It was only St. George's horse that worried him. Clearly, the horse was essential to the whole conception. Who had ever heard of St. George on foot? But even if he took riding lessons now, how could he be sure that no one would see him before he became proficient? How could he be certain that no one would guess that he had never ridden before? Not on a horse, that is. There had been a fortnight long ago at Broadstairs when he was quite small and his aunts had tried him on a donkey. But he had not persevered. There was something in the motion once the beast trotted, that had alarmed and terrified him.

But he was a man now, he reminded himself. Childish fears could play no part in his plans any longer. And surely there must be some quiet horses. It wasn't as though he wanted to do circus tricks. All that he was concerned about was that he should be able to ride in through the shrubbery, spear the cardboard dragon that Mr. Dawlish would have to make in the manual workshops—and so, out again—until the triumphal procession at the end when he would, of course, lead the whole company.

Dr. Trump's mind kept returning to the idea. Wouldn't Richmond be the place for learning, he asked himself? It was far enough away for no one to recognise him. And once inside the park there would be plenty of room in case the animal bolted.

I I

The physical restoration of Mrs. Warple and the discovery about Sebastian's chest were practically simultaneous—and, in prospect, almost equaliy alarming.

For a start, Mrs. Warple was almost completely recovered: every day was a good day now. She had not merely taken to coming down for breakfast, but she actually came down singing. Nor were the snatches of song the kind of thing that Dr. Trump liked to hear: only this week the words " Ta-ra-ra-bom-de ay " had reached him clearly from the bathroom landing.

Moreover, she was displaying a highly-developed and peculiarly maddening form of nervous energy. It was obvious—pathetically obvious—that she was trying to make herself useful, to take some of the strain off Felicity as she put it. In the result, Dr. Trump lived in a state of perpetual apprehension. His coffee cup was snatched from him at breakfast almost before he had been given time to put it down; his shaving-brush which he left always in full lather like a creamy white cauliflower was, on Mrs. Warple's instructions, carefully rinsed each morning under the cold tap; and the cushion of his chair which he preferred hard and flat was assiduously thumped and pounded into the consistency of a soufflé. It was like having a loving enemy about the place.

But all this was nothing compared to the news about Sebastian. It had, of course, been known right from the start that the child was delicate. A sudden change in the direction of the wind; the slightest dampness around the feet or legs;

the nursery door left thoughtlessly ajar; or a button come undone amid the several thicknesses of his chill-proof underwear, and Sebastian's snufflings and wheezings would inevitably begin.

In such circumstances, there would within any household have been precautions. A son and heir, especially where he is an only child, is naturally precious, not to say irreplaceable. There could be no argument about that. But when he had once raised the point, asking diffidently, even timidly: "You don't think, do you, dear, that perhaps we might try the other method—the hardening process, you know?" the effect on Felicity had been deplorable. It had roused the she-tiger and the vixen. For she had instantly rounded on him, demanding whether he wanted to lose Sebastian in just the way she had lost her own poor father and for precisely the same reason, too.

And then what made it so deeply humiliating for Dr. Trump was that Felicity's worst fear was suddenly confirmed. Expert, three-guinea opinion from Harley Street agreed in everything. The child's lungs were not yet actually affected: that much was agreed on by general practitioner and specialist alike. But at least there was a weakness. And the air of Putney, though bracing, was not apparently bracing enough. Switzerland was mentioned. There was talk of Montreux, Grenoble, Chamonix.

And, though very much to Dr. Trump's relief it was Broadstairs that finally was chosen, there was an uneasiness within his mind that he was powerless to dispel. For, from the moment when the truth about Sebastian's lungs had been discovered, Dr. Trump had been uncomfortably aware of being ignored, passed over, spurned. Whenever he had tried fleetingly to re-assert himself he had been brushed aside.

Try as he could, he could not longer conceal from himself the fact that, compared with his own son, he himself apparently did not exist. Even one sentence: "Much as I love my son, my place is still beside my husband," or: "But if I go off like this, who is to look after poor Samuel?" would have been sufficient. As it turned out, however, there was nothing. Just silence. Complete and deeply wounding silence.

There had, moreover, been a sudden marked increase in Felicity's affection for her mother. The two of them were always whispering together nowadays. And, on one occasion, it had been even worse. Felicity and her mother had been sitting there together, bunched occupyingly around the fire, when Felicity had turned her head slightly and remarked: " If you want to do anything, don't bother about us."

Spiritually, man is an animal lodged insecurely upon this planet: he is in need of constant cherishment and reassurance. And a terrible feeling of unwantedness passed through Dr. Trump as he heard the words. It seemed as though within the Warden's Lodging it was he and not Mrs. Warple who was the visitor, the object of compassion ; as though, to put it bluntly, he had been out-manœuvred and was in the way.

And now, suddenly, the whisperings were all explained, and the worst—the worst imaginable—had happened. While Felicity and Sebastian were wintering in the fine, preventive air of Broadstairs, Mrs. Warple was to stay in Putney to look after Dr. Trump!

It was all so matter-of-fact, so diabolically well calculated that Dr. Trump found himself sweating from its sheer inescapability. He demurred, he argued, he protested. But it was too late. Everything had been arranged, Felicity said, and there was nothing left to be discussed: he would merely, she added, have to be more considerate about little things because Mother wasn't so young as she had been.

III

Within the week everything had been arranged. It was February at the time and Felicity and Sebastian, accompanied by Dr. Trump, went down in a hired car at odious expense to install themselves in the private hotel that Felicity had selected.

It was the Ragusa that she had chosen. The rooms themselves seemed as comfortable as anything can be in the out-of-season wilderness of a seaside town. Indeed, so far as bead-mats and fancy stencilled runners could make them, they verged upon the lavish. But the position! As Dr. Trump sat muffled in his greatcoat during the return journey, he prayed that Felicity and Dr. Arlett and the specialists—the whole damn' bunch of them, in fact—had not blundered. It seemed to him, however, unthinkable that anyone, let alone a delicate child, should be carted off somewhere to a place where the wind came ripping in off the foreshore like a cascade of iced razor-blades, and a sea-fog like a wet Shetland shawl tucked the town up for the night immediately after tea-time. If he had been compelled to stay there for as much as a single week-end he did not doubt for a moment that it would not be merely his lungs but the very marrow in his bones that would be affected.

It was therefore with a kind of despondent relief to be back again amid the almost balmy air of Putney that he turned the key of his own front door—and was confronted by Mrs. Warple who had been sitting up for him.

CHAPTER XLVIII

IT HAD been one of Margaret's bad days.

An outbreak of summer colic had filled the sick-bay, and Margaret had been on her feet since early morning. She was tired now; very tired. And as she lay in bed, she rubbed one swollen ankle against another and tried to find softness between the ridges of the hard, unyielding mattress.

She ought to be asleep, that was certain. Fast asleep. She needed all the sleep that she could get. Because to-morrow was going to be quite as heavy as to-day. But there was too much on her mind for sleep. It wouldn't come to her. When the one thing that she wanted was to drift off and forget about things, all that she could do was to lie there restless, while the Hospital clock rattled out the hours somewhere just above her head.

It was either three or four now—she could not remember which had struck last. There was, in fact, only one thing that she could remember. And that was a letter that she had to write. Or, rather couldn't write because she didn't know what to say. It was her secret life catching up with her again, something that kept creeping in and intruding just when it looked as though everything was beginning to settle down again. And she hadn't got any more money left. At least, not enough to make any difference. Not enough to keep another human being going.

Because this wasn't blackmail. Or, at least, not blackmail in the ordinary sense. This was a sort of wheedling, insidious, emotional blackmail. The kind of thing where nothing unpleasant could happen even if you didn't pay anything— nothing that is except for another of those anguishing, cry-baby letters, and a hint of prison or suicide.

331

As it was no use trying to sleep, she put the light on again. It shone straight down into her eyes. But that didn't trouble her because she wasn't going to lie there looking up at it. She was going to read. Read what had been written to her. It was within arm's length as she lay there, in her handbag down between the bed and the wall.

The letter was written on that kind of thin, crinkly paper that people use overseas. It was as though it had been dried up in sunlight that had been too hot for it. Either that, or it was the cheapest that could be bought. Both, probably. And the fact that it was written in pencil did not make it any more encouraging. Harder to read that way, and with a suggestion of real poverty.

Holding it down so that the light didn't shine through, Margaret began to read: ". . . *just like my bad luck and when everything seemed to have turned the corner, too. If I'd had the capital and could have hung on a bit longer, I'd be worth something to-day. All the other lots showed a profit—eventually. As it was, I had to sell out for what I could get. And when I'd settled everything I was stony again, quite cleared out in fact. I think I shall go back up North where the competition isn't so fierce. It's really chronic down here, what with the Jews and everything. But before I see anyone I need a decent suit and a pair of shoes. It's no good going after a job looking like a beachcomber. I'd rather be on the land, but beggars can't be choosers and if I'm presentable enough, there's a new place opening down at . . .*"

Margaret did not read any farther. There was another full page asking her not to misjudge him and saying how he hated to seem like a sponger. But she had read all that before in his last letter and the one before and the one before that, too. In every letter, in fact. He never wrote to her unless he wanted something. And even though, somewhere towards the end, he always said that he loved her and that everything would turn out all right, and that he was living for the day when he could send her the money for the fare, it never came to anything. And what was worse she had entirely given up believing him. Given up years ago. She had even become reconciled to the fact that he was a waster—a no-good, a remittance man. But she still loved him, and that was all there was to it.

Not that she was going to send him anything. Not this time. She still had herself to think about. It wasn't the same
332

being at the Hospital as it had been with Dame Eleanor. The money wasn't so much for a start. And she wasn't getting any younger. It was all right slaving away for twelve hours a day at thirty. But what about ten years farther on, or fifteen, or twenty? She'd be fifty by then. And it wouldn't be such a good idea to find herself with nothing in the Post Office Savings Bank at fifty. Not with her other responsibilities, that is. She put the letter back into its envelope and thrust it deep down into the handbag alongside the other letters, all in the same handwriting. Then she lay there, still with the light on, staring up at the ceiling. Right into the glare of the bare bulb this time.

Why was she in this small upper attic, anyway, instead of in the big comfortable bedroom at The Cedars? Because of Sweetie. Sweetie wasn't like the other little girls. Other little girls could take care of themselves. But Sweetie couldn't. She was always getting herself into trouble. There was some trouble at the present moment about a bee and a letter. If she went on like that she would be in bad trouble one day. Really bad trouble. That was why someone who cared for her had to stand by and see that everything went right.

But how long could that go on? Sweetie was nearly twelve already. She had been born . . . well, say about ten days or a fortnight before she had been delivered on the Archbishop Bodkin doorstep. And she was twelve now: in two years the Hospital would have finished with her. She would be out in service somewhere. On her own then. Completely and absolutely on her own at last. Margaret couldn't go trailing all over London after her. Of course, she would try to see her, if the child wanted it. And if she could find out from Miss Phrynne where Sweetie had been sent she could keep an eye on her without Sweetie knowing anything about it. But it wouldn't last. Sweetie would change her situation. And her half day mightn't be the same as the Hospital's. Or she might take a place outside London. Somewhere right away in the country too far for Margaret to get to. After all, Sweetie had her own life ahead of her.

And when Sweetie left, Margaret realised that her real reason for being at the Bodkin Hospital would have been taken away from her. She liked to think that she cared for all children in the way she cared for Sweetie. But it simply wasn't true. When Sweetie left, she was going to leave too. She was going to earn all she could to buy that steamer

333

ticket. If her passage money didn't come from the other end, she was going to find it at this one. All on her own account, she was going to join the waster.

As much to rest her eyes as anything else, she thrust out her hand to put the light out again. And, as she did so, she found that the skylight pane of glass was shining, and that it was already morning.

CHAPTER XLIX

I

MARGARET need not, however, have bothered about the steamer ticket. At least, not yet, when if she'd had it all ready in her bag, she could not have used it. Because Sweetie suddenly showed how much she needed her.

In a sense, it was all Ginger's fault. He was missing. Been out all night—two nights, in fact. And, when Sweetie heard, she grew quite hysterical about it. It was this side of Sweetie's nature that alarmed Margaret: it revealed everything that she had feared for in the child. And it reminded her that no matter what happened, her place was beside Sweetie until she had grown out of that kind of thing.

In comparison with the fuss that Sweetie made, there had been little or no commotion about Ginger's departure. He had been on so many of these outings by now that routine had supplanted melodrama. He merely rolled his day clothes into a bundle, laid it carefully on the centre of the bed, pulled the sheet and blanket up round it and tucked in the pillow—not that Mr. Dawlish would have noticed anything amiss if Ginger had hung a placard " BACK IN HALF AN HOUR " on the end of his bedstead.

Apart from the counterfeit beneath the bedclothes, there was the little matter of the money. Ginger had drawn the whole of his savings for this expedition—eightpence, all in coppers. And not being accustomed to having so much loose cash about him he took extraordinary precautions. There was twopence in each trouser pocket and fourpence in a belt around his middle. What was more, the twopences were wrapped inside strips of old shirt because the holes in his trouser pockets were so large that the pennies by themselves would just have slipped through like quicksilver.

The good-byes were formal and deliberately casual.

" S'long, Ginger," was all that Spud said.

And " S'long Spud. See yer inner mornin'," was what Ginger answered. .

With that, he was gone: over the leads, down the drain-pipe, along the catwalk to the jumping-off place—with the jungles and gold-mines of London lying there waiting for him as soon as he chose to go among them.

It was June, and the night was fine and rather sultry. There was still a lot of daylight left hanging about in the heavens and there were more people in the streets than Ginger had expected. That was why he had to look so slippy. And once he got going he did not spare himself: Archbishop Bodkin Hospital to St. Mark's Avenue bus stop in under two minutes.

After the run, it was a bit slow, a sort of silly anti-climax, waiting for the bus. There had been two buses in the other direction by the time Sid Harris swerved in from the Wimbledon direction. He was driving worse than ever nowadays, Sid was ; not deliberately taking risks, but just swinging in and out of the other traffic as though there was no one but himself to think about. Nor, in a sense, was there. He was more self-absorbed and preoccupied than ever nowadays. He was still proud of his bus—it was the new model T, 40 h.p., double back-wheels that he was now driving—and still waiting for the surprise legacy to come along.

He almost overlooked the boy standing at the bus stop, he was thinking so hard about his fortune. But he wasn't callous or despotic ; not one of those wave-and-drive-on sort of drivers. Merely absent-minded. And as soon as he saw Ginger he slammed the brakes on hard and swung the bus into the kerbside. But not for long. He was off again before Ginger was properly on the step. But that wasn't callousness either ; he just wanted to get back home as soon as he could to see if anything had come by the second post. . . .

Ginger made his way on to the top deck and took the outside front seat. This was exciting, this was: he had never

been on a bus before. And it got better. There in front of
him was a river. A river—and, incredible fact, no one at the
Hospital had ever so much as mentioned it. What was more,
the river was behaving in the most enchanting way possible:
it was supporting shipping.

The bus was actually on the bridge by now. And there
below him was a barge, his first barge, a long black hull
piled high with bundles of something, and with a man standing on top of them. As Ginger looked, the barge slid silently
between the piles of Putney Bridge. Naturally Ginger got
up to see it out of the opposite window as it emerged. And
in doing so he bumped into Mr. Edward Musk, the conductor,
who had come up to collect the fares.

This was one of Mr. Musk's down days. Mrs. Musk was
still lingering on—even though it was obvious that the end
was due almost any day now. And what with the housework
and reading the Bible to her and seeing to pussy, Mr. Musk
was so tired he kept wishing that he were dead himself. That
was why he was rather short with Ginger. He couldn't forgive him either for dragging him right upstairs when the bus
was half empty inside, or for taking the very foremost seat.
And when Ginger held out twopence and asked for St. Paul's
Cathedral he thought that he was being fresh with him.

It was as a matter of fact a bad moment for Ginger, too.
Because when Mr. Musk said that they didn't go anywhere
near St. Paul's Cathedral, it left Ginger sullen and incredulous. Then, at the sight of the twopence held under his nose,
Mr. Musk suddenly asked Ginger if he was under twelve.

For all Ginger knew there was a law against people of
under twelve riding about in buses.

" I'm fifteen, wod'jer fink?" he replied.

Fifteen sounded better than thirteen; altogether more
manly and independent. And that settled it.

"Sarth Kensington, that's where you get orf," Mr. Musk
told him, as he punched a twopenny ticket. " An' if you don't
get orf when I say Sarth Kensington, I'll come up and put you
orf."

It was a nice ride and Ginger enjoyed every moment of it.
He had become very fond of public houses, and the route
seemed particularly rich in them. There was one on almost
every corner. And from the top of the bus he could see right
inside, with views of barrels and cash-registers and trays
of glasses and shining beer-engines all spread out below

him. Also, he had seen an unusually good cemetery on the way. But South Kensington itself was not very interesting. No better than Putney, in fact.

Standing afterwards at the corner of the Brompton Road he felt desperate. Desperate and lost. He paused to consider. Unless he did something definite, and did it soon, the expedition was going to be a wash-out. He was still in search of London, and the real trouble seemed to be that London was so big that he couldn't find it. There was a policeman opposite whom he could have asked. But he was keeping clear of policemen. So he tried a paper-seller instead. The paper-seller was altogether better: he looked the sort of man who might be keeping clear of policemen himself.

And he was very nice and understanding. He knew all about St. Paul's Cathedral and Paddington Station and Buckingham Palace and the Zoo. Buckingham Palace was easiest, he said: a penny bus to Hyde Park Corner and you were practically on top of it. After that, he added, Ginger had better ask again.

Not that things were going too well for Ginger. It was another bus ride to Hyde Park Corner—and there was more than a third of his capital simply frittered away on travel! Nothing to show for it.

And Hyde Park Corner itself was rotten. The rottenest place he'd been to yet. It was all open spaces, simply flat fields with street lamps strung across them. He turned his back on it. And because it looked brighter that way he set off, mothlike, down Piccadilly towards the lights. The farther he went, the better it got. The houses closed in and it became a town again. But what a town! Lights in the windows, the smell of scent and cigar smoke in the air, the noise of voices all round him. Long gleaming cars threaded in and out of the scarlet rows of buses, and some of them had lights on inside, so that it was like looking into other people's drawing-rooms as they slid past.

He noticed one car, in particular. There was a man just getting into it. The man himself was peculiar enough. He was dressed like a sort of monster penguin, with a shiny white front like polished enamel and little pointed shoes as bright as black diamonds. But it was at the lady who was with him that Ginger looked most. She seemed happy enough, not miserable and crying as Ginger would have expected. But there was nothing on her shoulders, absolutely nothing. Naked, in fact. At the sight of her, Ginger blushed. He

337

could feel a fiery wave of hotness passing right through him.
A sort of tingly shudder that left him a bit ashamed of himself because he hadn't expected it.

Then an entirely novel thought came over him. He felt
as though he had grown up suddenly. Perhaps until this
moment he had got things all wrong. Perhaps this was the
way ladies, real ladies, always behaved. Perhaps they didn't
mind if their men friends saw them undressed. Perhaps that
was only what boys in places like Archbishop Bodkin's
imagined. Perhaps they liked it. Perhaps . . . but what
was the use of thinking about it? The car with the penguin
millionaire and the naked lady had already been caught up
and swirled away in the rapids of the traffic.

And there were plenty of other sights just as remarkable.
Couples with arms entwined were strolling along together in
a kind of maudlin ecstasy, or lingering before the lighted
shop-fronts. Ladies, real ones again, wearing short fur capes
and heels that were like something out of a circus balancing
act, were standing about in the doorways, smiling politely
at everybody. Some of them even smiled at Ginger, they
were so friendly; and Ginger smiled back, conscious again
of that strange hot feeling inside him.

This was life all right, this was. Better than St. Mark's
Avenue. Better than South Kensington. Better than Hyde
Park Corner. A confirmed roué by now, Ginger allowed
himself to be swept away by the rapids in the direction of the
whirlpool that the current was making for, the great mael-
strom of Piccadilly Circus itself.

And once arrived there, the sheer intoxication of the scene
overwhelmed him. It was terrific. For a start, the whirlpool
arrangement made such giddy patterns of the traffic. Cars and
buses were sucked in from the side tributaries, sent twirling
round the rock in the centre and then slung contemptuously
away up one of the side canyons. And the noise. Noise on
every side. The lovely, discordant, melodious noise of a
great city. Motor horns. The clatter of passing feet.
Laughter. And paper-sellers shouting out about murders
and fires and rail smashes. There were strange surprises,
too, hidden in the midst of it all—like an old woman with
shoes tied on with string, who was selling bunches of lucky
white heather; and a man, rather a distinguished, smart-
looking man, wearing a paper-mask, who was trying to
interest passers-by in toy pomeranian dogs that yapped and

jumped about when he pressed a bulb that was hidden in the palm of his hand.

Then the ladies again, the real ones with the fur coats and the golden curls. There seemed to be a great many of them in this part of London. And, as though all this pageantry, this metropolitan pomp, were not sufficient, the front of the buildings blazed and danced and dazzled with a thousand lights. It was everything that Ginger had ever dreamed of. It was adventure. It was success. It was fulfilment. It was El Dorado. It was Alleluia.

"Cor," said Ginger. "Bet I've found it. Bet this is St. Paul's. Bet it's St. Paul's, if it isn't Paddington."

I I I

When at last there came a break in the traffic he made his way over to the centre and sat for nearly half an hour on the steps of the statue. And while he was sitting there he had a rather disturbing thought, something that shook the foundations of this whole expedition. By all ordinary rules and according to the Archbishop Bodkin clock, it should have been night-time by now. London ought to have been tucked down and sleeping. And instead of that, it was standing about at street-corners and getting into taxis and enjoying itself. The way it was behaving, it seemed as though it didn't intend to go to bed at all. But in a sense it made it easier. Because it meant that there would be a bus whenever Ginger wanted to return. That was rather a relief, that was. He was quite prepared to walk back to Putney if necessary. But he had come a long way already, and he was feeling rather tired. And sleepy. And hungry.

Because he was hungry, he started to look for a tea-shop. And straight away in Glasshouse Street he found what he was looking for—or thought he had. Not that he was quite sure, because it looked a bit expensive. It was a coffee-stall, the first coffee-stall that Ginger had ever seen. And the appointments, particularly the gleaming copper urn, seemed somewhat on the sumptuous side. But, now that he could actually see food, and smell it, his hunger returned to him worse than ever. Here was food on the most staggering scale. There were great piles of crusty meat pies, and ham sandwiches wrapped up in a clean white napkin with the layers of bright

339

pink ham plainly showing; and a bowl of hard-boiled eggs; and slabs of fruit cake and madeira as thick as hymn-books; and a couple of plates of fancies, mere tit-bits in the cake-line, with dense snow-falls of shredded coconut on top of the pastry.

Ginger edged up nearer so that he could find out what sort of prices the other customers were paying. And this wasn't easy because by the time he got there everybody was eating rather than ordering. And it was while he was standing there that a most extraordinary thing happened. He felt a hand—a friendly, loving sort of hand—pass over the top of his head, and a voice said:

" Hallo, Ginger."

The fact that the unknown person knew his name astonished him. It was mysterious and creepy. He swung round, hostile and defensive. And it was then that he saw that it was one of those real ladies who was beside him, smiling down at him.

" Having a good time?" she asked.

Ginger blushed. His whole face turned a deep fiery red. And at the sight of it the strange lady tried to stroke his head again. She seemed amused at the idea of anybody's blushing. But Ginger avoided her. He wasn't going to have anyone, not even a lady, messing him about like that. So he pushed his way up to the counter and gave his order loudly. Gave it for the first thing that his eye fell upon.

" Meat pie anner cupper cocoa," he said authoritatively, as though he never dined off anything else.

A moment later it was slapped down in front of him. Ginger took a bite. And then the awful thing happened.

" Sixpence," the coffee-stall proprietor said to him.

Ginger blushed again. He knew that the strange lady was listening and he could see that the coffee-stall proprietor wasn't the sort of man to stand any nonsense: he had a black waxed moustache and hard glinty eyes. But what could he do? It wasn't as though the meat pie was still intact. On the contrary, he could see his own teeth-marks in it. And the cocoa had been made specially for him.

" Please, I've only got fivepence," he said.

" Only got what?" the proprietor asked.

" Please, I've only got fivepence," Ginger repeated.

And it was then that the strange lady stepped forward.

" Thassallright, Sid," she said. " I'm paying for him."

And in the circumstances what could Ginger do? It wasn't

the moment to be proud when you'd got your mouth full of
something that you couldn't afford to pay for. And, in any
case, the strange lady had already taken a shilling out of her
little fancy handbag and flipped it on to the counter. There
was nothing for it, therefore, but for Ginger to be polite and
grateful.

"Fanks," he said. "Fanks very much."

It was quite a family party at the coffee-stall, and Ginger
liked the atmosphere. Everybody seemed to know everybody.
The proprietor, whom the lady called Sid, called her Violet.
And other friends kept dropping in. There was a tall thin
man with a velvet collar to his coat whom they all called
the Captain, and quite a few of the ladies—Mabel, Eve,
Doris, and others that Ginger couldn't remember. Not that
Violet didn't introduce him. On the contrary, she was most
punctilious about it.

"Meet my new boy-friend," she said to them one by one
as they came sauntering up. And when she wasn't saying
that she was inviting Ginger to have some more.

"Have a nice piece of cake, dearie," she kept on saying.
"Better make a good meal now. You never know where
the next one's coming from, do you?"

There was quite a crowd at the coffee-stall by now and
Ginger was pressed up close against her. She was soft and
cushiony, and she was using a thick, heavy kind of scent. It
was such strong scent that he wondered if he would ever get
it off him. But that wasn't the only thing that he was wondering. The thought that was uppermost in his mind was a simple
one. "Wonder what Spud'd say if he could see me now," he
was thinking.

IV

The rest of the night was a confused and jumbled memory
even to Ginger himself. After the social interlude at the
coffee-stall, Violet explained very politely to Ginger that she
had to meet a friend, and moved off into the darkness,
mysterious and unobserved. For a moment, Ginger felt quite
lost without her. Then, remembering that he had so to
speak had the freedom of the place conferred on him, he
decided to move off himself.

All the same, he left the Circus very reluctantly. It was

341

easily the best spot that he had struck so far; the best spot
in the whole world he reckoned. And the way he was walking, through Haymarket and Trafalgar Square towards
Whitehall, it was getting rottener all the time.

It was all right again on the Embankment. There were
trams, some of the noisiest trams that Ginger had ever discovered; and a boat of some kind was going down-river, her
navigation lights gleaming. He stood looking after her until
she disappeared round the bend by Blackfriars.

But Ginger had a new difficulty to contend with now. He
was sleepy again. With a meat pie and three pieces of fruit
cake inside him, he had a comfortably settled sort of feeling.
He decided therefore that he would take a short nap before
beginning the long journey back to Putney.

And it was then that he discovered a most extraordinary
thing. Purely by luck and without knowing it he had
stumbled on London's largest bedroom. There were sleepers
on all the benches, old men, old women and figures so non-
descript that he couldn't have said what they were unless he
had asked them. With their mufflers and their bundles and
their tin kettles and gaping shoes they were quietly dozing.
It was, in fact, right into the dormitory of the string population that he had stumbled.

There was even some difficulty in finding a bench for
himself—he didn't exactly fancy having any of these for a
bedfellow. But he found an empty bench at last and sank
down on to it with the rumble of Hungerford Bridge and the
rattle of the trams to soothe him.

" Only a short one," he kept saying to himself. " Just long
enough so I don't feel sleepy."

He was still saying this when he fell asleep. And it was
six o'clock next morning when he woke up.

CHAPTER L

THE NIGHT that Ginger spent beside the Thames was a notable
night also for another member of the Bodkin community.
It was in fact the night upon which Mr. Prevarius ultimately
prevailed.

After that disastrous episode in the Cannon Street Station
waiting-room with the dark red rose in his lapel wilting from

342

the sheer shame of it, it might well have seemed that everything would be up for ever between Sidney Prevarius and Desirée Standish.

But that would have been reckoning without Mr. Prevarius's remarkable powers of persistence. Indeed, rather than slacken, he redoubled all his efforts. And that was because he felt that he now had a double claim to the lady. He could not forget that, in addition to the tender, anguishing bonds of first love—or love at first sight, rather—he had already paid two separate fees of five guineas apiece for the strangely elementary privilege of meeting his own fiancée.

And so he applied himself. After discovering that letters, postcards, telegrams, even telephone-calls were contemptuously ignored or rejected, Mr. Prevarius resorted to the personal touch. In his best clothes and with a bunch of flowers held all ready in his hand, he started to haunt the Charing Cross Road.

He had already tried the simpler method of seeing Desirée by ringing up Mr. Spike Jerome and asking for an appointment. Mr. Jerome was always ready to see him, because Mr. Prevarius was not merely a song-writer but a song-hit writer by now. The reception side of the business, however, had been terrible. Desirée had shown Mr. Prevarius in as coldly as if he had been the sanitary inspector, and had kept her nose, her face, her whole being most offensively averted.

What was even worse was the fact that, as Mr. Prevarius emerged into the outer office, Desirée was always on the phone to some unknown, passionate admirer who was apparently offering her the choice of the Savoy, the Berkeley or Quaglino's, with Drury Lane or Covent Garden or the London Hippodrome thrown in as a make-weight.

In the result, Mr. Prevarius became desperate. He planned sudden encounters; shadowings; abduction even. And in the end it was a bunch of blue and green carnations—St. Vitus's Freak they were called—that did the trick. He had been standing out on the pavement for nearly half an hour when Desirée came down the front stairs. And, as soon as he saw her, he slipped forward and thrust the bundle—one dozen each of the blue and the green and ninepenn'orth of maidenhair fern—straight into her arms.

The whole thing was so sudden and unexpected that Desirée offered no resistance. She grabbed hold of the parcel instinctively. And it was there that she had made her mistake. Because, once it was in her grasp, there was nothing that she could do about it but stand there and go on holding it. It was too big for her to be able to see over it; and, if she simply let it fall, she was not sure that she would be able to step across it without stumbling.

So, firmly, she mustered all the professional charm she knew and fired off her entire social broadside. Without a quiver in her voice and speaking from somewhere hidden behind the enormous pyramid of damp tissue-paper, she said in her politest voice: "If a gentleman gives a lady flowers it is sometimes politer if he offers to carry them for her."

After that, of course, Mr. Prevarius knew that everything was going to be all right. And to show that he was ready to make things easy for both of them he pretended that each of them had really known who the other was all the time, and that the Fairy-Prince-and-Beggar-Maid stuff via the Eros Agency had just been so much innocent fun, mere nursery teasing.

Altogether, the whole reunion passed off most agreeably. It was not, indeed, until quite near the end of the evening, by which time Mr. Prevarius was beginning to wonder how he was going to account to Dr. Trump for his long absence, that he discovered why it was that Desirée had suddenly become so astonishingly forthcoming.

And, at first mention, the reason proved a rather disquieting one: it was simply because she happened at the moment to be quite unusually hard up. This time, moreover, there was no attempt at concealment—nothing about rethatching the stables at the old place down in Sussex; nothing about extra singing lessons for her kid sister in the ballet school; nothing about that brilliant young brother of hers, the sea-cadet who had just passed out of Sandhurst with all those diplomas and medals and things. No, it was all humble and straightforward and personal. It was the rent of her room, already three weeks overdue, that was worrying her. And the cause of the financial crisis was Mr. Prevarius himself. The fees of the Eros Agency were apparently the same for female clients as for male. And that Cannon Street assignation had cost her ten guineas as well.

As soon as the position had been fully explained to him, Mr. Prevarius patted her hand and told her not to worry: his knee was already pressed up hard against hers as he said it, and there was a pleasantly reassuring feeling of contact and intimacy to the whole encounter. He did not, however, speak again immediately, and that was because he was thinking hard. In his present-day prosperity as Mr. Berkeley Cavendish, the ten guineas was nothing to him: he even had enough notes on him to pay her then and there. But he checked himself. Wouldn't it be rather a waste? he reflected. Wasn't it simply pouring good money after bad? Why, in any case, should he pay the expenses for both sides in that tragic farce that the refined old lady had engineered for him.

Instead, he moved up closer still and, dropping his voice a little, he took Desirée's hand in his.

"It doesn't matter so much about the rent," he said. "That's only a trifle anyway. But it isn't just a room that a girl like you wants—it's a home, dear; somewhere that you can really call your own. I know that Deirdre Gardens isn't good enough. But it's yours, for the asking, sweety-pie—just so long as I can look in and see you sometimes."

When Desirée did not reply immediately Mr. Prevarius made no attempt to rush her. He just sat there whistling softly through his teeth; and finally, simply to bridge the gap and save her any embarrassment, he ordered two more Benedictines from the waiter. Indeed, he rather respected her for her indecision: maiden-innocence at the cross-roads had always seemed to him to be one of the most moving of all human situations, and he would not have missed a moment of it.

It was not, indeed, until Desirée had given him her answer —"Well, we eat to live and I suppose beggars can't be choosers, can they?" were her exact words—that he gave her the invaluable guidance of his advice.

". . . and if they've really been so horrid to my little popsy at the old place," he said, still in that same low, purring kind of voice, "I should think twice before paying up the arrears if I were you. There's Deirdre Gardens waiting for you just as soon as you want it. And you ought to be able to take most of your things out in the small attaché case: you can always iron them out afterwards. It doesn't matter how many journeys you make. It's a free country: they can't stop you going up and down stairs. The one thing you mustn't try to move is the big suitcase. So it all boils down to which costs more—three weeks' rent or another big suitcase. There's a sale on in a little shop in New Oxford Street. . . ."

345

CHAPTER LI

I

THE BENCH seemed harder and sharper than it had done when Ginger had lain down on it the night before. And colder. Even though the morning wasn't exactly cold, there was certainly a pretty bleak sort of draught blowing up between the planking. It came through in long cold slices like streaky ice.

Ginger got up and shook himself. And then he noticed something very interesting. The occupants of the other benches were getting up, too. It was still obviously very early because there was no one about in the streets yet. But already the newspaper bundles and the tin kettles were being gathered together, the soles of shoes were being tied on to the uppers again, and the old ladies, the bearded gentlemen and the younger ones who simply hadn't shaved, were on the move once more. Going heaven-knows-where to what daytime dust heaps. The string people, in fact, had begun its morning migration.

" Time I was gittin' back," Ginger told himself. " I mus' have overslep' a bit."

There wasn't a single important-looking person about in the streets yet. But London was getting a more lived-in appearance every moment. Newspaper sellers were undoing the tarpaulin wrappers of their kiosks, and a small café in Villiers Street was taking the shutters down.

" I'm late," Ginger told himself. " I've gotta hurry."

The words were still ringing in his ears as he reached the Strand. And that was where things became difficult. Because by daylight everything looked different. He paused for a moment to take his bearings. He still had a vague, generally right idea that he should be going northwards. But in his anxiety to keep moving, he turned right. And that was fatal. It brought him first into Chandos Street and then through Henrietta Street into Covent Garden.

Here it was all cabbages and potatoes and bunches of bananas, and it just showed how far off his rightful track he really was. Doubling back again, he made his way up Garrick Street and across Seven Dials still looking for St.

Paul's Cathedral or Paddington, or wherever it was there had been all those lights and nice people on the previous night. But he could see that he was wrong. And he was getting thoroughly frightened by now.

The streets, too, were filling up remarkably. Every time a bus stopped, a little crowd of people got off it. And not just workmen, either. The bosses as well, with their little attaché cases and their rolled-up umbrellas and their morning newspapers. And there were girls, swarms and swarms of them, getting thicker every moment. All dressed the same with their bobbed hair showing under their hat-brims, and not looking a bit as though they had got up specially early. That could only mean one thing: it was late. Really late. So late that by now the Archbishop Bodkin Hospital would be stirring, too, and he wouldn't be able to climb back unnoticed.

"Cor, bet I'll get copped," Ginger told himself. "Bet old Frump won't half beat me. Bet he'll be ratty."

Because the nearer that Ginger got to the Euston Road the less did it look like the part of London for which he was searching, he decided to ask someone. And he chose a crossing-sweeper. The man was a bit of a swell in his own line of business. You could tell that at a glance. His little three-wheel handcart, painted bright yellow and with the stiff-bristled broom and the long-handled shovel resting on top of it, might just have turned out of a livery yard.

But he was friendly all right and he knew all that there was to know about getting across London. He might even have made a special study of the Euston Road to Putney problem, he was so certain. Take a 14 bus, he said; a 14 bus was what was wanted. It was as simple as that: just take a 14 bus and it would put you down on your own doorstep. A 14 bus was the answer.

It was about this time that a rather awkward interview was beginning inside the Archbishop Bodkin Hospital. Mr. Dawlish had just been shown into Dr. Trump's study, and was clearing his throat in readiness:

"One of my boys seems to be missing . . ." he had begun.

Ginger thanked the crossing-sweeper very politely. He didn't stay long, however, because his luck had changed suddenly. There was a 14 bus drawing up nearly opposite. And nipping round the back of a taxi, he caught it just as it was moving away. But this time he wasn't going to risk any funny stuff from the conductor. He just held out his money —all that he had left of it—and said: "a fi'penny one."

Then he sat back and wondered. The No. 14 bus went chugging on endlessly through the streets. But it was all right, Ginger reckoned: the crossing sweeper had been so absolutely convinced of it. And it stood to reason that there must be more than one road leading to Putney. Perhaps it was simply that the driver was taking the other one.

Then finally the bus stopped and the conductor came up on top again to change the board in front. He seemed surprised to find Ginger still sitting there.

"This is as far as we go, son," he said.

"But this isn't Putney," Ginger told him.

He was suddenly cautious and wary again.

"Nobody said it was, son," the conductor answered. "You come the wrong way, that's what you done. You stay where you are, and we'll take you back again."

But Ginger's nerves were all on edge and he broke out suddenly.

"Gimme my money back," he said fiercely. "Just you gimme my money back."

The conductor, however, had met boys like Ginger before. He was a Hornsey man himself, and he knew the sort of tricks that they got up to down Hornsey way. He didn't even lose his temper.

"Like my mate to fetch a policeman?" he asked. "I'll wait here with you, sonnie."

That put Ginger in a difficult position. Getting a policeman was the one thing that he wanted to avoid. But he wasn't going to let the conductor know.

"I'll git 'im meself," Ginger said. "See if I don't," he replied.

It was only when he had actually set foot on the pavement, thereby surrendering his last claim to all possibility of a free return journey, that he said something that just for a moment made the conductor wonder whether perhaps Ginger was telling the truth after all.

"Where is this, please?" Ginger asked.

"It's Hornsey, my lad," the conductor answered, taken unawares. "And you know it is," he added, as he recovered himself.

But Ginger was too much confused by now to be listening. This was disaster. Sheer, irreparable disaster! Breakfast time over with no breakfast inside him, and with all his money gone, he was now marooned somewhere on the other side of London in a place he'd never even heard of.

Because there was nowhere else to go where he could think quietly, Ginger went across to the Public Lavatory that stood opposite. And he had just reached the conclusion that there was only one thing to do, and that was to give himself up and *ask* to be arrested, when he became aware of the sound of running feet. They were peculiarly noisy feet. And, amid the echoing tiles of the Public Lavatory, they sounded like nothing less than a cavalry charge.

The next moment he was being borne down upon. At the double came a horde of ruffians, all more or less about his own age and all dressed in rather dirty-looking flannel trousers. But unlike him they weren't in the least despondent. Most of them had sandwiches and oranges, and some had squeakers and paper teasers as well. And it was obvious that they were cheerfully and gloriously out of all control. Behind them, some twenty-five yards in the rear but travelling fast, came a young, sporting-looking curate in sports coat and flannels. There was a slightly breathless and apprehensive look on his face as he rounded the corner. And no wonder. It was the St. Botolph's Hornsey Annual Outing that had just arrived. And the curate was supposed to be in charge of it.

The idea of visiting the lavatory—of crowding every possible pleasurable sensation into a day that promised to be all too brief—had evidently occurred to all of them at once. The lavatory was now packed solid. And a moment later the breathless curate appeared in the doorway.

"Come along, boys," he said pleadingly. "Come along. We're just off. Button up! No loiterers."

Even then Ginger had not reckoned on the organising

energy of the young curate. Before Ginger knew what was happening to him he was being hustled out of the lavatory and into a bus, marked " Private," that was standing just outside. He tried to explain the mistake. Tried twice, in fact. The first time was on the step just as he was getting in, but the curate simply pushed him sharply up the stairs and told him that he would see about it later. And the second was when he had actually taken his place—but, on that occasion, a shrill and piercing sort of toy-siren was being enthusastically blown in the next seat, and the curate could not hear what Ginger was saying. He thought, indeed, that he was apologising for having kept the outing waiting. The curate, therefore, merely patted Ginger on the head, and went back inside again. He was new to St. Botolph's, this curate. It was his first annual outing, and he was anxious to make the best possible impression all round.

After his second attempt at explanation, Ginger reckoned that there was nothing for it, but to go through with the whole thing. In any case, this was not like an ordinary bus. It was a " Private " one: and it was a sight-seeing tour. Even if he had wanted to get off he could not have done so. So he just sat on while all round him the paper bags and the cardboard attaché cases were opened, and the first serious eating of the jaunt began.

In the matter of the taking of light snacks there is a strict protocol among boys. No one eats unless everyone is eating. The convention is respected everywhere; and in nowhere more than in Poplar. As soon as the boy next to him found that Ginger hadn't brought anything, he shared. Searching through his own picnic provisions, he selected what he liked least—a banana—and passed it over. The boy behind him observing this did the same. By the time the bus had reached the Bank of England, Ginger had breakfasted off a banana, a sardine sandwich, a piece of cheese, a jam tart and a fruit drop. He had also drunk half a bottle of Cherry Ciderette. And he felt better for it ; quite himself again, in fact.

Meanwhile the curate, who had chosen the seat nearest the door, was checking up on the numbers. At the third attempt he gave it up and put the list away.

"It says thirty-seven and I make it thirty-eight," he told himself. " But what matter? Better than losing one of the little beasts."

350

He broke off.

"Now, chaps!" he said in a voice that he hoped would combine authority with good-fellowship. "Go easy there. No ragging. Penknives away! Remember we're St. Botolph's. . . ."

But in any case Ginger was fully occupied. He and the boy next to him—the one who had given him a banana—were playing leg-locks, and he had got his benefactor gripped in a vice just below his left knee. Slowly but irresistibly he was forcing him off the seat and on to the floor of the bus.

With brief intervals for rest, the game continued fiercely and delightfully all along Newgate Street, across High Holborn and down the whole length of Gray's Inn Road. It was, indeed, only the arrival of the curate on the top deck with the announcement that they were nearly there and should begin getting their things together, that interrupted them.

IV

There was a policeman standing outside the gates of the Zoo.

By now, the news of Ginger's disappearance was known to the Force. And the policeman outside the Zoo had all the particulars. He was, in fact, on the look out. What is more, he was a young man, anxious for promotion and ready to pounce at sight.

But what happened? Instead of producing the handcuffs, he took two smart paces to the rear to avoid being trampled on, and let the procession, with Ginger within arm's length, surge right under his nose.

Not that he ever knew, of course. Standing upright and foursquare upon the kerbstone, he continued to keep a skilled and roving eye open for a missing boy, aged thirteen, five foot two inches, six stone five, red hair, freckled nose. . . .

Once inside the Zoo, there was for Ginger only one note of discord in an otherwise perfect and unblemished outing. And that note was hunger. Breakfast had evidently not been so satisfying as he had imagined and he became conscious of himself, not as a boy at all, but simply as a big rumbling emptiness. He ached. And the more he ached, the fainter and less interesting the animals became. The paths grew harder and longer. The seats less comfortable, with wider spaces between them.

By now, Ginger felt himself so much one of the party—a regular St. Botolph boy, in fact—that he would certainly have remained with them until closing time if it had not been for an unfortunate incident at a one-way turnstile.

The turnstile was placed in the thickness of a hedge dividing the Zoo from the rest of London. And in consequence, there was an air of mystery and enticement to what lay outside. At the mere sight of that turnstile the Zoo suddenly had become dull and commonplace, and the streets wonderful and rich in all surprises.

Ginger was first to pass through the turnstile, and he stood agreeably surveying the stream of traffic, the car park, the waiting taxis, the curved and sunny road. Then the awful thing happened. When he wanted to go back, the turnstile wouldn't budge.

If it had been a prison gate, it couldn't have been more massive and unyielding.

V

And he saw now that he had over-estimated the road. The traffic, after all, was just ordinary; the taxis hadn't even got their engines running; there wasn't a jeweller's shop or a public house in sight; in fact nothing worth looking at. Already, in retrospect, the Zoo seemed a vanished Eden, a corner of fairyland glimpsed for a moment in a dream, only to be snatched away and lost for ever.

But once he reached the Prince Albert Road on the far side he found something really worth while looking at. It was a daffodil-and-vermilion ice-cream wagon with the words " Luigi Rapporto, Pure Cream Ices " on the side. And it had broken down. The bonnet of the little car was up, and a man in a dirty white overall was fiddling with the engine. The presence of Ginger, standing appreciatively on the kerbside in the sunshine, appeared to irritate him.

" Getta along with you," he said. " You standa in da light."

Ginger moved back a pace. Then he stationed himself again. Any farther would have been unthinkable: the spectacle was too fascinating.

But after a few minutes' contemplation, Ginger decided

that the fat man was not very good at mending motor-cars. And evidently the fat man came to the same conclusion at about the same time. For, bringing down the bonnet with a crash, he thrust one arm into the driving compartment and began to push.

It looked a long way wherever he was going, and Ginger felt sorry for him. He hadn't, however, been particularly nice to Ginger. And Ginger didn't want to risk another snub. So he didn't say anything. He just went behind and pushed.

He had as a matter of fact been pushing for nearly quarter of a mile—the Prince Albert Road was entirely flat and the ice-cream wagon moved almost effortlessly—before Mr. Rapporto even noticed that Ginger was there. And when he did discover it he was not pleased. He had paused for a moment to wipe his brow, and the daffodil-and-vermilion vehicle, instead of remaining stationary, had mysteriously moved on without him. It was, indeed, only as it came abreast that he saw Ginger, head down, back bent double, pushing hard.

"Wotta you do?" he shouted. "You wanta make da collision?"

After that, Ginger just followed. He remained near, of course, so that he could still do a bit of pushing whenever Mr. Rapporto wasn't looking. But, for the most part, he merely followed. Whenever Mr. Rapporto stopped, Ginger stopped. And as soon as Mr. Rapporto moved on Ginger moved on, too.

He seemed a very excitable sort of man, this Mr. Rapporto, Ginger noticed. And expostulatory. He kept on shouting out things. Once when a bus passed a shade too close to him he pursued the conductor with insults ". . . and tella your friend in fronta he trieda da murder me," he was still saying, long after the bus was out of ear-shot. And again, when a policeman who was holding up traffic at Clarence Gate told him to hurry, Mr. Rapporto turned on him, too. "Wotta you thinka I am?" he demanded. "A bloody horsa?"

It was this little episode that made Ginger particularly respectful towards Mr. Rapporto. He had no idea that any-one ever spoke to policemen like that. Polite, almost obsequious, he drew nearer. And it was then that Mr. Rapporto had an idea.

" Whya you follow me?" he asked. " You lazy boy. Donta you see I braka ma back? Give da hand. Pusha. Pusha me hard."

That was all Ginger needed. It was acknowledgment. It cured that lonely and unwanted feeling. He pushed so hard, in fact, that all Mr. Rapporto had to do was steer. And with no pushing to do himself, Mr. Rapporto's spirits rose. He steered with one hand and waved to passers-by with the other. Soon he was singing as well.

It was fun, pushing: Ginger enjoyed it. But it was hard work, too. He was out of breath.

Then Mr. Rapporto stopped singing.

"Here we are," he said. "We gotta there. Thissa da garage."

With that he pulled on the hand-brake, and Ginger bumped his head.

But Mr. Rapporto was his friend by now, his guardian.

"Nevera mind da head," he said, consolingly. "I giva you da cornet. I giva you da cornet or da wafer. Da cornet or da wafer, becausa you pusha so good."

He kept patting Ginger on the back with his large hot hand. But he was still quick to take offence. And he was obviously disappointed, affronted even, by Ginger's answer.

"Please, I'd rather have the penny," was what Ginger said.

Mr. Rapporto stopped patting him.

"You Jewa boy?" he demanded. "You worka only for da money? Whata you wanta da penny for? To buya da ice-cream, ha!"

"Please I want it for my bus fare," Ginger told him. "I got to go to Putney."

"And if I no giva da penny, you walka?" Mr. Rapporto asked. "You walka from here to Potney?"

Ginger nodded.

"Yes, sir," he said.

It was then that the Mediterranean munificence of Mr. Rapporto's nature revealed itself.

"I goa to Potney, too. I driva you there," he said. "As soona da car she goes, I driva you. And I giva you da cornet. Anda da wafer. I doa everything. You gooda boy. You pusha me verra good." He paused. "I driva da Vicar once," he confided. "He jumpa about. Likea da monkey. He smasha everything."

354

And while Ginger was slowly eating his way through lumps of frozen custard, the drama of his absence was developing inside the hospital.

When Margaret went up to the dormitory last thing she found Sweetie crying.

"Ginger's dead," she kept saying. "Ginger's dead. And all because we didn't love him enough."

And when Margaret told her what nonsense she was talking, Sweetie turned on her.

"Go and find him," she said. "If you really liked him, you'd go and find him. I shall hate you for ever if you don't go and find him."

And after that it was Sweetie who was surprised when Margaret turned on *her*. She had never known Margaret so cross before—never known her cross at all, in fact—and certainly never known her cross with her. Instead of going off to look for Ginger, or even being all nice and comforting because Sweetie had lost her friend, Margaret took hold of her and shook her. Then twisting her round so that she was looking straight into her eyes, she went on being cross.

". . . and don't start getting interested in boys," Margaret said to her in a hard, bottled-up sort of voice. "It's wicked. Do you understand what that means? Wicked."

"It isn't wicked," Sweetie answered. "It isn't wicked to love Ginger."

"It's wicked to love anybody," Margaret repeated. "It's wicked to love anybody until you're sure you're going to marry them."

"But I *am* going to marry Ginger," Sweetie replied. "I'm going to marry him as soon as I'm grown up."

Then quite the most extraordinary thing of all happened. Because this time it wasn't Sweetie who was crying. It was Margaret. She held Sweetie close to her and put her head down on Sweetie's shoulder.

"Don't say such things," she said. "Don't say them. Why can't you be like other girls? Boys are bad, I tell you. Bad. They get girls into trouble. Terrible trouble. You don't want to be a disgrace to everybody, do you? You don't want to have to go away somewhere . . ."

It was late by the time Mr. Rapporto delivered Ginger on his own doorstep. The whole day had passed away by then, and it was evening again.

Ginger made his way back into the Hospital by the fire-escape route. It was not easy without Spud to help him. But there was a drainpipe that came in very handy. And Ginger had become pretty good at drainpipes. When, at last, he managed to get up as far as the gutter, the rest was easy. He could reach the coping from there. With both hands he grabbed hold of it and the next moment he was on the comfortable flat surface of the leads.

There was a bit of trouble with the window because it was locked on the inside. Spud was usually a heavy sort of sleeper, but to-night he might almost have been waiting for Ginger to turn up. At the second rap on the window-pane, he was out of bed. But, though prompt, he was not comforting.

" Where you been?" he asked. " You aren't half going to cop it."

" Garn," was all that Ginger answered.

He was tired and he didn't want to begin explaining things immediately. But Spud was not so easily put off.

" They've got the police out looking for you," he went on. " How d'you get past 'em?"

Ginger began peeling off his jersey.

" Shut up or I'll bash you," he said.

Spud shut up. It was nice hearing Ginger say that. It meant a lot to Spud having his friend back.

And Ginger was asleep a minute later. Fast asleep. In so deep and dreamless a sleep, that he did not wake up when the door of the dormitory opened and Dr. Trump appeared, dormitory register in one hand, electric torch in the other. Mr. Dawlish edged in just behind him.

Dr. Trump was highly professional. He did not, as Mr. Dawlish had done, rely on a quick glimpse in the pale light that came seeping in through the open doorway. Instead, he moved carefully from bed to bed shining his torch like a searchlight on to the sleeping occupant: it was a new drill

356

that he had instituted since Ginger's disappearance, and he was putting it into operation for the first time to-night.

He had already been down one side when he came to the bed on which Spud was lying. And here he paused. Had he —or was it only his imagination?—detected a movement, a tremor, beneath the bedclothes? He stood where he was without moving, carefully training the beam of his flashlight full on Spud's face. Then, breathing heavily, and with a faint look of disappointment, he moved on.

And when, in the neat circle of illumination that the torch made, Dr. Trump saw Ginger's head upon the next pillow, he was so surprised that he nearly dropped the torch. He simply stood there, staring.

"Look," he said to Mr. Dawlish. "Look, man."

It was his most terrible voice that he was using; a voice made somehow more alarming still because the words were spoken through clenched teeth.

"He . . . . he wasn't there last night," Mr. Dawlish said idiotically.

"Well, he's there now," Dr. Trump replied. "Arrest him!"

CHAPTER LII

I

ALTOGETHER, Ginger's disappearance was the biggest event of 1930. It started Canon Mallow writing again, and the affair didn't die down immediately, either. The Press got hold of it. And, after there had been a lot of irritating headlines of the "MYSTERY OF THE MISSING ORPHAN" and "POLICE INVESTIGATE 24-HOUR DISAPPEARANCE" variety, there were a whole lot more with a rather nasty sinister tone to them, as though the Press had turned against Dr. Trump.

"SENTENCE OF SILENCE," "THE MUTE ORPHANS OF PUTNEY" was how the new batch came out. And that was because Dr. Trump had imposed sentence of Coventry on the entire Hospital by way of punishment.

In the end, there had been a special Board Meeting to con-sider the situation. The meeting was longer than it need have been because of Miss Bodkin. She had reverted to Nature this morning, and was entirely instrumentless. In consequence, she heard nothing. And understood less. Every so often a stray word, as random and unpredictable as a meteor, would soar into her intelligence and the trouble would begin again.

" But why did Mr. Dawlish run away?" she asked. " Surely he wouldn't have done that if he hadn't been unhappy."

Then again.

" It still seems to me a pity that Dr. Trump ever wrote all those articles. If he hadn't written it nobody need ever have known what happened . . ."

But in the end it was, as usual, Dame Eleanor's meeting. She dominated. And her summing-up caused Dr. Trump to flush angrily and bite his lips. Indeed, it was only the knowledge of his hidden ace that enabled him to remain there, bitter and resentful, while Dame Eleanor proceeded.

" Well, I must say, things have come to a pretty pass when boys begin running away," she said. " It'll be the girls next, and then where shall we be? There's only one explanation of it all—slackness. The whole place needs tightening up. And now those ridiculous stories in the Press. If we go on like this we shall be a public laughing stock."

A shudder of icy coldness ran right through Dr. Trump at the words. Now, if ever, was the moment for him to play the ace. And when Dame Eleanor looked up impatiently he coughed.

" There is one other matter as the whole Board is assembled," he said, keeping his eyes down on to the blotting pad. " Normally I should have reported it next month. But in view of its importance I would not wish to withhold it. It is " —here Dr. Trump looked up, and the Board could see that, though his face was deathly pale, his eyes were blazing— " *the laundry has begun to show a profit.*"

I I

It was, indeed, his singular triumph with the laundry that provided Dr. Trump with his one consolation. For, with Felicity still down at Broadstairs with Sebastian, even his home was not his own. Life at the moment was being lived upon the lap of his mother-in-law. The sight of her sitting opposite to him at his own breakfast table enjoying, visibly enjoying, the first cigarette of the day, sent a shudder right through him. That, indeed, was one of her chief crudenesses: she enjoyed things so much. She even had a way of stirring the sugar in her teacup and scooping the marmalade on to her toast that verged positively upon the voluptuous; and more than once he had watched her mentally comparing the size of the egg in his egg-cup with the one within her own. Morning after morning, he sat there silently hating her.

But there were other qualities as well that he had not suspected—dangerous, seductive, feminine qualities. High-coloured and rather puffy as she now was, it seemed that in her youth she had been nothing less than a hunting nymph, a siren. The past revealed itself startlingly in stray sentences that popped up from nowhere.

"I could *sit* on my hair when I was first married," she had once confided after Dr. Trump had incautiously admitted that he was getting worried about his own. And another time, when she had arrived down to breakfast in a pink knitted jumper that Dr. Trump had carefully avoided noticing, she had suddenly remarked: "I've always looked my best in pink, and that's not just my opinion, either. There are some others you could ask, I can tell you."

Nevertheless, as the days passed, he was forced to admit that amid the cheapness, the tawdriness of her nature, there was a warmth, a geniality, that somehow had not been passed on in the inheritance to her own daughter. Dear Felicity, he had to confess, possessed simply none of it. Whereas, Mrs. Warple dedicated herself to him. She served, she slaved, she wooed. Her care for his comfort was overwhelming. What did he eat? What didn't he eat? Did he want quarter-rubbers when she sent his shoes to be repaired? Was his shaving-water hot enough in the mornings? Were there sufficient blankets on the bed at night? Why hadn't he told her that a button had come off his trousers and that it was this that was giving him that extraordinary, hitched-up sideways look? Wouldn't he rather change his study back again to a room that caught the sun?

But cautious, apprehensive, even hostile, as he was, there were advantages in so much solicitude that he would have been foolish to deny himself. It is so often the little things in life that count. Indeed, life on the material plane, he had to admit, was distinctly more comfortable with Mrs. Warple than it ever had been with her daughter. And it was obvious that Mrs. Warple for her part was enjoying herself thoroughly. With no one to gainsay her, she now exhibited a fierce technical efficiency, a kind of professional household competence that left him marvelling.

It was her nightly glass of milk stout that still made a main barrier between them. But, as her doctor had ordered it, what could Dr. Trump do to countermand it? Sipping his own cocoa and averting his eyes as soon as he heard the throaty *glug-glug-glug* as the noxious frothy stuff came thrusting out of the vile, black bottle, he nowadays sat quietly in the evenings, listening to his mother-in-law's conversation. And the later she went on, the more indiscreet she became. Not that she ever told him anything exactly. Hers was the conversational method of hints, pointers, and half-glimpses. Sometimes an entire evening added up simply to nothing, and then a chance remark dropped on the following night or a whole week later would explain everything.

There was, for a start, a lot of talk about the hotel business: it was the recurrent theme, the background against which Mrs. Warple's early life had apparently to be observed. There were no names, no addresses. Dr. Trump could not even satisfactorily determine the size of the hotel in which she had spent those early impressionable years. In the end, however, he concluded that it must have been quite a small one. How otherwise, he asked himself, could one young girl —even a girl of Mrs. Warple's youthful energy—have grown to know so much about its several sides, the dining-room, the open-air teas in summer time, the lounge, the room set aside for billiards, and the part that she referred to cryptically as " the Public "?

It appeared to be at this hotel that Mrs. Warple had first met her future husband—though whether she had been a permanent resident, or daughter of the household or even employed in some comparatively menial capacity, she did not enlighten him. There was no explanation either of what the late bishop had been doing there. There was, indeed, only one firm, unwavering fact to go on. And that had emerged just before bedtime one night as Mrs. Warple stamped out her last cigarette and remarked suddenly: " Archie's folk didn't approve of me, you know: they made that clear right from the start. If only they'd known ; my word, if only they'd known. But things being as they were, I couldn't very well enlighten them. It was Archie's job to do that, and I often wonder if he ever did."

And the significance of referring to Bishop Warple as

" Archie " was considerable. It served still further to loosen the last strings of reticence.

It was Archie's " bossiness," she said, that had first made an invalid out of her and induced her to keep to her bed for all those years. And, she added grimly, Felicity was every bit as bad.

" I don't mind telling you," she said, " the day of the funeral when she asked me to come and live here I said to myself ' good-bye liberty.' And I meant it. It's all right now. But when Felicity gets back, that's when the trouble's going to start. One word from me and up she goes like a sky-rocket, just the way Archie always did. . . ."

And on Saturday when Dr. Trump, with these disclosures still ringing in his ears, went down to see his wife and son, there was another revelation, just as startling, awaiting him amid the medley of bead mats and stencilled fancy runners.

Felicity, it seemed, was just as relieved to be separated from her mother: " She was always on top of me," she explained. " I know she didn't mean it. But when I saw her coming I could scream sometimes. Really, I could."

And then, slowly, the dreadful truth came over him. Despite the dead set that Felicity had made at him, he had been the means merely and not the end. It was not a husband any more than a mother that Felicity had wanted: it was a son. And having not only got a son, but actually got him with her, she asked for nothing more.

Dr. Trump and Mrs. Warple, the two unwanted ones, were high up on the self same shelf together.

CHAPTER LIII

I

DESIREE was at Deirdre Gardens at last. Had been there for nearly six weeks now.

And they had been radiant and blissful weeks. Finding that she had really no money of her own at all, Mr. Prevarius had been suitably indulgent in a coy would-kitten-like-to-put-her-paw-in-daddy's-pocket kind of way, and kitten's paw had dived in obediently every time. In the result, kitten now had a new fur wrap, two complete sets of silk negligée—one coral pink and the other amber—as well as a double row of pearls so highly cultured that they would have made a Cambridge don appear illiterate.

And then, without warning, into the very midst of this first-floor idyll came the bomb, the bolt, the thunder-flash. Mr. Prevarius's nerves were all on edge to start with. The presence of Desirée all alone in the flat, pining, unoccupied and defenceless, drew him like a magnet. He had now taken to slipping out of the Hospital almost every evening round about 6.30 and not returning until nearly midnight. And Dr. Trump, he could not fail to recognise, had begun to notice what was going on. Indeed, on the last two evenings in succession he had even been standing there at Sergeant Chiswick's lodge ready to say a cold " good-night " as Mr. Prevarius entered.

For the time being it was all right: Mr. Prevarius had put him off with an ingenious fabrication about carol practice at the B.B.C. But that wouldn't last for ever: to be precise it wouldn't last one day beyond December the twenty-fifth at the latest.

And there was another little matter that was worrying Mr. Prevarius. Up to the present he had always been so careful, so circumspect about his little affairs. Stray addresses in Maida Vale or Paddington are practically untraceable, and therefore innocuous. But this was different. This was so open, so obvious ; so positively defiant in its boldness. And the last thing that he wanted to do was to take any risks.

Indeed, in his position, he could simply not afford to do so. For more than twenty years now he had been concealing something, keeping a dark secret hidden. Successfully, too. The Archbishop Bodkin Hospital hadn't got so much as a trace of it in their dossier—Mr. Prevarius knew that for certain because he had once managed to distract Miss Phrynne long enough to take a peek at the records. His private card showed the typewritten entry " Single " against his name, without so much as a hint to suggest that it was inaccurate in the only way in which so important a particular can be.

And in any case, it had all happened so long ago. Mr. Prevarius could scarcely remember the lady. Certainly could not remember any motive that could possibly have induced him to marry her. She had been so genteel—at least he remembered that much. And so entirely sexless, too, in a tweedy, chilblainy kind of way. Even to remember that
362

awful wedding night when it was only the sound of her coughing that had kept him awake at all, was to plunge again into a whole ocean of melancholy.

It had been, he supposed now that he came to reflect upon it, a marriage of impulse ; and, what had made it worse, of *restrained* impulse. He had married her in order to save him from himself.

It had all taken place in Dumfries in a February. After the unfortunate affair of the dean's daughter, Mr. Prevarius had fled up north in order to escape the censure of malicious tongues. And naturally he had been lonely. He was still the Rev. Sidney Prevarius, B.D., at the time—the machinery of the Church was only slowly getting into motion—and he was acting as curate to the Rev. Phineas McTurk, the Anglican vicar of St. Crispin's. It was Miss Jeannie McTurk, the second daughter—the one who wore a black bandeau round her long, yellow hair, and gave music lessons—whom he had married. She was tall, a good six inches taller than he was, with a pathetic flowerlike droop to her long back ; and her hands, and feet too he discovered later, were always cold with a chill that suggested stone, metal, even ice itself— anything in fact except living flesh-and-blood.

The marriage lasted until mid-August, though even summer itself it seemed could not warm her. And then the ecclesiastical court uttered: Mr. Prevarius was suddenly in holy orders no longer.

Mr. McTurk, a bearded, whiskery old thing with fierce Celtish eyes, turned him out the same night. Mr. Prevarius had been living with Jeannie's people all this time. And Jeannie herself, urged on by her fanatical parent, swore that she hated Mr. Prevarius for ever, and would remain indissolubly married to him for life.

It was after this lamentable upset that Mr. Prevarius had slipped south across the border, alone, and after a spell in a preparatory school and another in canvassing for a popular encyclopedia, had reached Archbishop Bodkin's where Canon Mallow had been so guilelessly ready to take him in.

But that was why it was so important that he should continue at the Archbishop Bodkin Hospital. His miserable salary there was enough to persuade even a firm of Dumfries solicitors that he could not afford to make any contribution to a deserted wife. The only peril that he dreaded was that with one false move, he might somehow become involved in the sort of scandal that would lead inevitably to resignation, if not actually towards dismissal. Then the consequences might be terrible. The solicitors might even contrive to get their hands on some of the golden earnings of Mr. Berkeley Cavendish.

He had, right from the start, always been very careful as to what he should tell Desirée. And he had come to the conclusion that even so much as a hint of Jeannie McTurk would be an error. There seemed, after all, to be no point in worrying Desirée about something that was such ancient history. And so, whenever the topic of marriage cropped up, he treated the subject lightly and airily, brushing it aside and into the future somewhere.

Indeed, last time it had arisen, he had merely made a deprecatory sweep of the hand and said smilingly: "I may be anything my poppet says, but I don't think that she could accuse me of being old-fashioned. And I have never yet seen any evidence to support the theory that a wedding ring and marriage lines help people to love one another, dontcher know."

Not, of course, that Desirée was content to leave it at that. There were tears, misgivings, hesitancies. She had her good name to remember, she said. She demanded to know what her friends would think of them—which seemed strange to Mr. Prevarius because he had never met any of her friends. She wanted to know what kind of a woman he thought she was, and was not content when he replied: "But I've told you, dear. I've told you, I've told you so many, many times."

All the same, now that she had overcome her scruples, things were going along very smoothly. The one-room flat had proved to be a bit small for the two of them—largely because the grand piano and the Buddhist altar took up so much of the space; and Mr. Prevarius had taken the best bedroom as well; Miss Lewis's own best bedroom, in fact. Re-furnished in pale blond satinwood and with strip-lighting over the dressing-table it seemed somehow to provide Desirée with some solace for her own invidious position.

And it was at about seven-thirty one rainy Sunday morning in this very bedroom, with the pink curtains still drawn and Desirée's silk and swansdown dressing-gown draped negligently across the bed on top of Mr. Prevarius's blue-spotted one, that the incident occurred.

Mr. Prevarius declared afterwards that he had heard the fatal ring at the doorbell. But he had, he admitted, been far too sleepy to take any notice of it; in fact, had merely snatched an armful of the eiderdown back from Desirée and snuggled down again. A moment later, however, all thought of sleep was clearly impossible. There were trampling feet on the landing outside the bedroom and the sound of Miss Lewis's voice raised in shrilly protest. Then, without even a knock upon the panel, the bedroom door was flung open and a little man like a damp musk-rat, in a shabby bowler hat and brown overcoat, stood there.

It occurred later to Mr. Prevarius that he had seen the man somewhere before; and he remembered dimly that he had once or twice drunk beside him in the public house at the corner where he and Desirée used to drop in occasionally when drinking alone had become tedious. The man, he now recalled, had been noticeable for a kind of sideways stare that he had kept trained on them.

But this time there was nothing in the least sideways about the stare. It was one of the most straightforward stares in London, and it was directed full on to the bed. But not it seemed on to Mr. Prevarius himself. The trained, professional eye under the shabby bowler had already taken in the figure with the tousled hair and saffron and magenta pyjamas who was sitting up on one elbow goggling at him.

It was at the cluster of daffodil-coloured curls on the adjacent pillow that he was now looking. And when roused suddenly by Mr. Prevarius's indignant "What the blue blazes!" the daffodil-coloured head appeared above the bedclothes and Desirée showed herself, the man in the bowler and the brown overcoat appeared satisfied.

"Thank you both very much," he said. "I've got all I need. Sorry to disturb."

And before Mr. Prevarius could reply the man in the brown overcoat had closed the door in their faces.

But by then Mr. Prevarius had sprung out of bed: he was at the keyhole, listening. And what he heard appalled him. Above the noise of the heavy, clumsy feet descending the staircase he caught the words: ". . . my card . . . needed as witness . . . apologise for any unpleasantness . . ."

I I I

And after that, the whole Sunday morning was one of shame and turmoil. Mr. Prevarius had made his arrangements carefully and at 9 o'clock Miss Lewis was to have served a real party breakfast for the two of them—porridge, kippers, toast and marmalade, everything.

Now, instead of that, Miss Lewis still in an awful old dressing-gown was telling Mr. Prevarius that she had detected him to be a humbug from the very start and would have known Desirée for what she was even if she had washed the paint off. The revelation of so much coarseness in Miss Lewis's mind sickened him and in the end he was forced to lock the door on her simply so that he could explain matters to Desirée.

And it was then, and not until then, that Mr. Prevarius suffered the greatest disillusionment of his life. His faith in the whole of human nature was rudely, callously shattered, leaving him alone and defenceless in a deceitful and dishonest world.

For Desirée spoke first.

"Oh, well," she said, smearing some fresh lip-stick on to her face while she was still speaking. "If it had to happen, it's better to have got it over with."

"Then . . . then you expected it?" Mr. Prevarius demanded.

"I'm only surprised he still bothers about me," Desirée went on: she had put down the lip-stick by now and was busy on her nails with a polisher. "He must have been up to something himself or he'd never have forked up for it."

"*He,*" Mr. Prevarius repeated in a trembling, sickly sort of voice. "You mean . . ."

"Oh, forget it," said Desirée. "It's ancient history. We haven't seen each other for donkeys' years. I suppose a girl's entitled to some secrets isn't she?" She paused. "We were only married for a month or so. But it's nice to know

366

he's being so sensible about it. When I left him he always threatened he'd murder me if . . ."

But Mr. Prevarius was no longer listening. Face downwards upon the bed, his face cradled upon his forearms, he was crying like a child.

To think . . . to think that with more than a million other girls of the right age to choose from he should have selected —and, more than selected, pursued and hounded down—one who had turned out to be every bit as deceitful and contemptible as he was himself.

CHAPTER LIV

I

THE RIDING lessons had given Dr. Trump more trouble than he had expected. For a start, he saw now that he should have specified *private* lessons. But was he to have been expected to think of that? How was he to have known that every Wednesday the residents of Richmond would witness the spectacle of a grim-faced clergyman in pince-nez riding out in company with six little sprites in jodhpurs, and held on a leading rein by a big, glowing young woman like a kind of lustrous land-girl?

But he had persevered. He could not merely trot: he could canter. Once, on a large animal with the yellow and discoloured teeth of a chain smoker, he had even galloped. And he had persevered with other things as well. Detail by detail, he had gone over the various affairs of the Pageant— the final seating arrangements, the order of the triumphal procession, the size of the pieces of cake for tea, the discreet notices indicating the nearest route to the lavatories. In less than a week the tickets would be ready to go out.

As it happened, however, larger events intervened. And Dr. Trump, surrounded by little packets of pink and white and blue cardboard marked a shilling, half a crown and three and sixpence respectively, could do nothing but stare disconsolately out of the window at the spot where the marquees should have been. For, in view of what had occurred, the Board by a unanimous decision decided to postpone the Pageant. And by the time the episode was over, the entire course of Hospital history had been changed and the Archbishop's birthday was callously forgotten.

This time it was not Ginger's fault so much as Sweetie's. But what made it so much worse was that it was the fault of the two of them together. It came, indeed, as the first open declaration of their joint lawlessness. And it was no consolation to Dr. Trump to know that in a sense he had precipitated it.

It was one of his little tours of inspection that had started it all. It was evening, and he had got as far as the laundry block when he thought he heard voices. Low voices. Secretive voices. A girl's voice. And a boy's. This surprised him. Because, until that moment, he had imagined that he was alone. A sense of suspicion that expressed itself in stealth crept over him. He tiptoed up to the despatch counter and peered in through one of the windows.

And what he saw appalled him. There, seated on one of the baskets that contained to-morrow's deliveries, was Ginger. And beside him, so close that she was almost snuggling, was Sweetie. Ginger was holding her hand. No, now that he looked more closely he could see that it was Sweetie who had hold of Ginger's. She had Ginger's hand clasped firmly in one of her own and she was stroking it slowly, lovingly.

For a moment, Dr. Trump was on the point of shattering the window-pane, and tearing those two loving hands apart with his fingernails. But, with an effort, he restrained himself. Evidence, complete and damning evidence, was what he now demanded. And that he knew could be obtained only by waiting.

"Why don't you like me?" Sweetie was asking.

"I do," Ginger answered.

And Dr. Trump was glad, positively glad, to see that the wretched boy was endeavouring to remove his hand from the smaller, fondling one that encircled it.

"Then why don't you ever answer any of my letters?"

Letters! A clandestine correspondence! Was it possible? But already Ginger was speaking again.

"I got too much to do," he replied.

Also a good attitude, Dr. Trump decided. Really Ginger was showing up astonishingly well in the face of such temptation. Perhaps all those canings had done something to him.

"If you really liked me you'd find time," Sweetie persisted. "That is, if you *really* did."

"Wouldn't be any good," Ginger told her. "They'd only be stopped."

"Well, I seem to find a way, don't I?" Sweetie pointed out to him. "And you could if you wanted to. You could bring them to me at night. You did come once remember . . ."

But Dr. Trump had heard enough. And already he had decided. Because he could not trust himself to confront them face to face, he would take other measures. Sweetie and Ginger were both approximately fourteen by now. And in the morning he would send them both packing. As their spiritual as well as physical guardian, he saw clearly that it was his plain duty to put the greatest possible distance between the two of them.

I I

Dr. Trump wasted no time: he told them that same night of his decision. Normally, he said, they would have remained at the Archbishop Bodkin Hospital until the end of term ; as it was, however, he was making arrangements for them to leave immediately—to begin life's business upon the morrow, in fact.

And because of the admirable card-index system that he had instituted it was all wonderfully simple. Everything was down there in black and white: it was a butcher's in Hoxton to which Ginger was going, as for Sweetie, she had been very satisfactorily fixed up in a Finchley rectory with four children, an invalid wife and no other help. The rector had been delighted—yes, positively delighted, he told her—when he had heard that Sweetie could come at once.

When Ginger learnt that he was to leave to-morrow he was surprised. But not upset. He had been looking forward to the moment when he would leave. It was only that he was not prepared for the suddenness of it all. And for the fierceness with which Dr. Trump spoke to him.

"It is for your own good that I am sending you away," Dr. Trump told him. "Right away. Out of reach of temptation."

"Thank you, sir," Ginger answered, not knowing what Dr. Trump was talking about.

369

But the answer did not seem to satisfy Dr. Trump. He turned sharply and, gripping Ginger above the elbow, glared down at him.

"Beware," he said. "Beware of girls. Beware of young women. Above all, beware of yourself."

Even that did not worry Ginger. Remembering Sweetie, it seemed entirely sensible advice. Nearly all the trouble that he had got into at the Archbishop Bodkin Hospital had been because of Sweetie. So his answer was simple and direct.

"I will, sir," he said.

And immediately Dr. Trump began talking again.

"You will leave in the morning," he said. "Immediately after breakfast. And you will go out by the back way. I will be there myself to say good-bye. It is a butcher in Hoxton to whom you are going. An . . . er Christian butcher. You will become an apprentice. If you work hard you may become a butcher yourself one day. Avoid drink. Avoid gambling. And, above all, avoid women." Dr. Trump paused. "If you don't avoid women," he added, "you won't be able to avoid the police."

"I see, sir," said Ginger.

"And now go to bed," Dr. Trump told him. "And not a word to anyone. To-morrow will be time enough for that."

BOOK FIVE

The Runaways

CHAPTER LV

I

WHEN Ginger left Dr. Trump he was fed up. All that stuff about women was barmy. And the job he was going to sounded rotten. He didn't want to chop up bits of meat for people. He wanted to do something with cars. Wanted to drive cars and tend them and cherish them. If it had been a garage that he was being sent to, he would have volunteered to go off that same evening. It was his new enthusiasm, cars; and it was all-embracing.

And he was still wondering whether he had got to go on being a butcher for ever, or whether the police, or whoever it was who decided, would let him work in a garage if he wanted to, when he saw Annie approaching. She was wearing the stupidest of her expressions, the one that showed that she had secret and important news. And she made straight for Ginger.

"Sweetie wants you," she said. "She's down at the end of the kitchen garden. If you get on to the wall she can talk to you."

Get on to the wall! It was all right for Annie to talk like that. Getting on to the wall in broad daylight was madness. He'd be caught and caned for it. And then he remembered. He couldn't be caned any longer. At least not after to-morrow, he couldn't.

"Wot's she want?" he asked.

"It's something bad," Annie told him. "She's crying."

"Oh, orl right," Ginger answered, forgetting all about Dr. Trump's advice. "I'll go and see."

Mr. Dawlish blew his whistle for "all indoors," just as Ginger was setting out. But he didn't take any notice. He kept straight on, past the woodwork shop, past the boiler-room and on towards the gardener's shed. His favourite

371

plane tree stood there. And, even though the lower branch, the useful one, had been sawn off on Dr. Trump's orders, he could still manage the climb. That was where the leather belt of the Hospital uniform came in so handy: it could always be used for pulling yourself up in an emergency.

When he reached the top of the wall, Sweetie was waiting there sure enough. And he could see at once that she had been crying. Her upturned face showed up plainly enough. And it was all tear-stained and blotchy.

"Wozzermatter with you?" he asked.

"I'm glad you've come," Sweetie answered.

"Yus, but wozzermatter?" he persisted.

"I wanted to say good-bye," she told him.

"How d'yer know I was going?" he demanded.

"It's not you. It's me," Sweetie said with a break in her voice. "I'm being sent away to-morrow."

"Where to?"

"To . . . to a job," Sweetie answered. "And I shan't never see you again. Or Margaret. I shan't never see anybody I know."

Ginger paused.

"That's rotten," he said at last.

Sweetie was staring up at him, pleadingly.

"But what can I do?" she asked.

Ginger paused again.

"Dunno," he said. "Better go, I s'pose."

"I thought p'raps you could help me."

"Can't," Ginger told her. "I'm being sent off meself, termorrow."

It was this piece of news that was too much for Sweetie. She just laid her head upon her arm, up against the brick-work of the wall and began crying again. Then, quite abruptly, she stopped.

"I won't go," she said slowly. "I'll kill myself."

Ginger was aware of a strange emotion inside him. He had never seen another human being quite so distressed before. Certainly never seen a girl like that. And he wanted to jump down off the wall and put his arms round her.

But it was too late. Already through the gathering dusk he could hear Nurse Stedge calling. Her voice was shrill and anxious-sounding.

"Sweetie," it was saying. "Sweetie. Are you there? The bell's gone, Sweetie. Sweetie! Sweetie!"

372

"Good-bye," said Ginger.

There was no answer at first. Then Sweetie spoke slowly and distinctly.

"Good-bye," she said. "Good-bye for ever. I shall be dead by the morning."

Nurse Stedge, however, was coming nearer.

"Sweetie," she kept on calling. "Is that you, Sweetie? Can't you hear me? Sweetie! Sweetie!"

11

Ginger was lying in bed staring up at the ceiling. Chopping up bits of meat! Taking the skins off rabbits! "Good-morning, madam. Half a pound, madam. Certainly, madam. One and sixpence, madam. Your change, madam. Send it round this morning, madam. Certainly, madam. Good-day, madam . . ." that wasn't the sort of life he meant to lead: it wasn't like life at all, all this barmy madaming. Just thinking about it made him want to have a go at madam with the chopper.

And there was something else that made him feel miserable, too. It was Sweetie. She kept coming back into his thoughts just when he thought that he had forgotten about her. And he resented her.

"It's rotten enough already having to be a butcher when you could be looking after cars," he told himself for the fortieth time. "Rotten enough, without Sweetie bothering me. Wot's she think I can do to help her? Wot's the use of asking me? If I could help anyone, I'd help meself, wouldn't I?"

He followed this line of thought for some time. But there was another complication that he hadn't reckoned on. For he now found himself not only remembering Sweetie, but seeing her. She was so clear that it was as though he were still on top of the wall looking down on her. And every time he saw her that same, strange she-wouldn't-feel-so-bad-if-only-I-put-my-arms-around-her sort of feeling came over him again. But he wasn't going to do anything about it. He'd got himself into quite enough trouble already, because of Sweetie.

"*She* won't kill herself," he decided. "Not 'er. Killing yourself's potty. Bet she only said it to make me feel sorry."

373

And with that piece of consolation in his mind, Ginger rolled over and went to sleep.

He had not been asleep for more than half an hour when he woke suddenly. Really suddenly. So suddenly, indeed, that he sat bolt upright in bed all in one jerk.

He was being soft, that's what he was being. For the last couple of years he had told himself that he was going to run away, and here he was just waiting to be kicked around. It wasn't good enough. He wasn't going to stop there any longer. He'd run away good and proper this time—somewhere right away where Dr. Trump and the Hoxton butcher and the police would never find him. He'd be able to get on all right. He wasn't worrying.

But money! That was the first problem. The trouble was that he hadn't got any. And that two-day jaunt to Poplar had taught him the cost of things outside the Hospital. Then he remembered the half-crown that Canon Mallow had given him, the one that Dr. Trump had taken away again. If he'd had that, everything would have been right. And why shouldn't he have it? he asked himself. It was his, wasn't it? And it had belonged to him. And he reckoned he could get at it once again if he tried properly. No difficulty there. It was only in a wooden box with a padlock on it. And if the padlock wouldn't give way, he could prise it open. Bust up the hinges, and get at his half-crown that way.

"I'm goin' ter do it," he resolved. "Git me 'alf-crown, and clear out for good."

Because this was serious, not like the other times he had gone off, he didn't say anything to Spud. He just started dressing. He had no very clear plans in his mind as to where he was going once he had left the Hospital behind him. The important thing was simply to get as far away as possible. Into some quite different part of the country, so that when he began looking for a job, people wouldn't connect him with the boy who was missing in Putney. And as a final master stroke of concealment, he decided that he would even change his name.

"Yus, that's it," he told himself. "I'll change me name. Then I'll be somebody else and they won't never find me."

When he had put on the last of his climbing clothes, he paused for a moment to look round the sleeping dormitory.

"Bet Spud won't half be sick when he wakes up in er

morning an' finds me gone," he reflected. "Bet he won't half be sick."

But getting at the half-crown wasn't so easy as he had anticipated. For a start the Hospital collecting-box was in the open corridor leading to the hall. And, even in the dead of night, it seemed a pretty public sort of place in which to go rifling a treasure chest. Someone might walk through at any moment; and, if anyone did come, Ginger would be for it. That was because there was a lamp-post just outside the Archbishop Bodkin wall and the rays from it shone in through the Gothic windows almost like daylight. The box, too, was a strong one and the padlock had been made specially to prevent the sort of thing that Ginger was up to. There was nothing for it eventually but to break the hinges. And he had to use a poker out of the big fireplace in the entrance hall before he could make them even budge.

But, when they did go, they went abruptly. And with a bang. They made such a noise, indeed, as the thick iron bands came clean out of the woodwork that Ginger was afraid that the whole Hospital would wake up. He just stood there waiting while his heart went *dub-dub-dub-dub-dub* inside him.

The real difficulty came, however, when he looked inside the box. It contained three separate shillings and a piece of silver paper. That was awkward. If he took only two of the shillings, that would leave Dr. Trump with sixpence that wasn't his by rights. And if he took all three of the shillings, that would be stealing. But, in the end, he decided that for the moment he needed the odd sixpence more than Dr. Trump did.

"I'll only borrer it," he told himself. "I'm not goin' ter keep it. When I git a job, I'll post it back again. An' I'll pay for smashing up the box when I git me job. I'm only taking what's mine by rights."

And then, suddenly, Ginger remembered Sweetie. It seemed rotten going off like this without even saying good-bye to her. There was nothing, however, that he could do about it: he didn't even know which was Sweetie's dormitory any longer. But she was a soppy sort o' kid, he remembered. She'd probably been back at her place on the wall waiting for him ever since lights out. And, even if she weren't, he'd feel better about it somehow if he went along just to see. The three shillings safely in his pocket, he therefore started off round the Colet Block for a final check on Sweetie's stupidity.

He was still wondering whether he weren't being just as stupid about it himself, when he heard a noise—half hiss, half whistle—just above him. He started. Then he looked up. There was Sweetie on the wall already.

" I thought you'd come," she said in a whisper when he got near her.

" Did yer?" he asked lamely.

"I was sure of it," Sweetie answered. " Why are you wearing those clothes?"

" I'm runnin' away," he told her. " For good this time. I just come to say good-bye."

" That was nice of you," Sweetie said. " I'm glad you came because I wanted you to do something for me."

. " Did yer?" Ginger whispered back. " Wot was it?"

There was a pause. Only a slight one. But it was enough to warn Ginger that something important was coming.

" I wanted you to take me with you," Sweetie answered.

Then Ginger regretted that he had ever come at all. It showed that Sweetie was really barmy. Only somebody as barmy as Sweetie would ever have suggested it.

" You can't," he said firmly. " You're a girl."

" Girls are all right," Sweetie answered. " They're as good as boys."

She had raised her voice above the whisper of the rest of the conversation as she said it, and Ginger was alarmed.

" Shut up, can't yer," he said. " Somebody'll hear yer."

But Sweetie did not seem to be impressed.

" If you don't take me, I'll scream," she threatened. " I'll scream so loud that everybody hears. Then they'll find both of us. I will, if you don't take me."

She wet her forefinger and drew it across her throat as she was speaking. Ginger didn't like the look of that: it meant that Sweetie was in earnest.

" And I'll start screaming when I've counted three," she went on. " Go on Ginger? *One.* I won't be any trouble. *Two.* Please, Ginger. Will you take me? *Thr . . .*"

" Oh, orl right," said Ginger. " Come on."

Now he was in a mess. A real mess. He'd be copped for certain if he had a girl tagging along with him. And what's more he'd just remembered that he hadn't got any plans, any real plans, even for himself.

Hadn't the slightest idea, in fact, which way to turn once he had got outside the Hospital.

"Wot you goin' er wear?" Ginger asked when Sweetie had come slithering down off the wall and was actually standing there beside him.

"What I've got on," Sweetie answered.

Ginger looked. It was the regulation uniform of the Hospital that Sweetie was wearing.

"Too reckernisable," he said briefly.

Then he began to think. There was only one pair of flannel trousers in the whole Hospital, and he had got them on. But there was a blue boiler suit that Sergeant Chiswick used when he was doing the stoking. It was a bit on the large side, but Ginger reckoned that he could manage with it. And it would look businesslike, too, when he came to go after his job.

"You wait here," he said.

When he came back he had changed into Sergeant Chiswick's boiler-suit and was carrying the flannel trousers over his arm. He passed them across to Sweetie.

"You put these on," he said.

Politely, he turned his back on her as she changed.

The only thing that upset him was Sweetie's hair. It was soft and shining and wavy. Obviously a girl's hair. So long as Sweetie looked like that he need not have troubled about the flannel trousers. There was nothing for it, therefore, but to give her his cap as well. He resented that. The cap was part of his running away costume and he felt incomplete without it. But there was no other way.

"You put this on," he said. "An' shove all yer hair right up into it. Don' leave any bits showing."

"I won't," said Sweetie.

Ginger came close and inspected her. She looked better that way. Much better.

"Now you shut up, and do what I tell you," he commanded.

"I will, Ginger," she promised quietly.

Having got her own way, she was now meek, obedient, even humble.

It was a dark night and there was not much fear of meeting anyone in the courtyard. Ginger therefore took the quick route back across Colet and down towards the laundry. There was no point in climbing down drain-pipes when you could just open a gate by pulling the bolts back. Half a minute later, the two of them were standing in Ryecroft Gardens—free.

"You are clever," Sweetie said to him. "I wouldn't have thought of that way out."

But more to show that he was master of the occasion than for any other reason, Ginger ignored the compliment.

"You shut up," he said again. "We gotter get moving."

I I I

There aren't many people about at three o'clock in the morning. Cities are as dead as tombs at that time of night. The streets might be river-beds on the moon, and the buildings are just so many rock faces, blank and cold and unseeing. Sweetie had taken Ginger's hand by now and the two of them walked on together, not even talking. The main problem was Ginger's. He still hadn't got any idea of where they were going.

It was the coffee-stall at Hammersmith that gave him his first idea. Just to show how familiar he was with things like coffee-stalls, he led Sweetie straight up to it.

"You leave this to me," he said. And, in as loud a voice as he could manage, he gave the order.

"Two cups er coffee," he said. "An' er peecer cake."

He gave the piece of cake to Sweetie, shrugging his shoulders as he did so.

"I'm not hungry," he said.

It wasn't true. But he'd got his eye on those three shillings. He knew from last time the way money goes if you don't look after it.

While they were sipping their coffee, a lorry drew up. It was a big lorry with a row of double wheels at the side, and a thing like a caravan hitched on behind. When the driver climbed down from the driving seat it was like a man getting out of a first-storey window. Ginger stood there for some time admiring both the lorry and its driver. Then he happened to overhear what the lorry-driver and the coffee-stall proprietor were talking about. The lorry-driver seemed to be called Dave, and the conversation was about someone who lived up in Doncaster. When the coffee-stall proprietor asked to be remembered to him, that was the clue for which Ginger had been waiting. It meant that the lorry-driver was going

378

off to Doncaster. And it meant that Doncaster was where he and Sweetie were going, too.

"Give us a lift, guv," he said just as the lorry-driver was preparing to mount into that first-storey driving cab of his.

The lorry-driver scarcely paused. He was used to these pick-ups at all-night coffee-stalls, and he was suspicious of them: they usually spelt trouble. And he had no patience with people who just wanted to go anywhere. So he tried his stock question.

"Where d'you want to go to, son?" he asked.

"Doncaster," Ginger told him, adding in the sort of voice that clinches things, "My mate lives there."

The lorry-driver looked across again at Ginger's mate. He had been watching them out of the corner of his eye as they had stood at the coffee-stall, and he had noticed the way the smaller one broke the slab of cake up into small pieces before eating it and didn't simply take bites the way a man would have done. Girlish, he reckoned, it was; and where Dave came from they didn't like boys to be girlish.

On the other hand it was a long run from Southampton to Doncaster, and if he had someone to talk to it would be easier to keep awake. That was Dave's whole trouble with night driving. Whenever he got to one of the straight stretches where he could really let her rip, the need for sleep always came over him. He'd been clean through a hedge once and carried away a telegraph pole as well just because he had dozed off for a moment through not having anything to think about. And rather than drive alone, he would have taken a parrot with him if only he could have been sure that it would talk.

"Okay," he said finally. "Get in. But no monkey-business. If there's any monkey-business I puts you out. See? Puts you out wherever we are. See?"

"I see," said Ginger, and motioned to Sweetie for her to climb in.

Then he restrained himself. On the whole, he reckoned that it would be better if Sweetie didn't sit next to the driver. He had just noticed Sweetie's hands. It was the same trouble as with her hair. They were so obviously a girl's hands.

Looking back on it afterwards, Ginger couldn't remember anything that he had ever enjoyed more than that all-night drive. He enjoyed it so much, in fact, that he kept forgetting that there was anything else that mattered, kept forgetting that he was running away at all. The driving-cab itself was so fascinating that it satisfied him completely. There was a speedometer with a little light just over it, an ammeter and a radiator thermometer. It was best when Dave changed down to third. Then the engine sent vibrations like electric shocks all up his spine. Merely to be perched up there on the slab cushion was to have the sensation of privilege and purpose and effortless, inexhaustible power.

And it was even better outside. Dave had wormed his way through London at last. He had left the lamp-posts and the traffic-lights behind him, and was cruising down the main channel of the Great North Road. This was the real stuff, this was. They were alone now. Behind them lay London, all tucked-in and sleeping. And, in front, was blackness— plain inky blackness. It might have been on a journey into outer space that they were going. A trip into the heart of night itself. The lorry was all that mattered now. Inside, it was noisy, warm and rather fumey; outside was simply rushing, ebony air. The speedometer showed thirty-five, forty, forty-five . . .

"Go on talking," Dave said sharply. "I was nearly dropping off just now."

Not that Dave was taking things too hard. There were no grand endurance tests about his style of driving. He'd got something wrong with his stomach, he confided. It was the sort of stomach that needed a lot of food, and it needed it often. That was why he kept stopping. And his stomach seemed to know all the right places on the way—Charley's Bar, Eddie's Pull-Up, Cosy Café, the All-Night Tea-Rooms and Sandy's. The lorry drew up automatically at all of these.

They were pretty exciting sort of places. There were a lot of other lorries moored in a kind of little cinder-strewn harbour outside; and, inside, there was the smell of food and the noise of voices and the chink of slot-machines. They were all the same, too, Ginger noticed. It was as though Charley and Eddie and Sandy and all the rest of them had got together into one tremendous combine to supply meals after midnight. The furnishings were the same—the same cut-outs of big smiling girls, with pearly white teeth and open, inviting bosoms, the same shiny tops to the tables, the same bentwood chairs a bit too small for the customers that had to sit on them. And the food was the same as well—the same nut-brown, burst-open sausages and the same hot, greasy, slightly green-looking coffee. Even the customers were the same, a rather tired, sagging lot of men with shiny bottoms to their trousers from sitting all their lives in the driving-seat; and they all had Christian names only, no surnames—just Sid and Bill and Frank and Pat, and all the rest of them.

Ginger was only sorry that Sweetie was missing it all. But she didn't seem to mind: she was fast asleep whenever he went out to look at her. Had gone to sleep on his shoulder almost as soon as they had started, in fact. In the end, indeed, the very placidness of her sleep got on his nerves rather. He looked down at her all crumpled up on the slab cushion of the driving-cab, with his cap pulled down over her ears, and he pondered.

"She's takin' it pretty calmly, I must say," he reflected resentfully. "Just like a girl, leavin' it all to a fellow. She's takin' it calmly all right."

It was the same, too, in between the stops. Just the road and the blackness and the rushing air. Dave had only two remarks that he ever made. One was when he came on the red rear-light of another lorry in front of him. Then he would tighten up and thrust his chin out towards the windscreen. A new urgency would take possession of him, and he would start muttering. "Cor, you'd think 'e'd bought the whole flippin' road, the way 'e's flippin' well driving," he would begin. "Better git past him. That's the only thing to do with that flippin' sort of driver. Git past 'im." Down would go Dave's foot, and the eight-wheeler would begin to rock and sway as the engine roared under him. The other remark was kept all ready for whenever something passed him. He would tighten up in just the same way, but he would draw his chin back instead of thrusting it forward. "Silly flippin' bastard," he'd say, " 'e's arsking for it. That's what 'e's flippin' well doing—arsking for it. . . ."

Ginger must have dozed off for a bit himself because, when he woke, it wasn't dark any longer. Not really inky stuff.

There now was a slate grey light over everything, and he could see hedges and haystacks and the telegraph poles alongside them.

Sweetie woke up, too.

" Where are we?" she asked.

Her voice sounded more than ever like a girl's, and Ginger was worried. But Dave didn't seem to notice that there was anything wrong.

" Can'tcher see?" he asked. " We're nearly there. Putcher darn inside the 'alf-hour."

That made Ginger sit up. Doncaster was important. It was the place he was going to look for work. Then he frowned: he'd just remembered something. He'd have to get a room in Doncaster, a room for him and Sweetie. But it was too late to worry about that now. The thing to go after was a job. And Sweetie would have to go after one, too. It wouldn't matter if she had to live in. They could still see each other on her half days, if that was what she wanted.

Then just as Dave was putting them down, Sweetie spoilt everything.

" Where's Doncaster?" she asked.

That made the driver suspicious.

" I thought you said he lived 'ere," he remarked.

" So 'e does," Ginger answered. " 'E's forgettin'."

" Sez you," the driver answered. " I could tell you was on the run as soon as I see you." He brought the lorry to a standstill as he said it. " Now you 'op it, both of yer. If anyone asks yer 'ow you got 'ere, you don't remember, see! I don't wanner get mixed up in nothing funny, see! Take care of Sissy."

The driver pursed up his lips as he said it and made a rude sort of sound. That rather upset Ginger. It seemed a pity that such a nice, friendly man could have turned so unpleasant at the end of it. But he soon stopped worrying.

The one thing that mattered was that he and Sweetie had got there, and that no one knew who they were.

v

It was too early to start looking for a job straightaway, and Ginger and Sweetie spent the next hour or so hunting for a place to get breakfast. Not that Ginger really wanted it. With all those sausages and cups of coffee inside him, he had a full-up feeling already. It was Sweetie who wanted it: she had the appetite of a healthy schoolgirl. But it was too early even for breakfast. There was nothing for it, therefore, but to walk up and down the streets. They had one piece of luck, however. Right under their feet, too: in fact, Ginger nearly stepped on it. He saw suddenly something lying there and bent down to pick it up. It wasn't anything very much, just a gilt shamrock brooch with the single word " MOTHER " on a scroll across the bottom, but it was good luck finding it. Ginger cleaned it on his sleeve and examined it carefully.

" It's gold, I reckon," he said when he had completed his examination.

" Then we ought to give it to the police," Sweetie told him. " Gold's valuable."

Ginger looked at her contemptuously. " Don't be potty," he said. " I ain't goin' near no policeman."

He put the brooch in his pocket, and they walked on side by side in silence. When they reached the next street, however, Ginger took the brooch out again. The pin on the back needed straightening and Ginger used his teeth on it. Then when the brooch was wearable again he passed it over to Sweetie.

" You can 'ave it," he told her. " An' if anybody arsts yer say it was a present. Then they can't arrest yer, see?"

" Thank you very much," said Sweetie.

She was still thanking him when, for the second time, she nearly ruined everything. Just as they were passing the station she tugged at his arm.

" I want to be excused," she said.

It was only at the last moment that Ginger realised what she was doing: she was making for the LADIES.

He darted after her.

" You can't go there," he said. " An' you can't go in my side, either. You gotter wait."

Then he relented.

" Gimme my cap an' shake yer 'air out," he said. " Then you'll look more like a girl. Only don't ferget to put it on again. It's a boy and a girl people'll be looking for. That's why we gotter be two boys when we're togevver so they won't suspec' nothing."

" I'll remember," Sweetie promised.

While she was away, Ginger stood there biting his lip.

383

"I knew it'd be harder bringin' a girl along," he told himself. "I knew it was potty."

They had breakfast at an open bar by the bus stop. It was another and poorer version of the cafés of the night before: same sort of customers, but no pictures and no slot-machines. The man behind the counter looked decent enough and, in his position, he certainly ought to know Doncaster.

"D'you know where I could get a job?" Ginger asked.

The man pursed his lips.

"Got yer card?" he asked.

"Wot card?" Ginger asked him.

"That means yer ain't got one," the man replied. "No good trying round 'ere. You'd better go along to the Labour Exchange."

"Will they gimme a job?"

The man behind the counter shook his head.

"Say, was you born yesterday?" he began.

Then he was interrupted. Two teas and a coffee with ham-rolls turned up, and he couldn't spare any more time on Ginger.

Seen in broad daylight, Doncaster looked a pretty grim sort of place, Ginger reckoned. Hard and gritty, it had a pace and a purpose about it that didn't make it look as though jobs were easy to pick up there. But he was glad of that tip about the Labour Exchange and he decided to try it. He found the Exchange quite easily. But what he wasn't prepared for was the long queue of men already standing there. They were grown men, too: quite old, some of them. And he wasn't sure about Sweetie. There might be difficulties if they offered her the wrong kind of job, a man's job. So he told her to go down the road and wait for him.

"S'pose I've got to earn enough money for two of us," he thought gloomily. "Got to at first anyway until they stop looking for us."

The queue was a slow one. It was half an hour before he even got to the counter. And when he did get there he wasn't prepared for all the questions they asked him: he had been expecting something much simpler—just a slip of paper giving the name and address of someone who wanted a job of work done.

"Got your card?" the clerk asked.

"Wot card?" Ginger asked him.

"Third counter down," the clerk told him. "They'll see to you there. And don't stand here blocking everything up."

" No, sir," Ginger answered.

The clerk seemed a pretty important person. Ginger didn't want to do anything to offend him. And the clerk at the other counter was important, too. He scarcely looked at Ginger.

" Name?" he asked.

That was a stumper. If he said " Herbert Woods " the police would be on to him at once. He'd have to invent something. So he gave Mr. Dawlish's name.

" John Dawlish, sir," he said.

" Address?"

" I ain't got one, sir," he explained. " I only just got here."

" What was your last address?" the clerk asked.

Again the same problem.

" 'Ammersmith," he said: he'd seen the name Hammersmith above the coffee-stall on the night before.

" What road?"

" 'Ammersmith Road."

" London?"

Ginger nodded.

" Number?"

" Twenty . . . twenty-three," Ginger told him.

" First job?"

" Yus, sir."

" What school were you at?"

There was a pause.

" 'Ammersmith Boys'," he said. It sounded quite convincing when he heard himself saying it.

" Parents living?"

" No, sir."

" Guardian?"

Ginger didn't know what that one meant. So he said " no " again. But the answer didn't seem to satisfy the clerk.

" Got to have guardian," he said.

" Have I?" Ginger asked.

The clerk looked up for the first time. He had sharp, sneaky little eyes behind his spectacles, and Ginger didn't like the way they looked at him.

" You go and sit over there," the clerk said, pointing to a hard, deal bench up against the wall opposite. " I'll get some-one to deal with you in a minute. I'd like a few more particulars."

Ginger watched him closely. He was suspicious by now.

He saw the clerk deal with three other boys, all of whom had parents and addresses, and then the clerk looked up again.

"I'll be right back," he said.

"Yus, sir," Ginger answered.

But as soon as the clerk had disappeared inside a door at the end of the counter, Ginger scooted. There was a place marked "Exit," and Ginger went straight for it. By the time the clerk had returned, Ginger was half-way down the street towards Sweetie.

She smiled as he came up to her.

"Is it a good job?" she asked. "Is it to do with cars? Can I come too?"

"You shut up," Ginger told her. "We can't stand 'ere. They're looking for me. They haven't got no jobs."

Once they were down a side street, Sweetie turned to him again.

"Then we'll try somewhere else," she said. "I'll try next time. They won't think anything if I go alone."

But Ginger only shook his head.

"It's no good," he explained. "Not unless you've got parents an' guardians. An' you gotter live somewhere. The man inside said so."

"Oh," Sweetie answered.

It was certainly difficult: she had been relying on things being the other way round.

"But something's bound to turn up," she told him. "Somebody's sure to want something done."

They walked round Doncaster until after lunchtime. It was tiring, just walking. And Sweetie began to lag behind a bit. Once or twice she took hold of his hand as she walked beside him, but Ginger shook it off again. It would look barmy two boys going around hand in hand. People would guess at once that there was something wrong.

And there was that old trouble about feeling hungry. It kept coming over him in little waves of sheer emptiness. Their tour of the city had taken them longer than he had realised: it was nearly three o'clock already. And, when he could stand the feeling of emptiness no longer, he turned to Sweetie.

"Like sominker eat?" he asked.

"Whenever you feel like it," Sweetie answered.

She had been feeling sick and hungry herself for some time. But she hadn't liked to say anything about it. Above all things she didn't want to be a nuisance. She had made that resolution before she had asked Ginger to take her with him.

Going into a small shop, he bought some buns and a bottle of lemonade, and they sat on the canal bank. It really couldn't have been nicer, Sweetie thought, sitting there with Ginger close beside her, and their toes almost in the water. It was only the smell of the place that spoiled it. There was a factory just behind them that did tanning or something; and, to be comfortable, you had to keep your nose away from the direction the smell came from. But the buns and the lemonade made them feel better. When they had finished, Ginger bunged up the neck of the lemonade bottle with some old newspaper to make it watertight, and threw it into the canal. Then they threw stones at it until it sank.

And as soon as they got going again, their luck changed. It was Sweetie who saw the notice "BOY WANTED" over a door in a side street. There wasn't anything to say what he was wanted for, and it didn't look much of a business: it seemed to deal in broken-up boxes mostly. But it was a job. And while Sweetie waited outside, Ginger went into the shop.

He got the job immediately. Fifteen shillings a week it was, and nothing to it. All that he had to do was pick up the bits of wood that had been chopped up and tie them with pieces of tarred twine into bundles of firewood. It astonished him that anyone should really be paid for doing anything so easy. And he reckoned that if he showed himself good at it, he'd get promoted. He'd be on to the chopping-up next.

He had to go outside again to say a word to Sweetie.

"You just hang around," he said importantly. "I gotter job. Start right away. Meet yer 'ere at seven."

Sweetie smiled.

"I told you you'd find one," she said. "You go in and do it. I'll be back."

"You be all right?" he asked suddenly.

"Of course I'll be all right," she told him.

"Well, take this. But don't spend it."

He put his hand into his pocket and gave her one of the two remaining shillings.

"Just in case yer need it," he added unnecessarily.

He watched Sweetie as she moved off. She'd got his cap on again and none of her hair was showing, but even so he

387

still wasn't sure about her. The real trouble was that she *walked* like a girl. And he didn't altogether like the idea of a girl going off like that all by herself in a place where she didn't know anybody. It didn't seem right somehow. But he reckoned that she knew how to look after herself. She'd always seemed a pretty sensible sort of girl. And anyhow he couldn't go with her: he'd promised to get back into the yard and start faggoting.

It wasn't so much that the work was difficult: he'd been quite right about that. It was simply that it had to be done so fast. The choppers were hard at it all the time and the pile of bits beside him didn't seem to get any smaller no matter how quickly he tied. It wasn't all that easy, either: the little bits of wood kept slipping out of his hand until he got the knack of it. And the splinters. At first he stopped every time he ran a splinter into himself, and tried to get it out again. But he soon saw there'd be no time to go on like that—he'd be buried underneath the heap of bits that the choppers were piling up on him. And so he went straight on with the little slivers of wood sticking into him and the tarred twine biting into his skin as he pulled the bundles tight.

It wasn't a bad sort of place to work. They gave him a mug of tea when the others had it. But they certainly kept him at it. He was supposed to tie two bundles a minute: that was what the man said. And it took a bit of doing. He got up to a hundred an hour, and there he stuck. All the same, he had tied more than three hundred bundles by the time seven o'clock came round.

" What time to-morrow, please, sir?" he asked.

" Eight o'clock," the man told him, " and sharp at that, lad."

He spoke in a thick Doncaster sort of voice with a bit of a rasp in it that made him difficult to understand. But up here everyone seemed to speak like that. It was being so far from London that did it, Ginger reckoned.

And then Ginger put another question.

" Please, sir, when do I get paid?"

That seemed to startle the man. When Ginger had finished, he said. And rightly speaking, he added, he hadn't got properly started yet. That afternoon they'd merely been trying him.

But the job was too good for Ginger to start arguing about. He just said " Okay, sir," and started off to look for Sweetie.

Provided they didn't eat too much they'd be all right until pay-day. And after that there'd be nothing more to worry about. They could get a proper room. Then, as soon as the police had stopped looking for them, Sweetie could get a job of her own. The right kind of job. A girl's job.

As soon as he saw Sweetie, he knew that she'd been up to something. She was leaning up against a lamp-post and smiling. And when Ginger came up to her she reached into the pocket of his trousers—Ginger's trousers—and took out a paper packet. It was small and crumpled.

" Open it," she said.

And then, before he could unwrap it, she told him what it was.

" It's a tie-pin," she said.

She was smiling and excited and happy.

" But I ain't gotter tie," Ginger answered. And then he stopped suddenly. " You ain't blewed that shilling, 'ave yer?" he asked.

Sweetie avoided his eye.

" It's gold," she said. " It was sixpence."

But Ginger wasn't listening. With the shilling half spent he was wondering where breakfast and dinner and tea and supper were all coming from.

" But you've still got another shilling," Sweetie reminded him.

" No, I ain't," Ginger told her angrily. " Only sixpence. The uvver sixpence don't belong to me. I borrered it."

" I see," Sweetie answered. " I didn't know." She paused. " I only did it because you gave me the brooch."

" But I didn't pay nothing for it," Ginger pointed out.

He saw now that he should never have trusted her with the shilling. It wasn't safe to trust other people with your money. Not girls, at least. And certainly not Sweetie.

Slowly he counted out what was left. There was the shilling of which only sixpence was really his, and there was a penny left over from the shilling that had paid for supper and breakfast.

" We gotter shilling anner penny," he said at last. " An' we gotter eat."

Sweetie knew that she was in disgrace, and she wanted to make Ginger pleased with her again.

" I'm not hungry," she replied promptly. " Really I'm not."

But Ginger wouldn't listen.

389

"Gotter eat," he said stubbornly. "It's barmy not eating."

But as it happened, eating didn't prove quite so expensive as he had feared. Apparently they did things very cheaply and sensibly up Doncaster way. Fish and chips, for instance. He blamed himself for not having thought of fish and chips before. But he really didn't know much about eating out—at least not as much as he wanted Sweetie to think he knew. He was only now getting round to studying menus and price-lists.

He and Sweetie stood for some time consulting this one. There were things like plaice and rock salmon for people who were giving themselves a real blow-out, with money no object. But there were cheaper items as well like "Fish pieces, 3d." And best of all was "Chips, 1d." Ginger finally decided on that and, going inside, he ordered twopennyworth.

You could tell from the smell of the place how good the food was going to be. It was very nearly as satisfying as a meal, simply standing there washing your lungs in it. The shop provided their own newspaper, too, so there was no trouble about plates or anything.

Ginger and Sweetie went back to the spot on the canal bank where they had eaten lunch. There was no particular reason for choosing it—there were plenty of other places. But it had pleasant, picnicking memories about it, and they felt somehow that they belonged there. It is very important when you are on the run, that feeling that you belong some-where: it gives you assurance. But it was dark now, and cold. Little wisps of grey mist came reaching up from the surface of the canal, and they shivered.

"Don't let's eat it here," Sweetie whispered. "Let's go under the lamp."

It seemed warmer under the lamp. And it was a good meal, even though there was no lemonade to wash it down this time. Ginger felt better about things in general. With chips so cheap, he reckoned that he and Sweetie could just about last out. He began boasting.

"When I git me pay," he said, "I'll gitcher proper room somewhere. Only gotter wait a week. Then I can git a better job. Somink regular."

"I'll get a job too," Sweetie told him. "Then we needn't worry at all."

Ginger had licked his fingers clean by now and was read-ing the paper the chips had been wrapped in. It was a clean sheet, crisply torn off the noon edition. And he was reading carefully and laboriously through a paragraph that was staring up at him. "RUNAWAYS IN DONCASTER?" it ran. "*Two inmates, a boy and a girl, of the Archbishop Bodkin Hospital in London were reported missing last night. A clerk at Hythe Street Labour Exchange reports that a boy answering the police description applied for work at 10 a.m. this morning. The boy, who is red-haired, appeared agitated and ran away when questioned. . . .*"

The rest was torn off. But Ginger had read far enough. He passed it across to Sweetie.

"You read that," he said.

Sweetie looked serious.

"That's us," she told him.

"Then we gotter get going," he said. "We can't stop 'ere. We gotter get going now."

There was a pause.

"What's 'agitated'?" Ginger asked.

CHAPTER LVI

I

NEITHER of them remembered how far they walked that first night. They just kept on walking. It was a main road that they got on to and, though lorries, big trailer affairs like the one they had come on, kept passing them, they didn't try for a lift. A lorry-driver might give them away, Ginger said. There were rewards for missing people, he told her, and the lorry-driver might go to the police simply to get the money.

But nobody can go on walking all night even if the shoe leather stands up to it. And Sweetie's wasn't standing up to it very well. The heel on the right foot had come clean off and had been lost completely. And that meant that she had to walk with a kind of a limp.

"Do you mind if I have a rest?" she asked finally.

"Okay," Ginger told her. "But cut it short. We gotter be in a different part of the country by the morning. If we're in a different part of the country they won't know it's us, see?"

"I see," Sweetie answered.

And, while he was waiting, Ginger found that he needed a rest, too. He sat down beside her. Then he started yawning.

But he didn't want to admit that he was tired: that would look like giving up too easily. Instead he looked all round him, trying to inspect the black landscape.

"Might as well sleep round 'ere," he said. "Gotter sleep somewhere. It's a good sorter place. Nobody won't expecter find us 'ere. That's why I brought you this way."

There was the dark outline of a barn farther up the road, and they made their way towards it. But a dog began barking when they tried the door, and they went on farther up the road. It was under a hayrick that they finally dossed down. Ginger chose the hayrick because he had heard that hayricks were warm. But perhaps this was the wrong kind of hayrick. Because it wasn't warm at all. It was cold and damp. And when he lay down beside it, he found himself up against wet, icy spikes. Sweetie felt the cold, too. She was shivering again. He could hear the noise that her teeth made, chattering. He moved up nearer and put his arm round her.

"Gitcher warmer this way," he said.

"You are nice," Sweetie answered.

She was almost asleep by now.

It is very sudden waking up in the open air. There are no degrees to it. At one moment you are asleep and, at the next, you are wide awake with the sun splitting your eyes open. The sun itself too is brighter, with no blinds and curtains and window-frames to drain it on the way. That is, if you go to sleep facing east. And Ginger hadn't known enough to choose the west side. If he had done so, he would have found it warmer. Tramps choose the west side, always.

Sweetie wasn't awake yet, because Ginger's body had been protecting her. She was lying there, her head supported on one arm and her hair tumbled across her face. It was raven-black hair and, in the morning sunlight, it gleamed and shone at him. Suddenly, he wanted to stroke it. It was the first thought of that kind that he had ever had about Sweetie, and it surprised him. He got up stiffly and moved away.

"I must be going barmy," he told himself. "Clean barmy, or I wouldn't never have wanted to do it."

Then a different kind of thought came to him.

"Good thing I don't have ter shave," he reflected. "If I did, I'd look awful."

Because it was quite light by now—broad daylight, in fact —he went back and roused Sweetie. And the same curious feeling about her came over him. He didn't know where to touch her; suddenly felt shy about touching her at all. But he couldn't just let her lie there: that would be asking for trouble. So he used his boot, pushing it under her and poking her ribs and wriggling it. . . .

They moved on almost straightaway. But they couldn't go so fast as they had done on the previous night. Where the heel had come off Sweetie's shoe, the nails had been left showing and they had worked their way right up through the leather. Her heel was swollen now. It was as much as she could do to take the first few steps at all.

There was a stream at the bottom of the field and Sweetie stopped there, resting her foot in it. The water was as cold as though it had come from ice-bergs just melted. It was clear, too. Sweetie could see the pebbles on the bottom. And there were reflections of the trees on the surface of the water.

"Isn't it beautiful?" she said at last.

That remark made Ginger suspicious of her again. He was close beside her, squatting on the bank. And he had been thinking. Thinking hard. The one job that he had managed to get, he'd lost again before he had been paid anything. And the police were after them: he knew that from the paper. Being among fields wasn't so good, either. It was easier to find you when there were only a few people anyhow. A town, like Doncaster, was the proper place to get lost in—if you didn't make the mistake of going up to nosy clerks in Labour Exchanges. Only with Sweetie's bad foot he didn't see how they would get to the right sort of place. What with Sweetie and her foot, he reckoned that he might just as well never have run away at all. It was all Sweetie's fault, and all that she could think of to say was how beautiful it was.

"Gotter to be gittin' on," he said savagely.

"I'm ready," Sweetie answered, and squeezing her foot back into her shoe before her heel could begin to swell again, they started off.

It had been Ginger's idea that they should cut across country so that they could avoid any posse of policemen who might be lying in wait for them at the cross-roads. But with Sweetie's bad foot that was impossible. And, in any case, the precaution proved unnecessary. The roads were unguarded. It was a fine, golden empty sort of morning and they could have gone anywhere.

393

Because it was still so early, there was not much traffic about. Just small stuff mostly, going back into Doncaster. And the big ones, the six-wheelers, ignored them. They simply went on at a steady forty, massive and imperious, as though they were driving themselves, and hadn't got any flesh and blood and human feelings inside them anywhere.

"When we git to a shop I'll buy some biscuits," Ginger said at last. "We can eat 'em while we're still goin'."

The fear of Doncaster and its police force was still on him, and he felt anxious and apprehensive as soon as they stopped anywhere. Not that Sweetie seemed put out about missing her breakfast.

"Thank you," was all she said. "I like biscuits."

Then they had a piece of real good fortune. Without even having to ask for it, they got a lift. It was a lady who offered it to them. You could see at once that she *was* a lady, even though it was only a very old Austin Seven that she was driving. And from the way she spoke you had to be respectful to her.

"Jump in, boys," she said. "It's a bit of a squeeze. But we'll manage it. Careful there with that parcel. And mind the door-handle, it's broken. Don't bother about the back seat, it's always been like that."

And that they found was her trouble: she wouldn't stop talking. She was inquisitive, too—which was awkward. She wanted to know everything about them—how old they were, where they were going, whether they liked the pictures, what radio programmes they listened to, did they ever read books, or was it only magazines—anything on earth, in fact, just to keep the conversation going.

Ginger summed her up quite early. She was barmy; harmless, but definitely barmy. Perhaps it was because she was barmy that she was so kind: there was some milk chocolate in the front of the car and she gave them the whole of it. Just told them to divide it between them, like that.

They had a nasty shock at the end of the ride, however. Because she drew up right outside the police station.

"Here we are, boys," she said. "This is as far as we're going. No farther."

Ginger felt his mouth suddenly go dry.

"Wodjermean?" he asked.

But the lady didn't seem to notice any difference in his tone.

"You didn't know that you'd been driving with a magistrate, did you?" she asked cheerfully. "If you were local lads you'd have known it all right. Well, good luck, boys, keep smiling. Best foot foremost. No dawdling. . . ."

"Come on," Ginger whispered hoarsely to Sweetie. "Don't hang around 'ere. They're not all barmy."

I I

That was the only lift they got that day. And the food wasn't so good, either. Just biscuits. They bought the broken kind at one shop they came to because they were cheaper. But the broken ones were a mistake: there were too many sweet ones among them. And when you are hungry, really hungry that is, it isn't the sweet ones that you want most. It is something plain, like bread-and-butter. Or potatoes. Or meat. Sweetie and Ginger thought about all of those as they walked. And they thought about things to drink, too, like cocoa and milk or lemonade. Altogether they covered about five miles, thinking of food and drink all the way.

And they weren't so fortunate in the people they fell in with that day. It was a sour, bitter colony that they had stumbled on as though someone had just done the folks there a disservice. When they went into a field to rest, they were ordered out again by a man with a dog at his heels and a gun. He said that he had met their sort before, and didn't want to see any more of them. And then, when they went on down the road and came to an inn, the publican who was standing in the doorway regarded them through dubious half-closed eyes, and stood looking after them until they were out of sight again. He hadn't actually said anything. But he didn't have to say it. From the look on his face Ginger wouldn't have cared to ask him even for a drink of water. And a drink of water was what they both happened to be wanting at the moment.

The stops that they made by the roadside had grown longer, and the stretches of road between them had grown shorter. Sweetie just hadn't got the strength to keep going any farther. It was getting on for four o'clock by now, and they hadn't covered more than ten miles since the old lady had dropped them. That worried Ginger. All the time they were resting he could feel the police catching up with them. And once they had to crouch down in the hedge while a slow policeman cycled past them. He was out searching. Ginger

395

reckoned; scouring the countryside for the two of them. And he made Sweetie pull his cap lower down over her head so that even the little stray bits of hair at the side wouldn't show.

Because he was tired himself, Ginger's manners were growing a bit ragged.

"Yer oughter cut it off before we started," he said, after the second attempt to get the cap on properly. "It's potty muckin' everythin' up because of a lot of 'air."

"I'm sorry," Sweetie answered. "I didn't think."

"Well, yer should of," he told her.

And it was that last remark that made Sweetie cry. Ginger knew that she was crying. But he was determined not to take any notice, because he hoped that she would stop soon. Besides, he hadn't said anything to make her cry. Nothing at all that could have made anybody cry. But he felt ashamed about it all the same. And awkward, too. It was difficult walking with someone who was two paces behind him, and in tears.

When he could stand it no longer, he stopped and waited for her.

"Wot you crying for?" he asked.

"It's nothing," Sweetie answered. "I'm just sorry. I've made things difficult for you. I shouldn't never have come."

Ginger softened.

"Thassalright," he said awkwardly. "Dontcherworry."

Now that she was close to him, he could see how pale she was. Her face was dirty with dust, and the tears had run down it leaving channels. But, even under the dust, the skin still showed white—whiter than he remembered it.

"Yer not ill, are yer?" he asked.

"I'm all right," Sweetie said. "Only . . . only just a bit tired."

He put his arm round her.

"Got to go a bit furver," he said. "Can't stop here. I'll git yer some real food soon. Then yer'll feel better."

It was another three miles before they came on the next village. And Ginger kept his arm round her all the way. He could feel now how thin she was. There didn't seem to be anything to her inside that overall. He was surprised now that she had even been able to walk as far as this.

"Git yer some real food now," he said again. "Git yer the kind of food yer like."

396

But he was cautious all the same. He didn't want anybody in the village to get suspicious. So he made Sweetie wait on the outskirts, and he went into the village shop alone. It was a very nice little shop and it seemed to sell everything. He could have bought cough-cures and hair-brushes and leather bootlaces, and bunion plasters if he had wanted them. But he saw straight away what it was that he really wanted. There was a dish of real food on the counter, a thick rich-looking black pudding. At the thought of Sweetie waiting somewhere up the road he suddenly became extravagant.

"Threepennorth of that," he said, pointing. And, looking round the shop, he saw another of those thick, wonderful slabs of fruit-cake that he had met first at his Piccadilly coffee-stall. "And threepennorth of that," he added.

That was sixpence gone out of his one-and-a-penny. All at one go, too. But he still didn't feel that he had done enough for Sweetie—not after making her cry like that.

"Anner pennorth of those," he said, pointing.

It was bulls'-eyes that he had ordered that time. Then as the shopkeeper handed him the screw of paper, a wave of coldness passed through him. He realised what he had done: all the money that he now had left was the sixpence that wasn't really his. But he forgot about it again in thinking how excited and happy Sweetie was going to be when she knew what he had bought her for supper.

"Come on," he said. "Let's git goin'. Let's git goin' somewhere we can eat this." He paused. "An' you'd better walk in front," he added. "So that nobody won't know that we're together."

Because it was getting late there were lights in the cottage windows. Bright lights they seemed against the greyness of the sky, and Ginger could see everything that was going on inside. There was one room in particular that he looked into. It was quite a small room with a lamp standing in the middle of the table. The chairs were drawn up round the table and, as he passed, he could see the faces of the people who were sitting down there—warm, comfortable, smudgy faces, all eating. The top of a loaf of bread was showing just over the edge of the window-sill and he could see the teapot, too, a big, coloured, fancy one. Ginger paused, for a moment, because he felt envious. Not envious because of the loaf of bread and the teapot, but simply because everyone in that room looked so happy and secure. It was like peering into another world altogether, seeing them sitting down there. And he would have been ready to go on standing there, simply gaping.

But, remembering Sweetie, he started off again: she was still trudging on in front of him. The road in front led straight on to the moors. And as Ginger followed up behind he noticed how slowly Sweetie was moving. She might have been ill the way she was walking. It was her heel, he supposed. Perhaps it had got bad again after she had bathed it this morning. Then he noticed that she had stopped walking altogether: was simply standing there waiting for him to catch up with her. And that was silly, because it would naturally give the whole show away. He was all ready to tell her about that, too.

But as he got near, it was Sweetie who spoke first.

"Sorry, Ginger," she said. "It's no good. I can't go no farther."

"You're not bad, are you?" he asked anxiously.

Sweetie shook her head.

"Only tired," she said. "Just tired—and my foot hurts."

Ginger put his arm round her again.

"You'll feel better when you've had this," he told her.

When they had gone another half-mile or so, and the village looked quite small behind them, Ginger said that they could stop. There was a clump of trees just off the road and they made towards it. Compared with the bleakness of the moors in the dusk that was gathering round them, the shelter of the trees seemed friendly and comfortable. Ginger helped Sweetie pull her shoe off and then spread out the picnic that he had bought for them—there was the black pudding and the big chunk of fruit cake. He was keeping the bulls'-eyes for a surprise afterwards.

He divided the pudding carefully and then handed one portion to Sweetie. And it was certainly good; a bit on the rich side perhaps, but exactly what he was needing. He took another bite of it and felt better. When he looked up, however, he found that Sweetie wasn't eating. Hadn't so much as even taken a nibble to see if she liked it.

"Wozzermatter?" he asked.

"I feel sick," she said. "I couldn't eat anything. I just don't want it."

There was something in the way she said it that angered him. There he was, without a penny to his name because he had bought food for both of them, and all that Sweetie could think of to say was that she didn't want it. Just that. No thanks. Nothing.

" Well, if you don't, I don't either," he said suddenly.

And, as he said it, he threw the whole of his portion away from him. Three-halfpence worth of black pudding went sailing out through the tree-trunks. He was bending down to throw the cake away, too, but Sweetie stopped him.

" Don't do that," she said. " It's our breakfast."

It was six o'clock by now and the night was closing in fast. They saw the moor change from grey to purple and now to black. And, as the light faded, the mist began to rise. It lay like smoke in the hollows already. And long damp fingers began reaching into the little wood where they were sitting. Sweetie shivered.

" You cold?" Ginger asked.

Sweetie nodded.

" I am rather," she said.

" I'll come up nearer," he told her. Then, after a pause, he spoke again. " Have a bulls'-eye?" he asked.

He was glad that she accepted because they were good bulls'-eyes. And sucking the bulls'-eyes made everything seem better. They became friendly again.

" D'you see that house we passed?" Sweetie asked.

Ginger nodded. He knew which one she meant.

" Must be nice, having a house like that," she went on. " A house makes all the difference." She hesitated. " Where do we go to-morrow?" she asked.

" Oh, some place," Ginger answered. " Some place I can get a job. We'll be all right. I got that last job, didn't I? I can get another job any time I want it. Get one to-morrow, come to that. We'll be all right."

There was a pause.

" Do you know where we are?" Sweetie asked.

" Yus," was all that Ginger answered.

He was terse and not to be drawn on the subject: that much was obvious. And Sweetie did not press him. All the same, Ginger wished that she hadn't asked the question at all. He'd been wondering the same thing quite a lot lately. So far as he could see, they had come to the wrong part of England altogether. Nobody had ever told him that there was any bit of it like this—just fields without any hedges, and a road with telegraph poles beside it, and the mist. It might have been straight to the moon that this road was leading. Might almost have got there from the look of it. He began to wish that he had stayed in London. There were plenty of jobs in London. Compared with this, the whole place was full of them.

And more because he wanted to hear himself saying it than because he really believed what he was saying, he turned to Sweetie.

" It don't go on much longer like this," he said. " There's more towns over the top of the hill. Lots er towns. If we don't like the first one we can move on. I'll git a job all right once we've got over that hill . . ."

It was growing colder every minute as he was talking. But he'd got more on than Sweetie. Underneath the overall, she seemed to be wearing hardly anything. He could feel her shivers right through him. Then suddenly he got up.

" 'Ere, you 'ave my jersey," he told her.

But she wouldn't let him take it off. She was all right, she said. Even if he gave her the jersey she wouldn't wear it. So he sat down beside her again and put both arms round her. She seemed smaller than ever when he held her that way; smaller and somehow pitiable. Her hair was up against his face. It was soft, smooth kind of hair, and he started stroking it. He was sorry for her and, because he was sorry, he loved her. He had never known anyone quite so defenceless before.

" Cor," he said. " It mustn't half be rotten bein' a girl."

They didn't sleep much that night, because it was too cold for sleep. As soon as they moved away from each other even for a moment the coldness came striking at them. And they just lay there huddled against each other hoping that it would soon be morning. Their conversation was desultory and broken.

" Guess it'll be gittin' light again in a minute," Ginger remarked at last. " Then we can start movin' on."

That was about ten o'clock when he said it. And he found himself wishing that he really knew, that he had a watch—one of those good watches with luminous figures that you can read in the dark. But even without a watch he was still confident that at any moment dawn would be breaking and things getting warmer again.

" How long can people live without eating?"

It was Sweetie who had spoken and Ginger considered the point.

" About a munf," he said. " Fink of people on rafts."

There was a pause. Then Sweetie spoke again.

"Ginger," she said.

"Yus?"

"If I die, would you promise to go on without me?"

"What makes yer think yer dyin'?"

"I don't think so. Only I might. People do die out in the cold, you know."

"'Tisn't cold enough for that," Ginger answered. "At least, not yet it isn't."

And then, when it must have been nearly midnight, Sweetie asked another of those questions that Ginger would rather not have had put to him.

"Suppose you don't get a job?" she asked. "Suppose neither of us gets a job, what are you going to do then?"

"I've told yer I shall get a job."

"But supposing you don't."

"I'll go on looking."

"You can't go on looking if you haven't had any food."

"I'll steal some food."

Sweetie paused. She'd thought about stealing, and she'd wondered if it had occurred to Ginger, too.

"But suppose you can't, suppose it's all locked up," she went on. "We'd have to stop then. We'd have to tell a policeman who we are."

Ginger moved away from her.

"I shan't never do that," he said fiercely. "I'd rather be dead than git caught."

"Do you mean kill ourselves?" Sweetie asked.

The question put directly to Ginger startled him. He hadn't thought of it like that. But he didn't want to admit that there was anything that he hadn't considered. And, in any case, he supposed that killing yourself quickly would be better than slowly starving to death in some awful cold place like this one. So he shrugged his shoulders to show that he was prepared for everything.

"Yus," he said simply.

He had imagined that this would settle it, would frighten Sweetie off asking any more of her silly questions. But it didn't.

"How?" she asked.

And that really did irritate him. He'd just been planning to run away. Not to commit suicide.

"Oh, jump in a river or somefink," he said. "Now you shut up."

401

Sweetie could tell from his tone of voice that she had offended him.

"I'm sorry," she said. "I only wanted to know."

That pacified him, and he moved in closer again.

"An' go er sleep," he told her. "S'nearly morning any-'ow. Can't be more'n half an hour now. Guess it's gettin' lighter already."

It was light when he awoke again and Sweetie had spread her coat over him.

CHAPTER LVII

THAT WAS Sweetie's and Ginger's second night in the open. And it was their third night away from the Archbishop Bodkin Hospital.

In the course of a year quite a lot of children are missing for a single night. They drop off to sleep under a lilac bush in a public park, or slip round to auntie without telling mum, or even buy a platform ticket and lock themselves in the lavatory until the train reaches Glasgow. One night is nothing; you can't expect the police force to turn itself upside down just because a night's domestic arrangements have been a bit upset. But two nights' absence is serious. It means that the thing has been planned, calculated, fixed up in advance possibly: in short, it is thoroughly unchildish. Either that, or something bad has happened. And to be missing for three days means that the wheels start turning. All sorts of things happen—telephone calls, divisional conferences, photographs in the *Police Gazette,* door-to-door inquiries, newspaper paragraphs, appeals on the wireless.

And though Sweetie and Ginger woke, stiff and still shivery, to a peaceful October morning with a gentle mellow hush hanging over the whole landscape, that was only how it looked at first glance. In reality, it was a field day for the County Constabulary. The police were out hunting in real earnest by now.

Breakfast for Sweetie and Ginger didn't amount to much. And that was because the fruit cake had gone soggy in the night. After the bit of trouble about the black pudding, Ginger had forgotten to put the fruit cake back inside the bag again, and the dew had got at it. It was like a flat, wet sponge. They didn't break bits off: they scooped.

But having nothing to drink was the bad part. The Archbishop Bodkin seniors all had tea for breakfast—great amber rivers of it, poured out of big enamel jugs with the milk and sugar all ready mixed up with it. Even Miss Britt hadn't been able to put an end to that. And Sweetie and Ginger both remembered it as they sat there pecking at their handful of damp cake crumbs.

" Git a drink when we come to a river," Ginger observed at last. " When we come to a river we'll git a drink."

" I want one," Sweetie told him. " That's why I couldn't eat last night."

" Well, let's git goin'," Ginger said firmly. " Got to git over them hills."

But he had not reckoned on Sweetie's heel. She had walked on it for one day too many. And the heel was now red and angry-looking. Even with both of them pushing together they couldn't get it into the shoe. And, in the end, they had to stop trying because the pain of it made Sweetie feel sick again.

That beat Ginger. He squatted down on his haunches, wondering what to do. And finally it was Sweetie, not Ginger, who decided. She was wearing an Archbishop Bodkin petticoat and she tore a long strip off it. Then she made a bandage out of it. And finally, just to make sure that it didn't come off when she walked, she tied the two ends together round her ankle.

" We can go on now," she said.

Ginger looked at the bandage suspiciously.

" People'll notice," he said.

But Sweetie only shook her head.

" No, they won't," she said. " If anyone asks, I'll say I lost it. People do lose their shoes, because I've seen them."

All the same, it was slow going. Ginger made Sweetie keep to the grass verge where her feet wouldn't show up so much. And all the time they were walking Ginger was thinking.

" Knew I didn't oughterer let 'er come wiv me. Gotter stealer pairer girls' shoes now. Knew I didn't oughterer let 'er . . ."

It broke in on his thoughts when Sweetie spoke to him.

" Did you mean what you said last night about not letting the police catch us?" she asked.

" 'Course I meant it," Ginger answered. " Wot you fink?"

" I only wondered."

" If the police git me, they won't git me alive," Ginger assured her. " I'm not that kind."

Having made the remark, he forgot all about it. There was no particular purpose in it. It was simply that Ginger's sense of the dramatic told him that something of the sort was expected of him. And, as a matter of fact, it was strangely reassuring, merely uttering such words. They satisfied some deep male instinct for sheer boastfulness.

And Sweetie seemed to be impressed.

" I won't forget," she said. " I won't let you down."

" That's okay," Ginger told her.

II

When they had gone some distance they had to leave the verge and take to the road itself. Down the slope of the hill in front of them was parked a green Post Office van, and there was a man perched on the top of a near-by telegraph pole like a monkey up a coconut palm. Ginger paused. That was just what he wanted to avoid, having to go past someone. But the man up the telegraph pole seemed busy enough. He was bending over, concentrated on his work. It must have been windy up there, too. Ginger could see that the man had a leather strap round his waist but, even so, he swayed on his perch every time a gust blew. That decided Ginger.

" If he's doin' his job an' he's gittin' blown about, he won't 'ave time to bother about us," Ginger calculated.

And, turning to Sweetie, he said:

" Come on, we ain't gittin' nowhere."

" I'm coming as fast as I can," she said.

But the wind was against them. It was coming up the hill at them like little fists.

" Cor," thought Ginger. " It'll be rotten if it rains. She'll git wet."

And now when he looked he was conscious of another feeling, too. It was at her hair that he was looking, her hair that he had been stroking last night when they had huddled up together among the trees. But it was different hair now. It was loose and shining now, streaming back from her head like a comet's tail. Little wisps of it brushed across his face

404

as he walked. Then suddenly Ginger's heart gave a bump. This was awful: she looked like a girl and nothing else but a girl. There was no disguising her.

"Wot yer done with my cap?" he demanded.

"It's gone," Sweetie admitted. "It blew off. I couldn't help it."

"Why didn't yer say?"

"I did try to," she explained. "Only you wouldn't stop. I didn't know you'd mind that much."

Not mind! But it was no good saying anything now. They were too near to the man on the telegraph pole to be able to hang about any longer.

"Well, come on can't yer," Ginger said. "Don't stop talking. An' keep yer 'and over yer 'air. Yer don't want people to see yer."

It was the sight of a girl walking along with her hand on her head that first made the Post Office linesman take any real notice of them at all. Up there in all that wind and with a cracked insulator on his hands he had plenty to do without playing at being a sheriff. But when he looked he became interested. The girl seemed to have hurt her foot: she had a bandage or something round it. And then he remembered. There had been a paragraph about a boy and girl in the evening newspaper. And there they were to the life; boy with red hair, girl with black, and apparently trying to go north, just like the paper said.

He could get through to the exchange whenever he wanted to: the telephone instrument was hanging from a hook on his belt. So it was easy. He passed word up the line that he had seen the two runaways, or thought he had; and then got back to his broken insulator. He was not a melodramatic sort of chap; just sensible. He didn't go charging off in the Post Office van trying to collar them. Didn't do anything else in fact. Apart from reminding himself that it would be something to tell his wife, he forgot all about them.

But the police got busy straight away. Within five minutes, a blue Wolseley was drawing out of the yard of the police station, and was on its way towards the moors. Even so, Sweetie and Ginger had moved on by then, going across country again. And it is doubtful whether the two policemen sitting inside a saloon car on the main road would ever have found them, if it had not been for the Arkleydale and District Ramblers' League.

The ramblers were coming over the moor, thirty strong, with rucksacks swinging and bare knees glinting in the sunlight. At the sight of the police car they stiffened. They had been in trouble with the police before over rights of way, and they immediately suspected something sinister like a plot to close the moor to hikers. But when the sergeant merely asked them whether they had seen a boy with red hair and a girl out on the fells, they relaxed. And more than relaxed: they gloated. The fugitives, they said, were sheltering in a small copse on the way over to the reservoir. And suddenly becoming enthusiastic about the whole affair, the hikers suggested that if they fanned out across the moor, they could come down sickle-shape, cutting off all hope of escape while the two policemen took the direct path and made a neat arrest.

It was Sweetie who first noticed that something unusual was happening. She was seated beside Ginger in a small spinney, and wasn't looking at anything in particular. The bare moor extended on three sides of them, and down below in the valley lay a great lake walled in by concrete. The lake reflected the clouds and was beautiful. If only there had been some way of getting a meal, and if Ginger could have found a job in those parts, she would have been content to stay there for ever.

Then she noticed something moving, or rather a whole collection of somethings. As she looked closely she could see that they were people, a lot of people; and they were advancing in a long curved line.

She watched them with the casual interest of someone looking at something that can be of no possible personal concern. She was merely interested. And then she looked away. She did not even tell Ginger, who seemed cross and sulky about something. But when she looked again, the long line of people had come nearer. Much nearer. The nearest of them could not have been more than a quarter of a mile away by now. And it had become so interesting that she told Ginger.

She was surprised how excited he was immediately. He scanned the whole line of them and then looked directly behind them where Sweetie hadn't thought of looking. And what he saw he was prepared for. Climbing up the steep path to the spinney were two policemen.

"Come on," said Ginger. "It's the cops."

There was only one way clear for them, and that was the way towards the reservoir. It lay below them down the hillside, with its high stone wall cutting off the end of the valley. And the hillside fell away sharply. Sweetie and Ginger were not merely running now, they were falling and scrambling. He had hold of her hand, too, and was pulling her. As they ran, they heard shouts behind them. Then, when they turned for a moment, they saw the row of figures up against the skyline. The ground in front dropped away from them. It was a little ledge that they had come to.

"Can yer jump?" Ginger was asking. "I'll go down first and catch yer."

It was then that Sweetie really understood what it felt like to be hunted, knew why Ginger had said that he would never give himself up alive. Her heart was banging about inside her and her mouth was dry. But these were the only physical sensations that she was aware of. Even when she jumped and landed on her damaged foot, she did not feel it. All that she wanted to do was to escape from the shouting and the running feet that were behind her.

They had reached the grounds of the reservoir by now and a long row of spiked railings confronted them. But Ginger seemed to know all about spiked railings. He put his foot sideways between the spikes and jumped over as easily as if they had been made for climbing. He didn't even tumble when he landed. But he was breathless.

"Put yer foot up there," he said hoarsely. "I'll pull yer."

There was now nothing between them and the wall of the reservoir. It looked taller now than it had done from a distance. It towered. But there was a long flight of stone steps dwindling up to the summit, and they made for them.

"We gotter hurry," said Ginger. "I'll help yer."

They had reached the first landing before they looked down. And it was not so bad. The spiked railings were doing their work nicely. Only one of the hikers had got over, and the rest were clustered in groups trying to help each other. But one was enough for Ginger.

"Faster," he said. "We gotta go faster."

And as he ran, he remembered that time on the zig-zag fire-escape up to Sweetie's bedroom. He had known then what it was like to hear footsteps behind him on a ladder. But that time he hadn't had to drag someone up after him.

"Faster," he kept repeating. "We gotta go faster."

"I can't," Sweetie began saying. "I'm trying but I can't."
She knew then that it was hopeless. She wasn't as strong
as Ginger, she couldn't keep up with him. Because of her they
would catch him. And that must never happen.

"You go on," she said. "Leave me here."

"Shut up," was all the answer he gave her. "You hurry."
They had reached the top of the wall by now and they
were on a kind of level horse-shoe concrete road. It was
wide and level. On one side, ten feet below them, lay the
lake itself, dark and cold-looking. And seen close it wasn't so
placid as it had looked from the hillside. There were waves
on it, and spray where the waves came slapping against
the concrete. But it was better than the other side. There was
a forty-foot drop there, with rocks and boulders at the
bottom of it.

"Come on," Ginger was saying again. "Don't start
looking."

But no boy dragging a girl behind him can run as fast as a
man. And already there were others on the concrete road-
way. One of the policemen had got up there. And it was
obvious that he was in training. Even after his climb he
still seemed to have plenty of breath left in him. He was
fairly pounding along after them. In less than ten seconds
he was leading.

It was the sound of the footsteps closing in on them that
decided Sweetie. They were nearer now. Only ten yards
away. Or eight. Or five. In another moment he would be
on them. He'd be grabbing at her.

Suddenly, she snatched her hand away from Ginger's. She
was right on the edge of the wall now with the black water
breaking just beneath.

"You go on," she called after him. "I'm doing like you
said, Ginger."

Then she jumped.

CHAPTER LVIII

I

BUT THAT wasn't by any means the end of Sweetie. They fished her up again before she had even been down for the second time. Admittedly, she looked a pretty forlorn sort of figure in the policeman's arms, with her face deathly white and her dark hair plastered across her forehead. But she was still breathing, and that was the only thing that mattered.

It was Ginger who caused the real trouble. And that was because he had tried to do the gallant thing by her. When Sweetie jumped, he jumped in after her. And he was not so lucky as Sweetie. On his way down he struck one of the big stone bastions that projected into the water, and it stunned him. In consequence, when he reached the surface he simply disappeared under it.

They were nearly five minutes searching for Ginger and, when they did find him, it looked hopeless. They had to use artificial respiration, kneeling in the small of his back and squeezing the water out of his lungs before they could get a single breath to come into him. And even then it wasn't easy, without stretchers or anything of the kind, to get two half-conscious children down from the top of a forty-foot concrete wall, and up quarter of a mile of broken moorland to the police car that was waiting by the roadside.

The news that the fugitives had been found reached the Archbishop Bodkin while a Board Meeting was in progress. It was an emergency Governors' Meeting, called specially to discuss the two runaways. And already feelings were running high. There were rival factions. One, led by old Miss Bodkin, was for forgiveness; complete, unconditional forgiveness. The other, dominated by Canon Larkin, insisted on punishment, on bringing it forcibly home to the miscreants what trouble and anxiety they had caused to their elders and betters.

Dr. Trump, as it happened, had just been asked for his view, and, frowning, he had cleared his throat in readiness.

"I . . . I can see no other way," he was saying. "There is not merely the truancy and . . . er . . . all the undesirable publicity. There is also the theft. The three shillings, remember. I can see no alternative. I fear that we must proceed. That is, of course, assuming that they are both all right . . ."

It was at this point that the message from the local police station was brought into the meeting. Its effect was tremendous. For a moment there was silence—complete silence, as though the entire boardroom, chairs, tables and everything, had uttered up a sigh. And then, with the knowledge that Sweetie and Ginger were both living, the two sides, the forgiveness group and the punishment group, both started up again.

Finally, it was Dame Eleanor who tapped sharply on the table with the handle of her lorgnette and summed things up for the lot of them.

" Well," she said bitterly, " there's one thing that you may depend on, and that is that it's out of our hands now. We haven't heard the end of this yet, not by a long chalk we haven't."

And Dame Eleanor was right. The Press alone would have been enough to see to that: Sweetie and Ginger had been working their way steadily upwards. They were worth front-page banner headlines by now. And, though Dr. Trump did not know it at the time, there was still plenty in reserve to keep the item going.

Take Margaret's part in the affair, for instance. The moment she knew that Sweetie had been found she went to her. Leaving basins, and worse, unemptied, she went to her room, changed into her outdoor clothes and slipped out of the Hospital. Forty minutes later, with two pounds that she had drawn from her Post Office savings account, she had bought a ticket for Arkleydale and was already in the train on the way up there. It occurred to her only when the train had reached Rugby and was getting under way again in its journey north that perhaps she ought to have told Dr. Trump where she was going.

The omission, as it happened, was unfortunate. For the Press promptly got on to her story, too. And Dr. Trump, tired and nervous as he was, allowed himself to be trapped. Asked if it were true that Margaret was missing too, he replied that he had no idea of where she was. And, pressed on that point, he elaborated—always a fatal thing to do when answering Press inquiries. It was entirely without his permission, he said, if she had gone anywhere; and disciplinary action, he hinted, would certainly be taken as soon as she got back.

That was enough for the Press. By the time Dr. Trump opened his evening paper he was front-page news again. " RUNAWAY HALL " was the heading, and the mischievous black type continued gloatingly: " THIRD BODKIN FUGITIVE IN FOUR DAYS. WARD MAID MISSING."

There was, indeed, only one comfort anywhere. Canon Mallow had been ill again, and Mrs. Gurnett was keeping him in bed. That hadn't prevented him from writing—by almost every post in fact. But anything—*anything*, Dr. Trump repeated—was better than having Canon Mallow hanging about the Hospital at a time like this.

I I

Indeed, the strain of the past few days had been intolerable. Dr. Trump had not eaten. He had not slept. He had not done anything, in fact, except walk up and down his study wondering, waiting for the telephone to ring, praying.

And now, with the knowledge that Sweetie and Ginger were safe, a weakness that he had tried to fight against, had come over him. He felt tired, feeble, enervated. He was even angry with himself for having been so anxious. He despised himself.

But no matter how tired he felt, there was no opportunity for resting. The police alone would have been enough to see to that. They were round morning, noon and night, from ordinary police constables up to chief inspectors, with their big boots and their small notebooks, making what they called routine inquiries. And it was only Sweetie and Ginger in whom they were interested.

So far as Margaret was concerned, there was nothing to excite them there: she was merely someone giving her right name and an address that could easily be verified, who had gone off rather unexpectedly. They ignored her.

But about Sweetie and Ginger they wanted to know everything—ancestry as far as ascertainable, physical history, criminal tendencies, punishments. They examined the punishment book and took down an exact record of the number

411

of strokes that Ginger had received on each occasion; they
visited the cell in which Sweetie had been confined and
took measurements of the size, the height of the window
above the ground, the distance of the bed from the door.
They tramped through the dormitories. Walked imperiously
into the kitchens. Even went up and down the fire-escapes.

And, as soon as they had departed, there were other
visitors. An inspector called from a Child Welfare Society.
The governors began endeavouring to find out what really
was going on. Three probation officers, two male, one
female, arrived on the same day.

And, finally, just when everything seemed to be dying
down, the Home Office announced that it intended to hold
an inquiry.

III

It was this last communication that really shook Dr.
Trump. Think of the publicity! And all of it undesirable
too. Why, with an inquiry, the whole deplorable incident
would be kept alive and in the papers for weeks; even
months possibly. The blind, bureaucratic folly of it simply
staggered him. If only the Home Office had turned to him
for guidance, he could have explained to them how foolish
they were being.

And there was someone else who was every bit as angry,
bitterly angry, about the idea of an inquiry. And that was
Dame Eleanor. In all her thirty years of public service she
had never had any of her activities inquired into before.
And she did not intend to start now. She was, indeed, confident right up to the last moment that she could scotch this
one. Never so much as doubted it for a single moment. She
began simply and imperiously by writing to the Under-
Secretary telling him that the whole thing was ill-conceived
and should be called off immediately. And then when she discovered that the Under-Secretary was one of the obstinate
and upstart kind without the manliness to admit that he
had blundered, she tried other means. She marshalled re-
sources. She mobilised. She got her brother, the Bishop, to
speak personally to the Home Secretary and arranged for her
cousin, the judge, to drop a hint to the legal department.
Then as a final insurance, she arranged for a nephew who
was always in and out of the Central Office to say a word

inside the party. And having done as much she sat back, grim, confident, battleworthy.

"Pull yourself together, man," she told Dr. Trump. "We're not ruled by Whitehall. Take my word for it, we shall hear no more of this. They'll think better of it, if I know them."

And that was what made it so infuriating when she opened her paper the following morning and saw the name of Mr. Vivvyan Sparkes, K.C., who had been appointed to preside over the inquiry.

CHAPTER LIX

I

MR. VIVVYAN SPARKES, K.C., arrived punctually at the Archbishop Bodkin Hospital at ten minutes to ten on the morning of Tuesday, October the 23rd; and he arrived by taxi.

Dr. Trump saw the arrival. He was standing, restless and apprehensive, at the front window of the Warden's Lodging; had been there ever since nine-fifteen, in fact. And because his night had been an unusually troubled one and his nerves in a state of tension, he had been doing nothing but stand there, drumming with his fingers on the window-frame and telling himself that he must remain calm, unrattled, imperturbable.

He stopped drumming for a moment when the taxi drew up. But that was only because he was secretly rather surprised that K.C.s should go bundling about London by taxi: he had expected something very long and low and black to draw up outside; a Rolls or a Daimler or a Humber, possibly. But as soon as he saw Mr. Vivvyan Sparkes he realised that he was the sort of man who could have gone about by bicycle and still have contrived to remain dignified.

It was Mr. Sparkes's head that appeared first; then, a surprisingly long time afterward, the thin sloping shoulders; and after a further pause, the high narrow waist came into view. Mr. Sparkes was evidently a tall man: Dr. Trump felt that at least he had established that much.

And Mr. Sparkes was equally clearly in no hurry: the arrangement of arriving at nine-fifty had satisfactorily safeguarded against that. He paid the driver slowly and carefully, counting meticulously through his small change as though he were sorting uncut diamonds and expected to come upon one or two real little beauties if he searched long enough.

It was then that Dr. Trump noticed Mr. Sparkes's stoop. But, no. Stoop wasn't the right word at all. A leaning forward, rather. On the end of the long, flamingo-like neck, the head came pushing to the front as though for some reason it wanted to get there quickly.

Dr. Trump could not see his face at the time: for as soon as Mr. Sparkes turned and came forward, the top of the Archbishop Bodkin wall cut Mr. Sparkes clean off from him. But, later that same morning, Dr. Trump got to know the face. And, as he regarded it at close quarters, Dr. Trump understood why it was that the neck was unnaturally drawn out in that way. One glimpse at the face was sufficient to show that it would have drawn a coal-cart, let alone a neck, if it had happened to be attached on behind it.

By contrast with the nose, Mr. Sparkes's eyes, pale and slightly watery, seemed unusually deep-set. But with Mr. Sparkes's nose any eyes would have seemed deep-set. For the bridge came arching sharply outwards, as though the whole thing had been carved separately and then added some time afterwards. And this suggestion was further borne out by the fact that the skin of the face was only just sufficient to cover it. Even at that, it was clearly at full stretch: one size larger, or the bridge just one degree more steeply arched, and the bone would have been showing right through.

It was not until ten-fifteen that Dr. Trump's own presence was required. Some little clerk person in the Home Office had already written to Dr. Trump and told him so. The first fifteen minutes—from ten o'clock precisely—were to be spent with Dame Eleanor.

Dr. Trump had not moved away from the window when Mrs. Warple entered. And he could tell from her manner that she was in high spirits. Indeed her high spirits this morning had been positively unforgivable. All through breakfast she had been fairly spoiling for a fight—not with her son-in-law, whom she vigorously defended, but with his inquisitors and tormentors. And, now that the moment had come, she very nearly had her sleeves rolled up.

" They've just sent over," she said. " They're ready for you." She paused significantly. " My word, I wish it was me

414

they'd sent for," she went on. " I'd tell 'em a thing or two.
I'd show 'em where they got off."

She paused again and then to Dr. Trump's intense distaste, she patted him on the back. It was an affectionate
and encouraging pat ; the kind of pat that an owner gives a
nervous race-horse just before a big race.

" Don't spare 'em," she said. " After all, they can't hang
you."

I I

It was the Board Room that had been set aside for the
inquiry. And, as Dr. Trump entered, it seemed to him
unreal and somewhat nightmarish to see Mr. Sparkes installed
in Dame Eleanor's chair. But everything about the room
was unreal and nightmarish this morning. The little clerk
fellow from the Home Office was sitting, cocky as a robin, in
Dr. Trump's own chair ; and a strange, frowning stenographer, her pencil at the ready, was perched on the edge of
the seat where Miss Phrynne should have been.

The place reserved for Dr. Trump was at the far end, the
bottom end. And, at the sight of it, he shuddered : it was
the place normally reserved for people like Miss Britt, or
Miss Gurge, the laundry superintendent, when they were
summoned in person for their half-yearly reports. But what
was still worse was to think how else the place was going to
be occupied later on. Mr. Vivvyan Sparkes would see merely
a procession of faces with Dr. Trump's as one of them.

But already Mr. Sparkes had risen. With his head and
shoulders extended—he was more than ever like a flamingo
by now—he was waving a long thin foot—no, no, how silly
of me, Dr. Trump corrected himself : it is a hand, not a foot
that he is holding out to me—and inviting him to be seated.
Already, too, Mr. Sparkes was speaking. And, in place of the
harsh croak that Dr. Trump had expected he was annoyed to
find that the voice was full, mellow and rather gentle. It was
a churchman's voice.

" Ah, Dr. Trump," he was saying, " do pray be seated."

" Thank you, Mr. . . ." Dr. Trump began coldly, but
courteously, and then stopped himself. It was only now that
he had realised that despite all his rehearsals he did not know
how to address the man. Mr. Sparkes? Sir? Your Lord-
ship? What the deuce should it be?

Mr. Sparkes, however, did not appear to have noticed

anything amiss. In beautiful, cathedral-like tones he was addressing Dr. Trump again.

"Now this is not a Court of Law," he began saying . . .

"Quite so," Dr. Trump interrupted him.

". . . it is an inquiry instituted by the Home Secretary . . ."

"Quite so," Dr. Trump said again.

". . . with powers to invite witnesses, but not subpœna them."

Mr. Sparkes paused, and Dr. Trump attempted something in the way of a friendly and understanding smile that he hoped would serve to bridge the great gulf of polished pine, and the still greater gulf between witness and investigator, that at the moment divided them.

Mr. Sparkes, however, ignored him.

"You will not be called upon to speak on oath . . ." he continued.

Here Dr. Trump braced himself. He wished Mr. Sparkes to know from the very outset the manner of man with whom he was dealing.

"I always speak on oath," he said. "That is to say that . . . er . . . the force of my words is the same as if I were speaking on oath," he corrected himself. "I . . . I . . . I mean I always speak the truth."

The two pale eyes of Mr. Vivvyan Sparkes fixed themselves unwaveringly upon the Warden.

"It would never have occurred to me to think otherwise," he replied. "My object in reminding witnesses that they are not upon oath is merely to reassure any that may need such reassurance that in the event of error they cannot be committed for perjury."

Dr. Trump again braced himself.

"And if I choose," he asked, "am I free to refuse altogether to answer any question?"

"Quite free," Mr. Sparkes told him. "The choice is yours entirely." He paused. "Your refusal would, however, be noted. That is something I could not prevent."

Dr. Trump's eyebrows contracted violently, and his breathing suddenly became flutelike.

"I . . . I asked only in the spirit of seeking information," he explained.

"And it was in the same spirit that I gave my answer," Mr. Vivvyan Sparkes assured him.

They were getting on a bit faster by now. Mr. Sparkes,

after a whole battery of questions that had seemed impertinent and meaningless to Dr. Trump, was now devoting himself exclusively to Ginger.

"You are a believer then in corporal punishment, Dr. Trump?" he asked blandly.

"If the circumstances require it," Dr. Trump replied.

"And so far as this boy was concerned, am I to conclude that you felt that the circumstances always did require it?"

Dr. Trump nodded.

"That is so," he said. "Otherwise I should not have caned him."

"Can you remember how many times in all you have caned him?"

There was a pause.

"The details are all contained in the punishment book," Dr. Trump replied stiffly.

It seemed at that moment as though Mr. Sparkes's neck had suddenly become several feet longer. The pale, watery eyes were quite close to Dr. Trump's now, and they were staring into his.

"I am aware that the details are all there," Mr. Sparkes told him. "I have examined them myself. But what I am asking you now is whether *you* can remember."

Dr. Trump felt himself sweating. This was dreadful. Perfectly dreadful. Of course, he couldn't remember: there had been so many more important things to think about. But how could Mr. Vivvyan Sparkes possibly be expected to understand that? He might even attribute Dr. Trump's ignorance to mere callousness.

"I haven't the total in my head, if that is what you mean," he replied rather sulkily.

He looked away as he said it, and saw the frowning stenographer, frowning harder than ever and scribbling down his words after him.

"Yes, that is exactly what I do mean," Mr. Sparkes told him. "So perhaps I should refresh your memory for you."

"Thank you," Dr. Trump replied.

Mr. Sparkes paused.

"Would it surprise you," he asked, "to know that you have apparently chastised this boy upon as many as seventeen different occasions?"

Would it surprise him? Was there a catch of some kind here? Dr. Trump wondered. Remembering the stenographer, should he say "yes" or "no"?

"Yes," he replied at last.

"It would surprise you," Mr. Sparkes repeated, still in the same placid voice as though he himself had never been surprised by anything.

Dr. Trump thought again. Suppose that seventeen was right. How dreadfully slack it would seem if a simple fact like that surprised him.

"No. On second thoughts, no. That is to say . . ."

"Which *do* you mean, Dr. Trump?" Mr. Sparkes asked him, his neck held practically horizontally by now. "A fact must either surprise you or not surprise you. It cannot do both."

"It . . . it seems rather a lot," Dr. Trump replied lamely.

He was really sweating by now: the palms of his hands were so moist that they made little sucking sounds as he pressed them together.

"It may seem a lot to you, Dr. Trump," Mr. Sparkes resumed, "but I assure you that it is what the book says. Have you any reason, Dr. Trump, to think that the book may be wrong?"

"None at all."

"Thank you."

There was a pause.

"And before we leave this boy"—here Mr. Sparkes referred carefully to his papers, as though he hadn't been listening properly and had forgotten his name already—"this boy, Ginger," he resumed, "what were your feelings towards him? Did you dislike the boy?"

"No."

The reply was crisp and definite. This time, Dr. Trump was confident that he had read Mr. Sparkes's mind. And he had no intention of being accused of harbouring petty animosities.

"But you felt him to be a bad influence?"

"I did."

"And in your view he was a thief?"

"That is so."

"And he once showed physical violence to you?"

"He did."

"At least on two occasions he ran away and stayed out all night?"

"He did."

"And he illicitly associated with this girl?"—again the quick glance at the papers—"this girl, Sweetie?"

"I agree."

Mr. Sparkes's neck slowly withdrew itself. He appeared temporarily to be resting. At any moment now it seemed that he might be going to tuck his head out of sight somewhere underneath his wing, and go clean off to sleep in front of them. But instead of that he addressed Dr. Trump again.

"And even though you felt him to be a bad influence, and a thief, and physically violent, and a fugitive, and a forbidden associate with the other sex still under age, nevertheless you still did not dislike him?"

"That is difficult to answer."

The neck had come out again by now. The whole extent of it had shot right forward like a snake.

"But you have already answered it, Dr. Trump. You said 'no.'"

"I meant personally."

Mr. Sparkes nodded.

"I meant personally, too," he replied.

There was perspiration on the back of Dr. Trump's hands as well as on the palms by now: small beads of it were visibly clinging to them.

"In himself, he is a good boy," Dr. Trump explained desperately. "But bad . . . that is to say that underneath the badness there was something good. It was the goodness that I was trying to bring to the surface."

"By caning him?"

"If necessary, by caning."

"And do you feel satisfied with the result, Dr. Trump?"

"I do . . . I mean no, I don't. That is to say . . ."

It was five minutes to eleven by now. That meant that Dr. Trump had already had forty minutes of Mr. Sparkes's questioning to contend with. And there was no point in disguising the fact, he was disappointed in himself: he had, in fact, been his own betrayer—shifty, evasive, contradictory, even on occasion unintentionally rude. Whereas Mr. Sparkes had been consistently polite and gentle throughout, rather like a bland, insistent schoolmaster. He had not wavered. And his memory was apparently bottomless. When he really got going he was like a turn in the music hall. He was able, a full half-hour afterwards, to repeat word for word exactly what Dr. Trump had said even after Dr. Trump himself had long since forgotten it.

It was the matter of Sweetie that they had got on to by now.

". . . and so you decided to lock her up for the night in a room by herself?" Mr. Sparkes had just repeated after him.

"That is so."

"It was a rather unusual punishment, was it not?"

"I wished the punishment to fit the crime," Dr. Trump replied severely.

"And you felt confident that you could handle the situation?"

"I did."

"And could you?"

Dr. Trump recovered some of his earlier spirit.

"I don't understand you, sir."

"Then I will try to make myself clearer," Mr. Sparkes volunteered. "Did you persist in this punishment, this imprisonment, or did you end it summarily?"

"I ended it."

"Why?"

"I felt that it had gone on long enough."

"Long enough for what?"

"For . . . for the child's good."

"You mean that longer might have done her harm."

"Possibly."

"These timings must be very difficult to calculate, are they not?"

"Very."

"And you were not influenced by the views of other people who may not have agreed with your treatment."

"No."

"But there were those people, weren't there?"

"There were."

"How many?"

"Two or three."

"Anyone in particular?"

"One of the ward maids." Dr. Trump's lips tightened as he remembered the incident.

"You mean this woman "—again the quick glance at his notes—"this woman, Margaret."

Dr. Trump started. So that was known, was it? Evidently people had been talking.

"I do," he replied briefly.

"And what did she say, pray?"

"She threatened to interfere with the course of justice," Dr. Trump replied slowly.

Mr. Sparkes stroked the side of his nose as though whetting it.

"Justice, Dr. Trump?" he asked. "Do you possibly mean discipline?"

"I do. I mean orders. My orders."

"Thank you, Dr. Trump . . ."

And so it had gone on. Right on to twelve forty-five, in fact. In the result, Dr. Trump was so exhausted when he came away that he accepted the glass of sherry that his mother-in-law offered him.

Mr. Sparkes, however, did not seem to be susceptible to either exhaustion or hunger. He went straight on with other witnesses until nearly one-thirty. And then after a bun—left, merely with the mark of nibblings round the edges—and a cup of coffee only half drunk, he resumed at two o'clock sharp.

Annie was the first witness and she had been looking forward to this opportunity. She was determined to give all she had.

". . . crool, that's what it was, sir. Crool."

"Did you see the child?" Mr. Sparkes inquired. "Was she crying?"

"She was too frightened, sir. Her little face was set all rigid like a board."

"Where were you when you saw her?"

"I was in the kitchen, sir."

"Then you didn't see her?"

"No, sir. But I heard."

"What did you hear?"

"I heard the screams."

"Loud screams?"

"Terrible, sir."

"You're quite sure you heard them?"

"Almost-sure, sir."

Mr. Sparkes stroked his long nose.

"And has Dr. Trump ever been cruel to you personally?"

"Oh, yes, sir."

"In what way?"

Annie blushed. This was her moment. Her flat pink face assumed its happiest expression, and she dropped her eyes.

"I'd rather not say, sir . . ."

Mr. Prevarius's evidence also verged upon the unsatisfactory.

". . . as you understand, my dear sir," he was busy explaining, "cruelty, hardness in any form, oppression—these . . . these are anathema to me."

As he said it, he screwed his face up as though even the memory were too painful for him.

Mr. Sparkes's neck lengthened.

"And what did you do, pray?" he asked. "Did you protest to Dr. Trump? Or ask to see Dame Eleanor? Or inform the police, possibly? What action precisely was it that you took?"

Mr. Prevarius shook his head.

"Alas," he said. "I was too busy. Too much occupied by my professional duties. But I . . . I thought about it deeply . . ."

"Thank you, Mr. Prevarius."

The replies of Miss Britt and Nurse Stedge were in their separate ways both highly revealing. But they revealed more of Miss Britt and Nurse Stedge than of Dr. Trump.

When asked by Mr. Sparkes whether she felt Sweetie's punishment to be unduly harsh, Miss Britt did not hesitate.

"Matters of that kind are the prerogative of the Warden," she answered stiffly. "They are not for me to question—unless, of course, the health of the child is threatened. I satisfied myself that the room was clean and dry and that the ventilation was adequate, and then I withdrew . . ."

Nurse Stedge, however, was by no means so confident that she had done the right thing.

"I didn't like it, sir," she said. "Not a bit, I didn't. It seemed so . . . gruesome somehow. I ought to have spoken up, I did really. But I couldn't make myself. That's all there is to it. I did ought to have done something, but I didn't."

It was, however, Margaret's evidence that was the most remarkable. Mr. Sparkes had questioned her for quite a long time, and, with his neck withdrawn to the full somewhere right inside his collar, had then said in that quiet, easy voice of his: "Is there anything else that you would like to tell me?"

Margaret leaned forward.

"Only this, sir," she said. "I don't want you to think the
422

Warden's a bad man because he isn't. He means well: I'm sure of that, sir. And he works very hard for the hospital. And he doesn't spare himself, sir, not for a moment. It's . . . it's just that he doesn't understand children. That's all it is."

III

Mr. Vivvyan Sparkes had gone away again in another taxi, and Dr. Trump and Mrs. Warple were sitting on either side of the fireplace. It was still quite early; not yet eight o'clock in fact. But dinner—merely pecked at by Dr. Trump, and pushed away scarcely tasted—was already over. Mrs. Warple was just finishing her first after-dinner cigarette.

"I should," she said. "It's better than just sitting here moping."

"But I've told you: I never go to such places. I have never entered one in my life."

"Do you good for once," Mrs. Warple replied. "Have a good laugh or a cry. It's the same either way—makes you forget your own troubles."

"No, really, thank you."

Mrs. Warple came over to him.

"Well, do it for my sake," she asked. "Take me."

She was now using that husky, wheedling sort of voice that showed that she was really trying. And Dr. Trump began to feel alarmed: he was convinced that it was to just such throatiness that the late Bishop, his father-in-law, had once succumbed.

But why shouldn't he go to the pictures? he suddenly asked himself. After his encounter with Mr. Vivvyan Sparkes he was completely drained; washed out; good for nothing else. And there was nothing actually wrong in going to the pictures: Canon Larkin, he remembered, had once confided that he had been himself on several occasions.

"Oh, very well then," he said at last. "Just this once. But not in Putney. Nowhere that I am known. Let us try the City."

423

CHAPTER LX

I

THE MATRON of the Arkleydale and District Institution to
which Sweetie and Ginger had been taken was frankly
puzzled by her two new inmates. She was used to runaways
and juvenile outcasts in general, and she had expected
something far worse. By the end of the first week she was
on their side completely, and she went round telling everyone
that she knew quite enough about children to be able to tell
that they weren't the sort who would have run away from
anywhere without good reason. She even added that she
would like to have that Dr. Trump to herself for a few
minutes.

About Ginger she had not been quite sure at first. He
looked as though he might be rebellious. But as soon as he
was allowed out of the infirmary, she put him on to odd
jobs in the garden. And when she found that there was a
motor-mower for the large front lawn, he settled down
immediately. Ginger and the motor-mower came together
like Platonic souls. By the time he left, the approach to the
Arkleydale Institution was like a piece of worn-down billiard
baize.

As for Sweetie, the Matron lost her heart to her straight
away. She thought she was lovely—and lovely in a more
delicate, fragile way than the big-boned northern girls to
whom she was accustomed. Admittedly it was probably
Sweetie's big, dark eyes that won her—Sweetie's eyes usually
had that sort of effect on people when they met her for the
first time. But there was also the fact that the Matron felt
sorry for her. The child was so obviously miserable. And
the wound in her foot turned out to be worse than the doctor
had expected. More than a fortnight after she had been
delivered at the Arkleydale and District, she was still going
round in a wheel-chair with her bandaged leg stuck out in
front of her on an ankle-board.

That was why the Matron was so glad that Margaret was
still up there in Arkleydale with them. She had taken a room
somewhere in the village and practically had the run of the

institution by now. The Matron did not even quite know how Sweetie could have got along without her.

The effect on Sweetie of Margaret's arrival at the institution had certainly been remarkable. When Sweetie had first been brought there in a police ambulance she had been more dead than alive; and, what was more, she had persisted in saying that she actually *wanted* to die. There was even a lot of quite unaccountable nonsense about having *tried* to die.

It was the appearance of Margaret that changed all that. As soon as Sweetie saw her she held out her arms like a seven-year-old, and then burst into tears. Like all sensible women, the Matron was a great believer in tears. She knew that Sweetie would be all the better for them. What she did not know was how much better. Before the week was out Sweetie had recovered sufficiently to be able to persuade the Matron to allow her to see Ginger.

Not that it had been easy. At first the Matron had been opposed to the whole idea: it seemed to her that the two children had got each other into quite enough trouble already, without being brought together again. But there was an extraordinary persistence about Sweetie where Ginger was concerned. And, in the end, the Matron yielded. Sweetie could see Ginger for five minutes in the institution waiting-room, she said; for five minutes and no more, she added. What's more, she told Sweetie, she was going to be present herself the whole time just to make sure that they didn't get up to planning any more little jaunts together.

It was rather an awkward interview when it was finally arranged—Sweetie with her bad foot stuck straight out on the ankle-board, and Ginger standing stubbornly in front of the two of them and trying not to appear embarrassed. Ginger only looked at Sweetie twice, the Matron noticed. Once when he came in and then again on his way out. The rest of the time he seemed to be staring mostly at the bandaged foot. But it was very different with Sweetie. She didn't take her eyes off him for a single minute. Just sat there, staring. She even swung her chair round so that she could get a last glimpse of him as he went back out through the door.

It was some time before the Matron understood, and, when she did, truth came to her with a sense of shock.

"Good gracious," she told herself. "I do declare the child's in love with him."

And, naturally, after that, she wouldn't hear of any further meetings. Not that there would really have been time for any of them because Sweetie and Ginger were suddenly sent for.

The wheels that go round inside the machinery of the Children's Courts started turning, and the law was now ready for them. What was more, the law was taking the whole thing pretty seriously. There were to be no combined outings this time. Ginger was fixed up to go to a boys' remand home at Mill Hill, and Sweetie was booked for an institution at Blackheath. There was to be practically the whole width of London between the two of them.

They travelled down to London in separate trains, with Margaret following by the 4.45. And the Matron regretted that it was all over: Sweetie and Ginger had been about the most exciting thing that had ever happened in Arkleydale. As for Margaret, the Matron told her to her face that she was sorry that she was going. She could have done with her, and two or three more like her, at the Arkleydale and District, and, if at any time Margaret felt like returning, she had, as the Matron told her, only to say so.

II

But Margaret had no thought of going back there. Or back to the Archbishop Bodkin Hospital for that matter. Hadn't got anywhere at all to go to now, in fact. Sweetie's destination had been kept secret. The Matron herself didn't know where they were taking her. And when Margaret said good-bye to Sweetie up in Arkleydale, it was like losing her for ever.

She hadn't even got the money to go searching. When she had settled for her room in Arkleydale, she only had twenty-three shillings left in her handbag.

"I'll have to find some work," she thought anxiously. "I must have some money for when I find Sweetie again."

The one thought of finding Sweetie now filled her whole mind.

"They've taken her away from me. And I've got to find her. I've got to get her back somehow."

426

She was sitting upright and rigid in the corner of the compartment, a rather shabby figure in an old blue coat and a hat with a cheap ornament. Her hands were clasped tightly together in her lap. The other passengers were reading, dozing, looking out of the window. But Margaret did not appear to be aware of them. Her thoughts were running in the rhythm of the train wheels. "I've got to find her. I've got to find her. I've got to find her . . ." she was saying.

And when she reached London her mind was already made up. All the way down in the train she had been thinking of it. It seemed her last hope of discovering Sweetie.

"I'm going back to Dame Eleanor," she told herself. "She's the only one who can help me. And she's got to do it. She's got to help me get Sweetie back again."

It seemed strange going again up the long drive of The Cedars. And stranger still having to ring to be let in. It was all so familiar—the shape of the bell-pull, the way the curtains hung at the tall windows, the downward crescent of the steps—that she could not believe that she was no longer a part of it all. As she stood there, she could feel the beating of her heart . . .

"You can go up now," she heard the housekeeper saying to her at last. "But don't say anything to worry her. You can see that she isn't well."

The words came to her dimly. And, as she began to go up the broad staircase, she realised how tired she was. She had not eaten all day, and she was trembling. But she could not afford to be weak now. Everything depended on being stronger than Dame Eleanor.

And then, as soon as she went inside the room, she began to doubt herself. For Dame Eleanor looked so old. It was as though abruptly she had ceased even pretending that she was still only middle-aged. The bed-jacket buttoned across her shoulders was the garment of an old woman. Her hands without any of her rings upon them were old hands. Her hair was tattered and wispy around her shoulders. And her face had taken on all the lines and wrinkles that she had been smoothing and massaging and creaming away for years.

"I shouldn't never have left her," she began telling herself. "Not like this. Not old the way she is."

And, at that moment, Dame Eleanor began speaking.

"Did they send for you?" she asked. "I've been telling them to."

427

There was something helpless and pathetic about the question. This wasn't the Dame Eleanor that Margaret knew.

"I came myself," she said. "I wanted to see you."

Dame Eleanor smiled.

"I'm glad. I need you here. You mustn't ever go away again. I want someone who understands to look after me . . ."

Dame Eleanor looked different by now. Margaret had waited on her, brushing out her hair and rebraiding it into two thin plaits, smoothing the pillows, rebuttoning the bed-jacket, straightening the eiderdown.

Then she drew herself up.

"I want to ask you something," she began.

"What is it?"

"It's about Sweetie . . ."

But Dame Eleanor only shook her head.

"Not now," she said. "I don't want to talk about it. Not to-night."

"But I must talk to you," Margaret went on.

Again Dame Eleanor shook her head.

"Don't you bother yourself about Sweetie," she said. "They'll look after her. She'll go into an approved school all right. They'll find somewhere for her."

"But Sweetie mustn't go to an approved school," Margaret said suddenly, as though the words had been lurking there in her mind all the time. "She mustn't."

Dame Eleanor gave a little gesture of irritation. This wasn't what she had expected. She had never imagined that Margaret, too, would begin pestering her, just at the moment when the one thing that she wanted to do was to rest and forget about it all.

"She's got to go somewhere where she can be looked after," she said crossly. "There's no other way for it."

"There is," Margaret answered slowly. "That's . . . that's why I came here."

Dame Eleanor twisted her head so that she could see Margaret better. She remembered now that there had always been something mysterious about her, something concealed somewhere. But—Margaret's face revealed nothing. Under the shadow of the dark hair, it was smooth and placid as it had always been. Only a little tired, perhaps. But not a hint, not even the merest suggestion, of what was going on inside her mind.

"Well, what do you want me to do?" she asked.

"I want you to let me have her here," Margaret began

slowly. And then, before Dame Eleanor could reply, she went on quickly. "She wouldn't be no trouble to you. Really, she wouldn't. I'd see to that. And she'd grow up a good girl with me looking after her. I promise she would. If I had her to myself, I could manage her, I know I could."

Dame Eleanor arched out her neck from among the pillows that Margaret had arranged for her.

"Out of the question," she said. "I wouldn't hear of it. Simply couldn't hear of it." She paused. "Why don't you get married yourself and stop bothering about other people's children?"

She reached out for the glass of water as she finished, and Margaret rose and put it into her hand. When Dame Eleanor had drunk, Margaret took the glass from her and put it down again. She had made no reply but sat there quietly, almost as though waiting.

And, after a moment, Dame Eleanor spoke again. But her voice was fainter, the mere shadow of the voice that Margaret remembered.

"Just stay with me, dear," she said. "Put the other idea out of your head, and look after me instead. I'll make it worth your while. You need never worry about anything again. Be sensible. We aren't any of us getting any younger. It's something to have a home, remember. And I've told you how much it would mean to me. Say that you'll stop here and look after me."

Her hand was reaching out towards Margaret's as she was speaking. And Margaret wanted to take hold of it.

But she checked herself. She remembered why she had come and she knew that she would have to be strong. She got up out of reach of those tired, pleading fingers.

"Not unless Sweetie comes here, too," she said, backing slowly away from the bedside. "Not without Sweetie."

CHAPTER LXI

I

No ONE can go to the cinema every night no matter how worried he may be ; and Dr. Trump had not as a matter of fact enjoyed what he had seen on his first visit. The entertainment that was offered had seemed to him to consist mostly of sex, violence and a brightly-lit type of Californian callousness that left him shocked and horrified. What, indeed, amazed him was that Mrs. Warple—the widow of a bishop he could not help reminding himself—should apparently have been ready to sit there all night fairly lapping it up, the sawn-off shotguns, the ten-second kisses, the astonishing expanses of bosom seen suddenly in close-up, the screeching tyres in the car-chases, and all the rest of it.

But even if the cinema were spiritually closed to him, the need for it remained. For Mr. Vivvyan Sparkes seemed at least as leisurely in issuing his report as he had been in paying off the taxi driver. More than a week had elapsed since the inquiry, and so far there had not been so much as a single word from the Home Office. The suspense of wondering what Mr. Sparkes was going to say was indeed becoming unbearable. That was why Dr. Trump had suffered three entirely sleepless nights. In consequence, he was not able to settle down to anything. Even the composition of a sermon proved too much for him and he had, in the end, been forced to redeliver one of his old ones—a long, rather involved address about Free Will and its place in the Team Spirit.

This evening, the eighth evening since the inquiry, Dr. Trump was even moodier and more despondent than usual. He decided that he must have some fresh air and some real exercise. He wanted to be able to stretch his legs properly somewhere where there would be no chance of meeting anyone.

His first thought was of the cloisters. But Mr. Dawlish, pipe reeking, was there already, shuffling rather than walking, sloppily taking his own evening exercise. From the back he looked like a shambling ill-trained bear. Dr. Trump registered the point: to-morrow he would send for him and ask him politely—request him—to pick up his feet and avoid setting a bad example to the boys.

And with the cloisters occupied, Dr. Trump wondered about the boys' playground. But Mr. Rushgrove was already in possession. Dressed in almost embarrassingly brief running shorts he was doing his daily three times round. The kitchen garden? That too was inhabited. Miss Britt, smooth, placid and apparently unworried by the inquiry, was walking up and down in conversation with Nurse Stedge. Miss Britt held a piece of paper in her hand—a diet sheet probably—and kept pointing at it.

It was then Dr. Trump remembered the Tower. The esti-
mate had got through the Board at last, and the contractors
were already at work upon the job. Their scaffolding around
the Tower was like a giant constructional toy. Only his
excessive preoccupation with other matters had kept him
away from it for so long. And at the mere thought of what
a surprise visit of inspection might reveal his pulse quickened.
He was always at his best when inspecting.

He decided therefore to go straight up to the top balcony
and work downwards: there was a businesslike air to the
arrangement that appealed to him. And, as he emerged on to
the upper balcony, he drew in a deep breath of sheer content-
ment. The air was pure and uncontaminated up here. The
lights of London were coming on below him, and the infants'
block to the right was already a glowing honeycomb of
illuminated cells. Gazing down into the whole expanse of
the Archbishop Bodkin grounds that surrounded it, he found
himself loving every stone and corner of the place.

"There's old Dawlish," he began thinking almost affectionately. "He . . . he seems to belong there somehow . . ."

At the thought, Dr. Trump realised with a shock that he
himself did not belong there—not in the sense in which Mr.
Dawlish belonged. Dr. Trump was merely someone important who had suddenly arrived. Mr. Dawlish was a part of
the fabric. Compared to Mr. Dawlish himself, he was an
interloper . . .

He broke off, because suddenly a wave of faintness had
come over him, and he passed his hand across his forehead.
It was extraordinary this feeling, as though he and the Tower
were slowly toppling forward. He bit his lip in sheer
irritation.

"The stairs," he told himself. "The stairs. Perhaps I took
them rather fast. I must be more careful . . ."

He hated physical infirmity at all times; and at a moment
like the present, when he might need all his strength to deal
with Mr. Sparkes's report it was unbearable. He had, he was
forced to admit, been feeling on the edge of things for days.

But already the faintness had passed, and he was able to
stand there looking out once more. There was, however, none
of the exultation that usually came to him when he looked
out. Instead, he was aware of a strange emptiness, a feeling
of sadness and fatigue and loneliness; of failure, even.

"But this is absurd," he told himself hurriedly. "How
can I possibly think of myself as having failed? Why, the

laundry alone and . . . and this very Tower I'm standing in
. . . It must be simply that I'm tired. I've been overworking.
Perhaps I need a holiday."

Down below, the figure of Mr. Dawlish came into sight
again on the far side of the cloister, and Dr. Trump found
himself actually envying him.

"What does he know of worry?" he asked himself. "He
just does his job as I tell him to. He isn't waiting to have his
life's work condemned by . . ."

At the memory of Mr. Sparkes, Dr. Trump drew in his
lips tightly. This was the one thing that he did not want to do
—to think about the man. And this evening Dr. Trump could
not take refuge in his usual defence of feeling angry. He
was too tired for anger.

The vague sensation of faintness, of standing on a gently
rocking tower, returned to him and he looked round for
somewhere to sit. There was a pile of planking left there by
the contractors and Dr. Trump made his way towards it.
When he reached it he sat with his head bowed inside his
hands, almost as though he were praying. But they were
thoughts, not prayers, that kept passing across his mind; the
same miserable, disturbing thoughts that had been tormenting him for the past week. Only now they came tumbling
out with nothing to stop them. Dr. Trump at that moment
was ready to believe almost anything about himself.

"Perhaps I *am* to blame," he began. "Perhaps if I had
been gentler with Sweetie and Ginger they would never have
run away. But it wasn't only those two, was it? It's worse
than that; far worse. There was that Miss Wynne—the one
who'd lost her mother. I shouldn't have sent her off like that
—not in the circumstances. And Jeffcote. Poor old Jeffcote:
I wonder what's become of him. His eyesight was failing. He
was practically blind, I remember—it may have killed him
. . . And Margaret. After all, she only did what she thought
was for the best. She's a good person is Margaret . . . I . . .
I think I was in love with her once." The direction in which
his thoughts carried him amazed Dr. Trump: it seemed that
everything that he had been suppressing for years was now
coming to the surface and exploding in little bubbles in his
face.

He was aware now that he was shivering. It was always
cold up on the top of the tower, and to-night it suddenly
seemed arctic. His hands were numb and his knees were
beginning to knock together.

"I must go down," he told himself. "I have stayed too long up here. Early to bed. If only I could sleep . . ."

But, when he rose, the sensation of giddiness came over him again: he had to clutch at the ornamental iron-railing to support himself. He now felt sick as well as faint.

"I'm ill," he said miserably. "Really ill. I need a doctor."

The return journey down the tower took Dr. Trump over ten minutes. He had to cling on to the rail all the way, and whatever pieces of botched joinery or slipshod craftsmanship there were to find, they escaped him. When he reached the door, it was only the cross-bar that prevented him from falling. He stood there, swaying, his fingers fixed on to the Victorian waxed oak. The cloisters stretched ahead of him, wide and empty and forbidding. So long as this feeling of faintness remained, he realised that he could not possibly attempt to cross. He might do something unseemly like collapse, and have to be carried into his lodging by Sergeant Chiswick.

Then he saw Mr. Dawlish approaching and he realised that he would have to sink his pride.

"Dawlish!" he said in a thin, strained voice quite unlike his own natural rasping one. "Dawlish, I am unwell. I need your assistance."

It was not until Mr. Dawlish had given him his shoulder for support that Dr. Trump realised how far gone he really was. The almost suffocating odour of stale tobacco rose into his nostrils, but he ignored it. He was merely grateful, deeply grateful for a human being who could support him.

"You're a good fellow, Dawlish," he heard himself saying as though from the other side of a curtain. "I'm very much obliged to you. Very much obliged."

That was the last that Dr. Trump remembered until he was aware that he was half-way up the stairs with Mr. Dawlish, nearly purple in the face, and Mrs. Warple, similarly flushed but obviously delighted by her own importance, her necessariness, attempting to make a bundle of his legs.

11

He was still so shaken that he made no serious protest when Mrs. Warple insisted on putting him to bed herself.

It was only that he wished that she would not be so coarse, so frank about it.

"Don't you worry about me," she kept saying. "I'm an old married woman myself. I've put my own husband to bed before this, I can tell you."

And he did not feel strong enough to object when Mrs. Warple insisted on getting the doctor round to him immediately.

"I've learnt my lesson," she said grimly. "I'm not taking any more chances, thank you."

The only thing that he did try to fight away was the brandy. But even that was a battle that he lost in the face of her insistence.

"Go on, Samuel," she urged. "Get it down. What did God give us brandy for if it wasn't to drink? Do you all the more good because you don't take it regular. It's good brandy."

Dr. Trump was asleep when Dr. Arlett arrived. Almost in a coma. He was aware of having his pyjamas unbuttoned, and of the cold nose of a stethoscope as it was applied to his bare chest. Then he was conscious of hearing Dr. Arlett say almost casually: "Don't bother about this; it's only like a prick." It must, all the same, have been the jab of the needle that woke him up. Because he heard the next few sentences quite plainly.

"Have to get him away from here," Dr. Arlett was saying. "The strain's been too much. Send him down to Broadstairs and let his wife look after him. He'll be better once he gets away. He's got Sweetie and Ginger on the brain . . ."

CHAPTER LXII

I

DAME ELEANOR could feel all the loneliness of the years crowding in on her. As she lay there in the high, double bed, she knew that she had no one. It was loneliness of a kind that she had never known before, like being the last survivor on a fading and depopulated planet.

She remembered, though dimly, the figure of her dead

husband. It was all so long ago, however. And he had dwindled so in her memory. He was no more than a faint, lavishly whiskered figure, still steadily receding.

But it was not so with her son. He had never been away at all, really. If she went into any of the rooms downstairs, the billiard room particularly, she expected still to see him standing there, tall and high-shouldered and elegant, with his prematurely pouched eyes, and the weakness of his mouth concealed by the fine golden brown moustache that he always wore in full Guard's fashion. She knew that it was silly, of course. Because that was the way he had looked in 1921, and it was 1935 by now.

She lay back simply staring into the emptiness of the ceiling. For a while, motionless, she listened to the insistent *drub-drub drub-drub* of her heart. Then silently so that even the new companion should not hear, she began to cry. And, once started, she turned her head sideways on the pillow and went on crying like a schoolgirl.

After all, there was little enough to comfort her. Margaret was the one person on whom she had thought that she could rely. And Margaret had shown once again that she cared nothing for her; nothing for any single thing on earth except her own idiotic emotions—and these were all being squandered on that child that she was so foolishly anxious to adopt, to mother. Surely Margaret could see how much Dame Eleanor needed her. Wasn't it obvious that the whole episode of Sweetie and Ginger had disgraced her publicly? As one of England's leading social workers she was as good as ruined. And there is no pleasure in being an old woman whose public and private lives are both in complete collapse.

She would have to resign from the hospital: that much was certain. At her age, it was madness, sheer madness, driving herself so hard. There could only be one end to it, the doctor had said. And, each time, rather than describe what that end was, the doctor had simply spread his hands expressively wide open, leaving so much emptiness in between.

Not that she could give up everything all at once, not simply throw her hand in. There were her successors to be appointed. And who could possibly appoint them except herself? After all, they must be the right people. She couldn't have just anybody taking the chair at her committees, reversing her decisions, turning the accounts upside down, authorising the wrong kind of action.

At the mere thought of it, she roused herself. She must

435

begin straightaway writing letters, telephoning, interviewing the likely ones. The sooner the better, too, while she still had her finger on things. To-morrow morning at the latest.

Thump! Thump-thump! Thump THUMPetty-thump-thump! Her heart was pounding about inside her again. She could feel it shaking her whole body. And all the time she was waiting, waiting, waiting for that unspeakable moment when it would miss its beat altogether. Then, as she waited, the moment came. *Thump-thump, thump-thump, THUMP . . . thumpetty-thump-thump.*

Aaaah! She heard herself saying as the breath left her and she sank back. It was as though she were already actually dead for a moment, but still with enough life left inside her to know all the time what was happening.

The fool of a doctor wouldn't tell her how long she had got. He seemed to think that it was kinder, more professional, just to leave her there, wondering. But she didn't need any doctor to tell her: she knew. At the speed at which she was breaking up, she gave herself about another three months at the outside. Possibly less—say ten weeks. The one thing of which she was certain was that she would never know another spring. She had the picture of blossoming fruit trees in her mind and felt convinced for some reason that she would never see them. There comes a time, she reminded herself, when old people really do know that kind of thing.

That was why she wanted everything to be as peaceful as possible during the remainder of time that she had left to her. That was why she needed Margaret. Margaret was the only person who could look after her properly: she knew that from twenty years' experience. But, much as she wanted Margaret, she wasn't going to have her home turned into a reform school. And could anything be more absurd, she asked herself, than having a fourteen-year-old girl, and a problem child at that, suddenly introduced into the household when even the doctors said that the very things that she needed were absolute peace and quiet?

She paused.

"Of course, I suppose she *could* be put into the west wing," she reflected. "Or over the kitchens. I need never see her then. Or somewhere right at the top of the house. Heaven knows there are spare rooms enough. She could have Derek's room, for that matter. He's never going to use it again." She paused for a moment, and shook her head. "But it wouldn't work. Margaret would only be thinking of Sweetie

436

or whatever the child's name is, instead of looking after me. I don't want just a part of somebody's time; I need all of it." Again the pause, the hesitation. " But it would be nice to have Margaret in the house again. And she's so sensible, perhaps she could find a way. At least I could talk it over with her . . ."

She was still rambling on in her thoughts, half sleeping, half waking, when the companion came in. She was nearly five minutes late by now and she had been hurrying. The cup of Horlicks in her hand had spilled over into the saucer.

Dame Eleanor looked at it and turned away her head.

" Perhaps," she continued with her thoughts, " if I did allow Sweetie to come here, Margaret could make something of her. It's worth trying. I wish I'd had grand-children of my own. They take away the fear of death somehow, grand-children . . ."

II

It was nine-thirty next morning when the news of Dr. Trump's illness, his collapse, was phoned through to Dame Eleanor.

Miss Phrynne, the secretary, was first with the information. She was formal, diffident, polite: she did not like bothering Dame Eleanor, she said, or appearing to go behind Dr. Trump's back, but the Warden was very far from well and there were a lot of cheques that needed a second signature. Then Dr. Arlett came through, and what he had to say was most disturbing: it would be a month at least, he reckoned, before Dr. Trump was fit to resume—more, possibly, if he didn't get away from the place at once. And, finally, Mrs. Warple came on the line. In some obscure way she regarded Dame Eleanor as belonging to the other camp, an enemy; and she was short with her.

" So you see it's no good you asking him to carry on until you can get someone," she told Dame Eleanor, " because I'm taking him away to-night. And it'll be a miracle if I ever get him there. I'm only ringing you up now just so that you'll know what's happening."

That was enough. It meant that Dame Eleanor would have to stop being an elderly invalid and become an administrator a Chairman, once more. By nine forty-five, even though her poor old heart was going thumpetty-THUMP-thump again, she had been on the phone herself and had called a

Board meeting. What is more she called it immediately. For that very afternoon, in fact.

It was not an easy meeting. Everyone's mind had been full of Mr. Sparkes, and no one had given so much as a thought to Dr. Trump. In consequence, the Board met in an atmosphere of bewilderment. It was like having the principal actor fall ill before the final curtain.

It was, indeed, only Dame Eleanor who kept them to their business.

" It's no use saying we didn't expect it," she told them. " It's happened. And it's no use pretending that this hospital will run itself without a Warden, because it won't. We've got to appoint a *locum,* and we've got to appoint him to-day."

One by one, the names of the entire staff were considered, mauled over and dismissed. Miss Bodkin was the cause of some delay. Suddenly catching the name " Prevarius " just as he had been unanimously rejected, she thought that he was being proposed as Dr. Trump's successor and she opposed him. It took her nearly ten minutes to explain why and, in the end, she sat back wearing the exhausted smile of someone who has successfully carried her point in the teeth of fierce opposition.

After considering the staff, they next turned the searchlight on themselves. Dame Eleanor immediately made it quite clear to them that if it had not been for her other activities— the Unmarried Mothers, and all the rest of it—she would have taken over the vacant Wardenship herself ; would indeed, have jumped at it. And so would the others, but for their own peculiar commitments. Canon Larkin, for instance, had just been called in by the Polynesian Mission Officers' Association to advise on staff pensions and was more than fully occupied ; Mr. Chitt, the tract publisher, was taking practically full-time treatment for his rheumatism—had, indeed, emerged from a steaming seaweed compress specially for to-day's meeting, and had the tang of kelp and bladder-wrack still clinging to him ; Miss Bodkin couldn't even be made to understand why they were all suddenly talking about themselves ; and Mr. Chigwell had just got married.

The Board could probably have had Mr. Chigwell if they had really set their hearts on him. For, as soon as he found all eyes turned in his direction, he faltered. After a firm, rather romantic opening about a new bride, he now spoke as though, backed by a sufficiently strong resolution of the

Board, he would be ready to break up the marriage to-morrow if it were asked of him. But he need not have upset himself. Nobody really wanted Mr. Chigwell. And after that one dreadful moment in the limelight he was allowed to pass into obscurity again, fading slowly back from crimson into pink and so eventually to his own natural tallow pallid-ness again.

By then the conversation had turned to possible outside candidates, and even the rival masters of St. Christopher's were contemplated. But nobody got anywhere. The Board, indeed, was still hard at rejecting people when tea time came round and Canon Larkin took out his watch and began shuffling with his papers.

And then it was that Dame Eleanor showed herself at her most masterful, proved once again why she was Chairman and they were only Governors.

" Oh no you don't," she said, looking hard at Canon Larkin. "We're having tea served in here. We break up when we've found someone, and not before. As we're all busy people we might as well go on talking while we're eating . . ."

CHAPTER LXIII

I

IT WAS sheer kindness to Canon Mallow that he did not know what was happening up in Putney. As it was, he was sitting down to an after-dinner cup of tea in Mrs. Gurnett's private sitting-room, idly stirring round and round with the apostle spoon long after the lump of sugar had melted. Simply sitting stirring, and thinking about nothing in parti-cular.

Mrs. Gurnett was there on the other side of the fireplace. It was her one quiet time of the day, this moment when the doctors had gone, all the meals were finished and the trays had been collected. When the night-nurse took over, Mrs. Gurnett usually reckoned to have half an hour or so to herself. Or rather, half an hour or so with Canon Mallow.

It had gradually become a part of the pattern of the day that Canon Mallow should come down at this time. Not that there was anything crude and taken-for-granted about the arrangement. On the contrary, there was a delicately preserved air of refinement and surprise. Every evening at 7.25 the night-nurse knocked on Canon Mallow's door with the message that, if he wasn't doing anything particular, Matron wondered if he would care to join her in the private sitting-room. And, because Canon Mallow never was doing anything, he always thanked the night-nurse kindly and, after a decent interval of two or three minutes, he followed her down the stairs. What was so nice was that there was always the deeper of the two arm-chairs drawn up to the fire specially for him, and by about 7.29 he would be comfortably seated in it.

It was the cosiness of these moments that counted for so much. And now that he had experienced the real thing, he realised that up to the present there hadn't been very much in the way of cosiness in his life. In a muddled, disorganised, bachelor sort of way he had been too busy to bother about cosiness. But at present, with all the time in the world on his hands, he found himself rather liking it. And nowadays as 7.15 in the evening came round, he felt a kind of restlessness inside him as though all day he had been waiting for the knock on the door and the invitation.

To-night in particular the warmth of the little room enfolded him. It had the same quality as hot baths and fleecy bedroom slippers. He was a trifle on the tired side already because he had been at it pretty nearly all day sending off more of those innumerable replies to Old Bodkinians who kept writing to him. And it was pleasant, very pleasant, to sit there, with the heat of the fire on his knees and the standard lamp placed exactly in the right position—on the left hand side and about six inches to the rear.

The cup of tea was something else that he had been looking forward to. Mrs. Gurnett always insisted on making the tea herself, and there was a freshness to it as though the stuff had only just been discovered. And, come to think of it, it was funny that he and Mrs. Gurnett should have known each other for more than twenty years and, only within the past six months, have discovered that they both preferred China to Indian.

Then there was the evening paper. The night-sister made a point of bringing it in with her when she came on duty. And this was peculiar because apparently neither she nor Mrs. Gurnett really cared very much for what was going on in the outside world—both too busy probably. At any rate there it always was, ready on the occasional table beside the arm-chair when he got down there, as uncreased and new-looking as though it had just come off the press.

Mrs. Gurnett never seemed to mind either that it was to the evening paper rather than to her that Canon Mallow always turned. On the contrary, she encouraged it. A wise woman, she preserved her own silence. She was content to sit there, doing nothing mostly but brood over the small white-haired figure in the arm-chair opposite, watching for the moment when his cup was empty and he was ready for another one—just half a cup this time. And conversation, such as it was, never started until the cup had been put down for a second time and Mrs. Gurnett had rung for the maid to take away the tray.

To-night the silence was longer even than usual. Canon Mallow was drumming idly with his fingers on the arm of the chair, and Mrs. Gurnett was staring vacantly into the red honeycomb of the gas-fire.

Then, with her face flushed a little from the heat of the room and from her own proximity to the fireplace, she spoke.

"I've been thinking," she said.

And, having uttered as much, she stopped herself.

Canon Mallow looked up. There was a little half-smile upon his face; a mixture of friendliness and surprise as though even to be spoken to at all had taken him unawares.

"Yes?" he asked.

"It's about that room of yours," Mrs. Gurnett went on.

The smile left Canon Mallow's face.

"You mean you want it?" he asked.

Mrs. Gurnett's flush deepened.

"Bless the man," she answered, and flushed more deeply still realising that she had never spoken to him in that way before. "I don't mean anything of the kind."

"Then what do you mean?"

Canon Mallow's face was puckered into a frown now as he faced her. He wished that he could see Mrs. Gurnett more plainly, but with his reading-glasses on it was impossible. All that he could discern in the arm-chair opposite was a large square figure with what appeared to be an unusually bright pink face.

But already Mrs. Gurnett was speaking again.

"It's not healthy being cooped up in that one room all day."

"Oh, but I'm very comfortable there, I assure you," Canon Mallow replied. "I am really."

441

"If only things were different you could have this for a study," Mrs. Gurnett explained. "I need only be in here in the evenings."

The frown on Canon Mallow's face deepened.

"But . . . but how could they be different?" he asked at last. "I'm perfectly well content with everything just as it is. On the other hand, if you've got anything in mind you've only to mention it. I'm quite sure that I'll be able to fit in with whatever you suggest."

He paused, wondering what it was that had made Mrs. Gurnett quite so extraordinarily mystifying. In all the time during which they had been together he had never known her be other than straightforward and direct before. And her next remark was even more bewildering still.

"Well, if you can't see it, I'd better tell you," she said. "Really I had. And I don't care what you think of me."

At that Canon Mallow saw that he would have to take things seriously. He sat up very straight and folded his hands neatly in his lap.

"Whatever it is, I'm sure that I shall always think very highly of you," he replied. "Very highly indeed. I always have."

"You're not making it any easier for me," Mrs. Gurnett told him.

"But . . . but what do you want me to say?" Canon Mallow demanded. "I've told you, I'm ready to agree to anything if . . . if it suits your convenience."

"Well," said Mrs. Gurnett, bracing herself. "It's for you to decide, not me. But when two people who've known each other as long as we have don't seem to be able to get along without each other, and when there are no ties on either side, and when neither of them is getting any younger, and when there's a house and staff all ready and waiting . . ."

But she never reached the end of that sentence. For at that moment there was a knock at the door and the maid came in with a telegram. It lay there, orange-coloured and menacing-looking on the small electro-plated tray which Mrs. Gurnett insisted should be used for delivering all messages.

"For the Canon, ma'am," she said.

For a moment Canon Mallow said nothing. He was still too much confused and embarrassed to speak. It was only towards the end of Mrs. Gurnett's speech that he had realised the direction in which it was all leading, and he had no idea what reply to make. Mrs. Gurnett was such a

442

thoroughly sensible woman that if she wanted to marry him he had no doubt that it would be for the best all round. Indeed, now that he came to think of it he began to wonder why he had never suggested it himself. But even if it had occurred to him, he knew that he wouldn't have carried it any farther. He never had been the proposing kind, and seventy-four was a little too late in life to begin starting anything of the kind.

So, instead of attempting any kind of reply, he picked up the telegram from the tray that the girl was holding out to him.

" If you'll forgive me," he said. " Perhaps I'd better just see what it says."

Mrs. Gurnett noticed that, when he had seen it, he went so white that for a moment she thought he was going to faint. But, in the circumstances, perhaps even that would have been excusable. For the telegram was certainly a sensational one. It was from Dame Eleanor and it said everything that in silly, dreaming moments when he was just dropping off to sleep, he had imagined a telegram saying to him.

" IF HEALTH PERMITS CAN YOU RETURN IMMEDIATELY BODKIN HOSPITAL TAKE UP TEMPORARY WARDENSHIP DURING SUDDEN ILLNESS DR. TRUMP," it ran. " BOARD UNANIMOUSLY HOPES YOU ACCEPT. IMPORTANT REPLY BY RETURN."

When he had read to the end of it, he remained silent. Then, still without a word, he passed the telegram over to her.

Their eyes met.

" If there's a train, I really ought to go to-night," he said. " Perhaps we could discuss the . . . the other matter later. I . . . I do so appreciate what you were just saying."

II

It was poor Mr. Jeffcote's room that Canon Mallow chose for his own apartment.

There were two good reasons for this. In the first place, it was empty. And, secondly, after so many years spent right on top of himself in the twelve-by-ten of a bed-sitter, the Warden's Lodging seemed so vast, so ridiculously roomy. Indeed, now that he came to reflect upon it he could not imagine how he had ever contrived to occupy even half the space.

Besides, there was all Dr. Trump's furniture still there. And, even though Felicity had been charming, absolutely charming, about the whole thing—inviting him, *begging* him to make himself at home there—he somehow didn't fancy it. He was afraid all the time that in any manner of ways—like putting a cushion under his feet in the evenings and propping his pipe up on the glass shelf in the bathroom—he would be doing exactly the sort of thing that Felicity and Dr. Trump would have most disliked. And, after all, it was only a temporary arrangement. The last postcard with a Broad-stairs post-mark on it had said that Doctor Trump was getting on every bit as well as could be expected. In another month or two he would have taken up residence again.

But, in the meantime, there was far too much to be done for Canon Mallow even to think about being retired once more. And it wasn't ordinary sort of work, either. Not like going through account books and checking registers. All that side of things seemed to work perfectly without him, and Canon Mallow could only admire Dr. Trump for all the splendid organisation that he had introduced into the place.

No, it was on another plane altogether that Canon Mallow felt the need to do something. Vocational Training, for instance. Try as he could, he could not persuade himself that the girls really liked doing all that scrubbing and cooking; and, if they didn't like it, it seemed wrong to make them go on with it. Then there were the silent breaks and the no-playing-on-the-grass notices. Both of these seemed wrong, entirely wrong, to him no matter how he looked at them. And the overtime that was being worked by the ironers! Good gracious, it was enough to tire the poor girls simply to push those heavy irons about even for ten minutes.

The more he thought about it the more he realised that he would have to do something, whether he was temporary, or not. It just couldn't be right to leave things. And he was quite sure that it was none of it as the old Archbishop had intended. Certainly not as Canon Mallow himself had intended. Why, in his day the Bodkin Hospital for all its faults—for all *his* faults, he should say—had always seemed such a friendly, happy sort of place. And now, though he didn't want to be unfair to Dr. Trump, the place was more like a perfectly conducted barracks with a highly profitable steam-laundry thrown in as a side-line.

Come to think of it, he hadn't heard so much as the laughter of a single child ever since he had been there; and he remembered perfectly well that, in his day, the noise at playtime had frequently been so terrific that he had been forced to close the window if he had wanted to get on with things.

"There's a lot wrong with the place," he thought sadly. "Really there is. I shall have to speak to Dr. Trump when he gets back. I know he'll understand. It's just that I'll have to be tactful. . . ."

CHAPTER LXIV

AS THINGS turned out, Dr. Trump never returned to the Archbishop Bodkin Hospital.

For a start, everything that Dr. Arlett had said about his condition proved to be correct. The natural strains of Wardenship, coupled with the disappointment of the Pageant and the numerous re-organisations and dismissals and resignations had already taken their toll. He was an exhausted man even before the additional anxieties that Sweetie and Ginger had imposed on him. And just when what he was really needing was a six-weeks vacation to set him on his feet again, the dignified steam-roller of Mr. Vivvyan Sparkes had passed clean over him.

It was the middle of October when Fate chose to strike Dr. Trump down. And, in the end, he spent the whole of November and most of December down at Broadstairs with Felicity and Sebastian, even celebrating Christmas in the small private sitting-room of the Ragusa Boarding Establishment.

But there was more than ill-health behind it. For cut off as Dr. Trump was down there at the seaside, the ordeal of waiting for Mr. Sparkes's report became daily more tormenting. Dr. Trump went to bed at night and woke again in the morning—usually with any number of false dawns in between—with the single thought: "What is he going to say about me? Shall I ever be able to hold up my head again?" always racing through his mind.

And then suddenly the miracle occurred. Mr. Sparkes's report appeared and it vindicated Dr. Trump completely. Indeed, the findings of the report only went to show how appearances—even Mr. Sparkes's distinguished appearance— may be misleading. For Mr. Sparkes made it plain that he had been more than favourably impressed by Dr. Trump's

445

personality. He had found him—there the words were in the black-and-white typewriting of the Home Office—" High-principled. Conscientious. Efficient." Admittedly, the word " Old-fashioned " occurred a little later on in the report, and there were some references to need, apparently overlooked, for a specialist in child psychology to be attached to the hospital. But Dr. Trump was now in no mood for bothering about frills and afterthoughts. The bit about a specialist in child psychology was absurd anyway, because he did not believe in child psychologists. And " high-principled, conscientious and efficient " were quite good enough for him.

They were, indeed, what led him ultimately to offer Dame Eleanor his resignation. There was no pique and false pride about the gesture—nothing hurried, reckless, quixotic. It was merely common shrewdness and a sense of opportunism that prompted him. He had known for some time that the East India and China Missionary Society had been looking for a new organiser on the spot, a head man, someone who would be practically a bishop; and he had heard, too, before the deplorable affair of Sweetie and Ginger had blown up, that his own name had been suggested more than once in its connection.

That had been nearly six months ago, however; and, at the time, it had been the flattery rather than the prospect that had pleased him. It was the episode of the inquiry that had brought it all up again. Several times since he had first been threatened by an investigation, he had made cautious, exploratory feelers to see if the job, the important missionary headship, were still vacant. And it was. That heartened him. He had even got as far as practising a few good openings: " In the eyes of Whitehall I may not be all that a Civil Servant should be," he could say, lingering a little contemptuously on the words " Whitehall " and " Civil Servant " as he came to them. Or he might try something humble and disarming like: " I have no references to offer: all that I have to offer is my life." Or even the simple, manly one: " I'm afraid that I'm no good at talking about myself. I . . ." —he had become thoroughly proficient at the pause, the hesitation—"I . . . I have never had to do so before."

But now, armed with Mr. Sparkes's testimonial, what bliss it was not to have to get up to any of those tricks. The letter that he finally sent off was a corker, a real challenge to the whole missionary movement. *" Naturally,"* it concluded, *" I*

would not have considered even making known to you my
deep, indeed, life-long interest in your work so long as
there was any possibility of a smirch upon my own good
name. Publicly vindicated however, by one of our most
eminent K.C.s . . ."

CHAPTER LXV

THE NIGHT Margaret left Dame Eleanor, she had nowhere to
go.

As she made her way back down the long winding drive
she was crying. And when she reached the road and the
street lights, she saw people turn and stare as the shabby,
middle-aged woman, carrying the cheap cardboard suitcase,
went by them. But she was past caring what people thought
of her. She had her own thoughts and they were fully
occupying.

"I've got to get somewhere to sleep," she kept telling herself. "And then I'll find a job. And after that I'll start
looking for Sweetie again. I've got to find her somehow.
I've got to find her . . ."

It was over in Hammersmith that she found somewhere to
sleep. " BED AND BREAKFAST, 3/6 " the notice in the window
said, and she went to the house gratefully. There was no
difficulty there. The landlady preferred single ladies, provided they weren't the flashy kind. And when she discovered
that Margaret was hungry she gave her a cup of tea and a
biscuit. It was the first food that Margaret had eaten since
breakfast.

The bed wasn't a bad one as three-and-sixpenny beds go.
It was clean, and there was a comfortable groove down the
middle where the other three-and-sixpenny sleepers had
rested. But Margaret was too tired for sleep. Too tired, and
too miserable.

"I've got to find her," the words went on forming themselves inside her brain. "I've got to find her. I can't leave
Sweetie somewhere they don't understand her."

There was no one left to turn to now ; no one at all. What
she did not know was that, over in Putney, Dame Eleanor
had put the light on again.

"I shouldn't have let her go away again," she was thinking. "She's the only one that was ever any good. Even if she had the child here, it would be better than nothing. At least I'd get *some* attention."

Dame Eleanor had made up her mind. She couldn't exist without Margaret, and she was prepared to admit it. The last companion, after a singularly unfortunate little incident when she had upset a whole carafe of water over Dame Eleanor's morning correspondence, had been sent packing; and Dame Eleanor now had no one. She therefore needed Margaret at once. But where to find her? At the thought that, through her own stubbornness, she had allowed Margaret to slip through her fingers, Dame Eleanor became desperate. She tried the police; she wrote to Arkleydale; she pestered Canon Mallow; she inserted advertisements; she failed. And then, when the hunt was at its height, Margaret solved everything for her. She telephoned to ask if Dame Eleanor was better.

The response surprised her. Dame Eleanor asked her to come round at once.

It was the urgency of it all that bewildered Margaret. She began to fear that something had happened to Sweetie, that there was some alarming piece of news that they had to break to her. She did not guess that she herself was simply what Dame Eleanor wanted. And Margaret had a job to think of, too. She was now a kitchen hand in a restaurant and was getting two pounds a week. She was even planning to save on it.

Not that Dame Eleanor had been idle about Sweetie. On the contrary, so far as Sweetie was concerned, everything was practically arranged. For a start, she had sent for her brother, the bishop, and asked him to help her. He had come, a gaunt, vulture-like creature with long spatulate fingers and pale protruding eyes, and had sat beside the bed, fiddling with his ring and listening suspiciously to what his sister was saying to him. He had always hated getting mixed up in family affairs—it was somehow only in other families' affairs that he was so wise, so prescient, so episcopal—and what he disliked particularly was the way Eleanor always swept him along so. She was such a rusher. Unless he were careful, he had kept telling himself, he would find himself let in for something foolish—he had not yet forgotten the snub, the poke in the eye, from the Home Office when he had tried to forestall

Mr. Vivvyan Sparkes's inquiry. So, after saying for the third time: "Let me make some inquiries first, dear. Let us see how we stand," he had given her a dry, refrigerated kiss and withdrawn.

But this time everything had been quite simple. The family tentacles had reached out firmly, possessively. The chaplain of the Blackheath Remand Home proved to be an old pupil of the bishop's: he had in fact ordained the man. There were no difficulties there. The matter of public accommodation was, moreover, on Sweetie's side as well. The Blackheath Remand Home was already crowded out with a hundred-and-one other Sweeties all in need of a good home background and firm supervision; and, when the chance came of moving Sweetie on and so making room for still another one, the authorities jumped at it.. She could leave the Remand Home next Monday they said.

And then Margaret did one of those incomprehensible things that made Dame Eleanor wonder if she had done wrong even to think of having her back again. For Margaret insisted that she would have to work out her time at the restaurant. They had been very kind to her at the restaurant, Margaret told Dame Eleanor, and she would not like to think of leaving them in the lurch without proper notice. Sunday was the earliest that she could come to Dame Eleanor's.

It was as though, having discovered that Sweetie was alive and well and that in three days' time she was going to have her with her again, Margaret had lost all anxiety.

"I'll sleep here on the Saturday night, if I may, please," she said. "Just so that I can get everything ready for Sweetie when she comes. I don't want her to be a trouble to anyone."

CHAPTER LXVI

I

IT WAS five o'clock on an October afternoon when Margaret went across from Dame Eleanor's to collect Sweetie.

And all the way in the big, old-fashioned car, Margaret kept saying to herself: "It's going to come true. It's going to. Just like I knew it would. I shall have Sweetie for always now."

She made a strange figure as she sat there, amid the interior splendour of the tassels and ivory handles and little cut-glass bottles. She was sitting right forward on the very edge of the seat. But that was only because she was too excited to lean back, too excited to do anything but wait for the moment when she would see Sweetie again.

The light was already fading from the sky when they drew up at the high green gates outside the home. They were a blank, forbidding pair of gates, with a metal grille set in the middle of one of the panels. And, when they opened, Margaret could see into a stone-paved courtyard flanked on three sides by a high, brick wall. She shuddered.

"It's not right," she told herself. "It's like a prison. They didn't never ought to have sent Sweetie here."

The interior of the Home was just as prison-like. There was too much stone about. And there weren't enough lights. The corridor was merely a tunnel with occasional glints set down the length of it. And the waiting-room, with its plain deal chairs and the naked electric light bulb dangling from the ceiling, was like a cell.

It wasn't, however, so much the bleakness of the place that Margaret minded. It was the fact that when they brought Sweetie to her, the Matron had her arm round Sweetie's shoulders. She was suddenly jealous of the woman. It was only natural that other people should like Sweetie—she didn't see how they could help it, in fact. But it wasn't fair, to go shutting her away like this, and then start playing on her emotions. It was stealing something that by rights belonged to Margaret.

And now that she looked, she noticed that there was a change in Sweetie. It was less than a month since she had last seen her. But somehow she was different. They'd given her new clothes when she arrived at the Home: perhaps that was it. Or the way her hair was done. Margaret leaned forward. "They haven't been cutting Sweetie's hair, have they?" she asked herself.

But it was more than Sweetie's clothes, or the way her hair was done, that was different. And, as Margaret looked at her, she realised what it was. "She's growing up," she told herself. "That's what she's doing. She's growing up." For some reason the thought frightened her. "I only hope I'm strong enough to deal with her," she went on. "But I've got to be.

I'm going to *make* her grow into a good girl. That's what I'm going to do: I'm going to *make* her good."

Her eyes met Sweetie's for a moment. But only for a moment. It was as though Sweetie were avoiding them. There was that sudden pang again, a feeling as though something had been stolen from her. She started to reach out her hand; then she restrained herself.

"She doesn't love me any more," she began saying. "Something's happened to her. She doesn't."

It was the Matron's voice that startled her.

"There now," she said as she closed up the heavy black register with Sweetie's name in it. "If we get the signatures witnessed, I think that's everything." She patted Sweetie's hand. "Your tooth-brush and toilet things are in the little bag. And you can keep the magazine, dear, I'll give it to you."

She turned to Margaret. "I can see that Sweetie's going to be very happy with you," she went on in her cold, clear, Miss Britt-ish kind of voice. "You are, aren't you, Sweetie dear?"

Then back to Margaret again before Sweetie could answer.

"And, don't forget we want to hear from you once a week. Just for the first six months that is. Afterwards, once a month will be plenty. A couple of lines will be sufficient—just to say how our little friend is doing."

Finally she turned to Sweetie once more. Her arm, Margaret noticed, went around Sweetie's shoulders again as though it were accustomed to rest there.

"And remember everything I've said," she told her. "You don't want to be a disappointment to us, do you?"

The green gates had closed behind them, and they were alone together at last. Margaret was too happy to speak now: she was afraid that, if she said anything, Sweetie would know that she was crying. Crying from sheer happiness at having got Sweetie back again.

All the same, the ride back was not how she had imagined it. Unthinkable as it may seem, they quarrelled. It happened quite suddenly. At one moment there was Sweetie snuggled up against her, holding Margaret's hand in hers. And then, with the other, Sweetie had produced something from her coat-pocket.

"Look," she said. "One of the other girls gave it me. It's a lip-stick."

She was obviously proud of it. It was a treasure, a symbol. That was why it was so unforgivable when Margaret snatched it from her. And, having snatched it, she did worse. Pulling down the window of the car, she threw the lip-stick out into the street that was gliding past them.

" You're not to use lip-stick," she said. "You're too young."

Sweetie turned on her.

" Why can't you stop bossing me?" she asked. "I didn't ask you to come here. And I'm going to use lip-stick. As soon as I've got some money the first thing I'm going to buy is a lip-stick."

But Margaret was angry too, by then.

" Lip-sticks are wrong," she said. " D'you hear me, they're wrong. You're not never to use them. At any rate, not until I say so. Not until you're old enough to understand."

There was silence for a while. For so long, in fact, that Margaret was beginning to be afraid. She thrust out her hand towards Sweetie. But it was no use. Sweetie avoided her. She remained there, her body rigid, her head turned away, staring resentfully out of the window. Margaret could see the cold sullen face reflected in the glass.

" She's tired, that's what's the matter with her," she told herself. "And I ought to have been nicer. It's all my fault. I ought to have waited until to-morrow."

And she began to tell Sweetie about the new life that she was going to lead; about the bedroom that had been got ready for her—Dame Eleanor had decided finally on the little side room in the west wing, because the staircase led straight up past Margaret's own door.

". . . and it's going to be lovely," she said. "You won't never "—" won't ever " she corrected herself—" have to wear uniform no more. And we'll find you some friends of your own age, so you won't be lonely. And we'll go out walks together, and in the evening if Dame Eleanor's settled we can just sit together. My bedroom's just like a sitting-room, it is really. And you can come in there . . ."

Sweetie's hand was in hers by now. It was warm and soft and confiding.

" I'm sorry I was cross just now," she said.

Margaret squeezed her hand.

"That's all right," she said. "It's just that I don't want Dame Eleanor to think that you're one of the wrong sort. I want her to like you."

452

Sweetie moved close. She had been edging imperceptibly nearer to Margaret all the time and was leaning right against her now.

"Why's she doing all this for me?" Sweetie asked.

Margaret paused.

"Because she's good," Margaret answered. "She likes helping people. Don't you ever forget how good she is. It doesn't matter how cross she is on top; she's good underneath and that's all that matters. Good the whole way through, and just you remember it."

"I'll remember," Sweetie promised.

The car had reached Putney Common by now. Sweetie had been there nature-walking. It was pleasant, this, like coming home again. Then a shadow passed across her face.

"Where's Ginger?" she asked.

II

As a matter of fact, Ginger was miles away; right off the map somewhere at a farm school in Norfolk. And this was because the law, having summed him up, took a pretty serious view of Ginger. He had the twin charges of breaking open and larceny against him; and, as a potential criminal and menace to society, he was regarded as altogether too unstable for ordinary probation.

It was really Canon Mallow whom he had to thank for being sent to the farm school. Only he didn't know it. And Canon Mallow didn't know it either. Indeed, when the detective-sergeant came to see Canon Mallow and asked such a lot of questions about Ginger, he felt that he could hardly have given the boy a better all-round character. But what the detective-sergeant seemed to be chiefly interested in was a little matter of half a crown that he was supposed to have given Ginger. And here, if only the detective-sergeant had explained things properly, or if he had taken the trouble to make Canon Mallow realise that everything depended on whether Ginger had really believed that the half-crown was his or not, Canon Mallow's answer might have been different.

As it was, the detective-sergeant asked the plain question: Had Canon Mallow ever given Ginger a half-crown? And he received the plain answer: "No."

But can you wonder? Past seventy, the mind plays all

kinds of tricks. Whole episodes are erased sometimes. And, with not so much as a single clue to help him, Canon Mallow could not remember a thing. Simply not a thing.

Towards the end of the interview he did, admittedly, get the impression that perhaps he *ought* to have remembered, that perhaps he was disappointing the detective-sergeant, and he tried to make amends for it.

"I *may* have given the boy a half-crown," he said. "One can't be sure, can one? It's so long ago. But it's rather a large sum, half a crown, isn't it? If it had been sixpence or a shilling, I could have understood it. Of course, if he says so, I suppose I must have done. But I wonder why. I don't usually go about giving half-crowns away. At least not that I'm aware of. But I can't be certain that I didn't you know. It's only that I would probably have remembered it."

In the face of evidence such as that—and Canon Mallow repeated it all in Court in much the same terms until the Children's Magistrate had thanked him politely and invited him to stand down—it was decided that Ginger had really stolen the money. That he was a thief. And more than a thief—a burglar into the bargain. It was that bit about forcing the padlock with the poker that counted most against him. And with such a record, nothing less than a couple of years of institution life could be regarded as really tackling the problem.

That was how it was that Ginger came to be travelling up to Norfolk by train, in company with an elderly probation officer, rather like a dubious and despondent sheep, who kept one eye trained suspiciously on danger spots such as Exits and lock-up lavatories.

Ginger wasn't actually handcuffed; but that was the feeling. And he felt pretty rotten about things, just sitting there in the compartment with the jumpy old sheep edged up close on the seat beside him. The future at that moment just didn't seem worth living for. Even to have gone into a butcher's shop would have been better than having to go back to school again. And of all the barmy kinds of school, a farm school seemed to Ginger just about the barmiest of the lot of them.

But twenty-four hours later, he wouldn't have been anywhere else on earth. It wasn't the situation—bang in the centre of some of the flattest, dullest-looking country in the whole of England. It wasn't the house—a large, flat-faced sort of mansion like a . . . a . . . a, yes that was it: like a
454

school. It wasn't the Principal, a youngish curly-haired enthusiast, who embarrassed Ginger by linking arms with him straight away just to make him feel at home. It wasn't the food; or the games; or the companionship; or the animals. It was the tractors.

There were two of them, both Fordsons. One was practically new, with the gloss still on the paintwork; a veritable Beau Brummell among tractors. But it was the other one, ancient, discoloured, honourably-scarred, that tugged at Ginger's heart. And this was because its clutch had been taken down. Drawn up in the centre of the repair-workshop, the tractor stood there, degutted, its entrails spread neatly around it on the floor. And an instructor-mechanic was lecturing on the various parts, holding them out at arm's length as he did so, like a coroner carrying out rather an interesting post-mortem in public.

Ginger was right at the back for the first session. After the lunch break, however, he managed to work himself into the front row. And by tea-time he had been appointed assistant-demonstrator, and was allowed to pass the bits and pieces. He went to bed that night in the happy consciousness of a good day entirely well-spent. There had been virtue in it, and he fell asleep with his mind full of dry-plates and grease-washers and counter springs and Ferodo-facings.

His past life—dull, trivial and unrewardful, it now seemed in retrospect—slid from him. He forgot about the Archbishop Bodkin Hospital; and the reservoir in which he had so nearly drowned himself; and the Arkleydale Institution and the Children's Court; and all the rest of it. First-hand acquaintance with a reciprocating rocker-arm had temporarily banished all other memories.

Even the memory of Sweetie herself had slipped quietly away in the midst of them.

BOOK SIX

The Portrait and the Frame

CHAPTER LXVII

I

WELL, THERE you are: with Canon Mallow back at the Archbishop Bodkin Hospital where we first met him; and Ginger getting along nicely at the Farm School; and Sweetie and Margaret together again; and Dame Eleanor herself made thoroughly comfortable once more, the outlines of the pattern are beginning to appear. There is a certain discernible shape, even a shapeliness.

All lives, and indeed all collections of lives, are like that. If you withdraw far enough to get an angel's-eye view of things, as it were, and see the span of time as a whole, there is always the perfect and final pattern waiting somewhere. It may be something quite tiny—covering only a few years or months or weeks even; a mere design in miniature set inside the big untidy scribble of existence. The trouble is that so many people rush at it, kidding themselves that they have studied the whole plan when they have really only observed one small part of it. Then, at best, what emerges is a botch-up, lop-sided affair, a sort of badly-made picture frame that ten to one contains the wrong portrait altogether.

Indeed, that is just the way it would be if the Archbishop Bodkin chronicles were chopped-off somewhere round about at this point. The shape would be there all right. But, as it happens, it would be the wrong shape. It would be meaningless and, in places, downright misleading. To see the whole thing properly, to get the placid, uncrowded view to which the angels are accustomed, there is nothing for it but to withdraw still farther. Take in about another four years of it, in fact. And, even then, it is only somewhere towards the end where something happens to Sweetie and something else to Dame Eleanor, that the true picture jumps up at us.

It may be that the whole pattern is really a jig-saw. The little chunky bits have gradually been assembling themselves through the years—ever since 1920, in fact, when Sergeant Chiswick carried Sweetie in off the doorstep. But he didn't know then that it wouldn't be until nearly eighteen years later—with beer gone up ninepence and another world war just round the corner—that the final little twiddly bit, the key-piece itself, would be slotted into place and the portrait in the frame would be complete. Didn't, for that matter, know even whose portrait it was going to be, whether it was to be Sweetie's or Ginger's or Canon Mallow's or Dr. Trump's or Margaret's or Dame Eleanor's.

But it would not have worried him. For Sergeant Chiswick was never the thinking kind. And, in any case, by the time 1938 came along Sergeant Chiswick had backed his last loser and dropped quietly out of the pattern altogether.

I I

Meanwhile, the Archbishop Bodkin Hospital was in a state of confusion.

Dame Eleanor had been ordered by her doctor to rest and, with Margaret there to look after her, she was prepared this time to obey his orders. In consequence, it was Canon Larkin who, pro tem., presided at meetings. A born administrator, with a keen actuarial sense, he naturally spent a great deal of his time in discussing the nature of the hospital's financial settlement with regard to Dr. Trump. How long should full pay continue? he asked. What limit should be placed upon the half-pay period? Did sick leave count for purposes of pension? Was the Warden's Lodging a perquisite or an emolument? He was a great man for thoroughness and detail, and he succeeded finally in bewildering even himself. In the result, Dr. Trump continued to receive his full cheque every month and Canon Mallow, who was unable to get a word in edgeways, even when it was about hospital business, was left to direct the Bodkin fortunes single-handed.

And in small ways he managed to make his presence felt. Within the first month he got all the keep-off-the-grass notices removed ; and, by Christmas he had engaged a platoon of robust, old women to do the rough cleaning and so save the girls—some of whom were quite small Canon Mallow had noticed—from having to carry such heavy buckets about.

Then as a kind of extra Christmas present he relaxed the prohibition about masters smoking in their private bedrooms.

"I'm sure Dr. Trump won't mind," he kept telling himself.
"It's all so . . . so reasonable." But here it would have been
difficult for Canon Mallow to do otherwise, because he was
by way of being a rather absent-minded kind of smoker himself. Quite often he found himself with his own pipe in his
mouth, and the old briar drawing nicely, without so much
as the slightest recollection of having packed and lit it.

It was in the matter of the silent break-periods that Canon
Mallow failed most conspicuously. But Dr. Trump had been
a firm disciplinarian, and discipline dies slowly. Try as he
could, Canon Mallow was not able to get the children to let
themselves go properly. They walked when he felt that they
should have run, and they talked in whispers when he would
have liked to hear them shouting to one another. Altogether
it was as though they had just slipped out of the classroom
to attend a funeral.

Admittedly, things were a bit better already on the boys'
side since he had given permission for a football to be used.
And one of the ground-floor windows had gone already, lead-
lights and everything.

But Canon Mallow was quite frank about the whole position.

"It's going to take years, literally years," he said, "to
knock the discipline out of them. I don't know yet whether
I shall have time to succeed or not. But it's worth going on
trying."

III

But it was not at Broadstairs where Dr. Trump was still
waiting to hear from the Missionary Society, or at the Archbishop Bodkin Hospital, that the really important things were
happening. It was at Dame Eleanor's.

At first Dame Eleanor had been difficult. Convinced that
somehow or other the presence of Sweetie was going to
upset everything, she had sulked, refused to see the child,
ignored her. And her agitation, her misgivings, had revealed
themselves in a variety of ways. She was, for example, perpetually asking Margaret whether she was sure that she
wasn't overtiring herself, and then ringing the bell for her
unnecessarily just to make certain that she wasn't devoting
too much of her attention to Sweetie. Even that, however,
was in a sense excusable. Because the heart attacks, the

chokings, the palpitations, the feeling (to use Dame Eleanor's own description of it) as though an elephant had gone to sleep upon her chest while an entire string orchestra was playing in her ears, had grown no better. She was entirely confined to her bed nowadays.

Admittedly, she was making the most of her imprisonment. The bedside table was loaded with papers, minutes, reports; and her writing-case, red morocco outside and Russian leather within, was permanently open upon her knees. There was the illusion of still being at the hub of things. But she knew that it was only an illusion; knew that if the smallest thing went wrong—that even if her address-book or her fountain pen slid off the bedclothes on to the floor, she would have to start ringing that damn bell again in order to recover it. That was why she had to make sure that people were on their toes all the time, ready to come if she needed them.

But with her old possessiveness re-asserting itself, it was hardly to be expected that she would leave Sweetie alone altogether. Still keeping the child at arm's length—entirely out of sight, in fact, she began to manage her. She spoke of the need for friends of her own age. She hinted at idle hands. She recommended needlework and embroidery. She suggested that Sweetie might like to take lessons from the cook. She asked whether anything was being done about the child's music, and she reminded Margaret of the piano that stood there idle in the schoolroom. She became anxious that Sweetie's religious instruction was being scamped. She advised long walks. She wanted to know what books Sweetie was reading. She worried about her. She fretted.

The one thing that she did not do was to see her. But at last, curiosity overcame her. There was, however, more to it than mere idle curiosity. It was jealousy probably that was at the back of it. Margaret had just bought Sweetie some new clothes and Dame Eleanor suddenly decided that she must see them. She felt the need to know everything about them. What colour were they? Were they wool or a mixture? Where had Margaret gone for them? Had they got nice sensible hems that could be let down? Remembering Sweetie's age, was she sure that they were suitable? Were they winter weight, or summer, or just one of the in-betweens?

Then, when Margaret's answers all seemed to her so unsatisfying, so evasive somehow, Dame Eleanor resolved with equal suddenness that she must see not merely the clothes, but Sweetie wearing them. And, because at the back of her mind she knew that it was all a plot really, a subterfuge to insinuate herself, that the clothes as such meant nothing to her, she became self-conscious, even coy, about it.

". . . that is, if she doesn't mind coming to see a poor bedridden old woman," she finished up. "Some young people do, you know."

Directly after tea was the time that was chosen. Margaret in fact was already on her way to fetch Sweetie. She found her at the dressing-table when she reached the room. And as soon as Margaret entered Sweetie turned away and tried to conceal something. But Margaret had been too quick for her.

"What's that in your hand?" she asked.

"It's nothing."

"Yes, it is."

"No, really . . ."

"Show it to me."

"Oh, very well then."

Sweetie opened her hand and held it in front of her. In it was a pair of tweezers. Margaret took them from her.

"What are these for?" she demanded.

"Plucking my eyebrows," Sweetie told her.

Margaret thrust the tweezers away in the pocket of her house-dress. "Just you leave your eyebrows alone, d'you hear me. You don't want to go bothering about such things. Not at your age, you don't."

Sweetie shrugged her shoulders.

"I hadn't started yet," she said. "I was only choosing."

When they had reached the door of Dame Eleanor's room, Margaret paused.

"Now listen," she said. "Be nice to the lady. Say 'how-d'you-do' when she speaks to you. And if she wants to shake hands remember it's this one."

"I know that," Sweetie answered. "And about saying 'how-d'you-do'!"

Altogether, she could not make out what the fuss was about. She did not remember having seen Margaret so much agitated before. Did not remember even having seen her agitated at all in fact. But now she was trembling, actually trembling.

What Sweetie was not prepared for, however, was the size of the room and the smallness of Dame Eleanor. She had always thought of her as a large woman; the size of Mrs. Gurnett at least. Against the background of the Bodkin Hospital she had always seemed simply enormous. Whereas this was a tiny little old lady who was watching her out of the big pile of pillows. She looked as though she had been propped up specially for the occasion.

" I expect she's going to die soon," Sweetie reflected. " Perhaps that's why she wants to see me now."

But the little old lady still appeared to have plenty of life left in her. Her voice didn't seem to have changed at all. Sweetie remembered it from Speech Days and Founder's Days. And the voice wasn't even being particularly nice to her. It was the same old Archbishop Bodkin Hospital voice.

" Come nearer, child," it was saying. " I can't see you from right over there."

Sweetie stepped forward.

" How-d'you-do?" she said.

The reply seemed to take Dame Eleanor aback a trifle.

" How-d'you-do," she said, and extended a bony yellow hand on which the rings hung loosely.

" I hope you're better," Sweetie answered. " I'm sorry to hear you've been ill."

Dame Eleanor found herself looking at the child more closely. Practically every other child she had ever known, her own nieces and nephews among them, had a maddening and obstinate way of remaining silent and awkward when spoken to. But this child's manners were perfect. And she was certainly good-looking. Not a beauty by any means—beauties had gone out somewhere round about the time when Dame Eleanor herself had been a girl. But with those eyes and the shining blackness of her hair, she was undeniably good-looking. Dame Eleanor could understand now how it had come about that Ginger, or whatever the boy's name was, had been so much attracted to her.

" And there'll be plenty of others," she reflected. " You may be sure of that. You can see she's that sort."

As she looked, however, she became aware that Sweetie was studying her just as closely. There was a steadiness in the dark eyes that was strangely unnerving. And not a rude, staring steadiness, either. The mouth was creased up at the corners into the outlines of a polite social smile.

Dame Eleanor stopped regarding her.

461

"Do you like being here, child?" she asked abruptly.

"Oh yes, thank you," Sweetie told her. "I think it's a beautiful house you live in."

Dame Eleanor lay back against the pillows.

"I'm getting her sized up," she thought. "She's a little minx, that's what she is. The pretty ones mostly are. And what they need is taking down a bit. Everyone's too nice to them, just because they're pretty."

She paused.

"Better than sleeping under hay-ricks?" she asked.

Sweetie paused, too. But she kept her eyes on Dame Eleanor all the time. And the smile, the polite social smile had not even flickered.

"That was only tempor'y," she answered. "There wasn't anywhere else to go."

Dame Eleanor raised her eyebrows. Were all fourteen-year-old girls like this nowadays? she wondered. Perhaps it was something to do with progress and the spirit of the age. At fourteen, she herself had still been in the schoolroom; tall, silent, embarrassed whenever she came down if anybody spoke to her.

"Perhaps there *is* something unusual about her," she reflected: "I'll get Miss Phrynne to look up her record sometime. We have had children by girls of quite good families . . ."

She pulled herself up sharply. That was the worst of being old and ill, both at the same time: it made you lose your grip on your own thoughts. This wasn't in the least what she had intended. She had invited Margaret to bring Sweetie here simply so that she could see whether she was being dressed properly, and now she was just wasting her opportunity.

"Nearer, child," she said again. "I still can't see you properly."

Sweetie came right up to the bedside this time. And with the last step forward she had come suddenly into the focus of Dame Eleanor's lorgnette. Dame Eleanor took another long, quizzing look at her. And she had to admit it: yes, she had underestimated the child. There was more than ordinary good looks in that face. The eyelashes were as long as an actress's.

But she knew too much to spoil minxes by flattering them. And all that she said was: "You've got a pretty little face, dear. But you ought to do something about those eyebrows. They're all over the place: they're spoiling you."

She paused.

" And now let's see what Margaret's been buying for you."

The emphasis was obvious already: Dame Eleanor was speaking already as though Sweetie was hers, and Margaret had simply been carrying out a small commission on her instructions.

And even though the hand that shot out was old, it was still expert. Dame Eleanor had always claimed that she knew more about materials than any dressmaker. And what her fingers encountered now disgusted her. The dress—it was a blue one with white collar and cuffs, and white bows upon the pockets—was scarcely made of any material at all. It was the merest rubbish; cheap and smart-looking and nasty.

" Where did you get it?" she demanded.

" At a shop in Putney," Margaret told her.

Dame Eleanor shook her head.

" Shouldn't have gone there," she said. " Why didn't you go to Marshall's? They've got a proper juvenile department. They'd have looked after you."

" I'll remember next time," Margaret answered.

" And what did you pay for it?"

" Twenty-five and nine," Margaret replied.

It was a lot of money twenty-five and nine when it came out of a weekly wage of thirty shillings. And it was because there were so many other things that Sweetie needed that Margaret herself was still wearing the same black dress, the same shabby blue overcoat in which she had met Sweetie at the Remand Home.

But Dame Eleanor only shook her head.

" Simply throwing good money away," she said. " That's all it is—just throwing it away. I've told you before it's cheap clothes that cost the most in the long run. Look at me. Some of my dresses are ten years old, and they're still as good as when I bought them. Why? Merely because I paid a proper price for them in the first place."

She paused: her heart was fluttering again. That's the state she was in nowadays. She couldn't even discuss clothes without half-killing herself. And she didn't want to do anything silly, like fainting or having one of her really bad attacks, while the child was still in the room. So she pressed her left hand up against her heart to steady it.

But it was no use. She must get rid of the child somehow;

must be able to be quiet again. She didn't, however, want simply to send her away abruptly. All children are sensitive about that sort of thing, and don't forgive easily. And she wanted Sweetie to like her. She had always prided herself on the fact that she was popular with children; had, in fact, believed for years that if only things had gone differently with that son of hers she would have been the absolutely perfect kind of grandmother.

So she made a final effort.

" I'll give you a new dress . . . dear. A different one . . . For a present," she said.

Her breath was coming out jerkily by now, and she had difficulty in making the words sound natural.

" Margaret'll take you . . . You will, won't you, Margaret? Buy her the best . . . Tell them to put it down to my account."

" Thank you very much. That's very kind of you," Sweetie said before Margaret could speak.

Dame Eleanor had closed her eyes again by now. It was no use. The string orchestra in her ears was starting up again, and she knew that the real danger signal, the thumpetty-THUMP-thump was due at any moment now.

But she was still as anxious as ever that Sweetie should think kindly of her.

" Come . . . and see me again . . . one afternoon," she said huskily.

" Thank you very much," Sweetie answered. " I'd like to, any time."

Outside the door, Sweetie looked up at Margaret.

" Was I nice enough to her?" she asked. " Did I do what you told me?"

She paused.

" And now can I go and do my eyebrows, please?" she added.

I

THE LETTER from the China and East Indies Missionary Society had arrived at last. And Dr. Trump was jubilant.

He had already written five drafts of his letter of resignation to the Archbishop Bodkin Hospital, and was now busy on the sixth. This one was easily the best: it embodied all the key points from the previous five. But it contained one noticeable defect. For Dr. Trump had spent so much time in polishing up the prose that he had somehow missed the main point. Even after re-reading it, he could not himself quite make out whether after all he was actually resigning, or merely writing a letter to the Governors thanking them for past kindnesses.

His letter of acceptance on the other hand had been simple and emphatic. If the office boy had opened it he would have known at once that the job had been snapped up. And that was just what Dr. Trump intended. There were to be no fumblings, no dropped catches, this time. And already Dr. Trump was absorbed in missionary thoughts. He had done some pretty hard reading during the past fortnight. Naturally, until the job was definite he had not wanted to waste his time in picking up odd facts about outlandish places like Singapore and Hong-Kong. But for the last fortnight he had been making up for lost time. He now knew almost everything there was to know about population statistics, climatical conditions, means of communication, ethnological types, competitive religious systems, conversion rates. So far it was only the Tamil primer and the Ku-Yu Dictionary that had defeated him.

That is not to say, however, that everything was equally simple and straightforward on the domestic side. On the contrary, Felicity was opposed to the whole idea of his going. While all too obviously she did not mind—indeed, seemed rather to prefer—having her husband separated from her by some sixty-five miles of Southern Railway, she apparently could not bear the thought of having him separated by five thousand miles of P. & O. And she raised every objection she could think of to the whole project. She needed him, she said. His son needed him. Mrs. Warple needed him. Everybody needed him. It would be a loss to the country if he went away.

And with Sebastian's chest as it was, how, she demanded, could she contemplate either taking the youngster out there amid the fevers and high temperatures, or leaving him behind to be looked after by other and less loving hands? To all this Dr. Trump had been forced to make the most evasive of replies. Secretly—so secretly, in fact, that he scarcely admitted it even to himself—he was rather hoping that he would be able to go alone. He was not, even in his mind, disloyal to Felicity; there was nothing of the cheap or the fugitive about it. It was simply that the prospect of a job, and nothing but a job—no entertaining, no chest troubles, no womenfolk and, above all, no Mrs. Warple—seemed the kind of earthly bliss for which he had always longed. He wanted to be a busy, celibate missionary. And, flushed with the new enthusiasm, his whole being was now aflame with the desire to convert the heathen, baptise him, get him organised.

"What a field!" he reflected. "What boundless scope! Above all what an opportunity for modern methods—lectures and leaflets and lantern-slides and things."

11

And while Dr. Trump was guiltily, surreptitiously planning this new bachelor life under an Oriental sky, Canon Mallow was enjoying himself immensely, going round taking down notices, arranging extra free periods for the juniors, slackening things off generally. Another window, one of the stained glass ones this time, had gone during yesterday's morning break.

Apart from that, it was Miss Bodkin on whom most of the attention had been focused. By now, it wasn't only her hearing that was on the way out: it was her eyesight as well. At the last General Meeting she had first signed her name clean over the top of Canon Larkin's, and had then crossed out Mr. Chitt's in error when somebody had pointed the slip out to her.

But it was still Sweetie to whom most of the interesting things were happening. During her first six weeks with Dame

Eleanor she had merely been installing herself. It was the succeeding three months that really counted. And by the time these were over she had fairly turned things upside down.

Or rather, Dame Eleanor had turned them upside down for her. It had all started from the day when she had sent for Sweetie in order to see the new dress, the twenty-five and ninepenny one, that she had inspected and then said that she wouldn't have at any price. She had got herself so much worked up about it at the time that she had to spend three days flat on her back without seeing anyone. But, as soon as she was well enough, she sent for Sweetie again. And this time, having sent for her, she wouldn't let her go. She monopolised the child. Nowadays, Sweetie came in first thing in the morning, immediately Dame Eleanor had been tidied up, simply to say good-morning; looked in again before lunch; had her tea at the bedside; and came in last thing to say good-night.

There had been the brief experiment of getting Sweetie to read to Dame Eleanor. But that had been abandoned after the first attempt. Dame Eleanor was an exacting listener, and Sweetie read appallingly, with no pauses except for breath and, so far as Dame Eleanor could make out, no understanding of even the simplest words.

It was because of the revelation of ignorance—that Dame Eleanor would have put down to sheer stupidity if she had found it in any other child—that she decided to engage someone to keep Sweetie on with her school work in the mornings. Dame Eleanor did not consult Margaret. She did not even tell Sweetie. She simply engaged the woman.

In consequence, Sweetie now hated the mornings. From 9.30 to 12, she was closeted with the widow of a church schoolmaster and found herself right back in the middle of things—Scripture, English, History, Geography—that she had hoped that she had escaped from for ever. Progress was slow. There was complete agreement between Sweetie, Dame Eleanor and the schoolmaster's widow about that point. But as the woman was a dependent of Dame Eleanor's anyhow, it seemed to Dame Eleanor better that she should be paid for doing something—even though it was something useless—than for doing absolutely nothing.

And, if five mornings a week were now utterly ruined for Sweetie, there were still compensations. For a start, Dame

467

Eleanor, in a commanding, uncontradictable sort of way, was so unpredictably generous. Her sudden interest in Sweetie's clothes had not stopped at one new dress. When she discovered that the child had practically no underclothes, no nightdresses worth speaking of, no winter overcoat, no shoes, she sent Margaret off immediately, and told her to buy everything that Sweetie needed. Only they must be good, she kept reminding her; they must be good.

Then there was the matter of Sweetie's bedroom. As soon as Dame Eleanor could get up and move about again, she came up and inspected it. And immediately she found everything wrong. It was too small, she said; too dark, and it faced North. And, becoming suddenly sentimental about Sweetie she declared that a child of Sweetie's age needed all the sunlight she could get.

There was the blue bedroom, of course—but that looked over the drive and you could never be certain that you weren't going to be disturbed. Or the Chinese room—but, though it was never used nowadays, Dame Eleanor was very fond of its suite of lacquer furniture and felt sure that Sweetie would damage it somehow in the slapdash way young girls always do damage things. But why not Derek's room? It had stood empty for all that time. Indeed, there had been a time when she had thought of just leaving everything as it was and simply screwing up the door. As for herself it must be getting on for sixteen years since she had even been inside it.

And the fiery impetuousness that in her time had carried her roughshod through innumerable councils and committees now focused itself upon Derek's room. First there was the problem of re-decoration. A young girl's room, she explained, as though she had been designing young girls' rooms all her life, must be pale cream; with chintzes, not cretonnes; and the furniture kept as little like bedroom furniture as possible.

"What a fifteen-year-old wants is somewhere she can call her own; somewhere the rest of the household aren't bothering her all the time," Dame Eleanor declared, looking hard at Margaret as she said it. And she added as though she herself had been brought up in some kind of a crèche: "At least, that's what I always wanted when I was her age."

When, finally, everything had been settled to her satisfaction, Dame Eleanor put her hand on Sweetie's shoulder.

"There you are, dear," she said. "I've got it right at

468

last. That's the way you want it. It's always worth taking the trouble when it's something personal. It's your room, dear, and I was determined to have everything in it just the way it should be."

She paused.

"Thank you ever so much," Sweetie answered, squeezing Dame Eleanor's hand—they had got to the hand-holding stage about a month ago—"I think it's lovely. I never knew I should have such a beautiful room."

Dame Eleanor smiled contentedly. All her life she had been doing things for other people. It had become a dedicated purpose with her. She saw now, however, that what she had done was to make the mistake of doing things for people in the mass. In consequence, she had never known whether they were grateful or not; whether, in fact, they even realised. It had all been a one-way traffic. But this was different. To see the eager face, the shining eyes of this girl who had so surprisingly not only come into her life, but into the very centre of it, was the real reward. It made her feel warm and thankful just to think about the child's delight.

"And if there's anything at all you want," she told her, "anything you don't like, or anything that I haven't thought of, you've only to say so. Then we can forget all about getting it ready, and it'll be up to you to make it—a happy room. Is there anything you'd like?"

There was a pause.

"Could I have a gramophone, please?" Sweetie asked.

Margaret was angry afterwards when she heard about the gramophone: she insisted that Sweetie should not have asked for it. Asking for it had made her look greedy, mercenary, acquisitive, she kept saying.

"I don't like to see any girl growing up into a cadger," she told her.

She had been trying hard to bring Sweetie up properly. And to some extent, she supposed, she had succeeded. It had been easy to teach Sweetie how to dress properly and how long to spend on brushing her hair, and how to wash without leaving a brown horse-collar half-way down her neck. They had taught her most of these things at the hospital. But, after all, they weren't the most important things: and it was upon Sweetie's mind that Margaret was unable to make any

469

impression whatsoever. It seemed to be entirely self-enclosed. Appeals were useless, and Sweetie continued exactly as she was—selfish; self-confident; loving in a sprawling, desultory sort of way, and often rather bored.

It was Sweetie's boredom more than anything else that worried Margaret. And she was convinced that she was bored because she accepted everything so easily. It never even seemed to occur to Sweetie that instead of this room of hers with the pink-shaded light over the dressing-table, she might have been sleeping in a basement somewhere in Finsbury Park or Balham.

She took it all for granted, just as she took for granted the new dresses that Dame Eleanor had insisted she should have. Took them for granted. And then left them lying about in heaps on the floor as soon as she got out of them.

Part of the trouble was that Margaret didn't see enough of Sweetie nowadays: if she had seen more, she felt certain, she would have been able to have some effect simply by what she referred to as "keeping on at her." But Dame Eleanor was reserving Sweetie for herself. When she went for drives it was now Sweetie who sat beside her. And Sunday afternoons had suddenly been taken away from Margaret, too. At first, Margaret had been able to have Sweetie entirely to herself from lunch-time onwards. For the last three Sunday afternoons, however, Dame Eleanor had decided to have Sweetie downstairs with her. It would be good for the child, she said; give her confidence; take away her shyness.

In a sense, it was everything that Margaret had ever hoped for to find Sweetie made one of the family in this way. But there was one thing about it that she did not like: she kept hearing things about her at second-hand from Dame Eleanor. It was from Dame Eleanor that she learnt that Sweetie wanted to have riding-lessons; it was from Dame Eleanor that she first heard that Sweetie wanted to let her hair grow; and it was from Dame Eleanor that she discovered that Sweetie had not forgotten Ginger.

Dame Eleanor seemed merely to be amused by it. It even showed a friendly, childlike disposition, she said, to want to know how her old schooldays companion was getting on.

"After all, they did see a lot of each other during those three days together," she went on. "We must remember that. For my part I think it's wonderful the way she's got over it. Sometimes when I look at her I just can't believe it. She's a sly little puss, that's what she is," she added. "I know her: I can tell."

But Margaret was worried. And that night she spoke to Sweetie about it.

"What's this you've been telling Dame Eleanor about Ginger?" she demanded.

A half-smile crossed Sweetie's face.

"Oh nothing. Just that I'd like to see him again."

"Can't you think of anything but Ginger? You promised to forget all about him."

"You can't forget people just by promising."

"But why do you have to bother about him so much?"

"Because I like him, I suppose," Sweetie answered.

Margaret was silent for a moment. When she spoke again, she was quieter, gentler.

"You'll have to forget him sometime," she said. "You'll want to get married yourself, one day, and then you'll spend all your time thinking about the man you're going to marry. And he won't be a bit like Ginger either. Don't you see, things can't never be the same again. If Ginger came here now he wouldn't know you."

"I bet he would."

"He wouldn't. You're different now."

"Well, anyhow, I'd know him."

Margaret paused.

"But can't you see," she began again, "you'll meet lots of other people now. Nice people; people Dame Eleanor would like you to marry. Not people of Ginger's class."

"Well, it's my class, too, isn't it?"

Margaret did not answer.

"If you don't do nothing that's silly," she said, "you can be a lady for the rest of your life."

Sweetie shrugged her shoulders.

"There's no fun in being a lady if you've got to be bossed about all the time," she answered.

"You're an ungrateful girl, that's what you are," Margaret told her. "You just think of nobody but yourself."

"You said just now I only think about Ginger." Sweetie swung round suddenly. "Where is he, anyhow?"

Margaret flushed.

"I don't know," she said. "And if I did know, I wouldn't tell you."

"I can find out."

"That you can't."

"I'll write to Canon Mallow. He knows where all the old boys are."

"And he won't tell you because I'll warn him. I'll get Dame Eleanor to say that you're not to be told, not on no account."

Sweetie threw her head back.

"I shall find out soon enough when I want to," she said. "As soon as I'm ready I shall write and ask him to come here. I'll invite him. Dame Eleanor'll let me if I ask her. You can't stop that. She likes me better than she likes you."

Margaret got up and stood in front of Sweetie. She was pale and her hands trembled.

"I'm sorry I ever troubled about you," she said. "I'm sorry I didn't leave you to go into service. It's all you're fit for. You're just cheap and mean. Coming here and playing on an old lady's feelings . . ."

Sweetie drew in her breath sharply. She was calmer than Margaret.

"You got no right to say such things," she said. "You aren't anybody. You're just one of the servants . . ."

It was then, to Sweetie's great surprise, that Margaret smacked her face.

CHAPTER LXIX

I

IT CAME as a complete shock to everybody when Canon Mallow suddenly announced that he wanted to get rid of Miss Britt.

There had been no warning of any kind: no open clashes of authority; no rows; not even any sign of bickering. Canon Larkin, in particular, was entirely unprepared for it. He had just resigned his position on the Parochial Schools Central Finance Committee in order to succeed Dame Eleanor as the new Chairman of Bodkin's, and he was looking forward to an orgy of statistical analysis. Already he was a step or two ahead of Dr. Trump. Dr. Trump had merely been concerned with seeing the ha'pence come out right: Canon Larkin was intent on breaking everything down into man-hours. Man-hours are the secret of everything, one of England's leading industrialists had told him.

Then, on Canon Larkin's very first day in the new job, Canon Mallow delivered his ultimatum. Either Miss Britt went or he would have to go himself, he insisted. Canon Mallow was very nice about it, of course; he didn't want to put anybody to any trouble. He even offered to stay on until the end of the term whichever way the vote of the Board might happen to go. And when Canon Larkin asked him what had led him to arrive at his irrevocable decision, Canon Mallow was unable to give any very satisfactory reply. It was simply, he said, that he felt that the hospital needed someone who was warmer with the children; someone who didn't talk so much like a text-book, and cared for human beings for their own sakes. Someone, in short, who had a heart.

All that he did was to stick to his story: ". . . it doesn't matter so much about the qualifications," he persisted, " so long as she's a human being. There's no actual harm, I suppose, in vegetarianism: I'd just rather not, if you follow me. And I don't think kissing the little ones is wrong: I believe it's good for them. The children here might just as well be so many tadpoles the way that Miss Britt looks after them . . ."

But by then bigger things were happening at the Archbishop Bodkin Hospital. Mr. Prevarius had been cited as co-respondent in the divorce case of Twiddle versus Twiddle. And here Canon Larkin had felt compelled to act immediately. There was no hesitation. Scandal of any kind, and more particularly scandal connected with divorce, was anathema to him. As soon as he saw the paragraph in the evening paper—" TOP HIT-WRITER CITED " was the heading—he sent for Mr. Prevarius. And he was brutal. A more massive personality than Dr. Trump, he was also more commanding.

" Unclean," he said loudly and menacingly as soon as he had heard all the circumstances. " Distinctly unclean. Mr. Prevarius, you must leave us. We have no further need of your services. You may go to-night. Must go to-night, in fact. You positively shall go."

The speed of the dismissal was all deliberate and pre-determined. Above all things, Canon Larkin wanted to act before Canon Mallow's natural kindness of heart, his gentleness, could begin complicating matters.

Nor was there any appeal elsewhere. Mr. Prevarius, in fact, was finished. A ruined man, broken in spirit, not daring to look anyone in the eye, he crept out of the big Gothic gate and made his way back miserably to the mews-flat that he had taken, after he had been humiliatingly turned out of Deirdre Gardens by the outraged Miss Lewises. And even the magic of knowing that Desirée would be there in the mews waiting for him, in a complete set of salmon pink negligée that he had just bought her, seemed somehow to have evaporated.

But it was not the fact that he had been cited under his own name—apparently the musk rat in the shabby bowler had been a veritable Javert among detectives—that haunted him. It was the truth about Desirée's name that hurt.

There was something so silly, so damn' silly, he could not help feeling, about being cited by an injured husband called Twiddle. If it had really been " Manners " which is what Desirée had first told him, Mr. Prevarius would not have minded half so much. And there was still the danger that the other ridiculous name, McTurk, would come popping up again.

Twiddle and McTurk: Mr. Prevarius shuddered.

I I

Dame Eleanor was too much preoccupied by her own affairs to care very much about Mr. Prevarius when Canon Mallow told her.

" They're mostly bad eggs, those organists," she said cryptically. " You be careful who you get next time. Why not try a woman? There must be women who can play the organ. It's not hard work: it's all done by electricity nowadays."

And with that she dismissed the matter from her mind. It was something legal, something to do with her will that was occupying her thoughts. Margaret knew that much. Mr. Thring had been out to the house twice already. And he was coming again this afternoon.

The meeting proved to be an unusually long one. Mr. Thring called immediately after lunch and by five o'clock he was still there. He was a large elderly man like a sedate, grizzled buffalo, and, by teatime, he looked as if Indians

had been after him. His chief trouble lay in the fact that
Dame Eleanor had asked him to come alone. She disliked,
she said, having strange clerks and secretaries fussing about
in her bedroom. In consequence, Mr. Thring had to be
forced to write things down to her dictation. And this had
not been easy. Dame Eleanor was not the woman she had
been: her thoughts nowadays came in bolts and snatches
rather than in a continuous stream. And, when she wasn't
dictating, she was asking Mr. Thring to cross out what she
had just said. At the end of three hours, Mr. Thring's pad
looked as if he had been drawing maps of tube railways.

There was one little incident that left Margaret puzzled.
It happened around teatime. Dame Eleanor had just rung
for her to bring down the digitalis tablets, when Sweetie came
in to pay her regular afternoon visit. But this time, for
some reason, she appeared to have forgotten about the child
entirely. She brought down the lid of the writing-case with a
bang and told Sweetie to go away again.

"Outside with you, miss," she said. "Out you go. All in
good time. We don't want you here now."

It was all so sudden and unexpected that Margaret looked
up startled. Had something gone wrong, she wondered
anxiously. Had Sweetie been rude to Dame Eleanor? Had
they quarrelled? But it was all over as quickly as it had
begun. For as soon as Sweetie had got to the door, Dame
Eleanor called her back again; right back. Made her come
over to her chair, in fact. And, when she was within arm's
reach, she pulled her down and kissed her.

"My little Sweetie doesn't understand," she said. "But
how could she? This is my secret, not hers. Not yet. Now
say how d'you do to Mr. Thring, and then run away and
leave us. We're very busy, aren't we, Mr. Thring? We've got
our work to do."

It was nearly a week later when Margaret understood. Mr.
Thring was there again, and Dame Eleanor sent for Margaret. Spread out on the desk-flap was a document bound in
red tape, and with little red seals upon it.

"Come in," Dame Eleanor told her. "I want to talk to
you. It's about Sweetie." She paused for a moment to collect
her thoughts. "Have you ever wondered what would become
of Sweetie if anything happened to me?" she asked.

Margaret nodded.

" I have," she said. " Often. I've been worried about it."

The answer was just what Dame Eleanor had wanted to hear: she smiled contentedly.

"Well, you needn't worry any more," she said. " We've seen to all that. She's been provided for. Well provided for. Our Sweetie's a very fortunate young lady, isn't she, Mr. Thring?"

Mr. Thring nodded gloomily. There had been so many changes that it was difficult to remember precisely how fortunate Sweetie really was.

But Dame Eleanor was not bothering about Mr. Thring. She had kept her eyes fixed on Margaret's face while she was speaking. There was no change of expression there, however: it was the same smooth, placid face that Dame Eleanor had always known. And the far-off look in the eyes vexed Dame Eleanor.

"Well, aren't you going to say anything?" she asked sharply.

There was a pause.

"I'm too happy," Margaret told her. " Really I am. There isn't anything I can say. It's all so good of you."

She put up her hand and brushed away the tears that had come suddenly into her eyes. The gesture satisfied Dame Eleanor: she gave the same contented smile that she had given when she had shown Sweetie her room. But a moment later she drew her lips in. That was because the thumpetty-THUMP-thump of her heart was just starting. She had been talking too much. And she had to be careful. If she were snuffed out now she wouldn't have achieved anything. She beckoned to Margaret to come nearer.

"And . . . and there's something for you, too, dear," she said. "That's only fair. If it hadn't been for you I should never have met Sweetie. Besides, I want you to stand by her. Sweetie's one of the family now. If I go first there must be someone to look after her, someone who cares. And you've always seemed so fond of her. . . ."

476

CHAPTER LXX

I

SWEETIE was improving steadily. Dame Eleanor had put Sweetie's hair into the hands of a good hairdresser, and he had got some shape into it. But her eyelashes, without any help from a hairdresser, were every bit as good as her hair. And her eyes, deep and dark as a Madonna's, were really remarkable. The photograph of Sweetie that now stood on Dame Eleanor's dressing-table showed what magnificent eyes they were.

What was more important, however, was that Sweetie had outgrown her earlier restlessness. Even Margaret could see that she was settling down. It must have been a year at least since she had so much as mentioned Ginger. There were, of course, sudden crazes, sillinesses: she wanted to travel; run a riding-school; become a mannequin; be an air-hostess. But that is the kind of thing to be expected when a girl is getting on for eighteen.

And the real trouble was that she hadn't any friends. Dame Eleanor had done her best for her. She had invited some very nice girls from Cheltenham and Roedean. But it was no use. They wore the same kind of clothes; had the same manners; spoke with the same voices even, now that Sweetie had been given elocution lessons. There, however, it stopped. They had nothing, apparently, in common. It was all too plain that Sweetie wasn't very much interested in girls.

And, as for Dame Eleanor, she wasn't very much interested in young men; not for the present, at least. She changed her mind suddenly because of the young men whom Sweetie was meeting at her dancing-class. It was a thoroughly select dancing-class, with none but the nicest young men attending it. But Dame Eleanor decided that they were probably neither select nor nice enough. Slowly, carefully, she began admitting a trickle of young men of her own choosing. They arrived at The Cedars, pink, awkward, polite, self-conscious. They had the air of having been at Cheltenham or Roedean themselves. And Sweetie despised the lot of them.

Dame Eleanor was secretly relieved. It was not that she

wanted to keep Sweetie to herself for ever. On the contrary, she derived obvious pleasure from the thought that Sweetie would get married soon and have children of her own. It was the natural order of things, she kept telling herself. And for her part it was something to look forward to, something that would make up for the gap in her own life. All that she wanted was to be certain that it should be the right young man. There was her money as well as Sweetie's happiness to be considered. But they were absolutely interlocked, she could see that. She felt convinced, too, that if she could find someone who was worthy of the money, Sweetie's happiness would follow automatically.

It was late one evening, as Margaret was settling her down for the night, when Dame Eleanor first discussed the matter of Sweetie's marriage. There was nothing considered or deliberate about it ; just a casual reference. But that was the way Dame Eleanor always did speak to Margaret about Sweetie nowadays, as though Margaret were just an interested outsider.

"Eighteen's not too early for a girl," she said, as though it were another of those subjects on which she was an authority. "It's when she's in the late twenties that she finds it so difficult. The best thing a girl can do is to get married, and start having babies before she knows what's happening to her. That's the way it ought to be . . . ."

She broke off for a moment and seemed to be considering something. She did not appear to be worried by the fact that she was contradicting everything that she had said during her whole active life, that she was being a bad Suffragette. It was something else altogether that had distracted her.

Along the corridor, the strains of Sweetie's gramophone were coming. It was louder than usual and Margaret asked if she should go and stop it. But Dame Eleanor would not hear of it.

"I like to think of her enjoying herself," she said. "That's all that matters really ; making people happy."

II

The most persistent and also one of the nicest of the young men whom Dame Eleanor admitted to the house was James Sturgess, old Admiral Sturgess's son. James Sturgess was in the Navy himself, and was not so pink and awkward as the others. Perhaps that was because he was older: he was twenty-six. But the difference of a few years did not matter; all to the good in fact, Dame Eleanor considered. And, best of all, Sweetie seemed to like him. But that was no wonder. At Sweetie's age, Dame Eleanor would have been ready to like him herself. There was something about all the Sturgesses that women found attractive. The admiral, she remembered, used to cut in quite disgracefully at dances, and his partners had always forgiven him.

She kept telling herself, however, that she must not start getting sentimental about old times: it was not of herself but of Sweetie that she was thinking. And they made such a nice pair—James in one of those double-breasted dinner-jackets that his generation seemed to prefer, and Sweetie in the first of her proper evening dresses. Whenever she saw them together Dame Eleanor felt that she had steered things very well.

It was only Margaret who was worried. Dame Eleanor seemed to be taking so much for granted. She kept dropping stray remarks about it. " Couldn't get a steadier sort of man than James," she said. " Just what Sweetie needs. Someone to keep her on the rails," and, continuing with her thoughts, she added a moment later, " It's boy babies that always come first with the Sturgesses. Two boys and then a girl. I should know: I've seen three generations of them." And when Margaret asked Dame Eleanor if she thought that Sweetie was really in love with James Sturgess, Dame Eleanor shrugged her shoulders. " What does a girl of eighteen know about love?" she asked. " She's pleased when he rings up, and that's the main thing."

That night Margaret spoke to Sweetie. Not that it was easy. During the past year Sweetie had grown apart from her so much: she didn't seem to feel the need of her any more.

Sweetie was seated at the dressing-table spreading cream on her face when Margaret entered.

" Oh, it's you," she said over her shoulder, and turned away again towards the mirror.

Margaret waited.

" I want to talk to you," she said at last.

" What about?"

" About this James Sturgess."

479

Sweetie said nothing. But she raised her eyebrows. Margaret could see the gesture in the glass.

" Are you in love with him?" Margaret asked.

" Why do you want to know?"

" I do."

" Well, it's my business."

" But it's mine, too, Sweetie. I want you to be happy."

Sweetie turned and faced her.

" You may do now," she said. " You didn't always."

" What do you mean?"

" Nothing."

" Tell me."

" Well, you wouldn't say where Ginger was, would you?" Sweetie demanded. " You wouldn't say, just because you didn't like him. You always hated Ginger."

Margaret felt her nerves tightening. She got up and put her hand on Sweetie's shoulder.

" Are you still in love with Ginger?" she asked.

But Sweetie only thrust her away.

" Why do you come here?" she asked. " You're only trying to gloat over me. Leave me alone, can't you. I ask you. Please go."

I I I

Margaret told Dame Eleanor of her misgivings. But she was only laughed at; and, worse than laughed at, snubbed. Any talking to Sweetie about her marriage, Dame Eleanor told her, she would do herself.

" She doesn't want to be bothered at a time like this," she said decisively. " Leave her alone, that's the right thing to do. How can she possibly know whether she loves him until she's seen more of him? She's only a child: you're expecting her to behave like a grown woman."

Dame Eleanor paused.

" If it's the last thing I do, I'm going to see Sweetie married," she went on. " I know what's good for her: I've been studying her. Take my word for it "—here Dame Eleanor faced Margaret squarely—" a girl like Sweetie needs a husband. And if the right one comes along now, it's only common sense . . ."

" But she doesn't love him," Margaret interrupted her.

And it was then that Dame Eleanor lost her temper. She

was rude in that old imperious way of hers, not caring how many feelings she was hurting.

"You're all the same," she said. "Every one of you. Love, love, love as though there were nothing else in the world to think about. What do you know about being in love anyhow? If you'd ever been in love you'd have married somebody. It was children you always cared about, not husbands."

CHAPTER LXXI

I

CANON MALLOW—rather to his own surprise when he came to think about it—had succeeded in his purpose: he had got rid of Miss Britt. Or rather, Miss Britt had done it for him. She could not, she said, even consider being criticised by anyone so unscientific as Canon Mallow. After Dr. Trump's departure, it seemed, she had remained at the Archbishop Bodkin Hospital only out of her keen sense of duty towards the children. And now that she knew that she was not appreciated she would like to leave immediately. She had, she said, eleven days of annual leave, three days of special leave, heaven knows how many days of compensatory leave all owing to her and would probably have had a severe breakdown if she had remained there even one day longer. Then, rather illogically—for by now the volcanoes had melted the main glacier and everything was suddenly fluid and unpredictable—she added that if Dr. Trump had still been there he would never have allowed it. It was obvious as she said it that she had admired the man ; revered him ; idolised him ; even, in a chaste and chilly fashion, possibly, loved him a little.

But it was too late now to turn to Dr. Trump. In the P. & O. liner, *Sydney*, Dr. Trump was already approaching Suez on his voyage towards his brave new life. Violently sea-sick for the first five days, he was now steadying himself with rusks and bowls of hot beef-tea. And he was magnificently disdainful of infirmity. Even though it was hot, swelteringly hot, in the little cabin, he was making no concessions to the climate. With his chair drawn up directly under the electric fan, he was busy with the Ku-Yu dictionary; engrossed; absorbed in it. And every few minutes he would throw his head back and try actually to pronounce something.

He had put in more than two hours' work already. But work was easy on board; or, at least, comparatively easy. There were no interruptions from either Felicity or Sebastian. So far as they were concerned, it had all turned out just as Dr. Trump had intended. They had stayed behind in Broadstairs.

Admittedly, the leave-taking had been painful and distressing. Felicity had been convinced that she would never again see her husband alive and face to face; and on the quayside she had wept like one who is already bereaved. But, even in tears, she had still not budged.

"Sebastian's chest must come first," she had maintained firmly. "Sebastian's chest comes before everything."

And so, here he was, on the high seas and practically a bachelor again. But only practically. For, as he sat there on the hard, upright chair with his Chinese text-book resting on the ledge of the wash-basin, there came a knock upon the cabin door. Dr. Trump started, and looked agonisedly round the room until his eyes came finally to rest upon the clothes closet. But it was no use. The knock had come a second time and, if he did not answer, he knew that in a moment the door handle would begin turning.

Why, why, he asked himself despairingly, had Mrs. Warple positively insisted on coming with him to Chungking?

"Come in, mother dear," he said faintly.

I I

The significant thing is that nobody seemed to miss the efficient Miss Britt; or Dr. Trump himself for that matter. The gap that had been left closed, miraculously. Naturally, Nurse Stedge, when Miss Britt left, moved up one, and now held the Matron's post—the one that had once been Mrs. Gurnett's. But as for Miss Britt herself, nobody seemed to notice that she had gone. Indeed, apart from a visit of protest from the local greengrocer who suddenly found his turn-over cut by something like a half, Miss Britt's departure was entirely unregretted. Even there, however, the pleasure of the family butcher in the High Street, who began getting those nice orders again for forty pounds of stewing steak, or thirty pairs of rabbits, just about made up for the heartbreak of the greengrocer.

No, the real source of anxiety within the Archbishop Bodkin Hospital was the laundry. The laundry finances were giving trouble again. Convinced that the girls were being over-worked, Canon Mallow had been rather too easy with them. He had engaged eleven extra staff and the effect was beginning to be felt. The profits had declined steadily since Canon Mallow's return, and the Chairman, Canon Larkin, was now spending most of his time finding out why this should be. He had already got as far as determining that it took as much as .3 of a man-hour to wash, starch and iron a collar. And, by the following spring, he was convinced that he would have been able to stop the rot.

But there was more to it than mere statistical analysis.

"I fear, I very sadly fear," he found himself saying all too often nowadays, "that things will not come right until there have been further changes. After all, you know, Mallow is over seventy . . ."

III

There was one other ex-Bodkinian who had already faced change, and all the anguish that is implied in separation. That was Mr. Prevarius. Disgraced, shunned, ruined, a double outcast in ecclesiastical circles, he had just signed a twelve-week contract with the Leicester Square Majestic. Admittedly, the hours were long. But the pay was reasonable—the same as a Cabinet Minister's. And he was allowed to play his own stuff—Mr. Spike Jerome had stipulated that when he fixed up the contract.

At this very moment, Mr. Prevarius was on the job. Clothed in an all-white evening suit he was seated at the console of a mammoth Wurlitzer that was illuminated like an incandescent *bombe-glacé*. The *bombe-glacé* was rising from its pit, and a magenta light was being sprayed on Mr. Prevarius from the projector room. He was playing already as he came up—playing quietly, scarcely more than a whisper in fact; and mournfully; and with soul.

"Love's the Divinest Thing" the piece was called—it was his own latest number—and as he played he was thinking about his own divorce proceedings. It was Mr. Twiddle, not Desirée, who was in his mind as the deep vibrations of the Wurlitzer brought lumps into the audience's throat and started hands reaching out for hands everywhere from the two and fours to the nine and sixes.

CHAPTER LXXII

I

IT WAS Dame Eleanor's idea that Sweetie should be given a coming-out party. And it was her eighteenth birthday that was chosen for it.

"Dame Eleanor's giving you a new dress for it," Margaret told Sweetie. "It's going to be a white one."

She was pleased nowadays when she was able to tell Sweetie something. It showed that she was still in Dame Eleanor's confidence.

But Sweetie only smiled.

"I know," she said. "She told me." Then she turned to Margaret. "What are you going to wear?" she asked.

Margaret shrugged her shoulders.

"Don't you worry about me," she said. "I'll be too busy doing things to worry about what I'm going to wear."

"Have you got a party dress?" Sweetie asked.

Margaret paused.

"Not for that kind of party," she said.

Sweetie would not be put off, however.

"Borrow the blue one of cook's," she told her. "You'll look very nice in it. You're both about the same size." She paused. "And I've told you before," she went on, "it's silly of you, really it is, giving me a birthday present when you haven't even got all the clothes you want. You're too generous: that's the trouble with you. I want you to promise now that if I ever do get married you're not going to give me a wedding present."

Margaret smiled.

"I'm not going to promise anything," she told her. "It's too early. You may be glad of it by then. You never know . . ."

But there she checked herself. What she had said just now

484

surprised her. The words had come from nowhere, and she didn't know why she had said them.

Sweetie, however, hadn't taken them seriously. She was only laughing at her.

" I believe you'd like to see me poor again," she said. " Then you could do everything for me."

And, going up to Margaret, she kissed her.

It was not often these days that Sweetie kissed her. She seemed to have outgrown that sort of thing. And, at the party, Margaret could see how grown-up she really was. She was a young woman. And it was wonderful watching all these people, with Sweetie as the centre. James Sturgess was close beside her, and she was smiling ; smiling at everyone.

" I needn't have worried," Margaret told herself. " It's going to be all right. It'll all turn out just like I hoped."

Against the far wall, Dame Eleanor was seated on the couch alongside Admiral Sturgess.

" And she's one in a thousand," she was saying. " Whoever gets her is going to be lucky."

The admiral was non-committal.

" Damn' pretty girl," he replied. " Don't wonder he fell for her. Would have done so myself."

He was, as a matter of fact, still disappointed—and more than disappointed : fairly bowled over—by the fact that his son should have picked on a girl with no background. It seemed a sort of slight somehow on himself and the boy's mother. But he didn't want to start a row with Dame Eleanor this evening. So he merely repeated himself.

" Damn' pretty girl. Don't know that I ever saw a prettier."

" Or happier," Dame Eleanor reminded him. She had sensed a feeling of reserve somewhere, and she didn't like it. " Both of 'em, I mean. They're cut out for each other."

And it was Canon Mallow's view, too, that Sweetie was the happiest girl, as well as the prettiest girl, that he had ever seen. He pottered round the room telling everybody. And he went further with Sweetie : he insisted on kissing her.

" And it isn't the first time I've done it, either," he said smilingly. " I kissed you when you were only so big "—he spread his hands out, indicating something the size of a lap-dog—" That was just after you'd been brought in. I remember, it was a terrible night. The rain was coming down . . ."

And then he recollected that the one thing that he mustn't

do was to remember: it was only on condition that he did not refer to Sweetie's earlier life in the Archbishop Bodkin Hospital—and certainly not in front of any of the Sturgesses—that Dame Eleanor had invited him at all.

I I

Canon Mallow heaved a deep sigh of sheer physical relief when he got back to Mr. Jeffcote's old room.

"Aaah!" he said to himself as he pushed his shoes off and slid into his bedroom slippers. "That's better. Now I can breathe again."

He had never been much of a man for parties, and he had been thoroughly glad when it had come time to leave The Cedars. The noise of so many voices, the champagne, and meeting all those people had just been too much for him. And besides, he hadn't been able to smoke there. All round him at the party there had been people frantically snatching up cigarettes and lighting them and stamping them out again practically all in one motion, but a quiet, thorough-going pipe smoker like himself had been left completely out of it. That was why it was so pleasant now to get down his tobacco jar and fill his pipe and put his feet up.

Of course, he was delighted by the way things had turned out for her. It was wonderful; simply wonderful. Or, at least, he supposed it was wonderful. Everybody else certainly seemed to think it was. But now that he came to reflect on it he was not so sure. And the longer he sat there, blowing out blue, lazy clouds of smoke, and thinking things over, the more he found that he was convincing himself the other way.

"You can't help wondering," he told himself. "Really, you can't." This habit of addressing himself in the second person had grown on him since his retirement: sometimes he carried on whole conversations as though he were only in partial agreement with what the other part of him was thinking. "You never can tell," he went on. "It might have been better if Margaret hadn't bothered so much about her. A girl's got to stand on her own feet sometime. And most of my girls have been very happy in domestic service—provided they get into the right sort of family, of course. They like the feeling of being on their own." He paused and pressed down the tobacco in his pipe with the flat side of the match-box.

486

"You may say it's the chance of a lifetime if she marries that naval fellow. But he'll never understand her. I can't imagine what Dame Eleanor's thinking about to allow it. Now that other chap—what-d'you-call-him?—the one with the red hair: he'd have understood her. And she must have liked him at one time or they'd never have gone off together." Here Canon Mallow shook his head sadly. "I still think it would have turned out better if he hadn't been the naval fellow. I do. Really, I do. If only I'd thought of it earlier I'd have done something. I'd have told Dame Eleanor. Or Margaret. Or Sweetie. I ought to have tried to stop it. Say what you will, that's what I ought to have done. Tried to stop it."

But he realised that it was the unpopular view. Nobody would ever forgive him if he even mentioned it. And, in any case, it was too late now. Not that this surprised him: all his life he had been leaving things a bit too late.

III

Not so his predecessor. Dr. Trump was now busy making Chinese history. Already he had been able to report an unprecedented boom in Bible sales, and over seven hundred conversions in the Chungking postal area alone.

The most remarkable conversion of all, however, was one to which Dr. Trump had not even referred. But Felicity spotted it. The last issue of the mission magazine, unfortunately printed throughout in Chinese characters which meant that she could not read what it said, contained a picture of her own mother.

Actually it was Sebastian who spotted it.

"Look at Grannie," he said.

And Felicity looked. There was Mrs. Warple, wearing a plain cotton dress. She had discarded her pearls, and earrings, and was distributing what appeared to be hymn-sheets. Remembering the difficulty that Bishop Warple had experienced in getting his wife along even to choral evensong at home, Felicity felt that she had gravely underestimated her husband.

And, secretly, she was jealous. The moment, the very moment, Sebastian's chest was strong enough, she promised herself that she would go out to Chungking to be beside her husband. Cherish him, make him happy, win him back again.

CHAPTER LXXIII

I

YOU ARE not your own master in the Royal Navy. Until you are on half-pay and retired, things like private life and getting married have to take second place beside postings overseas.

And it was Lieutenant Sturgess's sudden posting to Malta that threatened to upset everything. Or rather, would have upset it if Dame Eleanor had not intervened. But she was adamant. Mediterranean Fleet or no Mediterranean Fleet, she was going to see something settled before young James went off anywhere. And when she found that Admiral Sturgess was inclined to the other view and to postpone things until he got back, she required no more persuasion.

Not that young James seemed reluctant. It was simply that Dame Eleanor would have taken a better view of him if he had *insisted*. She disliked seeing men in their late twenties completely under the thumb of their fathers; and she told him so. Frankly, she would have preferred him to be just a bit more impulsive.

"You and Sweetie seem to be very much interested in each other," she said to him. "If you want to get engaged to her before you go off I shan't put any obstacles in your way."

James Sturgess did not reply immediately.

"It's not me," he said. "It's Sweetie. I have asked her, you know."

"And she's refused you?"

"Sort of," he admitted. "She says she wants time to think about it."

Dame Eleanor drew in her lips.

"Leave this to me," she said.

She sent for Sweetie the same evening. She wasn't feeling well and she had to brace herself for what she was going to say. But it was in Sweetie's interest that she was doing it; she was sure of that.

"Now, listen, dear," she told her. "Nobody's trying to make you do anything that you don't want to do. It's only

488

your happiness that I'm thinking of." She paused. "But James Sturgess is a very nice boy, remember. And he comes of a good family. He's absolutely devoted to you, too. And he isn't the sort that falls in love easily. You could do a lot worse than James, you know."

"I know I could," Sweetie answered. "He's always been very nice to me."

There was something in Sweetie's reply that annoyed Dame Eleanor.

"And let me tell you something else, my girl," she went on. "It isn't everybody that would want to marry you, either. It's all very well being pretty and that kind of thing. But it counts for something having a family behind you. I've done what I could to give you a background. But it isn't the same thing. Some people put a lot of store by family."

"James doesn't. He told me so."

"Have you discussed it with him?"

"I told him just what you've told me now," Sweetie answered. "I was warning him."

"And he still wants to marry you?"

Sweetie nodded.

"Then why don't you accept him?" Dame Eleanor leant over and patted Sweetie's hand. "Don't you understand, dear, it's what I've been hoping for? I want to see you married and with a family of your own. I want to see—grandchildren." The word had slipped out unintentionally, but she did not correct it. Instead she went on quietly, "Think it over to-night, dear. And pray. It's always a great help praying when you're worried. And tell me the answer in the morning . . ."

Dame Eleanor was smiling when Margaret came in last thing.

"It's going to be all right," she said. "I've spoken to her. She'll come round all right. She doesn't dislike him, that's the main thing."

I I

It was late now; really late. Dame Eleanor had been put down more than two hours since, and all the servants had gone to bed long ago. Margaret was not asleep, however. She had just lain awake staring up at the ceiling ever since she

489

had gone to bed. She had thought a lot; remembered too much; cried once or twice; and prayed a little.

"Oh, God forgive me for everything," she had just said, "and let it be the right thing that I'm doing now. Make her love him more than she does, otherwise she won't never be happy. She's a good girl, really she is. Please, God, let her be happy. Don't let her do what I did. It's all worked out so wonderfully up to the present, thanks to you, God. Please don't let anything start going wrong now."

She heard the clock in the hall strike midnight, and then she got up. She decided to go down and kiss Sweetie goodnight. It was something that she had always done when Sweetie had first come there. Sweetie didn't know about it, but Margaret had often kissed her good-night without waking her.

Going over to the wardrobe she took out her dressing-gown. It was a thick dressing-gown, an old one of Dame Eleanor's, it made her look fat and shapeless. Her bedroom slippers were old, too. She had bought those for herself—cheaply: they were loose over the instep already, and the soles made a dragging sound as she walked. Because it was late and she would meet no one, she took no trouble with her hair. While she had been tossing in bed it had become unplaited at the ends and she thrust it into the collar of her dressing-gown. It was still rich, plentiful hair but it was becoming streaked with grey by now.

"I'll just kiss her good-night, and then I'll go back to bed," she told herself.

When she reached Sweetie's room, however, she saw that there was a light on. And she waited outside the door, undecided. Sweetie was so independent these days that perhaps she wouldn't like Margaret coming down to see her at this time of night.

"But I must go in," she told herself at last. "Perhaps she's worrying about what Dame Eleanor said to her."

She turned the handle of the door gently. Sweetie was kneeling in front of the fireplace, with a writing-case open on the rug beside her.

Margaret did not go over to her at once.

"Sweetie," she said, still standing over by the door. "Sweetie."

Sweetie turned suddenly. And, as she turned, Margaret saw how pale she was. She suddenly looked as young again as on the day when Margaret had first brought her there.

490

"You frightened me coming in like that," Sweetie said.

While she was speaking, she was shutting up the writing-case, trying to conceal what it contained.

"I couldn't go to sleep," Margaret told her. "I was thinking about you. So I thought I'd come down."

"I'm so glad you've come," Sweetie said slowly. "I needed someone."

Margaret came over to her.

"What's the matter, Sweetie?" she asked at last.

But Sweetie only shook her head.

"It's nothing. Nothing that I can describe."

"You'd better tell me."

"You wouldn't understand. Nobody would. Not even you."

Margaret put her arm on her shoulder.

"Perhaps I understand more than you think."

Sweetie looked up at her, puzzled.

"Not about this," she said.

"Is it that you're not in love with James?" Margaret asked her.

Sweetie did not answer immediately, but Margaret could feel her body stiffen as she heard the question.

"I love him all right," she said at last. "It's just . . . just that I love Ginger more. I wasn't going to tell you. But you might as well know. I love Ginger more than I can ever love anybody."

Margaret drew her breath in quickly. It was Sweetie this time who could feel the sudden, involuntary movement of the other person.

"You . . . you haven't been seeing him, have you?"

Sweetie shook her head.

"That's what's made it so dreadful."

"And do you know where he is?"

Margaret's voice had become hard and anxious now.

Sweetie shook her head again.

"I've been trying to find out," she said. "I've been trying all I could."

Margaret's hands were clasped so tightly that the knuckles showed white along the backs.

"Since you met James?" she asked.

"I tried again last week," Sweetie answered. "But it was no use. And I was writing again when you came in. He must be somewhere, and I know I can find him somehow. I shall go on trying—always."

Sweetie was crying now. And Margaret put both arms around her.

"But you . . . you do mean to marry James, don't you?" she asked, still with that same note of anxiety in her voice.

Sweetie paused again before replying.

"I . . . I don't know," she said slowly. "I've told him I don't love him, not properly, I mean. But he says he doesn't mind. You see, that's the trouble—he loves me really."

"And do you love him enough to marry him?"

"I suppose so."

"Well, be careful!" Margaret's voice had changed now. "Don't you go writing no more letters to Ginger," she went on. "When you're married, you're not to look at another man, d'you hear me? Not even at Ginger if you ever find him."

Sweetie turned away.

"I'm not afraid of myself."

"Then you should be."

"Why do you say that?"

"Because I know what happens when you're in love with somebody."

"*You* do?"

"Yes. And I know more than you think I do about you. I know what goes on inside your mind. That's why I've always tried to bring you up proper. There's a special reason why you've got to be careful. There's bad in you. You look out."

"I don't know what you mean."

"Then I'll tell you," Margaret said quietly, "I'm your mother."

Sweetie had got up and was facing her. What she saw was the tired shapeless figure in the old dressing-gown, the cheap bedroom slippers, the untidy hair streaked with grey.

"I don't believe you," she said.

Margaret's eyes were still fixed on her.

"I wasn't never going to tell you," she said. "Not ever. But if you feel this way about Ginger it's better you should know. That's the way I felt about your father once."

Sweetie was still standing apart staring at her.

"Do you really mean what you said just now?" she asked.

Margaret nodded.

"I can prove it to you if you want me to," she told her. "I've still got the other bit of card I wrote your name on.

492

I'm the one who called you 'Sweetie.' I called you that because I loved you so."

" Then why did you try to get rid of me?"

Margaret dropped her eyes.

" I couldn't afford to keep you. I wasn't never married, you see," she said. " That's why I'm warning you. And nobody else must ever know about it. Not James or Dame Eleanor or anybody. It's just our secret. I wouldn't have told you now if things hadn't been this way. But it's only fair to you. Now you know what you've got to guard against."

" Do . . . do I know my father?" Sweetie asked.

Margaret did not answer. She merely shook her head.

" Am I like him?" Sweetie asked.

Margaret, however, did not answer that question exactly. She seemed temporarily to have forgotten about Sweetie.

" He was such a lovely young man," was what she said.

She didn't say anything more ; just slid herself down into the chair that stood beside the fireplace and sat staring into the empty grate.

She was still like that when Sweetie came over to her.

I I I

Margaret slept no more when she got back to her room than she had before she left it. And she was angry with herself.

" I didn't never ought to have told her," she kept repeating. " That I didn't. I never meant to neither. But she made me. Sweetie's the same as I used to be. There's that streak in her. I can see it. I had to tell her. There wasn't no choice. Now that I've warned her she can be careful. She mustn't let nothing go wrong now the way I did. He's such a nice gentleman, the one who wants to marry her. And good-looking, too. She won't never get a chance like that again. And it'll be all right so long as she's watching out for herself. It's just that she mustn't never let herself go, the way I did. I wasn't going to tell her about me. Not ever. But I had to. It wouldn't have been fair on her if . . ."

Then upstairs she heard the maids moving about, and she knew that to-morrow had come.

CHAPTER LXXIV

MARGARET avoided Sweetie next morning. There are some things that can be said late at night that are unsayable, that don't even bear remembering, next morning.

And Sweetie herself went out quite early. When Dame Eleanor sent for her she wasn't there. But it wasn't far that Sweetie had gone. Only round to the Archbishop Bodkin Hospital, in fact.

The porter was new: Sweetie didn't recognise him. And it seemed strange having someone lead her to the Warden's room. As she went through the Cloisters past the Ridley Block, she felt suddenly as though she had never left the Archbishop Bodkin Hospital at all: as though all her life had been spent on those asphalt pavements; and as though there never had been a view beyond those walls. But somehow, now that she was back, it all seemed so much smaller. Smaller and shabbier and dirtier. The dormitories didn't appear so high as she had remembered them. Even the doorways were narrower. It was as though under the later layers of London soot that had descended, everything had been shrinking, dwindling, diminishing.

Miss Phrynne was quite overwhelmed when Sweetie came in. She had always shared Dr. Trump's opinion of Sweetie and had never approved of her in the slightest. Not at the time that is. So far as she was concerned, Sweetie was simply the girl who had disgraced Archbishop Bodkin's. But, naturally, Dame Eleanor's interest in her had changed everything. It was all quite different now. It was difficult to believe that there could be anything seriously wrong with a girl dressed as Sweetie was now dressed. So she greeted her warmly.

" This is a lovely surprise," she said. " Just fancy, it's our Sweetie come back to us. I may still call you Sweetie, mayn't I? I can't tell you how we've all missed you. And I must congratulate you. It's all been like a fairy-tale, hasn't it?"

" Just like a fairy-tale," Sweetie answered. " Is Canon Mallow in, please?"

There was an urgency, an impatience about her, that Miss Phrynne noticed immediately. But, even so, they couldn't find Canon Mallow. He was over in the infants' side some-

494

where, talking to the little ones. He came at once, however,
as soon as he heard who it was that was waiting for him. He
only hoped that it wasn't his advice that Sweetie had come
for. Supposing, for example, that she asked him outright
what he thought about marrying the naval chap, what on
earth was he going to say?

Sweetie was sitting there in his room when he got back to
it. And it touched the sentimental side of him as soon as he
looked at her.

"No, of course not," he told himself as soon as he saw
how slight and delicate she was. "It was quite wrong of me.
She couldn't have gone into domestic service. She's not the
right type at all. Most unsuitable." And he realised then
what a good thing it was that he hadn't tried to interfere in
any way.

Sweetie jumped up as soon as he came in.

"Hallo, Canon Mallow," she said.

"Hallo, Sweetie."

"I shan't keep you very long. I'm sure you're busy."

But Canon Mallow only smiled.

"Not really," he said. "They don't really need me here,
you know. It's just that it's useful to have someone about
when Larkin can't be here." He paused. He was sure that
Sweetie hadn't come to talk about him, or about Canon
Larkin, and he was just wasting her time. So he started
again. "What is it, Sweetie?" he asked. "What can I do for
you?"

"Do you remember I came once before?" she asked him.

Canon Mallow nodded.

"You wanted to know that boy's address," he said. "And
I wouldn't tell you. I remember. What is it this time?"

Sweetie smiled at him.

"I wanted to say 'thank you' for not telling me," she
replied.

"Say 'thank you' for not telling you . . ." Canon Mallow
repeated.

He was puzzled, frankly puzzled. But Sweetie was evidently
trying to explain.

"You see," she went on. "At the time I thought I was in
love with him."

"I know you did," Canon Mallow answered. "That's why
I wouldn't tell you."

He smiled self-indulgently at the memory of the deep
Levantine cunning that he had displayed. Some people had

accused Canon Mallow of being the sort of man who is easily duped. Perhaps he was, sometimes. But he had certainly seen right through Sweetie on that occasion.

"Do you know, I used to lie awake at nights just thinking about him," Sweetie continued.

Canon Mallow smiled again.

"Well, never mind," he told her. "You aren't the first girl to have done that. They all do it sometimes. Men, too, for that matter."

Sweetie paused.

"But it was you who saved me," she went on. "Because if I'd gone on thinking about Ginger "—Canon Mallow flipped his fingers suddenly. Of course, that was it: fancy his forgetting the name "Ginger"—"I should never have been going to marry James."

"Are you in love with him?" Canon Mallow asked rather abruptly.

Sweetie turned her large dark eyes full on him.

"If I wasn't, I shouldn't be marrying him, should I?" she asked.

As she said it, Canon Mallow felt the load of doubts and misgivings lifting from his mind. He got up and put his hand on Sweetie's shoulder.

"That's all I wanted to hear," he told her. "If a girl's really in love with a man it's worth all the rest put together."

"That's how I feel," Sweetie answered.

Canon Mallow began searching round for his pipe. This was being a far easier interview than he had expected.

"And, of course, it's just the same for the man," he went on. "A man's got to love the girl in just the same way to be happy . . ."

He stopped because something almost like a sob had come from Sweetie.

"That's why I came to see you," she said. "That's really what I want to talk about."

Canon Mallow broke off his search. His pipe must be somewhere. He had been smoking earlier this morning. But a pipe wasn't important compared with what Sweetie was saying.

"Do you mean you think he doesn't love you?" he asked. "Are you sure? It may only be his manner, you know. A lot of men are shy about showing a girl how much they really love her."

"Oh, it isn't James I'm thinking about," Sweetie replied.

496

"I'm not worried about James. Dear James loves me tremendously. It's Ginger."

"Ginger! But how does Ginger come into it?" Canon Mallow asked.

He was becoming confused again. If only he could have found his pipe it would have been easier. He could always think more clearly about important things if he was smoking.

"But he does," Sweetie assured him. "Ginger was in love with me once, you see."

Canon Mallow shrugged his shoulders.

"Mustn't take that too seriously," he said. "He was only a boy at the time. He's still only a lad now for that matter."

"He's nineteen," Sweetie answered.

"Well, what of it? He'll have got over it the same as you have."

Sweetie paused.

"I wish I could be sure of that," she said. "But you see I promised to marry him once, and he said he'd wait for ever for me. It just wouldn't be right if he thought that I was still waiting for him, somewhere."

Canon Mallow patted Sweetie's hand.

"I think you're worrying yourself about nothing," he told her. "Those sort of promises don't count for anything."

Sweetie smiled.

"That's what James said when I told him," she replied. Then the smile vanished. "But I can't feel like that. I feel I've got to break it off properly. If I write and tell him I don't love him any more, then I think I should feel better about it. It won't be an easy letter to write but I'd rather do it than not. I feel I owe it to James, too, somehow: he doesn't, but I do. I was awake all last night thinking about it."

Canon Mallow paused.

"Well, let's be sensible about it," he said. He had just found his pipe behind the blotter and was now wondering where the tobacco could be. "You don't think that perhaps it might upset Ginger hearing from you after all this time."

"I should be very careful what I said," Sweetie told him.

"Well, of course, you know best," he said. "But we don't want to revive a lot of old memories, do we? That might have quite the wrong effect."

"But I'm only doing it so that he shan't feel hurt."

"Yes, of course. I remember now. That's the whole idea, isn't it?"

The tobacco had mysteriously come into his hand some-how, as though it had grown up through the table-top like a mushroom while he was just sitting there. And as soon as he had started to pack his pipe, he felt better about everything; blander; more sure of himself.

"Well, if you've set your heart on it, I can't see much harm in it *now*," he went on, carefully emphasising the word "now" to show how circumstances had changed everything. "Or much good for that matter. But it's entirely up to you. Only keep it short and to the point, that's the main thing. He wasn't a very literary kind of boy."

"I'll remember," Sweetie promised.

Canon Mallow was at the filing-cabinet. It was a legacy of Dr. Trump's, this filing-cabinet; and because Miss Phrynne kept it up-to-date for him, it was really quite ridiculously easy to find whatever he wanted. Take Ginger for instance. There it all was in front of him.

WOODS, Herbert (" Ginger ") January 24th, 1933—June 12th, 1935, Thatford Farm School, Thatford, Norfolk. June 13th, 1935—March 10th, 1936, Fordson Tractor Works, Dagenham; July 14th, 1936, Pyramid Motor Garage, Dome Road, Brighton, Sussex.

"Well, that's the last address," Canon Mallow told her, as he copied it out for her. "Pyramid Garage, Dome Road, Brighton. I don't think he's left it. Of course, you could always phone up and make sure."

"Oh no," said Sweetie. "I think telephoning *would* be rather difficult."

"Yes, perhaps you're right," Canon Mallow answered. "I wasn't thinking."

As he gave the slip of paper to Sweetie, she kissed him. And this pleased Canon Mallow a great deal. It was nice being able to make people so happy; and it was nice finding someone like Sweetie who really cared about someone's feelings. Most girls in her position would simply have been thinking about getting married. So he kissed her back again.

"Well, that settles everything, doesn't it?" he said gently.

"Everything," Sweetie answered.

When she left the Archbishop Bodkin Hospital, Sweetie did not return at once to Dame Eleanor's. She went down to the High Street instead and walked over to the cab-rank.

"Victoria," she said.

CHAPTER LXXV

I

THERE COULD be no two opinions on the matter: it was
Sweetie's disappearance that finished Dame Eleanor. She
just never got over the shock of it. Or the shame. A sick,
tired old woman before it happened, she went all to pieces
afterwards. And the way things turned out, she did not even
see Sweetie again. Because by the time Sweetie, with a rather
embarrassed-looking Ginger beside her, had been found by
the Sussex Police it was too late for Dame Eleanor to see
anybody.

Not that Sweetie deliberately kept her in suspense. It was
not until after 10 o'clock that morning when Sweetie saw
Canon Mallow, and by 6.30 the same evening a telegraph
boy was already cycling up the long drive to The Cedars.

The telegram itself was simple, terse, laconic. "HAVE
FOUND GINGER AND AM GOING TO MARRY HIM," it said.
"PLEASE EXPLAIN TO JAMES AND DAME ELEANOR AND DON'T
WORRY. LOVE SWEETIE." That was all. It was as though in
some strange fashion she had never really doubted that things
would turn out in that way and was merely confirming what
had happened.

And, from the moment Margaret saw that telegram, she did
not doubt what it contained. That didn't mean, of course,
that her hands did not tremble as she opened the envelope.
She knew that the telegram stood for the complete ruin and
destruction of everything that she had planned. It meant that
Sweetie would never be a lady now, and that her own last
solemn warning, the admission that had meant humiliating
herself in front of Sweetie, had been ignored completely.
But, as she read, there was another feeling altogether inside
her, a fierce, illogical, happy feeling. "That telegram was
addressed to me," she told herself. "I'm the one she turned
to. It's me she wanted to know."

Dame Eleanor insisted on seeing the telegram, though she
might just as well have taken Margaret's word for what it
said. For she was too far gone by then to be able to make
out post-office handwriting on a post-office paper. The whole
of the past six hours had followed a course of mounting

anxiety, and she was now exhausted. She had rung up the police and the hospitals; and she had talked incessantly of murder, kidnapping and the white slave traffic.

Then, when everything had failed and it was apparent that Sweetie was lost completely, she sent for James. She had deliberately left him till last, she explained, because she did not want to worry him. But there was another and a stronger reason. And that was where the shame of it came in. She did not want to have to admit in front of a Sturgess—especially in front of one of the *young* Sturgesses—that something had gone wrong, alarmingly and disastrously wrong, with her own carefully made arrangements.

James, of course, came immediately; was actually in the room, in fact, when Margaret brought in the telegram. And Margaret felt sorry for him. He was such a thoroughly nice young man. Too nice. He just stood silent, biting his lip and looking down at his feet. He even remained nice when Dame Eleanor started to act as though something had gone wrong in one of her committees.

"Well, it's no use just standing around," she said suddenly. "You'd better go and tell your father."

James Sturgess shifted from one foot to the other.

"But isn't that all making it too definite?" he asked. "We can't even be sure that Sweetie really means it. Don't you think that if I went down and saw her . . ."

Dame Eleanor shook her head.

"If she'd wanted you, she'd have told you where to find her," she said. "And if you did go you'd only be making a fool of yourself." She paused. "You're well out of it, young man," she went on. "Better now than later. Take my word for it. You're well out of it."

Young James looked up from his feet for a moment. Ever since he had come into the room he had behaved as though he had just seen his feet for the first time and was fascinated. It was now with a wrench that he tore his eyes away from them.

"Mind you, Dame Eleanor," he said, still speaking quietly, nicely, "we don't even know for certain that Sweetie sent the telegram. It could be a fake, you know."

But it was obvious that Dame Eleanor was anxious no longer about murder, kidnapping and the white slave traffic.

"Don't you go trying to comfort yourself," she said. "That telegram's from Sweetie all right." As she spoke she faced

500

round towards Margaret. "What do you say?" she demanded. "Is that telegram a fake, or isn't it?"

Margaret could not answer: she merely shook her head.

But there was no question about the telegram. It was from Sweetie all right. If anyone else had sent it, the telegram would have read "WE ARE GOING TO GET MARRIED": as it was it had said: "AM GOING TO MARRY HIM."

And that was precisely what Sweetie had been saying for the last twelve years.

II

There were two people, a girl and a young man, sitting in the corner of a Brighton café. The police were looking for them. They were seated side by side and the girl was holding the young man's hand. In front of them on the marble table-top was a brooch: the girl had just put it there.

"Don't you remember it?" she asked.

He picked it up and looked at it, disengaging his hand from hers in order to do so. The brooch was obviously a cheap one. It was of silver-gilt in the shape of a shamrock with the word "MOTHER" inscribed across it.

The young man shook his head.

"You gave it me," the girl told him. "That time up in Doncaster. I've kept it ever since. Have you got your tie-pin?"

"What tie-pin?"

"It doesn't matter."

The young man took hold of her hand again.

"Don't you worry," he said. "I'll get you a better brooch than that. Something you can really wear. I've got a good job now, I have."

III

Dame Eleanor's attack, the first of the two really bad ones, came on that same night. When Margaret went in to her she thought that Dame Eleanor was actually dying. But Dame Eleanor was not ready for dying just yet. She had too much on her mind. She was sitting up in bed leaning so far forward that the pillows no longer supported her, and she was trying

501

to speak. Margaret went over and put her arm round her. It was like putting her arm around a child, Dame Eleanor had grown so thin.

"You lie still," she said. "I'll fetch the doctor. I'll go for him now."

But Dame Eleanor reached out and caught her by the arm. The old fingers fastened there.

"Not the doctor," she said. "I . . . don't . . . don't . . . want the doctor. I want . . ."

She was too weak to say any more and for a moment she simply lay there, still feebly holding Margaret's arm so that she could not go away from the bedside.

"It's . . . it's Thring I want," she said at last.

Margaret looked at the clock.

"But Mr. Thring can't come now," she said. "It's too late. I'll get him to come in the morning."

"I mayn't be here in the morning," Dame Eleanor replied. "He's got to come now. If I die . . ."

"You're not going to die," Margaret told her. "I'll give you your tablets, they'll make you feel better."

She measured out the dose into the little tumbler and held it to Dame Eleanor's lips.

"I'll get the doctor first and then Mr. Thring," she said. "You want to be strong enough to talk to Mr. Thring when he comes, don't you?"

"I want Thring," was all that Dame Eleanor answered. "I want Thring. Tell him he's got to come. Say that I'm dying and I want him. Say it's about Sweetie."

I V

It was 9.30 next morning when Mr. Thring called. And it was obvious that he knew what he was in for. He had his brief-case all ready, and he wore a drawn, harassed expression.

But he need not have worried. After last night's attack, Dame Eleanor was now at her quietest and most lucid. There was no need for any crossing out and writing over this morning. Dame Eleanor came straight to the point. And it was a simple one—to erase all mention of Sweetie: to make quite certain that there was no loophole through which any of Dame Eleanor's money might get to her.

502

The only trouble was the time. This was will-making with the scythe waiting. Dame Eleanor would not hear of Mr. Thring's going back to his office to get the thing typed out properly. Nor would she agree to having a secretary come out to the house—even that was wasting precious, invaluable time; cutting things too fine for her liking. Mr. Thring had to sit down then and there and make a fair copy.

It was the doctor and Canon Mallow—he had come round to say that he did hope that he had done the right thing in giving Sweetie Ginger's address—who witnessed it. And as soon as the paper was back in Mr. Thring's brief-case, Dame Eleanor closed her eyes. There was nothing more she wanted, she said. Just to have the light out and be given another hot-water bottle and be left alone.

Margaret sat with her all that afternoon. Most of the time Dame Eleanor dozed. But for quite long stretches she lay staring up at the ceiling, thinking. They were scattered, muddled sort of thoughts. Sometimes the past came near completely extinguishing the present, so that there was all that terrible trouble with Derek to contend with again; and sometimes the present receded almost indefinitely and Sweetie became just another of the Bodkin girls, one among so many, who, despite everything, had obstinately gone wrong somehow. She had been a pretty little girl, Dame Eleanor remembered, with large eyes and dark, shining hair, and only about half the size of the other children.

There wasn't much difference between sleeping and being awake by now. People came and looked at her and gave her sips of things and re-arranged the bedclothes and went away again. The doctor kept on coming. Derek looked in a couple of times, once in his uniform and once in that big check sports coat of his that she had never really liked, and he had a different girl on his arm each time; Sweetie came in to say good-night—she was looking pale again, Dame Eleanor thought, and seemed to be worrying about something; and that red-haired boy who was always running away came to borrow half a crown.

Then, quite unannounced, God Himself dropped in just to see how she was getting on. He was passing, He said, in a voice like Mr. Vivvyan Sparkes's, and it was no trouble really.

"Are you better?" He asked. "Feeling all right for the journey? If you'd like an angel to carry your things you've

503

only got to say so. Everything's ready. We're expecting you, you know."

And Dame Eleanor made a supreme effort. She dropped one of her Court curtseys—which wasn't easy, having to do it in bed.

"It's very gracious of You to call," she said. "Very gracious, indeed. If I'd known, I'd have made a point of being up. There are one or two facts You ought to know about me, but if You don't mind I'll dictate something when I get there because I'm rather sleepy at the moment. And please don't bother about an angel. I shall be coming just as I am—in my night things . . ."

At nine o'clock, the doctor thought that her brothers ought to be sent for. But when they came, she didn't appear to know them, however. She was worried by a sort of veil, a thin, invisible cobweb that had drifted across her face, and she kept trying to brush it away again.

There was one more lucid moment, a completely lucid one, shortly after midnight. The nurse had arrived by now but it was Margaret who was sitting at the bedside holding Dame Eleanor's hand. Dame Eleanor suddenly opened her eyes and looked at her.

"This is just the way I wanted it, dear," she said. "It's such a comfort having you." She paused. "I've been thinking," she went on. "We're not really to blame about Sweetie. That's what happens when the stock's bad. If only we knew who the mother and father were we should probably be able to understand everything." There was a longer pause this time. "Don't you worry, dear," she said at last. "I've remembered you in the will, Mr. Thring knows all about it."

Dame Eleanor did not speak again except to say that she was cold and that the lights were flickering. But it was only a mumble by now, and even Margaret could not make out what she was saying. She sat there with the thin, chilly hand —practically bone already—held tightly in hers, and thought about Sweetie.

"Perhaps it's better that way," she was trying to tell herself. "If she loves Ginger, I didn't ought to have ever tried to stop it. And it's only her father who's different. She's the same sort as Ginger, really. Perhaps it'll work out all right."

The next thing that Margaret remembered was the nurse

telling her that it was all over. She still had Dame Eleanor's hand in hers, but it didn't belong to Dame Eleanor any longer. The bed was empty really. Dame Eleanor herself, with all her cares and wills and committees left behind her, was living her last dream. She was far out in space somewhere, on the other side of the moon already, making for a star shaped like a cross, and growing smaller and smaller every minute.

"No, really, He shouldn't have bothered you," her last words had been: they were addressed silently to the angel. "I said I was coming just as I was. I've brought nothing with me. Perhaps He can lend me something . . ."

And, as she said it, she felt about fifteen again; fifteen, and at her first fancy dress party where she had been so excited that she had forgotten even to feel self-conscious.

CHAPTER LXXVI

THE FUNERAL was over and done with now, and the blinds were up again.

But the air of funerals and dissolution still hung about the place. There was a half-finished feeling to everything, as though the house itself were going to be buried next. It was quiet, too, with an unnatural tomblike quietness. The hush of the undertaker's mutes still hung about the staircase; and, in the drawing-room, there were dust sheets over all the furniture. But it was at night-time that it was at its worst. Nobody seemed to have the heart to turn on enough lights any longer. Not that there were many of them left to turn on anything. Out of the whole staff only Margaret and a caretaker now remained.

Margaret herself had been prepared to go along with the others. But Mr. Thring stopped it. It had been Dame Eleanor's wish, he said; and the bishop and the judge both confirmed it. They wanted someone, he explained, to go through all Dame Eleanor's personal belongings.

Margaret, however, was not thinking of Dame Eleanor any longer. Or even of Sweetie. She was thinking of herself. She had heard again from Mr. Thring, and Dame Eleanor had been true to her word all right: she had remembered her. "*To my companion, Margaret Hart, three months' salary and the sum of two hundred pounds if still in my employ,"* it ran.

And, of course, that altered everything. She could really begin to live now. It wasn't as though she were old yet; or at least not really old. Only just forty. She still felt like a woman. And the letters that she had been getting had always been full of that one idea.

Even the last one that had come less than a month ago had mentioned it:

> ". . . *if only I could raise the money somehow I'd send you your fare so that you could join me out here,"* it had said. *"I've had about enough of knocking around without even a home to come back to in the evenings . . ."* And there was more in the same vein. *"The hotel job didn't turn out quite as I expected,"* it explained, *" but I've gone in with one of my own sort now. It's a riding academy, and though yours truly is only a sort of glorified stable boy the life's all right—see photo enclosed. And don't forget that two can live as cheaply as one out here—a damn' sight cheaper in some respects; all the boarding-houses rook you if you're single. So here's still hoping, even though I'm not exactly flush at the moment. Your last two pounds was a real godsend: I don't know what I would have done without it: you've been a brick all through, and I feel a worm taking your money. There isn't another woman . . ."*

Margaret put the letter down and took up the photograph. Up against a stable door it showed a tall, rangey man, still with that same handle-bar Guards moustache, and those shining, smiling teeth. He was dressed in a sweat shirt, and his body, she noticed, seemed to be dark all over. But that was the only change. The last twenty years didn't seem to have aged him. There wasn't a wrinkle anywhere on his face—just the linings that come of being out in all that sun. And the carefree look was still there despite the bad times he'd been through.

"He's a lovely man," she suddenly said aloud. "That's what he is—he's lovely."

It was the reply that wasn't so easy to write: but she blamed herself for that—she should have written to him sooner. As it was, she had to tell him everything.

" Dear Derek," she wrote. *" Your mother died peace-fully last week. I was with her at the end and she wasn't never in any pain, I can vouch for that. I didn't tell her about us so, of course, she died without knowing. It would only have upset her, so I thought better not. Now I've got a big surprise for you, Derek. You've got a grown-up daughter. I swore I wouldn't tell anyone while your mother was still alive. I was only one month gone when you sailed so of course I couldn't be sure. And I never told you because I was afraid you'd do something silly like trying to come back and then you'd have been arrested like you said. She's getting married soon so she won't need me any longer. And, Derek, your mother left me two hundred pounds and I'm coming out to join you the way we always said I would. It isn't much Third, which means we'll still have something over when I get there. What happens about your allowance, have you heard? Oh, Derek, write and say you're glad. I won't actually sail until you've written because I want to be sure you weren't just being nice about wishing I could come, because I really can now . . ."*

She broke off because her fingers ached. Writing letters had always been difficult and this was the most difficult that she had ever tried to write. Her eyes were burning and she went across to the wash-basin to bathe them. Then she looked at herself in the mirror. On her face there were plenty of lines. And round the mouth, too, it was more than lined: it was saggy. There were cups under her eyes that she could see as she stared at the image of herself. Frowning only made them deeper, and she turned her head sideways. But then the light caught the hair at her temples: that was the worst of dark hair—it showed the grey so. And at the temples there was more than grey: there was white. She bit her lip and went over to the cheval-glass. She had put on weight since she had been back at Dame Eleanor's and the blouse that she was wearing seemed too tight for her. It bulged. But it wasn't only the blouse. It was the way she was standing. She did bulge nowadays. And throwing her shoulders back wasn't the answer, either. It didn't feel natural any longer, and she wouldn't be able to keep them like it anyhow.

Then she looked down at her feet. She was wearing her old bedroom slippers. Those bedroom slippers were just what she was made for nowadays. They were right for a tired, sagging sort of woman of forty.

She turned suddenly and picked up the letter that she had just written. And, when she had picked it up, she began to tear it, first into wide strips, then into narrow ones and finally across and across so that the sheet of notepaper was like confetti when she dropped it in the basket.

" He don't want me, not like I am now," she told herself. " What he wants is me like I was when he first had me. I'd rather that's how he went on thinking about me. I don't want to see his face when he finds out. It wouldn't be fair on him. Not when he's kept himself so lovely."

BOTH OF Margaret's secrets are out by now: you know all that there is to know about her child, and about the father of her child. The woman in the raincoat isn't one of London's mysteries any longer.

She is putting on her raincoat again at this moment. Not the same raincoat, of course ; even with all her care, the old one wore out about fifteen years ago. But it's still the same sort of thing ; shapeless and clingy and mildly waterproof. She's got her suitcase—a reddish hardened cardboard affair with reinforced corners—packed already, and she is drawing on her gloves as she stands there. Her job's over. The three months are up and all Dame Eleanor's things are disposed of. It's time she was moving on.

Looked at in one way, there isn't very much to show for having stayed there. In her handbag, she's only got three pounds ten and a picture of Derek that she took from Dame Eleanor's dressing-table drawer. She found it right under the lining of the drawer, as though Dame Eleanor hadn't wanted to risk coming upon it suddenly but couldn't on the other hand bring herself to part with it altogether.

The three pounds ten is all Margaret's fault, of course. There was the two hundred pounds ready and waiting for her. But she gave the two hundred pounds to Sweetie for a wedding present ; felt that Sweetie needed it more ; and, in a way, had more claim to it.

That's why Margaret's going after another job. It is in a Children's Home again. And general help is what the job is called. Not that Margaret minds ; she knows just what that means. It means stairs and nappies and floors and crockery, and odd cups of tea for the Sister and a bedroom somewhere right under the tiles again.

" But it's better that way," she keeps thinking. " Plenty to do. Keep my mind off myself. Stop me brooding."

There is no one, except the housekeeper, to say good-bye to as she leaves The Cedars. And because she isn't the sentimental kind, she doesn't go round the house having a last look at everything. She just goes straight down the stairs, putting the corner of the mat straight in the hall as she passes it, and out through the big front door, closing it behind her for the last time.

It is a long walk down the drive and the cardboard suitcase is heavy with all her winter things. But that can't be helped. There is nothing for it but to walk. It is right down to the bus-stop that she has to go. And the bus-stop is nearly half a mile from Dame Eleanor's.

Because of the time of year—it was late summer when Dame Eleanor died, just as she knew it would be—it is getting pretty dark now by teatime; and Margaret had drunk a cup of tea with the caretaker before she had left The Cedars. The street lamps are on already, and a faint drizzle that makes the pavements shine is beginning to come down. While she waits for the bus, she turns up the collar of her raincoat. You can't even see her face any longer. She is just anyone by now. The original mysterious woman in the raincoat. The one we followed. And lost in the darkness. And finally caught up with again.

She's the one the picture frame was made for. And the portrait is finished now. Margaret had used up all the emotion in her life. She'd got to content herself with the memories of it from now on. And deep inside herself, she knows it. If she'd been in any real doubt in the matter she'd have bought that steamer ticket and gone out to South Africa, white hairs and felt bedroom slippers and all.

But the bus is drawing up in front of her. And Margaret is glad to be inside it. The drizzle has turned to rain, and it is coming down properly by now; bouncing up again off the road blocks in real Putney fashion. It is the corner of St. Mark's Avenue where the bus has stopped. But she can't see anything because the windows of the bus are streaming. Then, as the driver moves off again, she catches a glimpse of the lime-trees, the outline of the gatehouse, set in the high stone wall, the gas-lamps and the tracks of watery light leading up to them. But that, too, vanishes and she is left to the rain and the darkness. She is thinking of Sweetie. And all the time the bus is carrying her away from us.

Then the bend in the road comes. And she is gone for ever.

THE HOUSES IN BETWEEN
Howard Spring

A brilliant novel by one of the most widely read contemporary authors. A picture of England during that most interesting period in our history—the years between 1848-1947.

FROM HERE TO ETERNITY
James Jones

A great deal of the raw violence of Jack London, the mighty loneliness of Wolfe and the pounding word-rhythm of Hemingway make this a book of genuine literary importance.

MY EARLY LIFE
Sir Winston S. Churchill

The story of the first 25 years in the life of Sir Winston Churchill—the key to an understanding and appreciation of this most dominant character in our history.

THE STRUGGLE FOR EUROPE
Chester Wilmot

The book that explains how we won the war and lost the peace. How the problems we face to-day arose not from what happened since the war but what happened during the war.

LONDON BELONGS TO ME
Norman Collins

With Dulcimer Street as the centre, this is a story of London and Londoners told with humour, understanding and, above all gusto. *A Book Society Choice.*

PILLING ALWAYS PAYS
Thomas Armstrong

As a business man Sam Pilling is highly respected. He rescues his father's bookmaking business from bankruptcy and builds it into a large and prosperous concern. But as a father he is a failure. His children, given everything they want, grow up foolish, selfish and hopelessly spoilt. Finally Sam makes a great sacrifice to bring his children to their senses. The carrying out of his plan makes an absorbing story.

KNOCK ON ANY DOOR
Willard Motley

Nick Romano, a sensitive young American boy, is sent to a reformatory for a petty crime which he did not commit. The treatment he receives determines the path of crime he will inevitably pursue. His philosophy is crystallised *live fast, die young and have a good-looking corpse.* He is not merely one boy of to-day. His type, unhappily, is legion. You will find him in any low street in any big city. *Knock on Any Door* is Nick's story, engrossing, exciting, powerful and compassionate.

THE EYE OF LOVE
Margery Sharp

Only the eye of love, in this case, Mr. Gibson's, could have transformed the lady known as Old Madrid into a Spanish Rose. Only her reciprocal eye of love could transform fat Harry Gibson into Bluff King Hal. For ten years their slightly ridiculous bliss has been complete: now it is threatened by a depression in the fur trade. How Mr. Gibson steers his way between ruin and a politic marriage must be left to Miss Sharp's ironic and compassionate pen.

THE BISHOP'S MANTLE
Agnes Sligh Turnbull

The Rev. Hilary Laurnes came of a line of distinguished clergymen —sincere, clever, courageous and handsome. To these attributes he added a beautiful and wealthy wife, so that his appointed living —the prosperous parish of St. Matthews—should provide a most successful career. But we are shown how he needed all his qualities to overcome his own blessings, which were in reality a great obstacle.